The Reluctant Rect

The Father Tom Mysteries, Books 1

By

J. R. Mathis and Susan Mathis

CW00796672

First Printing, October 2021

Contact: mercyandjusticemysteries@gmail.com

HALLELUJAH, Words and Music by LEONARD COHEN, © 1984 Used pending permission from copyright owner.

Cover Photo: Adobe Stock Photos

Cover: Millie Godwin

Editing: Anna Palmer Darkes

Also by J.R. and Susan Mathis

The Penitent Priest

The Father Tom Mysteries, Book 1

One

It has always struck me as odd that people believe that priests don't have pasts, that they are somehow born full-grown men with Roman collars around their necks.

People don't think this about their accountant, or their lawyer, or their doctor. But they assume their priest knew he had a vocation from the moment he was born, and grew up in some kind of preschool seminary before actually landing on the steps of their local parishes.

Of course, the truth is completely different.

No man can even enter seminary until he is at least 18 years old, and it's rare that any do so that young. Most have probably tried some sort of illegal drugs, almost everyone has driven too fast, gotten drunk at least once, and disappointed his mother on numerous occasions. One or two may have spent time behind bars, perhaps even outside the country.

It's also fair to say that many—if not most—are not virgins, though there is no record kept concerning this. Most of those who are not have slept with women, though a few have slept with men. The requirement is chastity from the day you choose this life—or more precisely, decide to see if God has chosen you for it—going forward, no matter what you have done in the past.

But a few of us, like me, don't have to be asked for details. The fact is right out there, because we have been married before.

Yes, I am one of the few people now on earth who, at the end of my life, will have received all seven sacraments of the Roman Catholic Church—assuming someone's around to give me last rites, which I certainly hope they are. But it's not really the kind of thing you can plan for too much.

Because people assume that we don't have pasts, people also assume their priests don't have emotional triggers—events that cause them flashbacks or discomfort. But of course we do. There are priests who still get a little sentimental about a song on the radio, or some for whom the smell of a certain food brings him back to Mother's house.

For me, being back at Saint Clare's today is one of these triggers.

The last time I was here I was not standing behind a font but instead, in front of a casket, that of my much loved, much too young wife, Joan, who had died in my arms just a few days earlier.

Today could not be any more different than that dreadful day, for while then it seemed that my life was ending—and in a way a part of it was—on this day the life of little Benedict James Reynolds is just beginning, and it is my job to welcome him in to the arms of the Holy Mother Church.

And that's what makes me nervous.

To make bad matters worse, little Benedict himself is something of a trigger, clad as he is in a family heirloom baptism gown. It's not unlike the one my mother passed on to me when I took my first fiancée to my family home in Florida to meet her. Strangely enough, Mom didn't ask for it back when that engagement ended in a heated argument in a cheap apartment, instead of sacred vows in front of an altar. Instead, she waited until after I did marry—and lost—Joan, with the child who might have worn that gown, to ask for it back. Of course, by then, my sister Sonya had had numerous pregnancy scares and, as Mom said in her usual way, "You've already lost two women, Tommy. God only knows if you'll ever find anyone else."

Apparently God did know, because I never did find anyone else. Instead, I found Him and a very surprising vocation to the priesthood.

That is why I am standing before this altar now, about to pour holy water over the forehead of this squirming infant in the arms of his proud mother.

We get to the part I have been dreading, as I carefully take little Benedict James from his mother and hold him over the font. I pick up the silver shell, dip it in the water, and pour the water over his head. The little boy is still and peaceful, looking at me with wide-eyed wonderment. I have worried for days that he'd scream the entire time, and prayed that he wouldn't. Fortunately my prayers are answered, and I hand Benedict back to his mother, breathe a sigh of relief, and turn to the assembly.

"Let us welcome Benedict James Reynolds into God's family."

The crowd applauds, punctuated by the cries and screams of the dozens of children in the pews.

The 10:30 a.m. Mass is a lively, well-attended one. From what I can tell, the church is full almost to capacity—primarily with young families, though all ages are represented. I recognize some of the people from years ago. Anna Luckgold, my mother-in-law, is here, third row from the front. Glenda Whitemill, the parish secretary, sits in the front row studying my every move.

She was also at 8:00 a.m. Mass.

I make it through this, my first Mass with more than an audience of five since—well, ever. Everything is fine until the end. I have just finished the prayers before Communion when I see movement out of the corner of my eye. Glenda Whitemill has left her seat and moved to the altar with the other Eucharistic Ministers.

Instead of lining up with everyone else, Glenda comes right to my elbow and whispers, "Remind the parents to keep their children in the pews."

"What?"

"They only come up if they're old enough to receive Communion. Otherwise they have to stay put."

I look at her and shake my head slightly. "I'm not going to do that. The parents can bring their children up for a blessing if they want to."

"But Father Anthony—"

"Is not here," I say, firmly. "Now, please go back with the others."

She looks at me, her eyes burning with indignation.

"Yes, Father," she says quietly. She walks back and stands with the others.

After the final prayers, I say, "Please be seated for just a moment."

The congregation sits down, mothers and fathers wrestling reluctant toddlers and older children back into their seats.

"Before the final blessing," I say, "I just want to say how happy I am to be here at Saint Clare's. I look forward to the next four months with you, and please know that my door is always open if you have any need or concern. I'll do my best, but I'm not planning on making any major changes, since I've never been in a parish on my own before, so please bear with me as I find my way."

I hear a wave of murmurs through the church, intermingling with the sounds of fussy children. I try to read people's faces. I think they look approving—except, of course, for Glenda Whitemill.

I let the murmuring die down. "Most of you are newer to the parish." I pause before going on. "Some of you may remember me from—from my previous life here in Myerton."

Glenda jerks her head up at that. I hear more murmuring and think I notice a couple of signs of recognition. "I look forward to renewing old acquaintances and making new ones in the short time I'm here."

That's not true. My real hope is that my brief return to Myerton will be quiet and uneventful. I am only at Saint Clare's because Archbishop Knowland ordered me here to fill in for Father Anthony. I have no more desire to stay than I had when I left everything behind fifteen years ago.

I give the final blessing, the final hymn starts, and I proceed down the aisle with the altar servers, led by a pair of very serious young men who look so much alike they must be brothers. Back in the vestibule, I thank everyone, introducing myself to Vincent Trent and his younger brother, Dominic.

Vincent shakes my hand firmly and informs me, "Father Greer, this is my last Sunday here before I leave for college, but Dominic is well trained and completely up to taking my place as head altar server."

I say casually to Dominic, "Is altar service a family apostolate for you?"

He surprises by answering me with complete seriousness, "It was at first. When Vincent started out, he and I were about the only little boys in the church. It's only been in the last ten years or so that the Lord has blessed us with so many young families. Father Anthony brought to the parish a wonderful combination of orthodoxy and family support."

With this piece of information ringing in my ears, I go outside.

***

The day is one of those sunny, clear days in mid-September that have the last taste of summer and the first taste of fall. It is warm, but with a cool breeze that makes being outside in full Mass vestments tolerable.

I place my hand against one of the six white marble columns that line the portico. Saint Clare's is an imposing structure, said to be one of the largest churches west of Baltimore. The white Ionic building was constructed in the 1850s to replace the earlier brick parish that had burned. Funded by the small donations of Irish immigrants who had made their way into the Allegheny Mountains to work on the railroad, as well as the larger ones of the Myer family who employed them, the church has seen untold numbers of baptisms, as well as weddings and funerals.

Joan and I stood under its soaring vaulted ceiling the day we married. She wore white, looking impossibly beautiful, her veil covering her chestnut brown hair and her lace-covered shoulders. Father Anthony, whose place I am taking, officiated that day, and then said her funeral mass just a few years later.

People begin coming out. Children run past, chased by frazzled moms hastily saying, "Thank you, Father," as they hurry by. I shake hands, saying, "Thank you very much," to people who say, "We're glad you're here" and "Good homily, Father." I am surprised at the number of people who pass by whom I have no memory of. Then, a large man about my age stops. With him are two twin teenage boys. Leaning on a cane, he extends a beefy hand. I laugh, grasp his hand, and give him a hug.

"John Archman," I say, "how are you?"

"Good to see you, Tom," says this big bear of a man. "Or maybe I should say Father Tom?"

"Tom's fine. I didn't know you were still living in Myerton?"

John nods. "Chloe wanted to raise the kids here; it's near her parents. And I like it, too."

"So, what are you doing now?"

"Consulting," Archman says. "The new Tech Center outside of town."

"Bit far from D.C. for consulting, isn't it?"

"Internet, teleconferences, you'd be surprised how little face-to-face time is required in IT consulting." John turns to his boys. "John, Mark, say hello to your godfather." The twins say hello, then ask their dad if they can hang out with their friends until it's time to leave.

"Don't make me come look for you," John says as they run off. When he turns back to me, he grimaces.

"You OK?" I ask.

"Yeah," he replies. "My leg still gets to me sometimes. I'll have to get back into physical therapy."

Soon after 9/11, John enlisted in the army. He served two tours in Iraq. During his second tour, an IED exploded as his squad was on patrol. He was the only survivor and was himself severely wounded.

"So," he says, looking me up and down. "You're a priest now. I've gotta tell you, I didn't see that one coming."

"You're not the first one to say that to me. Is it that remarkable?"

"No, not remarkable, it's just—I remember what you and Joan were like together. You were inseparable. I envied you two that. Chloe and I—I've never seen two people in love as much as you two were—I know how devastated you were after her—" John pauses. "Joan was special," he whispers.

"Yes, she was," I say quietly.

"Then you left and didn't tell anyone where you were going. No one heard from you for a while. Then when Anna told us—none of us could believe it. " He pauses. "So how did it happen?"

It is a question I hear frequently, especially when people learn how old I was when I was ordained. Granted, most priests don't discern their vocations when they are in their late 20s. Even fewer receive the vocation after they are married. But my situation was different. So, I keep getting the question, one I am getting kind of tired of being asked.

"It's kind of a long story," I reply. "I don't want to get into it right now."

He holds up his hands "OK, OK. No problem. But you say you weren't in a parish before here? What have you been doing?"

"I've been the archivist for the Archdiocese since my ordination, so I've been at the main office for eight years."

"Well," he says smiling. "It is good to see you. Chloe will be sorry she missed you. Home with a sick kid. Hey, we'll have to have you over for dinner. Catch up."

I hesitate. "Maybe when I get the time. But give Chloe my best."

John's smile fades. "Sure, sure Tom. When you get the time. I'll tell Chloe you send your best." I watch as John, leaning on his cane, goes off to find his boys.

"So you've seen John," Anna says, having come up behind me. I turn.

"He's missed you," she says. "You were his best friend."

"And he was mine."

"He could have used a friend like you over the last few years."

I look at her, puzzled. "He hasn't had an easy time since you left," she explains.

"He seems fine to me, except for the cane."

"Looks are deceiving. He's struggling. Chloe tells me these last few years have been hard."

I remember how John was after he came home. The physical wounds were slow to heal. The emotional wounds festered. Joan and I were as supportive as we could be, but after a while, John just withdrew.

I look at her. I don't know how to answer.

"Anyway," she smiled. "Good job. Everyone seemed really pleased."

"Except Glenda."

"Oh," she waves her hand, "don't worry about Glenda. She's had the run of this place for years. It's about time someone stood up to her."

"I didn't want to cause a scene."

"You didn't. You did what Father Anthony should have done a long time ago. But Father Anthony isn't inclined to confront her. And Glenda is—"

"Yes, she certainly is."

The day I arrived, Glenda Whitemill made it very clear what she thought of me.

"I don't know why the Archbishop sent you," she had said. "Father Anthony's coming back. He doesn't need to be replaced."

"I'm not replacing Father Anthony," I said. "I'm just here for four months while he . . . rests."

"We can get along just fine having a priest show up for mass," she went on like I hadn't said anything. "When I spoke to the Archbishop—"

"You called the Archbishop?"

"—I told him we didn't need a resident priest. I asked him just to send one around for mass on Saturday nights and Sundays. He gave me some hogwash about a parish needing to have a resident priest. I told him exactly what I thought."

She went on like that, all the while showing me through the rectory, a two-story house sitting next door to the church. A walk from the front door led to what I assumed was the side door of the church. Another path led to the sidewalk. The first floor had a living room, dining room, kitchen, guest bedroom and what would be my office and Glenda's office. Upstairs were two bedrooms—Father Anthony's and another guest room, where I would be staying. The furnishings looked like rejects from Mike and Carol Brady's home, frankly hideous in shades of brown, yellow, and that tried and true staple of the 1970's color scheme, avocado.

There was a worn and threadbare quality to the whole place, much like Whitemill herself.

I realize I have not seen Glenda coming out of the church. Not knowing where she is makes me nervous. I look around in the crowd and finally spot her. She is standing on the corner, speaking to a man about my age. He is also about my height but wears a pullover hoodie and jeans that hang loosely about his frame, showing he is quite a bit skinnier than I am.

"Who is that?" I ask Anna.

She turns. "Who?"

"That guy over there talking to Glenda." They are too far away to hear, but she is shaking her right finger in his face, and he is shaking his head emphatically.

"Hmm," Anna says. "I'm not sure. I know Glenda has a nephew, and that could be him, but I can't say for sure. Not sure I've ever seen him."

The man storms away from Glenda, who just stands there looking after him.

"He's not a member of the parish?"

"I don't know—he could be. Maybe he just comes to the earlier Mass or only shows up at Christmas and Easter, I really can't say. I don't know everybody, Tom."

Glenda turns. She looks upset. Looking around to make sure no one had observed the scene, she walks quickly down the sidewalk to the Rectory.

The crowd has thinned out so there are only a couple of small groups talking to each other, their children running up and down the steps. Some have started an impromptu game of tag on the grass between the church and the parking lot. Two brown-haired twins start wrestling for reasons only known to them. A young woman, trailed by a little girl with brownish-blond hair, rushes to the two boys and pulls them apart. They're soon joined by a large, muscular man who takes both boys by the arm and leads them away, either for a firm talking-to or for a more painful exhortation.

"Why don't you come over for lunch?" Anna says. "Nothing fancy, just sandwiches."

I hesitate. "Anna, I'm kinda tired—"

"I'm going to see her this afternoon," Anna goes on. She pauses to let that settle in.

"It's been a long day," I say. "I'm really drained. Maybe another day."

She looks at me, but says nothing. I see the accusatory look in her eyes and brace myself. Then, she smiles.

"It's OK, Tom," she pats me on the arm. "Some other time." She begins to walk away, then turns and says, "I'm sure she likes them."

"Likes what?"

"The carnations," Anna says. I shake my head. "The peppermint carnations?"

Peppermint carnations. Joan's favorite flower.

"What about peppermint carnations?" I say, thoroughly confused.

"You really don't know what I'm talking about?" Anna asks. "You haven't been sending peppermint carnations to her gravesite once a month?"

"No, it wasn't me," I say. "Sorry."

Anna sighs. "Oh. I just assumed. Guess it's one of her friends." She begins to walk away.

"For how long?" I say after her.

"It's been a long time. Almost fifteen years," she says over her shoulder. "I thought it was you. Guess I was wrong."

With that Anna walks away. I walk back into the church. In the sacristy, I take off my vestments and turn the lights off.

I look around. The only light comes through the stained glass windows and from the candles. Incense still hangs in the air; I can also smell the oil on my hands from anointing the Reynolds baby.

The building is at peace.

I am not.

Two

Monday is a parish priest's traditional day off. Since arriving at Saint Clare's I have not had the time to learn about the parish, so I decide to spend it in my office. There are files on the desk, put there by Glenda, I assume, that I need to go through. After my first cup of coffee and Morning Prayer, I sit down at the desk and begin to familiarize myself with my temporary assignment. I know I will have a couple of hours of silence because Glenda is out.

After thirty minutes, my eyes begin to glaze over. I've never had much of a head for numbers, and trying to make sense of Saint Clare's financial statements is taxing my limited powers to the utmost. I can't tell if the parish is running a deficit, has a surplus, or is breaking even. From what I know of other parishes around the Archdiocese, the truth is probably somewhere in the middle.

I plow ahead with another folder labeled "Baptisms and Confirmations." While Saint Clare's does not have a lot of money, it is rich with people. Since January, ten babies have been baptized into the Church; also, four adults entered the Church the previous Easter and five more are preparing to join the next. The folder on religious education also shows healthy numbers.

Whatever is going on at Saint Clare's, it is good.

The doorbell rings. I don't get up at first, because I think Glenda will get it. By the third ring, more insistent this time, I remember she is still out. I open the door to find the man I saw Glenda talking with the previous day.

He seems surprised to see me. "Good morning," I say.

He doesn't speak at first. He looks like he is in a daze. I can't tell if he is high or just confused. I try again. "Can I help you?"

"Huh?—Oh, yeah, sorry, Father," he finally says. "Is, ah, is—is Glenda here?"

"No, she's out right now. She should be back soon. Would you like to come in?" I open the door wider to make it more inviting.

"No, no, no, that's—that's OK, Father. I'll, ah, I'll just call her later—"

"—Is there something I can help you with?"

"You?" He seems shocked by the question.

"It's kind of what I'm supposed to do, help people. Comes with the collar." I smile, hoping the joke will put him at ease.

It doesn't work. "No, no, I'll just get Glenda later. Sorry to bother you." He turns and walks off, looking back over his shoulder at me.

"What's your name so I can tell her you stopped by?" I call after him. He doesn't answer me so I just stand looking after him before going back to my desk and picking up where I left off.

I have only been back at work for about a half hour or so when the doorbell rings again.

"Some day off," I mutter as I go answer the door.

This time, there is a woman at the door, one I recognize.

"Hello, Chloe," I smile.

Chloe Archman smiles the smile of a person who has the choice of either laughter or tears, and chooses laughter only because it isn't as socially awkward.

"Hi Tom—Father Tom," she said.

"Tom's fine, Chloe. Please, come in." We hug, and I show her into the living room. She sits on the edge of the couch, hands folded in her lap. I sit opposite her in an ugly seventies-brown armchair. A spring pokes me in the back.

"Sorry I missed you at Mass," I say. "John told me one of the kids is sick. Are they better?"

"Oh, yes, she's doing much better. A twenty-four hour thing. The kids are at home. We homeschool but someone comes in to watch them a couple of mornings a week. I teach one class per semester at the college."

"So you're back teaching? English lit, isn't it?"

"Yes." She pauses. "So, how have you been?"

"Fine, fine."

"Good, good."

There are a few moments of silence while we just look at each other.

"Can I get you something to drink? Water, coffee?"

"No, I'm fine." She sighs. "Sorry, this is harder than I thought it would be."

"What is?"

"Coming here. Seeing you—my best friend's husband—for the first time in fifteen years. You know, I thought about what I'd say when I finally saw you—oh, I had some choice words in mind for you. Leaving without saying good-bye. Not coming back even one time. Not a card, not an email, not so much as a text. The only thing we ever heard was from Anna—we couldn't believe it when she told us you'd been ordained to the priesthood—so at least we knew you weren't dead. I am so, so angry, with so many things to say. But I can't say any of it now because you—" she gestures with both arms "—are now a priest. Worse, you're my priest. So, is it a grave sin to be angry at a priest?"

"No graver than being angry at anyone else," I answer.

"Oh, OK, well—I'm angry at you, Tom. Really, really angry. You left Anna, you left John, you left me. You were the only connection I still had to my best friend. I was devastated when she was murdered. I was devastated when you left. But you know what, not nearly as devastated as John."

"John?"

I can see tears beginning to form in her eyes.

"Oh, Tom!" She cries, and buries her face in her hands. I grab a nearby box of tissues and hand it to her. She takes out a couple and wipes her eyes.

"Anna told me he's had some problems."

"Not just some problems, Tom. Oh, you don't know, but then how could you—you weren't here."

"Well, I'm here now. Tell me what's going on."

She exhales. "After he came home from the hospital, he seemed to be doing well—I guess as well as could be expected. He was still in pain, but the physical therapy was helping and he was working hard at it. He got stronger, he was seeing a therapist to help him process what happened, he was becoming the John I knew again. Well, you remember how he was."

"I remember. After a while, he seemed like the old John."

"He was doing so well," Chloe says. "Then, he began to change. He became withdrawn, spending more and more time by himself. He didn't want to see anyone or do anything. He spent all his free time either locked in his office or taking long walks by himself." She pauses and wipes her eyes as the tears return.

"Oh, and by the way, you and Joan were not much help," she continues, rage now strengthening her. "It seemed like every time we wanted to do something, Joan was too busy with her new business."

What she says is true. Joan was busy back then, trying to get a new design business off the ground. But I also remember a few times when I tried to get John out for a boys night, only to have him turn me down. There were also plenty of times they cancelled plans with us. In the months before Joan's murder, we spent very little time with the Archmans.

I am wrestling with these thoughts while Chloe continues, now in the voice of spent, rather than active, rage. "Not long after Joan's death, his leg began bothering him—he reinjured it somehow, he thinks when he tripped on the back stairs while taking the trash out."

"That's why he uses the cane," I say.

Chloe nods. "But before that," she goes on, "his mood changed. His depression got worse and he began having nightmares. He started drinking. When he reinjured his leg, he couldn't get around without the cane. He's been in pain ever since. He won't do physical therapy anymore—says it's voodoo, doesn't work. I don't know when he decided that—just takes painkillers and drinks." A tear snakes its way down her cheek. "But I can handle the physical pain. That doesn't worry me as much as the other."

"What other?"

"The moods. The depression," she said. "He'll be happy one minute, then screaming with fury the next."

That doesn't sound like the John I knew. "Has he ever hurt you or the kids?"

"Oh no, no, he's never laid a hand on us. He has the presence of mind to go scream in the garage when he's really angry. I think he knows I'd leave if he ever did anything like that."

"He needs to get help, Chloe," I say, "before he hurts someone."

"I'm more concerned about him hurting himself. When he's really down, he begins to talk about how he's responsible. That it's his fault people died. He says he's a coward, how he should have done something to help instead of hiding, about how he betrayed them, about how the wrong people always die."

"But that makes no sense," I say. "He received a commendation. There's no way any of that in Iraq was his fault."

"I know. But he's been carrying a big load of guilt for a long time."

Guilt. I cringe at the very word. It seems like most of my life has been shaped by things I could have or should have done. But Chloe doesn't know that, can never know that, and anyway, this isn't about me, it's about her.

"Is he seeing anyone?" I ask, trying to apply what we're taught in seminary about dealing with parishioners suffering from depression.

"No, not anymore," she said. "He did for a while, saw both a therapist and a psychiatrist, right after he came home. It was helping." She shrugged. "Then he stopped."

"Why'd he do that?"

"Well, he told me he doesn't need to go anymore, but I don't know the real reason." She sits back and sighs. "I'm about at the end of my rope and am hoping you can talk to him."

"I'll try," I say. "But I don't know what I can do."

"You were—are—his friend. He used to listen to you. I've run out of ideas. Besides, you're a priest."

"That's true, but still, he'll have to want to talk to me, he'll have to want help. Do you think he does?"

She thinks for a moment, then, "I don't know. I really don't know."

I sigh. "OK, Chloe. I'll try talking to him. In the meantime, I'll keep you and your family in my prayers."

She smiled, a real smile this time. "Thank you, Tom. Thank you so much."

After she leaves, I settle back into my study with another folder, this time on the Knights of Columbus, when I hear the front door open. What sounds like two people come in.

"There's no reason to bother the Father about this," Glenda says.

"I just want to ask him if he would mind if we had one this year," a young woman replies.

"Father Anthony has said no each year for the past five years," Glenda continues. "It would be just too disruptive."

"Well Father Anthony's not here, and it will not be disruptive. We're just talking about a small, simple production—"

"You will not talk to Father about this because—"

By this time, I am standing in the doorway. The young woman with Glenda is one I recognize from the 10:30 a.m. Mass sitting with her husband and three children, a girl and twin boys.

"Glenda," I interrupted. They look at me.

"Oh, Father," Glenda says. "I was just telling Miriam that—"

"Thank you, Glenda, but why don't you let Miriam talk? Miriam, you have something you want to ask me?"

"Well—yes, yes, Father Tom," Miriam says. "I want to ask—well, some of the other moms in the parish think—you see, Christmas is in a few months—"

"Yes, that seems to happen every year," I say. Smiling, I add, "What would you like?"

Miriam takes a deep breath. "We are wondering if you would allow us to organize some of the children to do a Nativity pageant."

"You mean with the children playing the various parts? Mary, Joseph, shepherds, kings? A few toddlers dressed as sheep?"

Glenda interjects. "I told her it would be impossible, Father."

"Really, and why is that, Glenda?" I ask.

She seems stunned that I would question her statement. "Well . . . well—it just would be. The Advent and Christmas season is already so busy, and the children would disrupt everything."

"Now Glenda, if Saint Clare's could survive being used as a hospital during the Civil War, I think it can survive a small Nativity play." I turn to Miriam. "Sounds like a fine idea, Miriam—what is your last name?"

"Conway. Miriam Conway. Thank you, Father, thank you so much. Now we thought maybe Saturday, a week before Christmas?"

"Actually I have an idea. Isn't there a Christmas Eve Vigil Mass, Glenda?"

"Yes, at 5:00 p.m."

"Good. Why don't you do it at the Vigil Mass?"

Miriam smiles. "Really?"

"At the Vigil Mass?" Glenda is not smiling.

"Yes. I would think that Mass would have a lot of children attending, with parents wanting them to get to bed early. It would be fun for them. We'd do it instead of the homily. What do you think, Miriam, do you think everyone would go for that?"

"Absolutely! Thank you, thank you, Father. This means a whole lot to us—more than you can know."

Miriam shakes my hand, looks at Glenda, and leaves. After she is gone, Glenda turns to me.

"Father Anthony—"

"Is not here, Glenda. Let me ask you, just between you and me, did he ever actually tell the ladies he didn't want a Nativity play?"

Glenda hesitates. "Well, well, not exactly—"

"I thought so." I pause. "Glenda, I understand that you spent a lot of time acting as Father Anthony's gatekeeper. I'm sure he appreciated it. But you don't need to do that with me."

"You cannot spend your time talking to every parishioner who wants your attention."

"I know, but I can speak to most of them," I say. "From now on, I'm available for anyone who wants to talk to me during office hours."

"Father Anthony didn't keep office hours. People had to make an appointment."

"Well, they can still make an appointment, but if they stop by and I'm here and I'm not in the middle of something critical, I'll be available to them. Understand?"

Glenda stiffens. "Yes, Father. If you'll excuse me, I have to put the groceries away and start dinner. You're having chicken tonight." She grabs her bags and storms out.

"Oh, Glenda," I call. She stops in the doorway and turns slightly. "Someone stopped by to see you."

"Who?"

"I don't know his name. I saw you talking to him yesterday after church. Anna thought it was your nephew."

The blood rushes from her face. "He . . . my . . . he stopped by the Rectory while you were here?"

I furrow my brow. "Yes, it was while you were out. Is everything OK, Glenda?"

"What—yes," she said, squaring her shoulders. "Oh yes, Father, everything is fine. I'll call him after I finish lunch. I'm sorry he bothered you."

"It was no bother, Glenda. Does your nephew live with you?"

"Yes, yes. Roger, he's my sister's son," she says quickly. "He's staying with me while he works a construction job at the college. I'll call him in a bit."

She has just cleared the doorway when the phone rings. I look at the clock. It's just 11 a.m. I have to be in the church by 11:30 a.m. to get ready for the Noon Mass.

"Lot more lively place than I thought it would be," I mumble to myself. I pick up the phone.

"Hello, Saint Clare's Rectory."

"May I speak to Father Tom Greer, please?"

"Speaking."

"Oh, Father Greer, good. My name is Nate Rodriguez. I'm a freelance documentary filmmaker."

"What can I do for you?"

"I'm hoping I can interview you for my next film project."

"Me? Why would you want to interview me?"

"Well, you see, my project concerns the unsolved murder of Joan Greer."

Three

"I know this was short notice, but I really appreciate you agreeing to talk to me," Nate Rodriguez says.

"Let me be clear, Mr. Rodriguez—"

"Nate, please call me Nate."

"OK, let me be clear, Nate," I say. "I have not agreed to anything. I only said I would meet with you."

Only two hours after he called the Rectory, I find myself sitting across from this very earnest young man with auburn hair at The Perfect Cup, a little coffee shop across Main Street from Myer College. The stone archway people consider the main entrance to the campus is just opposite where I sit.

Dominating the scene is the statue of Winthrop Myer, founder of Myerton and the College. Myer had arrived in the western Maryland mountains having gained and lost his first fortune in Baltimore. On the frontier, he built another on lumber and the railroad. He dreamed of the mountain town rivaling Baltimore or Pittsburgh in size and wealth, with Myer College becoming the Johns Hopkins of the Alleghenies.

I look at the young boys and girls, books in hand, backpacks on their backs, walking to class or back to their apartments. It was at a spot very much like it, but at another college campus a couple of hours east of where I sit, where I met the first woman I ever loved.

***

I was finishing my sophomore year at the University of Maryland. One day in early March, I was walking along, not paying attention to where I was going—I was reading something, don't remember what—when I walked into a young woman, knocking her down and sending a large stack of books flying out of her hands. Worse than that, there was a three-ring binder in the stack, and it broke open on impact, allowing the pages inside to blow in every direction.

"What the hell is wrong with you?" she yelled, "Are you blind or stupid or both?"

"I'm sorry," I said, before deciding to try to get back the moral high ground. "It's just that I haven't seen too well since that tear gas went off near me."

She froze at this and said, "Wait, what?"

"Yeah," I continued, warming to my story. "I was protesting poverty in Baltimore, and some fascist counter-protesters attacked us. The police had no choice, I understand that now. But still . . ."

I started staring over her shoulder blankly, even as I reached my hands out toward her. She quickly grabbed them, grasping one of my fingers particularly hard. She began to bend it back when I said, "Wait, it's a miracle. I can see."

She let go, laughing in spite of herself. "I'll help you get them back," I said sheepishly.

"Damn right you will," she replied as she began chasing after her notes. I follow after her, grabbing notes of various types cartwheeling across the lawn, all the while keeping my eye on this woman.

Unlike most of the female students and faculty on campus, she didn't wear jeans; instead, she wore a long straight denim skirt that coyly accented her delightfully round figure. That day she had paired it with a red turtleneck. Her black curly hair was pinned up and a few stray curls framed her soft face.

But it was her eyes that caught my attention.

They were like no eyes I'd ever seen before, blue sapphires floating in shining bowls of white.

We managed to get the papers gathered up. As I handed her my stack, I said lamely, "I hope they're OK."

She didn't take any time to look at them but instead just shoved them into the space between the binder's covers. "I sure they are," she said over her shoulder as she began to rush off.

I just stood there on the sidewalk, students passing us on their way to or from classes, looking after her. Then, I called out, "Are you hungry?"

She turned. "No, but I am late," she yelled back, then hurried on to wherever she was going before we collided.

That was the last I heard of her until the following fall, when I found myself comfortably seated in a class that had just started when she rushed in. If anything, she was ever more beautiful than she had been in the spring. The next class, I got to the room early, took a seat near the door, and placed my backpack in the seat beside me. When she arrived, late again, I was ready.

The rest was—or more precisely, should have been—history.

It took me two weeks to work up my courage, but I finally asked her to lunch.

We wound up at Marlowe's, a restaurant in a small Victorian house not far from campus. She had the Cobb salad. I had the tomato bisque and four-cheese grilled cheese.

We were engaged six months later, and parted ways a couple of years after that. I never saw her again.

They say you never forget your first love, and for all that I loved my wife dearly and would give anything to have her back, no, you don't forget.

***

"I'll be glad for any help you can give," Nate says, bringing me back to the present.

"Let's just slow down a bit," I reply.

"Sure, sure, OK."

I stir my coffee. "So, you make documentaries?"

"Yes, that's right."

"Anything I might have heard of?"

He shakes his head. "No, no, nothing—well, actually, I've only done a few small projects for my classes at Myer, so this is the first big project I've worked on."

"I see," I reply. "You went to Myer?"

"Uh-huh, graduated two, three years ago. Got my degree in journalism."

"Are you working for the Myerton Gazette?"

"Ah, well, not exactly." He takes a drink of coffee. "I actually work here."

"Here," I repeat. "At The Perfect Cup. As a—?"

He shrugs. "Whatever my uncle tells me to do—wait tables, bus tables, barista. Listen, Father, can we get on with this? I only get thirty minutes for lunch."

I wonder even more what I am doing there. "Let me see if I understand correctly," I say. "Your project is to investigate—"

"OK, well, investigate is probably too strong a word. I'm not really investigating your wife's murder—can I call her your wife, I mean, with you being a priest?"

In spite of myself, I hesitate. It's been so very long now since she was my wife. I've been without her longer than I was with her but, yes, she is still my wife. She just lives somewhere else, with Someone who will not fail her like I did.

"Obviously I was not a priest when I was married to Joan," I say. "You can call her my wife."

"OK, OK, well, your wife. So the project isn't to try and find who killed her—though I gotta tell you Father, that would just be so cool." He stops himself when he sees the expression on my face. "I'm sorry, I don't mean cool-cool, just, you know, finding justice after all this time—"

I hold up my hand. "So what exactly is your project?"

He takes a deep breath. "I was looking for a project for my next film and was doing research in the files of the Myerton Gazette when I came across stories about the murder. You know, Myerton is a pretty small town. Murders don't happen every day. The way it happened, no one was caught—it got a lot of attention."

I nod. He is right. At the time, Joan had been the first person murdered in Myerton in almost a year. The paper covered it extensively and reporters from as far away as Baltimore came to do stories for a few days afterwards.

"So it got me thinking," Nate continues, "about what happens after the news cameras leave and the paper stops writing articles. What about the people left behind? How do they cope? How did it change them? I mean, in your case—"

"Yes, yes, I see what you're getting at."

"So I've already done several interviews, researched the case, looked at the police file—"

"You got a copy of the police file?"

"Oh yeah, you can get almost anything through a Freedom of Information request. There's some portions blacked out, but it's been helpful. So I have that."

"Who have you interviewed?"

He pulls out a notebook. "Let's see, some people who knew her from college, her mother—"

"You interviewed Anna?" I wonder why she hasn't given me a heads up about this guy.

"Yeah, Mrs. Luckgold was great—very helpful. Gave me some great pictures and videos to use." He looks through his notes. "The owner of the gallery up the street, The Painted Lotus, did an interview."

"Bethany Grable's still in town?" She was a friend and colleague of Joan's from Myer's Fine Arts Department.

"Yeah, she gave me all sorts of insights about who she was."

One name is conspicuously absent. "Did you interview Chloe Archman?"

Nate sighs. "No. She refused to talk to me."

"Really? Did she say why?"

"No," he shakes his head. "She just said she doesn't want to talk to anyone about Joan Greer."

I find that very odd. They were best friends, after all. Practically inseparable. Chloe was Joan's matron of honor at our wedding, like John was my best man. If Anna would agree to participate, why wouldn't Chloe?

And if Chloe didn't, why should I?

I take a sip of my coffee. I've let it get cold.

Putting my mug down, I say. "Nate, I wish I could help you, but—"

"Oh please," he says, looking at me anxiously. "Don't say 'but.' Look, I've done a lot of work. It's good, I mean I think it's good, but there's a big hole in it. That's why I was so glad when Mrs. Luckgold called and told me you were back in town."

"Anna told you I was back in town?"

"Yes, and I am so glad. I have tried to track you down, but after you left Myerton, you kind of disappeared for a while."

"Yes, I wanted it that way."

"So then you came back here, and I thought, wow, just in time, he's exactly what I need to really finish this. The victim's husband. The man whose arms she died in."

The night is a blur. Joan lying in my arms, gasping. The blood. Cold steel against my forehead. A painful throbbing in my temples. And the sound.

Click. Click. Click.

"I really, really need you for this, Father Tom," Nate concludes.

I shake my head. "No. That night is not something I want to talk about. If you have the police report, you have my statement. I can't help you." I get up to leave.

Nate stands. "Father, please, just think about it. You know, there's one thing I keep coming across. Everyone I've talked to says how much they need closure, how her murder not being solved never gave them any. What if this film, well, maybe jogs someone's memory? Maybe it could give the cops a lead? Who knows, maybe this film could help finally solve your wife's murder?"

I look at the young man. "No," I say quietly. "I gave up that hope years ago. Her murder will never be solved and her murderer will never see justice in this life."

"Are you so certain of that?"

"Yes, I am," I say. "I have to get back to Saint Clare's now. Good luck with your project."

"Father," he says as he stands up. "Just think about it. If you change your mind, please call me."

I look at him and nod.

"OK, if I change my mind. But I'm not going to."

***

Walking back to the parish, I call Anna.

When she answers, I say, "I just spoke to Nate Rodriguez."

"Oh, he got in touch with you?"

"Yes. Why didn't you tell me about him? Why didn't you tell me he interviewed you?"

"Because if I had, you probably wouldn't have spoken to him."

"I would have appreciated a heads up."

"I'm sure you would have."

"So why didn't you give me one?"

"Because you wouldn't have talked to him."

I'm not sure what Anna is trying to do with this circular argument so I decide to go forward.

"Well, it doesn't matter. I heard him out, but I'm not going to talk to him."

Anna doesn't say anything.

"I don't want to talk about Joan's murder. Not with him, not with anyone. It's not like it would do any good."

"What do you mean?"

"Anna, it's not going to bring her back, it's not going to help find her killer—her killer is never going to be found. It was just a senseless, random crime. The guy tried to rape her, I got there before it got too far, there was a struggle, the gun went off, Joan was shot, then she died. That's it."

"There's no need to shout, Tom."

I stop. I have forgotten where I am. I don't realize I've been yelling into the phone. I look around, but no one seems to have taken notice. Surprising, considering you don't see a priest yelling into a cell phone every day.

"I never knew there was a struggle," Anna says.

"Huh?"

"You said there was a struggle. I never knew that."

"Yeah, yeah," I say. "There was a struggle. I thought I told you that."

"You've never told me anything about that night."

"Oh, I'm sure I have."

"No, not a word. The police told me Joan was killed. They didn't say anything about a struggle. And I always thought you two were together when she was attacked."

I hesitate before answering, and when I do, I don't answer her question. "Everything happened so fast, I was in shock—listen, I don't really want to talk about this right now."

"OK, OK," Anna says. I hear resignation in her voice. "By the way," she says, "Bethany Grable called me today. She heard you were back."

"Nate said he interviewed her about Joan."

"Really? I didn't know that. Anyway, she still has Joan's things."

"What things?"

"You know, her art stuff. Joan had a studio there, remember?"

How can I remember something I didn't know about? If Joan had a studio at Bethany's, this is the first I'm hearing about it.

Instead of saying this, I say, "Why didn't she give it to you in all these years?"

"She tried. I told her you'd be back."

"For fifteen years?"

"I can be very persuasive. Besides, she loved Joan."

"I'll give her a call. Thanks."

"How about coming to dinner on Wednesday?"

I hesitate.

"I thought I'd invite Chloe and John," Anna prompts.

"I don't think so, Anna," I say. "Not right now. I'm still trying to get settled in. Can I have a raincheck?"

"Of course," Anna says with evident disappointment. "Any time. Maybe Sunday afternoon. Can't imagine you feel like cooking after two Masses."

"By the way," I say, wanting to change the subject, "did you know Nate Rodriguez tried to interview Chloe and John?"

"Of course. I put Nate in touch with them."

"Why didn't they do it?"

I hear Anna sigh. "I don't know. Joan told me before she was killed that things were strained between them. She never told me why. Chloe won't talk much about her. As for why John won't talk, you'd have to ask him." She pauses. "Please think about it, Tom. Doing the interview."

"Anna, why are you doing this?"

Slowly, she replies, "Because Joan deserves not to be forgotten."

I'm not sure what she means by that, if she means it as a criticism or just a general observation, that other people should remember she was murdered and no one brought to justice. I don't believe she thinks I have forgotten Joan. I haven't forgotten about her. How could I? I have just decided to forget about her murder. I don't see why that has to be remembered, especially since remembering it is not going to bring her back or bring her killer to justice. Nate and Anna can cling to the belief that someone might have their memory jogged, that someone out there might remember the One Clue that would lead to her killer.

I can't do that.

I won't do that.

All I want is peace.

Four

Thursday afternoon, I am sitting at one of the outside tables at The Perfect Cup, finishing up my coffee and one of their famous chocolate doughnuts, when I hear my name. I turn just in time to be embraced by a flood of fabric.

"I thought that was you," the flood says. Engulfed in a paisley hug, I catch a familiar whiff of incense. I know who it is.

"Hello, Bethany," I say as I return the hug.

After a moment, she breaks the hug and kisses me on both cheeks. Bethany Grable has always been physically demonstrative, a heady combination of earth-mother and shrewd businesswoman. She is artistic, but not artsy. She takes her art very seriously and makes sure she is well paid for it. She is probably very comfortable, but her outfit looks like it has been thrown together with thrift store and fabric shop rejects. Bethany is one of those rare souls who is both older and younger than she appears. When she was in her fifties, when I first met her, she looked to be in her sixties. Now that she is in her sixties, she has all the appearance of a woman in her forties.

"I have been meaning to come see you," she says, tugging on the canvas tote bag slung over her shoulder.

"Anna told me you called about Joan's studio."

"Yes, but not just that," she says as she calls Nate over to the table. "Nate, dear, bring me a chai tea, please." Nate scurries off and Bethany settles back, looking me over.

"I can't believe it's been fifteen years," she says. "A lot's changed."

I nod. "You look the same."

She laughs. "Oh, Tom, you always were a charmer. I'm doing OK, a little older, a little fatter, a little more arthritis, but I'm good. And you're a priest."

"That I am."

She folds her arms. "How exactly did that happen?"

"It's, ah, complicated."

"I bet it is. I'd like to hear the story some day."

"Someday I'll tell you." Nate brings her tea. "So how's the gallery?"

"Oh, the gallery, really good. I had a show last week for a couple of new local artists, made some good sales, made a good commission on each. My own art sells now and then, but these days I'm content to make money off of people who're younger and more talented." She sighs. "Like Joan. She had so much talent. It's just a shame."

"I know she enjoyed painting. She didn't do too much of it after we married, just the occasional canvas. Joan was too focused on teaching and trying to get her business off the ground."

She looks surprised. "You didn't know, did you?"

"Know what?"

"She kept painting," Bethany says. "That's why she had the studio."

"I thought it was for her design business?"

"Well," Bethany says, "She did do some of that. But mostly she worked on her own art."

I nod. That explains a lot.

"And you've kept all her things?"

"Oh, yes. I've had to rent out the space, but I kept everything she had. I meant to contact you about it, ask you what you wanted to do with it, but by the time I was going to get around to it, you had gone. I mentioned it to Anna, but she put me off, saying you'd be back." She sips her tea. "Just as well. I don't think she likes me very much."

This is true. While she was consistently very civil and polite to her, I always got the impression when I saw Anna interacting with Bethany—which was very rare—that Anna was jealous of Bethany's friendship with Joan. I thought Anna saw the flamboyant artist as a rival for her daughter's affections, something I couldn't understand, given how close Joan and Anna were.

"Would you like to see her things? I'm not busy now. I was just headed to the thrift store to see if I could find something interesting when I spotted you."

I hesitate. Memories of Joan are not something I want. Not today.

"Unless you're too busy this afternoon," she says. "We could make it another day."

I have nothing the rest of the day, and to say otherwise would be a lie. After I tell her I'll meet her at her gallery, I walk back to the Rectory to get my car. The gallery is just up the street from The Perfect Cup but I figure I'll need the car to haul everything in. Also, it buys me a little time to think.

About ten minutes after we part, I pull into a parking space next to Bethany's car in the alley behind her gallery. She is standing at the back door, fumbling with her keys.

She finally gets the door open and I follow her in. "Joan's studio is up this way," Bethany says as I follow her up the narrow flight of stairs leading to the second floor. She leads me down a hallway, saying, "Be careful," as she lets me into one of the rooms. "He's into industrial; don't trip over something. It's either junk or his next piece."

I can see what she means. The brightly lit studio, with sun streaming through the windows, is dominated by a large object that resembles a wrecked automobile. Looking more closely, I can see that this is exactly what it is—a wrecked automobile. Only this one is covered with Barbie dolls painted red.

I look at Bethany. "He calls it 'American Carnage.'" She shrugs. "Someone will buy it, I guess."

Picking my way through the room, being careful to not trip over the numerous objects scattered on the floor, I follow Bethany to the back of the studio.

"I put her things in this storeroom," she says, unlocking the door. "I've kept everything safe."

She pulls open the door and reaches in to flick the light on. I peer inside. Shelves line one wall and the back of the room. I see it is mostly covered with paints and Joan's sketchbooks—she always seemed to have a sketchbook with her, though until this moment I never realized where they all were—with a few bankers boxes. I also see a small pink suitcase I recognize as her laptop.

"How long did she have the studio?"

Bethany thinks for a moment. "Hmm, she had just graduated from Myer with her bachelors and was starting her MFA. She asked me if she could rent the studio space. I asked her why, since students in the MFA program were given their own space at the college, but she said she wanted a private space to work. I didn't ask any questions, and I didn't charge her anything."

She had the space before we met. "Did anyone else know?"

"I doubt it," Bethany says. "She really wanted her privacy."

A bell rings. "That's someone downstairs," she says. "Take whatever you like and close the door behind you."

After she leaves, I walk further into the room, to the shelves. I peek inside the banker's boxes. At random I take one of the sketchbooks off the shelf and open it. Joan had dated it. She started it a month before her murder.

I flip through it rapidly. Some are pencil and charcoal, others pastel, all things that had caught her eye or potential studies for paintings. The book was only about half full.

I flip to the middle. Stuck in the center is a folded piece of paper, about five inches by eight inches, the kind traditionally used for letters.

I smile. I'd often leave Joan notes, little things saying "I love you" or "thinking of you." I open it, wondering what I had written her on what day.

But I hadn't written it.

My grip on the letter loosens and it floats to the floor. My knees buckle and I grab onto the shelves for support. There is a chair nearby and I collapse into it. I can hardly breathe. I pick the letter up off the floor and stare at it, reading it over and over.

It takes me a few minutes to catch my breath. I shake all over and look up at the other boxes. Jumping up, I grab one, tear the lid off, and begin rifling through the contents, pulling handfuls of papers out and flipping through them, looking for the same notepaper, looking for more letters. I take a second box, then a third, repeating the same process. I go through all the boxes in the same frantic manner. But I find no more letters. Joan was a pack-rat, usually unwilling to get rid of anything. The papers were a mix of old bills, receipts, student lists from her classes at Myer. But no more letters on cream-colored note paper.

I shake my head. It must have been a letter from a student of hers who had developed a crush on her.

In my haste, I drop a plain manila envelope, unsealed but clasped. I peek inside. I can see it is a marriage license. I smile and pull it out.

My smile quickly turns to a frown.

It isn't our marriage license. It has her name on it. But not mine.

I collapse back in the chair, a wave of nausea passing over me. There is a sink with a mirrored cabinet over it. I make it just in time.

I rinse the sink out and splash my face with cold water. Looking around for a towel, I open the cabinet.

There are three prescription medicine bottles. I pick one of the bottles up. The date is fifteen years old.

Joan's name is on it.

***

I get back to the Rectory about an hour later, slipping inside with a box and Joan's laptop, before carefully closing the door.

Glenda calls from the kitchen, "Is that you, Father?"

I stop dead in my tracks. "Yes, it's me."

"Just in time. I didn't know where you had gone. Your dinner will be ready in ten minutes."

"OK, thank you," I say, walking to the kitchen and peering inside. She is at the counter, working with her back to me. I have to admit, it smells good even though I'm not very hungry.

"You have some phone calls to return," she says. "The messages are on your desk."

I furrow my brow. "Calls don't go to voicemail?"

She turns to look at me. "Yes, they do. I check it and give you the messages. Or if I'm here and you're not, I answer the phone and take a message. Parish secretary. It's my job."

On this, I have to admit she's right. "Thank you," I say, "I'll return them after dinner."

I walk away before she can say anything else. I go to my room, put the box and laptop on my bed, and go back downstairs to the kitchen. Glenda is putting food on my plate as I walk over to the refrigerator and get a soda.

"Anything I can do to help?" I ask.

She turns and looks at me with her 'what is this strange life form' look. "No, I've got it," she says with a tinge of irritation. Then, "Thank you," she adds as an afterthought. She walks to me with the plate in one hand and a knife, fork, and napkin in the other.

"Since you're here," she says, handing them to me. I stand there as she washes and dries her hands. Glenda notices me still standing there. "Anything else?"

I shake my head. "No, no, this is fine. It looks and smells really good, thank you." It seems rude to tell her I'm not hungry.

"I will see you tomorrow, then. Good night, Father," she says as she walks past me out of the kitchen. When I hear the front door close, I put the silverware back in the drawer and the plate in the refrigerator. If she asks why I didn't eat anything, I'd come up with an excuse.

I go back up to my room and look at the box, then at the time. I need to say Evening Prayer. I pull out my phone and open my Breviary app. Usually, I'd go into the church. Tonight, I don't want to go anywhere. Instead, I pray with a confused and distracted heart.

I finish Evening Prayer and look at the time again. It's only 7:30 p.m., but it seems like midnight. I am drained from the last few hours so I change into my pajamas, move the box to the floor, and crawl into bed, lying for a moment looking at Joan's picture, in a small frame on my bedside table.

When we were married, I always made sure she was the first thing I saw in the morning and the last before I turned out the lights. After her murder, I framed this picture, because it showed her as I always wanted to remember her—the laughing eyes full of life, the flowing chestnut hair, the red lips whose feel I still remember. For fifteen years, I've told her I love her every night and every morning, just as I did when she was alive.

Tonight, I just turn the light out and roll over.

***

As tired as I am, I can't go to sleep. Instead, I keep thinking of Joan. And that night.

I have run the entire scene in my head hundreds—thousands—of times. Tonight is no different. I replay everything that happened again and again. I can't stop it, no matter how much I try. It is as if I am forcing myself to relive it over and over again to punish myself. The only way it stops is if I sleep.

Tonight, though, other thoughts run through my head.

Questions I have no answers to.

Questions I'm not sure I want the answers to.

I get up, turn on the light, and go through my bag, pulling out a bottle of sleeping pills filled six months ago, a 30-day dose. There are still 20 pills in the bottle. I open it and look at the pills. I put the lid back on and the bottle back in my bag.

Not tonight.

Instead, I decide to read, since reading usually relaxes me. I get my e-reader and pull up one of Chesterton's Father Brown mysteries.

Forty-five minutes later, I am no closer to sleep. I put the e-reader on the table and just lay in bed, staring at the ceiling. When I close my eyes, I think of the box, feeling it pull at me, call to me to open it, to look inside.

I don't want to, because I don't want to know anything else.

After another 30 minutes, I give in. I sit up and pick up the box, placing it on the bed beside me. Opening the lid, I pull out the pill bottles.

Lithium, Risperdal, Lexapro. To my knowledge, Joan hadn't been on any medications. I don't know what these were for. A quick internet search answers the question. They are all treatments for bipolar disorder and anxiety. I have no idea why Joan would have these.

I toss them back in the box and pull out the manila envelope, unclasping the flap and reaching inside to pull out the one piece of paper it contains: a marriage license.

From the date, Joan would have been sixteen. There's her name, Joan Luckgold. And a man's name. Randy Earl.

Who was Randy Earl?

I just sit on the edge of the bed, staring at the official piece of paper in my hand. Joan had been married before. She had never told me. It didn't come up in our premarital counseling sessions with Father Anthony. What did it mean? Why didn't she tell me? Was our marriage even valid? Or was everything—the wedding Mass, our lives together—a sham?

I lay the envelope on the bed beside me and pick up the folded cream-colored note. I open it and read again the short letter to Joan, in handwriting I don't recognize but know isn't mine.

My love, I don't know why you won't return my emails, or answer my calls. Don't you realize yet I'm the only man for you? Haven't I sent you enough notes and cards, pouring my heart out to you? You don't love him. You couldn't. He's nothing like me. I'm the right one for you.

Maybe I haven't done enough. Maybe I need to do more.

Maybe I need to show you.

Five

Maybe I need to show you.

I read the words over and over again, trying to figure out what I'm looking at. Had Joan been having an affair? Was there another man? I can't see how. We were so happy.

Or were we?

Had I missed something? Was what I thought was a happy marriage in fact a lie?

I look at the box. Joan hadn't told me she was on medication. She hadn't told me about being married before. So there are already two lies I knew of. Now three. But a lie about what?

I read the whole note. There is a tone of desperation and longing mixed with a vague hostility and threats.

It is stalkerish.

Was Joan being stalked? Had she become the target of a deranged person? Who had sent this? The letter is unsigned, the handwriting tight and precise but I can't place it.

One thing I am certain of though, even fifteen years later.

She had never mentioned this to me.

At all.

Why?

Why had she kept this from me?

Maybe it was just a one-off, I think.

But the note refers to other cards and notes. This was the only one I have found. Are there more?

A few moments later, I am looking at the login screen of Joan's laptop. Fortunately, Joan always valued ease of memory over security. I type "Password 1," and her desktop comes up.

Her background image is a picture of us, one from our honeymoon. She has photo editing and design programs for her design business, along with the standard word processing and spreadsheet software. There are also folders on the desktop related to the classes she taught at Myer as an adjunct. The summer before her murder she taught a still-life class. Her design business was supposed to help pay the bills, but she really loved teaching.

I click on her email icon and see the last opened email, the one I sent the day of her murder.

I got the reservation. You wanna just meet me there? It was about dinner that night.

There is another email, right below it. The subject line catches my attention.

Why won't you talk to me? The email address is "artluver57@myer.edu." Whoever sent the email was at the college. Was it a student, a colleague? "Artluver"—art lover. Someone in the Fine Arts department? But who?

I scrolled through her inbox. In the month before her death, there were about fifty emails from artluver57. I clicked on the first one.

Did you like the flowers I sent you?

Joan had responded, *I told you, you need to leave me alone.*

I don't care if you're married. I love you. Can't you see that?

I'm telling you, please stop this. I thought I made that very clear to you.

What is clear to me is you don't know me very well, you don't know my heart. I'm gonna show you. Then you'll see. You'll fall in love with me.

You know I love Tom. There is no way that's going to happen.

We'll see.

That was the last of that thread. There were dozens of others after that, none of which Joan had opened, except for one with an attachment.

Why can't you be this happy with me? It reads. *Why don't you smile that way at me? I want you to smile that way at me.*

I click on the attachment. It is a photograph, taken at some distance, of Joan and me. We are walking across the commons at Myer. I must have said something funny, because her head is thrown back and she is laughing.

The date of the email is a week before her murder.

None of the other emails, up to three or four per day, were opened. One says, *You're not answering my calls. Why? Please talk to me.* Another says, *I can't believe you're ignoring me for him! If he wasn't around, you'd have time for me. Maybe I need to do something about that. What do you think?* The next one, sent ten minutes later, says, *I'm sorry, please don't be mad. I don't want to hurt anybody. I just get so desperate. I love you so much, I need you so much. Please, please just talk to me.*

The emails alternate back and forth between pitifully pleading for her attention and veiled threats.

But not against Joan.

All his threats are against me. And Joan had just ignored the emails—even the one with the photo of us. She never told me about them and I can't figure out why. Had she told anyone or did she just think they were something she could ignore, that whoever it was would go away, or was just saying things?

Then two thoughts burst into my mind.

What if Joan's murder wasn't random?

What if he meant to kill me?

I stand up and start pacing—I often pace when I am trying to figure things out.

What do I have?

I have a letter from an unknown man, one Joan had not told me about, that was vaguely threatening to me, and definitely showed an obsession with her.

I have unsigned emails, probably from the same person. I pick up the letter again and study it closely. There was no clue who wrote it.

I look at the prescription bottles again. And her marriage license.

Joan hadn't told me about any of it.

What else hadn't Joan told me about?

As I pace, I realize I don't know a lot about Joan's past. I know her mom, of course. I know her father had died when she was in her early teens, but she never told me how. I know she entered Myer a year late, but she had alluded to taking a gap year to travel. I know her grandparents, aunts and uncles lived out of state—I only met them at the wedding—and she had cousins she didn't particularly care for.

To be fair, I hadn't shared much about my family. She did question why I didn't invite my mother to our wedding, but not very deeply, sensing correctly that my mother was a topic I didn't want to talk about.

But does any of this tie into her murder? I put my head in my hands, the question turning around and around as I feel tears welling up in my eyes. I replay the scene in my head, trying to remember the look in the man's eyes. Through fifteen years of time and grief, I try to focus on his eyes, and try to remember the look. What was there?

Suddenly I know.

It was anguish.

Had he said something? Had he screamed, "No!"? I can't remember. It is all so foggy. Then he put the gun to my head and pulled the trigger.

Click. Click. Click.

I don't remember much else after that. I came to, he was gone and Joan was dead beside me.

I push the box to the floor and collapse back on the bed, finally drifting off to sleep.

***

A ringing phone wakes me with a jolt. .

I grab my cell phone and see it's just after midnight, but that isn't the source of the noise. As the fog lifts, I realize it is the Rectory phone. If someone is calling for a priest at that time of morning, that can mean only one thing: someone has died.

I lift the receiver and say, "Saint Clare's Rectory, Father Greer speaking."

"Tom?" says a woman with panic in her voice. It's Chloe.

"What's wrong?" I ask.

"I don't know," she said. "It's John. He . . . he's not home yet. He should have been home hours ago. I've tried calling his cell phone but it goes straight to voicemail."

"Have you called the police?"

"He hasn't been missing for more than 24 hours so they won't do anything. They did tell me no accidents have occurred involving him. I called the hospital and he's not there." She pauses. "He used to do this all the time, but it's been a while. The last few days, though, he's been . . . different."

"Do you have any idea where he might be?"

She sighs. "One. But he promised me he'd never go there again."

Six

The Hoot-n-Holler is off of Highway 62, north of Myerton. The sign out front advertises all-you-can-eat boiled shrimp and a crab cake po' boy. I doubt many of the pickups and sedans in the parking lot belong to people there for the food, not at 1 a.m. The place has the heavy smell of beer, liquor, and desperation. The polished wood bar parallels a mirrored wall, with shelves holding dozens of bottles—tequila, whisky, scotch, bourbon. Behind it stands a man in his late thirties, wearing a t-shirt pulled tight across a muscular frame, pulling a mug of beer heavy with foam while country music plays from the loudspeakers. John isn't at the bar so I look around the half-filled room and spot him alone in a booth, nursing a shot of something.

I walk up to him and stand at the table for a minute. He doesn't appear to see me, or at least he doesn't acknowledge my presence. "John," I say.

He glances at me, then back at his drink. He picks it up and downs it in one gulp. Then he looks back at me with eyes heavy with intoxication, his hair mussed, his tie undone, his suit rumpled. He has a plate with the remnants of the boiled shrimp.

Apparently, some do come for the food.

"John," I say again.

He looks at me and smiles, but not in a 'glad to see you' way. "Well, hello there, Father Tom. If it isn't Father Tom, used to be just Tom, not a priest or even much of anything."

"Come on, John, it's time to go."

He stares at me then goes back to picking through the plate, looking for more shrimp. Then he holds up his glass, shouting at the bartender, "Hey, Steve, another one. And one for my friend."

"No, thanks, I'm good," I say over my shoulder. Turning back to John, I say, "Look, Chloe's worried about you—"

"—I know she's worried about me. I know better than *you* she's worried. I even know *why* she's worried."

A young woman with her red hair pulled back in a ponytail, wearing tight jeans and a tight low-cut t-shirt from Luray Caverns, brings him the drink, placing it and a cocktail napkin on the table. John says, "Thanks. Put it on my tab."

"Uh-uh," the woman says. "Tab's closed. Pay up."

"Aw, cummon, Lola—"

I say, "You've had enough, John."

"Listen to your friend," she says. "Cash or card?"

"This," John points to me, "is not my friend, at least not now. He is my priest!"

"Listen, I don't care if he's the President," Lola replies. "He's right, you've had enough, now pay up." She crosses her arms. "Or am I going to have to get Steve over here?" She indicates the heavily muscled guy behind the bar.

John puts up his hands. "OK, OK." He fumbles for his wallet and pulls out a card. "Here."

Lola takes the card and John downs his drink. "Well, I guess I'm going. You gonna drive me?"

I nod. "We'll pick your car up later."

He reaches into a pocket and pulls out his car keys, tossing them on the table in front of me. Lola comes back with his card and receipt. "You need a pen?"

"Do I look like I need a pen?" He fumbles in his coat pocket and pulls out a silver ballpoint. He adds a tip and scratches out his signature. Putting his card back in his wallet and his pen in his pocket, he says, "OK, lead on, Padre."

I've seen John drunk only a couple of times but I don't remember him being an angry drunk, more quiet than anything else. I don't like this side of John, and I realize I don't know him anymore at all. I have been away too long.

He is only a little unsteady on his feet, leaning on his cane, so I only have to help him navigate around a few tables, chairs and bodies before getting him outside. I walk him over to my car and get him in the passenger seat. He fumbles for the seat belt, but I reach in and buckle him in place. I get in the car and soon we are heading south to Myerton.

We drive in silence for a few moments and I think for a time he has fallen asleep. Then I hear John say, "Chloe shouldn't have bothered you."

"It's no bother," I say. "Glad to be of help."

"I guess it's your job now, helping, right?"

"I'm not doing it because it's my job," I say. "You're my friend."

"Friend," he says, letting out a short laugh. "Yeah, I'm your friend you haven't seen or spoken to in ten years."

I have nothing to say to that. "I know," I say after a minute, "But I'm still your friend and still care about you."

"Save it for Sunday, Padre."

"Now look—" I stop myself and drive in silence while John sits leaning his head against the window.

After a while, John speaks again. "Why'd you come back, anyway?"

"I was assigned to Saint Clare's for four months."

"I know, I know, that's what you say. But why did you come back?"

"I had no choice. When the Archbishop makes an assignment, you can't say no. He's like my superior officer. You were in the Army, you know that."

"Yeah," he says quietly. "Yeah, I know that." He looks out the window. "So why did you leave?"

I sighed. "Does it matter?"

John looks at me. "Yeah, Tom, it does, to me and a lot of people. You know, you left so suddenly—people had a lot of questions. Rumors flew around for a while."

I look at him quickly, then back to the road. "Rumors? What rumors?"

"The kind of rumors that your friends spent a lot of time putting down. Rumors like you had gone crazy with grief and had checked yourself into a mental hospital. Rumors that you had killed yourself—that was a good one. Rumors about some coed at the college. There were some whispers that you were responsible for Joan's death and you had run before you could be caught."

"What?"

"You heard me," John says. "That the whole story of the attempted rape, that you made it all up to cover the fact that you killed Joan. Didn't help that the police started asking questions."

"What kinds of questions?" I grip the steering wheel as my face gets hot and beads of sweat erupt on my forehead.

"The kind of questions the police ask about a husband and wife when the wife winds up dead."

I am quiet for a few minutes before slowly asking, "Did they question you?"

"Me? Oh, yeah. I'm your best friend, remember?"

"What did you tell them?"

"That you and Joan were the perfect couple, the absolutely perfect couple, without a flaw or problem in the world. You know, the truth." He snorts.

"John, you make one really mean drunk."

"That," he says, "is why I don't drink at home."

"I don't remember you drinking at all, well, not like this."

"Lot's changed," he mumbles. "A whole lot's changed."

"What's changed for you?"

He looks out the window. "I don't want to talk about it."

"You can talk to me."

He shakes his head. "Nope, not interested."

"I'm your friend," I press. "And as you pointed out, I'm your priest."

"What do you want me to do?" John says, turning to look at me. "Confess my sins to you, so you can absolve me?" He turns back to the window. "No thanks."

"Nothing like that, just talk to me, tell me . . . "

"Just drop it."

"But John—"

"I. Said. Drop. It."

We drive in silence, then suddenly John says, "Tell me something—tell me about the night Joan was murdered."

I don't say anything. "Thought not," he says, then closes his eyes and leans back against the window.

I turn my attention to the road. We have just passed back into town and I make the turn on the street that will take me in the direction of his house.

"Tell me something," John says.

"What?"

"Why did you become a priest?"

I sigh. Not this question again. "It's complicated."

"How complicated could it be? You were a married man. Your wife died. Now you're a priest. I just want to know what happened between the wife dying and becoming a priest."

"It isn't that simple."

"Was it grief? You couldn't live a normal life without her, so you went into the Church? Guilt, like you had to do penance for something you did or didn't do—"

"Drop it, John."

"I'm just asking—"

"I said drop it." I say it louder and more forcefully than I mean to.

John just looks at me. "We're not that different. You have your pain, I have mine. We keep it private. I drink, you pray."

I say nothing the rest of the way to his house. When I pull in the driveway, Chloe is waiting. I get John out of the car and he walks to her, steadier on his feet than I thought he would be. I guess that the alcohol is finally wearing off.

"Do you need help getting him inside?" I ask Chloe.

She shakes her head. "No, I've got it from here. Thanks again."

I nod. "John, take care." As I turn to walk off, he touches my arm. "Hey Tom?"

"Yeah?"

"I, uh, you know—sorry. Thanks."

I smile and pat him on his shoulder before turning and walking back to my car.

By the time I get back to the Rectory, it's about 3 a.m. As I begin to walk up the path to the door, I have a sudden sense that someone is behind me. I spin around, and in the dim light from the streetlamps, I think I see a figure dart behind the corner of the Rectory.

"Hello?" I call. "Is someone there?"

No one answers so I continue up the path. Then I hear leaves rustling, even though there is no wind.

I turn again.

No one.

I am at the door and putting my key in the lock when I hear the plod-plod of running feet. I turn in the direction of the sound and see a hooded figure running down the sidewalk away from the Rectory.

"Hey! Hey!" I call, running after the figure.

Why I run after them, I don't know. But by the time I reach the edge of the yard and look down the sidewalk, they're gone.

Seven

The next day, Friday, is a busy one. In the morning, I visit the hospital and give communion to some parishioners who are there, then go over to the nursing home and do the same thing. After Mass, I have meetings with three parishioners. The evening is taken up with a facilities committee meeting where the discussion of painting the classroom areas takes up more time than it should have because Glenda keeps insisting that the rooms don't need to be painted, that they were just painted five years ago, and we really should wait until Father Anthony comes back so he can weigh in.

"What she means is," one of the committee members whispers to me, "is so he can agree with her."

"Does that happen a lot?" I ask.

He nods. "Eventually, he always agrees with her."

Saturday morning is the first time I am able to call and check on John.

"He's better," Chloe says. "Slept most of yesterday, still asleep now. He sleeps a lot," She pauses. "Thanks again for going to get him."

"It was the least I can do. Don't mention it."

I hesitate for a moment. "I want to ask you something."

"Sure, what is it?"

I take a deep breath. "You and Joan were close, right?"

"I like to think we were."

"You two talked about things?"

She doesn't answer right away. "Yes, we talked about a lot of things."

I decide to dive right in. "Did she say anything about anyone giving her unwanted attention?"

Slowly, she says, "I'm not sure what you're talking about. What do you mean?"

I tell her about the letter and the emails, the tone. "I just want to know if she mentioned anything about them to you."

"Did she mention them to you?"

"No," I answer. "That's why I'm asking you."

"Why do you think she'd say something to me when she didn't mention anything to you about it?"

"I don't know, I just thought because you were her best friend—"

"And you were her husband," she interrupts. "I don't see why you would think she would mention them to me when she didn't say anything to you."

I'm getting a little exasperated as I say, "I told you, Chloe—since you were her best friend, I thought she might have said something to you when she obviously didn't feel comfortable telling me about it."

"Tom," Chloe says, "did it occur to you that she didn't tell you because she didn't want you to know?"

"Well, obviously she didn't want me to know. I just want to know why."

"No, you don't," she says, then stops herself.

"Why?"

"No, Tom. I can't say anything. I promised her I would never—"

"She's dead, Chloe. It doesn't matter now. And it might be important."

"How?" she whispers.

"Because—because I'm beginning to think her murder wasn't random. That whoever sent those letters was responsible."

After a minute, Chloe answers, "That's not possible."

"Why? Why isn't it possible?"

Chloe hesitates. "Because it just isn't, OK? You need to trust me on this."

"For heaven's sake, Chloe—"

"—Please, Tom—"

"—don't you care about finding Joan's killer?"

"It was a long time ago," Chloe says, her voice suddenly hard. "Besides, when did you get so interested? You left town. You got on with your life. Some of us had to stay here with it."

I don't respond, but hear something in the background.

"I'll be right there," Chloe calls. "One of the kids needs me," she says. "I've got to go."

"Chloe—" But she has already hung up.

***

I hear confessions that afternoon. Business is brisk; apparently, people have been saving up sins. There is a line of about four or five people, all young moms, waiting when I arrive. The benefit of being new is that I haven't had time to really learn who people are, which I think helps people feel comfortable confessing to me. I have no doubt business will drop off.

The confessions are pretty standard. "Yelled at my children too much." "Yelled at my husband." "I was gossiping about her." "I lusted after him." "Used the "f" word in talking to my mother-in-law." "Used the "f" word talking about my mother-in-law." One penitent, an older man from the sound of his voice, tells a long story about himself, his brother, and a fishing boat that apparently began ten years before and is still a problem between them. I tell him for his penance he needs to sell the fishing boat and give his brother half the money. Apparently, that is the wrong answer, since he leaves before I can give him absolution.

I look at my watch. 3:45 p.m. Fifteen minutes, then I have to get ready for the 4:30 p.m. Mass.

All's quiet for a few minutes. Then, I hear the door on the other side close and I open the screen.

I can only see a shadowy figure on the other side. "Let us begin," I say, "this sacrament of God's mercy in the name of the Father, the Son, and the Holy Spirit."

I hear nothing from the other side of the screen. For a second, I think I have made a mistake, that the door hadn't closed. Then I hear a sigh.

"Do you want me to hear your confession?" I prompt.

Still nothing. I have never experienced anything like this.

"Take your time," I say. "I'm here when you're ready."

But there is still no sound coming through the grille. Suddenly, I hear movement, the door opening, and footsteps on the marble floor leading away from the box.

I shake my head. *I guess they changed their mind*, I think.

Looking at my watch, I see it is just after 4:00 p.m.. I leave the confessional and check the penitent's side to turn the light off, when a glint catches my attention.

A gold ring lays inside. I pick it up and look at the inscription.

It's my wedding band, the one I left on Joan's headstone the day I left Myerton.

Eight

I spend a restless Saturday night tossing and turning, pacing in my room, reading the notes and emails over and over again for some clue—any clue—to the sender's identity. But there is none.

I have no proof that the person who wrote the letter and the emails is in fact the person who came to the confessional. But that person left my wedding ring there, which means they had taken it from Joan's headstone.

Sunday mass is a fog as I find myself looking out over the congregation and wondering, *Are they here? Are they watching me?*

As I stand on the steps greeting the parishioners as they file out, I sense a change in the mood. As people speak, I hear sympathy in some, pity in others. I see little clusters of people speaking in whispered tones, with occasional glances in my direction.

I know what they are talking about. Myerton is a small town and there are enough people in the parish who remember what happened. As much as I might wish it, Joan's murder was never going to be a secret for long.

Anna stops and says, "You're a big topic of conversation, Tom."

I sigh. "I can guess why. Everyone's heard the story by now."

We start walking back through the church towards the sacristy. I have many questions for her about Joan, but I don't know where to start. Or how.

"I wouldn't worry about it, Tom," Anna says. "It was a straightforward random crime."

"That's what I told the police," I say.

Anna stops. "Was it something else?"

I look at her. "No," I say quickly, "No, of course not." I pause. "John told me the police asked about me, after I left?"

She nods. "Yes, they did. I don't think they ever took you seriously as a suspect. But after you left so quickly, I guess they wanted to cover all their bases. And it's not like anyone thought it was you. Everyone knew how in love you two were."

"Things weren't perfect," I say slowly. In the sacristy, I take my Mass vestments off. "We had our problems."

"What young couple doesn't? Drew and I fought constantly the first two years we were married, and we stayed together until the day he died." She pauses. "And I only thought about killing him once or twice."

Drew. Joan's father. I decide to probe a little. "I wish I could have known Drew. Joan always talked about how they would do everything together."

She smiles. "They were pretty much inseparable. She was only thirteen when he died and she took his death very hard."

"I don't think Joan ever told me how he died. He was rather young, wasn't he?"

"Yes, he was," she says, a guarded expression passing over her face.

"What was it, an accident?"

"Yes," she says quickly. "It was a hunting accident. He was out in the woods deer hunting when he fell over a fallen tree and his gun discharged. Killed instantly."

I am shocked. "Joan never told me her daddy hunted. That must have been awful."

"Yes," she says, "But it was a long time ago. Oh, look at the time. I'm sorry, Tom, I have to take a casserole to one of the new moms. We'll talk later, OK?"

She walks quickly out of the sacristy. So now I have another mystery about Joan, her father's tragic death. Yet another fragment of her life that floats in my mind.

***

It was Sunday afternoon that I decided to go to the police. Which is why I'm sitting in my car Monday morning in front of the Myerton Police Department.

I think I have enough to interest them in taking another look at the case.

But what do I really have?

I have a letter and emails from an unidentified person who showed an obsession with Joan, but no explicit expression of violent intent.

I also have Chloe's cryptic statements, but I can't bring her into this yet.

The only solid thing I have to go on is the mysterious person in the confessional—and I cannot mention them.

And the ring.

But the more I think, the more I doubt that I'm doing the right thing, or even just the sensible one. I think about driving back to the Rectory, tossing the emails in the trash, and just getting on with my life, like I have tried to do for the past fifteen years. My coming back to Myerton has stirred things up enough. People in the parish now know about Joan's murder. Nate Rodriguez's documentary is floating around out there. Going to the police will just stir things up more.

If I let it alone, it might just go away. I'll be gone in four months, away from Myerton, away from Saint Clare's, away from the memories of that night.

Away from Joan.

On the other hand, if I do nothing, the police might never have a chance to catch her killer. Don't I owe it to Joan to find him?

But I have to wonder what exactly I owe this woman who shared my life for four years, but never told me she'd been married before. Or that she had some sort of mental health issue. Or that her father had died suddenly and tragically. What do I really owe her?

I am pondering this when I hear a baby cry. I look up, startled, to see a woman lifting a small pink bundle out of a stroller, clutching the baby to her and singing softly as she shifts to push the stroller with one hand while holding the baby with the other. This scene is enough to remind me what my duties truly are to the dead.

I take my keys out of the ignition and get out of my car. I walk across the parking lot to the front door of the police station.

***

The Myerton Police Department is a concrete and glass structure with all the charm typical of mid-20th century Brutalist architecture. It could have been a professional office building for doctors, lawyers, and dentists. The only thing that sets it apart are the metal letters that spell out "Myerton Police Department" over the concrete-covered walkway leading to the glass doors.

The inside is no more appealing than the outside, white walls contrasting to a white and black speckled floor of formica tiles. While the walls look like they were painted relatively recently, overall it doesn't look like much has been done since the original was built.

A uniformed officer is behind an elevated horseshoe desk in the lobby. To his left is a metal detector and x-ray machine of the type that have become ubiquitous in government buildings at all levels in the years since 9/11. There was much talk just after the attacks about the need to install better security, and no small amount of controversy in town, if I remember correctly. The city council had voted to install them temporarily but they have since become a key part of the decor.

I'm wearing my clericals, thinking that a priest in a collar will get a little more attention, if not respect, than someone dressed as a civilian. The officer looks up from the computer screen that has been occupying his attention. We both have an instance of recognition.

"Oh, Father Greer," the officer says, breaking into a smile. "Good morning. What brings you here?"

I don't know the name, but I recognize him as a young father of three from 10:30 a.m. Mass, the husband of the organizer of the Nativity play. I return the smile, "Good morning, Officer, er—" I can't read his nameplate.

He laughs. "Conway. Dan Conway. I'm one of your parishioners. You know, 10:30 Mass, the three brown-haired maniacs, right side rear pew."

I chuckle. "I know, I just didn't have the name. How are you? How's the family?"

"All good. Just found out number four's on the way. Miriam's thrilled. I'm hoping for a promotion. You know, just the basics."

"Four," I say. They all seem to have no problem having multiple kids, I think with a surprising pang as I remember for a second how Joan and I struggled to conceive.

"Well, congratulations. I'm sure Father Anthony will be glad to have another baptism."

The smile fades a bit. "Yes," he says. "Father Anthony's a good man." He pauses. "Anyway, what brings you here?"

I clear my throat. "Who would I talk to about the Joan Greer case?"

"Joan Greer—Oh!" he says. "Of course, Father, of course."

"It probably happened before you were on the force."

"Yes, fifteen years ago, right? I was in the Marines in Iraq, actually. Only heard about it the other day."

I nod. "It wasn't going to remain a secret forever. Anyway, who would I talk to?"

"That'll be Detective Parr. She's the chief detective—well, the only detective."

"What's she like?"

"Detective Parr? Well, she's a really good detective, been here for a couple of years. Tough, but good. Can be a little—difficult, let's say. She was a detective in D.C. Pretty high up from what I understand."

"Oh? What's she doing here?"

"Well, I don't really know. I've heard things. But gossip is a sin, you know."

"Venal at worst," I smile.

I would usually not want to hear rumors or gossip, being the current target of both myself, but something tells me that I need as much information about Detective Parr as I can get.

"Well," he leans forward. "Apparently, she clashed with higher-ups about a sensitive high-profile investigation. She raised a ruckus, and they got rid of her."

"Fired her?"

"Not exactly. From what I've heard, the Chief of Police in D.C. is an old friend of our Chief. They did a transfer, so to speak. She didn't take it too well. The first six months or so she was here, she'd take her displeasure out on the nearest person. But she's settled down a lot since then. She and I get along really well, but I've learned how to handle her. Trust me, she is not a woman you want to cross. When she gets riled up—I'll tell you, Father, she reminds me of some drill sergeants I knew."

"Thanks for the warning. Can I see her?"

"I know she's in. Let me check with her." He picks up the phone. "Yes, Detective Parr. Officer Conway at the front desk. I've got someone here who wants to see you about a cold case."

Conway pauses as Parr speaks on the other end. "The Greer murder," he says. Another pause. "It's—" he looks at me "her husband?" Short pause. "Yes, sorry, Detective, I'm sure it's her husband."

There's a long pause as she says something to Conway. Finally, he says, "Uhm. OK. Ah, when? Sure, let me check."

Looking at me, the officer says with a tinge of embarrassment, "Ah, Father, Detective Parr says that she can meet with you tomorrow morning at 9 a.m. Will that work for you?"

"Sure," I say, not at all happy that after psyching myself up to finally do something about this, I'm going to have to wait until tomorrow.

Conway nods, then says into the phone, "He says that's fine. OK, thank you."

When he hangs up, he says, "I'm sorry about that, Father."

I shake my head. "It's OK, Officer—"

"Dan," he says. "Please, Father Greer, call me Dan."

"OK, but you need to call me Father Tom," I say. "Like I was saying, it's fine. It's been this long. I doubt one day's going to make a difference at all."

***

I'm back at the station at 8:45 a.m. and Dan's again at the desk. "Hi, Father," he says. "Listen, about yesterday, I don't want you to think Detective Parr was avoiding you or anything. Apparently she had some errands she needed to run because she left right after you did. In fact, she was gone the rest of the day."

At Dan's thoughtful look I ask, "Is there a problem?"

"No, it's just that I cannot remember a time Detective Parr took a day off. She's pretty much a workaholic, if you ask me. Single. No family. No relationships of any kind really. This job's her whole life."

He shakes his head, then picks up the phone. "Detective, Father Greer is here."

Hanging up, he says, "She'll see you now, Father."

I walk past the front desk and down a short hallway, taking a right into a longer hallway. As I walk, I hear an oddly chipmunk-like voice coming from an office. It's uncharacteristically loud and I catch, "new dress and shoes, wow," as well as "you look great," and "must be someone special."

Just then a young woman in a wheelchair comes out of an office at the end of the hall and rolls toward me. Her hair is the most shocking shade of blue and she wears turquoise-rimmed glasses. I can't even describe the dress she's wearing, except that it looks like something from a 1960s catalog.

She stops when she sees me and just stares, forcing me to squeeze past her as she rolls to one side and turns. As I walk past, I hear her say softly with a sigh, "Oh, it all makes sense now."

I reach the door that has "Helen M. Parr, Detective" on the nameplate. I hesitantly knock.

"Come in," the Detective says from the other side of the door.

That voice. It—it sounds—she sounds like—

No, it's impossible.

There is no way it could be.

Still I hesitate, pushing the impossible thought out of my mind,

I turn the knob and open the door. "Detective, th—"

I stop in my tracks.

It's just not possible. But, there she is, standing in front of me.

For a moment, time freezes and then speeds backwards twenty years, to before I was a priest, before I loved and lost Joan, to a time when I was still young and this woman before me was a girl of 22. The last time I saw her, her stunning blue eyes were ringed in red, caused by hours of arguing and crying between us. She was thinner then, but still soft and gently round, as she is now, clad in an emerald green dress that is in harmony with the sapphires in her eyes and the rubies on her lips. I catch myself before I can wander any further, as she looks up at me and I see a look of amusement at my shock.

"Hello, Tom," she says, sitting back in her chair, with a tight smile on her lips.

"Helen?"

We just look at each other. I don't know what to say next. There are so many possibilites.

"So, you're a priest?" she says, breaking the silence.

I nod. "Yes," I reply. "You're a detective?"

"That's what it says on my door," she says. "What are you doing here?"

What am I doing here? *A good question,* I think. *Maybe I should just leave before this goes any further.*

"Tom," she says. "Did you hear me?"

"Oh," I say, shaking myself. "Sorry, yes, what am I doing here?"

She leans back in her chair, and folds her arms before saying with a laugh, "That's my question." She indicates a chair in front of her desk.

I sit down and say, "I'm here to talk to you about the Joan Greer case."

The detective looks at me for a moment. "She was your wife?"

"Yes, I was married to Joan at the time of her murder."

"I am so sorry," she says with a softness not in keeping with her current reputation. "That is a terrible thing to go through."

"Thank you."

"So obviously, you weren't a priest then."

"No, I entered holy orders after her death."

"Why?" Her puzzlement seems genuine.

"It's complicated."

"Hmm," she said. Her fingers dance across the keyboard.

"So I take it Parr's your married name," I say. "Congratulations. How long?"

She stops and looks up from the keyboard, then keeps typing. "Two years," she says quietly, "but I'm not married now."

"I'm sorry," I say.

"So am I," she replies, sounding strangely distant.

"Any kids?" I ask.

"No," she says, "no kids. OK, let's see. Greer, Greer—here it is, Joan Greer, assault, attempted rape, murder, case still unsolved—not a lot of those around here." She moves her mouse and clicks.

Helen stands, and I avert my eyes as she walks to a file cabinet and pulls out a file. She's in her early forties, but her figure—

"OK, Joan Greer, let's see what we have," Helen says as she sits down, opening the folder. She flips through some pages, takes out a photograph and looks at it, flipping through some more pages, pauses and looks up at me, then back down and reads another page.

"We haven't done much with this in almost ten years," she says. "I've got notes here that Detective Keifer looked at the file a few times, but the last case notes are dated about eight months after her death." She looks up at me. "That was about two months after you left town?"

I nod and prepare myself for further interrogation, but she moves on. "And now you're back, and you say you have new information. Tom, why don't you share that with me?"

"This," I say, pulling out the letter and printouts of the emails and handing them to her. I tell Helen how Joan had not told me about receiving them, how I thought maybe the person who sent them had something to do with her death.

She takes the stack, reads through it, then places it back on her desk. She says nothing but instead just looks at me.

"Is this all?" Helen finally asks me with just the slightest hint of irritation.

"No. I also found out Joan was married before she met me." I show her the copy of the marriage license I have found.

"She never told you she was married before?" Helen asks after she looks at it. "Never mentioned this Randy Earl? Never said anything to you about it?"

I shake my head. "Never."

"Let me see if I understand you," Helen begins as she leans back in her chair. "You have an anonymous letter and emails your wife didn't tell you about. Your wife also didn't tell you she had been married before you met." She pauses. "Look, I don't want to be unkind, but I have to wonder how well you actually knew your own wife."

The question stings. But it is one I've started asking myself.

"At one time, I would have said well, but now, I really don't know." I look at her now, anxious in spite of myself to hurt her like she has hurt me. "Of course, this is hardly the first time I've not understood the choices of a woman I love."

If this barb hits home, she doesn't say anything. Instead, we just look at each other across the four feet of desk that separates us. But I know that isn't the only distance between us.

No, it is time. Time and the decisions we had made.

"Well, what do you think?" I finally say to break the silence.

"What do I think? What do I think?" she repeats. Then she looks at me with a wry smile. "Well, if this were a *normal* situation, based on the history of the parties involved, I might think that you are using this situation with Joan as an excuse to make contact with me."

"Excuse me?" I reply, infuriated at her bluntness. But I shouldn't be surprised. Her bluntness in the past had led to more than one fight between us.

"You heard me," she said. "Though listening was never your strong suit—but I guess you've had to learn that, huh?"

Ignoring the jab, I say, "Helen, the last I knew you were going to be a lawyer in a big firm in New York or D.C. or somewhere. I had no idea you'd become a detective, much less that you moved to Myerton."

"Well, since you're a priest now and I'd doubt you'd lie to me, I'll choose to believe you. Still, Tom, this 'evidence' you have is useless. There's nothing here."

"You don't think—"

"—no, I don't think the incidents are interesting or relevant at all," She leans forward. "What I see here are notes from a man—presumably a man—who seems to have had a serious attraction to your wife. Stalkerish? Yes. Creepy? Definitely. Evidence of murderous intent? Not by a longshot."

"But her marriage—"

"So she was married before? What are you saying? That this Randy Earl wrote these to your wife, that he was still in contact with her? There's nothing to tie this to him—or anybody."

"There's a Myer College email address."

Helen shrugs. "A student, faculty member. It was fifteen years ago. Unless you think Randy Earl enrolled as a student just to stalk her."

She leans back and picks up a pen, drumming it on the desk. "You know, on second thought," she says. "I do find something interesting."

"What's that?"

She stops drumming her desk. "I find it interesting that you claim you never knew about any of this."

"Why is that interesting?" I ask. "It's the truth, just like I told you."

"Yes," she says with a touch of sarcasm, "I know what you told me. You told me that after having been away for fifteen years, you return to town—why did you come back?"

"I'm assigned temporarily to Saint Clare's."

"I see—you return. You get a bunch of stuff out of her former art studio. You find a letter stuck in a sketchbook and a marriage license in a box. You find these emails on her laptop. And from them," she concludes, "you get the idea that they're connected to her murder." She pauses. "Am I missing anything?"

I look at her. My idea—what had been my idea?—had been to show the notes to the police and get them interested in giving the case another look. That clearly is not going to happen with what I have shown Helen.

"Well, Tom?" she prompts.

I reach in my pocket and finger my wedding band. I hesitate, then pull it out and hold it up.

"There's also this," I say and place it on the desk in front of her.

She looks at it, but doesn't pick it up.

"Your wedding ring?" she asks.

"Yes."

"What about it?"

Slowly I say, "When I left Myerton, I left it on Joan's headstone."

"How typically dramatic of you," she says. "OK, so how did you get it back?"

I exhale. "Someone—gave it to me."

"Someone gave it to you," she repeated. "Who?"

"I—I don't know," I say. "I found it."

Helen sighs. "This conversation brings back so many memories," she says wearily. "Where did you find it?"

"At Saint Clare's. In the church."

She picks it up and looks at it. "So let me see if I understand you. You're telling me that you left this ring on Joan's headstone when you left fifteen years ago."

I nod.

"And fifteen years later it turns up at Saint Clare's."

"Yes," I say, smiling. "I know it sounds strange."

Without further comment, she hands the ring back to me. "Anything else, Tom?"

Taking the ring, I shake my head. "No," I say.

She slowly nods her head. "OK," she says. "Let's go over this again. You claim you knew nothing about these," she holds up messages.

"No, absolutely nothing."

"Nothing about a student or faculty member making unwanted advances."

"No."

"Joan didn't mention being followed or stalked."

"Not a word."

"Didn't tell you she had been married."

I shake my head.

She pauses. "Just out of curiosity, did you ever tell her about us?"

I look at her, then off to the side. "No," I say. "I never told her about you."

She considers this for a minute, then asks, "Were you two close?"

"Yes, very close. We had been married just over three years when she died. We were inseparable. Ask anybody."

"If you two were so close," Helen goes on, "then why didn't she tell you?"

"I really don't know. I've been asking myself that."

"Can you think of a reason she wouldn't want you to know?"

"No, honestly, not one."

"Were you the jealous type?"

"Jealous? No, I don't think so."

She looks at me. "Come on, remember who you're talking to," she says bitterly. "We both know better. Shall I review that with you?"

She doesn't need to.

***

In a flash, we are back at her apartment, the last time I ever saw her before today. She was insisting that we could make a long distance relationship work, that we could see each other every weekend, that she loved me and was committed to our future together.

And what was I saying?

Oh, how I wish I could forget.

I was accusing her of losing interest in me, of wanting to find someone else before she turned loose of me for good.

"After all," I screamed, "why else would you be holding out on me? If we're getting married anyway, why aren't we sleeping together?"

Her face went completely white at this. "Tom," she said, quietly, "I thought we were on the same page, that we agreed with the teachings of the Church."

"No, I never agreed. I just went along with what you said because I figured, if you really loved me, you'd give in."

"Really loved you? Is that your only barometer, Tom Greer? How soon will I sleep with you? So that other girl, back home in Bellamy, you were really in love with her?"

"Well, no, but we were in high school. Everybody was doing it. It didn't matter."

"Didn't matter? Well, maybe not for you but it did for me, and for the guys I dated."

"Oh, yes, how could I forget the marvelous young men of Future Monks of America who showed up once a month for a dance at St. Monica's School for Girls? You mean none of them ever tried to make a move?"

"Not more than once," she growled.

"Well, Helen, since that's obviously what you want in a man, I sincerely hope you find it at Duke, though I wouldn't hold my breath if I were you. Unless, of course, that's what turns you on."

She slapped me then, hard. I knew I deserved it but I didn't care. I turned and walked out the door. As I closed it, I heard a clink of metal hitting metal.

Her engagement ring.

She had taken it off and thrown it at me.

***

When I don't answer her question, Helen says, "From my experience, if a wife doesn't tell her husband that another man has expressed an interest in her, it's for one of two reasons. Either her husband is prone to jealousy and would react badly, possibly violently, against her or the other guy, or the attraction is mutual. So tell me, Tom, which was it?"

I sigh. "Look, Helen, I see where you're coming from, why you'd think I'd be that guy. But you know I would never hit a woman, especially one I loved."

Wistfully, she says, "Yes, I know that, Tom."

"As far as the attraction being mutual, that is one of the things I guess I'm most afraid of."

"I can understand that."

I want to ask her if that's what ended her marriage, and then, for reasons I can't explain, I want to hunt down the guy in question and hurt him badly. But instead, I continue, "I can't tell you which it was, since I have no idea who sent those."

"These, and," she picks up the printouts, "cards, notes and flowers. Pretty big expressions of his feelings, don't you think, and she didn't tell you. Could she have been having an affair?"

"I don't know!" I answer sharply, causing Helen to raise an eyebrow. I calm down and say, "No, I'm sure she wasn't having an affair."

"With all due respect, you didn't know about any of this. How can you be sure?"

"Because I knew my wife."

She looks at me. "Apparently not, Tom," she says quietly. We sit in silence until Helen finally says, "Is there anything else? Because if not, I do have other cases, ones that I can do something about."

"I do have one more thing," I say quietly. "I'm sorry about how I left things between us all those years ago. I was the one who was too immature to deal with everything. You didn't do anything wrong."

"Look, Tom, it just wasn't meant to be," Helen says, shaking her head. "We're fortunate that we found out when we did."

"That's certainly true, though I doubt we'd have made it through pre-Cana." I say the latter with a smile because I know better than she does what that would have entailed.

"I doubt I would ever have gotten you to go." She pauses, and then says with an expression that I quite can't decipher, "Did you go with Joan?"

"Yes," I say, "she wanted to get married in the Church."

"Oh, so she was Catholic?"

"Yes, uhm, but not like you." Why am I telling her this? It's none of her business.

"Oh, I see," she says with a smile. "Obviously she had more influence on you than I did."

In spite of myself, I say, "No, not really. We married in the church because that's what she wanted. But we didn't really go to Mass, mostly just Christmas and Easter." I swallow the lump in my throat, and add, "Her funeral of course."

"Then how did all this happen?" she says, waving her hand at me.

I smile sheepishly. "That's a long story. But, after her death—not right away, but after I left—I found God again. Or I guess I should say, God found me."

Something occurs to me, and I sit back, thinking I'm about to gain the upper hand. "I've been here two Sundays, and I haven't seen you at Saint Clare's."

She nods. "I don't go to Saint Clare's. I go to Saint Aloysius near Frostburg. I will admit, John wasn't much of anything by the time we met. He'd been raised Catholic, but had stopped going years ago for . . . various reasons. We were married in the Church, and I'd go by myself occasionally, but while he was—we were together, I fell away from my faith."

"I'm sorry to hear that."

"Well, after . . . everything happened with John, I started going again. I'd go to the Basilica of the National Shrine of the Immaculate Conception in D.C. on Sundays, and there was a parish near police headquarters where I'd go to daily Mass when I could."

"But why don't you attend Saint Clare's?" I ask. "It's not far from here, and we do have daily Mass, you know?"

She sighs. "A friend of mine from D.C. lives in Frostburg, she attends the parish. When I moved here, I started making the drive to go with her. I have nothing against Saint Clare's, Tom. Sergeant Conway and his family attend, and speak highly of the parish. But other than them, I don't know anybody, and frankly when I first got here, I wasn't planning on hanging around very long."

"Well," I say quietly, "you know someone now."

She says nothing for a moment, then says, "Do I, Tom?"

I open my mouth to speak, then realize I'm not at all sure what to say. I want to tell her she does, that I'm the same person she knew over twenty years ago.

But we both know that's not true. I'm very different than I was, as she probably is.

And besides, what does it matter anyway where she goes to Mass? It's not like I'm going to be here after December.

I suddenly realize that I have lost track of why I came here today and say, "As far as Joan's case is concerned, you're not going to do anything, are you?"

"No. There's nothing to do."

I sit back and stare at her. She stares back.

"Helen, please—"

"Is there anything else, Father?" she repeats.

I smiled ruefully. Standing, I say, "No. I guess not. Thank you for your time. I'll let you get back to your bike thieves."

I leave her office, struggling to keep calm.

Inside, I'm a mess.

I can't believe how she dismissed my concerns, then turned around and talked so pleasantly to me. She doesn't believe I didn't know, she doesn't believe it when I say Joan didn't have an affair. But beyond that, she isn't going to look into Joan's case. Nothing I have said or could say has moved her.

I hope our past isn't coloring her judgment, but I suspect it might be.

I drive back towards the Rectory, arriving with just enough time to get ready for the Noon Mass. Once in the sacristy, I yank off my coat, fling it on the table and quickly pull on my vestments.

As I walk past the table, I see that my phone fell out of my pocket. I pick it up to put it back in my coat when I stop. Opening the call log, I scroll down until I see Nate Rodriguez's number. I look at the time. I have just enough. I touch the number and hear the phone dial.

"Hello," the voice on the other end says. In the background, I hear people talking and dishes clattering. Apparently, Nate is at work.

"Nate, this is Father Tom Greer. Listen, I have to go into Mass, but I've thought about it some more."

I take a deep breath. "I'll do the interview for your documentary."

Nine

"I can't believe this," Nate says as he looks through the emails. "This is great! You see this, Father?"

When I called Nate and told him I'd do an interview, he was happy. When I told him about what I had found and Helen's response, he was practically speechless. Meeting him at The Perfect Cup the next day and showing him copies of the emails, he is jumping up and down in his chair like a little boy on Christmas morning.

"Don't you see, now this has everything. It's not just a cold case of a senseless murder," Nate goes on, holding up the emails. "This is a cold case of a planned murder. She was stalked, and whoever was stalking her killed her—"

"Now, really, we don't know that," I interrupt.

"—and we have the police doing nothing when new evidence is shown to them." He inhales and exhales. "Now we have a story."

"I thought you had a story before?"

"We did," he answers. "It's a better story now. And you'll do an interview on camera?"

"Yes," I say, "but who's we?"

"We," Nate repeats. "My partner and I."

"What partner?"

"My partner in the film," he replies. "Oh, did I forget to mention her? She's meeting us—oh, here she is now." Nate stands and waves at someone. I turn around to see who.

She is young, blond, pretty, and earnest. Very earnest. I recognize her from one of the local stations in Baltimore. She does those human-interest stories that really interest nobody. She leans into Nate and gives him a quick peck on the cheek.

"Katherine Shepp," Nate says, "Meet Father Tom Greer."

She smiles and extends her thin, well-manicured hand. "So nice to meet you, Father," she says, her voice as silky as her hair. I take her hand as she covers mine with her other hand and looks into my eyes.

"I'm really looking forward to working with you," she purrs.

I settle down to my usual coffee with cream and two sugars as she sips on her decaf soy latte. Nate is there until his uncle comes over to remind him that his break is over.

After he excuses himself, Katherine says, "I'm glad you've agreed to help me with the story."

Me? "Yes, I decided that Joan's story needs to be told."

She smiles, showing perfectly white teeth behind her expertly colored lips. There is no lipstick on her cup so it is either very good lipstick, or she has had her lips tattooed.

"When Nate told me about the story of your wife's murder, I was just so . . . so . . . moved, I guess is the word I'm looking for. And then when he told me you came back, and you are now a priest, well, that's just wonderful."

"I guess an unsolved murder is a bit of a change from doggy beauty pagents."

She guffaws. "Yeah, that. Not why I went to J-School, that one. I tried to sell my boss on an animal cruelty angle, but he said no one would believe that dog owners who spend $500 on a custom tailored tuxedo for their pedigree German Shepherd were guilty of abusing their pets. I guess he's right. But this is my ticket out of that crap and into real, hard-hitting stuff."

"I don't know how hard-hitting this is," I say. "Nate's tells me you're working on the human interest angle, how her murder has affected others."

"Well," Shepp says with a slight eye roll, "Nate and I disagree a little on our view of the project."

"What's your view?"

She sits back with an air of triumph. "I intend to solve the case."

It is so ridiculous I have to laugh a little. She frowns, and I clear my throat. "Sorry, Ms. Shepp—"

"Please, call me Katherine."

"OK, Katherine. Why do you think you'll be able to solve a fifteen-year-old murder when the police haven't been able to?"

Her eyes narrow. "Because I'll have your help." Then she leans forward. "Nate told me about the new information you have. The emails the police ignored. I'm not going to ignore them. I'll figure out who sent them. Are these the emails?" she says, picking them up.

I drink my coffee and watch her read through the stack. The further she gets, the more she smiles. Katherine puts the papers down and drinks from her latte. "OK, Father, yes, I definitely think that there is a connection between those emails and your wife's murder."

I smile in spite of myself, swept up in her enthusiasm and flattered that someone is finally taking me seriously.

"Now," she goes on, "we've got work to do. I'll need to lay the groundwork."

"I've told Nate I'll talk about that night on camera."

"Well, yes, of course we'll need that, but there's more, too."

"What do you mean?"

"I want to get the background, you know, the story behind the story," she says. "I want to learn everything you can tell me about Joan, your relationship, the days and weeks leading up to her murder. Did anything stand out in her behavior? Did anything unusual happen? Was there tension between the two of you?"

"Now wait—"

"I'll need to talk to Joan's mother and her friends."

"I thought Nate already interviewed them?"

"He did," Katherine nods.

"Then why—"

"Well," she leans towards me, conspiratorially lowering her voice, "if I can be candid, Father Tom, Nate's really a behind-the-scenes person. Not an on-camera one. Oh, he's sweet and technically really good, but he doesn't have the," she pauses looking for a word, "presence that someone who's on-camera all the time has."

"Someone like you," I say.

"Yes, someone like me," she says, leaning back and tapping the table with her nails.

"I have the copy of the police file Nate got," she continues. "It's so redacted it's practically useless. Fortunately, I know someone who can help get more information on what the police have."

"How?"

Katherine smiles. "Old boyfriend. He's an officer and married now, but I think I can, you know, persuade him."

I squirm. "Listen, Katherine, I'd rather you didn't do anything—"

"Oh," she waves dismissively, "I'm not going to break any commandments, Father. Maybe bend a little, but not break." She drinks. "Besides, you want the truth, right? Sometimes getting to the truth means getting your hands a little dirty. Sometimes the truth itself is dirty. In fact, it usually is." She paused. "I'm not sure people know what they're going to get when they say they want the truth. I think they'd be happier if they never knew the truth."

"I want the truth," I say with more certainty than I felt. What if she is right? What if the truth—the whole truth about Joan's murder, about Joan, about our relationship—is messier than I imagined?

She smiles the same white-veneer-perfect smile. "Now, when can I get you on camera?"

I return the smile, even as one thought runs again and again through my head.

What am I getting myself into?

***

A few days later I am standing in front of the restaurant where we were eating the night of Joan's murder. It is still a restaurant, but the name is different. It had been La Petite Maison and served French food; it is now called Pasta Primo and serves Italian. The decor is also completely different and the exact table we were sitting at is no longer there, but I can still see the area of the restaurant where it had been. The table for two was by the windows overlooking Main Street. It was the same table in the same restaurant where I had proposed to her a few years earlier.

I turn away from the window. Nate has set up a camera on a tripod and is looking through the viewfinder. He looks up, telling Katherine "All good here."

She nods and looks at me. "You can start whenever you're ready, Father."

I exhale, having been holding my breath unconsciously until that moment. I am nervous, more nervous than I remember being the Sunday of my first homily.

What are you doing? I think. *You've spent years avoiding talking about that night. And what are you going to do? Talk about that night. On camera. Your every word recorded. Everyone will hear what you say, and see how you look when you say it. And for what? What are you hoping to gain from this?*

"Peace. Justice," I mumble to myself.

Are you sure? You don't really want to talk about it. You know why.

I shake my head to still the thoughts.

You know why.

"Where should I begin?" I ask.

Nate presses a button on the camera and looks through the viewfinder. He adjusts a knob on the sound recorder slung over his shoulder, listening as I speak into the lapel mike. I am dressed in my clericals at Nate's suggestion.

"Wherever you're comfortable starting," Katherine says. "Why were you at the restaurant that night?"

"That night," I repeat. "That night was a special night."

"What made it special?"

I smiled. "It was the anniversary of our first date. Which was also the anniversary of the night I proposed. We sat at the same table where we sat when I proposed to her, in this restaurant—well, not this restaurant, it was La Petite Maison back then."

"So it was a happy night."

"Yes, very happy. But it got happier."

"How?"

"Joan had been to the doctor that day," I continued. "We had been trying ever since we got married to have a baby. But things hadn't gone well. She had problems getting pregnant. There were a couple of miscarriages along the way. We had just about given up, talked about exploring adoption, even IVF—she was an only child and I just have a sister, so we wanted to have a large family. I was looking forward to being a dad." I pause a moment.

"Anyway," I continue, "a few days before, Joan had taken a home pregnancy test. We'd had false alarms before so she scheduled an appointment with her doctor for a more accurate test. She told me what the doctor said over dinner."

"What had the doctor said?"

I smile, even as I feel a lump in my throat. The beginnings of tears sting my eyes. Even fifteen years later, the memories of that night bring up huge emotions in me. I swallow and clear my throat. "That we were going to have a baby."

"How did you feel about that?" Katherine asks quietly.

"Feel? I was ecstatic. I knew that there would be a time when it could all go wrong—we'd been down that path before, like I say—but at that moment I was the happiest man on the planet."

"What was Joan's reaction?"

"She—she was happy. But guarded, looking back. She had been through a lot. I guess she didn't want to get too excited, not while she could still lose the baby."

"What did you two do then?"

"I ordered champagne, and then realized that it needed to be sparkling cider. We laughed over that, that joyful kind of laugh you do when the whole world seems bright. While we ate, we discussed baby names, how to decorate the nursery, talked about whether we were going to need a bigger house. We had started looking at places; at the time we were living in a two-bedroom apartment that was adequate but we knew we'd need a bigger place for kids. We wanted a place with a backyard and enough space for lots of kids."

"Anything else?"

"Oh, just work stuff. I told her about the latest project I had at work—I wasn't a priest then, obviously. I was an archivist at Myer in their Archives and Manuscripts section, actually the archivist, there was only one, and I was it. I had just started a preliminary list of the papers of a former Senator who had been an alumnus of the college. I remember because it had been a very big deal, the largest collection ever donated to Myer at the time. I told Joan that I realized that day how big a job it was going to be, and that I might be able to get the college to hire an assistant. She told me about her work. She was getting her design business off the ground and had a few clients. She told me about one client of hers who was proving to be a problem."

"Didn't she work at the college?"

"Yes, she was an instructor in the fine arts department. Joan had received her art degree there and they hired her as a part-time instructor. Joan was good—her students loved her, and the department thought highly of her. The job gave her enough time to work on her business. But she had also hoped the department might take her on as a full-time instructor."

"So, you finished dinner. What happened next?"

I look at her. "After dinner and dessert, it was getting late, so we left."

"Where did you go?"

"We walked back to the car."

Nate stops the camera and looks up. "That's great Father, heard everything loud and clear. What we'll do now is walk down the sidewalk to the parking lot—it's that one over there, right?" He indicates a small lot between the two rows of shops, the one where the restaurant is and the next one with a used bookstore, antique store, and crystal shop.

I nod. That was the parking lot where it all happened. "Do you want to film me walking?"

Before Nate can answer, Katherine says, "No, that won't be necessary." Nate looks irritated.

We get to the lot. It hasn't changed much since that night it seems, but it had been dark and the lot was not very well lit, so I couldn't see much. I look up. There are more lights now, and cameras.

There hadn't been cameras that night. There was no video of what happened. All the police had was my story.

I lead them to the part of the lot where I remember we parked, not too far in from the street. Nate sets up his tripod and camera. After a few minutes he says, "OK, when you're ready."

I nod and he starts the camera.

"We had parked about here," I say. "We took our time walking here, the night was warm and clear. Just strolled together hand in hand. I remember Joan leaning against me, holding me by my upper arm, resting her head on my shoulder. It was late so there were not a lot of cars on the street. By the time we got here, the lot seemed empty except for us."

I pause. Now is the hard part. I say a quick prayer for strength.

"What happened next," I went on, "is foggy. I'm not sure I remember everything that happened. I remember we arrived at the car. We walked around so I could open her door—Joan liked that, she teased me when I forgot, which was quite often. I heard footsteps coming behind us. I looked up, and there he was. Just standing there, holding a gun on us."

"What did you do?"

What did I do? What did I do? "I—I froze. I just stared at him. Joan stared, too."

"What did he say?"

"Nothing. That was the strange thing, nothing. He held the gun on me and grabbed Joan. Started dragging her away."

"What did he look like?"

"I'm not sure. The light wasn't very good. I couldn't make out any features. I could see his eyes but he was wearing a hoodie. A mask maybe."

I stop and stare at the spot in the parking space where my car had been. I am trying to remember what I told the police about what happened next.

"Joan started screaming, hitting at the guy, trying to pull away. But he was too strong. He said something, I can't remember what. I darted after him. I remember jumping on him, trying to wrestle him away from her. He let go of Joan and she ran back to the car, I think. Then he threw me off."

I stop, feeling tears welling up again. "Can we stop for a moment?"

Nate looks up from the camera. Katherine says, "Sure, Father. Take the time you need."

I walk away from the spot. My mind is spinning. I know what happened next. I have lived with the memory every day since it happened. The images swirl through my head every night when I try to sleep. I hadn't talked about what happened to anyone, not since the police interviewed me. Now I am being asked to tell the story again. I close my eyes and say a quick prayer, open my eyes, and walk back to Nate and Katherine.

"OK," I say. "I'm ready now."

Nate looks through the viewfinder. "OK, Father."

I exhale. "He pointed the gun at me. I ran at him and grabbed his arm. I guess I was trying to get the gun away from him. We fought for a minute." I stop and swallow. "Then it happened."

"What happened?"

I stopped. I couldn't form the words in my mouth. I have lost the ability to speak.

"What happened?" Katherine repeats.

"A—a shot," I whisper "There was a shot. He must have had his finger on the trigger. For a second, I thought I had been shot. I didn't feel anything, didn't see any blood. He looked shocked, like he wasn't expecting it." I pause. "Then I looked at Joan."

I close my eyes, tears welling up again. But I can't stop now, I just have to get through it.

"Even in the dim light I could see. Her blouse was white. It was very easy to see the blood. She hadn't screamed or cried out. She just stood there, blood slowly spreading crimson across her front. She began to sway. I ran to her and caught her as she sank to her knees. I started screaming for help. I looked in the guy's direction. He was still standing there. It was like he was transfixed or something. Like he couldn't believe what he had done. I thought I heard him speak, I can't be sure. I was holding Joan, cradling her in my arms, telling her, begging her to hold on until help came.

"Then suddenly, he walked up to me and held the gun to my head. He looked me right in the eyes. I saw—"

"What did you see?"

"I saw—anger, hatred, rage. Murderous rage."

"Did he say anything to you?"

I shake my head. "He just stared at me, pointing the gun right here," I point to my forehead, between my eyes. "I closed my eyes. I thought to myself, at least we'll die together. I won't have to live without her. Then, I heard a click. Then another click. A third click. Not a shot. Just clicks. Something must have happened to the gun. He moved it away from me. I opened my eyes. He was looking at the gun with disbelief. Then he looked at me and screamed, drew his arm back and slammed the gun into my head. I only remember searing pain, then darkness."

"What's the next thing you remember?" Katherine prompts.

My breathing is ragged. "I came to," I say, "and Joan was on top of me." The tears were hot on my cheeks. "I rocked her slowly, talking quietly to her. I looked her in the eyes, willing her to be alive. I held her tight, sobbing, asking God to bring her back. But there was no life in her eyes. They stared blankly into mine. She was gone."

I stop and lower my head, squeezing my eyes tight against the tears that were about to overwhelm my ability to control them. I squeeze my hands into fists, gritting my teeth, using every fiber of my being to control the emotions welling up from inside me. I feel I am drowning in a sea of my own sadness. It is just like before. It hasn't been this bad in a long time.

I shouldn't have done this, I think. *This was a mistake.*

I have lost all awareness of where I am. I am no longer standing in the parking lot, feet from Nate and Katherine and the video camera. I am adrift in a cold void created by the overwhelming pain I have brought back to the surface.

I don't know how long I am like that but the next thing I know, I'm back. I look up. Nate and Katherine are just staring at me.

"That's everything," I say. "That's what happened. That's how Joan was killed."

***

That evening, I kneel in Saint Clare's before the tabernacle. I have just finished Evening Prayer. I am physically and mentally exhausted.

I look at the crucifix, then the tabernacle, comforted by the knowledge that Christ is here with me.

I slowly shake my head. One thought keeps repeating over and over again. It started after we finished filming and I still can't stop it.

It's been fifteen years. You still can't face the truth.

Ten

Sunday's Mass begins as they all do, with me progressing down the aisle behind a ramrod straight Dominic Trent swinging the incense burner—the thurible—by a long chain, sending light gray clouds of fragrant smoke into the space around us. Behind him, the crucifix is held aloft by another teenage boy who I haven't met yet, red-headed with freckles. He in turn is flanked by two younger boys carrying candles. A woman in glasses, wearing a skirt and sweater with her salt-and-pepper hair pulled back into a ponytail—who just happens to be Dominic's mother—carries the silver bound Gospel in front of me, holding it aloft. We all proceed up the steps towards the altar, each bowing in our turn.

I come in last, my eyes fixed on the altar. Today I'm wearing the flowing green vestments of Ordinary Time, trimmed with a tapestry pattern down both the front and the back. My hands are folded in front of me in an attitude of prayer, and indeed my concentration remains unbroken as I genuflect, then walk around the altar, bend, and kiss the marble surface.

I turn to Dominic and take the thurible from his hand, bowing slightly, then turn to the altar. I walk around it, swinging the thurible in small circles. Soon, the entire sanctuary is shrouded in an aromatic haze that smells of a musty pine forest with hints of citrus, spice, and rosemary.

The hymn finishes just as I move to my seat. I adjust the microphone, then spread my arms wide, saying solemnly, "The Lord be with you."

"And with your spirit," comes the response.

"My friends, let us—" I pause for a split second as I catch sight of the young woman with blue hair from the police station. She is sitting in the front row in her wheelchair, dressed in a yellow suit right out of the 1960s, complete with matching gloves and a pillbox hat, with a matillia over the hat.

But in spite of her outrageous attire, she is not what causes me to stumble.

Sitting next to her, in a long navy blue dress made from some sort of wrinkled, sheer fabric, is Helen.

She seems amused by my momentary discomfiture, and I quickly collect myself, continuing, "—acknowledge our sins and so prepare ourselves to celebrate the sacred mysteries."

Mass continues without any further incidents. The closer we get to the elevation, the stronger my focus as I place my hands over the bread and the wine, saying the prayers that turn them into the body and blood of Christ. My eyes fix on the large white wafer as I hold it aloft, barely holding it by the tips of my fingers. A moment later, I elevate the chalice, grasping it with one hand while supporting the base with the other.

More prayers, then it's time for everyone to receive communion. I move about the altar giving plates of communion hosts to the Eucharistic Ministers, taking the big one myself. Throughout the church, people slide out of their pews into the aisles. Helen remains seated beside the young woman as I approach her, always offering communion first to those who might have trouble making it to the front.

I stop in front of the young blue-haired woman and, leaning forward slightly, I whisper to her, "Would you like to receive?"

She has a glazed look on her face. Her lips move as she tries to speak but she only shakes her head, so I ask, "Would you like a blessing?" Wide-eyed, she nods. So, using my thumb, I make the sign of the cross on her forehead. I am a little concerned when she looks like she might pass out.

Still, I move on to Helen. Instead of raising her hands to me so I can give her the host, she folds them together in an attitude of prayer and tilts her head upward, signaling that she wants to receive on the tongue.

Her simple action, taught to children when they are preparing to receive their first communion, hits me like a lightning bolt.

My fingers are still poised above the plate of communion hosts, but my heart is beating so loud it's drowning out all other sounds. I half expect it to leap out of my chest and start running around while a dozen toddlers chase after it. Unbidden comes a flash of a memory of Helen's ruby-red lips in a much different context.

I manage to gain control of myself and take one of the consecrated hosts from the plate. Holding it before her to adore, I say, "Body of Christ."

"Amen," she says quietly. I place the host on her tongue, then go to give the other people their piece of Christ.

By the time Mass is over, I have made up my mind that I need to try to reconnect with Helen and make amends. I greet those passing through the doors briefly, moving them along as best I can. I notice that Helen does not come out the front door, but I assume she went out the side and down the ramp with the young woman in the hat. I step outside into the soft fall day to find them.

At first, I don't see them. I look at the children running up and down the stairs, oblivious to their mother's cries to be careful. Over on the lawn next to the church, where the Rectory is, there's a group of older boys tossing around a ball that someone must have brought from home.

I finally spot them and see Helen speaking earnestly to the woman. I wonder momentarily if she might be part of some sort of program designed to help the differently-abled get jobs.

I walk up to them, but hesitate when I hear Helen hiss, "Gladys! There are children around!"

"I know," the young woman whispers. "So many. Aah." Her expression of ecstasy dissolves into an other-worldly smile.

"Gladys." Helen says, obviously embarrassed. When she doesn't respond, she bends down and speaks directly in her ear. "Gladys!"

She starts and looks up. "Huh? Oh, sorry Chief. What were you saying?"

They both laugh at this and Helen continues. "I was about to ask if you wanted to grab coffee at The Perfect Cup?"

"How 'bout lunch at The Bistro instead?" Gladys says. "My—" she stops in mid-sentence, her mouth open, her eyes filling the frames of her glasses as I approach Helen from behind.

"Good morning, Detective," I say.

She turns. She seems a little flustered but responds. "Good morning, Father," We stand like that for a moment until I hear, "Ahem." The young lady is looking at Helen expectantly, a grin on her face.

"Oh! Sorry, Father. This is Gladys Finklestein. She's the department's forensic data analyst and computer expert."

When I step towards her and extend my hand, Gladys looks like she's going to topple backwards. "Nice to meet you, Ms. Finklestein," I say.

"Nice-ahem-nice to meet you, H—Father Greer," she gushes.

"Your first time at a Mass?"

"Yes. No. I mean. Not in a long time." Then, breathlessly she adds, "Is it always like this?"

This takes me aback a little but I continue to smile, saying, "The Mass itself is pretty typical but with this many kids, it's often loud."

"No," she shakes her head. "That's not what I mean. I mean, is what just happened normal?" At my confused look, she says, "You're kidding? You didn't feel it?"

"What are you talking about?"

"The whole Mass," she says, gesturing back to the church. "It was so . . . the only word I can think of is passionate. Like I was watching the tenderest act of lovemaking I've ever seen. The way you held that wafer so loving and gently and showed it to us. And then, when you touched me with the same fingers that had just held God—I felt . . ." Her eyes close and her mouth drops open slightly. "I've never felt anything—and I mean *anything*—that good!"

I laugh and say, "Well, I hope to see you next week."

"Uh-huh," Gladys nods, still looking at me.

"Gladys?" Helen says firmly, "Why don't you go get us a table at The Bistro? I'll be there in a minute."

"Huh? Oh, sure, Chief, I'll meet you there. Bye, Father," she says, then wheels herself towards the ramp to the sidewalk.

"Is she OK?" I ask.

"Gladys? Oh, yeah, she's fine. But," she turns to me and smiles, "she can be as socially awkward as someone I once knew."

"Oh? And who would that be?"

She sighs. "Just someone."

We both chuckle. "I was surprised to see you," I say. "Especially after the other day."

"I decided to give Saint Clare's a try," she says. "I mean, since it doesn't look like I'm leaving Myerton anytime soon, it doesn't make sense to drive thirty minutes each way when my apartment is less than ten minutes away."

I nod. "Well, I am glad to see you, Helen. I'd like to talk to you sometime, but not here, not now, not like this. Would you be willing to stop by my office sometime?"

"Sure."

"What about this afternoon? I need to get a few things off my chest and I'd like to do it sooner rather than later."

"My, it must be important if you're willing to miss Darlington for it."

I smile at this. She always hated NASCAR, or at least had very little interest in it, so I am curious how she knows about todays' race. As if reading my mind, she admits, "They were talking about the race on the radio when I was on my way over."

"Ah," I say, in spite of myself. "So you still refuse to embrace the one true sport?"

"I suppose so," she says, but guardedly now.

"Could you stop by after your lunch with Gladys? You'll have to pick up your car anyway. I promise I won't take long."

"OK. Sure. I'll see you then." She turns on her surprisingly high heels and walks away. In spite of myself, my eyes linger, but not where most men would. I'm looking at her hair, glistening in the sunlight like the wings of a blackbird, the light turning her black tresses blue as it bounces off.

Recovering, I remind myself of where and who I am and turn resolutely to continue to speak to the people around me.

***

Back at the Rectory, I find myself unable to eat the obviously delicious stew Glenda left for me to warm up. I'm glad she's not here to see me reject yet another of her meals, but I just can't face it.

I know what I need to do, what I want to do, and yet, I am still incredibly nervous about facing Helen and admitting all the ways—big and small, recent and ancient—that I have mistreated her.

I spend the hour or so that passes between when she leaves and when she returns alternatively pacing and flipping channels on the TV. I can't even enjoy the fact that there has been a rain delay and so I won't miss the race.

It's no surprise, then, that I jump when I hear a knock at the door. I rush to answer it with a stupid amount of speed and stop myself just short of snatching the door open.

Helen's standing there on the steps, looking more than she has any right to like—what?

The woman I abandoned? No, that implies a certain helplessness, which was never the case with her.

Betrayed? Again, not exactly that.

Walked out on twenty years ago? Yeah, that's the only way to describe it.

She's obviously less vulnerable than she was then as she says confidently, "I didn't know which door to knock on."

"This one's fine," I say, letting her in and then escorting her through to my office. "Like most priests, I work from home."

I thought this would sound funny but it doesn't at all so we just sit down in wing chairs placed across from each other. Not knowing where to start, I say, "So, what did you think of the Mass? You certainly had a good seat."

She looks uncomfortable at this and rushes to say, "That was never my plan, I can assure you. Frankly, I had planned to sit in the back but there was no room."

"Yeah, those back pews fill up quickly with families with little kids. And I'm sure you noticed there are a lot of those."

"I really could not believe how crowded the church was. I mean, the parish in Frostburg is usually less than half full, and I'm one of the few people there under the age of 60."

"I know. We have a very young congregation, at least at the 10:30 Mass."

"Before I walked in I was afraid I would stick out like a sore thumb. But honestly, I dealt with protests in D.C. as a street cop that were less chaotic."

"Speaking of sticking out, your friend Gladys is certainly . . . exotic? Classic? Odd? In her taste in clothes., I mean."

"Oh, yes," Helen manages to laugh. "Apparently, she watched an old movie to find out what she ought to wear to Mass."

"Well, it's charming to find someone willing to make that level of effort. I wonder, though, where she found that outfit around here."

"Oh, I can assure you, it came right out of her closet and she'll probably wear it to work tomorrow—sans the veil and gloves, of course."

"Really?"

"She does all of her shopping at vintage clothing stores. I doubt she owns anything made after 1965."

"That is interesting."

Our conversation is beginning to peter out, and I realize that I need to get to the reason why I asked her here today.

"Helen," I say, "I want to apologize. I was an ass the other day. I was just upset, when you said the things you said. I thought it was because you were still angry over what happened between us."

"Tom, no, it had nothing to do with that," She shakes her head. "I was just doing my job."

I nod. "I know. I just got angry. And you may remember what I can get like when I get angry."

"You act like a petulant child, if memory serves."

"Ah, yes." I look at her. "No hard feelings?"

"No hard feelings," she says with a slight smile. We just sit in silence looking each other in the eyes.

I clear my throat. "Helen, there's something else. I'm sorry for leaving the way I did. I shouldn't have done that. I was hurt and angry. But it wasn't right to do that to you."

She seems taken aback by this but then says, "You were young. We both were. We were kids who thought we knew everything."

I nod. "Yes. I was a fool. We had something good, and I threw it away."

Helen looks at me, eyes no longer colored by anger or resentment. "Well, Tom," she says quietly "it worked out well for both of us, in the end."

I am suddenly discovering that it is hard when dealing with Helen to find the boundary between priest and former fiancée. I am afraid I have crossed it when I ask, "Were you happy with him? Your husband? Was he good to you?"

Her eyes begin to water as she whispers, "Yes. We were very happy together. You would have liked him."

"I'm sure."

She catches me off guard by asking, "Were you happy with Joan?"

"Didn't you ask me that already?" I ask.

"I want to hear your answer again."

"As Detective Parr?"

She shakes her head. "No. As me."

Now it's my turn to develop moist eyes. "I was. I thought we were happy together. But since coming back, since finding what I found . . ." I slowly shake my head. "I don't know anymore."

I see her arm flinch, as if she was going to reach toward me but then changed her mind. Instead, she says, standing, "This has been very nice, Tom, and I am glad we're friends again. But I really need to go. And anyway, you surely want to catch some of that race."

"Yes, of course." I say, walking her to the door.

She turns to me. "Good-bye, Tom," she says. "I'm sure we'll be seeing each other around town."

"Good-bye, Helen," I say. She starts down the steps. Trying to make my priest-self speak loudly enough to drown out the former lover, I say, "It was good to see you today. I hope you'll come back."

She just smiles and nods, walking down the sidewalk toward her car, a beam of sunlight briefly making her dress transparent.

I step back inside quickly and close the door behind me, subconsciously locking out—what?

Temptation?

Perhaps.

As I lean against the door, I hear the lover ask the priest, *And what will we do if she does come back, Father?*

Eleven

The address Glenda gives me for the sick call is not so much an address as a series of directions which take me out of town and onto a series of left turns, right turns, and curving mountain roads. As I get further from Myerton and into the surrounding mountains, I am struck by how beautiful the fall color is.

I'm not a fan of autumn as a rule—autumn leads to winter, which is my least favorite season. But I do love the fall colors.

Joan and I would drive up into the mountains around Myerton at this time of year to enjoy the color, and there is one overlook where we'd always stop, which has a spectacular view of Myerton surrounded by the mountains, displaying bright splashes of reds, golds, browns, and oranges.

The last time we did that was a couple of weeks before her murder.

I set up a canvas chair and sat a short distance away, reading a book. Every so often I'd look up. Joan was working steadily, stopping every so often to look at the scene, then back to her canvas.

Then, suddenly, Joan began screaming. I looked up to see her stabbing her painting with a pallet knife.

I threw my book down and ran over to her. Grabbing her, I looked her full in the face and shook her. "Joan! Joan! What's wrong?" I cried.

"It's shit!" she screamed at me. "It's just shit! Can't you see it, or are you too blind to see what a pile of shit it is!"

I looked at the remnants of the canvas. I held her close, stroking her hair. "I see it," I whispered. "I see it. It's breathtaking. One of the best things you've ever done."

What I thought would calm and reassure her had the opposite effect. In a flash, she went from leaning against me sobbing to screaming at me, beating my chest with her fists.

"Don't lie to me! You're such a liar! Why don't you just tell me the truth, huh, Tom, why?"

I grabbed her wrists and looked her in the eyes. "I am telling the truth," I say, trying to stay calm. "The painting was—is—great." Then, "What's wrong Joan? Why are you doing this?"

"Wrong? Wrong?" She started beating her chest. "I'm wrong, Tom! I'm wrong! I'm all wrong!" She collapsed to the ground, heaving with sobs as she repeated, "I'm wrong," over and over again. I knelt by her and held her against me as she cried. After a while, I gently helped her get up and led her to the car.

We drove back to our apartment in silence. When we got home, I helped her inside and tucked her into bed. Then I sat in the room, watching her as she slept. I didn't go to sleep for hours, my mind trying to make sense of what had happened. She slept all night and well into the morning.

When she woke up around 11 a.m., she greeted me with a cheerful "good morning," kissed me, and went about her day. She was fine. There was no explanation, not even an acknowledgment that anything had happened.

I decided not to press, to just leave it alone.

As I drive through the mountains fifteen years later, I think how different things might have been if I had.

***

After what seems like an eternity—travel on winding mountain roads always seems to take longer than it actually does—I arrive at the address. The house is a two-story farmhouse, painted a startling shade of reddish-pink that makes it stand out against the surrounding hills. The farm looks like it is still worked, for the fields look as if the corn has just been harvested. In one of the enclosed fields are a few cattle—I can't tell if they are steers or milk cows—and a short walk from the house is a chicken coop and a pig sty. The house has a wrap-around covered porch with three rocking chairs; the porch itself fronted by two beds of flowers struck down by an early frost.

I hear the sound of running feet when I knock on the door. Three children opened the door, two girls and a boy, who look under ten, each with sandy brown hair and hazel eyes. "Hi," I say. "Can I see your mom or dad?"

"Hope, Faith, John Paul," I hear a slightly frazzled voice call from inside. A woman, also with sandy brown hair and hazel eyes comes to the door. "What have I told you about opening the door to strangers—Oh!" she says, when she sees me. "Sorry, Father."

"Hi, um—"

"Serenity," she says, offering her hand. "Serenity MacMillan. Thanks for coming, Father."

"It's my pleasure to meet you, Ms. MacMillan," I say, taking the offered hand. "I'm here for your—-mother?"

"Please, Father, call me Serenity. It's my grandmother-in-law, actually," she says. "She hasn't been to Mass in a few weeks. I've offered to have a priest come to give her communion but she always says, 'Oh, I don't want to bother him, he's too busy,' until yesterday when she said, 'Call Saint Clare's and get the priest over here.'"

"Any idea what changed her mind?"

Serenity shakes her head. "No idea."

I don't have enough experience to speculate. I've heard that people will often call for a priest when they feel the end is near. I assume this was the case, that the person I am there to see can feel she is in her final days and wants to receive the sacraments one last time while still relatively clear. I prepare myself to minister to a frail elderly lady.

"Who is that at the door?" I start at the voice that booms from one of the downstairs rooms, more like a command than a question. The voice of a general or an admiral. I look at Serenity.

"Who is that?"

She smiles. "That's Gloria."

"Gloria? Your—your grandmother-in-law?"

She nods. "She's a force of nature. Always has been."

I have never met a force of nature before, so I steel myself for the experience. Serenity shows me down the hallway to a snug, well-lit room. In the bed, underneath a hand-crocheted afghan, is the force of nature herself, resplendent in a white bed jacket and long gray hair pulled back in a bun.

"Grandma, you have a visitor," Serenity says.

"Well I can see that, silly," she snaps. "Next you'll tell me he's a priest. I can see that, too!"

Serenity looks at me. "I'll leave you two alone. Good luck," she whispers as she slips from the room.

"Ms. MacMillan—" I start.

"Mrs." she interrupts.

"Excuse me?"

"What, can't you hear?" she says. "I say Mrs. Not Ms. Never liked Ms. Never was ashamed of being married to my Harry, though he could be a bit thick at times. Always went by Mrs. Not going to change now."

"OK, sorry, Mrs. MacMillan. I'm Father Greer."

She looks at me as if really seeing me for the first time, squinting through her round wire-rim glasses. She studies me for a few moments.

"You're not Father Anthony," she finally says.

"No," I say. "No, I'm not. I said my name is Father—"

"I heard you just fine, young man, nothing wrong with my hearing, I hear everything worth hearing just fine. Anything I can't hear, well . . .," she waves dismissively.

I smile in spite of myself. Gloria MacMillan is a handful.

"What I mean is, you're the new priest." It is a statement not a question.

I nod.

"So, they finally caught up with him, did they?"

"Finally caught up with who?"

"Father Anthony, of course, who do you think I mean?" she says. "I've spent years trying to get someone at the Archdiocese to listen to me about his shenanigans, and I guess they finally decided to take me seriously and do something about him."

I sat down in the chair next to the bed. "What shenanigans?" I ask hesitantly.

She points a bony index finger at me. "Bingo."

I have been with her for five minutes and am totally confused. "Bingo?"

"Bingo. You know, bingo. The game with the cards and the numbers. Bingo."

"What does bingo have to do with it?"

"What does bingo—why, everything young man!" She slaps the bed with her hand.

I look at Gloria MacMillan, convinced she is completely senile. What am I to do with this elderly woman carrying on about bingo?

"For the last twenty years," she goes on, "Saint Clare's has had a monthly bingo game on the last Saturday night of the month. The Knights serve spaghetti—absolutely vile if you ask me, Tim Horton can't cook to save his life—and run the game. They have Father Anthony call the numbers. Guess they figure you could trust a priest to be honest." She harrumphs.

I nod, vaguely remembering Glenda telling me about this when she told me about parish activities. I am dreading having to get involved with it.

"So, Father Anthony," she says, "calls the numbers. I play five or six cards at a time and I always have bingos for the smaller prizes—I've won a slew of backscratchers, don't know why they had so many, I only have one back. The last round of the night is always for the big prize—an electric blanket, a coffee pot, you know, something like that, do you see what I'm saying?"

"Oh, yes, absolutely," I say, when in reality I have no idea what this is about.

"And every month for twenty years, in all that time, I have never gotten a bingo for the big prize." She crosses her arms in triumph. "And now they've got him."

"Got him? For what?"

"For rigging the game, of course! The winner is always one of his favorites. That housekeeper-slash-secretary of his, Glenda, she's won a coffee pot and an electric blanket. I've complained to Father Anthony, but he just smiles and pats my hand and says, 'Well, better luck next month, Gloria.'" She points at me. "So I've written to the Archbishop several times. Never heard anything. Well, I guess they finally listened to me. So young man," she points at me again, "you better be careful. I'll be watching you."

"Mrs. MacMillan," I say, "Father Anthony hasn't been removed for—rigging bingo."

"Oh? No? Why?"

"He's not been removed, per se. I mean, he's still officially the parish priest at Saint Clare's. I'm just temporary. He's had some health issues—"

"Oh, fiddlesticks," she says, dismissing the idea with a wave of her hand. "Health issues? He's younger than I am. They're just trying to cover it up. I promise you," she hits the bed again with the palm of her hand, "I'm going to contact my lawyer and sue the Archdiocese."

"Mrs. MacMillan, please. I didn't come here to discuss this. I don't think you need to sue anyone—"

"But it's wrong, taking advantage of a defenseless old woman like me," she pouts.

I stifle a laugh. I've only just met her, but defenseless hardly describes Gloria MacMillan.

I change tactics and get a serious look on my face. "Mrs. MacMillan, I don't know what has happened in the past. But you have my solemn promise that in the four months I'm here at Saint Clare's, every bingo game will be run with the utmost propriety."

She looks at me. "Really?"

I nod.

"You promise?"

"I promise."

"Well, good. About time." She adjusts herself in the bed, then looks at me.

"So, are you going to give me Communion or not?"

I smile and proceed to do just that.

***

I leave the MacMillans and begin the drive back to Saint Clare's. Just outside of town my cell phone rings. It's a number I don't recognize.

"Hello?" I answer.

"Tom? It's Helen."

I say nothing for a moment. "Helen," I finally say.

"Did I catch you at a bad time?"

"I'm just driving back from seeing a parishioner. What can I do for you?"

"I just wanted to let you know I'm taking another look at your wife's case."

"Really," I say, the amazement in my voice apparent even to me. "Thank you, but I thought you said—"

"Oh, it wasn't my call. I stand by what I said to you the other day." She pauses. "You've been a busy little priest, Father."

I note the sarcasm in her voice. "What do you mean?"

"A reporter called yesterday, started asking questions, wanting a comment for her story. Said she is working with you. I sent her over to Public Affairs, which told her that the investigation was ongoing and we couldn't comment. But since the investigation wasn't really ongoing, the

Chief thought it would be a good idea to work on it." She pauses. "So I'm working your wife's fifteen-year-old murder."

"Sorry it's taking you from your bike thieves," I say, immediately regretting it. She is trying to do the right thing, whether she wants to or not, and I shouldn't respond with sarcasm.

"I've begun reading through the file," she goes on, choosing to ignore my comment. "There wasn't much in the way of physical evidence, but what was collected is stored off-site. It will take a couple of days to get it here. I've got some questions about your original statement."

"OK, well what are they?"

"No, not now, not over the phone," she says. "I'd like to do it face to face."

"When would you like me to come down to the station?"

Helen says nothing for a moment and I think the call has dropped. Then she says, "What are you doing tomorrow night?"

"I think I'm free. What time?"

"I thought maybe we could discuss things over dinner?"

I am stunned and don't know what to say for a moment. "Do you think that's a good idea?"

"Why not? Afraid I might attack you?"

"No, of course not, that's not what I mean."

"Look, I just thought a more informal atmosphere would be better." She pauses again. "And I thought we could catch up."

I hesitate, then say, "I don't think that's a good idea, Helen, do you?"

I hear her sigh. "No, Tom," she replies. "I guess not. I'll call you in the next couple of days, arrange a time to meet at the station."

"Fine," I say. "Looking forward to it."

We hang up just as I pull up to the Rectory. My phone rings again. It's Katherine Shepp.

"I hope I'm not interrupting anything," she says.

"Not at all, I'm just getting back to Saint Clare's."

"I was hoping you'd have some time Thursday for an interview."

"I thought we'd already done an interview?"

"No, that was you telling your story," she says. "An interview is where I ask questions and you answer them."

"Oh, OK, what time do you and Nate—"

"Nate won't be there. Just me and a cameraman from the station. For this, I need a little more professionalism than Nate. Is 2:00 p.m. all right?"

"I don't have my calendar with me, but it should be fine."

"Great." She pauses. "This is going to be really good, Father. You'll see."

Twelve

Thursday afternoon arrives and after the Noon Mass, a van with a satellite dish emblazoned with the call letters and logo of Katherine Shepp's television station pulls into the driveway of the rectory. Katherine gets out and walks towards me, her hair perfectly coiffed and wearing a light blue dress. She smiles that same perfect smile I noticed when I first met her.

After we exchange pleasantries, I say, "You're a little early. I haven't even had time to change out of my vestments. We said 2 p.m."

"Oh, I know," Katherine says. "We're going to shoot some B-reel."

"B-reel?"

"Yes, shots we can use to illustrate the report," she explains. "We want shots of the exterior of the church, you walking to the front, of you inside—"

I shake my head. "Not inside, no."

"Really? Why not?"

"I'd have to get permission from the Archdiocese first. There's not enough time."

"Oh, OK." She walks back to the van. "Sam, let's set up at the front to begin with, I'll do my intro standup there. Father," she turns back to me, "why don't you change and come out in about twenty minutes. We'll do some exterior shots of you." She then busies herself with her equipment.

I go back inside the church to the sacristy and get out of my vestments. I then go to my office and lean back in my chair.

After talking to Anna the day before, I am slightly uneasy about agreeing to the interview. Katherine had talked to her, and Anna was not impressed.

"Why did you agree to talk to her?" Anna had asked me. The irritation in her voice came through the phone loud and clear.

"She's interested in Joan's case," I said. "She wants to find out who killed her. I thought you wanted that, too."

"Of course I do, you know that. But Tom, I'm telling you, I don't trust her. Whatever she wants to do, I don't think it's finding out who killed Joan." She had paused. "You need to be careful around her."

"Anna, I appreciate it, but I think you're worried for no reason. I admit she's a little intense—"

"No," she had said. "A thunderstorm is intense. Hot sauce is intense. That blond thing is dangerous. Just be careful."

I had promised her I would be, but at the time I didn't really give her concerns too much thought.

Now, however, I begin to turn them over in my mind.

What if she's right? What if Katherine really isn't that interested in Joan's case? And if she isn't really after Joan's killer, then what is she after? According to Nate, she sees a story on Joan's murder as her way of moving up in her profession. What if that is all she cares about?

There's a knock on my office door. I close my eyes and shake my head. There is only one person it can be.

"Come in, Glenda," I call.

The door opens to reveal a very vexed-looking Glenda. "Father Greer," she says, "are you aware that there is a news truck outside?"

"Yes, I am aware of that."

"And," she goes on, "a reporter—I guess that's who she is, though by the way she's dressed it's hard to tell—from one of the Baltimore news stations?"

I nod.

"Why is she here?" Glenda says, walking towards my desk.

I look at her. "She's here to interview me," I say.

"You?" Glenda sits down in one of the chairs in front of my desk. "Why would she want to interview you?"

"She's doing a story about my wife's murder," I say, "and she's here to do an interview. I've already talked to her, but she had some other questions."

The look on her face changes from puzzlement to—something I can't describe. "Oh," she says quietly. "That was about fifteen years ago. The crime was never solved, right?"

"That's right." I have a hard time believing she has not heard.

"So why is she here?"

"I just told you, she wants to do an interview for a story she's doing on Joan's—my wife's—murder. She hopes—we hope—that it will spark interest in what happened. Apparently, it already has. The police have reopened the case."

"They have?" Glenda says, a little too loud. She startles me.

"Yes, they're taking another look at it." I look at her, confused about her reaction.

"Well that's—that's good," she says. She swallows, then draws herself up. "What did the Archbishop say when you told him?"

I get a sinking feeling in the pit of my stomach. "The Archbishop," I say to myself.

"You did tell him about the interview request," she goes on. "To get permission."

"I, ah, well—"

"Father Greer," she says in her typical imperious tone, "You know full well that the Archbishop would not want you talking to the press without his permission."

"I am not speaking as a representative of the Church," I say. "This is a personal matter. I don't believe I need his permission."

"Perhaps not," she replies. "But I would think the Archbishop would appreciate a heads-up, at least."

I have to admit that she has a point. "You're right Glenda. I should have contacted the Archbishop before now. I'll call him after the interview to let him know what's going on."

"I guess that will just have to do," Glenda says as she stands. "By the way, I have to go take my nephew to an appointment. May I leave early?"

"Oh, of course Glenda. How are things going with him?"

She hesitates for a moment, and I see a crack in the stern veneer she hides herself behind. "Fine, thank you," she says curtly, cutting off any more inquiry.

A few minutes after she leaves, there's a knock on the Rectory door. I guess that Katherine is ready for me.

But when I open the door, Katherine isn't standing there. It is Nate, dressed better than I have ever seen him, wearing a white shirt, blue striped tie, and a sportcoat. The fact he's also wearing jeans and tennis shoes is besides the point.

"Hi, Father, am I late? For the interview?"

"No, we haven't started yet," I answer. "Come in, Nate." I show him into the living room and he sits in one of the easy chairs while I take the one opposite.

"I wasn't expecting you," I say. "Katherine hadn't—"

"Oh I know, I know, but I thought since it was my early work that got her attention, she would want to have a few words from me. Also, since we're working on this together, I thought I oughta be here."

"Well, I'm sure since you're here, she'll want to talk to you."

There is another knock. This time it is Katherine.

"OK, Father," she says as she sweeps past me, "we're ready to shoot some footage. What we're going to want you—oh, Nate, you're here." She doesn't sound happy to see him.

"Hi, Katherine," Nate says, grinning from ear to ear.

"What are you doing here?" she says, an even tone in her voice.

"I thought I could help," Nate says with unabated enthusiasm. "Since I started all this, you know."

She smiles. "And I'm so thankful for all you did. It really gave me a place to begin. But," she pats his arm, "why don't you leave this to the professionals?"

She turns to me before Nate can answer, leaving him with his mouth slightly open. "Shall we, Father?" She heads to the door. I look at Nate apologetically as I follow her out. Nate stands in the entryway for a minute then follows.

We spend the next half-hour with me walking back and forth in front of Saint Clare's, standing on the steps looking at the camera, standing with the church behind me gazing into the distance. Several people walking by stop to look at the spectacle. I feel self-conscious and at one point I look in the direction of the Rectory. Nate is still there, standing on the bottom step, his hands in his pockets, looking forgotten and forlorn.

We finish the filming and go back to the Rectory. Katherine and her cameraman spend the next half-hour rearranging the furniture in the living room and setting up lights. I stand by, trying to stay out of the way, imagining what Glenda will say when she sees the parish's furniture rearranged.

"Why don't you sit here, Father," Katherine indicates the better-looking of the two armchairs. She has set the other one up for herself directly across from me, the lights arranged on either side. I have seen enough television interviews to recognize the arrangement.

I sit. "Do I need makeup?"

Katherine looks at me and gives a small laugh. "No, Father, you'll be fine."

She sits up straight and arranges herself in the chair. "OK, Father, here's what's going to happen. I'm going to ask you questions and you're going to answer while looking at me, not the camera. Got that?"

"Sure, I've got it."

"Good," she says. Then she turns to look at the cameraman. "You can start."

The cameraman looks through the viewfinder, presses a button, and a red light comes on.

Katherine turns to me and smiles. "Father Tom Greer," she begins, "Thank you for agreeing to speak to us."

I return the smile. "My pleasure, Katherine." Both the smile and the response comes more from habit than honesty.

"A few days ago," she begins, "I filmed you talking about your wife's murder. That murder, for our viewers who may not be aware of the story, was never solved."

I nod, "That's correct. No one has ever been arrested for Joan's murder."

"And you describe to me what happened in great detail, right?"

"Right," I reply. I'm not quite sure where she is going with these particular questions.

"According to you," Katherine looks down at her notes, then back up at me, "Joan died in your arms."

I swallow. "Yes," I say quietly.

"A very touching story," Katherine says with what sounds like feigned sympathy. "Truly, very touching."

I take out a handkerchief and wipe the beginning of tears from my eyes.

"So Father," she continues, "tell me what happened next."

"Next?" I say. "Well, we had her funeral. Her Funeral Mass was in this church. She's buried at a cemetary outside of town."

"Were there a lot of people at the funeral?"

I search my memory. "I think so, yes."

"You think so?"

"Well, it's been fifteen years," I answer, "and I don't remember much about that day."

"You don't remember much about the day of your wife's funeral," she says, "but you remember the details of your wife's murder?"

"It's burned into my memory. What I remember is burned into my memory. Most of the details are hazy."

"But it's been fifteen years. Do you think you may have forgotten some details? Or embellished them, perhaps?"

"No. Absolutely not."

"Hmm," Katherine says. She looks down at her notes again. "So according to my interviews around town, you left town shortly after Joan's funeral. Is that correct?"

"It wasn't exactly shortly after her funeral. It was about six months later."

"OK, six months after her funeral. Why? You had a job at Myer College and had lived here for a number of years—"

"That's true" I say. "I was hired by Myer College as an archivist. That's where I met Joan."

"So you lived here for several years, were married in this church, and your wife was buried here," Katherine continues. "Why did you leave?"

I take a deep breath. "I just—it just became too much. The memories. Joan and I had a lot of good memories here. But I couldn't stay here, not in the town where she was murdered. It was just too much."

There is another reason—one no one except me, the administration of Myer College, and the other person involved knows about—that I pray she doesn't bring up.

"So after six months, you left."

I nod.

"According to your ex-mother-in-law, you didn't tell anyone you were leaving. Is that correct?"

"Not quite," I say. "I resigned from my position. I sent an email to Anna—Joan's mother, my mother-in-law—telling her I was leaving. But I didn't let anyone else know. I just wanted to leave quietly, without a fuss."

"You didn't want anyone to know you were gone," she says.

"No, I wouldn't put it that way."

She looks down at her notes again. "Were you aware that after you left, the police continued investigating your wife's murder?"

"I'm not surprised," I say, "since the crime was unsolved."

"No, I don't mean that," she says. "Were you aware that the police began investigating you?"

I look at her, a little stunned. Anna's warning comes back to me. Slowly, I say. "I only became aware of that after I came back to Myerton."

"Oh, yes," she says, "your sudden and mysterious return to Myerton."

"It may have been sudden," I reply, "but hardly mysterious. Saint Clare's needed a temporary parish priest. The Archbishop assigned me here."

"He assigned you to the parish where your wife's funeral was, in a town you had left fifteen years ago because of the pain you felt surrounding your wife's murder."

"That's exactly right."

"If this place has so many painful memories as you claim," she asks, "why would you ever come back?"

"Would you refuse an assignment from your boss?" I ask. "It was a question of obedience. I had no choice. By my vows, I'm obliged to obey my superiors."

"Still, you can see how odd it is, given the story you tell."

"It's the truth."

"Is it? Is it really?" Katherine looks at me, then back at her notes.

"Let's talk about something else," she goes on. "Were you and your wife close?"

"Yes," I say. "Very close."

"No problems?"

"I wouldn't say that. We were a young married couple. I don't know of a young married couple that doesn't have a period of adjustment."

"Let's go back to the night of her murder," Katherine says. She flips through her notes. "You say you and your wife were having a celebration dinner, right?"

"Yes," I say. "Joan had found out she was pregnant. We'd been trying for a while. We were both happy."

"Really?" she says. "So it was a happy time for both of you."

"Yes, very."

"You laughed, probably toasted each other, talked excitedly about baby things, maybe names for the child."

"Yes," I say quietly.

"All very expected." She pauses. "Does the name Tony Armando ring a bell?"

I think, then shake my head. "No, should it?"

"Probably not, though he was the owner of La Petite Maison fifteen years ago. Retired now, living in Florida." She pulls out a document. "Here's a copy of his police interview. Do you know what he told the police?"

"I haven't the slightest idea." The knot in my stomach says otherwise.

"Are you sure, Father?" she says, a tight smile forming on her lips. "Are you quite sure?"

I stare at her but say nothing.

"Maybe this will jog your memory," she says. She pulls out a small digital recorder. "I located Mr. Armando and interviewed him on the phone. Here's what he said."

She presses play and turns the sound up. Through the recorder's small speaker, I hear an older male voice.

"They had just ordered dessert, I think," Armando says. "All of a sudden I heard her yell at him. I looked over. She had stood up, waving her arms like a mad woman. He was trying to calm her down, get her to sit down. She threw her napkin down, grabbed her bag, and stormed out of the restaurant. He watched her leave."

"Did he go after her?" Katherine's voice said.

"Yeah, he went after her, ran out of the restaurant after her."

She clicked the recorder off. I am feeling hot. Beads of sweat have formed on my head.

"Well?" Katherine asks.

I try to be as nonchalant as possible. "We had a fight. Young couples have fights."

"But," Katherine says, leaning forward, "wasn't it more than that?"

I look at her. "No, just normal young couple stuff."

"Really, Father?" She reaches down and pulls out a stack of papers. I recognize them. They are copies of the emails.

"Then," she goes on, "how do you explain these emails?" She hands them to me. I take them and look through them. They are the emails I had given her.

"These," I say as I leafed through the pages, "are emails Joan received in the weeks leading up to her murder." I look up. "They appear to be from a man who had some kind of obsession with her, who was stalking her."

"Did you know about these emails?"

I shake my head. "No. Nothing. Joan never told me about them. She never told me she was getting unwanted attention from a man and never said anything to me about being stalked."

Katherine sits back in her chair, a look of triumph on her face. "Come now, Father. Do you expect anyone to believe that your wife was receiving these emails, was being stalked, and she said nothing to you about it?"

"It's the truth."

"Or," she says, "isn't the truth actually much different than you've said." She pauses, I suppose expecting a comeback of some kind.

When I say nothing, she goes on. "I have here," she says, showing me another paper, "a copy of a marriage license. Isn't that your wife's name?"

I look and nod.

"But that's not your name, is it, Father?"

"No," I whisper. "No, it's not."

"This license," she says, "shows that Joan Luckgold married a Randy Earl in 1996. I have here," she says, pulling out another piece of paper, "a decree of annulment dated six weeks later. Am I right that you claim you knew nothing about your wife's marriage and annulment?"

"It's the truth," I say quietly.

"What about this?" she says, presenting another document. "This is a document showing that Joan Luckgold was admitted to Gentle Brook Treatment Center six months after the annulment."

I grab the paper out of her hands. It's an admissions paper showing Anna signed Joan into Gentle Brook Treatment Center.

I have heard of it. It is a private mental hospital.

"How did you get this?" I ask.

"I have my sources," she says. "Well, Father, did you know anything about this?"

"No, nothing," I say, handing it back to her.

"Seems there's a lot you didn't know," Katherine says. She looks at me.

"So what really happened that night, Father?"

"I already told you," I say, my voice firm and even. "It's what I told the police fifteen years ago."

"You didn't tell the police about the fight, did you, Father?" Katherine says. "Why?"

"I didn't think it was important."

"Really? Or was there another reason." She leans forward. "Was there really an attack, Father? Was it really a mysterious hooded stranger with a gun?" She pauses. "Or was it you?"

I leap from my chair and snatch the lapel mike off. "Turn the camera off."

Katherine protests, "We're not finished, Father Greer."

I look at her and scream. "I said turn that camera off, now!" My pulse is racing, I can feel heat rising in my face. My chest is heaving. Katherine looks at me, startled, and then smiles.

"Fine, Father," she says. "I have everything I need."

Thirteen

"What I fail to understand, Father Tom, is why you are telling me this now, after the proverbial horse has left the barn!"

I knew it was not going to be an easy conversation when I called Archbishop Walter Knowland to tell him about my interview with Katherine Shepp. I have put off telling him for a week after the interview, telling myself it is in order to find the right words.

In reality, I was avoiding him.

I couldn't foresee how upset he would be. I have never seen or heard the Archbishop angry, and he's always very jovial in our conversations. I have heard rumors of a fiery temper when he is provoked but discounted them.

Standing in the Rectory office with my phone in my hand, I realize that had been a mistake.

I've made a lot of them recently.

"I'm sorry, Your Eminence," I say.

"Don't you think," he bellows, "it might just have been a good idea to ask before you had any dealings with the press? Or are you completely unaware of how the press has treated the Church in the last few years?"

"To be fair, the Church has brought a lot of that on itself."

"Don't get smart with me, Father," he snaps.

"With all due respect," I go on, "this has nothing to do with the Church. This is about something that happened before I even had a notion of becoming a priest."

"Father Tom," the Archbishop says, more patiently this time, "you need to remember that you represent the Church all the time. Even if this interview has nothing to do with the Church or your activities as a priest, people will see you as a priest. Anything you say, anything this reporter chooses to highlight, will be seen by people as being done by a priest of the Catholic Church. I don't mean to come across as hurtful, but no one will care that your wife was killed before you became a priest."

I really haven't thought about that. I have only thought about my situation. I see my life as having two parts. The first part was my life before I became a priest. The second part was my life after I became a priest. For years I have kept my former life in a box, locked away and separate from my life as a priest, or at least I have tried. Coming back to Myerton, I thought I could be here as a priest without having to open up that box.

But that's what I did. I did it in the most public way possible—on television. And I did it without thinking about the impact on my priesthood.

"Father? Father? Are you still there, Father?"

"Yes, yes, Your Eminence," I reply. "I'm still here."

"I asked you how bad it was?"

I hesitate. "Well, it could have been better." Which is the truth. Maybe not the whole truth. But not an outright lie.

The Archbishop does not respond right away. "I could ask you to be more specific, but I don't think I will. Do you want our attorney to intervene? Ask the station not to run the story?"

"No sir, I think that might make things worse."

I hear him sigh. "I suppose you're right. When will it air?"

"I'm not sure. She didn't say."

"Well, we'll just wait and see, I suppose," the Archbishop says. "Maybe it will all be OK."

I hang up. Given what has happened, I can't see how.

Glenda knocks on my door. "Do you have a moment, Father?"

"Of course," I say, indicating the chair.

"My nephew," she begins as she sits. "He needs a job."

I have stopped being surprised by her bluntness. "I thought he had a job working construction at the college?"

Glenda nods. "Oh, he did. They fired him. Got into a disagreement with his supervisor. But he needs work, so I had a thought. There is a lot of grounds work that needs to be done, with all the leaves and everything, and the beds need to be mulched. The parish could hire him as groundskeeper."

"Well," I say, "do you think that's a good idea?"

"Why wouldn't it be?" she says, slightly indignant.

"You just told me he lost a job because he got into a dispute with his supervisor," I say. "Will he do what he's supposed to do? You know, without complaint?"

"You leave him to me," she says. "He'll do what I tell him. He always has."

I think for a moment. It is such a small thing she is asking. And the work needs to be done.

"I'll need to speak to the parish council," I say.

"I already have," Glenda says. "They all say they are fine with it. They just need your say-so."

I look at her with a slight smile. "Well, then, when can he start?"

"He'll be here tomorrow morning," she says, standing. "And thank you, Father. He really is a good boy. You'll see."

***

The next evening, Friday, I am preparing to go into the church to say Evening Prayer when my cell phone rings. It's Anna.

"Hi," I say, answering. "What's up?"

"Tom," Anna says. She sounds strange.

"Is everything OK, Anna? Is something wrong?"

"Why didn't you tell me that woman's report was going to air tonight?"

"What are you talking about? I haven't spoken to Katherine Shepp since my interview. That was over a week ago."

"It's on right now," Anna says. "You better turn it on."

I hang up and run down the stairs to the living room. I turn on the TV.

". . . recently retold the story of that night," the disembodied voice of Katherine Shepp says. On the screen is the video of me recounting the night of Joan's murder. It goes on for about a minute, then cuts back to a shot of Katherine standing in front of the Church.

"That's the story Tom Greer, now Father Tom Greer," she says as a still of me appears in the corner of the screen, "told police. But is that the real story?"

I get a sick feeling in the pit of my stomach.

She holds up some papers. "I-Seven has obtained copies of internal police documents showing that authorities during the original investigation considered Greer a person of interest. The investigators found evidence of financial difficulties between the young couple, and there were reports of arguments between the Greers over money."

The report cuts to Bethany Grable. "Joan was trying to get her business started," she is saying, "and things weren't going well. Tom was constantly bailing her out. Things were tough."

"Police could never find solid evidence tying Greer to his wife's death at the time," Katherine continues, "and did not believe that money was a motive because there was no life insurance or savings that would have gone to Tom Greer in case of her death. So the case has remained unsolved for fifteen years."

I breathe a sigh of relief. It wasn't as bad as I thought it would be.

Then Katherine says, "But this reporter has uncovered new evidence that sheds some new light on this case, light that spotlights one person—Father Tom Greer."

I feel the oxygen leave the room as my photo fills the screen.

The picture cuts back to Katherine. "I-Seven obtained emails that Joan Greer received in the weeks leading up to her death, emails that are from an unnamed man who, by all appearances, Joan had recently ended a relationship with."

The picture cuts to a clip from the interview. There I am, sitting in the Rectory.

I know what comes next. The insinuations. The accusations. My reactions.

I put my head in my hands.

This is bad. So, so bad.

A reporter just accused me of murder on live television.

Katherine Shepp used me. She used my desire to find Joan's killer to further her career.

"That was some reaction from Father Greer," the in-studio anchor is saying. "Any comments from the Myerton Police?"

"Ted, a spokesperson for the department says the case is still considered an open investigation so they have no comment. But a source inside the department tells me that, because of this reporting, they are taking a closer look at the case."

I turn off the TV and stare at the blank screen. I don't know how long I sit there. Time has stopped. My mind whirls. I have not expected this—though I should have from her line of questioning. She had decided that I would make the most likely suspect. Of course, there wasn't much evidence pointing in another direction. All I had were the emails, the fact that Joan had not told me about them, and my vague suspicions.

I also have the knowledge that I did not kill her. But at this moment, that is little comfort.

On the other hand, the one thing I have worried most about, the one thing about that night I have hidden for all these years, the one thing I am most ashamed of, still remains my secret.

Unless, of course, Helen has figured it out.

And while I have no idea what kind of detective she is, I know her—or at least I did. Determined, stubborn, persistent—she is all these things. I fell in love with her because of her stubborn persistence in helping me with Elementary Statistics.

Again, my mind goes back over twenty years.

***

"Tom, you're not paying attention."

She's right, of course; I wasn't. Instead, I was caught up in the scent of her hair: vanilla, like a fresh-baked cookie at my grandmother's house, or the vanilla cola my dad always ordered at the diner. But still, I have my pride so I say, "Yes, I am."

"OK, then what did I just say?"

"That you find me irresistible and want to go out with me?"

"No, that is not even close. Had I said anything so personal, it would have been that I need to leave for Mass in an hour and, while I'm glad to pray for you there, I am dubious about how much it will help if you don't focus."

"Wait, why are you going to Mass? Have I been so captivated by your charms that I've lost a day or two? Did I miss Friday and Saturday entirely?"

"No, doofus," she said playfully, "I try to go to daily Mass during Lent. The church is right on campus, so it's not hard."

"But Helen," I said, trying to cajole but instead whining, "wouldn't saving my grade be of more value to humanity than praying?"

"Actually, no, Tom. You see—and I am going to use little words here so you can understand—God is God and you are, well, you."

I pretend to pout as I said, "I still don't get it."

Then I had an inspiration. "What if I go with you to Mass and then you go to dinner with me. After all, you've got to eat and I sort of owe you for helping me."

She contemplated this for a minute and then said, "All right. I'll do that."

And that's how my 22-year-old self agreed to spend 30 minutes with the God of the universe in return for two hours with a woman.

If they ever perfect time travel, I'm totally going to go back and shake that guy until his teeth rattle.

***

I close my eyes and lay my head back in the chair.

I must have dozed off—when under stress, I often fall asleep, a defense mechanism I learned growing up—because the sound of my phone jars me back to consciousness. I look at the Caller ID.

The first person to call me is the last person I would have thought of.

"Helen?" I say.

"Tom, are you OK?" She sounds worried and angry at the same time.

"I'm really not sure," I chuckle. "I've never been accused of murder on TV before."

"I can't believe you agreed to an interview with her!"

"Look," I say, "I believed her when she said she was interested in Joan's case. It was a mistake. Frankly, Helen, I'm surprised you're not knocking on my door right now."

"Oh, don't be silly," she says. "I'm not about to arrest you for Joan's murder. Unlike a reporter, I actually look at evidence. And the evidence doesn't point to you."

I let out a sigh of relief. "Thank you. So, why did you call?"

"Because I wanted to make sure you're OK," she says. "And also to assure you that bitch did not get that file from me."

I smile in spite of myself. "Helen, I never believed that for a minute. But someone in your department gave it to her."

"And I'm having Gladys check every log-in to our system to see who was the last person who accessed that file. The original's still locked in my office. Just to make sure, I checked."

"You were looking at the original when I saw you," I say. "But the files have been scanned? Why didn't you just look at that?"

"I prefer paper," she says. "I like the feel of it. Also, I could look at you, see your reaction. I couldn't do that if I was looking at my screen."

"Makes sense, actually," I say.

"So when I find who did this to you, Tom, I promise you, I'm going to have their damn badge!"

"Look, I appreciate your position, Helen. You need to find out the person who leaked that file," I say. "But frankly, no one did this to me. I did this to myself. Even if someone hadn't given her the file, she'd have made the same accusations. This is no one's fault but my own."

There's silence on the other end of the call. "Wow," she says quietly. "Tom Greer taking responsibility for something. Never thought I'd hear that."

"I'm not the same person I was back then, Helen," I say quietly.

"You know, Tom," she says. "I believe you're right."

***

Helen no sooner hangs up than my phone rings again.

I'm surprised it took him this long to call.

"Good evening, Your Eminence."

"Father Tom," the Archbishop says. "Can you please tell me how things could be any worse?"

"You saw the news."

"No, no, I was at a fundraiser for the Retired Priests and Religious Fund when it aired. I got a call from Father Wayne about it. I saw it myself online when I got back to the Residence. You were not completely forthcoming with me, were you?" the Archbishop says.

"No, sir, not entirely."

"So you knew when we spoke that this reporter was going to accuse you of murder. On television."

"No, that I did not know."

"I saw the end of your interview—everybody saw the end of your interview! That didn't give you some idea?"

"No, I just thought—"

"No, Father, the problem is that you didn't think. At all. About any of this. You agreed to the interview without consulting me. When you told me about it, you didn't tell me everything. And now, the entire Baltimore-D.C. area thinks the Archdiocese has a priest under suspicion of murder!"

"Your Eminence, the accusation is completely—"

"False, I know, I don't believe it for a minute. But what I think doesn't matter. What the truth is doesn't matter. This is a bad look for the Church. We don't need this publicity, not after—well, everything that has happened over the last several years." He pauses. "I want you to come back. To the Archdiocesan office."

I sit up. "What?"

"Yes," he said, "back here. You don't need to be in the public ministry with this swirling around. I can find another priest for Saint Clare's."

"No, sir, respectfully, no. Your Eminence, don't do this."

"It's for the best, Tom. You'll be no good at Saint Clare's."

"If I leave Myerton now, everyone will think I'm guilty. My friends, my family—they won't know what to think."

"I can't keep you there, Tom."

"Yes, you can," I say. "I need to see this through. Besides, you just mentioned what's happened over the last several years. Do you think moving me will make the Church look good? Right now, this is just about me. I know how it reflects on the Church, but Joan's murder happened before I became a priest. You can argue that it has nothing to do with my position now, that the Church has no involvement, you will let the authorities make the final decision, whatever you want to say. You don't have to say anything about my guilt or innocence. But if you move me, it will look like the Church has something to hide."

There is silence on the other end of the phone. I realize what I have done. I just gave the Archbishop a way out. He can protect the Church by disassociating from me.

And I can stay at Saint Clare's.

"You know," he says slowly, "I could make you. You are under obedience to me."

I nod. "I am aware of that, sir. But you won't. Because you know I'm right."

He is silent for a moment, then says, "All right. You stay at Saint Clare's. For now, Tom, for now. But," he continues, "if anything else happens, you're back here. That will be an order."

He hangs up before I can thank him. I hold the phone in my hand, then toss it on the couch. No other calls come in, and I need to think. I leave the phone on the couch and walk upstairs to my room. I throw myself on the bed fully clothed. I am tired, tired to my bones, even though it is only eight o'clock. I don't want to think, but I know I have to.

I have brought this on myself, I know. I should have left it alone. Joan died fifteen years ago. No one else had found her murderer. I thought I was content with that, that I had found peace. I had my papers and my boxes and my folders and my lists of records. I had my vocation. I had the Lord. Joan was in the past, still part of me, but in the past. Her murder was still a part of me, but in the past.

But it isn't really in the past. And I don't really have peace. Because I know the truth about that night—the whole truth. I have hid the truth from everyone for fifteen years—from the police, from Anna, from our friends. It was easy to avoid the truth when I was away from Myerton.

Then I returned. I found out Joan's secrets. I convinced myself that those secrets had something to do with her murder. I had to find out more, because I thought it would lead to her killer.

Instead, I wound up accused on television of her murder.

Not to mention, seeing Helen again after twenty years has stirred up feelings and emotions I'd buried long ago.

I don't know what to do next.

Fourteen

In my sleep, I hear a pounding.

I wake up with a start. Light streams through the windows of my room. As I sit up in bed, I catch a look at myself in the mirror. I still have on my clothes from the night before, including my shoes. I sit up and run my hand through my hair. I fell asleep without realizing it.

There's a pounding again, and someone at the front door is calling my name. Pulling myself together, I go downstairs and open the door to a very flustered and somewhat angry Anna.

"You pick today not to answer your phone, Tom?" she says, brushing past me.

I rub my face. "Sorry, I left it downstairs. Have you been trying to call for long?"

"Since seven this morning," she says, looking at me with her hands on her hips.

"What time is it now?"

"Almost nine," Anna says. She pauses and looks me up and down. "You look awful."

"Then I match how I feel."

"I wouldn't have come," Anna says, "except Nadine called to tell me no one showed up to celebrate the 8:00 Mass and there was no answer at the Rectory—they called and knocked, too."

I close my eyes and sigh. "I slept through Mass."

"Hmm-hmm," she says. "They were close to calling the police, but apparently someone thought that might be inappropriate considering..."

I look at her. "What are people saying?"

Anna turns around. "Come on, I'll make you some coffee," she says, walking to the kitchen. "Glenda not here today?"

"She doesn't work on Saturday anymore," I say, following her. "About last night," I press, "what are people saying?"

She turns around and crosses her arms, asking "What does it matter what people are saying?" There is an edge of defiance in her voice. Anna is obviously in full mama bear mode.

"Unfortunately, it matters a great deal. It's OK. Tell me."

"Well," she begins. "Look, I really haven't talked to that many people, and the ones I have, well, they really don't know you, and—"

"Anna, please!"

She turns back to the counter and pours coffee into two mugs. Handing me one, she says, "People don't know what to think. Many of the people in the parish weren't living in Myerton when Joan was killed." The ones who were here, on the one hand, know how hard you took it, and on the other how suddenly you left. A few remember the police asking about you." Sitting down with her coffee at the table, she says, "It's mixed, I'd say."

I sit with her and look at the cup. "I had a call last night from the Archbishop."

"I bet that didn't go well."

"You win the bet."

"Mad?"

"Furious." I take a sip of coffee. "He wanted to transfer me out of Saint Clare's."

She stares at me and I look at her. "I told him I wanted to stay."

Anna exhales. "Good, I'm glad to hear it."

We sit in silence for a few minutes drinking our coffee. Finally, Anna speaks.

"You didn't tell me about the emails."

"No, no, I didn't," I say. "I don't even know what they mean."

"What do they say?"

I tell her about the emails, about how they seem to be from a man who had some kind of obsession with Joan. How they were sent in the weeks before her death. How a couple seem to be vaguely threatening. How none of them were signed, only had the email address.

"And you think they're connected with her murder?" Anna asks.

"I wasn't sure, until I got this." I pull my wedding band out of my pocket.

Anna's eyes get big. "Where?"

"In the church." I hesitate before I say, "I left it on Joan's headstone the night I left. Someone picked it up and kept it all this time, then left it where I'd find it."

Anna stares at me. "And you have no idea who?"

I shake my head.

"Why didn't you go to the police?"

"I did, right after I found it. Showed them to Hel—Detective Parr. She didn't seem interested at the time. But they reopened the case when Shepp started poking around."

"Hopefully, she doesn't have you in her sights," Anna says, getting up. Walking to the sink with her cup, she turns on the water to rinse it out.

"I have a question," I say quietly. "Why didn't you—or Joan—tell me about her marriage to Randy Earl?"

She says nothing. She turns off the water and dries her hands. Then, she walks to the table, pulls out a chair and sits. She looks at me, her hands folded on the table in front of her.

"I told her you'd find out someday," she says.

I exhale. I don't know what to say next. I just sit there.

Anna speaks first. "Tom, you have to know, Joan didn't tell you because she loved you."

"Loved me?" I spit out. "Loved me? How could she keep such a big secret from me? Not to mention one that calls into doubt whether or not our marriage was valid in the first place?"

"Now, Tom," she begins, "Everything was handled properly. It was no impediment to you getting married in the Church. We made sure of that."

"But I didn't know. It never came up in our pre-marital counseling."

She nods. "I know, I know. I told her she should talk to you about it. She didn't want to risk losing you. It was a bad time in her life."

"Did Father Anthony know?"

"Yes, he knew. He said that since her marriage was a civil marriage and had been annulled not long after, it was never valid to begin with. It was like it never happened. Joan took that to mean she didn't have to tell you." Anna pauses. "Joan was bad about that, not facing things that were difficult."

"And what about the other," I went on. "She was in a mental hospital when she was sixteen?"

"That wasn't the first time, Tom." Anna sits back. "By the time you two met, Joan had been hospitalized several times. That's where she met Randy. They were patients in the same hospital."

"She never told me that, either," I say. "Why did she hide her illness from me?"

Anna swallows. "You don't understand what it's like, Tom. Not just for the person who has the illness, but for the people who love them. Joan knew the toll her illness had taken on me, and she wanted to spare you that."

"But she could have told me," I say. "I would have understood."

"She couldn't take that chance. She'd told other men about her illness, that she was taking medication and had it under control. But it was always the same story. They'd dump her soon after. When she met you, and you two hit it off so well, she knew you were the one she wanted to marry. And she wasn't about to jeopardize that."

"I would have married her anyway," I say. "I loved her. We would have carried the burden together. She didn't have to do it alone."

Anna sighs. "I told her that. But she wouldn't listen."

We sit quietly in the kitchen for the next few minutes. Finally, I say, "Her father, Drew. What really happened, Anna?"

Anna puts her cup down and folds her hands. "They say there's a genetic component to Bipolar Disorder," she says quietly. "Poor Drew struggled our entire marriage. Hospitals, medication changes, the roller-coaster of manic highs and deep depression. Outbursts of irrational anger. I loved him, Tom. But it wasn't always easy. You say you would have stood by Joan, and I believe you would have. But only a fool or a saint wouldn't consider leaving in the face of all that. In the end, I stayed with Drew. Years later, I still haven't decided which one I am."

I put my hand on hers. "Anna," I ask quietly. "How did Drew die?"

She takes a deep breath and whispers, "Suicide, when Joan was fourteen. Overdose of sleeping pills. I was at work." She closes her eyes as tears flow down her cheeks. "She found him. She called me, said her Daddy wouldn't wake up. I told her to call 911. They were taking him out to the ambulance when I got home. He died on the way to the hospital."

I close my eyes. I was twelve when I came home from school to find Dad dead. That's something you don't just get over.

"Do you think that triggered Joan's problems?"

Anna nods. "She had a major manic episode about six months later. That's the first time she was hospitalized."

"How long was she in the hospital?"

"Oh, only a couple of weeks. Just long enough to get her stabilized and started on her first medications. By the time she left, she seemed better again. She went back to school, and she started seeing a psychiatrist as well as her therapist. There were months of trying to get her medications adjusted so they'd balance out her moods. Her moods, even when she was doing well between episodes, were unpredictable."

I nod. I don't want to remember that about Joan, but Anna is right. When I knew her, her moods could change on a dime.

"So we went on, more or less good, for about a year. Then she had another really bad episode. I don't remember what exactly it was, I think it had something to do with an art competition she entered that triggered it, but it was the first time she tried to harm herself."

"She didn't try to kill—"

"No, no, not suicide. I found out she had started cutting herself, on her upper thigh where no one could see. I don't even remember how I found out. So, another hospitalization for a month because of self-harm."

She gets up and started pacing again. "It was during this hospitalization that she met Randy."

Randy. Her first husband.

"Who was he?" I ask.

Anna smiles ruefully. "Tom, who do you think a patient in a mental hospital is going to meet? I'll answer that—other mental patients. Some as bad off as you are, many worse off. Randy was the latter."

"What was he in there for?"

Anna shrugs. "To this day, I don't really know. Joan told me he was bipolar, but I suspect there was more than that. Maybe some schizophrenia, one of the other disorders, who knows. It doesn't really matter. He may have been mentally ill, but he wasn't stupid. He was shrewd and clever, even charming. And he charmed Joan."

She sits back down and folds her hands. "Joan called him her boyfriend, said they were getting married when they got out of the hospital. I thought she was just being delusional. I should have paid closer attention."

Anna goes on. "So another round of meds, more intensive therapy, and she was released. By this time her sophomore year had come and gone, and she was so far behind that she and I spent the summer doing schoolwork. At first it seemed like things were going OK. Then I found out that she was in contact with Randy."

"How did you find out?"

"I caught her talking on the phone with him at 3 in the morning," Anna replys. "I blew up and we had the first screaming argument we'd ever had. I forbade her to have any contact with him again. She screamed and cried that they were in love and there was nothing I could do about it. She ran to her room and locked the door. I didn't go after her, figured I'd just let her calm down. The next morning she came out of her room, all calm, said she was sorry, we hugged, and got on with our day. I thought things were OK again." She shakes her head.

"About a week later, I went to get her up. She was gone. Joan had left a note, saying that she and Randy were going to get married and live together and I'd never see her again."

"What did you do?"

"I screamed. I cried. I fell on the floor and beat the ground with my fists. I cursed like a sailor. And yes, in the midst of all that, I cried out to God. I asked the Blessed Mother to protect her, to keep her from doing anything she couldn't take back. Then I called the police, reported her as a runaway. I even got in the car and drove around town, hoping I would catch sight of her. But nothing. Every day for two months, I waited for her to call. Nothing."

I just listen to her talk. There is nothing I can say.

"So for two months, I was in limbo," she continues. "I wouldn't do anything except go to work and come home. I'd go to Mass on Sunday, but I dropped out of everything else I was doing. I didn't tell anyone what had happened, I was too ashamed. I told people Joan was off at art camp, that she was doing fine. Looking back, I think people knew there was something wrong, but no one asked me.

"Finally, after two months, I heard from her. It was late one night. The phone rang. She was sobbing, almost hysterical."

"What had happened? Where was she?"

"Baltimore," Anna answers. "I could barely understand her, it took me forever to get her to calm down. She and Randy had had some kind of fight. He had left her alone on the street in one of the worst parts of the city. I later found out they had been sleeping in an abandoned row house for about a month. I still didn't know what they had been doing, what had happened since they left. But I didn't care. She begged me to come get her, to send someone to come get her. Tom, I had no one I could call, so I told her to get to a safe place and stay there, to call me back with the address. I waited for half an hour, scared to death she wouldn't call back. Finally, she called. She was at an all-night diner. The owner had let her call using his phone. I put some clothes on and drove as fast as I could to Baltimore. It was after sunrise by the time I got to her."

She shuddered slightly. "I barely recognized her, Tom. Her clothes were dirty and torn, she had everything in a plastic garbage bag, and smelled like she hadn't bathed in weeks. It looked to me like she had lost thirty pounds, she was almost skin and bones, like she hadn't eaten well. Before we left, I got her something to eat. She downed it so quickly I was afraid she'd get sick. The kindest thing that happened was that when I went to pay, the owner told me it was on the house, that he was just glad to see a girl get back with her family, that it didn't happen often." Anna looks at me. "Made me wonder, how many other Joans were out there.

"I drove her home. She slept the entire trip. She got a shower, and must have stayed in there for an hour. Got some clean clothes on, then crawled into bed. She slept for two days."

"Did you find out anything?"

Anna shakes her head. "Not then. She was too traumatized to talk, and I knew I'd get nothing if I pressed. No, I was just glad to have her back and safe. I knew there would be time enough. I didn't want to push her away by pressing too hard. I also needed the time to prepare myself. She was a mentally ill sixteen-year-old girl who had been, from what I could figure, living on the streets of Baltimore for the better part of two months. You can imagine what I thought had happened. The fact that she hadn't been alone didn't give me any comfort. Randy was worse off than she was, from the little I knew."

By this time it is close to one o'clock. Anna notices the time and says, "I bet you're hungry. I know I am." She gets up and goes to the refrigerator and starts pulling out sandwich makings. I hadn't realized until she mentioned it that I hadn't eaten that day.

I take my wedding ring out and look at it, remembering her smile, the brightness in her eyes on our wedding day.

Was it true? Did she really feel that way? Or was it all a lie?

Anna places a sandwich in front of me. "Tom," she says firmly, "no matter what you learn from me today or anyone else in the future, know this. Joan loved you and was happy with you.

Chewing a bite of sandwich, I say, "Not always."

Anna nods at this and adds, "I know she still struggled. But more often than not, she won."

"So you got Joan back," I say, anxious to get the conversation back on track.

"Once she had rested and eaten some, she was ready to talk. She said they got married and then hitchhiked and walked to Baltimore. Randy had told her he had a job, had friends they could stay with, and Joan believed him."

"He was lying?"

"Not exactly. There were friends they could stay with, but no job. Joan said he kept looking, would work day labor sometimes, but more often than not, he'd just sleep all day. Eventually, he had a fight with his friends and they kicked them out. So they started living on the streets, eating at soup kitchens, sometimes staying in a shelter. Joan told me she wanted to leave after a week, but she was afraid of Randy, afraid that he might hurt her. Then one day, they had a fight and he left."

"And that's when she called you."

"Yes," Anna says. Swallowing, she continues, "She cried while she told the story, cried after the story, cried herself to sleep in my arms. As she lay there, I accepted the reality that she needed to be in a hospital for a while.

"It took a lot of persuasion, but I was finally able to get her to go." She sighs. "She refused to see me the first couple of times I went to see her. Finally, we started talking again. It took three months, but by the time she got out, things were better. They had come up with the right combination of meds, along with the right therapeutic approach. She came home and got her life back on track.

"She got caught up with school, and managed to graduate. Then she got accepted to Myer, in their art program—she and I both wanted her to stay close to home, to make sure that she kept up her treatment." She smiles. "She excelled, she was stable and happy. Then she met you."

I sit back, still trying to absorb what I have heard. "But she never told me any of this," I say.

"I tried to get her to tell you, even after you were married, but she wouldn't listen. She was very careful to make sure you never knew she was on medication. She found a therapist out of town and saw her weekly."

When she says this, I remembered Joan would take a weekly day trip out of Myerton, saying she had to buy things for her clients. It makes sense now.

"And she was on meds through our entire marriage?"

Anna hesitated. "That," she says slowly, "I can't say for certain. She may not have been for the six months before her death."

"Why not?"

"Because she wanted to have a baby—you both wanted to have a baby. She was worried about her meds harming the baby, or that they would keep her from carrying one to term. The miscarriages didn't help. She told me she wanted to taper off them while she was trying to get pregnant. But I don't know."

"If I had known," I say, "We could have done something else. There were always options. We could have adopted. Certainly, she knew it didn't matter to me."

"But it mattered to her, Tom," Anna says. "All she wanted was a normal life, to be a normal wife and mother, to be a normal person. That's all she wanted."

I lean forward and put my elbows on the table, resting my head in my hands and staying that way for several minutes. It has been a long few hours, I am tired and my head hurts. It is a lot to take in but there is one more thing I need to know.

"What about Randy?"

She shrugged. "I never met him, and as far as I know, Joan never saw him again. I think I saw a picture of him once, but I don't think I'd know him if he appeared on my doorstep."

Fifteen

"What are you going to do now?" Anna asks.

I look at the clock. "Take a shower, get some fresh clothes on. I have confessions at 3 p.m. and Mass this afternoon."

"That's not what I mean," Anna says, a tinge of irritation in her voice. "What are you going to do about that—reporter?"

I open my hands. "I don't see anything I can do. You can't unring a bell."

"But you heard what she said at the end of her report. She's going to keep digging into this—into you."

"Oh, she's probably left by now."

"No, she's still at the Myerton Inn."

I am surprised. "How would you know that?"

"Ellie Hooper's son has a part-time job there. Shepp's paying by the week. No, Tom, she plans to stay a while."

"Wonderful," I say.

***

Anna leaves and I decide to get on with my day. I take a shower, put on a fresh set of clericals, and walk up the block to The Perfect Cup for a coffee. The day is bright and clear, cool but not cold, unusually warm for the middle of October. Glenda's nephew is raking near the garage when I walk down the sidewalk from the Rectory. He has done a good job, I think, as I look at the piles of brightly colored leaves dotting the grass. I walk up the sidewalk past the front of the Church towards the coffee shop, passing several people on the sidewalk. Some turn back and stare, apparently recognizing me from the news report.

When I get to The Perfect Cup, the crowded cafe is buzzing with conversation and the sounds of coffee cups and spoons clinking. By the time I get to the counter, the talking has stopped. I don't turn around, but I sense that every eye in the place is on me.

Nate's Uncle Pete is behind the counter. "Hi, Padre, the usual?" he asks cheerfully.

"Thanks, Pete." He hands me a steaming cup of coffee and I hand him a five dollar bill. I find a table in a far corner, sitting so I can see the whole room. When I do, the people in the cafe restart their conversations.

I drink my coffee and look around. People seem to be going about their business, talking with each other or looking at their phones. Occasionally, though, people look over in my direction, then quickly go back to what they are doing. Couples stop their conversations to look, then lean in closer to talk to each other.

Is this going to happen every time I go out in public? Are *people going to look at me like I am some kind of sideshow freak, or like I have a scarlet M on my forehead? Maybe the Archbishop was right. Maybe I should leave town. If people in a coffee shop are going to look at me this way, what will people in Church be like?*

"Can I get you anything else, Padre?" I look up to see Pete looking down at me, a fatherly smile on his face.

I return the smile. "No, thanks, Pete. I'm fine." I look past him. A bespeckled co-ed is looking at me over her laptop. She catches me looking at her and furtively looks down.

"I seem to be attracting some attention," I say.

"What?" Pete looks over his shoulder. "Ack, don't worry about them. They've got nothing else to do. So they look, and they go on their phones, and they send their Twits, and their Handbooks, and all that social crap. I mean look at them—half of them are sitting with someone they aren't even talking to, they're on their little phones. Now me, I don't have any of that. I've got real friends, I talk to real people."

"Must be nice."

"You Father, you have friends. You used to live here, right?"

"A long time ago," I say. "But everyone knows what happened."

"They think they know," Pete says. He leans over and looks me in the eye. "They don't know the truth. They only know what they see on the news. You—you know the truth. You, and God, and that's all that counts." He stands up. "Stop by on your way out, I'll give you one to go."

I watch him walk away, his words reverberating in my head. *You know the truth. You, and God, and that's all that counts.*

That's the problem.

I know the truth.

***

I leave the cafe and walk back to the church, going straight to the sacristy and grabbing the small purple stole I wear for confession. The church is empty, but it is almost three, and I want to make sure I am in place before anyone comes in. People are nervous enough about confession as it is without there being a chance the priest might be able to place a face with a sin.

I sit in the confessional for a while, waiting for the first penitent. I pass the time saying a Rosary and reading prayers in my Breviary. But no one comes, which is odd, I think. There had been a line the previous Saturday. Are people reluctant to confess their sins to a priest accused of murder?

For the second time today, I wonder if the Archbishop was right. Staying in Myerton seems to be more trouble than it is worth.

After about 45 minutes, I hear the sound of soft footsteps on the marble floor. They get louder as they approach the confessional box. I hear the door open and close and the person sits down.

I say, "Let us begin—"

"Liar."

I stop. I don't recognize the voice.

"Liar," the voice repeats. "You're a liar."

Lowering my voice, I say, "Why do you say that?"

"You know. You know. I saw you on the news. You lied."

"I don't know what—"

"I was there. You lied."

I don't say anything.

"You lied to that reporter," the voice says. "Did you lie to the police?"

I sit quietly.

"You did, you lied to the police about what happened." There is a low laugh. "That's great. So they don't know, they don't know what you did."

"I didn't do anything. You shot Joan, not me."

"Only because of what you did. You know that. You're a liar. Isn't lying a sin?"

I just sit and listen.

"I shot her, but you killed her. That's the truth, Father. You know that."

I hear the person get up and go out the door. Instead of walking this time, I hear the person jog out of the Church.

This time, I don't try to go after them. I just sit. I am having trouble catching my breath.

Staying in Myerton was definitely a bad idea.

Sixteen

After the interview debacle, I fully expected Saint Clare's to be virtually empty Sunday morning.

Boy, was I wrong.

People pack the pews at both Masses. Familiar faces jockey for places with newcomers, most of whom look somewhere between confused and horrified at the chaos of 10:30 Mass. At communion time, most of the new people stay in their pews. I want to believe it's because they hadn't been to Mass in a while and hadn't gone to confession first. But really, they probably aren't Catholic anyway. They're just here to see the priest accused of murder.

Well, at least they are in church. That's a good thing, no matter the reason.

I get through the Mass without any problems, give the final blessing, and begin the recessional. As I am walking down the aisle behind Dominic Trent and the other altar servers, one of the ushers waves at me frantically. I no sooner clear the doors then he grabs me by the arm and pulls me off to one side.

"You don't want to go out there, Father," he whispers.

I look down at his name tag. "What is it, Norman?"

"That reporter's outside. Has a camera set up and everything. I tried to get her to move, but she said something about it being a public sidewalk and freedom of the press."

I sigh. "I think she's right about that. It is a public sidewalk, and unless she steps on church property, we can't ask her to leave." I square my shoulders. "However, I'm not going to cower in here."

Hoping I look more confident than I feel, I walk outside.

Katherine Shepp, camera and microphone at the ready, stands on the sidewalk right in front of Saint Clare's. When she sees me, she actually smiles and waves, calling, "Good morning, Father."

I return the smile. "Good morning," I say before I turn to greet the first parishioners coming out the door. Everyone smiles, shakes my hand, says the usual pleasantries people say to their priest—good Mass, nice homily, thank you—and proceed on their way.

While I am talking to a young couple, I hear a small commotion behind me. I turn around to see Katherine Shepp going from person to person, sticking her microphone in people's faces.

At the sight, something inside me snaps.

I know I should ignore her.

She is, after all, just doing her job.

But this is too much.

I start down the stairs, my vestments flowing behind me. "Ms. Shepp!" I yell. "What are you doing?"

She turns to me. "I'm just trying to get some comments from the members of the church."

"What sort of comments?"

"Oh, just how they feel knowing their priest might be a murderer," she says. A small smile plays on her lips. "You know, the human interest angle."

"No, no, this is too much," I say with an emphatic shake of my head. "You can film all you want to, but I must ask you not to harass my parishioners."

"Harass? Really, Father, I'm not harassing anyone. I have every right as a journalist to ask questions, and they can answer or not. Also, I'm on a public sidewalk, so—"

"Yes, I know you're on a public sidewalk, and I know you have the right, I'm just asking you to respect the privacy of—"

I notice the camera. The red light is on.

"Wait, are you—are you filming this?"

She nods. "It will make great footage in my next report. The accused priest greeting his unsuspecting flock after church. The confrontation with the press. Really good stuff."

"No, no, absolutely not!" I say, lunging at the camera. I manage to grab it out of the cameraman's hand and throw it to the ground. The camera breaks, the lens separating from the rest of the mechanism.

Katherine and her cameraman stare at me. "You—you'll pay for this, Father!" Shepp sputters. "That's station property!"

"Send me the bill!" I yell. "And get out of here! Now! Or the camera won't be the only thing broken!"

I am shaking. The blood rises in my cheeks. My hands clench into fists as I move toward the reporter. Shepp backs up, looking genuinely frightened.

"Father Greer," a familiar but authoritative voice behind me says. I turn.

Helen's standing there, looking at the scene.

"Oh, good," Shepp says with a sinister smile. "Detective Parr, I'm—"

"I know who you are, Ms. Shepp," Helen says, crossing her arms. "Now, what seems to be the problem?"

"You saw!" she says. Waving at the crowd of onlookers. "Every person here is a witness to Father Greer's unprovoked attack on me and my cameraman."

"Unprovoked attack?" Helen says, a tight smile playing on her lips. "I saw no attack on you."

"You can't be serious, detective!"

"What I saw was Father Greer asking you to leave his parishioners alone—a not unreasonable request—and to stop filming him. When you did not comply with his perfectly reasonable request, he knocked the camera to the ground while attempting—clumsily—to turn it off himself," Helen says.

"But—But—" Shepp sputters, "He threatened us with physical violence! It's on the tape!"

"I did not hear him threaten anyone."

"Are you deaf as well as blind, detective!" Shepp yells.

"Nooo, my hearing and eyesight are perfect, according to my last physical," Helen says, taking a step towards the reporter. "Father Greer said, and I quote, 'or the camera won't be the only thing broken.'" She shrugs, then adds, "Could have referred to anything, but he clearly did not mention you or your cameraman."

"I want him arrested!"

"Oh, come now, Ms. Shepp," Helen says calmly, breaking into a grin. "You don't want that. I mean, right now you've got a good story. Accused priest loses his temper in front of his entire parish. But if I arrest him, when you have no injuries and no witnesses to back up your claim, how petty will that look, hmm?"

Shepp just looks at Helen for a few minutes. Then finally, she holds up her hands. "OK, OK, we're leaving. Let's go, Pete," she says as she walks to the news van. Pete looks at me, gathers up the pieces of his camera, and follows after her.

I am breathing heavily, my pulse beating in my ears, as I watch the reporter and cameraman climb into their news truck. Helen turns back to me and says, "Are you OK?"

I nod. "Yeah. Thanks."

"I couldn't very well arrest my priest on a Sunday in front of everyone, now could I?" Helen says. "That wouldn't make me too popular around here. Come on. I'll buy you a cup of coffee."

She starts up the steps, and I scurry after her. "I didn't see you at Mass," I say, finally catching up to her just inside the door.

"I was here," she says. "In the back corner. I didn't want to distract you this time."

"You didn't distract me," I say.

"Isn't lying a sin, Father?"

"I wasn't lying. I wasn't distracted, I was . . . surprised to see you."

I walk up the steps to the altar and bow. I head for the sacristy, when I notice Helen's stopped just before the bottom step.

"I, ah . . . I'll just wait here for you, OK?" Helen says nervously.

I smile. "Of course," I say, and hurry into the Sacristy. Shedding my vestments quickly, I emerge only a moment later.

But Helen is no longer alone. Dan Conway is standing with her.

"Dan?" I say.

"Hello, Father," he says nervously. Looking furtively at Helen, he rubs the back of his neck and says, "I—I need to—well, you see, Father, there's something—"

"Of course, Dan," I say. "Hel—Detective Parr, if you'll excuse us. I'll catch up with you at The Perfect Cup."

Helen nods and is about to leave when Dan stops her. "No, Detective—ah, I was going to see you tomorrow morning about this. Might as well rip the bandage off and get it over with."

I walk down the steps and place my hand on his shoulder, aware that Helen's eyes are flickering with something. "How about we go to my office? This sounds like it could take a while."

***

"Well? What do you have to tell us, Dan?"

Dan looks at me, then at Helen, then at his hands. He takes a deep breath, and says, "I'm the one who gave the unredacted case file to Katherine Shepp."

I sit back in my chair, surprisingly calm at this news. Helen, however, sits up straight and yells, "What! Dan!"

"I know," he says, swallowing. "It was a stupid thing to do. I'm ashamed and I'm sorry."

"A stupid thing—ashamed—sorry!" Helen sputters. "Sorry! Dan, you could lose your job over this! It's a violation of department policy, not to mention Father Greer's privacy!"

"I just didn't feel like I had a choice," he says, shaking his head.

Helen's about to yell some more—I remember the look—when I hold up my hand to stop her. "Katherine Shepp told me she had dated someone in college who was now in the police department. That someone was you, right?"

"We didn't exactly date," he sighs. "We slept together a few times. Back then—well, I wasn't always who you see now. God and Miriam are responsible for that. But anyway, yeah, I knew her. She was manipulative back then, too. The other night, she was waiting for me when I left work. She asked me for a drink. I didn't see any harm. I should have just gone home. But we talked about old times, and she reminded me of some things I'm not proud of." He paused. "She threatened to tell Miriam if I didn't get her the information she wanted. I told her to go ahead, that I'd told Miriam about my past years ago. So, she upped the ante."

"She threatened to tell Miriam you'd slept with her that night, didn't she?" Helen says.

Dan nods. "So, I printed the case file out and gave it to her. Oh, Father, Detective Parr, I am so sorry."

"Wait," Helen says. "I had Gladys pull the logs. There's no record of you accessing the Greer file."

"That's because I snuck into your office and used your computer," Dan says softly. "You have a bad habit of leaving your system open, Detective."

Helen's jaw clinches at that. "I see," she says coolly. "Officer Conway, I will be speaking to the chief about this. I don't know what he'll do, but you should prepare yourself for the worst."

Dan just nods. As he stands up, I stand and extend my hand to him. "Dan, I just want you to know," I say, "I forgive you. If there is anything I can do to help, please let me know."

The big man swallows as he wipes a tear from his eyes. "Thank you, Father Tom. That means a lot to me. Detective, I'll see you tomorrow. I . . . I need to go home and have a talk with Miriam."

Dan walks from my office, shoulders slumped in defeat. When the door to the Rectory closes, I sigh and sit back down. "Well, that's one mystery solved."

"Frankly, I'm surprised," Helen says, sitting back and shaking her head.

I shrug. "Dan didn't believe he had a choice."

"No, that's not what I'm talking about. I'm surprised at you. Forgiving him so easily. I mean, Tom, he made things worse for you."

"As I've said, she'd have done it anyway," I say. "He didn't do it out of malice. He was being blackmailed."

She stares at me. "You really aren't the same person, are you?" she mutters.

I smile. "Neither of us are, Helen."

We sit quietly for a few minutes, then I say, "So, what's going to happen to Dan?"

"Well, it's up to the Chief, but he'll probably be fired."

"Oh, Helen, he can't fire Dan. He's got a wife and kids—and another on the way, in case you haven't heard."

"The Chief is not a man inclined to be merciful," Helen says.

"Can't you do something? Put a good word in for him?"

"Put a good—Tom! He broke department policy!"

"Not out of malice."

"Doesn't matter, he still broke the policy."

"OK, then punish him, whatever that looks like. But he shouldn't lose his career over this."

Helen opens her mouth to say something, then stops. She slumps down in her chair. "You know, I happen to agree with you. Dan did something stupid. But he's a good cop. I've seen his record—service in the Marines in Iraq, college here in Myerton, then the State Police, then here. Never even a hint of a problem, not a single civilian complaint—and these days, that's rare. He shows real promise."

"So you'll help him?"

"I'll try, Tom. Maybe I can use my powers of persuasion on the Chief."

I can't help but smile. "If I remember, those were rather formidable."

A wistful look passes across her face. "Not formidable enough in the end, Tom."

That not-so-subtle rebuke hovers in the air between us. Finally, trying to break the tension, I say, "You know, my secretary/housekeeper doesn't work on the weekends, so I usually fend for myself. And I haven't eaten since this morning. How about lunch at The Bistro?"

Helen smiles sardonically. "Well, well, Father Greer. No longer afraid to be seen with me?"

"It's not that," I say. "I just—I don't want there to be any misunderstandings."

"Tom," she sighs. "You're a priest. I know what that means. It's just two old friends eating together."

"Oh, of course," I say. "I agree. Let me run upstairs and change into some regular clothes."

Helen nods and I dash up the stairs to my bedroom. I look at myself in the mirror over my dresser and pull my collar out and place it on the top. I stare at it for a moment. I've always appreciated it as a symbol of my calling. When I wear it, even the most hardened sinner knows who I am.

But until today, I've never realized everything else it symbolizes. Just as a wedding band shows the world I belong to one woman, my collar shows I belong to God, forsaking all others.

"We both know what that means," I say to myself. "We're just old friends. Just having lunch. That's all."

But in spite of that, the former lover whispers, *Yes, that's all. But will it always be enough?*

Seventeen

Ten minutes into lunch with Helen, I have the uneasy feeling I've made a mistake.

After a somewhat awkward walk from the Rectory to The Bistro where I tried to keep at least six inches between us, we manage to find a quiet table in the corner of the restaurant. Not hidden, exactly, but out of easy sight of anyone who might see us and wonder what a priest is doing having lunch with a single woman.

Or any woman for that matter.

It's not like I'm doing something that's forbidden, exactly. We were taught in seminary to be careful with our relationships, to not give any cause for scandal and to avoid the near occasion of sin. But, we were also told we shouldn't avoid friendships, even with members of the opposite sex. We should just take care that they didn't develop into . . . more.

And if Helen were just another woman, close to my age, who happened to be a member of my parish, then I'd have no real reason for unease.

Even if she is a beautiful woman.

But Helen's a beautiful woman who I once loved. Who I was ready to spend the rest of my life with. Who I have very fond memories of, even if how I ended things was horrible.

And she's sitting three feet away from me, chin resting on her hand, looking at me with azure blue eyes that I so often lost myself in.

Yes. I'm definitely in trouble.

"So," she says after we order, "I know what happened to Joan. How did you two meet?"

I chuckle. "We met here, on campus."

"Oh, I know that from interviewing a few people. Your ex-mother-in-law for one."

"Anna? You interviewed Anna? Why?"

"Just part of the investigation. But don't worry. She's a big fan of yours."

"And I of her," I say. "She's been as much of a mom to me as my own Mom—more so, actually."

"Oh, and how is Nola?" Helen asks sarcastically, no doubt remembering our one trip to visit her in my home town of Bellamy, Florida after our engagement.

"She's Mom," I sigh.

"Your sister?"

"The same," I say. "Mom says she's been clean and sober for a while, but . . ."

"I'm sorry."

"Me too." I clear my throat. "Anyway, remember how we met the first time? I was walking along and I ran into you?"

"Yes, I—wait," she says with a grin, "you're kidding me!"

I shake my head. "Nope. I was walking along, reading something, and ran right into her. Only instead of a binder, it was her portfolio. We spent about half an hour chasing sketches and watercolors as they blew through the commons. After we gathered them up, I asked her to lunch."

"Unlike me," she says, "Joan said yes."

I nod. "There was a lot about Joan that wasn't like you."

"Oh? Did she let you sleep with her before the wedding?"

I stiffen. The words are no sooner out than her hand flies to her mouth, a look of horror in her eyes.

I feel my jaw tighten.

This was a mistake.

"Oh, Tom!" she whispers. "I'm—I'm so sorry. I—I don't know where that came from. Please, forgive me. That was horrible."

Looking in her eyes, already filling with tears, I realize I'm not the only one who's changed.

Twenty years ago, Helen wouldn't have apologized for that. She often spoke before she thought, then spent time arguing about how she was right to say what she said.

I take a deep breath. "Helen," I say slowly. "To my shame, I will admit that was one of the things I liked about Joan. She didn't have your ... concern for the niceties of Church teaching. So, yes. We slept together before we were married. And I've come to regret that, especially recently."

"Why recently?"

I clear my throat as my eyes begin to burn with tears. "Because maybe if I hadn't been so anxious to get her into bed, and then get married ..." I shake my head.

"I've seen the file, Tom," Helen says. "Your anniversary. Almost a year to the day after we broke up. You didn't waste any time."

I shake my head. "No. I have no excuses."

"You don't need to make any excuses to me," she says quietly.

"No, but I do need to apologize."

"Tom, you've already—"

"No, you don't understand," I say. "When we were together, I put pressure on you to sleep with me. I pretended to agree with you to wait until we were married, but I believed if I kept at it, eventually you'd give in. I didn't respect your wishes. And for that, I am sorry. You were right. I should have listened—really listened—to you."

Helen looks at me with something akin to astonishment. "I don't know what to say, Tom."

"Well, that you forgive me would be nice," I say, breaking into a grin.

"Oh, that goes without saying," Helen says. "I'm sorry, I'm still not used to this."

I nod. The server brings us our food—hamburger and fries for Helen, grilled cheese and tomato bisque for me—and we eat quietly for a few minutes.

Finally, I ask, "What about you and John?"

She stops and looks up at me. With a slight smile, she says, "Well, for one thing, I didn't make him wait."

My heart drops to my stomach. This, I didn't expect.

I take a sudden interest in my soup, even though I'm no longer hungry. "Oh," I say, because I can't think of anything else to say. It's not like I have any right to say anything. After all, I left her, and she met John long after me.

People change. Helen obviously did.

"Tom," she says finally, "let me explain."

"You don't owe me an explanation," I say, continuing to study my soup. It's creamy with crunchy croutons floating on top—not quite as crunchy anymore because of the soup.

"I know," she says quietly. "But I think you deserve one, after everything."

I look up at her. Staring into her eyes, the lover in me is hurt and angry, not to mention jealous. The priest is screaming at me, reminding me I have no reason to feel any of those things.

Oh, lunch was *such* a bad idea.

I should just get up and leave, forget we ever had this conversation, and spend the next few months avoiding her. She can attend Mass, she can investigate Joan's murder—not that she's going to get anywhere—and I can have little contact with her. After all, it's not like I'm going to be part of her life again.

But instead of leaving, I say, "OK. What happened, Helen? You spent our entire relationship keeping me out of your bed. What was it about John? Did you find him more attractive than me? Maybe he was just more persuasive. Was that it?"

Really, really mature, Tom, the priest says. *Watch her slap you again. You really deserve it.*

For just a moment, I think that's what she's going to do. Her eyes flash with anger—not that I blame her—but then she takes a deep breath.

"I can see why you'd think that, Tom," she says quietly. "But it wasn't anything like that. John was a handsome man, yes, but I didn't find him more attractive than I find you."

The lover in me takes note of what she just said.

Find. Present tense.

Don't go there, Tom, the priest says. *A slip of the tongue, no more.*

"Frankly, Tom," Helen says, "I don't have a good reason or explanation. Looking back, I'd become disillusioned with the Church—not God, not even the Mass or anything like that, but the rules. It didn't help that the friends I went to Mass with at Duke didn't seem to care what the

Church taught about sex and marriage. Most of them lived with their boyfriends, some of whom attended Mass with them, and they took communion like it was no big deal."

"It was—it is—a big deal," I say.

"I know, I know," she says, "but I reached the point where I didn't care." She pauses. "Then, I met John."

"Was he a student?"

She laughs. "Oh, no. John was older than I was by about ten years. He came down from D.C. my last year of law school to talk about opportunities with his firm. Afterwards, we got to talking, then he invited me out to dinner."

Before I can stop myself, I ask, "Did you sleep with him that night?"

"No," she says. "He was only there for a few days, but after he left, we began a long distance relationship. After about a month of that, he invited me up to D.C. to visit. It was then that we . . . Anyway, he asked me to marry him a few weeks later, and we were married six months after that. I joined his firm, he was already a partner, and we began our brief life together."

She's given me the opening to ask a question I've been wondering about since that day in her office. "What happened?"

Helen's blue eyes begin to fill with tears. Instinctively, I reach across the table and take her hand. I've done it numerous times, with the grieving, with the sick. But this is not the hand of an elderly dying person, rough and worn with age.

It's Helen's hand. It feels exactly as I remember. Soft, with long fingers and manicured but close-cut nails. I used to joke that she had man -hands, and the truth is they are larger than mine. But when we'd walk along together, we'd just . . . fit so perfectly.

She's startled by the gesture, and her expression causes me to pull my hand away.

"He died. On 9/11," she whispers quietly.

"Oh, my God, Helen!" I say with real sorrow. "How horrible. Was he in New York on business, or something?"

She laughs bitterly. "Oh, no. Nothing like that. He was in D.C. just trying to get home to me. I had a bad cold, so I hadn't gone into the office that day. After the plane hit the Pentagon, the firm sent everyone home. I mean, no one knew if there were going to be further attacks that day or not. The office was only four blocks north of the White House, and we lived in Georgetown. So John was trying to get home. We lived in the city, so we either took Metro or taxis.

"Of course, everyone else had the same idea. The roads were gridlocked, the sidewalks packed, buses full to the brim, the Metro running full cars. It was chaos. Everyone was scared."

"Here, the college closed for the day after the first tower fell," I say quietly. "Joan and I were glued to the news. They showed D.C."

"The pictures didn't do it justice. I was waiting, praying for John to get home safe. Hours went by. I tried calling, but cell service was just overloaded. I didn't know anything until around midnight, when I got a call from the hospital."

She takes a drink of tea and clears her throat. "I still don't know what happened for sure, but John was hit by a car while he tried to cross the street. Ironically, he was only about two blocks from our apartment. People on the scene tried to help, but traffic was a nightmare; it took an ambulance too long to get to the scene." She dabs her eyes. "Apparently, he was gone by the time they got there."

"Oh, dar—Helen, I'm so sorry."

She nods. "Well," she sniffs. "After that, I kinda lost it for a couple of months. I didn't go into work. I barely ate. I thought my life was over. I mean, I wasn't even thirty and I'd lost the two loves of my life."

That stabs at my heart.

"But I finally recovered. I started going to Mass again, and gradually got back to work. But my heart wasn't in law anymore. Everything changed that day. Not just for the country, but for me personally. I couldn't see the point in filing briefs about patent infringement or negotiating settlements of class-action lawsuits over defective tricycles."

"So you decided to become a cop?" I say with a smile.

"I decided to become a cop," she says, returning the smile. "Part of me wanted to do something useful with my life. But another part of me thought, if there had been just one more officer on duty for traffic or crowd control that awful day, John might not have died."

She folds her arms. "So, I managed to pass the physical requirements, entered the Police Academy—I was the oldest rookie on the force for a time—became a patrol officer, and eventually made detective."

"And you wound up here."

Helen sighs. "And I wound up here. Not my decision really. It was either accept the job here or be fired."

"What in the world happened?"

She smiles. "Well, you know me, Tom. I can be a little stubborn."

"Oh, really? I never noticed."

"Ass," she mouths. "Yeah, there was a case involving someone rather prominent. I clashed with my superiors. OK, I disobeyed a direct order. Fortunately, the Chief in D.C. owed the Chief here a favor—Lowden saved his life, or something like that—so I was strongly encouraged to accept the job as Chief Detective with the Myerton Police Department, a jurisdiction which included a town of around 20,000 people and the surrounding county."

"So," I say, raising my glass, "we're both here against our will."

She raises her glass in turn. "Well, I've been here a while. I actually like it. I like being a big fish in a small pond. Who knows? Maybe I'll be chief someday."

"I can certainly see that."

"So, you know my story," she says, resting her chin on her hands. "Now I have questions, Tom."

I sigh. "Look, why I became a priest—"

"No, not that," she says, "though I am still curious about that. But I have a more pressing question."

I have a sick feeling in my stomach. I know what's coming.

"It's about the night of Joan's murder."

And, like that, the oxygen goes out of the room. "I've been waiting for you to call me down to the station," I say as calmly as I can.

"Do you have something you want to tell me?"

"You mean, like a confession, that Shepp was right, I did kill Joan in some kind of jealous fit?"

"Did you?"

"No, absolutely not."

Helen crosses her arms. "I really didn't think so, Tom. You learn something about the man you're going to marry. That reporter's full of it, trying to pin the murder on you."

"Thanks, I appreciate that."

"But, I also know when you're hiding something," she says. "Oh, I know you didn't mention the fight, I've known that since I read the file. But that led me to believe that there is something else about that night, something you didn't say at the time, something you've been hiding all these years. So I ask again. Do you have anything you want to tell me about the night of Joan's murder?"

I return Helen's penetrating gaze. There it is. A direct question. A chance to come clean. To tell the truth I've been hiding for fifteen years. To relieve myself of a burden I've carried since that night.

I look at her and she looks at me. I can hear my heart pounding in my head. Can she hear it, I wonder? Can she see my face getting red as a flush runs through my body?

Suddenly, strangely familiar music starts to play, causing me to jump.

Helen blinks. She bends down and digs through what has to be the largest tote bag I've ever seen while her phone continues to play a tune I can't quite place.

She finds it, and as she pulls it out, I recognize the song.

"'Eye of the Tiger'? Really?"

She puts her finger to her lips to quiet me.

"Yes," she says into the phone. She listens to the voice on the other end, then looks at me. "I see. When was it called in?" she asks as she pulls a pen and small notebook out of her enormous tote bag. "Uh-huh, OK. When's the ME going to get there?" She listens to the answer and makes a face. "I know it's a Sunday, what does that matter?" The person on the other end responds, causing Helen to sigh. "OK, start questioning people and keep the scene secure. Call the techs. I'm on my way." She puts her phone, pen, and notebook back in her tote bag.

"What is it?" I ask.

She looks at me and sighs. "Well, Tom, it's a damn good thing we've been together all afternoon. Otherwise, you'd be my prime suspect."

"Prime suspect for what?" I ask, surprised.

"The murder of Katherine Shepp. She was found dead in her hotel room about thirty minutes ago."

Eighteen

"I want to come with you," I say as she pays the check.

"No, absolutely not," she says.

"She should receive last rites."

"She's dead, Tom."

"Her body is dead. I'm concerned about her soul. I need to do this."

"You don't even know if she was Catholic."

"You don't know she wasn't."

We stare at each other. Helen looks like she was leaning towards continuing the argument.

"Look," I say finally, "I wasn't very kind to her the last time I saw her. It's the least I can do. Please, Helen?"

Finally, she shakes her head and holds up her hands.

"Fine. Your guilt wins. But," she points her finger at me, "stay out of the way. Don't touch anything."

"I have to touch the body, for the anointing. But only the forehead."

"OK, but nothing else," she says as we walk out of The Bistro.

***

I manage to keep up with Helen on the way to the hotel, in spite of the fact that she always drives like she's on the road course at Le Mans instead of the quiet streets of a small town nestled in the foothills of the Alleghenies. Somehow, we arrive at the same time.

"You still drive like a bat out of hell," I say.

"And you still drive like an old woman," Helen says.

"There is nothing wrong with my driving," I pout.

"God, Tom," she says, taking a deep breath and marching to the entrance, "just don't do that."

"Do what?" I ask, trotting to keep up with her. But she doesn't answer me.

The Myerton Inn is on the outskirts of town, and markets itself to the families of students at the college and businessmen visiting Myerton. The layout is all interior rooms with one main entrance through the lobby, but stairways allowing exits to the parking lot.

When we get to the scene of the crime—Shepp's room is on the third floor of the five-floor building, halfway between the elevators and the stairwell—there are police in the hallway holding back a few curious onlookers. What strikes me when I get to the hotel is the lack of news people. The murder must not have gotten out yet. But the word will spread, the news will get to Baltimore and D.C., and news crews from both cities will converge on Myerton like locusts.

Like they did after Joan's murder.

"Stay right here," Helen tells me before going under the crime scene tape into the room. "And get these people out of the hallway," she adds to the police officers. They move the onlookers down the hallway and a couple of them turn back to look at me, either wondering what a civilian is doing at a crime scene or, as is more likely, recognizing me from the news reports.

I realize I'm not wearing my clericals. I didn't have time to change at the Rectory, stopping only long enough to get my purple stole and anointing oil. No wonder people are looking at me.

I turn my attention to the hotel room. Helen's looking around the room, following the officer inside as she points at different things. The elevator doors open and a man and a woman in dark-blue jumpsuits carrying cases approach. I have seen enough police shows on television to suspect they are the crime scene technicians.

I move to allow them to pass, but Helen holds up her hand. "Father," she says, "you can come in. Watch your step."

The two technicians look at me puzzled. I dip under the tape and walk into the room.

Suddenly, I realize I can't go any further. The vision of Joan's dead body flashes before my eyes. Here, I am about to see another dead body, another woman violently taken from this life.

I couldn't help Joan then, but I can help Katherine Shepp now.

"Father," Helen says insistently. She looks both irritated and concerned. The irritation is obvious—she wants me to do what I need to do and get out of the way. I have no idea why she is concerned.

I walk slowly around the bed to where Katherine liess. Her body, except for her feet, are covered with a sheet. Near her lies a lamp. The lamp is all white ceramic, except for the base, which is red.

Blood. The red base sits in a blood-soaked carpet.

I squat down by her head and look up at Helen. "May I uncover her head, Detective?"

She nods. "Mike, can you please?" she says to the officer.

The officer bends over and uncovers her head.

I inhale sharply.

I knew there would be blood, but I'm not prepared for what I see.

Katherine Shepp had been a young attractive woman. Thanks to her murderer, she is no longer. They had smashed her head to a shapeless mass of blood, brain, and bone. A wave of nausea washes over me.

I turned my head to look in her eyes. People think it's like in the old movies, where people die with their eyes closed. But no, if someone is awake when they die, their eyes are open. If they die suddenly, violently, you can read their last thoughts in their eyes.

When Joan died, her eyes expressed love and sadness. Katherine's eyes had something different. Very different.

Surprise.

"She didn't see it coming," I mumble to myself. I look at the mass that had been her head. "So violent. More than one hit. Who could you have made that angry?"

I pulled the vial of oil out of my pocket. Quietly saying the rite, I make a small sign of the cross on her forehead, being careful to disturb the body as little as possible.

My work done, I stand up and say to Helen, "Thank you." She nods and motions to the two crime scene techs. They dip under the tape and come into the room. Opening their cases, they get to work.

Helen and I move out of their way. "What do you think?" I ask.

"Too early," she replies.

"I'd think it was obvious. This is somehow related to her story about Joan's murder."

"We don't know that. It could be a robbery gone bad. There's nothing—"

"Helen" I interrupt, "you don't believe that, do you?"

She pauses and looks down at the lifeless reporter. "No, Tom, I don't. She was killed because of what she was doing. And because you were with me, it was someone other than you."

"Joan's killer."

"What? The man who killed Joan? Tom, I know you think he's in town—"

"I don't think," I interrupt. "I know."

"Because of your wedding ring mysteriously appearing at the church?"

"Not just that," I blurt out. Helen starts.

I freeze. I have said too much.

"What else Tom?" she asks quietly.

I shake my head. "I—"

There is a commotion at the door. "I'm telling you I need to get in there now!" I recognize the man arguing with the officer standing guard as the cameraman. He catches sight of me. "You!" he screams and points at me. "You did this. Arrest him!"

Helen walks towards him. "Calm down, sir," she says as she shows him her badge. "Father Greer is here as a priest. Now who are you?"

He stops. "I'm Pete. Peter Rawls. Her cameraman."

"Where have you been?"

"To Baltimore to get another camera." Rawls glares at me. "You'll be getting the bill."

"Baltimore? You've been all the way to Baltimore and back since the incident at Saint Clare's? You made good time." There is more than a hint of sarcasm in Helen's voice. Baltimore is at least a two-and-a-half hour drive.

"Traffic wasn't bad," he says. "I have a bit of a lead foot."

"So when did you last see her?"

"I left about 12:30 p.m. Then she called just before I got to Baltimore."

"Why did she call you?" Helen asks.

"She told me I had to come right back once I got the camera," Rawls says. "I had planned on staying at home overnight and driving back tomorrow. But she said I needed to be back that night."

"Did she tell you why?"

"No. She just wanted me back here, no explanation. My wife wasn't happy when I told her. But that was Katherine. She expected to get what she wanted, and she usually did."

"What time did you get the call?"

He pulls out his phone. "She called me at 2 p.m."

Helen thanks him and tells another officer to take him to get a formal statement. As Rawls is leaving, he looks at the desk. "Wait," he says, rushing toward it before the officer can stop him. "Where's her laptop, her research? All the files?" He looks up. "It was all right here this morning." He looks at me. "What did you do with it?"

Helen places a hand on his chest. "What exactly is gone?" she asks.

Rawls looks at Helen. "All the background research and documents about this story. It's all gone."

Nineteen

After one of the officers takes Rawls to get his statement, I ask Helen, "Do you believe him?"

"It's easy enough to check, but if he's telling the truth, we know when she was killed."

"What do you mean?"

She looks at her notebook. "There was an anonymous 911 call about a dead woman in a hotel room about 4:00 p.m." Helen looks up. "He says he spoke to her around 2:00 p.m. Which means she was murdered sometime between 2:00 p.m. and 4:00 p.m."

"But we only have his word about the call," I point out.

"As I say, easy enough to check." Helen looks at the evidence technician. "Let me see her cell phone."

The technician looks up. She had been photographing the murder weapon. "Cell phone, boss?"

"Yes, her cell phone."

"I didn't bag a cell phone," she answers. "Danny?"

A young blond man pokes his head out of the bathroom. "Yeah?"

"Did you bag a cell phone?"

He shakes his head. "No, not me. Don't think I've seen one."

The other technician looks at Helen. "Sorry, boss, we didn't find a cell phone."

Helen shakes her head and runs her fingers through her hair. "Well, that's great. Whoever killed her took her phone."

"Must be something on there the murderer didn't want us to see," I say.

"You think, Father Brown?" Helen snaps. Then she sighs. "Sorry, Tom. "

I smile. "You still get sarcastic when you're stressed."

She doesn't reply but instead pulls out her phone and places a call. "Gladys, find a judge. We're going to need a warrant to pull cell phone records. Yeah, I'll get the information to you. Thanks." She hangs up and says to me, "It won't be as quick, but we'll find out who she spoke to in the last hours before she was murdered."

I look at the desk, which is empty. "The cameraman says someone has taken her laptop and all her research," I say. "She must have found something the killer didn't want revealed."

"A secret?" Helen says.

I turn to look at her.

"You said something right before Rawls got here," Helen continues. "Something about your ring not being the only thing that makes you think Joan's murderer is in town. What was it?"

I hesitate. What can I say?

"Tom!"

I jump.

"Tell me!"

"All I can tell you is that I know he's in town because I've talked to him," I say quietly.

Helen looks astonished. "What?"

"Yes, he's spoken to me."

"And when were you planning on telling me this?"

"I wasn't."

She goes from astonished to angry. "And why not?"

"Because he came to me in confession," I say. "I can't tell you what he said because it's protected by the seal of confession."

"The seal—Tom, you know you're protecting a murderer. Your wife's murderer. Maybe Shepp's."

"I know," I whisper. "But I can't tell you anything."

She glares at me. Like she used to right before—

"Officer Scott," she calls to the young man guarding the door. "Take Father Greer down to the station."

"What are you doing," I ask, astonished.

"Do you want me to arrest the Father?" the young officer asks, a wary look on his face.

Helen says nothing, but she looks like she's considering it.

"No," she says finally, "just do what I say and put him in an interview room. Keep him there until I get there."

I stammer, "Helen—Detective Parr, I—"

"Don't," she snaps, holding up a finger. "Not a word. Not one little word. You've brought this on yourself, Tom."

***

The officer drives me to the police station and takes me to an interrogation room, with one metal table and two chairs. One wall has a window that looks like a mirror but I know it has to be a two-way mirror.

They haven't taken my watch or my Rosary, I suppose because I'm not being charged. I begin to pray for Katherine Shepp's soul.

Then I pray for the soul of her killer.

Then I pray for Joan's soul.

I don't pray for Joan's killer. I never have, though I know I should. As people so often say to me in confession, and as I have said to my own confessor, I'm working on it.

After several hours, the door opens. Helen walks in, looking perturbed, and stands in front of me with her hands on her hips. She doesn't speak for several minutes but just stands there, looking at me.

Finally, she says, "OK, Tom, you can go."

I look at her. "You mean, that's it? No questions? No interrogation? You've kept me here for hours, Helen!"

"I know."

I wave my hand around the room. "So all of this—"

"Yeah, sorry."

"Sorry? Sorry!" I stop. "Is there anyone behind there," I say pointing to the glass.

"No, it's just us."

"You have me dragged down here for no reason. I've been sitting in this room for hours with no explanation. And you're sorry?"

"Listen," she says, slamming the table with her palm. "I'm doing my job!"

"How is any of this doing your job?"

"You are a witness—a witness who's proven not to be entirely honest."

To my questioning look, she says, "Oh, don't give me that. One, I know there's something you're not telling me about the night Joan was murdered. Two, you didn't tell me her murderer contacted you in the confessional—wait," she says. "Yesterday wasn't the first time, was it Tom?"

I look at her.

"No, no, it wasn't, was it?" she continued. "The ring. Oh, you found it in the church all right. In the confessional. Am I right?"

"I don't know if it was the same person," I say. "They never spoke."

She put her hands on her hips. "You priests and your damn seal of confession."

"Now wait just a minute," I say.

"No, Tom, you wait just a minute," she points at me. "It's a great phrase, nice and high sounding, but what it really means is you can shield evil people from people like me."

She crosses her arms. "Do you know why John was so non-religious when I met him? Oh, he wasn't always that way. In fact, he was raised a Catholic. He was an altar boy. And you know what? His priest molested him."

I close my eyes. "Oh, my God!"

"Yeah, that's right," she says. "It went on for months before John finally had the courage to tell someone. Then, the priest was just quietly moved. But you know the real kicker, Father Greer? One of the places John was molested by the old bastard was in the confessional."

I shake my head. "That is awful, truly horrific. But it doesn't change the fact that the seal of confession is sacred, anymore than someone being molested in a library means that books should be censored. The seal keeps the sacrament pure. Penitents need to know they can receive absolution without their sins being advertised."

"What about the victims?"

"It gives the priest the chance to pray for them."

"Well, prayers didn't do John much good," she says bitterly.

"You don't know that," I say.

Helen goes to the door and yanks it open. "You're free to go, Father," she says to me as she goes out, slamming the door behind her, leaving me alone in the stark gray room.

***

It is well past two in the morning before I get back to the Rectory. I don't sleep well, but doze fitfully as the events of the past forty-eight hours play in my head. One thought goes through my mind over and over again, like a song on repeat.

That's two people whose blood is on your hands.

I can only hope that the morning will see things begin to turn for the better.

Twenty

After 8 a.m. Mass, I go back to the Rectory. Glenda is there waiting for me with a newspaper in her hand. I recognize it as the daily out of Baltimore. She shoves it in front of me, pointing with her bony finger at a headline below the fold.

INVESTIGATIVE REPORTER FOUND MURDERED IN HOTEL ROOM.

I grab it out of her hand and begin reading it as I walk into the office and sit down at the desk.

Katherine Shepp, investigative reporter for Baltimore's WQDJ, was found dead in her hotel room outside Myerton. Police say the evidence points to murder.

Shepp, 28, was in Myerton working on a story concerning the unsolved murder of Joan Greer fifteen years ago. In a recent story, she confronted Greer's then-husband, Thomas Greer, over evidence that indicated his complicity in her murder. Internal department sources indicate that Thomas Greer, now Father Greer of Saint Clare's Catholic Church in Myerton, was questioned and remains a person of interest.

According to reports, Father Greer had a confrontation with Ms. Shepp after services at Saint Clare's in the hours before her body was found. A parishioner who witnessed the confrontation says Greer was angered that Shepp and her cameraman were stopping parishioners on their way out of the church and attempting to interview them about Shepp's allegations. Greer, the parishioner said, grabbed the camera out of the cameraman's hand and threw it on the ground, then yelled at them to get off church property. WQDJ apparently has video of the confrontation. A spokesman for the network says local police were notified.

A spokesman for the Archdiocese had no comment.

Glenda sticks her head in my office. "The Archbishop called while you were in Mass. He wants to see you. Today."

"You mean he wants me to return his call."

"No," she replies. "He wants you to come to the Residence to meet with him." She pauses. "He said you should plan on staying." She turns and leaves me staring at the empty doorway.

I pick up the phone and call the Residence.

"Yes, Father Tom," Father Wayne, Archbishop Knowland's assistant, says gruffly when he answers the phone. "The Archbishop was expecting your call."

"Good, well—"

"—and he told me to let you know he'll be happy to talk to you when you arrive this afternoon. He'll expect you at 1 p.m."

"But I have sick calls to—"

137

"He also told me to let you know that he's already assigned a priest to handle your duties at Saint Clare's. He'll be arriving later this morning." With that, he hangs up, leaving me holding the receiver.

Glenda comes back to the office. "So, you'll be leaving?"

I look at her, then get up and walk past her out of the office without saying a word.

"Don't forget to leave your keys," she says as I stomp up the stairs.

Going to my room, I sit on the bed and look around.

For somewhere I didn't want to be in the first place, St. Clare's has become somewhere I don't want to leave.

Not yet.

Not like this.

I guess the Archbishop saw the headline and decided things had gone too far. I am being taken away from Myerton for the greater good of the Church.

I can see that.

I still don't like it.

My phone rings. It's Helen. Reluctantly, I answer.

"Tom," she says.

"Helen."

There is a pause. "Listen, Tom, I'm—well, that is,—look, I was out of line. I just wanted to say I'm sorry."

"It's OK. Look, I understand your feelings, but it doesn't change anything. We'll just have to disagree on this."

"And I want you to know that I understand the seal of confession," she says. "I really do. As a Catholic, I even appreciate it. But as a cop, it's just difficult for me to get my mind around. So, really, we don't disagree. We just have a different point of view."

"Yeah, I guess we do," I muse. "My job as a priest is to show a penitent God's mercy—Saint Maria Faustina actually called the confessional the great tribunal of God's mercy. Your job as a cop is to see that justice is done for the victims of crimes."

"So, Tom," she says, a trace of amusement in her voice, "are we on opposite sides?"

"Oh, hardly," I laugh. "Mercy and justice are two sides of the same coin. You can't really have one without the other. The Cross shows that."

We're silent for a few moments, then slowly Helen says, "How about I buy you breakfast? You know, to make up for yesterday."

A big part of me wants to say yes, to take what might be my last opportunity to spend some time with her.

But another part of me knows, especially after yesterday, that more time with Helen Mason Parr would not be good for me.

I take a deep breath and say, "Sorry, I can't. You caught me right before I started packing."

"Packing?" she asks with—what is that, panic?—in her voice. "Are—ahem—are you taking a trip?"

"Yes, a one-way one apparently. The Archbishop saw the paper."

She says nothing for a moment. "So you're being punished?"

"I guess you could put it that way, yes."

"Do you want to go? I mean, do you want to leave?"

"No, not really."

Helen doesn't say anything for a minute. "I'll call you back," she says, then hangs up.

I look at my phone, shake my head, get my suitcase out and begin to pack. I open the top drawer of the dresser and am clearing out my socks and underwear when my cell phone rings. Helen is calling me back.

"OK, done," she says.

"What's done?"

Just then my call waiting beeps. I check the number.

"Why is the Archbishop calling me?"

"Call me back," she says and hangs up.

I answer the call. "Hello?"

"Father Greer," Archbishop Knowland says in a grave voice.

"Your Eminence, I am just packing."

"Yes, well, about that. I just got a call from a Detective Parr."

My eyebrows go up. "Oh?"

"Yes. She's very—forceful."

I smile. "I've noticed that about her."

"She made it clear that you cannot leave Myerton while the investigation is ongoing," the Archbishop continues. "Detective Parr says because you are a person of interest, you need to stay in town."

"I see," I respond. "So I'm staying at Saint Clare's?"

"No, you're not. I can't make you leave Myerton, but I can remove you from Saint Clare's. Consider yourself on paid leave. I will see you back here when the investigation is over. Until then," he sighs, "try not to wind up in the newspaper again, Tom. Please?"

"I'll try, Your Eminence. And thank you."

"Hmm," he says and hangs up.

I dial Helen back.

"You're welcome," she says when she answers.

"I'm not sure if I should thank you or not," I reply.

"Hey, you told me you didn't want to leave. So, you can't leave." She pauses. "You're welcome."

I sigh. "OK, thank you, I guess. I still need to pack, make room for the new priest."

"Where are you going to stay?"

"Probably with Anna. She has room."

"Do you think she'd have a photograph of Joan's first husband?"

It stings to hear that phrase 'first husband.' "Why?"

"Well, if he's in town, it would be nice to know what he looks like, or looked like twenty years ago. So do you think she has a photo?"

"I doubt it," I say.

"Could she give a description to our sketch artist?"

"She told me she'd only seen him once or twice and wasn't sure she'd recognize him if he was standing right in front of her." I pause. "I can look in Joan's things at her studio. I'll try to get over there today."

"Sounds good. Keep me posted."

Helen hangs up. I call Anna and bring her up to speed.

"Of course you can stay here, Tom," she says. "I'll fix up the guest room."

"Don't go to any trouble."

"Oh, don't worry. It's no trouble. I've got a list of things that need to be done around here that you can help me with."

I finish packing my things and toss the keys on the desk in the office.

As I leave, I pass Glenda's nephew working in one of the beds. He looks up at me. I smile and nod but he does nothing, says nothing, just goes back to work.

I get in my car and sit, looking at Saint Clare's.

***

Later that afternoon, I am in the middle of cleaning out Anna's garden shed when my phone rings. It's Helen, so I say as soon as I answer, "No, I haven't had time to look through Joan's things."

"That's not why I'm calling," she says. "I've been looking into Randy Earl."

"What have you found?"

I hear paper rustling in the background. "Turns out Randy Earl was quite well known in Baltimore twenty years ago, at least among police and mental health professionals. Several arrests for disturbing the peace, assaults, several psych holds. And he was hospitalized for several weeks at a time over the course of several years." She hesitates. "He was definitely in the same hospital Joan was at the same time she was, like Anna told you. That's where they met."

"Where is he now?"

"No idea. Fifteen years ago, he just dropped off the face of the earth."

"Fifteen years ago?"

"Yeah," she says. "Not long after Joan's murder."

"What about family?"

"Mother and father are both dead. No other family listed, either in Maryland or anywhere else."

"What do you think happened?"

"Who knows? He may have left the state. He could be living on the streets and somehow managed to keep out of trouble, though I find that highly doubtful."

"But we know he's in town," I say. "We have to find him."

"We? I didn't realize the department had given me a partner."

"Hey, you called me Father Brown. Besides, I don't have anything else to do right now. Might as well make myself useful."

"Wasn't he kind of a pain?"

"I will do my best not to interfere."

She pauses before saying, "OK, but here's the deal. You don't do anything on your own. You can help, but you can only do what I tell you to. You stay in the background. If I'm interviewing someone and you're there, you don't say anything. Understand?"

"I understand. Where shall we start?"

"Right now, we've got two cases that overlap somehow—Shepp's murder and your wife's murder. There has to be a common factor."

"The same killer."

"Maybe. Or another connection. I think if we find the connection, we'll find either Shepp's or Joan's killer. Maybe both."

"OK, so what do we do?"

Helen pauses. "I've got a lot of evidence from Shepp's murder to go through. We're still waiting for the surveillance footage, but that should come in today hopefully."

Today. Something clicks. "What's the date?" I ask.

"The fifteenth. Why?"

October 15.

"I've gotta go," I say quickly.

"Tom, what—" but I cut Helen off before she can finish.

It's the anniversary of Joan's murder. I have almost forgotten.

There is someone else in Myerton who knows what day it is, and that's what I am counting on.

Twenty-One

The cemetery is just outside Myerton, about twenty minutes from Anna's house. I haven't been here since the day I left. But I know exactly where I'm going.

I park my car not far from Joan's grave. Up a slight rise, underneath the broad branches of a tall oak tree covered in golds, reds, browns, and oranges, is the simple and tasteful white marble headstone. Anna did a good job picking it out. I had let Joan stay buried under the tree, her final resting place unmarked, for two months after her funeral. I couldn't bear to think about it. So her mom had commissioned the stone.

I saw it for the first time when I left.

I walk up to her along the path I'd taken in leaving her fifteen years earlier. Fallen leaves crunch underneath my feet. I can see the top of the hill. I see the tree and the white headstone gleaming in the fall sun.

I look around, hoping I'll see someone by her grave, someone holding a bunch of peppermint carnations, and hoping that person will turn out to be Randy Earl.

But no one is there.

I reach the top of the hill and stand, staring at the headstone, where I had stood years earlier when I said good-bye. I stroke the marble lightly, my finger lingering on the spot where I had placed my wedding ring.

"Hi," I say. It's odd. I pray for her soul and ask for her prayers. But now words fail me.

She isn't really here, I know. Just a dead, lifeless body, more dust than anything else. Her soul is alive. I feel her presence often and reap the benefits of her prayers for me. Still, I feel guilty for not visiting her grave, like I have abandoned her.

"I know you're not here, Joan," I say to the stone. "But I'm sorry I haven't visited." I pause. "It's hard. It's so hard." I feel a lump in my throat as a tear comes to my eye. "I'm so sorry." I pull out a handkerchief and wipe my eyes.

"You OK, Father?"

I turn. The groundskeeper has come up behind me. I hadn't noticed him working.

"Yes, yes, I'm fine."

He points at the grave. "You knew Ms. Greer?"

I look. "Yes, I knew Joan. A long time ago."

He nods. "Yes. Very sad story. She was murdered, you know, died in her husband's arms." He leans on his rake. "The guy was never caught." He shakes his head. "Why would someone do something like that, Father? Do you know?"

I shake my head. "No," I whisper. "I don't."

He shrugs. "Some people are just evil, I guess. Anyway, she must have been a special young woman."

"She was. Very special."

"A woman comes all the time, I guess it's her mom. She comes, talks to her for a few minutes." I nod. Anna.

"And her husband, once a month, like clockwork," he says as he resumes his raking.

"Her husband?" I grab his arm, a little too firmly. Startled, he looks at me.

"Yeah, Father," he says, looking at my hand on his arm, then at me. Embarrassed, I let him go.

"Her husband visits her? Regularly?"

He nods. "Yeah. Every month. Like clockwork. Brings those puffy flowers, the white ones with the red stripes."

Peppermint carnations.

"What does he look like?" The groundskeeper looks at me. "I knew Joan when we were younger," I say quickly. "I'd like to meet the man she married."

"Oh, well," the groundskeeper shrugged. "He's a big guy, taller than you, dark hair. About your age. A veteran."

"How do you know he's a veteran?"

"Just carries himself like ex-military. Oh, and the cane."

I look at him. "He uses a cane?"

"Yeah, looks like he may have—"

I don't hear the rest, instead I run towards my car. About halfway I stop and turn. "Has he been here today?" I call.

The groundskeeper looks up from his raking. "Today? No, he hasn't. You know, that's odd. What's the date? The fifteenth? Huh, he usually comes in on the fifteenth of the month. Like clockwork."

I thank him and hurry to my car.

I sit behind the wheel and think about calling Helen. I pull out my phone, then put it back in my pocket.

No, I have to check this out myself.

I pull out of the parking spot and turn the car in the direction of Chloe and John Archman's house.

***

I hesitate before ringing the doorbell. The lights are on, and John's car is in the driveway, so I know at least he's home. I hope that Chloe isn't. I need to talk to John, but I'm not sure what I would say or if Chloe knows what I suspect. I'm not entirely sure myself what I suspect.

I steel myself and ring the doorbell. After a minute, the door opens.

It's Chloe, and my courage sags.

She seems both surprised and pleased to see me. "Tom, hi. What are you doing here?"

"Can I come in, please, Chloe?"

"Of course," she says as she stands aside to let me in. I thank her and walk into the hallway. She shows me into their living room.

Sitting down, I ask, "Is John here? I really came to see him."

"He's here, but he's not doing too well," Chloe says. She sits in an armchair opposite me.

"I'm sorry. Has anything happened?"

"He won't tell me, but something had to have to trigger something this bad. It started a couple of days ago, and if it's anything like his other episodes, he'll be fine in a couple of more days. Trust me, Tom, I've been through this enough times. Now," she says sitting back, "what did you come over for?"

I hesitate. "I want to ask John about something." I pause.

"Well?" She asks. "What is it?"

"I just want to ask him why he visits Joan's grave every month on the anniversary of her murder."

The smile disappears as the warmth in her eyes cools. Her brow narrows. "What?" she whispers.

I tell her what the groundskeeper told me and give her the description of the man. "It's John, isn't it, Chloe?"

She stands. "I need a drink, you want one?" Before I can answer, she walks into the kitchen and returns with two glasses of red wine. "Here," she says, handing me a glass. "I don't keep anything stronger in the house, on account of John."

I take the glass as Chloe sits back down and immediately takes a big swig of her wine. She sits the glass on the table and folds her arms.

"Well?" She stares at me. "What do you want to know?"

I think, *What do I want to know? Why do I want to know it? Where to begin?*

"It all began," Chloe starts, reading my thoughts, "when John signed up for one of Joan's classes at Myer."

"I had forgotten that," I say.

"It was his therapist's idea, a way of reprogramming his brain after his injuries. She suggested that he do something creative to develop those parts of his brain he never really used before. So he decided on painting." Chloe takes another drink. "At the time, it seemed like a good idea. Turned out he had some natural talent, no idea where it came from. He took a couple of extension classes, then he wanted something more intensive, he said. So he signed up at Myer. For Joan's class."

"Makes sense, we were friends."

"That's what I thought," she says. A small laugh erupted from her. "If I had only known."

"Now, Chloe, you told me that Joan never cheated on me."

"Oh, Tom," she says, smiling. "No, Joan was always faithful to you. That's not what I'm talking about."

I sit with this for a minute, turning her words over in my mind, slowly realizing what she's saying.

"Was John Joan's stalker?" I ask.

Chloe sighs. "Why does it matter, after all this time, why? Why can't you just leave things alone?"

"Just tell me, please!" I snap. "I'm tired of secrets, tired of people not telling me things. I just want to know the truth!"

"OK, OK." She takes another sip of wine. "It was partially my fault, I guess, looking back. I wasn't the most understanding wife after he got back from Iraq. I was just glad he was still alive. After he was wounded, I just wanted to forget everything that happened. I couldn't understand why he didn't just get on with his life. Things were strained between us. He needed patience and understanding, compassion. I was short of all three, busy carrying the burden of the kids while he healed."

She drinks some more of her wine, then goes on. "He found it with Joan. It started innocently enough apparently, coffee together after her class. But they began to see more of each other, talk for a long time. They'd meet for lunch. John would go to her studio to watch her work. She'd give him advice and pointers with his work. They became very close."

The silence is heavy between us as we look at each other for a while. My wine sits untouched, while Chloe drinks the rest of hers. I am a mix of anger and jealousy and hurt. Joan had let John into her studio, a world she never told me about, a world I never knew existed. And I can't understand why.

"But nothing physical happened between them?"

Chloe shakes her head. "No. Joan swore to me it never went that far."

"She told you about it?"

"Oh, yes, she told me everything after she realized what was happening."

"John was becoming obsessed with her," I say.

"Yeah, he was. Joan told me he was becoming intense, leaving notes at her office in the art department, sending flowers, calling and texting her. She told him firmly to stop, that she only had feelings of friendship with him, that she would never betray you or me."

"He sent the emails and the note, didn't he? You've known this whole time." I am angry.

"Yes, I've known!" she cries. "And I lied when you asked me. I just wanted to forget about it, and I didn't want you to be hurt, knowing it was your best friend."

"Best friend," I spit. "I'm wondering if anyone is my friend in this town. You, John, Anna, all keeping Joan's secrets after all these years. Especially when the secrets may have kept her murderer from being caught."

"I told you that John had nothing to do with her murder."

"But I saw." Chloe and I stand up and turn toward the hallway. John, haggard and disheveled, stands there leaning against the wall.

"I saw," he repeats.

"John," Chloe says, walking towards him. "Go back and rest,"

"I saw what happened that night," he says looking at her. He sways, leaning harder on his cane. "Joan. I'm sorry, Chloe. I loved her."

She nods and pats his shoulder. "I know you did. We all did."

"I did," John repeated. He looks at me. "I loved her, my friend. I know you did, too. But I couldn't believe what I saw."

I stiffen. "What?"

He points at me. "I saw, Tom. I was there. No one saw me. But I was there. I saw the whole thing. I saw. I saw." John sways and pitches forward, falling to the floor in a heap, not moving.

Chloe screams as I rush to John, dropping to my knees by him. "John! John!" I call as I shake him by the shoulders. I lean over to listen.

"He's not breathing," I say. "I can't find a pulse. Chloe, call 911!" I say as I start CPR.

"John! John! What did you do!" Chloe cried.

"Call 911, now!" I order firmly. While I do compressions, I pray for John, that the ambulance will get here before it is too late, and that I'll be able to keep up CPR until they get here.

"They're on the way," Chloe says. "They asked what he took."

"Go see if you can find out," I say. "Come on, John, Come on. Hang in there buddy."

I can feel my back and arms getting stiff. Finally, after what seems like hours, I hear a banging on the door.

"Paramedics," a voice calls.

"Get in here!" I yell, still pumping. I hear the door open and a second later, feel a strong hand on my arm.

"Sir, I'll take over," says the paramedic. He takes over CPR while the other paramedic puts the oxygen mask on John.

"What happened?" the second paramedic asks.

I shake my head. "He was talking, then he just collapsed."

"Is he taking anything?"

"I don't—"

"Here," I hear Chloe say. "He took these. It was a full bottle."

The paramedic takes the bottle and says, "Sleeping pills, just filled yesterday."

Both move quickly. One places heart leads on John's chest and when the screen shows a flatline, the other charges the defibrillator and shocks him, John's body convulsing as the voltage shoots through him. They look at the screen. What had been a flat line now has peaks and valleys, a rhythmic beeping keeping time with the line.

"He's back," one paramedic says.

"He's breathing on his own," says the other. "But his blood pressure is low."

"Let's get him on the bus."

"Can I come with him?" Chloe asks, her worry on full display.

"You can ride with us," one paramedic says.

"I'll follow you and meet you there," I say.

They get him on the stretcher, roll him out of the house, and lift John into the ambulance. The paramedic riding in the back helps Chloe inside; the driver closes the doors and runs around to the front. Lights flashing and sirens blaring, the ambulance pulls away from the curb and races down the street.

I hurry to my car, my mind full of questions. What has driven John to try to take his own life? It wasn't an accidental overdose, it wasn't an overdose of pain meds. He deliberately swallowed a bottle full of sleeping spills. He meant to die. But why now?

Why hadn't Joan told me about John? Why hadn't John told me about things? And what about what John said? He was there that night? He saw what happened? He saw what really happened? What am I going to do about that?

I thought the secret of that night was known only to me and Joan's killer. But no. There is another person who knows.

As I drive, I struggle with what to do next. But there is only one thing I can do.

I am within sight of the hospital when I pull the car over and pick up my phone.

"I was just about to call you," Helen says when she answers.

"We need to talk," I say.

"Yes, we do," she says. "We're finally getting the surveillance footage from the hotel. The camera in the hallway outside Shepp's room wasn't working properly, so the video's going to have to be cleaned up before we can see anything."

"Oh," I say. "What I want to talk to you—"

"But the cameras in the parking lot got something."

I stop. "What did you find?"

"Someone coming out the stairwell exit into the parking lot. It's too far away to see who, but the time is close to the time of the anonymous call to 911. They got in a sedan and left. The camera caught the licence plate. The car is registered to a John Archman."

Twenty-Two

Helen arrives at the emergency waiting room of Myerton General about half an hour later. Chloe is with John in an exam room.

"Any word?" she asks as she takes the seat next to me.

I shake my head. "He was alive and breathing when they got here, but I don't know anything else."

"So tell me what happened again? You didn't get into too much detail on the phone."

So I tell her about John coming out in the hallway collapsing, Chloe finding the empty pill bottle. I do not tell her what John had said.

"Good thing you were over there," she says. "Why were you there?"

"They're old friends of mine, they were in our wedding. John's been having problems since coming home from Iraq. I was checking on him." All of this was true. But I don't tell her what I learned about John and Joan.

I will, just not now.

Helen looks at me. "You know you're a bad liar, Tom, right?"

I feel my face flush but I smile. "What do you mean?"

She points her finger at me. "You know exactly what I mean. You've been lying to me about things. Or at least you haven't been completely honest. And you're lying now. This isn't going to work, Tom, unless you let me know what's going on. Now tell me the truth. All of it."

I hold her stare for a moment. Then I slump in my seat. There is really no sense going on.

"OK, I'll—"

Just then the doors of the Emergency Room slide open and Chloe walks through. We stand up as she approaches me.

"How's John?" I ask.

"Better," she says. "He's stable. They pumped his stomach. Fortunately, not all the pills had dissolved."

"Is he conscious?" Helen asks.

Chloe looks at her, the irritation evident on her face. "Who are you?"

Helen takes out her identification. Chloe looks at it, then me. "Why did you call the police?" she asks me. "Trying to commit suicide isn't a crime."

"Technically, it still is in this state," Helen says.

"That's not why she's here, Chloe. It's about something else."

"Oh, what is it?"

I turn to Helen. "Maybe this isn't the best time, Detective."

152

"I'm sorry, Mrs. Archman," Helen says, "but this is important. Do you know where your husband was Sunday afternoon?"

"What, this past Sunday afternoon? I don't know," Chloe answers.

"You don't know where he was?"

"What, no, of course not. I know where he was."

"Was he at home?"

"No, not in the afternoon. After lunch, he said he needed to go to the hardware store, said he needed some leaf bags, and he wanted to look at snow blowers."

"Did you go with him?"

"No, I had to stay home with the kids."

"So," Helen says, "you don't know if he went to the hardware store."

"Actually, I do know that. He brought the bags back with him."

"Did he stop anywhere else?"

"I don't think so. What's all this about, Tom?"

"Just answer the questions, Chloe."

Helen continues, "About what time did he get back?"

"I think it was around 5 p.m., maybe 5:30 p.m."

Helen and I look at each other.

"Will someone please tell me what this is all about?" Irritation has been replaced with confusion and worry in Chloe's voice. She is not holding up well.

"Maybe you can ask more questions later," I say to Helen.

She shoots me a warning glance. She has no intention of waiting. "I know this is a very distressing time for you," she says to Chloe, "but I wouldn't ask these questions if they weren't important."

Chloe inhales and nods. "Make it quick, please, I'd like to get back to my husband."

"Just a couple more questions, Mrs. Archman. When he got back, did he seem distressed or unusual in any way?"

Chloe gets a serious expression on her face. "Now that you mention it," she says, "he did act like something was wrong. I asked him if he was OK, but he told me he was fine. He suffers from depression, anxiety, and PTSD, so I'd seen him bad off before. But this seemed different somehow."

"Different how?"

"Like something had rattled him," she explains. "Something had upset him. When he couldn't get out of bed the next day, I knew he was having one of his episodes."

"But he didn't tell you anything."

"That was not unusual, Detective. John keeps his struggles to himself, pretty much. Not for my lack of trying. Whatever it was, you'll have to ask him when he wakes up." She looks back towards the emergency room entrance. "If he wakes up."

Helen nods. "One last question, Mrs. Archman. After he got home, what did he do?"

"What did he do?" Chloe repeats. She thinks for a moment, then answers, "Oh, he took a shower."

"He took a shower?" I say.

Chloe nodded. "Yes, he went straight to our bedroom and took a shower. About twenty minutes later, he comes back in a t-shirt and sweatpants."

"What was he wearing when he came home?" Helen asks.

Chloe shrugged. "Khakis and a green polo, I think."

"Where are those clothes now?"

"Why—"

"Just answer her, Chloe," I say, gently placing my hand on her shoulder.

"Those clothes?," she repeats. "In the dirty clothes hamper, I guess." She pauses. "Wait, that's odd."

"What is?" Helen asks.

"I was doing laundry this morning. I'm almost certain that those weren't in there."

Helen and I look at each other, then at Chloe.

"What about the leaf bags?" I ask.

"The leaf bags? I guess they're in the garage. He went there before he came into the house." Chloe looks at us. "Now will one of you please tell me why all these questions?"

Indicating an empty area of the waiting room, I say, "Why don't we sit down over there?"

***

It is the first time I have ever told someone that a loved one is a suspect in a murder case.

I am not entirely prepared for the range of emotions Chloe exhibits: denial, anger, fear, rage, despair—she shows all of them in a matter of moments. She is adamant that John couldn't have had anything to do with Shepp's murder. I don't believe it either, but the evidence shows he had been at the hotel around the time of the murder. Chloe cannot give us a reason why he would be there. I can only think of one, but I can't figure out why John would have killed Shepp.

After Chloe goes back to check on John, I begin to tell Helen what I had started to tell her in the waiting room, about John and his obsession with Joan. About his monthly visits to Joan's grave. About how Chloe told me John sent the emails. I leave out what John says about witnessing Joan's murder.

"Archman was stalking your wife?" Helen says to me as we walk to our cars. Chloe has agreed to let Helen and me search the house. The Archman kids are staying with friends. "That gives him motive."

"I don't see—"

"Shepp was investigating Joan's murder. It's the overlap we keep coming back to."

"Are you thinking now that John had something to do with Joan's murder? Impossible."

Helen stops and looks at me. "I've got a lot of experience with this sort of thing, Tom. One thing I've learned is that when it comes to murder, nothing is impossible."

"But I was there, remember?" I say. "John was my best friend, my best man. I would have recognized him."

"Your own statement says it was dark and he may have been wearing a mask," Helen points out. "Isn't he about the same height as the person you described?"

"Well, yes, but—"

"For that matter, his wife's about the same height," Helen says as she continues walking.

"What, now you think Chloe killed Joan?"

"Jealousy is one of the seven deadly sins, Tom, you know that. She had motive."

I shake my head. "No, I was there. It wasn't her, and it wasn't John, either."

We are at Helen's car. Before opening the door, she turns to me. "I'd have a much easier time believing you if you were being honest with me."

I feel my face get warm. "I'm not sure what you mean."

She points towards the emergency room. "Before Chloe came in, you were going to tell me something. Something about the night of Joan's murder. Something you haven't said before in fifteen years. You kept it from the police that night, and you're keeping it from me now. You know, I can arrest you for hindering a police investigation. Is that what you want?"

"Of course not."

"Then tell me," she demands, but not in her cop voice. "What are you hiding?"

I look at her. She stares at me and then throws up her hands. "You know, never mind. Don't tell me now. Are you coming?"

I nod and turn to walk to my car.

"But this isn't over, Tom," I hear her call after me.

***

I let Helen and myself in using the key Chloe gave us. Things are as we had left them, the unfinished glasses of wine in the living room near where we had been sitting. Helen looks around, not picking anything up.

"If you find anything," she says, "don't touch it. Crime scene will have to photograph and bag it. Where is the bedroom?"

"Back this way, I would think." We walk down the hallway. The house is two stories, with the kids' rooms upstairs. The master bedroom is downstairs, a good-sized room, light and airy. Or it would have been if the blinds and curtains hadn't been drawn. With the sun having gone down an hour before, it is pitch black before Helen flicks on the light switch

The bed is unmade where John had been. An empty water glass and an ebook reader is on the bedside table along with a smartphone. The room is neat and tidy except for the bed.

"What are we looking for?" I whisper.

"His clothes for one," Helen answers in a normal voice. "Other than that, anything that might tie him to Shepp."

I look at the bedside table and pick up the phone. It is fingerprint and pin locked.

"What did I tell you about not touching anything?"

I turn to Helen and smile sheepishly.

"Sorry," I say, putting the phone back, as close as I can, to the same place I found it. She is looking through the drawers while I wander out of the bedroom and down the hall. I want to check the garage to see if the leaf bags are actually there.

The garage has a workbench, garden tools, a lawn mower, and some other yard equipment. It takes me a minute to spot the leaf bags. John had put them under the worktable so I have to bend down to pick them up.

Underneath the paper bags is a stack of neatly labeled file folders and a laptop. They have to be Shepp's.

I pick them up. There is a folder labeled, "Greer, Joan—Background." Another labeled "Greer, Thomas—post-murder." Inside, there is a printout of a page from the Archdiocese website, showing the new seminarians. Each face is young and eager. Except mine.

There are about a dozen folders in all, Shepp's research. The folders had been taken from Shepp's room.

By John.

I open a folder labeled "Myer College." It contains a print out from the Myer College registrar's office listing the students in Joan's class from the summer before her murder. For each student the list has their name, year in school, and email address. I scan the list until I find John's name. Then I find what I already know.

John was "artluver."

I hold the proof in my hands. Shepp had gotten this list from the college, somehow, and found out John had sent the emails.

And John had taken it from Shepp's hotel room.

I close my eyes and let the knowledge sink in.

"Well, I've called the crime scene—what do you have, Tom?" I turn to Helen. She looks exasperated with me.

"I know, but I had to pick them up to see what they were," I say, pointing to the stack of folders.

She looks at them. I hand her the printout and point to John's name. She looks at it and the stack of folders.

"Well, this, along with what I found, places Archman in Shepp's room."

"What did you find?"

She looks at me. "A green polo and a pair of khakis along with a pair of size ten walking shoes buried in the back of the closet. I didn't pick them up, but it looks like blood stains on the khakis. And if I was a betting woman, I'd say it's even money that those shoes match the bloody footprints we found." She pauses and looks at me. "Sorry, Tom, but it's not looking good for your friend."

Twenty-Three

I leave Helen at the Archman home to wait for the crime scene technicians. Once in my car, I call Chloe to find out how John is, but the call goes straight to voicemail. Either she has bad reception in the hospital or she is declining my calls. I don't blame her. I'd be mad at me, too, if I was in her position.

I drive back to Anna's and let myself in. Anna has already gone to bed, and it is after 11:00 p.m. I realize I haven't eaten since lunch, but in spite of that, I'm not hungry. Just tired, tired down to my bones, mentally exhausted from everything that has happened in the last few hours—it is just hours, isn't it? It seems like days. I get to my room, take my shoes off, and collapse on top of the covers.

I must fall right to sleep because I start dreaming. It is the same dream I always have, about the night of Joan's murder—at least, it is the only dream I ever remember. I usually don't remember my other dreams. But this one is different. In this one, I grab the killer and pull his mask off. John's face stares at me. The next thing I know, the mask is back on. I pull it off again. This time, it's Chloe. The mask goes back on again. I pull it off again. This time there is no face, only darkness. From the darkness I hear a voice, the same voice I heard from the confessional. "You should have died. I meant to kill you. It's your fault she's dead." In the dream, I feel the figure's hands grip my throat and squeeze. I can't breathe.

I wake up with a start and sit up. The clock says 12:30 a.m. I have been asleep for an hour.

I collapse back on the bed, not sure I'll be able to sleep and certain that I don't want to.

I lay in the darkness, staring up at the ceiling. I should never have come to Myerton. I should have pushed back against the Archbishop sending me. Nothing good has happened. I couldn't leave well enough alone. Now another person is dead and a friend is a suspect.

I feel trapped.

I need to get out.

I need to leave Myerton.

Twenty minutes later I am in my car, driving east out of town, towards the one place I might have peace.

***

Around 3:00 a.m., I turn off the main road just south of Emmitsburg. I take the narrow paved road deep into the woods of western Maryland, the way illuminated only by my headlights. There are no signs of habitation anywhere.

159

I finally see what I am looking for. Two stone pillars indicating a driveway, both topped with lights that burn low and orange in the night. I had not thought before I left Myerton that the gate might be closed, as is usual at night.

Tonight the gate is open, inviting me in.

I turn onto a dirt and gravel drive that is barely wide enough for the car. The trees are so close on both sides that if I meet another car coming the opposite direction, I'm not sure what to do. But I also know that possibility is remote. It is rare to see a car leave this place, for this is the kind of place that once you find it, you don't want to leave.

I left, somewhat against my will, but am now finding my way back.

The drive ends in a large open space dominated by a low stone building. It looks ancient, as if it has sprung from the mountain whole. It is old, about two hundred years, I suppose, but men had built it from the stones provided by the earth, men determined to build a sanctuary for God on this mountain where they could serve him through prayer, enriching their souls in the process.

I stop at a small building adjacent to the stone structure, one that is newer by about a hundred years. It is small, more of a cabin than a building, constructed of logs harvested from the forest surrounding the great stone piece. There is a single light burning in the window, a beacon that pierces the darkness, welcoming any visitor who needs comfort, solace, and peace.

I found all of those when I first saw the light, so many years ago. That is why I am there now.

I knock on the door. After a moment, I hear movement, a slow shuffling from inside as someone comes to the door. I also see an orange glow moving through the window. The door opens, squeaking on its rusting hinges. A hooded figure carrying a kerosene lantern stands before me.

If I didn't know who it was, I would run screaming back to my car, thinking I was being chased by the apparition in my earlier dream. But I recognize the kind eyes, the soft features, the gentle smile that greeted me as a stranger fifteen years ago. Older, more wrinkled, but the same person.

He comes a little closer to me, holding the lantern by my head to better see my face. The smile broadens.

"Father Tom," the hooded man says. "I've been expecting you."

I smile. What he says doesn't surprise me. "Brother Martin, you look well."

He beckons me inside. A fire is burning in the stone fireplace in the one room that comprises the entirety of the dwelling. In one corner is a bed that hasn't been slept in, opposite another bed that hasn't been slept in. There is a small table with two chairs, a small desk piled with papers, and a kneeler with a crucifix hanging on the wall over it, on one side an Icon of the Blessed Virgin, on the other an Icon of Saint Joseph.

He closes the door behind me. I hear a click, and light from an electric lamp illuminates the space. I turn in surprise.

"Electricity?"

"A necessary innovation," Brother Martin says. "These days, I order our supplies online. Just as well. My days of going into town once a week are pretty much over."

"Finally gave up driving?" He had been in his early seventies when I first met him, and his eyesight hadn't been the best then.

"Gave up? Nah," he says with a gesture of disgust. "One little three-car accident and Father Abbot ordered me to hand over my driver's license. Said one of the younger brothers could drive me when I needed to go into town. But they wired this place, ran the Internet to the cabin, and got me a computer so it wouldn't be an issue."

The monastery had both electricity and an internet connection to the outside world when I first came there. It was necessary for the brother's business, the production of truly wonderful jellies and preserves as well as books and pamphlets about the Church. But Brother Martin's cabin had neither when I first met him.

"An old Luddite like you?"

"I've adjusted. Sit down and I'll make you some tea." Brother Martin shuffles to a hot plate where a tea kettle has just started whistling. "They also made me give up my wood stove for this thing," he comments as he pours boiling water into two mugs. Dropping tea bags into each, he sets one down in front of me on the table.

"I don't have milk or sweetener," he says as he sits down.

"This is fine, thank you." I absentmindedly dip the teabag in and out of the hot water, letting it steep for several minutes. Brother Martin does the same, neither of us saying anything. The only sounds in the cabin are the crackling of the fireplace and a faint clicking as Brother Martin fingers his rosary beads.

When the tea looks strong enough, I put the cup to my lips and take a tentative sip. It's hot and bracing, herbal, with a hint of mint, burning a little bit as it slides down my throat.

"You say you were expecting me?" I finally say.

Brother Martin smiles serenely. "For some time now."

"I didn't even know I was coming here until about an hour and a half ago. I decided on the spur of the moment. I didn't tell anyone I was coming."

He shakes his head slightly. "You didn't need to. I just knew you'd be coming."

I look at the old monk. Even though he is not one of the cloistered brethren, as an extern and doorkeeper for the monastery, he is by far the most mystical. Had he seen a vision in a dream or in one of his long times of prayer in the nearby grotto?

"No," he says as if reading my thoughts. "I saw no vision, received no inspiration in prayer. I just always knew you'd be back."

"Really?"

"Yes. That and we do get newspapers here, you know."

I chuckle. "So you know what's been going on."

"Only what I've seen in the papers. I wasn't aware you'd been assigned to a parish in Myerton. Why don't you tell me how that came about?"

Over the next hour or so, I tell Brother Martin everything. How the Archbishop had assigned me to Myerton for four months. About Nate Rodriguez and Katherine Shepp. About being contacted by Joan's murderer. About Helen reopening the case. About Joan, the emails, what her mother told me, about the secrets she had been keeping from me about her illness and her first marriage. It all comes out in a tumble, as if I have been carrying a wheelbarrow piled with stones up a hill, and having reached the top, I dump it out all at once. Hearing everything out loud leaves me exhausted, on top of the fact that it is almost 5 a.m. and a faint pink glow on the horizon shows that dawn is near.

"And that's it. I needed a break. So I left."

Brother Martin leans back in his chair. His smile never softens, but his eyes grow firm. "Just like last time."

I think for a minute before responding. "Yes, I guess it is just like last time."

"You ran."

"Yes."

"But you didn't leave it. You brought it with you." He looks at me over his cup. "Just like last time."

I don't respond. Brother Martin gets up and pours himself another cup of tea. "I used to make my own blend, you may remember. But," he says, flexing his hand, "really can't do it anymore because of the arthritis. So, now it comes in a box from Amazon." He takes a sip and considers for a moment. "Not bad, but not the same either."

He turns to look at me. "I never told you this, but I was not in favor of you leaving."

I look at him surprised. "But at the time you said—"

He cuts me off with a wave of his hand. "I know what I said, and I meant it. A man like you isn't meant for this life, having lived so much in the world and having experienced so much tragedy. You need to serve the Lord out there," he gestures with his cup, "among His people, saying Mass, baptizing babies, marrying and burying, walking alongside them in their darkest times. No, your call is real. It wasn't a figment of your imagination."

It comforts me to hear him say this. I have wondered often since if I had dreamed it all. What I consider my call to the priesthood was so unusual that I sometimes doubt the reality of it.

Brother Martin was the first person I told of what I experienced those years ago at the grotto. It had been he who encouraged me to tell Father Abbot. That was the beginning. I went from never wanting to leave the monastery to preparing for a life as a diocesan priest.

"But," Brother Martin continues, "that didn't mean you needed to rush out like you did. I didn't think you were ready. You still had too much of the world you were carrying, too much on your shoulders, too much guilt. And guilt is not a reason to become a priest, ever. You needed more time here for your mind and soul to heal before you were ready to serve others. That's what I told Father Abbot."

"What did he say?"

"Ack, what he always says to me when he thinks I'm overstepping, that I am the extern and the care of the souls in the monastery is his responsibility, not mine. I'm just the doorkeeper, remember?"

I smile. Brother Martin is the monastery's contact with the outside world, but he is much more than the doorkeeper.

"So, I kept my mouth shut and saw you off to seminary," he gestures in the direction of the seminary. "But I always thought you'd be back. Not for forever, no. But you'd be back to finish healing."

"I am healed," I protest.

"No, you're hiding. If you were healed, you wouldn't be here." He sits in the chair opposite me. "You still have the guilt over your wife's murder. Now that's been joined by guilt over that reporter's death and your friend's suicide attempt. Mixed in, too, is your anger over Joan's secrets."

My tea has gotten cold.

"It was guilt that brought you here the first time," Brother Martin continues. "It's guilt that brings you here now. The question is, what are you going to do?"

"I thought I'd stay here a few days, ask Father Abbot for one of the retreat cabins."

"Which he'll grant you, but that's not what I mean." Brother Martin's smile disappears. He leans towards me, asking, "You know why you feel guilty still. You know what you need to do. When are you going to do it?"

I know what he means. Besides being my confessor, Brother Martin is the only person on earth I've ever told what really happened the night of Joan's murder.

I look at him and nod.

Twenty-Four

I finally fall asleep as the sun is rising. Brother Martin prepared the other bed for me before answering the monastery bell summoning the Brothers for Morning Prayer. I am so exhausted I sleep soundly, so deeply that no dreams disturb my sleep. When I wake up, the sun is high in the sky. I check my phone. It is 1 p.m. I am no longer exhausted, but I don't feel rested.

On the table is a covered tray. Brother Martin is not here, so I assume he is off working somewhere else in the monastery. On the tray is a bowl of soup and a small loaf of crusty bread with a glass of water, the ascetic but flavorful noon meal of the brothers. There is also a note in Brother Martin's familiar, but now shaky, handwriting.

Talked to Father Abbot. You can stay as long as you like. Cabin One.

I am hungry, so I eagerly eat the soup and bread. The water is crystal clear and lacks the chemical taste I've grown used to in the city. It is from a natural spring that both feeds the grotto on the monastery grounds and supplies water for the brothers.

After eating, I walk outside. It is a clear and crisp fall day. In daylight, the monastery looks inviting in spite of the fieldstone construction. Except for the parts that have been cleared for the buildings and the paths, the area is surrounded by trees that are still holding on to their brightly colored leaves. The sun shines through their branches, making the colors seem alive. I look down the path which leads to the cabins the monastery maintains for individuals who want to come and make a retreat, either with the brothers or alone.

I'll take the belongings I brought with me there later. There is someplace I want to go first.

A five minute or so walk through the woods, my steps crunching fallen leaves on the path, leads me to the grotto. Some decades before, one of the brothers had discovered a small spring among an outcropping of rocks. He decided to create a reproduction of the grotto of Lourdes, where the Blessed Mother appeared to Saint Bernadette and revealed herself to be the Immaculate Conception. Using only hand tools and manual labor, over several years he created a scale model of the site of the most famous Marian apparition in the world.

In the grotto is a statue of the Blessed Mother as described by the Saint; looking up from the ground, a statue of Bernadette kneels in prayer. Benches have been hewn out of logs. Not many people know it even exists, but the brothers do allow the public to access the site, and every week, individuals and small parish groups come for prayer and to fill bottles with the water that a priest has blessed.

I sit on one of the benches near the front and look at the statue of Our Lady. Her hands are outstretched, a slight smile on her lips, as if to welcome me back. I have a feeling of déjà vu.

Everything, including the shadows cast by the trees, reminds me of the day I experienced my calling to the priesthood. Like this day, I had come to pray and meditate alone for a while.

I take out my Rosary and have just begun the prayers when I hear the sound of crunching leaves behind me. I stiffen, not wanting to turn around. The area teems with wildlife, so I'm not sure what is behind me.

If it is a deer, I have nothing to worry about.

But bears do live in the area.

Whatever it is comes closer, crunching leaves under its feet—or hooves—or claws. Then it stops.

"Thanks a lot for making me drive all this way to bring you back," a woman's voice, heavy with exasperation, says. I turn around to see a very angry Detective Helen Parr standing in the clearing.

"How did you find me?" I ask.

"I'm a detective, remember?" she says as she continues to walk towards me. "I had Gladys ping your cell phone. She says hello, by the way."

"There's no phone reception out here."

"GPS locator still works." Though only of average height, she towers over me, clearly unhappy. "You want to tell me what you're doing here? Why you left town without telling anybody? Against my orders, mind you. I could arrest you, you know?"

"And charge me with what?"

"I'll think of something—hindering an investigation. Answer the question," she says as she sits on the bench next to me.

"I needed to get away, to think."

"You couldn't stay in Myerton and think."

"Everything got to me. It was too much. I needed distance."

"So you left town without telling anyone, just like last time."

"You're the second person in the last 24 hours to make that same comment."

"What is it with you, running when things get tough? I guess *some* things haven't changed." She glares at me.

"I wasn't running," I protest. "I just needed to get away for a few days. I have a lot to put together. I was planning on coming back."

"Really? When?"

"A few days. A week, tops."

"And what did you think would happen in the meantime? That everything would stop until you got your act together?"

"I haven't thought about what would happen while I was gone. I'm not sure I care."

Helen takes her shoes off and rubs her feet. "If I had known I was going for a hike, I would have worn different shoes. I've been walking around here for an hour looking for you."

"Why didn't you ask at the monastery?"

"I did. They said you'd be in one of two places. Unfortunately, I chose the wrong place first."

"Sorry. Why are you here anyway?"

"I tried contacting you, but your phone went straight to voicemail. I called Anna Luckgold and found out you'd left—by the way, she's pissed off at you, too. When Gladys figured out where you were, I decided to come after you."

"But why?"

"Two reasons," she says, putting her shoes back on. "First, John Archman's awake."

"Have you talked to him yet?"

"No, that's one reason I was trying to get in touch with you. I thought you'd like to be there when I do."

"I would. What's the second reason?"

She looks at me steadily. "I wanted to finish the conversation we were about to have at the hospital."

I look at her and sigh. "Right."

"Joan's not the only one who kept secrets. You've been keeping some for a long time. Some you're keeping from me right now."

She stops talking and looks around. "It's beautiful here," she says. "Very peaceful. Lourdes, right?"

I nod and say with a smile. "I used to love coming here, and I came here a lot after I got here. I'd still be here if—" I trail off.

"If?"

I turn to the statue standing in the grotto, showing the Virgin Mary as Saint Bernadette described her. "If I hadn't been called away." I sit quietly for a minute, gazing at the statue.

I look back at Helen. "But that's for another time."

"So," she asks quietly, "are you ready to tell me?"

"No, but I will. You're right, it's time."

I tell her about John hearing Chloe and me talking. About him coming out of the room. And I tell her what he said.

"He said he was there the night Joan was killed," she says with surprise. "Why did he never come forward?"

"You'll have to ask him; he passed out before I could."

"Did he say anything else?"

I exhale, my mouth tightening into a line. I nod. "Yes. He said he saw what really happened."

"And here we are," she says quietly. "What did he mean, Tom?"

I feel tears falling down my cheeks. I have reached the point of no return. I have no choice now. It's time.

"He saw the truth," I whisper, closing my eyes and dropping my head. The tears are coming faster now. I clench my hands together and feel Helen place her hand on mine.

Fighting against the emotions I feel coming up from within me, I raise my head to look at Helen, this woman I once loved. I look into her eyes and see pity, sympathy, and determination.

"Tell me, Tom," she whispers. "Everything."

I know she'll accept nothing less.

So, I tell her.

Twenty-Five

"So," I say quietly, wiping the remaining tears from my eyes. "Now you know."

I don't know when I started sobbing, if it was during or after. But by the time I finished, I was doubled over on the bench, my body wracked by sobs and screams that came from a place deep within me. Years worth of pain and torment, of guilt and self-loathing, burst forth in a flood.

Through all that, Helen held me. She wrapped one arm around me and stroked my head, her warmth and the ever-present smell of vanilla reminding me of another time she held me like this. The time I told her about my father's death.

I needed her then, but not as much as I need her now.

"Oh, Tom," she says quietly. "I'm so sorry."

All I can do is nod.

We sit together quietly for a few moments, then she says, "I need to get back to Myerton."

We stand and walk the path from the grotto to her car in silence.

At her car, Helen says, "You do know I could charge you with making a false statement to police?"

"I know you could."

"Why didn't you just tell the truth at the time? Pride?"

"Pride, guilt, some combination. I didn't want people to know how I failed her."

She starts to say something—probably about the fragility of the male ego—but apparently thinks better of it. Instead, she says. "You'll have to make a formal statement revising your original statement."

"I know."

"And I'll have to mention this to the State Attorney, but," she says, "I'll go to bat for you. I'll make the point you've suffered enough, and in the end, it probably didn't affect the investigation that much. I doubt he'll want to prosecute the husband of the victim of a cold case who's now a Catholic priest."

"Thanks, Helen."

She puts up her hand. "Don't thank me. I'm still mad at you." She gets in her car and starts the engine, then rolls down the window.

"When are you coming back?"

I smile slightly. "I'll be back tonight. I want to speak to Father Abbot first, thanking him for his hospitality, explaining that I won't be staying."

"Then be at the hospital at 10 a.m. tommorrow or I'll ask the State Police to bring you in. In handcuffs." The window goes back up and she puts the car in reverse, turns it around, and speeds down the driveway.

I watch her drive off and then look up at the sun overhead. I close my eyes and smile as I feel the warmth on my face.

Telling Helen has been painful, but for the first time in years, I feel light. I have tossed a great burden from my shoulders. I am no longer hiding from the truth.

"And you shall know the truth," I whisper. "And the truth shall set you free."

"Father Greer?" I turn to see a young brother walking towards me. "Father Greer? Father Abbot would like to speak with you when you're free."

"I'm free now. I was going to ask to see him anyway. Why does he want me?"

"He did not share that with me. He just told me to come find you."

I follow the brother through the entrance to the monastery. I haven't passed through these doors in a long time. The last time, I was on my way back out into the world, into my second life as a priest. I follow him down the hallway to Father Abbot's office.

The brother knocks quietly on the door. "Come in," I hear from the other side as the brother opens the door. Father Abbot Anthony is sitting behind his desk.

"Ah, Father Greer," he says, waving me into his office and pointing to one of the chairs off to the side. "Let's sit over there, so much more comfortable and informal than here." He gets up slowly, grabbing a cane to steady himself. He walks with a slight limp to the other chair.

"Old age," he responds to my questioning look, "nothing more. Arthritis in the hip, in the knees. Some days are better than others. But the Lord has given me a good life in His service, so I try not to complain."

He sits and looks at me. "If I remember correctly, you arrived in the middle of the night the first time you visited us, too."

"And you welcomed me in then, as well."

"Brother Martin has seen to your needs."

I nod. "All of them."

"Yes, Brother Martin has told me of your circumstances," he leans forward. "I'm sorry to hear you continue to suffer because of your wife's death."

"This, I'm afraid, I brought on myself," I reply.

"Perhaps, perhaps. But you're here now and you can stay as long as you need."

"Actually, Father Abbot, I was going to speak with you. I need to go back much sooner than I anticipated. Like today."

His eyebrows go up. "Oh? Well, that's a shame. It kind of negates why I wanted to talk with you. I wanted to ask a favor. Well, I'll still ask, since you're here."

"I'll do anything I can for you. You have been so kind to me in the past."

"It's not really for me, it's for the monastery. You see, the doctors have told me to slow down. They're concerned about my balance. In truth, I have more bad days than good ones. I need the cane all the time just to stand and get around. Which makes saying Mass rather difficult."

He sits back, shifting in the chair to get comfortable. "I've applied to the order for another priest to be assigned, but there is no one available right now. And none of the other brothers here are in holy orders. We have one taking seminary classes up the road, but he won't be ordained for a couple of years. I have been praying for a solution. Then you showed up, and I thought—well, never mind."

"I'd be happy to help if I could, Father Abbot, but I'm under the Archbishop's authority. He'd have to—"

"Oh, I can take care of the Archbishop. It wouldn't be for forever, he'd get you back eventually."

"How long?"

He shakes his head. "I don't know. As long as a year, maybe more, maybe less."

A year in the monastery. Withdrawn from the world, living a life of prayer with the brothers. At the moment, the idea appeals to me.

"I can't right now," I finally say. "I have to take care of things first."

"Well, I need to get the Archbishop's approval anyway. Is this a yes?"

"It's a maybe. I need to consider this."

"Of course, of course, take the time you need. Pray, seek God's counsel. I will do the same. Who knows, maybe another priest will show up looking for peace." He smiles serenely. "Now let me give you a blessing."

I bow my head while he says the words of a blessing and makes the sign of the cross. I stand up and thank him. "I pray it all works out for you," Father Abbot says as I leave.

I go back to Brother Martin's cabin. He is sitting at the table, drinking a cup of tea and offers to make me one.

"No, thanks. I need to go."

"So the woman detective found you?"

"How did you know—"

"She stopped here first looking for you. Attractive young lady. Seems very smart."

"She's good at her job."

"I'm sure. Just—be careful. Remember who you are."

Brother Martin looks concerned. "I'm not sure what you mean," I say.

"She's an attractive woman."

"Brother, I assure you, there's nothing going on or going to go on. She's just the detective investigating Joan's murder."

"She's a woman who drove over an hour to find you and get you to go back to Myerton. Why do you think she did that?"

"I shouldn't have left, I'm considered a witness, she came to get me."

"She could have sent someone else. She came herself." He pauses. "She likes you, Tom."

"Well, I like her, too." I don't tell him that Helen and I have a history.

"There's more there than you're seeing," Brother Martin says. "Listen, I'm not saying either of you are doing anything wrong or will do anything wrong. Just remember your vows."

Later on the road, I turn over the conversation with Brother Martin in my head. As far as I'm concerned, Brother Martin is wrong.

You are fooling yourself, Tom, the lover inside me whispers. *You know how you feel. You know how she feels.*

"No," I say out loud. "Any feelings I have for Helen, or she has for me, are in the distant past. We are just—well, I don't know exactly what we are. But whatever it is, that's all we are."

Are you really sure about that? the lover asks.

I also think about Father Abbot's proposal. I'm not sure what to do about that either. When I first arrived at the monastery, I was broken. The brothers took me in, and I was healed in their midst. After a few months there, I decided I would never leave. I talked about entering the novitiate to become a full-fledged brother and enter their life of prayer and work.

Then came my call to the priesthood. That call took me out of the monastery and back into the world. But I wasn't really part of the world, not really. I had turned my job at the Archdiocesan Archives into my own little monastery.

Archbishop Knowland knew that. He told me as much when he assigned me to Saint Clare's.

***

"Father," he had said, "do you know what one of my responsibilities is? It is to see to the spiritual welfare of the priests in my charge. That's what I'm doing in your case."

"I don't understand," I said. "My spiritual—there's nothing wrong—"

"I'm not saying you're neglecting your obligatory prayers and Masses." He had leaned forward and rested his chin on his hand, his elbow on the desk. "The priesthood is not a way of hiding from the world." He had slapped the desk with his hand. "No, sir, it is not."

"But, I'm not hiding."

The Archbishop had sighed. "Tom, I know your background."

I looked away from him. It was the first time in our many conversations that he had even alluded to Joan's death. His tone was gentle, father-like.

"I don't doubt the sincerity of your vocation or your devotion to God or the Church. But your entry into holy orders was—unusual." He paused. "The loss you suffered—I can't even imagine. Out of deference to your age and previous occupation—your skills were needed, there's no doubt about that—Archbishop Gray did not assign you to a parish. Heaven knows I'm not questioning his decision. The more recent records in the Archdiocesan Archives were in horrendous shape and you have done a fantastic job that you are to be commended for."

"Thank you."

"But," he had continued, "I think your position has served you ill. You work by yourself, without any help except for the odd intern or seminarian. It's become your cloister. Your escape from the world. You don't escape from the world when you become a priest. You're called to bring Christ to the world. That's how you serve our Lord. You don't run from the world no matter how bad it is."

***

He had sent me to Saint Clare's to force me to do the work proper for a priest. From all appearances, I have messed that up badly. Maybe—maybe I needed to return to where it all started?

But do I really want to do that? Would I just be running again?

But where do I belong? I'm not sure.

I start to pray for guidance. As I pray, I think more about Father Abbot's offer.

I also think about Helen.

By the time I am at the outskirts of Myerton, I know what to do.

***

It is after 10 p.m. by the time I get back to Myerton. I stopped on the way back for dinner, realizing I hadn't eaten anything except the soup Brother Martin had left for me. I'm surprised to see the light still on and even more surprised to find Anna sitting in the living room.

"So, you decided to come back this time," she says when I open the door.

"I should have let you know I was leaving town. Sorry."

"That's OK. I'm used to you leaving without warning," she shoots back. "At least you didn't wait fifteen years to come back this time. I guess Detective Parr found you?"

I nod. "I needed space to pray so I went to Emmitsburg. She pinged my cell phone, came there and threatened to arrest me."

"Good. She should have brought you back in handcuffs." She turns and looks at the fireplace. I just stand there, not knowing what to say.

Finally, she turns back to me, her expression softer. "Well, you're back now. Do you know how John is doing?"

"Helen—Detective Parr told me he's awake. She's going to question him tomorrow. I'm going to be there."

Her eyebrows go up when I call the detective by her first name. Her brows go up again when I say I'm going to be at John's interview.

"Any idea why he did it? I talked to Chloe, but she is being very vague. Said it had something to do with that reporter's death?"

"We really don't know," I say. "Detective Parr wants to ask him, talk to him about some other things."

"What other things?"

"Just part of her investigation, I don't think I can say anymore."

She looks at me and shrugs. "OK, I guess I'll find out when everyone else does. Oh, why don't you sit down? I'm not going to bite you; I'm not even that mad anymore."

I sit down. "I really need to get to bed."

"So do I, it's way past my bedtime. I just wanted to stay up in case you came back tonight." She takes a seat across from me. "Detective Parr, she seems very competent. A very good detective."

"She is," I say.

"Pretty, too."

"I guess."

"You guess?"

"I hadn't really noticed, Anna."

"You hadn't really noticed?"

I look at her. "What are you implying?"

"Me? Implying? Oh, nothing, nothing. Just making a couple of observations."

Anna holds my look.

"Well," she finally says, getting up. "As you pointed out, it's late. I'll see you in the morning." She leaves the living room, leaving me sitting there looking after her.

I turn out the lights and go to my room. Undressing, I crawl in bed and set my alarm for 6 a.m.

It doesn't take me long to go to sleep. The last thing I remember thinking is one word.

A name.

Twenty-Six

On my way to the hospital the next day, I stop by The Perfect Cup and get a large coffee with a double shot of espresso, cream and sugar, and a chocolate doughnut. I rarely eat breakfast, but I need the extra sugar and caffeine to get going.

As I stand at the counter, I ask the young lady serving me, "Nate's not working today?"

"Nate hasn't been here in a few days," she says. "Not sure what's going on. His uncle says he's sick."

I drive by Saint Clare's. Glenda's nephew is working in the yard, raking more leaves. He's wearing the same sky blue hoodie he always wears, pulled up over his head. He turns in my direction. I am caught short for a moment, realizing I can't see his face. Then I realize it's his beard.

I pull into the parking lot at the hospital a little before 10 a.m. John has been moved out of the ICU into a regular patient room. I find Helen seated in the waiting area, flipping through a magazine.

Closing the magazine and tossing it on the table, she says, "So you did come back."

"I told you I would. Did you doubt me?"

"In a word, yes," she stands up. "Shall we?" She turns and takes a step forward.

"Wait," I say. She turns back, a questioning look on her face. "I never thanked you."

"For?"

"Yesterday. Listening to me. Giving me the opportunity to unburden myself."

"You've told people before."

"Yes, my confessor and my spiritual director," I say. "But not someone outside, out here."

"Well, don't thank me yet," she says. "I still have to talk to the State Attorney and persuade him not to prosecute."

"You said you'd be able to."

"And I probably will. Brian likes me," she smiles. "We've been out a few times. In fact, he even asked me to marry him once."

A flash of jealousy shoots through me. "Oh?"

She shakes her head. "Don't look at me like that, Father. We were only engaged for a few weeks, never even got to the point of picking out a ring."

I blush like a schoolboy.

"He's a good lawyer," she goes on. "He can be a boring conversationalist. His hobby is restoring old furniture. He spent an entire dinner telling me in great detail about an armoire he is stripping. Do you know the difference between a butt joint and a dovetail joint?"

"Not a clue."

"Yeah, well, I do. Come on, let's go talk to your friend." She turns and walks down the hallway, with me following. We stop outside one of the patient rooms. Helen knocks softly on the closed door.

A woman's voice answers. "Yes?"

Helen opens the door. John lays in bed, looking better than the last time I saw him but still haggard. Chloe sits beside him in a chair, holding his hand. They both look at us.

"Mrs. Archman," Helen says, nodding at Chloe. "Mr. Archman, I'm Helen Parr," she flashes her ID. "If you feel up to it I have a few questions."

"Can't this wait?" Chloe asks, the irritation heavy in her voice.

"I'm afraid not, Mrs. Archman," Helen says.

"I can't believe you're having anything to do with this," Chloe says looking at me. "He's your friend Tom. You're his priest."

"Chloe, please," I say.

"It's all right, sweetie," John says, patting Chloe on the arm. "I want to talk. I need to do it."

"But John—"

John shakes his head. "Why don't you run home, get some rest, come back in a few hours? I'll be fine."

Chloe looks at her husband, as if she's afraid to leave him. John knows it, too. "Really, I'll be fine."

Chloe looks at us, then back at John. "Should I call a lawyer?"

"You have the right to do that, Mr. Archman," Helen interjects. "I was going to Mirandize you before we started."

"No, that's OK. I'll talk to you." He turns to Chloe. "Go on."

Chloe hesitates, then stands up and kisses John. Without looking at us, Chloe walks out of the room and Helen closes the door.

John looks at me. "Tom, I'm so sorry."

"Shush, John, you have nothing to be sorry about," I say. "I'm sorry things got so bad for you."

"No, I'm sorry about Joan."

The sentence hangs in the air between us, the following silence thick. Helen breaks through it. "One thing at a time, Mr. Archman—"

"Just call me John," he says, indicating the chair by the bed. Helen sits down. I stand by the wall, in a corner near the window. The shears are drawn, filtering the bright October sun.

"I know you said you'd talk, John, but I need to read you your rights anyway," Helen says, and then does.

"I understand," John says. "What would you like to know?"

"Tell me what happened Sunday afternoon."

"I'll need to start earlier than that," John says. "Late last week—I think it was Thursday—I got a call at my office from Katherine Shepp. She explained who she was, what she was doing. But I knew who she was. She had called Chloe for an interview, but Chloe wouldn't speak to her. I had dreaded hearing from her myself."

"You had been expecting her to call?"

"I knew eventually she'd come across something that linked me to Joan." John looks at me. "I want you to know that I never, that Joan never—"

I nod. "I know John, it's OK."

"Go on," Helen prompts.

"She had been digging and digging, and like I say, I knew she'd come across something eventually. When you found those emails and that note, I just about died. All these years, I thought Joan had gotten rid of them. I thought I was safe. But you found them. And then you shared the emails with Shepp."

"If we can get back to the call from Shepp," Helen interjects. "Please, what was Shepp calling about?"

"What do you think? She had the emails I sent Joan from my Myer College email address. Somehow she had gotten hold of the student list for Joan's class and my records from Myer. I don't know how she got a hold of that. I always thought they're supposed to be private."

"They are. We're looking into that. Go on."

"She wanted to interview me about my relationship with Joan. I told her there was no relationship, I tried to explain. She says I could explain on camera for her story, or she'd run the story without my help. So I agreed to an interview."

"When did it take place?"

"It was supposed to take place yesterday. When I got off the phone with her, I was fine. I had resolved in my mind just to tell the truth. It happened so many years ago, and Chloe knew about it all, I didn't think anyone would care. But the closer Monday came, the more anxious I got, the more scared. I began to think all sorts of things, about how people would look at me differently, whisper things behind my back, how you'd find out," he looks at me, "and what you might say. Then I saw her interview of Tom and knew what I had in store. For all I knew, she was going to say you found out about Joan and me and killed her in a jealous rage, or say I was going to kill you and Joan got in the way. By Saturday night, I realized I couldn't go through with it. I called Shepp and said I was pulling out of the interview."

"How did she react?'

"Not well. She said if I wanted to give up my chance to tell my story in my way, she'd tell it in hers. I pleaded with her not to, but she hung up. I lay awake that night trying to figure out what to do."

"When did you decide to go to her hotel room?"

"After Mass on Sunday, I needed to get out of the house and think. I told Chloe I had to go to the hardware store, but I drove around. I found myself at the hotel. I sat in my car for a while, then decided that I needed to talk to Shepp face to face and plead with her not to run the story. So I went inside to see her."

"Did you stop at the desk to get her room number?"

"She had already given it to me, the interview was going to take place there. I got up to her room and knocked. She didn't answer, so I knocked again, a little harder that time. The door moved, it wasn't completely shut. I opened the door and called her. I stepped in the room. That's when I saw her—well, not all of her, just her foot. I went around the bed and saw her—or, what was left of her. Someone had smashed her head with a lamp. I knelt down and tried to check for a pulse." He pauses and looks at Helen. "She was already dead when I got there."

"Why didn't you call the police?"

"I did."

"Not right away you didn't."

"No, no, you're right. It was my first impulse, then I realized I had no explanation for why I was there. I decided to leave and then call anonymously. Then I saw the files on her desk. I grabbed the whole pile and her laptop and cell phone and left."

"You went out of the hotel by the stairwell at the end of the hallway," Helen says.

John nods. "I called 911 from my cell phone."

"The call came up as an unknown number; they couldn't locate it."

He shrugs. "I'm a tech guy. I disabled the GPS and masked my number."

Helen nods. "OK, what did you do next?"

"I stopped by the hardware store, got some leaf bags, and went home."

"Pretty cool of you. When did you realize you had blood on your shoes and on your clothes?"

"When I got out of the car at home. I hadn't seen it before. I went inside and took my clothes off. I hid the files in the garage—I was going to take them to work, we have a crosscut shredder for classified documents, I was going to put them through there—and the clothes in the back of my closet. Then I took a shower."

"The papers were still in the garage."

"I haven't been to the office," John explains. "The whole thing, seeing her dead, all the blood, it just triggered me, brought back things I'd seen in-country. I have dreams, blending everything together." He looks at me. "I even dreamed about the night of Joan's murder."

"We'll get to that in a minute," Helen says.

"Finally, I just had enough. I was tired, tired of living. So that's when I took the sleeping pills. I didn't leave a note for Chloe, figured it would just make things worse. I was lying in bed waiting for them to work when I heard Tom and her talking. That's when I came out of the room. Talked about being there that night" John looks at me. "I'm so sorry, Tom."

"OK," Helen says. "If you feel up to it, why don't you tell me about the night of Joan Greer's murder? You saw what happened? You never came forward as a witness."

"I couldn't, I couldn't let anyone know I was there. I couldn't let Tom know. I had told Chloe I'd stopped."

"Stopped what?"

John looks at his hands. "Following Joan."

The words hang in the air. "You were following Joan that night," Helen says.

"I was following her every day," John says, "making up one excuse after another to Chloe. I had to see her every day, or my day was just empty. I was obsessed with her. And I was jealous of Tom. I could barely stand to see the two of them together." Looking at me, John asks, "Didn't you wonder why Chloe and I stopped coming over on Saturday nights?"

"Joan said Chloe said you couldn't find sitters."

"That wasn't the truth. I couldn't stand being in the same room with you two together. Chloe knew that, so she made the excuse. I guess Joan believed her, but I don't know. She knew my feelings for her, she had to suspect that had something to do with it."

Joan, I knew by then, was very good at hiding her feelings. She could have known the truth and just decided it didn't bother her.

"Anyway," Helen prompts, "You were following her the night of Joan's murder. What did you see?"

He lays his head back and looks at the ceiling. "I was in my car across the street from the restaurant. I could see Tom and Joan in the restaurant, your table was near the window. I watched you two eat, talk, laugh. You seemed happy. At least most of the time."

I knew what he meant.

"You got a call," John continues "I could tell from your face, that whatever it was, you weren't happy."

It was from a collection agency, about money Joan owed for a design job. She had told me it had been taken care of. I had given her the money to pay the bill. Apparently, she hadn't.

"You got off the phone and said something to Joan. I don't know what you were saying, but I could tell you were angry."

I had asked her about the bill, if she had paid it. She claimed she had, said it must have been an accounting mistake on the company's part. I accused her of lying.

"Joan started waving her arms, banging the table."

Joan had gotten angry and loud. She started hurling accusations against me and saying the most hurtful things. She was nearly hysterical. I went from angry to trying to calm her down.

"I saw you put your hand on her shoulder, trying to calm her down, I guess. She jerked away, got up, grabbed her jacket and purse, and stormed away from the table. You grabbed her arm to stop her, she pulled away."

I tried to stop her, to assure her that we could work it out, that it would be OK. She was beyond reasoning with at that point.

"Why didn't you go after her, Tom?" John says, now looking at me. "I've wondered that for fifteen years."

I had learned it was best just to let her cool off before trying to talk more.

"What did she do then?" Helen prompts.

"She walked out of the restaurant and up the sidewalk," John says. "She was walking really fast, gesturing with her arms. She looked like she was talking to herself." He hesitates. "I did something stupid."

"What was that?"

"I got out of the car and followed her."

"Why did you do that?"

"She was upset, I thought I could calm her down. Besides," he looks at me, "Tom wasn't going after her and it was dark. Something could have happened to her. Something did, didn't it, Tom?"

His words sting.

"Where did she walk to?" Helen asks.

"She walked to the parking lot in the alley by the restaurant. She got to the car and tried to open the door. I heard her curse when it wouldn't open."

I had locked the doors when we parked. I had the key. I had asked for the check and was in the process of paying it while all this was going on.

"I was about twenty feet behind her or so. I had slowed walking when I realized what I was doing. I was trying to come up with an excuse as to what I was doing there—you know, out for a walk downtown, just happened to be passing by. I realized what I was doing was stupid and had decided to just go back to my car when I heard someone calling her name. I looked around and saw a hooded figure standing about five feet behind her."

"What did Joan do?"

"She turned around. I ducked behind a tree so no one could see me. There wasn't a lot of light. The lot had a couple of street lights, so I could see both of them but not a lot else. But I could hear pretty well."

"What did you hear?"

"She asked, 'Who are you? What do you want?' I heard the figure speak and knew it was a man. 'Don't be scared, Joan, it's me.' I saw him lower his hood. 'It's me.'" I saw Joan walk toward him. She whispered something I couldn't really hear, maybe something like 'What are you doing here?' I didn't hear his answer. She started waving her arms, she stomped her foot. 'Why'd you come! I'm married to a good man! I have a good life!' He turned and walked off a couple of paces then turned back. 'Married? How can you be married to a guy when you're already married to me.'"

Helen and I look at each other.

Randy Earl.

"You could hear all that?" I say, ignoring Helen's look.

"They were yelling at each other. Joan said, 'Not anymore. After you left me on that sidewalk, I called my mom, she came and got me, and we got that mistake annulled.' 'No, no, we're still married, you're coming with me.' He grabbed her arm and tried to drag her off. She shook him off. 'Don't you touch me,' she yelled at him. 'Just get out of here. I don't want to see you.' That's when I heard Tom."

When Joan hadn't come back after a few minutes, I left the restaurant and went after her. As I walked toward the car, I heard Joan yelling. I couldn't hear what she said, but I ran towards her voice. I turned the corner.

"You know what happened next," John says.

"Go ahead and finish," Helen prompts.

I lean back and listen to John. While he speaks, I run the scene through my mind.

"I heard Tom call her name. Joan turned away from the guy and started to run towards Tom. The guy said something like, 'Oh, no, you don't!' and grabbed her arm, pulling her back. Joan jerked herself free again and ran to Tom. She grabbed at Tom, Tom held her. The other guy ran up and tried to pull Joan free from him, yelling, 'She's mine not yours!' while pulling on her. He pulled Joan away and started to walk away, pulling Joan behind him. Joan was struggling. Tom leaped on the guy's back, started to hit him. The guy let go of Joan, threw Tom off his back, and turned on him. Tom lunged at him—I don't know what Tom was thinking, the guy was about Tom's size but looked like he had been used to fighting—and the guy struck him across the face, knocking him to the ground. Tom was down, the guy standing over him. The guy reached around back and pulled out a gun—it must have been in his waistband, and pointed it at Tom. He said something I couldn't hear, all I could hear was Joan screaming. Before the guy could fire, Joan grabbed his arm—I think she bit him, I'm not sure—but he screamed. It threw his aim off." John stopped and looks at me. "Tom was lying there, not getting up. He just—he just didn't move."

I heard the accusation in his voice. I have no clear memory of what he described. Just grabbing at the guy I thought was assaulting Joan. Him slamming me across my head. Me going down. Everything else is a blur. Could I have gotten up if I wanted to? Could I have done anything to help Joan, to prevent what happened? Even now, fifteen years later, I'm not sure.

That's the guilt that I've carried all these years.

I had done nothing to prevent Joan's death. I hadn't gone after her when she left. And I hadn't gotten up off the ground.

"What happened next?" Helen says.

"The guy recovered himself, pointed the gun at Tom. I heard Joan yell and saw her run to Tom—then I heard the gun."

John stops talking. I stop breathing.

"What did you see next?"

"I saw—I saw Joan, laying on top of Tom. She—she wasn't moving." John starts crying. "She wasn't moving. Do you realize what she did, Tom?"

I do.

"What did her killer do?"

"He just stood there. I think he was stunned. Then I heard him scream, 'NO!' He walked forward, screaming, 'NO, NO, NO!' He stood right over Tom and Joan and pressed the gun to Tom's head."

I can still feel the cold steel of the gun pressed against my forehead.

"I heard the gun click. Just a click."

There were three clicks. But no bang. No bullet blasting through my brain, exploding the back of my skull.

"I saw the guy back up, look at the gun, look back at them. It was like he didn't know what to do next. Then came the sirens. He looked in the direction they were coming from and ran off."

"What did you do? "

He sighs. "I ran back to my car, drove home, and got drunk."

My eyes snap open. Helen moves towards me, but she isn't quick enough.

Before I know what I'm doing, I grab John by his hospital gown. "You—you were my friend—you said you loved her!" I scream at John, shaking him. "You were there—you saw all this happen—you, you didn't do anything!"

"I couldn't, I couldn't" John pleads. "I was trying to get my life back together, trying to fix things with Chloe, repair my marriage. She would have found out I'd been following Joan."

"You kept this all to yourself, this information from the police, all these years, allowing her killer to stay free!"

"Besides, I already knew he wasn't going to hurt her," he says as he grabs at my wrists, "and I didn't care what he did to you!"

I stop shaking him. John looks at me. "I'm sorry," he pleads. "I wanted you to die. You had her. I wanted her. I thought if you were dead . . ."

John looks away from me. My breathing is heavy, my grip on him firm. I feel a hand on my shoulder. I turn. It's Helen. She gestures with her head for me to move. Letting my old friend go, I throw myself into the nearest chair and stare at the wall.

"When you came back to town," John says, "I struggled with telling you. I tried that day in the confessional."

My head snaps around. Helen asks, "Which day?"

"The first Saturday Tom was here," John says. "I had every intention of coming clean. But I couldn't. I just couldn't."

I look at him. "The ring," I whisper. "You had it."

"Yes," he said. "I've kept it for fifteen years."

"How?"

"I saw you the day you left, at Joan's grave. I saw you leave it there. I had no idea why you'd do that. I took it. You left her alone, Tom, all this time. I made sure she wasn't lonely."

John lapses into silence. No one speaks for several minutes.

"I'll have someone come and take a formal statement—statements, I guess," Helen finally says. She closes her notebook and puts it back in her shoulder bag. "That's all for now. Thank you. We'll let you rest now."

I take that as my cue, so I stand up. John and I locked eyes, then turn from each other.

At the door, Helen turns back. "Oh, one more thing, Mr. Archman," she says. "You say Shepp was already dead when you got there?"

"She was, I swear."

"Did you see anyone in the hallway, maybe going out the exit to the stairway?"

John shakes his head. "No, but maybe Glenda did."

I turn. "Glenda? Glenda who?"

"Glenda Whitemill."

"Wait, who's Glenda Whitemill?" Helen asks, pawing through her bag for her notebook.

"She's the parish secretary and the housekeeper at the Rectory," I answer. "John, Glenda was there? What was she doing there?"

"I guess working," John says. "I was about to get off on Shepp's floor. When the doors opened, there was Glenda with a housekeeping cart. She seemed surprised to see me. I asked her what she was doing there. She said she'd started working there on the weekends, to pick up a little extra money. We chatted for a moment, then she got on the elevator. If anyone knows something, maybe Glenda does."

Twenty-Seven

"Do you believe him?"

We are outside the hospital when I speak.

"About what?" Helen asks.

"Shepp. Do you believe him?"

She thinks and shrugs her shoulders. "I don't know. All the evidence is circumstantial. We don't have any other witnesses. He could be telling the truth. But by his own words, he had motive and opportunity."

"But John's not a killer."

"He was a soldier, right? He's killed before."

"That's different. That was in war. This—he's not capable of cold-blooded murder. I know him."

"Tom," she jabs a finger in my chest. "He was your best friend, but he was obsessed with your wife and watched while you were attacked and she was murdered. He just admitted not caring if you lived or died. Would you have guessed that?"

I pause and shake my head. "No, I wouldn't have." I sigh. "What about what he said about the night of Joan's murder?"

"What he saw of you and Joan at the restaurant matches what you told me, right?"

I nod.

"And," she goes on, "what he says happened after you got to Joan in the parking lot matches up with your account—your account now, that is."

"Yes, it does."

"The only part we don't have any other witness to is from the time she left the restaurant to the time you arrived. And I see no reason he should make it up."

"So it was Randy Earl that night."

"Maybe, Tom, maybe. All we have is John's fifteen-year-old memory of what he could hear."

"But it makes sense," I say. "Earl shows up, wants Joan back. She spurns him. He gets angry. Tries to kill me. Kills her instead. Stunned, he runs away."

"It does make sense," Helen agrees. "But we have no evidence. The only other living person who knows what happened that night is Earl."

"Then we try to find him. We know he's in town."

"I've tried. I can't find any trace, remember? We don't even know what he looks like." She shakes her head. "One murder at a time. I've got to talk to this Glenda person. Where would she be now?"

I check the time. "Now? Probably at the Rectory."

"Come on, let's go," she turns and starts walking.

"Go? Where are we going?"

She stops and turns back to me. "Going? To the Rectory to interview Glenda. You can make the introductions, you know, ease the way."

"She doesn't like me," I say as she walks away.

"I'll meet you there," she calls to me over her shoulder.

***

Glenda doesn't open the door when we ring the bell at the rectory. Instead, a young, redheaded priest answers.

"Yes, can I help you?" he asks.

I smile. "You must be the new priest."

"Yes, I am just assigned to Saint Clare's. I wasn't told I have any marriage counseling appointments." He looks puzzled. "At least I don't think so. Glenda," he calls back in the Rectory, "am I supposed to do any marriage counseling today?"

"There's nothing on the schedule. Maybe it's a crisis," Glenda calls from inside the Rectory.

"Ah," the priest says. "Well, I have time now if you'd like to—"

"I'm Father Tom Greer," I say, extending my hand. "This is Detective Helen Parr." Helen displays her identification to the befuddled young man.

"Oh!" His eyes widen. "Sorry! So sorry!" He grabs my hand and smiles. "Father Greer, nice to meet you. I'm Father McCoy. Leonard McCoy. You're not wearing clericals, and you two look like a couple, so I just assumed—"

"We're here to see Ms. Whitemill," Helen interjects.

"She's here," he says, his smile vanishing. "She's always here."

I try to suppress a smile. "I—I didn't mean that the way it sounded," Father McCoy says quickly. "Glenda is wonderful. Very—very efficient."

"She is that," I say. I pause, then look at him. "Wait, your name's Leonard McCoy?"

The young priest sighs and shakes his head. "Yes, my parents named me Leonard. They were Star Trek fans."

"I bet your childhood was rich," Helen says.

"You have no idea," Father McCoy says as he shows us in. "I'll get Glenda for you." He takes a couple of steps, then stops. "Is Glenda in any trouble?"

"No," I say. "Detective Parr just has some questions for her."

"Questions," he says. "Just questions." Then he whispers something that sounds like, "Pity." In a louder voice, he says, "You know where the living room is, Father. I'll bring Glenda to you."

As we sit down, Helen whispers, "Glenda sounds like a piece of work."

Before I can answer, Father McCoy returns with Glenda. She does not look at all happy.

"Here she is," Father McCoy says. "I'll leave you three to it." He takes a step backwards, gently shoving Glenda towards us.

"Father," Glenda says. "You have sick calls to make. The list is on your desk."

"I know, Glenda, I know," Father McCoy says wearily. "I was just going to attend to them."

"You'd better go to Gloria MacMillan first. She's all the way out in the mountains, and you don't want to be driving those roads in the dark, not your first time out."

"Tell her I said hello," I say to Father McCoy. "You'll find her delightful."

He nods, looks at Glenda, then leaves.

"Now," Glenda says, turning to us. "What's this all about? Why do you want to talk to me, Detective?"

"I just have a few questions related to the murder of Katherine Shepp," Helen says.

"Shepp? Shepp? Oh, that reporter," she waves her hand dismissively. "I don't know anything about that. You can go now." She turns to leave.

"Glenda," I say gently. She turns to look at me. "This won't take too long. Just sit down and answer Detective Parr's questions."

She huffs. "Oh, all right," she says and plops herself down in an armchair. Looking at Helen, she says, "Ask."

I see Glenda's nephew outside. He isn't raking leaves or doing any lawn work. He is standing on the sidewalk, looking towards the Rectory. He wears a hoodie, earbud cords snaking into his pocket.

"Were you at the Myerton Inn last Sunday afternoon?" Helen asks.

"Is that any of your business?"

Helen sits on the edge of her seat. "Ms. Whitemill, let me be very clear about something," she says quietly. "This is a murder investigation. The questions I'm asking you are part of this investigation. This can happen in one of two ways. You can answer them here, now. Or I can take you down to the police station, and it will soon get around town." Helen smiles. "You don't want that, do you/ Ms. Whitemill?"

Glenda's imperious expression softens into a tight smile. "Why didn't you just say so, Detective? Of course I'll answer your questions."

Helen smiles. "Thank you. Now, were you at the Myerton Inn last Sunday afternoon?"

"I was at the Myerton Inn last Sunday, yes," she answers.

"And what were you doing there?"

She pauses before answering. "Does that matter?"

"Ms. Whitemill, please answer," Helen says with irritation.

"Oh, all right," Glenda crosses her arms. "I work at the Inn on weekends when they're short-handed. As a housekeeper. The extra money helps." She looks at me. "The parish really should pay me more."

"So," Helen continues, "you were working there Sunday afternoon?"

"No, not in the afternoon. I mean not all afternoon, I finished about 3:30 p.m."

"Did you see Katherine Shepp at all that day?"

"Oh, yes," Glenda nods. "I remember. It was near the end of my shift. Ms. Shepp had called down to the front desk to ask for towels. They asked me to take them to her."

"What happened?"

"I took them up, knocked on the door. She opened the door and I handed her the towels."

"Was she alone?"

"I assume so. I didn't see or hear anyone else in the room."

"How did she seem?"

Glenda shrugs. "Fine."

"She didn't seem upset or afraid or anything?"

Glenda shakes her head. "Like I say, she seemed fine to me."

Helen makes a note, then looks up. "Did you run into anyone as you left the floor?"

"No, no,—wait, yes. I did run into someone."

"Who?"

"Oh, I don't remember the name, he has twin teenage boys, you know the one, Father, I think he's an old friend of yours."

I feel a little sick. "John Archman."

Glenda points at me. "Yes, that's the one. John Archman."

"OK, Ms. Whitemill," Helen says. "Just to review. You brought Katherine Shepp towels, a little before 3:30, right? And she answered the door, you spoke to her. There was no one in the room with her. On the way out, you ran into John Archman coming off the elevator. Does that just about sum it up?"

Glenda nods. "That sounds right, Detective." She stands up. "If that's everything, I have work to do." With that, she turns and leaves the room.

Leaving the Rectory, I see Glenda's nephew again. He is pacing along the sidewalk, his hands in the pockets of his hoodie, watching us.

"What do you think?" I ask.

"That things look really bad for your friend, Tom," Helen says.

"But I'm telling you, John's not a murderer."

She stops. "Now look," Helen says, jabbing me again in the chest with her finger. "I'm not saying he made some kind of plan to kill her. Probably happened on the spur of the moment. He tried to persuade her not to run the story about him and Joan, she refused, he got angry and bashed her skull in. Second-degree murder, manslaughter. With his mental health history, a jury would buy it."

I shake my head. "No, it just doesn't add up."

"Motive, means, opportunity," she counts off three fingers. "He had all three. He's our only real suspect, unless," she points to the rectory, "you think that woman murdered Shepp?"

"As much as I think Glenda's capable of anything," I say, "I admit that's highly unlikely."

"We only have Archman's word that she was dead when he got there," Helen continues. "The word of a man who kept secret what he saw the night of your own wife's murder for fifteen years. A man who's good at lying and keeping secrets. For crying out loud, Tom, it's so obvious."

"So you believe Glenda's story?"

Helen nods. "I believe her story more than your friend's." Then she pauses. "But I will tell you, I got a bad vibe from her."

"She has that effect on people."

"No, I don't mean I found her irritating, which I did. It's something else."

"What do you mean?"

"I don't know. Something just doesn't sit right—who's that staring at us?"

I look. "That's Glenda's nephew. He does yard work around the parish.

"Have you ever met him?"

"Yes."

"Spoken to him?"

"Tried a few times. He's not very talkative."

Helen looks at Glenda's nephew and takes her notebook out of her bag, jotting something down. I try to read her handwriting, but her script is indecipherable. Had she not been a detective, she could have been a doctor.

"What is it?" I ask.

She shrugs. "Probably nothing."

"Are you going to arrest John?"

"Right now? No, it looks bad but I don't have enough. Just two contradictory stories. I need hard evidence. I'm waiting on fingerprints, lab results. These things take a lot longer than they do on TV, you know. In the meantime," she says, looking again at Glenda's nephew, "I think I will look into your parish secretary's background. Just to make sure."

"What about Joan?"

Helen looks at me. "I'll add Archman's statement to the file. Right now, I don't have much else to go on. I'll make some more inquiries about Randy Earl. And besides, we only have Archman's word about what he heard. You know, maybe if you found a picture of him in Joan's things? Aren't you supposed to be doing that?"

I nod. "I'll get back to it."

"You do that."

"I want to be there when—if—you arrest John."

She nods. "OK, I'll let you know."

***

I drive back to Anna's house. There is a bicycle laying in the driveway, so I have to park on the street. I am already in a foul mood, and having to park on the street doesn't make me feel better.

As I opened the door, I call out, "Anna, whose bicycle—", then stop in the doorway.

Nate Rodriguez and Anna are sitting in the living room. They both stand up.

"Tom," Anna says, "thank goodness you're home. Nate—"

"Father Tom!" Nate says as he rushes towards me. He grabs me by the shoulders. "I need your help! I need your help! I—I think I'm in a lot of trouble."

Twenty-Eight

It takes about a half-hour and a couple cups of herbal tea to calm Nate down.

"What happened?" I ask Anna in the kitchen as she makes the tea.

"He got here about fifteen minutes before you. I heard him banging on the door, ringing the doorbell, calling for you. I thought there had been some kind of accident. Nate rushed in when I opened the door. He was breathing hard, saying he needed to talk to you, over and over again, he needed to talk to you. I would have called you but I tried to calm him down first, tried to get him to tell me what was wrong. He just kept saying he needed to talk to you, he is in a lot of trouble. What do you think he is talking about?"

I shake my head. "I don't know. I know he hasn't been at The Perfect Cup for a few days. Maybe he had some kind of falling out with his uncle. I guess I'll find out."

"Well, good luck," Anna says, handing me the tray with a tea cup and tea pot.

Nate and I sit in silence in the living room. I hear Anna puttering around the kitchen.

Finally, Nate looks at me. "If I confess something to you, Father," he says, "you can't tell anyone else, right?"

"The seal of confession is absolute," I say. "I can't tell another living soul on pain of excommunication." Hearing the movement in the kitchen stop, I raised my voice slightly. "In fact, anyone who hears what you tell me has to keep it secret, too." A second later, I hear the whir of the mixer.

"No matter what it is?" Nate implores.

"That's right, no matter what it is."

He swallows. "Even murder."

I sit up. "Yes," I say warily.

Nate exhales. "I—I think I killed Katherine. I'm sure I killed Katherine." He looks at me, his eyes pleading for me to say something.

Outwardly, my face is impassive. Inwardly, I am in turmoil.

"Go on," I say gently. "What makes you think you killed Katherine?"

"Because I—"

I hold up my hand. "Slow down, Nate. Why don't you begin at the beginning?"

"The beginning. OK. The beginning." He sits back and thinks. "Since the interview aired, I had been trying to get in touch with her, but she wouldn't answer my calls. I mean, I called, I texted, I emailed. She ghosted me. I mean, not so much as a 'sorry, too busy, will talk to you later.'"

"Why had you been trying to get in touch with Shepp?"

"Because I was angry," he cries. "I mean, I'm the one who started this whole thing. I started looking into your wife's cold-case. I'm the one who got the interview with you. I'm the one you showed the emails to. I'll admit, I wasn't going to get as far as she was, but I deserved credit for something."

"And she didn't give you any."

Nate shakes his head. "Not a word. She aired the footage of our interview without giving me credit on air—I mean, I don't expect overwhelming praise for my work, but honestly, I expected at least an acknowledgment."

I nod. Shepp hadn't mentioned Nate in her report, and the report didn't indicate that the footage of me recounting the events of the night of Joan's murder was made by him as well as her. I can understand his anger.

"But it wasn't just that," Nate goes on. "I didn't like how she interviewed you, implying that you murdered your wife that way. I mean, without any evidence, just conjecture, speculation. It was rotten. An absolutely rotten thing to do. Unethical. I wanted to tell her that."

"How many times did you try to contact her?"

He thinks a moment and shrugs. "I don't know, a couple dozen."

That isn't good. When Helen finally gets Shepp's cell phone records, those calls will stand out.

"So you decided to go over to see her."

"Yes, I had had enough of being ignored. So I went to her hotel room. She wasn't happy to see me. Asked me bluntly why I was there. I told her I thought it wasn't right to air the footage without giving credit, and I wanted it corrected. She laughed—she laughed, Father. She said she wasn't about to do that, that she had told her producer she had filmed the interview outside the restaurant with you herself—"

I hold up a hand. "Wait, wouldn't the cameraman be able to back up your story?"

"Maybe, but she was probably sleeping with him and he was probably married so she had a way of keeping him quiet."

"Oh, I see," I say, mentally adding the cameraman and his wife to the list of possible, though unlikely, suspects.

"She said she'd get fired, and she wasn't about to let that happen, not when she was so close to getting what she wanted. Apparently, she had been contacted by one of the cable news channels and offered an interview. I told her that it was my work as much as hers, and it was important to my career, too, that it was my entry into documentary filmmaking. She laughed more. 'Career? What career,' she said to me. 'Your career is serving coffee in your uncle's coffee shop in this two-bit town. You're not going anywhere. You're certainly not going to pull me down on my way to the top.'"

"But you still have the original raw footage you shot. That would be proof."

"No," Nate said, shaking his head. "I gave her everything I had."

"You didn't keep a copy?"

"Wouldn't do any good, she'd just claimed she gave me the copy."

He slumps back, looking at his shoes. I am quiet for a few minutes. The only sound is Anna in the kitchen.

"After she said that to you, what did you do?"

"That's when it happened," he says quietly, his voice just above a whisper, still looking at his shoes. "I got angry—I never get angry, Father, never did when I was a kid—but I got so angry at her. I grabbed her by the shoulders and threw her to the floor. She must have hit her head on the bedside table or something, because she went down." He looks up, his eyes welling with tears. "She didn't get up. I said her name. I shook her. She didn't move. I panicked. I ran out the door and down the hallway. It took forever for the elevator to get there. I leapt into the elevator when the doors opened and went down to the lobby. I got in my car and drove back to The Perfect Cup. I was supposed to work but I told my uncle I thought I was getting the flu. I went up to my room and locked the door."

"Did you check to see if she was breathing?"

He shakes his head. "No, I thought she was. But then I heard the news. I've been hiding in my room ever since, trying to figure out what to do."

"Do you remember anything else?"

He shakes his head, then says, "Wait. I did hear the other elevator doors open as the doors on mine closed."

I sit back. "Why come to me now? Why not go to the police?"

He extends his hands plaintively. "I don't know, I trust you."

I sit with Nate's story. He looks like he is telling the truth, but he has kept little things from me, so I know that he is capable of lying.

I don't believe he is lying, but something isn't adding up.

He did not mention using the lamp to bash her head in. But that's how Shepp was killed.

Glenda had said she had brought towels to Shepp's room a little before 3:30. So Shepp was apparently alive at that time. Glenda hadn't said anything about Shepp seeming hurt or groggy, but it seems possible that Shepp had recovered shortly after Nate had left and gotten up off the floor.

John said Shepp was dead when he got to the room, which contradicts Glenda's account and makes John look guilty.

Now we have Nate's account.

Something is wrong somewhere.

I look at Nate. "You need to go to the police."

He winces as if I've punched him in the arm. "Can't you just tell them?"

"Me? No, this has to come from you. Besides, I can't tell them."

"Can't I give you signed permission? I can even get it notarized—I know a notary."

"It doesn't work that way, Nate. Even if I could, the police are going to want to hear your story from you."

Nate closes his eyes and swallows. "All right."

I don't have to look at the time to know it's late. I am bone-tired. I haven't slept more than four hours in the last forty-eight and it's beginning to catch up with me.

"Go back to your room," I say standing up. "I'll come by and get you around 9:30 a.m. We'll go see Detective Parr together."

"Will you be in there with me?" He asks.

"You should have a lawyer."

"I don't know any lawyers. One of the baristas dropped out of law school to start a marijuana dispensary. Maybe I can ask her?"

I put my hand on his shoulder. "Maybe not your best plan, Nate. I'll be there."

***

"What do you think?"

Helen and I are in the break room around the corner from the room where she just finished interviewing Nate. He's in there writing down a formal statement.

She looks back in the direction of the interview room. "What do I think? I think he's an idiot."

"That's a bit harsh, don't you think?"

She shrugs . "Maybe. But he's not exactly blessed with common sense, is he?"

On that one, I have to admit she's right.

"But what do you think of his story?"

"Well," Helen puts the coffee down and looks at her notes. "It doesn't really change anything. We know Shepp was still alive after that because we have Glenda Whitemill's testimony. So clearly, Nate didn't kill her."

"Unless Glenda was lying," I say.

She gives a snort. "You really don't like her, do you, Tom?"

"That has nothing to do with it," I say.

"So you're saying you believe Nate killed Shepp?"

"No, I really don't see him as a murderer. His story fits with his personality."

"So what are you saying?"

I shrug. "I don't know, Helen. Something's not right here. I can feel it."

She rolls her eyes. "OK, Father Brown."

"Don't," I say a little more firmly than I mean.

She looks at me, holding up her hands. "OK, OK, sorry." She sighs. "Listen, Tom, I know you don't want to believe your friend killed Shepp, and I admit Nate's story complicates things a little, but we have a witness that says Shepp was alive before 3:30 p.m. And if you're going to tell me that a parish secretary is less credible than a man with known mental health issues and a history of deceptive behavior, then you're the idiot, Tom. Which I don't believe for a minute."

I slump against the counter. "OK, you're right. It doesn't look good. But are you going to check out Glenda's story? We only have her word that she was working that day."

"So what, she lied about working? Why would she do that?" I look at her. "OK, OK, fine. I'll check with the hotel to make sure she was supposed to be there."

We are interrupted by Gladys, who rolls in saying to Helen, "You said you wanted to see this when it came." She turns to leave but then sees me and freezes. "Oh! Oh, hi, Father. How are you?"

"I'm fine, thanks."

Before I can ask how she is, she says with a grin, "Yes, that's obvious."

"Gladys," Helen says tersely, "don't you have something you're supposed to be doing now?"

Gladys looks at Helen a little stunned, then confused, and then defensive, saying "Yeah, bringing you these papers, Chief."

"Thank you, then," she says, nodding toward the door. Gladys rolls away as Helen opens the folder and looks through the pages.

Helen then looks at me and says again, "I'll check on her story. But there's something I need to do first. Come on."

"Where are we going?"

"To the hospital to arrest John Archman for Katherine Shepp's murder. That was the fingerprint report. There were two sets of prints on the lamp—Shepp's and Archman's"

"What?" I say, incredulous. Helen puts her hand on my arm.

"I'm sorry, Tom. Your friend's a murderer."

Twenty-Nine

Chloe is in John's room when we arrive. She starts crying hysterically as Helen arrests her husband and reads him his rights. I hold her as she sobs, her head buried in my shoulder, me patting her back. She doesn't see Helen handcuff him to the bed or have a police officer placed outside his door.

I ask Chloe if there is anyone I can call for her. It takes a while, but before I leave with Helen, she has pulled herself together and is on the phone with a lawyer—their family lawyer—and she is asking for a good criminal attorney.

"I doubt he'll do much serious time," Helen says as we walk down the hospital corridor. "A good lawyer will have him plead down to manslaughter. He won't spend the rest of his life in prison."

"He shouldn't spend any time in prison," I say. "I still don't believe he did it."

She shrugs. "The evidence says otherwise."

"The evidence is wrong." I quicken my pace to pass her.

She stops, grabs my arm, and pulls me back. "Listen, Tom," she snaps. "I know you don't like it, but the evidence is what it is. OK, maybe some of it is cirumstantial, but the fingerprints on the murder weapon are pretty damning if you ask me. Remember, I'm the detective here. This is what I do. I've appreciated the help. I really have. It's been fun, but this case is over."

She pauses, releasing her grip. Then she surprises me by gently rubbing my arm. "As is Joan's murder case."

"What do you mean?" I say as we get on the elevator.

"I probably couldn't make an arrest based on Archman's statement," Helen explains, "But it's pretty clear now what happened. Randy Earl killed Joan and tried to kill you."

I stand staring at the stainless steel doors of the elevator as the numbers count floors down to the ground level. I say nothing. I am processing what she has said.

The doors open and we step into the hospital atrium. "You told me there wasn't enough," I finally say.

"There isn't, not enough to make an arrest. All I really have is his statement. Even your revised statement—which you still need to make, by the way—can't corroborate his because you didn't hear what he did. But I believe his story, and believe he heard what he heard. I have a suspect now."

"A suspect you can't find."

"A suspect I can't find yet. So really, I'm not closing the case. I'm just putting it back in the drawer. Joan's case may never technically be closed," she puts her hand on my arm, "but at least now you know who did it. And why."

I nod. I do know who murdered Joan. And why.

"More importantly, Tom," she continues as we walk, "you can let go now."

I say, "Let go of what?" But I know what she means. .

"Let go of your guilt." She stops as I keep walking. "It wasn't your fault, Tom. You're not responsible."

I stop and stare ahead. Then I turn. "If I had followed her out of the restaurant when she left instead of waiting—"

"Randy Earl would still have been there."

"But he might not have come out if it were both of us."

"True," Helen says, walking slowly towards me. "But then again, he might have."

"If I had just gotten up," I whisper.

"He knocked you down. You were stunned."

"I should have protected her."

"He shouldn't have decided to shoot you," Helen says.

She stands in front of me and places her hands on my shoulders. "Tom, you can continue to blame yourself if you want to. I can't stop you. But from where I stand, there is only one person responsible for Joan's death. And that is the man who shot her."

I look at her. How many times had I heard Brother Martin say the same thing to me? How many times had I heard a fellow priest hearing my confession say it? I hadn't been able to accept them saying it. Would I accept it now, coming from this woman detective? This woman I once loved? This woman I had once planned on marrying?

I don't know.

***

The news of John's arrest for Katherine Shepp's murder makes the evening news that night and is on the front page of the Baltimore paper the next day. I am sitting in Anna's kitchen, reading the story on my phone, eating pancakes that she had made for me. I have just wiped a mix of butter and syrup from my mouth when my phone rings.

"Good morning, Archbishop," I answer.

"Father Tom," comes His Eminence's bass voice over the phone. He sounds a lot more jovial than the last time we spoke.

"I assume you saw the news."

"Yes, yes, I did. Do you know him, this Archman?"

"He was the best man at my wedding."

"Oh," he says . "Well, I am sorry. Sounds like a crime of passion."

I don't blurt out that he didn't do it, that the police have made a mistake, everything I really think.

"Tragic for his wife and family," he continues. "So sad. I will pray for them. And the victim." He pauses a moment. "I suppose you know why I'm calling."

"I've been expecting it."

"With this case over, you're no longer needed in Myerton," the Archbishop says. "Before you protest, I've already spoken with Detective Parr. She says that, while you may be needed for the trial, you're no longer needed as a witness, so you're free to leave."

I listen without saying anything.

"So with that," the Archbishop says, "I expect you back here now."

"Yes, Your Eminence," I reply. "I'll return right away."

"I'm not unreasonable. Take a couple of days to get your affairs in order. But by the end of the week."

"Thank you," I say.

"Of course. Oh," he continues, "by the way. Had a very interesting call from Father Abbot at Our Lady of the Mount. Says he's spoken to you? Apparently you paid them a little visit?"

"Just an overnight one, as it turned out. I had—things I needed to think through. Needed a little solitude."

"That's what he said. Anyway, he asked me about lending you to them temporarily as their priest"

"Yes, he spoke to me about it and said he would talk to you."

"Well, he spoke to me. Has been speaking to me. Father Abbot can be persistent."

I smile. *Not unlike someone else I know*, I think.

"What did you tell him?" I ask.

"Frankly, first I told him no, that I needed you here. But," the Archbishop sighs, "he wore me down. Last thing I told him when he called me yesterday was that I have no objection but I would give you permission to make the decision. He is agreeable to that. So, Father Tom, is this something you'd like to do?"

I think for a moment before answering. "No, Your Eminence, at least not right now," I say. "I need to be available for the trial, and I'd like to be able to visit my friend. I can't really do that from the monastery."

The Archbishop says, "I'll let Father Abbot know."

***

A few days later, I say my goodbyes to Anna.

"You will be back," Anna says, "this time."

"Of course," I say. "To see you. I'll be back for John's trial."

"Have you seen him since . . ."

I shake my head. "No, he's still in the hospital. I spoke to Chloe—well, sort of, she's not too happy with me right now—and she told me he's going to be released from the hospital today, but taken into custody. There'll be an arraignment and hopefully, he'll be released on bail. I'll come back in a week or so and see him then."

She nods. I see her hesitate. I know what she wants to ask me. It was what she has asked me repeatedly since I returned to Myerton.

I smile. "On my way out of town, I promise."

She smiles and hugs me.

***

The trees are bare of their leaves, the victims of a windstorm a couple of nights before. The late October sun shines unfiltered through the gray branches against the crystal clear blue sky. The brown carpet of leaves crunch beneath my feet as I make my way up the slight hill through the rows of white tombstones towards the majestic oak tree.

I stand in front of Joan's grave. I stroke the stone. It feels cool underneath my touch in spite of the sun shining directly on it.

"Sorry I haven't been here," I say.

I pause, thinking about what to say next.

I want to ask her all the questions I have, about everything I have learned about her that I hadn't known when she was alive. It still hurts that she didn't share parts of her life with me.

But I think I am beginning to understand why.

Standing there, looking at her grave, I realize my asking won't give me answers. She took them with her when she died. So I will be left with my questions and no answers. It is the way things have to be.

"I've been away," I say, "but then you know that." I pause. "I need to leave again," I continue, "but I'll visit the next time I'm back."

I pull out my book of prayers and start reading Saint Paul's words from Romans.

"I am convinced that neither death, nor life, nor angels, nor principalities, nor present things, nor future things, nor powers, nor height, nor depth, nor any other creature will be able to separate us from the love of God in Christ Jesus, our Lord."

I finish, saying, "May the love of God and the peace of the Lord Jesus Christ bless and console us and gently wipe every tear from our eyes: in the name of the Father, and the Son, and the Holy Spirit, Amen," while making the sign of the cross.

I stand there for a few minutes in silence, then I bend down and kiss the stone.

"I love you, Joan," I whisper.

***

A couple of weeks later, the Archbishop gives me permission to visit Myerton. A mild October has given way to a chilly November, and the wind whips down Main Street as I drive past the storefronts and Saint Clare's Parish. I make a mental note to check on Father McCoy before I leave. The Archbishop has assigned him to the parish permanently, and I want to see how he is settling in. And by settling in, I meant getting along with Glenda. Before I do that, I have a stop to make.

The county jail is about twenty minutes from downtown, nestled in a small valley between two mountains. From a distance, it looks like a school, or maybe a small hospital. It's only when one gets closer that you see the ten foot fence topped with razor wire. Used to house offenders serving time for minor offenses as well as those awaiting trial, it's where John Archman has been since his release from the hospital.

I park my car and get out. Walking across the lot to the jail, I hear a familiar voice call my name.

Looking up, I see a smiling Detective Helen Parr walking towards me, bundled in a heavy overcoat against the wind, which blows curls of her raven-black hair around her face, causing them to catch the sunlight.

For a second, I'm back in time twenty years to a different windy fall day, in a different place. She's a younger version of the woman I see, same black hair catching the sun, same curls blowing across her face, same smile.

You've got to stop this, Tom, the priest in me says.

It's just a memory, replies the lover.

The priest and the lover begin to argue—again—as I stop and return the smile.

"Tom," she says. "Good to see you."

"Good to see you, too, Helen. I'm surprised. What has you all the way out here?"

"Two reasons, actually," she replies. "The shooting range is almost next door. I come up every couple of weeks to squeeze off a few rounds to keep up my proficiency."

"I didn't know you liked to shoot," I say. "I don't think you ever did when we were together."

"Remember, I grew up in Nebraska as an only child," she laughs. "My dad taught me to shoot. There just wasn't an opportunity in College Park. But, it turns out being able to shoot well is kind of important for a cop."

"Yes, I can see that," I say with a smile.

"Besides," she says. "It's a great stress reliever."

"And what exactly do you have to be stressed about?"

At my question, a wistful look passes across her face. She tilts her head to one side and brushes a curl behind her ear. "My job's very stressful, Tom," she says quietly. "And I've had a lot on my mind recently."

I don't know how to respond to that, but fortunately, Helen continues, "And since I was out this way anyway, I stopped by to get some paperwork. I assume you're here to visit John Archman?"

"Yes, it's the first chance I've had to get away."

"Archbishop keeping you busy, huh?"

"I've got a lot to catch up on," I explain. "How is John, do you know?"

"Sorry," she shakes her head. "I haven't seen him since the arraignment. You know he entered a plea of not guilty."

"I heard. I also heard bail was denied?"

She holds up her hands. "Hey, not my fault, Tom. Bri—the State Attorney opposed and the judge agreed. It's an election year next year. Neither of them want to be portrayed as soft on crime."

I could protest, insist that John isn't a criminal. But I decide against it.

"Well, I need to get going," she says. She stops and turns slightly. "Are you here long?"

"No, just for the day."

"Awfully long drive just for the day."

"The Archbishop is keeping me on a short leash."

"I just thought, well, we—" she stops. "I mean, there is still the issue of the revised statement," she resumes. "I let you get away without it. I still need that, Father."

I shrug. "I should have time this afternoon."

She nods. "Good, I'll see you at my office at 1 p.m. I'll bring lunch." She walks off, stops, then turns.

"Tomato bisque, right?"

I smile. "You remember."

Helen returns the smile, hers small and wistful. "I remember a lot of things, Tom."

***

Because I am in my clericals, the jail staff allows me to meet with John privately. The room has all the charm of a utility closet and is about as large, constructed of cinderblocks. There is one metal table, bolted to the floor, and two chairs. A heavy door with a window is on one wall. The lights are harsh, incandescent.

I wait for a few moments, then John is brought in by one of the guards. I have seen prisoners on TV with wrists and ankles shackled, wearing orange jumpsuits. John wears a khaki jumpsuit and is unshackled.

The guard seats him in the chair. "Father," he says, "I'll be right outside if you need me."

"I'm sure we'll be fine. We're old friends."

The guard looks at me, then at John, then leaves the room, closing the door behind him. He takes his position outside so he can keep an eye on us through the window.

"I'm glad you still consider me a friend," John says, smiling. "I'm not sure I have too many of those left."

"Of course I still consider you a friend," I say. "Nothing's changed. Why would it?"

John rubs his face. "Oh, I don't know, let's start with the fact I stalked your wife. Hid while someone killed her and tried to kill you. Kept secret what I saw for fifteen years. Told you I didn't care if you lived or died. Let's start with that."

"That was a long time ago. You told the truth eventually. The police now know what happened that night."

"Can they make an arrest?" John asks.

I shake my head. "No. They don't know where he is. We're not even sure what he looks like."

"I'm sorry, Tom."

"I didn't come here to talk about Joan," I say. "How are you doing?"

John manages a slight smile. "OK, I guess. It's not as bad as you'd think. Food's not too bad, and they've got a pretty good library. I'm doing a lot of reading. And praying."

"Good. Has Father McCoy been by?"

John grins. "You mean Reverend Bones? Yes, he's been here several times. They let him bring me Communion."

"Reverend Bones?"

He shrugs. "Some of the teens call him that. He's a good priest, nice, but a little stiff. Nervous. Afraid of his own shadow."

We exchange chuckles and lapse into silence.

"What's your lawyer think of your case?" I ask after a few minutes. "You know, the evidence is circumstantial, even though your fingerprints are on the murder weapon, but I'm sure you've explained—"

"I must have touched the lamp when I checked on Shepp," he says. "They found my fingerprints on the folder, on the desk, on the door. I said I was in the room."

"Yes, you were in the room, but you should be able to convince a jury at trial—"

"There's not going to be a trial," John says quietly.

I look at him dumbfounded. "What?"

He shakes his head. "No. No trial. I don't want to put Chloe and the kids through any more. My lawyer's cut a deal with the State Attorney. I'm pleading guilty to manslaughter. In return, the State Attorney will recommend I serve the minimum at the Patuxent Institute over in Jessup." He pauses. "They're taking into account my PTSD and my drug and alcohol abuse."

"John, you didn't do it."

"It doesn't matter," John says. "I don't want to take my chances. And like I say, I can't have Chloe and the kids go through that."

I sit and look at him. "Is there anything I can do?"

"Thanks for coming by. Are you going to be here when I plead?"

I nod. "Yes, I'll come back."

***

After I leave John, I still have about an hour and a half before my meeting with Helen. I decide to go to Saint Clare's to see how Father McCoy is doing and catch the Noon Mass. When I arrive, he is already in the sacristy.

He has his back to me when I knock on the open door. He jumps and gives a little cry, spinning around.

"I told you I'd take care—Oh!" I obviously am not who he is expecting.

"Thought I was someone else?" I ask, unable to hide my amusement.

"What? No, no, yes, I mean—you startled me," sputters the flustered Father.

"She doesn't usually knock, you know."

He grimaces. "I have noticed that. Is there a trick to locking the office door?"

"The trick is there is no lock," I say. "I think she removed it."

"I can believe it," he nods.

"She's not a bad person," I go on. "Glenda is just—intense."

"She's a nightmare," McCoy mutters. Then, realizing what he said, his eyes get big. "Oh, I mean, well, she has many fine qualities."

I decide to put him out of his misery. "Yes, Father, yes, she does." I advance with an outstretched hand. "I just wanted to see how you were doing."

He shakes my hand. "Good to see you, Father Greer."

"Tom, please."

"Tom, it is. Leonard."

"Are you settling in, Leonard?"

"Oh, yes, I suppose," he says. "I wasn't sure I was ready for my own parish when the Archbishop assigned me here. He didn't give me much time."

"It was an emergency," I say slowly. Leonard looks at me.

"Yes, I realize that. Still, to go from where I was to here—I mean, there are just so many people. And children." I think I detect a slight shudder.

"Sunday Mass can be lively."

"Someone is always screaming," McCoy whispers. "A baby or older child."

"Most of the time," I smile. "There is the occasional mom."

He looks at me. "Joke," I explain.

"Ah," he nods. "Don't get me wrong, children are a blessing, and I'm gratified to see so many people open to life and all that, it's just not what I'm used to."

"Where were you before Saint Clare's?"

"I was chaplain at Saints Joachim and Anna's."

I nod. That explains it. Saints Joachim and Anna's Assisted Living is a much quieter posting than Saint Clare's.

"Well," I say, "the children's nativity should at least be—"

"Oh, I've cancelled that," Father McCoy says.

"What?"

"Yes, Glenda explained to me what a bad idea it was, and in this case I have to agree with her."

"She was against the idea in the first place," I say. "I bet the moms were disappointed."

"I've only heard from one," he whispers. "The director. Miriam Conway. She seems like such a sweet person. But she threatened to have me arrested!"

"Her husband is a police officer, though I doubt she'd actually do it."

"Well, that is a load off my mind."

"Anyway, I'm in Myerton for the day," I say, "and wanted to stop by."

"Why are you in town? It's not a short drive from Baltimore."

"I was visiting John Archman."

"Oh, of course. He is a friend of yours. Poor man. I've visited him several times. First time visiting a prisoner. I took him Communion, heard his confession, we chatted. Very nice man.

Troubled. I can tell that. His experiences in Iraq. My father was a First Gulf War veteran. Hardly the same, I suppose. He doesn't seem like a murderer."

"He's not," I reply with perhaps a little more force than I mean. McCoy blinks.

"Oh, of course, I didn't mean to imply, it's just that he is going to plead guilty, and the police wouldn't have arrested him without evidence."

"The evidence was all circumstantial," I say. "I understand why he's pleading guilty. But I know the man, Leonard. He didn't do it."

Not knowing how to reply, the young priest says . "Well, as you can see, I am getting ready for the Noon Mass. Would you care to celebrate with me?"

I smile. "I would be delighted."

***

After Mass, I say goodbye to Father McCoy. I still have plenty of time to get to the police station, but I don't want to risk being late.

On my way out, I bump into Glenda.

"Oh, good afternoon, Glenda," I say with a smile.

"Father," she says curtly.

"I didn't see you in Mass."

"Trying to catch up on some parish affairs," she says. "Father McCoy's an adequate priest but has no administrative ability. He'll learn, though. I'm bringing him along."

The vision of Glenda leading Father Leonard with a leash and dog collar flashes through my mind, an image I quickly dismiss.

"Why are you here?" she asks in an accusing manner.

"I was in Myerton visiting John Archman. I have time before another appointment, so I thought I'd come to Mass."

"I see, I see. Well, as a priest, visiting prisoners is your job."

"It is one of the corporal acts of mercy," I say. "We all should."

She looks at me. "Well," she says, "I won't keep you." She turns to leave.

A question pops into my head. "Oh, Glenda?"

She stops and turns around. "Yes?" she asks with a tone of irritation.

"You told the police that you spoke to Katherine Shepp and gave her fresh towels the afternoon of her murder."

"Yes, what about it?" she snaps.

"Did she seem all right?"

"Did she seem all right?" Glenda repeats. "I suppose. I didn't notice anything. I didn't ask about her health, just gave her the towels."

"She didn't seem groggy? You didn't notice any bumps on her head or anything?"

"Oh, what nonsense is this?" she says with a dismissive wave. "I told the police she was alive when I left."

"But I'm just—"

"Wasting my time," she says. She turns around and walks off.

I walk back to my car to drive to the police station. Sitting behind the steering wheel, I think for a few minutes.

I can't shake the feeling that something isn't adding up.

Nate said when he threw Shepp down, she hit her head on the table and was knocked unconscious. As far as he knew, she hadn't gotten up when he walked on the elevator. He said he heard the doors of the other elevator open as the doors of his elevator were closing.

Glenda says Shepp was alive when she gave her towels. But she didn't appear hurt.

Did Shepp have enough time to recover from when she was knocked out by Nate to when Glenda brought her the towels to appear fine? Was it possible that Glenda simply didn't notice if Shepp was hurt?

I shake my head. It doesn't matter. John has decided to plead guilty. The police are satisfied. It isn't my job to try to prove otherwise.

Thirty

John's next court appearance is the first Wednesday in December. Myerton has decorated Main Street with green, gold, and red for Christmas. In the square in front of the courthouse, the town Christmas tree is festooned with lights and large gold balls, topped with a silver star that reflects the early winter sun. In-ground speakers pipe Christmas music through the square to complete the festive holiday scene. There had once been a Nativity scene, but a threatened lawsuit caused the City Council to remove it.

The courthouse itself is decorated with wreaths on the door, a Christmas tree, a Menorah, and a Kwanzaa candelabra in the atrium. I walk down the hallway to Courtroom Three, where John's hearing is scheduled.

The room is crowded, with some members of the press lining the back wall. Two tables are up front. At one sits a man who I assume is the State Attorney, a man about my age in a grey pinstripe suit.

Brian.

Helen's—what? Boyfriend? Former fiancé?

A small wave of jealousy washes over me at the thought of Helen with him.

Stop it! the priest yells at the lover.

I turn my attention to the other table, where John sits with his attorney.

I survey the room, looking for a seat. I see Chloe seated right behind John. I start to walk forward to say hi when I hear my name. I turned to see Helen, indicating the seat next to her.

"I'm surprised to see you here," I say as I sit down. "Your job is done."

"It probably is," she says. "I'm here just in case the judge has a question the State Attorney can't answer."

She swallows and looks away from me. "I also knew you'd be here," she says quietly. "And I wanted to see you."

In spite of myself, I feel a thrill shoot through me. "Oh?" is all I can manage.

She clears her throat and squares her shoulders. "Yes," she says. "I wanted to be able to tell you in person that you're in the clear."

I look at her, puzzled. "The State Attorney decided not to prosecute you," she explains.

I sigh with relief. "I had forgotten about that. Thanks."

"You can thank me over lunch after this is over," she says.

"Are you buying?"

"I bought it last time, remember?"

"All rise," says the bailiff. We stop our banter and stand with the rest of the courtroom as the judge ascends to the bench.

"Please be seated," the judge says, which we obediently do.

It is over in about thirty minutes. John pleads guilty to manslaughter, the State Attorney recommends no more than ten years to be served at Patuxent due to his history of mental illness. The judge accepts the recommendation and formally sentences John. He gavels the hearing adjourned, everyone rises, and he walks out of the room. John turns to hug Chloe, who is visibly sobbing. The guards approach him and quietly lead him away. The crowd begins to thin. Chloe sits down and stares straight ahead.

"Shall we go?" Helen asks, slinging her bag over her shoulder.

"I'll meet you outside," I say. "I want to see Chloe."

She pats my shoulder and leaves the courtroom. I walk to the front and stand by Chloe for a moment.

"Hi, Chloe," I say. She stares straight ahead.

"May I sit?" She turns to look at me and nods.

We sit together in silence for a few minutes. The only other person in the room is a clerk gathering papers from the Judge's bench.

"John told me you visited him," Chloe whispers. "Thank you for that. He really appreciated it."

"It was the least I could do," I say. "He is my friend."

"Yes, your friend. My husband. You know he betrayed us both," she says with a hint of bitterness.

"No, I don't see that—"

"That's because you're blind," she says to me, the anger coming out with every word. "Or too holy now that you're a priest. His obsession with Joan back then betrayed me. Oh, I know nothing happened between them—but emotionally, it was her he wanted and not me. He was too big of a coward to help you that night. Think about it, Tom. Don't you realize that if he had jumped in, Joan might be alive today?"

That thought hit me one day when I was working at the Archdiocese. I felt like someone had punched me in the solar plexus. I felt a boiling rage welling up like a volcano from deep within me, anger I had never felt before. I sat at my desk, gripping the edge. The intern was working quietly at a desk in the corner, oblivious. In my mind's eye, I began to scream, picking up the papers on my desk and hurling them into space, throwing my chair, knocking boxes off the shelf.

With herculean self-control, I left my office, then the building. I walked across the parking lot into the woods. I kept walking until I couldn't see the offices anymore.

Then I screamed.

And screamed.

And screamed.

I don't know how long I screamed. Finally, I ran out of screams. I went from screaming to crying. I fell to my knees in the dirt and leaves and sobbed.

And sobbed.

And sobbed.

"Yes, Chloe, yes, I do," I whisper.

She leans toward me. "Doesn't that make you angry?"

"I was angry," I say. "But I'm not angry anymore."

She crosses her arms. "You're a better man than I am."

I pat her shoulder. "You need to forgive him, Chloe."

I see a tear travel down her cheek. "I know, Tom. I—I just can't right now." She turns to me. "I love him. I'm angry but I love him. Now he's gone from me. Gone from the kids."

"He told me why he pled guilty," I say.

"He pled guilty because he did it."

That stuns me. "Did he tell you that?"

"No," she says. "He still insists he's innocent, that he's just pleading guilty to spare me and the kids a trial. But I don't buy it. I hate to think my husband is a murderer. But he went there because of what she knew about him and Joan. He must have lost control, hit her with the lamp they found his fingerprints on."

"I can't believe that," I say, shaking my head. "I won't believe it."

"Then who, Tom? Who did it, huh? Do you think that woman detective who's attracted to you would have arrested him if she really didn't think he did it?"

"What do you mean, attracted to me?"

"You heard me. I've seen the way she looks at you. You can't be that clueless." Chloe gets up and grabs her bag. "I've gotta go. I'm going to visit John. Where are you going, back to Baltimore?"

"Not yet, I'm having lunch with—" I stop myself.

Chloe smiles. "Tell Detective Parr I say hello. And no hard feelings. I'm trying for forgiveness."

She walks out of the courtroom, leaving me sitting by myself. I shake my head and follow her out.

Outside the courthouse, I meet up with Helen. She is on her phone.

"All right, I'll be right there." She hangs up and looks at me apologetically.

"Problem?"

"No, the Chief wants to see me about something related to a case. I can't do lunch." She sighs. "Raincheck?"

"Of course," I smile.

"When will you be back in Myerton?"

I shrug. "I don't know. I'll probably come back around Christmas, see Anna for a couple of days."

"You're not going to Florida?"

I shake my head. "You remember what it's like when I'm there," I say. "Nothing's changed."

She nods. "I remember," she says as she strokes my arm. "Good to see you."

I pat her hand. "You, too, Helen."

I watch her as she walks away. I think about what Chloe said. About what she sees in Helen. She had said I couldn't be that clueless.

Sadly, I'm not. Not about Helen's feelings.

Or my own.

My phone rings, breaking me out of my daze. It is a Myerton number I don't recognize. "Hello?"

"Hello, Tom, this is Bethany Grable. Did I catch you at a bad time?"

"No, not at all. What can I do for you?"

"Well, I didn't get a chance to see you before you left the last time, but I am wondering if you could finish getting the rest of Joan's things out of the studio? I don't mind holding onto them, but I could use the storage space."

"Sure, I'll come by and grab some things. I can't take everything today in my car."

"Anything you could do would be great. I'll see you in a bit."

***

Bethany unlocks the door and opens it, reaching around to turn the light on.

"I'll leave you to it," she says. "I have someone coming to look at American Carnage."

I look at her with surprise. Smiling, she says, "Told ya someone would buy it."

She leaves me standing in the doorway, looking at Joan's things in the storage room. I'll take her canvases and sketch books, I decide right away. Her sketchbooks are stacked on the shelf, but I look around and can't find her canvases. I make a mental note to ask Bethany about those; she must have moved them for safekeeping. I go to the boxes on the shelves and lift the lids, peeking inside. Mostly art supplies—paints, brushes, pencils. If they are still any good, I'll tell Bethany she can keep them, maybe donate them to a school.

I look through box after box. Some contain papers that I don't want to go through right away, so I take those off the shelf and carry them to the door. There is one box left on the shelf. Looking inside, I see more papers.

As I lift the box off the shelf, the bottom gives way, the contents of the box falling to the floor.

I utter a scatalogical expletive and toss the remnants of the box to the side. I look around and find an empty intact box. Crouching down, I start picking up the papers—a mix of what looks like scrap paper, pictures torn and cut out of magazines, even entire issues of old magazines. Underneath the pile is a padded binder.

It is a photo album, fallen open to a picture of a very young Joan. She must have been eight or nine years old. She is sitting on a carousel horse, holding a big cone of cotton candy, a look of absolute mirth on her face.

I smile. Our daughter—if it was a daughter—would be older, a teenager by now. I hope she would have looked like her mother.

I slowly flip through. There are pictures of Joan with her Mom and Dad, confirmation pictures, pictures of Joan with groups of boys and girls the same age looking like they were taken at a summer camp. All show Joan happy, laughing, smiling, having fun.

The album is only half full. The last photo shows Joan sitting between her Mom and Dad, blowing out the candles on a birthday cake. From the number, it was her thirteenth.

The last birthday before her father killed himself. She and her Mom are smiling, happy. I look at her Dad's picture. He is smiling, too. Was he really happy, I wonder, or was he hiding his pain, keeping it a secret from those he loved? Is that where Joan learned to keep her pain a secret, that you kept it from your husband to keep from hurting him, so he wouldn't think less of her?

I dismiss the thoughts and decide to drop the album off with Anna on my way out of town. It rightfully belongs to her.

I close the album. As I start to place it in the box, a loose photo drops out and falls face down in the box. I reach to pick it up, then stop.

Written on the back was a month and year. March, 1996. The month and year on her marriage license.

I hesitate, then pick it up. I slowly turn it over. The picture shows Joan at sixteen, looking very different from her birthday picture. Gone is the light in her eyes, the joy-filled smile. Her smile is joyless, her eyes dark.

With Joan is a young man, slightly older looking, with the same expression on his face, a scruffy beard, and longish hair that looks like it hadn't seen a comb or soap and water in a while.

I stare at the man. I bring the picture closer, studying it, looking at the eyes, the shape, the spacing.

In a flash, I know.

Leaving the boxes, I run to my car. On the way, I call Helen's number. It goes to voicemail.

"Helen," I say quickly, "I'm sending you a picture. Call me back as soon as you get this." I take a picture of the photo and send it to Helen's phone.

I get in my car and squeal out of the parking lot towards Saint Clare's.

***

I speed all the way there and blow through at least one stop sign. I park and run to the door of the Rectory. I press the doorbell, and bang on the door.

"Glenda, it's Father Tom," I call, knocking again.

A very irritated Glenda throws the door open. "For heaven's sake, Father Greer," she says.

"I need to talk to you, Glenda. Right now," I push my way inside and spin around to face her.

She closes the door. "You're in a state, Father," she says. "Father McCoy is at the hospital—"

"No, it's you I came to talk to." I show her the picture. She doesn't look at it, and kept her arms crossed.

"What is that?"

"Please look at it," I say. "Take a good look."

"Oh, why should I waste—"

"Just look at the picture!" I scream.

She looks stunned by my outburst, but does as I ask. She brings it close to her eyes. She studies it for what seems like a long time.

"The girl is Joan," I say quietly. "I think you know the boy. He's younger and thinner, but there's no mistake, is there?"

She looks up from the photo. She shakes her head. "No," she whispers.

"It's your nephew, isn't it? His real name is Randy. Randy Earl. Am I right?"

She hands the picture back to me. "Sit down, Father. I'll get us some coffee." She leaves the room.

Before I can sit down, my phone rings. It's Helen's number—not her cell phone, her office phone.

"Did you see it?" I ask as soon as I answer.

"Wait, what are you talking about?" she asks.

"I sent a photograph to your phone. Listen, Helen, I've—"

"I haven't looked at my phone, haven't had time. I have to tell you—"

"Well, look at your phone. It's important."

"So's what I have to tell you," she went on. "Listen, I had an officer go interview the hotel manager. Somehow, we hadn't done it and I wanted to add his statement to the file. The officer asked if Glenda was working that day."

"We know she was. Listen, Helen—"

"No, she wasn't, Tom. In fact, the manager says she doesn't work for the hotel at all."

Stunned, I look to the kitchen. I turn around and walk to a corner of the room. "What?" I say, being careful to keep my voice low.

"She lied, Tom. She lied about why she was there. And there's something else. I've got more information on Randy Earl."

"That's what I've been trying to tell you. I know who he is."

"So do I," Helen says. "Randy Earl isn't his real name. I mean it is his real name, but not his birth name."

"Birth name?" I whisper. "Wait, are you saying he was adopted?"

My mind begins to race. Something is beginning to come together.

"Yes, usually adoption records are sealed, but this was an open adoption. He was adopted shortly after birth by his married aunt, whose last name was Earl. His mother was her sister." She pauses. "You'll never guess."

But I don't have to guess. I already know. It's in the eyes.

"Helen," I whisper, "you need to come—"

"Put the phone down, Father," I hear Glenda say behind me.

I turn around.

Glenda stands in the doorway of the living room, a gun trained on me.

Thirty-One

"Tom, Tom, are you there? Where are you?" I hear Helen say.

"Don't say anything," Glenda says firmly. "Just hang up and give me the phone."

I do as she says. She points to the couch with the gun. "Sit," she says. I take a place on the couch. She sits in a chair, still pointing the gun at me.

"Yes," Glenda says. "It's the same gun. My father's. The only thing he left me when he died."

"He's your son, isn't he?"

"Oh, Detective Parr told you that, did she? Yes, he's my boy. I'll tell you everything. But first." She makes the sign of the cross. "Bless me, Father, for I have sinned," she begins.

"No," I say.

"It has been six months since my last confession." She smiles.

I know what she is doing. Making sure I can't say anything. Anything she says is now under the seal of the confession. I am pretty certain now that she'll let me live, but if she does, she doesn't want me to be able to tell anyone what she told me.

"It won't work," I say. "They already know you lied about working at the hotel."

"This is my confession, Father," she says. "Shut up and listen."

I settle back. And pray.

"You're right, of course," Glenda begins. "Randy is my son. I got pregnant at 15—I was troubled, I'll admit that, I am a later-life child and I'm still not sure my parents really wanted me. I got drunk one night at a party and some boy, I don't even know who, well, took advantage of the situation. I didn't tell my parents at first, but after I missed a period and started throwing up every morning, I had to tell them. The doctor confirmed I was pregnant."

"How did they react?"

She shrugged. "Not too badly, I suppose. My mother was mainly upset with herself for not putting me on the Pill. They were Catholic, but not too Catholic—mainly just Christmas and Easter, making sure I had all my sacraments so they could check the boxes. They were Catholic enough not to have me get an abortion. In fact, they saw my situation as a solution to another problem."

"What problem was that?"

She frowns, her eyes grow darker. "My older sister," she says bitterly. "The good one. She and her husband had been trying for a baby for five years, but had had no luck. After several miscarriages, her doctor told her she might never be able to carry a baby to term. So, they all sat down and agreed that when I gave birth to my baby, my sister and her husband would adopt him or her and I'd become Aunt Glenda."

"How did you react to that?"

"I was fifteen," she says. "I didn't want a baby. It made sense to me at the time. I'd have the baby, my sister would raise it, and I'd go on to have a life. Besides, I thought I'd get married and have other babies." She paused. "It didn't work out that way, though."

"What happened?"

She exhales slowly. I think I can see a tear welling up. "I went into labor about a month early. I started bleeding. They had to do an emergency Caesarian to save Randy. They wouldn't let me hold him. They couldn't get my bleeding to stop, so to save my life, they had to give me a hysterectomy." She sniffs and wipes away a tear. "So there would be no more babies."

I feel a tinge of sorrow for young Glenda.

"I was only sixteen, Father, and I'd never have children. The only child I would ever have would never be mine." She shakes slightly. "I lay in that bed for days, knowing I would never have a baby of my own and hating my sister and my parents for taking mine away from me. I never forgave them for that," she whispers.

"Did you tell them how you felt? Maybe they would have changed their minds."

"You didn't know my parents," she laughs. "No, they were determined to have no single moms in their family. They brought me the papers to sign and I signed them. I put a smile on my face and kept it there. Over time, I buried my anger deep inside until I wasn't even aware it was there. I played the role of the dutiful younger aunt, seeing Randy as often as I could in the early years. After a time, I grew used to it and didn't see him as much. I went off to the university and got my teaching degree. That's how I wound up here, in Myerton. I took a job at one of the high schools in the county. I started attending Saint Clare's, I even began to date—though I knew I would never marry."

She looks so sad. If she hadn't been holding a gun on me, I would have felt pity.

"I'd still see Randy occasionally," Glenda continues. "Christmas and birthdays."

"He never found out you were his mother?"

"No, dear sister did a good job of keeping that from him. It wasn't until much later. Anyway, time passed. Then I began to hear about Randy."

"He was beginning to act out," I say.

"Very good, Father, you know the lingo and everything. Yes, my sister started telling me about his episodes, the mania, and depression, the uncontrollable rages, all of it. It began when he was thirteen or fourteen, I guess. They had to hospitalize him after he tried to kill himself the first time. After that, he was in and out for a couple of years before they put him in a special residential school in his senior year."

"That's where he met Joan," I say.

Glenda shrugs. "I suppose. I didn't know about her until much later, about them being together."

She pauses for a long time. "At first, I blamed myself. I thought that it was my fault he was sick, that it was because I gave him up and somehow deep inside, he knew. Or I thought I gave it to him, that I have it in my genes, or the guy who made me pregnant was that way and gave it to him. The anger returned." She smiles ruefully. "About the time he graduated from that school—he was, he is a very bright boy, Father—I was fired from my job at the high school."

"Why?"

She looks at me and smiles. "One day I got tired of my students not paying attention. So I sprayed my class with a fire extinguisher." She laughs. "I didn't hurt them and it got their attention. But the principal thought it was a bit excessive, especially after the parents sued the school district. My going was part of the settlement."

I just sit quietly, taking it all in. From the way she is talking and from what I am seeing, I have no doubt where Randy's illness comes from.

"So, I was fired," she goes on. "I couldn't get another teaching job, so I just remained in Myerton. I was able to get a couple of administrative jobs—glorified secretaries and office clerks—so I got by."

"What was Randy doing at this time?"

"Well, he graduated from the school, he was eighteen and a legal adult. But he really couldn't handle keeping a job. He lived with his parents and tried to work. Occasionally, he'd leave home for months at a time, go back to living on the streets, pick up odd jobs. His medication kept his bipolar disorder under control, but he still wasn't well. Frankly, I doubt he ever will be. This went on for several years. Then, his parents died in a car accident."

"Where was Randy at the time?"

"Let's see, I think he was living at home. They had gone out to dinner, it had snowed, and the temperature had dropped. They hit a patch of ice and slammed into a tree. My brother-in-law was killed instantly. My sister lasted for a few days at the hospital. I visited her before she died. The last thing she said to me was, 'take care of Randy.'" She pauses, looking at me over the gun. "So that's what I've done."

"He came to live here with you. When did he find out you were his mother?"

"That happened by accident. He has this habit of rummaging through things. One day he was in the basement and he started going through a box of old photos. There were several of me pregnant, with my sister who obviously was not. Like I say, he is very bright. He figured it out."

"How did he react?"

"He accepted it, started calling me Mom almost immediately. He was doing well those first few months." I see a shadow creep over her countenance. "That's when he saw her."

"Joan," I say.

She nods. "I remember him coming home, excited, talking a mile a minute, saying over and over again, 'Mom, I saw her, I saw her, she's here, she's here, she's come back to me.' It took me forever to calm him down. Then he told me the story, about how he and Joan had met at the school, how after he had graduated and she had left, they had run away together to get married, and how she had just up and left him a couple of months later. He was so excited."

"She didn't leave him," I say. "He left her alone on the streets in Baltimore."

She shakes her head. "That may be what she said, but my Randy wouldn't do that. Such a good-hearted boy."

Looking at the gun, I decide not to press the point. "Where did he see her?"

"I'm not really sure about that, I couldn't get a clear answer from him. I think he saw her just walking down Main Street one day when he was working on a construction job or something. It's been so long, I don't remember." She sighs. "After that, Joan was all he'd talk about. He lost that job because he couldn't focus. He started roaming around Myerton, looking for any chance to see her."

"He didn't attend Saint Clare's with you? We attended once in a while."

"No, he didn't want to go and I wouldn't make him. I couldn't tell him you and she even attended Saint Clare's. I didn't know myself until that first Sunday you were here. Well, eventually he saw her again and he followed her." She looks at me. "He saw her with you one day, I guess you were walking together arm in arm. He came home devastated; he cried for two days. I really thought he was going to kill himself. Then he pulled himself together. But that's when he started stalking her."

She exhales. "He somehow figured out where she worked and where you two lived. He started following her everywhere she went. He'd stay out all hours, sometimes all night—I think he'd sleep outside where you lived. That went on for weeks. Then it happened."

The room is quiet. "So you knew," I whisper. "All these years."

She nods. "I didn't realize until it was too late that he had gotten Daddy's gun. He came home late that night in the worst state I'd ever seen. He just kept repeating. "I didn't mean to do it, it's not my fault, it's his fault, I didn't mean to do it." It took me forever to calm him down to get the whole story."

"Why didn't you call the police?"

"And betray my boy!" she cries. "I couldn't do that, not again. I had betrayed him when he was born. No, I needed to help him. It wasn't his fault anyway."

"He shot her, Glenda. He had the gun."

"He didn't mean to shoot her. He meant to shoot you. She got in the way. If she had just gone with him, like he wanted, she'd still be alive. So Father, it really is your fault, not my boy's."

I look at her, dumbfounded. She really believes what she is saying.

"Once I got him calmed down," Glenda continues, "I had to come up with a plan. I had to get him out of town, somewhere far from Myerton until everything settled down. He didn't want to go, but I was able to get him to do it. I knew someone who was looking for men to work the Bakken shale oil fields in North Dakota—the boom was just starting, and they were desperate for men. It was perfect for Randy, hard work outdoors, he'd learn a skill, and it was far from here. So a couple of days after the incident, I put him on a bus to Bismark." She sighs. "It broke my heart to send him away, but I had to do it. To protect him."

"You stayed here, knowing the whole time."

She nods. "I had no problems with what I did. I was protecting my son. Doing what any mother would. I hadn't been a mother to him when he was growing up. It was the least I could do. It was a great plan. And it worked. They never figured out it was him."

Glenda smiles, pleased with herself.

"It would have gone on working, too, if you hadn't come back," she says bitterly.

"When did Randy come back to Myerton?"

"Only about six months before you did," she says. "You may know, the oil boom in North Dakota went bust about three or four years ago. He was laid off, and he wasn't able to get into another job. That triggered his symptoms. He had been doing fine, keeping on his meds and everything, without a major manic episode. He lost his job, he lost his health insurance, and couldn't afford his medication. He wound up in the hospital again."

"What happened?"

"He tried to kill himself again. Didn't succeed, really didn't even hurt himself, but it was enough. It was the start of a cycle. He was in and out, when he wasn't living on the streets, for a long time. And North Dakota isn't a place you want to live on the streets."

"Did you know what was going on?"

She shakes her head. "Not really. He'd call me occasionally, write some. There were weeks—months—where I wasn't sure where he was. I would have gone and looked for him, but that wasn't practical. No, all I could do was pray, so I did a lot of praying. I found real comfort in prayer."

The irony of a woman holding a gun on a priest while speaking about prayer is not lost on me.

"Eventually, he was stable long enough to work and earn money for a bus ticket back here. Like I say, he got back about six months before you did. People had forgotten about the murder, so I thought it was safe for him to stay. I got him a construction job, which he lost after six weeks, then another job, which he held onto for a little bit longer, but mostly he slept a lot and played video games." She sighs. "It wasn't easy. I had forgotten how high maintenance he could be. But he's my boy and I am so glad to have him back. And everything was fine. Until you arrived."

"He recognized me that first Sunday," I say.

"Yes. He had come to meet me after Mass when he saw you standing outside greeting everyone. Somehow, he recognized you immediately. It really sent him into a panic."

"You were trying to calm him down, weren't you? I saw you talking to him."

"He wanted to talk to you," she said. "I don't know about what. I told him to go home. It took a lot of persuasion. But he did what I said."

"He did talk to me later, you know," I say. "Did he tell you that?"

"Oh, yes, he told me. I am so angry with him for doing that. Everything was getting stirred up again. It was bad enough when that waiter was running around wanting to do his video about the case and that reporter started poking around. Then you had to get involved and do that interview. I had to do something."

"Why did you kill her?"

She blinks. "Why? To keep her from figuring out what happened."

"You knew the police were looking into it."

Glenda dismisses my statement with a wave of her hand. "They hadn't figured it out in fifteen years. No, she was the danger. I knew it when she waved around those emails."

The emails. The ones that John had written. "You thought—"

"I just knew Randy had written them," she says, "and it'd only be a matter of time before she figured that out. I had to get them from her."

"They were just copies. I have the originals."

"I'd figure that out later," she says. "No, she was investigating. She was beginning to put two and two together."

"Did Randy tell you he'd written them?"

"Oh, he denied knowing what I was talking about. But I knew he was lying."

"But he wasn't lying."

"No," she admits. "No, no, he wasn't. I know that now."

"You pretended to be a housekeeper at the hotel so she'd open the door. Did you plan on killing her?"

"No, I don't think so. I was just going to find those emails and steal them. If I had to, I'd knock her out or something. I am really clever. I grabbed a cart from another floor, put gloves on—no one pays attention to staff—so I was confident no one would take notice of me.

"But when I got to her room, the door was cracked. I called out that I was housekeeping and opened the door. I found her lying on the floor, face down, moaning and trying to get up." She shrugs. "Seemed like an ideal opportunity. So I picked up the lamp and bashed her head in."

"But Glenda," I say. "You left the emails."

"I couldn't find them," she says. "I started looking for them on the desk, but I thought I heard someone in the hallway. I had to get out of there."

She stops. We look at each other for a while.

"Where is Randy now?"

"Oh, he's at home."

"You know the police are going to figure it out."

"We'll be gone. Our bags are already packed. As soon as we're done here, I'm going and we're leaving Myerton for good."

"They'll find you."

"No, I don't think so, not where we're going."

I look at her. "What about me? Are you going to shoot me?"

"Oh, don't be ridiculous, Father Tom. I'm not going to shoot you. I'm not a killer. No, this is what's going to happen." She leans forward. "We're going to finish here, you're going to get up from that couch, and leave. I know you can't reveal to anyone what I told you. So I have nothing to fear from you."

"You need to turn yourselves in, Glenda, you and Randy."

"No, that's not going to happen."

"Aren't you the least bit sorry for what you've done?"

"Hmm, no, not really. I did what had to be done. To protect my boy."

"If you have no contrition," I say, "I can't grant you absolution."

She raises the gun a little higher. "Oh, I think you can, Father. You will. Do it now."

I look her in the eyes. Slowly, I shake my head. "No."

She stands up and takes a step forward. "Do it now, Father," she screams, "or I will shoot!"

Suddenly, I'm back in the parking lot. Joan is dying in my arms and the gun's to my head.

What if it hadn't misfired? What if she hadn't jumped in front of me? I'd be with her now. We'd be together again, with our child, the little one I've never held. Maybe Glenda would be doing me a favor. After all, "to be absent from the body is to be present with the Lord."

Justice would be served, and all this pain would be gone.

It's not a suicide. I am just standing firm for my vocation.

I'm thinking about this when I hear the Rectory door quietly open.

I am afraid that Glenda will hear it, but she doesn't react. I've noticed before that her hearing is not really good.

Behind the crazed woman, Helen steps quietly into view, training her gun on Glenda. I try not to look at her, but keep my eyes fixed on the woman in front of me.

"You're wasting time, Father!" Glenda screams.

Helen is close now and I give in to the temptation to look at her. Her eyes meet mine. They radiate confidence—and something else.

Suddenly, I realize that I want to live.

I do want to be with Joan and to meet our baby, but not yet.

"OK, Glenda," I say, trying to buy Helen the time needed to get across the room. In my best priest's voice, I say firmly, "Bow down for the blessing."

As I expected, this elicits an automatic response. As Glenda drops her head, Helen steps forward and places the gun against the small of her back. In a firm, calm voice she says, "Give me the gun, Glenda. It's all over."

After only the briefest of hesitations, Glenda drops her hand and Helen takes the gun. She hands Glenda off to another officer and looks at me, asking, "Are you all right?"

I nod. "It took you long enough."

"Hey, I've told you these things don't work as fast as they do on TV." She offers me her hand. "Come on, let's have the paramedics look you over." I take her hand and she pulls me up.

I wind up standing very close to her—not touching, but close enough to smell the scent of vanilla in her hair. We look into each other's eyes. Again, I'm captivated by hers, a deep azure blue. Her hand is so soft in mine. Her hair—oh, her hair, so black. There's a curl dangling down. I resist the urge to brush it behind her ear.

Helen's lips part as if she is about to speak.

"What in the name of—what is this?"

We turn to see a very confused Father McCoy standing in the doorway. "Father Greer, what are you doing—what, what are all these police cars doing?"

"Father McCoy, you remember Detective Helen Parr? She'll be glad to explain everything to you." I incline my head. "Detective, I think you wanted me checked out by the medics?"

She nods, with a slight smile. "Yes, Father Greer, that's right."

"Well, I'll go do that," I walk towards the door. "Oh, Father McCoy?"

"Yes?"

"You'll need to hire a new parish secretary."

***

"We're getting the prisoner now, Father. It will be a couple of minutes."

I thank the guard. After he leaves, I stand a moment, looking around the room. It's the same one in which I visited John.

A couple of minutes later, the door opens. The guard brings the prisoner in, clad in a khaki jumpsuit, hands and feet shackled. The prisoner shuffles along the floor, hampered by the ankle cuffs. The guard helps the prisoner to the table and fastens the handcuffs to a metal loop on the stainless steel surface.

"I'll be right outside, Father, if you need anything," the guard says.

"Thank you, we'll be fine."

He nods and then takes his place guarding the door, though he looks through the window instead of at the hallway.

I look at the seated figure. The prisoner is an image of despair. Shoulders slumped, head down. Helen told me they haven't gotten much since the first night, that the prisoner has spent most of the time in the cell staring at the wall.

"You can visit if you want to, Tom," she had told me on the phone. "I'll clear it. But don't be surprised if you're the only one doing the talking."

"That's fine," I said. "I just need to say a few things."

Now, sitting across from the prisoner, I'm not quite sure where to begin. So I decide to keep it simple.

"Hello, Randy."

Randy Earl doesn't look up, but stares at a spot on the table.

"Are they treating you well? I hear the food isn't bad."

He continues to stare at the table.

"I want to thank you for seeing me. We've never really had a chance to talk." I smile. "That day in the confessional, you did most of the talking."

I pause and look for a reaction. Nothing.

"When you killed Joan," I say quietly, "you ripped my heart out. I didn't—I wasn't sure I wanted to go on. I loved her so much, and missed her so much, that I could hardly stand it."

I pause and take out my handkerchief, catching the tear that's beginning to make its way down my left cheek. "I couldn't eat. I couldn't sleep. I could barely work. I cut myself off from everyone. I made one really bad decision that cost me the little I had left. I left Myerton and didn't come back for fifteen years."

I stop and clear my throat. "I left her here because I didn't want to remember. I thought I could run away from my pain. But it was with me wherever I went. They say time heals all wounds, but they're wrong. It's not time. Do you know what heals, Randy?"

Randy stares at the table.

"Forgiveness," I say gently. "God's forgiveness and man's forgiveness. My problem wasn't that I couldn't forgive you—though I'll admit, I couldn't do that. I couldn't forgive myself."

I take a deep breath and slowly blow it out. "You told me it was my fault she is dead, that I am the one who should be dead. That's what I believed, too. And I carried that guilt with me, not forgiving myself and not being able to forgive you."

I stop and look for any kind of reaction from Randy, but there is nothing. He just sits quietly. I'm not even sure he's listening to me.

"But now, I can," I say. "I'm here to tell you that I forgive you, Randy. And that God will forgive you too. But you also need to forgive yourself."

I reach out and put my hands over his shackled hands. "I know you didn't mean to kill Joan. I believe you loved her, and that killing her was an accident. And it's eaten you up since that night. I can forgive you, Randy. But God, through his forgiveness and infinite mercy, can help you forgive yourself. And help you heal."

I sit with him for another minute, looking for some kind of sign. His hands are still beneath mine. There's not a flicker of movement.

I squeeze his hands and remove mine. "I just wanted to tell you that, Randy. I will be praying for you." I stand and walk to the door.

"Father?"

I stop and turn back. Randy's looking at me.

"Will you hear my confession?"

I smile and go back to the chair. I get out my book and my scapular, kiss it, and place it over my shoulders.

Randy's looking across the table at me now, his eyes filling with tears.

With a smile, I say, "Let us begin."

Epilogue

April has grown sunny and mild after a cold and rainy March. The sun is bright in the cloudless sky. Birds sing, and the flowers in the planters lining the sidewalk along the grounds of Myer College are beginning to put forth their blooms. I walk down Main Street past storefronts, past The Painted Lotus Gallery, where a sign advertises a show of new works by the creator of "American Carnage," past a small yarn store that is having a two for one sale, and past the used book store.

I'm in sight of The Perfect Cup when I see Helen seated at a table.

I take two more steps, then stop.

She isn't alone.

Sitting with her is Anna.

I pick up my pace again and walk up to the table. "Well, hello."

They look up at me. "You're late," Helen says.

"Really?" I check the time. "Sorry, I got delayed."

Anna finishes her coffee. "Well, I need to get back to Saint Clare's. I've got to arrange things for Father McCoy for the Parish Council meeting tonight."

"I take it you're settling into the parish secretary's job?" I ask.

"Yes, but I only agreed to do it on a temporary basis until they could find someone else. He's conducting interviews this afternoon. I really like one of them; she's a young single woman, really active in the parish. Pleasant personality. I think it will be a nice change of pace for Father. I don't think he's fully recovered from the shock of having the last parish secretary arrested for murder."

I laugh. "Well, he's lucky to have you."

She looks at me. "Can you stop by on your way out of town?"

"I probably won't have time. I'm expected at 3:00 p.m. and it's after noon now. I've just got time for coffee."

She nods. "Well, I'll see you when I see you," she kisses me on the cheek and gives me a hug. "Don't stay away too long. Promise me."

I nod. "I promise."

She breaks the hug and turns to Helen. "And I'll see you on Sunday, right, Helen?"

"See you then, Anna."

As Anna walks off I sit down across from Helen. "You two have become friendly," I say. "I didn't know you knew her."

"Well, I met her when I interviewed her after I re-opened Joan's case," Helen says. "It was a tense conversation, to say the least. But she brought cookies to me the week after the arrests to

229

thank me. We got to talking, and she wound up inviting me to Christmas dinner at her house with a bunch of other single people from the church. I was the youngest one there, as it turned out, but still it was nice to meet some other people from the parish. She's made me feel welcome."

"Anna's a mom at heart," I say. "She tends to adopt us strays."

She laughs. "Well, I'm not sure they know what to make of me, yet. A woman my age, not married, with no kids. It is taking me a while to get used to all the kids."

"You don't like children?"

"I like children fine. Just maybe not so many all in one place. But I will say, Officer Conway's kids are amusing. Especially that Catherine."

The mention of Dan's name leads me to ask, "I never found out, what happened with Dan?"

"Well," Helen says. "I was able to persuade the Chief not to fire him. He was suspended without pay for a month, which he's already served. He's still on the force, back out on the streets instead of behind a desk. I'll be honest, Tom, I've had my eye on him for a while. He's a good officer. He made one mistake. Now, he gets a chance to prove himself."

"Well, I'm glad to hear that," I say. I pause for a moment, looking for the right way to ask a question I have on my mind. "Um, Helen, does Anna—"

Helen shakes her head. "No, I haven't told her about us."

Nate Rodriguez brings me a cup of coffee, heavy cream and sugar. I look at him. "How's it going?"

"Great," he says. "You caught me on my last day."

"Oh, you have another job?"

"I've sold the documentary," he says, "About Joan, about the investigation. I'm going to New York to sign the contracts."

"You're moving to New York?"

"Oh, no," Nate says. "I'm coming back to Myerton. I'm just not going to work here anymore."

He leaves us alone. I look at the sun reflecting off her hair. A years-old memory flashes through my mind, one I quickly pushed out.

"How's Glenda?" I say.

"Difficult, from what I hear."

"She confessed to Shepp's murder and pled guilty to second-degree murder," I say. "When is she going to be sentenced?"

"It's coming up soon. With no criminal history and her age, she'll probably get the minimum." She takes a drink of her coffee. "I was surprised you weren't here the day John Archman was released."

"I couldn't get away, but I am glad your boyfriend supported his motion to withdraw his guilty plea."

"First, Thomas Jude Greer," Helen says somewhat testily, "Brian Dohrmann isn't my boyfriend. We dated. We were engaged briefly. But that's over. Our relationship is strictly professional. "

"Sorry," I say. "I didn't mean—"

"Second," continues Helen, "he really didn't have much choice."

"Randy's competency hearing is coming up too, isn't it?" I ask, trying to get the conversation back on track.

Helen nods. "End of May. Considering he knew what he was doing when he confessed to everything the night we arrested him, I'm not sure his public defender will succeed in getting the confession thrown out. That's good, because the only thing we really have to tie him to Joan's death is the gun Glenda used on you. He'll probably enter a plea of not criminally responsible. I doubt he'll spend any time in prison. Probably the state hospital, maybe for the rest of his life."

"That's probably the best thing for him," I say.

Helen sits back. "So what are you going to do now? Go back to Baltimore?"

I trace the rim of the cup with my fingers. "No, I'm not. I have a new assignment."

She sits up straight. "Oh?"

I look at her. She looks at me with expectation.

I shake my head. "No, not Saint Clare's. The parish is in good hands with Father Leonard."

She slumps a little. "Maybe, but he's no Father Tom. So, where are you going?"

I tell her about my new assignment. Her eyes widen.

"Well, that is a change. Does that mean you're never coming back?"

I laugh. "Oh, I'll be back. Anna's the only real family I have. Joan is here." I hesitate, then add, "I have friends, too."

She smiles. "I hope you consider me one, Tom."

I nod slowly. "Yes, Helen. I do."

She leans forward and looks at me. "Tom, I want to ask you something. If you say no, I understand, given our history together and your position now. But could we stay in touch this time?"

I take a deep breath. "Helen, I—"

"It's OK," she says, shaking her head. "I understand."

"No, I wasn't going to say no," I say slowly. "I'd like that. But it'd have to be email. Where I'm going, the cell service isn't great, and talking or texting—I just don't think that's a good idea."

"OK, sure, email's fine. You can send things to my work email."

"And," I add, "because of my position and our past relationship, anything we send to each other, I'll show to my spiritual director. I want you to understand that."

She smiles slightly. "Of course. Tom. Keep everything proper and above board."

"Exactly," I say. I don't add, *because I'm afraid of what I might say otherwise.*

"Well," Helen says, gathering her tote bag, "I need to go. And you need to be getting along, too, I suspect."

"Yes," I nod. "I do."

She looks at me, then leans down and kisses me on the cheek.

"I'll miss you, Father Tom," she says. "Don't stay gone too long."

I look at her as she walks off, my heart beating rapidly.

It's a good thing I'm leaving Myerton.

But I will be back.

***

I turn off the main road onto the gravel drive, making my way through the open gate. I follow the drive up the slight hill, twisting through the woods with trees casting deep shadows from the green leaves that had burst forth with the coming of spring.

I pull up to the hand-built cabin. I get out of the car and look around. I walk to the door of the cabin. I knock softly.

It opens.

"Welcome, Father," Brother Martin says with a smile. "We've been expecting you."

***

The Framed Father

The Father Tom Mysteries, Book 2

Prologue

Dear Tom, I hope you are well and still enjoying your life behind monastic walls. Sometimes I envy the quiet you must enjoy there, but just as often, I wonder how you stand it. Not that life in Myerton is anything like walking a beat in DC, but at least I get the occasional robbery to keep me busy.

Parish life at St. Clare's is also pretty interesting. I have not yet followed your suggestion to join the Ladies of Charity, but I do attend parish functions occasionally. Most of the time I'm working so Dan can attend with his family. It makes a lot more sense for him to be there with Miriam and the kids than it does for an old widow like me to go. I've only met Miriam once or twice, but I admire how devoted she is to her family.

Oh, Gladys wants me to be sure to tell you 'Hi.' She still has a huge crush on you, so watch your back if you come into town. I'm not sure what she might try if she caught you in a dark corner, and she's pretty fast in that wheelchair. I admit I'm a bit worried about her. She seems to have a very active social life—a little too active, if you know what I mean. As her supervisor, it's none of my business, but as a friend, I wonder if I should say something to her. Another thing you can pray for me over: discernment.

Speaking of social lives and discernment, this thing with Brian is beginning to get out of hand. He just won't leave me alone. In fact, I'm about to the point of saying I'll go out with him once just to prove that it won't work out. I mean, I don't think he's a bad guy, but he's very ambitious politically and as you may remember, that is something I do not care for at all.

So, is there anything new at Our Lady of the Mount? I saw something in a supermarket tabloid about a secret Vatican takeover. Do you know anything about that? I suppose you couldn't tell me if you did. Anyway, please write back when you get a chance. I do look forward to hearing from you.

Helen

One

I begin to reply to Helen's latest email when there's a knock on the door of my cell.

"Come in," I say, quickly closing my laptop.

"Excuse me, Father Tom," a young brother says.

"Yes, Brother Thomas?"

"There's a call for you on the main line," he replies, somewhat out of breath. "The Archbishop."

"Did he say what he wanted?"

Brother Thomas shakes his head. "No, he didn't say. He just told me to get you as quickly as possible. Apparently, he's been trying to call you."

A summons like this is not to be disobeyed and I follow Brother Thomas quickly down the dimly lit hallway to the office. The blinking hold light shows the line the Archbishop is waiting on.

Lifting the receiver, I begin, "Hello, Your Eminence what—"

"Father Tom, I need you to go to Saint Clare's immediately," he orders before I can finish my sentence.

"Excuse me?"

"How soon can you leave?" he asks.

"Well, I don't know," I reply. "I have several—"

"Let me clarify," the Archbishop interrupts. "When I say immediately, I mean today. When I ask how soon can you leave, I mean how long will it take you to pack?"

"I don't understand," I say. "Why the urgency?"

He hesitates. "A . . . A situation has arisen that needs to be addressed quickly and quietly."

"What kind of situation?"

The Archbishop sighs. "One involving Father McCoy."

I furrow my brow. "What kind of situation could Father McCoy be involved in?" Having met the young priest, I have a hard time coming up with one that would agitate the Archbishop so much. I like Father Leonard McCoy, but he seems too scared of his own shadow to be involved in anything that might be termed "a situation."

"Something has come to my attention," the Archbishop continues. "I need you to look into it."

"With all due respect, Your Eminence, you haven't answered my question. Are you going to tell me what you want me to look into?"

Silence. "Hello, are you still there, sir?" I ask.

235

"Yes," he says. "I'm here." A pause. A sigh. "We've received an anonymous allegation of misconduct against Father McCoy."

"What kind of misconduct?"

"Father Greer, are you being obtuse on purpose? What kind of misconduct do you think? All right, I'll come right out and say it. We've gotten an anonymous allegation of sexual misconduct involving Father McCoy and an adult member of the parish."

I pause, then burst out laughing. "You're joking!"

"Do I sound like I'm joking?"

"But really, Your Eminence. We're talking about Father McCoy. Leonard McCoy? The same Father McCoy who is pastor of Saint Clare's Parish in Myerton? That Father McCoy?"

"Yes, Father, the one and only."

"But have you met Father McCoy? I mean, it's absurd! He's the walking definition of milquetoast. This has to be a joke."

"I do not find it the least bit funny."

I pull myself together. "No, sir, of course not. We need to take the allegation seriously."

"We can't afford not to," the Archbishop says. "We're still trying to recover from our past behavior and we can't discount something like this or sweep it under the rug."

"I agree," I say. "So, who is he alleged to have . . . committed this misconduct with?"

I hear papers rustling. "The parish secretary."

I burst out laughing again. "But I know the parish secretary," I say. "She's my mother-in-law. Anna's an attractive woman for being in her early sixties, but she's—"

"I am certainly not talking about Anna—Mrs. Luckgold, Father," Archbishop Knowland says.

"But she was serving as parish secretary when I left Myerton four months ago."

I can hear the Archbishop shuffling papers. "According to the allegation, the parish secretary's name is Rachel Watson."

"Before I left Myerton," I say, "Anna told me they were interviewing for the position but I hadn't heard that Saint Clare's had hired one."

"Is there any reason why you would have heard, Father?"

I think of my weekly emails from Helen Parr, an old friend whose acquaintance I had renewed during my brief time as Rector of Saint Clare's parish in Myreton last year. In keeping with our commitment to avoid personal entanglements, her emails typically concern goings-on in the parish and in the town of Myerton itself. She has not mentioned the parish hiring a new secretary, but then again, I guess she might not have noticed unless she had to go into the office for some reason.

"No, sir. There really is no reason." I answer.

"This says that Ms. Watson," the Archbishop continues, "is a single woman in her late 20s."

"Hmm," I say. "Not your typical parish secretary. Not like the last one."

"Exactly, which is why we have to get on top of this," the Archbishop says. "I need you to go to Myerton to sort this out."

"What do you—"

"Talk to Father McCoy, get his side of the story. Interview this Watson woman, see if anything alleged is true."

I hesitate to ask the next question I have, but it needs to be asked. "Have there been any other similar allegations against Father McCoy in the past?"

"No, not one," the Archbishop says. "I had his file pulled the moment I finished reading the letter. He's squeaky clean, not so much as a hint of scandal at his previous assignments."

Considering his last assignment was at the Archdiocese assisted living facility, I'm not surprised.

"What exactly are the allegations?" I ask.

He hesitates. "I don't want to get into them over the phone," he says. "I sent a copy by email to Saint Clare's."

"So Father McCoy knows about the allegations?"

"Yes, I called him last night to tell him."

"I bet he had a restless night."

"He's not the only one!" Archbishop Knowland exclaims. "This hasn't been good for my blood pressure or my ulcer!"

"Does he know I'm coming?"

"He knows someone is coming. Frankly, you were not the first name on my list. You've shown a tendency to, well, get a little too involved."

"I hardly think being involved in one murder investigation—"

"—two, Father, if you include your wife's."

I pause. The Archbishop says, "Sorry, Tom. I shouldn't have said that. It wasn't fair. But you got too involved last time you were at Saint Clare's. Because of that, you weren't my first choice. But I got to thinking that your familiarity with the parish, with the town, with the authorities could come in handy."

I furrow my brow. "Are the police involved?"

"No," the Archbishop insists. "No, not yet anyway, since the letter does not imply anything illegal has happened. That's one thing I want you to look at." He paused. "If Father McCoy did something egregious to this woman, something that broke a law, then I want you to find that out, and I want you to report it. You know the Myerton Police's lead detective, correct?"

I'm careful before answering. "Yes, I got to know Detective Parr fairly well. She's a good detective."

"What kind of person is she? In other words, will she give the Church a fair shake?"

"Oh, definitely," I say, remembering our relationship of 20 years ago. "She was raised Catholic and may have stumbled in her faith as a young adult, which most people do, but it's my understanding from her own words that she never stopped attending Mass completely. But she has not been involved in a parish since the death of her husband. Still, last I spoke to her, she had begun attending Saint Clare's."

"Well, hopefully, this will not be an issue. If the police need to be involved, involve her. We're not sweeping another problem under the rug. But don't do it unless you uncover something that is a crime."

"I understand."

"Oh, I should also say you'll be taking over the public ministry of Saint Clare's until this matter is cleared up."

"But what excuse will I give?"

"I'm sure you and Father McCoy will think of something appropriate."

I sigh. "What do I tell Father Abbot? We'll be leaving him in a bit of a lurch."

"That's not my concern," the Archbishop yells. "He'll have to manage for a while. We've got to get this taken care of. Pack up and get on the road to Myerton. I'll be waiting for your call." He hangs up, leaving me looking at the receiver.

I ask Brother Thomas if Father Abbot is free. "I think I saw him go in the Grotto's direction. He'll probably be back soon."

"That's all right," I say quietly. "I'll go to him there."

***

I find Father Abbot at the reproduced Grotto of Lourdes, seated on one of the rough-hewn wood benches. The elder monk looks deep in prayer. I approach him quietly, stepping softly on the warm summer grass. It's just after 9:00 a.m. and the early July sun is already hot. I'm sweating by the time I get to the Grotto. The sun is glistening off the white marble statue. I stand a respectful distance away so as not to disturb him.

After a few moments, he looks at me and smiles. "Come, Father, sit by me," he says, patting the seat next to him."

"Sorry to disturb you, Father Abbot," I say, sitting down. "I wouldn't have if it wasn't important."

He shakes his head. "It's perfectly all right, my son. I just come here to meditate. It's often the quietest place on the property. The enclosure gets too noisy sometimes."

I smile inwardly. The monastery is too quiet for me sometimes, and he finds it noisy.

"Now, what is it you need to say to me?" he says, turning to face me.

I tell him about the Archbishop's call. "So he's taking you away from us?"

"Only temporarily," I say, "only until I can get this situation at Saint Clare's straightened out."

"Temporarily," he repeats. "But he gave you no idea how temporary this would be, did he?"

"No," I say hesitantly, "but I can't imagine it would take very long. It's ridiculous, these allegations, and it should only take a week or so to wind up."

He considers what I say, turning to the statue of the Blessed Mother. "Well, I suppose we have no choice," he sighs. "You're still under the Archbishop's authority, and I think we can manage for a few days without a priest. I can still say Mass; one brother will help me move around."

"I'm sorry," I say. "You, the brothers, everyone has been so good to me since I came. It's been a real blessing to me."

He smiles and places his wrinkled hand over mine. "You've been a blessing to us, Father . . . to me." He pauses. "Have you gotten what you came here for?"

"I came here to serve, to help the monastery, to repay you for what you did for me years ago."

Father Abbot smiles. "Yes, I know that's why you say you came. But that's not why you came. You know that. So, I ask again, have you gotten what you came here for?"

I look at the statue of Mary, then the statue of Saint Bernadette. Often my thoughts have returned to this spot, to this place of prayer and solitude, to the day—the moment—I received the call to the priesthood. Out of the depths of my despair over my wife's murder, out of the depths I had sunk to in trying to numb my pain, I had found myself in the monastery all those years ago, wanting peace. What I found then was peace—and a new life.

What had I come back for? After Helen arrested Joan's murderer, after I saw him convicted and locked away, after all the events of last fall, I needed to find peace again. Have I found it? Maybe. But after four months in the quiet and solitude, I am feeling restless and am secretly not sorry to be called to go out again.

"I think so," I reply. "I guess I really won't know until I leave."

"The guilt you once carried, do you still carry it?"

I take time to consider this before I can admit the truth. "No," I whisper. "That's gone, but I still grieve for Joan, for what I lost, not just when she died, but when I learned all that I did last year. It still hurts, even after all this time."

"You wouldn't be human if it didn't," Father Abbot says. "We never really get over our losses. A loved one dies. A favorite pet runs away. Our innocence is taken from us." He pauses and smiles wistfully. "Someone you love marries another person."

I look at him, my mouth open to speak. He looks at me and smiles. "I wasn't always a monk, Father Tom. But that was a long time ago. I never—well, rarely—think about it. So when I say we never really get over loss, I know what I'm saying. Loss isn't something we get over. It's just something we learn to live with. Some people suppress it, others replace it, and others allow their losses to consume them. It's those last who have the hardest time."

"What have you done with yours?"

He smiles. "I'm still figuring that out."

***

"It's ridiculous. It's absurd. It's preposterous. It's . . . it's scandalous!"

I watch the agitated, red-headed cleric pace up and down in the Rectory living room. He's been this way since I arrived, only four hours after the Archbishop's conversation with me at the monastery.

He hadn't greeted me when I knocked on the door. Much to my surprise, Anna answered.

"Tom, thank God," she had said. "I can't get him to calm down."

"What's going on? What are you doing here?"

"What am I doing here? He called me," Anna explained. "At six o'clock this morning he called me. Fortunately, I was up. He asked—begged me to come over. He sounded agitated, so I came right away. He's been in the living room the whole time. Sometimes, he'll sit and stare at the wall, then he'll get up and pace back and forth, mumbling to himself, gesturing with his hands. Then he got a call and when he hung up, he looked at me and said, 'Father Greer will be here around noon. Can you make sure the guest room is ready, please?'" She stopped. "What's going on, Tom? Why are you here?"

I'm not sure how much to tell her. "The Archbishop called me. He asked me—ordered me—to come."

"Why?"

I choose my words carefully, admitting, "I can't say, really. He asked me to look into a . . . complaint against Father Leonard."

She looks confused. "Who could have a complaint against Father Leonard? He's the least offensive person I've ever met."

For Anna to call someone the least offensive person she's ever met is high praise. She has firm opinions about most people, many sharp, few incorrect. It is a trait I have found comes in handy.

"That," I say, responding to her question, "is what the Archbishop wants me to look into. He wants me to see if there's any merit to the complaint."

Anna's countenance turns serious. "Is Father Leonard in some kind of trouble?"

I sigh. "I don't know, Anna, that's what I'm here to find out. Listen, I can't say any more, the Archbishop asked me to be discreet."

She puts her hand up and insists, "Say no more, I won't ask anything else. Though," she smiles, "you know I can find out if I want to."

"And I'm asking you, Anna," I say firmly, "not to."

She nods. "Okay, Tom."

The first words out of Father Leonard McCoy's mouth when Anna shows me into the living room are, "Father Greer, I've done nothing inappropriate with Rachel Watson!"

Anna's eyes get big. *So much for discretion*, I think. I glance at Anna and get a look that is a combination of surprise, concern, and assurance. Surprise at the accusation, concern for Father Leonard, and assurance that I can trust her not to say anything.

"Why don't I go make us some coffee," she says. Returning a while later with a tray holding a coffee pot and two cups with a creamer and sugar bowl, she says, "I'll be in the back cleaning if you need anything." A moment later, I hear the door to the kitchen close, music coming from her phone, and the exhaust fan over the oven running. When Anna has to stay out of the loop, she does it, no matter what the temptation.

Father Leonard spends the next half hour continuing to pace up and down the living room, sometimes quietly, sometimes uttering words of protest, all the time agitated, just as Anna had described.

"Please sit down, Leonard," I say finally, exhausted by his exertions. "Calm down. No one is saying you've done anything wrong."

"Then why did the Archbishop send you? Why is he removing me from public ministry?" He runs his fingers through his mop of hair, grabbing a handful and pulling. "Oh, what would my mother say if she were alive to hear about this?"

"The Archbishop," I say, trying to sound as soothing as possible, "sent me to look into the allegations. Discreetly, quietly. He wants me to take over your public duties, well, to give you a break."

"But what will we tell people? You're not supposed to be here. Everyone knows you're at Our Lady of the Mount."

"I don't think we need to make a big deal of it," I tell him. "I'm here in town for two weeks, visiting family and friends, and I'm helping at the parish. A vacation, we'll say."

He slumps back in his chair and I shift on the couch. I'm pleased to see new—or at least newer—furniture in the rectory. Someone has gotten rid of the sixties vintage thrift-store rejects and replaced them with much more comfortable, much less threadbare furnishings. I recognize a couple of pieces as ones from Anna's house. She must have done it when she was parish secretary.

"Why don't I get us a fresh pot of coffee," I say standing up. "Give you a chance to calm down. Take a few minutes and we'll continue talking when I get back. Okay?"

Father Leonard looks at me, his mouth in a firm line, and nods. "I'd prefer tea if you don't mind."

I carry the tray into the kitchen. Anna turns to me, eyes wide, and exhales.

"Well," she says, "that's something."

"Now, Anna," I say as I empty the coffee pot and fill it with water.

"So that's why the Archbishop sent you here," she whispers. "You're replacing Father Leonard?"

"Oh, no, no, not at all," I say, pouring the water into the coffeemaker and scooping coffee grounds into the filter basket. "Can you put on a kettle of water for Leonard? He wants tea."

"Of course he does," she mutters, then fills the kettle. "So if you're not here to replace Father Leonard, what are you here for?"

"To look into it," I say. "To see if there's any merit."

"I can tell you there's no merit," Anna scoffs. "I mean, Father Leonard? Inappropriate? I doubt he's ever done anything inappropriate, or even thought anything inappropriate."

"I told the Archbishop as much, but he insisted I come and investigate immediately. He says the Church can't be seen as taking any accusation lightly, no matter how improbable." I shake my head. "I have to say I agree with him."

"Well, I see his point. But why you?"

I shrug. "Not sure. He said I wasn't his first choice, but decided I was the best person for the job."

"Well," she says as the kettle whistles. "If you can find Joan's killer after fifteen years, you can get to the bottom of this."

"Well, that wasn't me, that was mostly Detective Parr."

Anna looks at me and smiles. "Don't you mean Helen?"

I glance her. "Oh, don't look so surprised," Anna says. "I know there's something there, though I'm not saying you're in any spiritual danger. Still, it's in your eyes when you say her name. It's in her eyes when I mention you."

I open my mouth to speak when Anna goes on, "So who made the allegation?"

"No idea. It was anonymous."

"Well, whoever did it either doesn't know Father Leonard and Rachel, or really has it out for one or both of them." She hands me Father Leonard's mug, a bag of Earl Grey already steeping in it. "You will not find anything."

"I hope not," I say. "I really hope not."

Two

Father Leonard adds three teaspoons of sugar to his tea when I set it in front of him. He seems calmer, but his red hair is all over the place, like he had continued running his fingers through it while I was out.

"Feel better?" I ask.

"How would you feel if you were in my position?" he replies. "I feel attacked. Assaulted. Betrayed."

"Okay, all understandable. But I'm here to figure all this out. Now just calm down, take a deep breath, and let's talk this over."

He does what I ask. "All right. What do you need to know?"

I pull out my phone to take notes. "Why don't we start at the beginning. When did you meet Rachel . . ."

"Watson," he says. "Rachel Watson. I met her back in April, for the first time. Well, I should say that's when I officially met her. She started attending Saint Clare's just after Christmas."

"Okay."

"I noticed her at 10:30 a.m. Mass, I think on Epiphany Sunday it was." He stops then adds quickly, "I don't mean I noticed her-noticed her, like I took any special notice of her, more like I saw her and thought, 'oh, someone new,' not that I really thought of her then or later, I mean—"

"Father McCoy," I say, holding my hand up. "Leonard, please, I'm not here to trap you. Just go on. So Epiphany was the first day you saw her."

He nods. "It's the first time I saw her at Saint Clare's. I had not seen her here before."

"When did you meet her?"

"Well, you know we needed to get a new parish secretary, after everything that happened," he says. "Ms. Luckgold was wonderful, a valuable person. I asked—practically on my hands and knees—if she'd take the position permanently. But she declined. So we advertised." He sighed. "We got two applicants. One was an old widow, a long-time parishioner, a solid person. The other was Rachel."

"Why did you choose Rachel? It seems like an unusual thing for someone her age to apply for the job of parish secretary and housekeeper."

"I thought so too when I first saw her resume—she was the only one to send a resume. The other woman just left a note in the offering basket. College degree in business management, experience in retail and customer service, quite over-qualified. But I interviewed her, anyway."

"What was that like?"

His eyes brighten, and a slight smile appears on his lips. "Wonder—" He obviously catches himself. "Quite good," he replies. "She was very impressive in the interview. She explained that she wanted to work in the parish because she was discerning a vocation."

I raise my eyebrows. "Really? That's good."

"I thought so too. I thought it was a great deal for everyone. She told me she thought working at the parish would give her the opportunity to be closer to our Lord—more time to pray and attend Mass daily. Her current job was at the office park outside town, so she couldn't make daily Mass and she wanted to adopt that discipline."

"So you hired her, but of course she didn't live here in the Rectory."

"Oh, no, Father, no, she rents a townhouse in one of the recent developments on the edge of Myerton."

"Have you been to her home?"

"What—oh, no, certainly not. I just know where she lives because I drove her home when her car was in the shop and I thought it was too late for a single woman to take an Uber."

"She would work late?"

"Occasionally."

"You'd spend time alone with her, here in the Rectory?"

"Yes, of course, she worked here after all. But nothing inappropriate ever happened."

I look at my notes. "I haven't seen the complaint, so I don't know exactly what the accusation is."

"The Archbishop sent it to me by email," Father Leonard says, getting out of the chair. "I'll go get it for you." He leaves the living room and Anna darts in from the kitchen with a plate of sandwiches.

"I thought some food might help," she whispers. "I'm not sure he's eaten today."

"Could you hear anything?" I ask, taking a sandwich off the plate.

"Oh, Tom, I wouldn't listen to a private conversation."

"I didn't ask if you listened. I asked if you could hear anything?"

She hesitates. "These walls are kind of thin, Tom."

I nod. "Any thoughts?"

She leans closer and whispers to me, "There's more here than he's saying."

"Here," Father Leonard says, brandishing a piece of paper as he returns from the office. "This is—oh, Anna! I forgot you were here. Sandwiches. Thank you. They look delicious."

"I'll leave you two," Anna says. "The . . . kitchen floor needs mopping. I'll just go do that." She hurries from the room as Father Leonard resumes his seat.

"This is the allegation?" I say, taking the paper from him. It's the printed scan of a handwritten document. "It wasn't sent by email?"

"Apparently not," Father Leonard says. "It arrived at the Archdiocesan Office late last week by regular mail. No return address, a Myerton postmark. It wasn't signed. It's a tissue of lies and slander!" He's getting agitated again.

"Father Leonard, I very much want to find out the truth in this situation, and if you are as innocent as you say you are, then to prove that. But to do that, I need to see for myself what's in this letter and I cannot do that with you blathering over me," I say as I try to read the letter.

Only when I've read it through twice do I ask, "Is any of this true?"

Father Leonard shakes his head vigorously. "No. Not a jott. Not a tittle."

I roll my eyes slightly. Why he insists on speaking like a character out of a Dickens novel, I don't know. "So nothing in this is factual? Nothing at all?"

"Not a word of it."

"But you told me you'd work late with her here at the Rectory and," I look at the letter, "it says right here, 'Father McCoy and Ms. Watson are often at the Rectory late at night alone.' So this is true, isn't it?"

"Well," he sputters, "well, yes, I suppose if you put it a certain way, that is strictly accurate. But it's the implication that's incorrect."

"I'm not seeing the implication, Father."

"The person who wrote that," Father Leonard explodes, "is clearly implying that Rachel and I are engaged in some kind of inappropriate behavior here late at night. The whole letter is like that, one unfounded accusation after another. Preposterous." He plops in an armchair and brings his clenched fist down on the arm.

"The letter also says, 'Father McCoy engages Ms. Watson in intimate conversations.'"

"I've offered her spiritual direction," he barks. "She's discerning her vocation. We'd pray together. She'd ask for guidance. I'd offer it as best I could."

I look at Father Leonard. Slowly, he's changing from frantic and anxious to visibly angry. I continue reading, "'They've been seen dining alone together.'"

"We've had dinner a few times at The Bistro, the restaurant up the street," he says. "People have to eat."

"'Several people saw them together at the parish Memorial Day picnic.'" I look at him.

His face turns red and sweat beads on his forehead. A look of panic passes across his face. He swallows and clears his throat. He clenches and unclenches his fist, rubbing it with his other hand. "That—" he squeaks, then clears his throat. "There were a lot of people at the picnic."

"'Father and Ms. Watson disappeared for about half an hour, then someone saw them engaged in deep conversation apart from the rest of the group. Father at one point kissed her.'"

"She had gotten something in her eye," he explodes, standing up and beginning to pace again. "Rachel wanted to discuss something with me, so we went off a short way—a very short way, I could still see the games the children were playing—and sat together to get away from the noise. You know how noisy it is here, all the time, with all the children. We sat together under a tree. She got something in her eye, so I was trying to get it out. I got close to her face, you know, to see her eye."

I regret how lame this excuse sounds. One the one hand, most people know that it's the oldest excuse in the book. A sophisticated man would never use it. But Father Leonard is anything but sophisticated, so it's just possible that that's what actually happened. "What did you and she talk about?" I ask.

Father Leonard shakes his head. "No, I can't tell you that. It's under the Seal."

The Seal of Confession. The shield that can be a sword. "In general, then," I continue. "What did you and she discuss?"

He exhales. "She wanted to discuss her call to religious life. She was having doubts, and she talked to me about them."

"Why at the picnic? Seems an odd place for spiritual direction."

"It was my idea," he says. "I noticed her looking distracted, somewhat upset. I asked her if anything was bothering her. She said there wasn't, but I insisted we go off together to talk."

"What did she tell you?"

Leonard shakes his head. "You know I can't tell you that, Father. You must ask her."

There's a soft knock behind us. "Excuse me," Anna says. "Father Leonard, you have sick calls this afternoon."

"Oh! Oh my, I completely forgot," he says. "I suppose I can't do that now, can I, Father?"

I shrug. "I don't see why not, Leonard," I say. "The Archbishop said nothing to me about your visits or hearing confessions, just saying Mass. I'll be glad to go in your place if you don't feel up to it."

"No," he says, squaring his shoulders and straightening his collar. "No, thank you, Father. These scurrilous accusations have deprived me of saying Mass. I will not let them keep me from my flock. No, my mother always told me, 'When people speak ill of you, go out among them with your head held high.' If you'll excuse me." He starts out of the living room, then pauses.

"I was just trying to help Rachel," Father Leonard says. "We became friends. I've never had that many. It's difficult for me to make friends. Rachel, well, she and I are a lot alike." He sighs. "It's just nice to have someone who understands."

"That's all you are. Friends," I say.

Father Leonard looks me in the eye. "Yes. Friends."

***

"There were many people at the picnic, Tom," Anna says. She squeezes the mop out into the bucket, then leans it against the counter. She dries her hands and looks at me. "I was helping with the kids' games so I saw nothing in particular I thought anything about."

"Have you heard anything? I mean, I know you keep your ear to the ground."

Anna wipes the counter with the towel. "Nothing specific. Just murmurings about how close they seem." She looks at me. "I've heard nothing that would warrant someone writing to the Archdiocese."

"Do you have any idea who would write anonymously?"

She shakes her head. "I can't think of a single person, Tom. Everyone in the parish likes Father Leonard. I mean, we all think he's a little odd sometimes—the way he speaks, his homilies can be a bit long-winded, he sometimes lapses into untranslated Greek or Latin, the fact he's named after a science-fiction character, you know the teens call him Father Bones—but he's been good for the parish. The young people like him. He's done a lot of talks to the Catholic student group on campus. Overall, a nice, calming presence."

"Someone doesn't think so," I point out.

Anna sighs. "Well, I'm sure you'll get to the bottom of it."

"That's what the Archbishop wants me to do." I think for a minute. "So tell me about Rachel Watson."

She shrugs. "There's not much to tell about her. Her family has lived in Myerton for years. They're members of the parish, but not active; if they attend more than Christmas and Easter, I'd be surprised."

"She attended Myer College?"

"No, she went to school in Emmitsburg. Got her degree in business, according to her resume, and took a job with a firm in Pittsburgh. Worked there for a few years, then moved back to Myerton. She's been attending Saint Clare's since January."

"How did she come to be interviewed for parish secretary?"

"She applied," Anna says matter-of-factly. "Simple as that. We put a note in the bulletin asking for applicants. She and Fern Grumly were the only two that applied. Fern just didn't cut it; Father McCoy didn't like her, though I think she would have done a good job. But," she adds slowly, "he took to Rachel right away. Came out of the interview having offered her the job. Only took about fifteen minutes."

"You weren't in the interview?"

"Oh, of course I was," she says. "Had an entire list of questions for her. We kept Fern in there for about 45 minutes—may seem like overkill, but parish secretary is a sensitive job. They're privy to all sorts of information about members, and work intimately—" she stops. "Maybe not the best word under the circumstances, but I mean closely with the priest. They need to get along, have discretion and sensitivity."

I chuckle. "The last full-time secretary had none of that," I say.

Anna guffaws. "Yes and look what happened. Anyway, 45 minutes with Fern, about fifteen with Rachel. I got through three or four questions when Father Leonard offered her the job."

"Didn't you think it was strange?"

"At the time I did. When we received Rachel's resume, he had a negative reaction. Nothing specific, mind you, but I could tell from the way he looked and the tone of his voice when he talked about her he wasn't too excited about her interest. So it surprised me when he offered her the job so quickly. But I said nothing. Rachel was much more qualified. And her reason for applying made perfect sense in one respect."

"But not in all respects?"

Anna shakes her head. "In working here, even full time, she's making less than half what she did in her previous job."

"Leonard told me she has her own townhouse," I say. "Does she still have family in town? Why doesn't she live with them?"

"From what she's told me," Anna says, leaning forward, "she's not on great terms with her family. They're not exactly thrilled that she is considering entering religious life."

"So no support, huh?"

She shakes her head. "No. Oh, her mother and father are decent people. Her father is a CPA in town. I think they just had something different in mind for their daughter. Rachel has a twin sister, Rebecca, who is married." She pauses. "Her husband is Winthrop Myer IV."

I whistle. Winthrop Myer was the founder of Myerton, the founder of Myer College. The Myer family is still a prominent family in town, and Myer Holdings owns much of the surrounding mountains. "So Rachel is related by marriage to the Myer family?"

Anna nods. "There is one other thing I should mention about Winthrop Myer. It's probably nothing. But I think you should know."

I lean against the counter. "What is it?"

She looks out the window over the sink, then turns to look at me. "Not long after Rachel's resume came in, Mr. Myer paid Father Leonard a visit. They were in his office for about half an hour." After he left, Father Leonard gave me a check to deposit in the Parish's account. It was for $15,000, signed by Winthrop Myer IV."

I stare at her. "Do you think Myer persuaded Father Leonard to hire his sister-in-law?"

She shakes her head slowly. "I don't know, Tom. It could just be a coincidence. You know, the Myers have been patrons of the parish for generations. His great-great-grandfather helped pay for rebuilding Saint Clare's after the fire. He's continued to be a frequent donor, though rarely under his own name. Maybe he threatened to turn off the money?"

I exhale. "I'll ask Father Leonard about it. What can you tell me about Rachel and her sister? Do you think the sister would have sent the letter?"

"Rachel and her sister still seem close, from what I've seen and what Rachel's told me. But even her sister doesn't seem to understand her vocation. But to answer your question, I really don't know."

She folds the dish towel and places it on the counter. "So what are you going to do now?"

"Well, I suppose I must interview Rachel. I'll contact her and try to get that done in the next couple of days. First, I'll get settled in here. The Archbishop wanted me to let him know when I arrived, so I guess I'd better call him."

"I've got the guest room all ready for you," Anna says.

"Thanks." I pause. I wonder if I should ask what's on my mind. "How's Helen?"

"I don't really know," she replies. "I have seen little of her lately."

"But I thought she started attending Saint Clare's?"

Anna shrugs. "With three Masses, she's probably just not there at the same time I am. I mean, there hasn't been a murder since you left, and I can't think what else would make her miss Mass."

I note the sarcasm and laugh. "Well, that shouldn't be a problem this time."

Three

After getting my bag out of my car and taking it to the Rectory guest room, I take a walk. It's a beautiful day and I need the time to think about Father Leonard's situation.

I walk along Main Street, enjoying the July warmth. The street is still decorated with the red, white, and blue streamers and American flags the city put up for the annual Fourth of July parade and fireworks extravaganza. Though warm, it's not too humid, one benefit of being in the mountains. Downtown Baltimore would be unbearable, the concrete and asphalt acting to absorb every bit of the heat and magnifying it. Just thinking about it makes me perspire.

Myer College is on summer break, so there are only a few students on the college side of the street. There are quite a few people out, though, a combination of town residents and tourists who enjoy the surrounding mountains for the hiking and the downtown for its quaint shops. The historic railroad offers daily excursions through the mountains, so some are probably here during a layover.

As pleasant as the weather is, I'm getting thirsty as I walk. Up ahead is The Bistro, a charming restaurant very much like a Parisian cafe, right down to the wrought-iron tables and chairs along the sidewalk. The day is so nice that I'm looking forward to sitting outside and having a nice tall lemonade. Up ahead, the place looks crowded, but I think I see an open table. I quicken my steps, hoping to get there before it's taken.

Then I catch sight of dark black hair shining in the sun. My pace slows.

It's Helen. Helen Parr. Detective Helen Parr. The detective who arrested the man who murdered my wife. She is also the woman I was in love with many years ago. The woman I meant to marry until we took different paths. Her path led to law school in North Carolina, mine led to a master's degree in Maryland. She wanted to be a lawyer and became a police detective. I wanted to be an archivist and wound up a priest.

She doesn't see me. I smile and quicken my pace. I'm trying to figure out what I'll say. The last time I saw her, she had whispered in my ear she missed me. Did she still? Will she be happy to see me?

Why do you care? I think to myself. A good question. I realize now that I have thought of her more often than I should and I make a note to discipline myself to stop.

Our weekly emails, by mutual agreement, avoid any talk of the past. Anything that might be considered intimate. On the surface, they are messages between friends.

That's all we are. Friends, the priest inside me says.

Isn't that what Father Leonard just said? the lover counters.

She throws her head back, laughing. She always had a great laugh. Not like Joan's. No one had a laugh like Joan's. Joan's laugh was a ringing bell, clear and melodic. Helen's was boisterous, almost muscular. I smile, then stop when I see her looking in my direction. She sees me and looks surprised.

I walk up to the table. "Hello," I say with a smile. "Fancy meeting you here, Helen."

"Tom?" she says, standing up. We look at each other awkwardly. Do we hug? Do we shake hands? We do neither. We just stand there, looking.

"I didn't know you were back in town," Helen says, sitting back down. "Your emails didn't mention you were coming."

"I just got in a couple of hours ago," I say, avoiding her statement. "I thought I'd go for a walk, such a nice day."

"Are you visiting Anna?" Helen says.

"Yes, but I'm staying at the Rectory. I'll be saying Masses for a week or so, to give Father McCoy a break." I smile. "I hope to see you there."

The waitress interrupts us. "Will you be joining her, sir—Father Tom! What are you doing here?"

The face is familiar. "Visiting," I say.

"Are you going to be celebrating Mass Sunday?" she asks.

"Yes, Father McCoy's taking a break for a couple of Sundays. The Archbishop thought he could use a rest."

"Oh," she replies, a slight frown on her face. "But he'll be back, right?"

"Oh, yes, he's not going anywhere."

"Oh, good!" she says with enthusiasm. "I'll let everyone know. We'd be really upset if Father Leonard was leaving. He's been so good to us."

"Who's we?" I ask.

"We're the Catholic Students Club at Myer College. I'm Vicki. Vicki Morgan."

"Well, while I'm here, I look forward to seeing you and your friends."

She smiles. "Oh, well, thanks." She turns and walks away, then stops and comes back. "I'm sorry, a little scatterbrained. Will you be joining her?"

I look at Helen. "Sure, why not," she shrugs.

"Lemonade and a menu please," I say. "I'm feeling a little hungry."

Vicki goes off. I turn to Helen as she asks, "So why are you really here?"

I am about to repeat the excuse I gave Vicki when I remember that Helen is, after all, a detective and is particularly adept at spotting lies. I also remember that, unfortunately, I've lied to her a few times and so she knows what that looks like, too. So, I decide to tell the truth and say, "I can't really say."

"Is it about Father Leonard and his church secretary?"

I nearly choke at this and sputter, "What do you know about that?"

"Not that much, just that I got a call at the station a couple of weeks ago from some woman who gave her name as Jane Doe and asked me if he could be arrested for seducing her. I said not if she was an adult, and it was consensual, and the woman hung up on me."

"Do you know who it was?"

"I could find out but I won't. It came in on the anonymous crime report line and that's, well, you know, Tom, anonymous." She says the last with a smile made only slightly less attractive by the dripping sarcasm in her voice.

Vicki sets my lemonade down and hands me a menu. I look through it. "I'll have the Monte Cristo," I say, handing her back the menu.

"Right away, Father," she says and practically skips off. I look back at Helen.

"So do you think there's anything to it?"

She pauses and looks away, not meeting my eyes. I sit there, wondering why this seems to bother her so much, when she says, "I don't know."

"Is that why you haven't been to Mass in a while?" I say. Helen looks at me, surprised. "Anna told me she hadn't seen you in Mass."

"Tom, don't lecture me," she says with exasperation. "It's difficult getting back into parish life, and really, it's none of your business. You're not my priest and Father Leonard doesn't seem to care."

I'm about to ask what she means by that when she slumps back and looks at me. "Look at us. Haven't seen each other in four months and we're already bickering."

I smile. "Wanna start over?"

Helen returns my smile. "I'd like that. You're irritating, Father Tom, but," she leans forward, "it's good to see you."

"You, too, Helen," I say.

"When you left, I didn't think I'd see you so soon. You seemed intent on staying at that monastery."

I sigh. "I was."

She looks at me questioningly. "Is it not what you expected?"

"Oh, it's everything I expected. I'd been there before, remember. The brothers' routine, the prayer, the silence. I have plenty of time to pray, to read. I've been doing both a lot. I've been able to deal with some things I've avoided for a while."

"About Joan," Helen says.

"Yes," I say. "And other things." I pause. I'd thought a lot about Joan, about her murder, working through my residual guilt. Also, I came to terms with the things I found out about her mental illness and her first marriage, both of which she had kept secret from me. I also struggled with feelings about Helen, feelings I had buried long ago but that resurfaced during my previous time in Myerton.

"But recently," I continue, "I've been getting a little antsy, I guess you could say. I'm glad to get out of the monastery for a while. Spend time with Anna." I pause. "Visit Joan . . . and others."

We look at each other for a moment. "Well," Helen says to break the silence, "I am glad to see you. Things haven't been the same without you. I haven't had to arrest anyone at the Rectory in months."

"And I hope that doesn't change," I laugh. "You look good."

She smiles and nods. "You, too. So you'll be here for a couple of weeks? Then what?"

I shrug. "The monks still need a priest, so I guess I'll go back there. It really depends on the Archbishop."

"Well," Helen says, standing. "I need to get back. I'm sure I'll be seeing you."

"Yes, Sunday, right?"

She stops and looks at me, hesitating. She nods. "I'll be there." She walks past me. I touch her arm. She stops and looks down at my hand, then into my eyes. A memory passes between us.

"Helen," I say, "I don't think I ever thanked you for that night at the Rectory, getting there when you did."

She moves her arm away from my hand. "Just doing my job, Father. I can't have a dead priest on my record. I think it'd be bad for my career." She moves toward me as if to kiss or hug me, then stops. She straightens up and I turn to find Vicki standing there with my Monte Cristo. Her eyes are enormous.

"I'll see you, Father," Helen blurts, then walks away.

Vicki sets my Monte Cristo in front of me. "Thank you," I say. "Looks delicious."

She flashes a smile and walks away, though at one point she looks over her shoulder in my direction.

I pick up my sandwich. Before I take a bite, I look over my shoulder. I see Helen, about half a block away, also turn to look over her shoulder. Our eyes meet. Quickly, I turn to my sandwich.

I take a bite and a drink of my lemonade. I'm about to take another bite when my phone rings. It's Anna.

"Hello?" I say.

"Tom, I know you just left," she says, "but you better get back here. Father Leonard just got back from his sick calls. He's upset about something, he won't tell me what, but I can't get him to calm down."

"Has he said anything?"

"Only one thing, over and over again." She pauses. "He keeps saying, 'She's ruined me.'"

Four

I hurry back to the Rectory with my partially-eaten Monte Cristo. Father Leonard is exactly as Anna described him. I find him pacing in the living room again, muttering "she's ruined me" repeatedly.

"He got back here quickly, didn't he?" I say. "How many sick calls did he have?"

"Six. Five at the nursing home and one—" she sighs "—one at Gloria MacMillan's."

"Oh," I mouth. I only had the pleasure of visiting Gloria MacMillan once. She spent most of the time berating me about the supposedly crooked bingo game run for years by Father Anthony, the former pastor of Saint Clare's. She was liable to say anything and I'm certain she was the source of Father Leonard's distress.

"You'd better get in there before he has a stroke," Anna says as she shoves me into the living room.

He doesn't see me at first. He's stopped pacing and is leaning with his forehead against the wall, his fists gently tapping the surface. He's still muttering something I can't quite hear, but sounds like, "I'm so sorry, I'm so sorry."

I walk up behind him and touch him gently on the shoulder. He jumps and yells, startling me and causing me to back away from him. His face is contorted with a combination of anger and distress, his red hair is wild, and he's sweating profusely.

"Leonard," I say as I recover myself, "what happened?"

"Have you stopped screwing your secretary!" he yells. "That's what she said to me. Just as matter-of-factly as if she was asking about the weather! Have. You. Stopped. Screwing. Your. Secretary."

"Who?" I said. "Who said this to you?"

"Gloria MacMillan, of course!" He circles the living room. "That senile old hag," he mutters. "She's been a thorn since I got here. Her and her bingo. She's had it in for me since the electric blanket incident."

I groan. "Don't tell me she didn't win it."

"Not the electric blanket, nor the toaster, nor the complementary dinner buffet at the casino off I-70!" he cries. "She's had it in for me the entire time. But I never thought she'd stoop to repeat gossip." Father Leonard stops and looks at me. "You know what this means, don't you Father? I'm finished here. It's all over the parish, this accusation."

"The accusation says nothing about you and Rachel Watson having sexual relations."

"No, no, it doesn't, but someone is spreading a rumor to that effect." He runs his fingers through his hair, gripping a bunch and pulling. "What am I going to do? I need to leave Saint Clare's." He heads to the entrance to the living room. "I need to call the Archbishop."

"Stop, Leonard!" I say, a little loudly. He turns back to me. "Just stop it right now and get a hold of yourself." I approach him and grasp his shoulders. "Do you think you're the first priest in the history of the Church to have rumors spread about him?"

"But, but—," he pleads.

"You can't pay attention to what Gloria MacMillan says. She's a loose cannon who says the first thing on her mind. We don't know what she's heard, or if she's heard anything from anyone else. She's out there on that farm, she doesn't get to town that much, and I doubt she has many people left alive who'll talk to her. Maybe she heard something, maybe it's all in her head. We don't know."

"But it just seems—"

"And if there is such a rumor going around about you and Rachel Watson, what do you think would be worse? Staying, letting me sort this out, seeing it through with courage and dignity? Or leaving? What do you think people will say then?"

He hesitates, then says, "They'll say I left because it's all true."

I nod. "That's right. The last thing you want to do is leave. It fixes nothing and only makes things worse. Trust me. I know."

Leonard looks at me and sighs. He smiles slightly. "Thank you, Tom. I needed that."

"Now," I say, "why don't you go take a shower and rest the remainder of the day. I'll have Anna give me the list of calls and I'll finish them for you." I pause for a moment. "Did you give her communion?"

He closes his eyes. "I just did that before I ran out. I'm sure the family thinks I've gone insane. I didn't even say goodbye, I just ran through their living room and out the door."

I pat him on the shoulder. "They live with her, I'm sure they thought nothing of it."

Anna comes in as Leonard leaves. She hands me a slip of paper. "Here are the remaining calls. They're all at Mountain View Nursing Home. You remember where that is."

"It hasn't been that long," I say, looking at the list. "I'll get right on it."

She looks at me and blows out a breath. "You've got a big problem here, Tom."

I nod. "I know, I know. A huge one."

"You don't really believe she made it up in her head, do you?"

"No, not really," I admit. "She heard something that made her think it. No, Anna," I say, looking at the direction where Leonard went. "There are rumors going around about that young man. I've got to get on top of this, and fast."

"What are you going to do?"

I look at her. "Can you do me a favor and call Rachel Watson for me?"

"Of course," she says.

"See if she can meet with me tomorrow morning, here." I pause. "Are you free? I'll want you nearby."

Anna smiles. "I'll clear my schedule."

***

The next morning I tell Father Leonard to take the day off and drive to Our Lady of the Mount. "Spend the day in prayer," I say. "Ask Our Lady for guidance. Visit her at the grotto." I pause. "I think you may find it helpful."

"You're going to speak to Rachel?" he asks. "What are you going to say?"

I shrug. "Say? Probably not much. I will ask her some questions about the things alleged in the anonymous note to the Archbishop, see if she has any idea who may have sent it."

"How could she when I can't figure out who may have sent it?" he protested.

"She may know something you don't," I point out.

After he leaves, I settle in with a cup of coffee and look over the letter again. Reading carefully, none of the allegations are very specific, just the fact they spent a lot of time alone together and were frequently together at night. The most specific thing mentioned was the Memorial day picnic.

I sit back and think. Father Leonard's explanation for the picnic was plausible, but delivered with a little too much vehemence. He was agitated when we first talked, so that was probably all it was.

Or was it guilt?

I shake my head. The more time I spend with Father McCoy, the harder time I have imagining him doing anything inappropriate, much less breaking his vow of celibacy. It just doesn't fit with the scared, perpetually nervous, and excruciatingly upright prelate I know. I know nothing about Rachel Watson aside from what Father Leonard and Anna have told me, but based on that, I don't think she'd be the type to make accusations out of whole cloth on the one hand or act inappropriately with a priest on the other. A young woman in this day and age wanting to become a nun wasn't likely to do that.

But I have been surprised before.

Right at 10 a.m., there's a knock at the Rectory door. I hear Anna answer the door, then come into my office. She looks perplexed.

"Father Tom," she says, "Your, ah, appointment is here."

"Good," I smile. "Send Rachel in."

She hesitates. "What is it, Anna?" I ask.

"She's not alone," she whispers, moving closer to the desk. "Her mother and sister are with her."

"But I want to talk to her alone," I whisper. "What are they doing here?"

"I guess moral support?"

"Well, can you ask them to wait in the living room while I speak to Rachel?"

Anna nods and goes off. A moment later, I hear a woman say, "No, we will not wait in the living room." A flurry of steps precedes a woman in her late forties, blue dress, blond hair, tall, sweeping into my office.

"Father Greer," she says with calm authority, "I'm Marjorie Watson, Rachel's mother, and I will be right here while you speak to my daughter."

I stand. "Nice to meet you, Mrs. Watson. I understand your desire to be supportive. I just think it would be better if I spoke to her alone. These are serious allegations, and I think Rachel might be more comfortable—"

"Father," she sighs. "For obvious reasons—of the Church's own making, let me point out—I don't trust you not to manipulate her into saying they're all a bunch of lies." She pauses. "I mean nothing personal by that, Father. I'm sure you're a decent enough man, but you are here because the Archbishop sent you, am I right?"

"Yes, that's correct," I say, "and he told me to—"

"Get this to end quietly? Sweep it under the rug? Make it go away so the Church doesn't have another black mark?"

"No, Mrs. Watson," I say firmly. "He told me to look into these allegations thoroughly and follow the evidence no matter where it leads. And that's what I intend to do."

She regards me with scepticism. "Do you think they're lies?"

Before I can answer, a voice behind her says, "But Mama, they are."

For the first time, I notice three other people in my office. Aside from an apologetic-looking Anna are two young women with the same height, same blond hair, and same face. Twins. In fact, from their height and blond hair, mother and daughters could be triplets. But beyond that the similarities end. One twin outweighs the other by a good 10 pounds, has her shoulder-length hair in a short ponytail, and wears a grey cotton jumper that practically brushes the floor. The other's blond hair is styled, also cut shoulder length; she wears a red dress that goes just below her knees. In contrast to her sister, who wears no makeup, she is well made-up and sports well-manicured nails. Even the shoes are different; one sister wears simple comfortable flats, the other, strappy heels. Two more different people I cannot imagine. But I see the red-dress sister place a comforting hand on the grey-jumper sister and pat her gently. A genuine expression of care and concern.

"Rachel, let me handle this," Mrs. Watson says. She gently takes her daughter's hand. "You've shown you don't know what's best for you."

"Mama," the woman in the red dress, "that's not fair. Rachel just—"

Mrs. Watson is about to speak, then stops herself. She smiles. "You're right, Rebecca," she says, though I'm not sure what Rebecca was right about since she didn't finish what she was going to say. Mrs. Watson turns to me, a smile on her lips.

"My apologies, Father Greer," she says, her voice dripping with graciousness. "I didn't mean to question your integrity. I'm just concerned about my daughter, you understand. This is all so distressing for our entire family. "

"I assure you," I say, "it is for all of us."

"This is our parish and has been for years. I know my husband and I don't attend as often as we should, but we have great affection for Saint Clare's. Both Rachel and Rebecca were baptized and received their sacraments here. Rebecca was married in this church. The thought of a priest, especially here, taking advantage of my daughter is just more than I can stand to think about." Her eyes well up with tears.

Rachel pats her mother's shoulder. "I've told you, Mama, Father Leonard never took advantage of me." She looks at me earnestly. "Father, he did nothing wrong!"

"Why don't we let Father Greer ask his questions, my dear," Mrs. Watson says quietly to her daughter, then sits down in one of the two chairs.

"Mama," Rebecca says, "I think Father Greer wants us to wait outside." When Mrs. Watson doesn't move, the sister looks at me. "If it's all right with Rachel," Rebecca says to me, "can we stay? We'll be quiet. We won't say anything. Right, Mama?"

Marjorie Watson looks at Rebecca and smiles. "Of course, dear." Turning back to me, she says. "May we, Father, if Rachel doesn't object?"

"Is it okay with you, Rachel, if your mother and sister say?" I say to Rachel.

She looks at me and nods. "Yes, it's fine, Father," she whispers, "they can stay."

I nod and look at Anna. "Let's get some more chairs." I excuse myself and leave my office. I hurry to the kitchen and grab a chair. Anna is on my heels.

"I don't think it's a good idea to have them in there, Tom," she whispers.

"I don't either, Anna. But I don't see that I have a choice," I say as I walk with the chair back to my office. Anna nods her head to indicate she'll be at her desk if I need her. I nod discreetly.

I close the door. The three women follow me with their eyes as I go around the desk to sit down. "Now," I say, folding my hands together and leaning forward, "Rachel, thank you for being here."

Rachel starts to speak but her mother says, "I'm just thankful the Archdiocese is not just sweeping things under the rug like it did in the past."

I try to look reassuring. "We've made mistakes in the past in dealing with situations of wrongdoing. We're trying to rectify that. That's why the Archbishop sent me here, to look into what's been alleged and see if there's any merit to these allegations and take steps if necessary. However, there will be no rush to judgement."

Rachel starts to speak again when Mrs. Watson says, "Father Greer. If there was nothing to these allegations, do you think they would have been made? I mean, my daughter's seen her good name dragged through the mud. Not to mention the reputation of Father McCoy. Why would someone do that if there was nothing to this?"

"That's why I'm here, as I say, to look into these allegations, to see if there is anything to them, and," I add slowly, "if there is nothing to them, try to figure out why they were made." I pause. "Making false allegations, bearing false witness is a sin. If they made it up for reasons of spite, for any reason whatsoever, your daughter and a good priest have had their reputations besmirched."

"Father," Rachel finally says, "I'm so glad you're here. Leon—Father McCoy's always been perfectly proper with me."

Mrs. Watson opens her mouth to speak again. Rebecca places a hand on her knee. Mrs. Watson closes her mouth and settles back.

"Well, let's just begin at the beginning," I say. "The letter is anonymous, and there's nothing very specific in here—nothing alleging Father McCoy took advantage of you or assaulted you in any way—but there are allusions to inappropriate behavior. I want to ask you about a few of the things in here. Is that all right?"

She nods, but her mother says, "She'll answer your questions. I'm sure she's eager to get this matter taken care of." Mrs. Watson pauses. "What will happen to Father McCoy, if you find out it's true?"

"I don't think we're anywhere near that yet," I say. "But if there's no criminal activity, they will transfer the priest out of the parish, have to undergo counseling and a period of penance, and then the decision will be made about whether to put him in another local parish. But if a priest commits a crime—in this case, a sexual crime like rape or assault—then, well, we'll let the state take over."

A slight smile plays on her lips. "So either way, he'll be gone?"

"Only if he did something wrong."

"He didn't!" Rachel protests.

"Now, Rachel," Mrs. Watson says.

Rachel opens her mouth to retort, but Rebecca says. "Mama, let's let Father Greer do what he's here to do, and let Rachel answer the questions." She turns to me. "Sorry, Father. This has been very upsetting for everyone, especially Mama. Rachel's the baby of the family, so someone taking advantage of her—well, it's just upsetting."

"I'm not a child!" Rachel says to Rebecca. "I wish everyone would stop treating me like one!"

"Maybe if you'd stop acting like one," Mrs. Watson says. "Fantasies, always fantasies with you."

I hold up my hand, desperate to get the conversation back on track. "Ladies, please." Looking at Mrs. Watson, I say. "I have let you and Rebecca stay here because I thought you were here to support Rachel, that she wanted you here. But if that's not the case, you must leave. I have questions for Rachel, and I want her to answer them without interference or commentary. I have a job to do and I will do it. Am I clear?"

Mrs. Watson looks at me, her eyes betraying a desire to unload on me a stream of invective. Instead, Rebecca says, "Yes, Father Greer. Very clear. We'll just sit quietly while you talk to Rachel. Isn't that right, mother?"

"Yes. Father Greer," she says, "you can ask Rachel any questions you like. I won't say a word."

I incline my head. "Now, Rachel," I say, leaning forward, "how would you describe your relationship with Father Leonard?"

"My relationship?" she says. "He's my boss. I'm the parish secretary, you know, so I work for him. Well, technically, I guess I work for the parish, but he gives me the work to do."

"But beyond that," I say. "How would you characterize him?"

"He's my spiritual director. My confessor." She pauses. "Father Leonard is my friend."

"How did you two meet?"

She looks at me, a flash of panic crossing her face. She recovers quickly and asks, "What do you mean?"

"I think I'm clear," I say. "When did you meet Father Leonard?"

"I met him at Saint Clare's," she says slowly. "One of the first Sundays I started attending Mass here."

"I understand you're discerning a vocation to religious life?"

"Yes," she says. She cuts her eyes to her mother, who looks at her out of the corner of her eye.

"Her father and I," Mrs. Watson says, "have been trying to discourage this. We raised both of them in the Church, made sure they had their Sacraments at the appropriate time and all that. But we want them to make something of themselves. We just don't understand why a young woman as accomplished as Rachel would do something as extreme as becoming a nun."

"I've tried explaining, Mama," Rachel says. "You and Daddy just won't listen."

Mrs. Watson opens her mouth to speak when she sees me shake my head slightly, then closes it and folds her arms.

"I see," I say. To Rachel, I say, "Are you working with a particular order?"

"There's a convent near Emmitsburg," she says. "I've done a few discernment retreats there. I'm hoping to enter as a postulant within the next couple of years. I have some debts to pay off before I can do that."

"I understand from Mrs. Luckgold that you have a background in business?"

"Yes, I got my degree in business management and finance. I had a job at a company just outside town. I quit to take the job at Saint Clare's."

"You took a big pay cut to do that. If you wanted to pay off debt, why would you want to work for less salary?"

She looked at her hands, folded in her lap. "The work environment was . . . difficult. Also, I didn't have the time to pray, and I couldn't attend daily Mass. When I found out about this job, I jumped at the chance. I could work here at the parish, serving God, and I'd have the chance to go to Mass every day and pray." She smiled. "The money wasn't important."

"It was important enough," Mrs. Watson comments, "when you wanted to go to Emmitsburg for college."

"I would have been satisfied," Rachel says, "coming back home after graduating high school and attending Myer." She pauses and looks at Rebecca. "But that was not an option, was it?"

Rebecca puts her hand on Rachel's shoulder. Rachel looks at her hands, but allows Rebecca's hand to stay there.

I sit quietly looking at the three women. So much is going on in front of me, but I don't understand what it is, or what—if anything—it has to do with the issue at hand.

"If we could get back to the reason we're here, please," I say, hoping to steer the conversation back to the allegations against Father Leonard. "Rachel, I will ask you a direct question. Has Father Leonard ever touched you inappropriately?"

She jerks her head up and looks me square in the eyes. "No, Father Greer, absolutely not. Father Leonard never touched me in any way that was inappropriate or unwelcome."

"He never made an unwanted physical advance? Never engaged you in any kind of suggestive conversations? Made no kind of lewd propositions?"

She shook her head. "Absolutely not."

"And the descriptions of you two spending time alone together here at night?"

"We were working," she says. "Sometimes we'd talk." She smiles. "Father Leonard is very easy to talk to."

"What would you talk about?"

"Oh, everything. God, faith, the Church, the Scriptures, theology. Also books—he's one of the most well-read men I've ever met. He's a very interesting person. We'd also talk about . . . " she paused for a moment.

I raise an eyebrow. "Yes?"

She took a deep breath. "Nothing, Father. We'd just talk about many things." Rachel glanced to her right and left. "I'd rather not say."

"Things one might say to a confessor?" I ask.

She hesitates, then nods her head.

"One allegation is very specific," I say. "There's the matter of the Memorial Day picnic?"

"That was nothing!" she blurts. I sit back. She composes herself, then says, "We were just talking, that's all. It was crowded. He doesn't like crowds of people, the children were running around, and he knows I don't like crowds either. He suggested we go off to have some peace and quiet."

"There's a claim that someone saw you two physically close?"

She blushes. "I had stumbled on a root. He caught me, making sure I didn't fall."

I sit quietly. "So you're saying that the allegations are false."

"Absolutely, Father. I don't understand why someone would accuse a man as good and as holy as Father Leonard of something so heinous."

"Do you have any idea who might have sent this letter to the Archbishop?"

Rachel shakes her head. "I don't know who could hate him, or me, that much." She begins to cry.

Mrs. Watson grabs her daughter's hand and pats her on the shoulder. "There, there, dear. It's okay." She looks at me. "You see how upsetting this all is for Rachel. My question to you is, Father, what are you going to do about it?"

I fold my hands. "I don't know if I need to do anything. They both deny the allegations and have offered reasonable explanations for what's described in the letter. Because it was sent anonymously, I can't ask the person who wrote it." I spread my hands. "It looks to me that there's nothing here."

"But Father Greer," Ms. Watson says, "you can see that that priest has a great deal of influence over Rachel. He could have gotten her to say anything. Not to mention this idea about becoming a nun."

"Mama, I've tried to tell you," Rachel says through her tears. "That has nothing to do with Father Leonard. I've felt the call for a long time now."

"But it makes no sense, Rachel," Ms. Watson says. "You've got so much potential, and to throw it all away—"

"I'm not throwing it away!" Rachel stands up and looks down at her mother. "You understand nothing about me! Besides, why do you care what I do? You've got everything you've ever wanted with her." She points to her sister.

"Rachel!" Rebecca says, looking hurt.

Rachel turns to her sister. "It's not your fault," she says. "It's just the way it is. Excuse me, Father," she says, then dashes out of my office. I hear the front door close.

I'm left in my office with Mrs. Watson and Rebecca in an uncomfortable silence. Finally, Mrs. Watson says, "I'm telling you, Father, he needs to leave." She sits back. "Do you know who my son-in-law is?"

I nod slowly. "I understand Rebecca is married to Winthrop Myer."

"That's right. Winthrop Myer. You know, the Myers built this town, the College, owns most of the land around the town. I even believe they built this Church."

"His great-great-grandfather donated to have it rebuilt after a fire, yes, that's true."

"Well, then, I guess you see my meaning," she says with a smile of triumph.

I return the smile. "Thank you, Mrs. Watson, for the history lesson." I stand and say, "But I think we're done here for today. Anna," I call, "please show the Watsons out?"

"But, but what are you going to do?" Mrs. Watson asks.

"Do? I'll keep looking into it, but it seems to me right now that the allegations in the letter are unfounded. However, I am getting more interested in who sent the letter. You wouldn't know anything about that, would you, Mrs. Watson?"

She glares at me. "Are you asking me if I sent that letter to the Archbishop?"

I nod. "Did you?"

"Father Greer," Rebecca says indignantly, "Mama would never do that to Rachel! Make up stories, put them in a letter, send it to the Archbishop."

Mrs. Watson places her hand on Rebecca. "Dear, it's all right."

Rebecca looks at her. "But Mama, you wouldn't do that!" She looks at her. "Would you?"

Mrs. Watson looks at her daughter. "I was worried about your sister."

"Oh, Mama!" she whispers.

"Father Greer," Mrs. Watson says, turning to me. "I admit it. I sent the letter. But I made up nothing I wrote. They were all things that were told to me, based on rumors in the parish."

"Who told you these things?"

"I have friends who still attend here," she says. "They were concerned about some things they heard. Some things they saw themselves. After hearing it, I got concerned about Rachel—she's the baby of the family, after all—so I did something." She paused. "My son-in-law kept an eye on her."

"What?" Rebecca exclaims. "You got Win involved in this?"

"He offered to do it," she says. "Someone needed to look after your sister, and Win was worried about her."

"I just bet he was," Rebecca mutters.

"So, you know who sent the letter," Mrs. Watson says. "Now, what are you going to do?"

I shake my head. "Both Father Leonard and Rachel say nothing improper happened. Until I find evidence to the contrary, I won't be advising the Archbishop to take action."

She stares at me. She's a woman not used to being told "no." Without saying a word, she turns on her heels and marches out of the Rectory.

Five

"He's just so unreasonable," she says from behind the grill. "I can't get him to listen to me. He does whatever he wants to do, he doesn't care about the effect it has on me or the other children. I'm at the end of my rope, Father, I just get so angry with him. I hate the thoughts that go through my head. For these and my other sins, I am very sorry."

"I understand your frustration," I say quietly. "But you need to remember he's only five years old. He won't always be this way. He'll grow out of it. Keep in mind you are the adult and he is the child. You must treat him firmly but kindly. But frustration is a part of being a parent sometimes. Look to the example of Our Lady who, as sinless as she was, expressed frustration at her Son when he went missing. My advice to you is when he is pressing your buttons and you feel your frustration giving way to anger, just look to Our Lady in prayer and ask for her to pray that you'll have the strength to treat your son with love in your frustration. Now for your penance, I want you to say two Our Fathers and two Hail Marys. Now say your act of contrition."

I listen as she says the words of the penitent, then I speak the words of absolution while making the sign of the cross. "Go in peace, your sins are forgiven. Have a pleasant week."

"Thank you, Father," she says. I hear movement, then the door opens. I sit back and exhale, checking the time. Four o'clock. A busy Saturday. Mostly moms talking about their kids. It's the middle of summer, kids are out of school or homeschooling's suspended, children have time on their hands, and the entire under-18 population of Saint Clare's appears determined to drive their mothers crazy.

I don't have that many men so far today. Boat Man, as I call him, came to confess the same sins against his brother over the same boat story he told me about nine months ago. I gave him the same advice then that I gave him today—for his penance, he needed to sell the boat and give his brother the money. And again he left before absolution. I wonder if he'd been to confession with Father Leonard, and what the other priest had given him.

I think about Father Leonard and the reason I'm sitting in the confessional at Saint Clare's. The meeting with Rachel Watson, her mother, and her sister was interesting. I wasn't surprised when Rachel denied that anything inappropriate happened; the letter itself specified nothing in particular, beyond their behavior at the Memorial Day picnic. But her story about the picnic differed from Father Leonard's version; he said she got something in her eye, but she said she stumbled over a root. The more I thought after the meeting, the more that inconsistency troubled me.

Then Miriam Conway stopped by the Rectory.

"Father Greer, we're so glad to have you back," she said breathlessly as Anna showed her into my office. She had stopped by unannounced, but I had almost finished my homily for Sunday, so I was more than glad to talk to her.

"It's good to see you, Miriam. How are you getting along?"

"Well, Catherine's just getting smarter and smarter, the twins are driving me crazy, and Andrew's beginning to walk, so I'm keeping busy."

"And how's Dan?"

Her smile faded a bit. "Fine, fine," she said. "They suspended him for a month after . . . "

I nodded. "He told me about it, how Katherine Shepp manipulated him into giving her my wife's case file."

"After the suspension, things seemed to go fine for a while, but he was just passed over for a promotion. He thinks he's still being punished."

"How d'you take it?"

She shook her head. "Not very well, I'm afraid." Miriam lowered her voice. "His job wasn't the only thing he was suspended from, if you catch my meaning, Father. But we got through it. We're doing fine now."

She sighed and smiled again. "But we—the moms—are just so glad you're back, which is why I'm here. You know Father Leonard cancelled the nativity last year—because of that witch Whitemill—and we've been asking if we could try again this year. He's resisted, but now that you're here—"

"Wait, Miriam, just wait," I held up my hand to stop her. "I think y'all are under a misunderstanding. I'm only here for a very short time."

She looked crestfallen. "Really? How short?"

"Only a couple of weeks," I said. "The Archbishop thought Father Leonard could use some time off." Father Leonard had taken my suggestion and gone to Our Lady of the Mount. He was still there, having stayed through the weekend. "I'll probably be leaving a week from Monday."

"So, asking if we can have a nativity . . ."

I shook my head. "I'm sorry, Miriam. I'll talk to Father Leonard, give him my advice, tell him I think it would be a great thing for the parish, but that's all I can do."

"But when we heard you were back, we thought you were here to replace him because of all the—" she stops and puts her hand to her mouth. "Maybe I shouldn't say anymore. It's gossiping."

I raise my eyebrows. "What's being said, Miriam?" I said, motioning her to sit down. "Why don't you tell me why people think I'm here."

Sighing, she said, "Well, people think you came to replace Father Leonard, that the Archbishop is removing him from Saint Clare's because he found out about him and Rachel Watson."

I tried to look neutral, but I doubt she missed the look of distress that passed over my face. "And what do you know about Father Leonard and Rachel Watson?"

I raised my finger as she opened her mouth to speak. "Now, Miriam, be very careful. Tell me only what you know, what you saw. Not what you heard. Not what you think. Just what you've seen with your own eyes."

"My own eyes," she said. She thought for a minute. "They spend a lot of time together. I mean, I know she's the parish secretary, so it's natural they would work together. But they spend a lot of time together outside of work. I was at the park a few weeks ago and I saw them walking, not quite arm in arm, but close to each other. They were talking and laughing, like . . . oh, I shouldn't."

"Like what, Miriam?"

She sighed. "Like a couple," she said. "Other than not holding hands or anything, and him wearing a collar, they looked no different from any other man and woman their age walking together if they were in a relationship."

I nodded. "Anything else you've seen?"

"She hovers around him after Mass on Sunday," she said. "She's with him at every parish function, always sitting next to him. Sometimes when you want to talk to him about something, she runs interference like—well, like I do sometimes with Dan." She took a deep breath, steeling herself. "Then there was the Memorial Day picnic."

Everything went back to the picnic. "What do you know about that?" I asked, settling back in my chair.

She looked guilty as she said, "Probably more than anyone, since I'm the one who found them."

I sat up. "What did you find them doing?"

"Nothing like that, Father," she blurted. "And I'm sure there's a perfectly innocent explanation."

"Miriam," I said slowly. "It's very important that I'm told what people know for sure—not rumors, not innuendos—actually observed. So I need you to tell me what you saw."

She took a deep breath, then nodded. "Okay. Well, I had just finished with the children's games and everyone was gathering to get the food. We needed Father to lead the blessing, but no one could find him. Someone, I forget who, said they thought they saw him go off. I volunteered to go look for him." She swallowed. "I must have walked about a hundred yards away from the main group when I saw him—saw them, I should say." She paused, an embarrassed look on her face.

"What were they doing?" I asked slowly.

"They were standing together under a tree. They had their arms around each other, it looked like they were dancing." She exhaled quickly. "They were whispering and laughing, he was cradling her, they were rocking back and forth. Then . . . then I saw them kiss."

"Did they see you?"

She shook her head. "Maybe, I'm not sure. When I saw them I ducked behind a tree. I didn't know what to do, Father Tom, I just had seen nothing like that before—well, not with a priest. I couldn't just walk back to the picnic and tell people I couldn't find him. So I had to think fast. I walked about ten yards back in the direction I came from and started calling his name—with my back to where they were, so they wouldn't suspect I'd seen anything. After twice calling him, I heard him say, 'Yes, here I am,' and turned to see him jogging towards me. I said to him, 'Father, it's time for the blessing,' and he said, 'Oh, thank you, I just went off to get away from the noise for a bit'—the man can't stand children, it's a good thing he's a priest, I guess, not being able to have any of his own—then jogged back to the picnic. I turned to where he had come from and saw Rachel standing under the tree." Miriam paused. "I don't think Father Leonard knows I saw them, but Rachel knew. I could tell by the look on her face."

I sat back, leaning my head on the back of the chair and looking at the ceiling. Miriam was a cop's wife and from what I could tell, an honest person. If she said that's what she saw, I had little reason to doubt her veracity, but one thing occurred to me.

I sat up and looked at her. "You were the only one to see this, Miriam?"

She nodded slowly. "Yes, no one was with me."

I smiled at her and gently asked, "How then did a mention of an incident involving Father McCoy and Rachel Watson get around town?" I paused for a moment to see her reaction.

She lowered her eyes. "I told her to keep it quiet. You just can't trust some people, Father, you know?"

"Oh, Miriam," I sighed.

"I'm sorry, Father, I really am, but, well," Miriam sputtered, "I have a weakness."

"How many people did you tell?"

She smiled weakly. "Only one. Jenny Reynolds."

I recognized the name. She was the mother of Benedict James Reynolds, the first baby I baptized during my last stay at Saint Clare's.

"Blabbermouth," Miriam muttered.

"I don't think you're in any position to cast aspersions," I said. "You told one person, she may have told another person. It's a terrible cliché, but it only takes a spark to set a forest fire." I lean back. "That's what's happened here. Somehow it got all over town"

"But I didn't tell Jenny everything I saw," she protested. "I just said I saw them together alone, not that they were doing anything wrong."

"Be that as it may," I say, "your lack of discretion has caused this to go all over the parish, it appears. It's very difficult now for Father McCoy. And for Rachel."

"But Father Greer," Miriam whispered, "it's true. There is something going on between the two of them. What are you going to do?"

I had asked myself that question repeatedly since the conversation. Now, sitting in the confessional, I am still uncertain. Miriam saw them holding each other, whispering, talking, laughing, and kissing. They weren't having sex. They weren't doing anything anyone would consider truly wrong. But for a priest? For a woman who wants to become a nun? Clearly not permissible. But what am I going to do about it?

I know I don't have the full story. There are only two people who do know. Father Leonard and Rachel Watson. And so far, they haven't been completely honest with me. I need to talk to both of them again. I am going to have to get Father Leonard to be honest with me about his behavior—and his feelings. I will have to do the same with Rachel, but I'll have to do it without the presence of her mother and sister. I'll have to tread carefully.

I hear steps on the marble floors approaching the confessional. I collect myself and prepare to meet the penitent on the other side of the grill. But instead, the knob to my door is turned. It opens.

In the doorway is Rachel Watson.

"Father," she says.

"Rachel," I say.

She comes in and closes the door. Taking the seat opposite me, she looks at me expectantly.

I say, "Let us begin this sacrament of God's mercy in the name of the Father, the Son, and the Holy Spirit, Amen."

"Bless me, Father," she whispers, her voice heavy with emotion, a tear snaking its way down her cheek. She lowers her head and continues, "Bless me Father, for I have sinned. It has been a month since my last confession."

I nod. I can feel the emotions, thick in the room. I sense what she's feeling and have a good idea what's coming.

At least I hope I do.

Or do I?

She takes a deep breath. "In the past month, I have lied. To a priest." She looks at me. "To you."

I smile and nod. "I know, Rachel. I know."

She shakes her head. "I didn't mean to. I mean, I did mean to, but I didn't want to. I just couldn't tell you the truth."

"Why don't you tell me now?"

She sobs. I grab a box of tissue and hand it to her. She sobs for several minutes. "I'm sorry," she croaks through her crying.

"It's all right, just take your time."

"I've just felt so guilty since we talked," she says "I haven't been able to sleep, I haven't been able to eat. I knew that I needed to come here today and confess to you, but I've spent the last hour in my car in the parking lot, debating whether or not to come in."

"Why don't we begin at the beginning," I say, leaning forward and taking her hand. "What did you lie about?"

"All of it," Rachel whispers. She looks at me. "No, I don't mean that I lied when I said that Father Leonard did nothing inappropriate or forced himself on me." She smiles, a dreamy look in her eyes. "There was nothing wrong or forced about it. I liked it. I liked every moment we spent together. I liked everything we did."

"What did you do?"

She blushes. "He was tentative, very gentle," she said. "I'll be honest, Father. It was my first time."

Now I blush. I was married at one time, and I wasn't always a priest even when I wasn't. I have a good idea what she's talking about. Frankly, it's the part of confession that leaves me the most squeamish. Sex within marriage is sacred, part of God's plan, nothing to be ashamed of. But even then, I've always been a little uncomfortable talking about it. Outside of marriage, well, it's even worse.

"Neither of us wanted it to happen, we didn't plan it or anything," she continues. "It just happened." Her smile fades. "He was so upset afterwards. He cried. He kept saying he was ruined, that we had sinned, that he had broken his vows. I cried for him. And for myself," she ended with a whisper.

"You want to become a nun," I say. "Or you did."

"I still do," she says firmly.

"When did this happen?"

"The first time was Memorial Day," she said with her eyes downcast. "At the Rectory after the picnic."

"The first—there's been more than once?"

She nods. "Three times. Twice in the Rectory, once at my apartment."

I close my eyes and sigh. "Rachel, how?"

"After the first time," she says, "we were both upset, regretful about what happened. We avoided each other for a week. I called in sick, I just couldn't face him, and I wasn't sure he wanted to see me. I even wrote my resignation; I decided to leave Myerton and enter the convent. Then on a Friday evening, there was a knock on my door."

"It was Father Leonard," I say.

Rachel nods. "He came, he said, to apologize, to say it was wrong and it must never happen again. It tortured him, I could tell. He was going to leave right after saying that, but he wound up staying. Then we—"

"I get the picture," I say, holding up my hand.

"That just made matters worse," she continued. "We weren't sure what to do after that. But to me, deep inside, it didn't matter. The fact he was a priest. The fact I thought I was being called to religious life. It didn't matter." A tear rolled down her cheek.

I say, slowly, "You were falling in love with him."

"It wasn't that difficult. Leonard is so kind, so gentle, such a sweet man, it's very easy for a woman to fall for him. I'm surprised, frankly, that every woman in the parish doesn't have a crush on him."

This is a woman truly in love, I think.

"So one day I screwed up my courage and went to the Rectory and told him." She paused. "And showed him."

I react with surprise. "I know," she smiled shyly, "I surprised myself, what I did. But I just couldn't help myself." She sighed. "But it didn't help."

"How did Leonard react? What happened afterward?"

She sighed and shook her head. "He said nothing to me. Just got up, dressed, and left me in his room. I thought he'd come back, but he didn't. After a while I got up and dressed myself, went looking for him." She looked down at her hands, twisting in her lap. "I found him here, on his face in front of the altar, crying. He was whispering something over and over that sounded like, 'I'm so sorry, I've let you down again.' "

I sit back. "When did this happen?"

Still looking at her hands, she says, "About three weeks ago."

"Did you tell anyone about this?"

She hesitates. "I . . . told Rebecca what was going on. I had to. I had to tell someone. But she's my sister. She wouldn't do that, betray my confidence."

I sigh. She's told me a lot and is emotionally spent. "What are you going to do now? Are you still intent on entering religious life?"

She takes a deep breath. "After everything that happened, I wondered. I prayed, and I thought about it a lot. But I still feel God pulling me to him. I love Leonard, and I always will, but I have to follow the longing of my heart. Besides, Leonard is a priest and always will be. He can no more give that up than he can cut off his right arm. Mother Superior is expecting me early next week. I'll be leaving Myerton Monday morning." She smiles. "That will put an end to everything."

***

I get through the 4:30 p.m. Mass and retire to the Rectory. I throw myself into a chair, emotionally exhausted. I'm still trying to process what Rachel Watson revealed in confession. She's put me in an unpleasant situation. What she told me in confession, I can't tell anyone. I can't even tell Father Leonard that I know the truth. But Rachel gave me everything I needed to tell the Archbishop that the young priest broke his vows of celibacy and needs to be dealt with.

Leonard can't stay at Saint Clare's. Not because of the rumors, as bad as those are, because if they moved a priest every time there were rumors in a parish about them, there wouldn't be a priest in a parish for more than six months at a time. No, Leonard can't stay for his own sake and the sake of his calling. He needs counseling. He needs to spend time in prayer and penance. He needs time to heal.

If he wants to stay a priest. That is the other thing. Rachel seems determined to follow through on her call to religious life. But is that genuine? I had absolved her because she expressed genuine contrition. I believe she is sorry for what she did, but part of me wonders how sorry she is. I believe she loves Leonard and am concerned that her going into the convent is running from the truth.

Running from the truth is something I know a little about. Eventually you have to stop, turn, and face the truth. What will happen if later in her religious life, she wakes up one day and realizes she made a terrible mistake? What would that do to her spiritual life?

And what about Leonard? Does he still want to be a priest? He had said nothing to Rebecca to indicate anything other than remorse and sorrow for his sins. I needed to speak to him; I needed to get him to admit the truth, and I needed him to do that for the sake of his own soul. Beyond that, there was nothing I could do to help.

But he's at the monastery. I need to talk to him.

Anna comes into the living room with a glass of ice water. "Here," she says, "I bet you're thirsty."

I take it gladly and down it in one gulp. "That's just what I needed," I say, handing it back to her. "Thanks."

She tilts her head to one side. "Rough afternoon?"

"Not one of my better ones."

Anna knows not to ask anymore, so she says, "There was a message for you. From Winthrop Myer."

I sit up, surprised. "Did he say what he wanted?"

Anna shakes her head. "No, he just asked you to call him when you get the chance. I wrote the number on your blotter."

Getting up, I say, "Thanks," and walk out of the room.

"Dinner's in half-an-hour."

I stop. "You didn't have to make me dinner, Anna. I could have just grabbed something at The Bistro."

"Nonsense, you probably haven't had a home-cooked meal since you were last here—actually, you never came for dinner when you were here the last time—so I did some shopping and made your favorite."

I smile. "Lasagna. You remember."

She nods. "Bring your appetite. I made enough for you and Father Leonard, but if he will not be here, I guess I'll have a bit."

I walk to my office and pick up the Rectory phone. The first number I dial, I don't have to look up.

"Our Lady of the Mount, how may I help you?" says the familiar old voice.

"Brother Martin, good evening."

"Good evening, Father Tom," he replies. "How are you?"

"Fine, thank you. I was wondering if it would be possible for me to speak to Father Leonard. Would it be too much trouble if you could see if he's available?"

"I'll check to see if he's in his cabin." He pauses. "He seems very troubled."

"Did he tell you why he was there?"

"He said nothing to me, but he's been talking to Father Abbot. Father Abbot was glad to have him this morning; he said Mass to the community. But I can tell he's carrying a substantial burden."

"That," I say slowly, "he is."

"Hmm," he says. "I won't ask any more. I'll find him and have him call you. It will be about twenty minutes."

After hanging up with Brother Martin, I dial Winthrop Myer's number. A woman answers.

"Hello?" I recognize Rebecca Myer's voice.

"Rebecca?"

"Yes, this is Rebecca."

"Good evening, Rebecca, this is Father Greer at Saint Clare's. Am I calling at a bad time?"

"No, no, we had not sat down for dinner yet. What can I do for you?"

"Well, I'm returning your husband's call."

There is silence at the other end of the phone. "What?"

"Yes, your husband left a message for me at the Rectory and asked me to return his call. Is he available?"

She doesn't answer right away. "Yes, Father Greer. I'll get him." She puts the phone down and I hear her walk away. A few minutes later, I hear quick footsteps. "Hello?" a man's voice says pleasantly.

"Mr. Myer, this is Father—"

"Ah, Father Greer, Rebecca told me you were on the phone. Thanks for calling me back."

"I apologize for the delay," I say, "but I was hearing confessions and then had—"

"Oh, I understand how busy you are," he says. "I just want to talk to you about this situation with Father McCoy and my sister-in-law."

"Well, as I told Marjorie, I am looking into it and will make a recommendation to the Archbishop based on my findings."

"Yes, yes, I understand," he replies. "I just thought you and I could talk, you know, man to man, to clarify things. I just want to make sure things are handled properly. I don't think the Church in this state can handle another scandal, do you?"

"I agree, but if you don't mind my asking, why are you interested?"

"Why, well, why—Rachel's my sister-in-law," Myer says. "I care about her welfare."

"I understand, but what do you want to talk to me about?"

"I just want you to understand where I'm coming from. I find this entire situation very upsetting."

"Understandable. It is for all of us."

"Yes, I'm sure." He pauses, then says. "Why don't you come to our house tomorrow for lunch?"

I sigh. Lunch after two masses on top of what I've already gone through. But I don't have a good excuse to refuse. That they're racing at Michigan doesn't qualify as a good excuse. Anyway, there's a sixty percent chance of rain in the Irish Hills, so it will probably be delayed.

"That would be fine," I say. "I can be over there at about 1:30 p.m., is that too late?"

"No, no, 1:30 p.m. is fine. I look forward to it."

After I hang up, I look at the clock. It is a little after 6:00 p.m., and from the smells coming from the direction of the kitchen, dinner must be about ready. I start to leave my office when the phone rings.

"Father Tom," Brother Martin says, an edge of concern in his voice.

"Brother Martin, is anything wrong?"

"I don't know," he says. "I looked for Father McCoy at his cabin, but he wasn't there. I noticed his car was gone. I asked around and one of the novices said he saw Father McCoy leave about an hour ago. He didn't tell anyone where he was going."

Six

Mass the next day is uneventful. I am distracted. After speaking to Brother Martin, I had tried calling Father Leonard on his phone, but it went straight to voicemail. He was either out of range—not unusual in the mountains—or had turned his phone off. I'm concerned about why he left the monastery without telling anyone he was leaving or where he was going. I have no idea where he is, but he had not returned to the Rectory by morning. Under other circumstances, I wouldn't be concerned.

But circumstances are far from normal.

The crowds at the 8:30 a.m. and 10:30 a.m. Masses are what I had experienced during my last time at Saint Clare's. The former Mass is smaller, older, and quiet; the later is larger, younger, and loud. There seem to be more children than last time; I count at least four new babies and twice that many pregnant moms. Miriam and Dan Conway are in their traditional pew, along with their four children. Anna is where she always is. Helen is there, in the front pew.

After Mass I stand on the steps greeting the parishioners as they filed past me. Anna comes up. "It's like you never left," she says.

"I'm kind of distracted, to be honest. I'm glad it didn't show."

"Still no word from Father Leonard?"

I shake my head. "No. Not a word. I don't mind telling you, I'm getting a little concerned."

"I'm sure he's fine," Anna says. "How about coming over for lunch, something to take your mind off of things? It's just the leftover lasagna from last night."

I shake my head. "Sorry, I'm going over to the Myers' for lunch, remember?"

"Oh, that's right," Anna says. "I forgot. I'm planning to go to see Joan this afternoon."

I smile. "I'll meet you there, about 4:00 p.m.?"

Anna returns the smile. "That sounds fine. See you then."

I watch her walk off. More people file past, shaking my hand and saying how glad they are to see me. Dan, Miriam, and their kids all stop by to say hello. After about twenty minutes, the crowd has thinned out. I turn to go back inside when I see Helen.

"I'm glad you came," I say to her as she walks up to me.

"I told you I'd be here," she says with a smile. "It was good to see you in action again. As a priest, that is."

"What did you think?"

Helen cocks her head to one side. "Honestly, I still have difficulty seeing you on the altar. Too many memories, you know. But . . . it suits you. It's where you belong."

I smile and nod my head. "It's where I'm happiest, honestly. Saying Mass, being close to the Lord. I feel at peace."

She looks at me quizzically. "Are you, Tom?"

I stiffen a little. "What makes you ask that?"

"You seemed distracted today," Helen says. "Like something is bothering you."

"You still know me too well," I sigh. "This situation with Father Leonard has gotten—well, it's more complicated than I thought it would be."

She shakes her head. "I'm not surprised, Tom. Everyone else here may think he's harmless, but there's something about him that's always struck me as a little . . . off."

"Off? How so?"

"Oh, nothing that would hold up in court," she says with a wry smile. "It's just a gut feeling, I guess you'd say?"

"Well," I say with a frown, "I can't go with a gut feeling."

"Sometimes a gut feeling is all a cop has," she says.

"Really? What does your gut say about me?"

No, I don't know what makes me ask that question. Helen seems as surprised to hear it as I am to have said it.

"Hmm," she says, narrowing her brow. "I'm not sure, yet, Tom. I'll let you know."

We just stand there, looking at each other. Finally, Helen says, "It was good to see you, Tom, but I'm meeting someone for lunch."

"Oh? Anybody I know?" I say with a smile.

She hesitates for a moment before saying, "Brian."

My smile fades in spite of myself. "Oh, yeah. I remember your last email."

"It's just lunch, Tom," she says. "I've just got to put a stop to his constantly trying to get back together with me. I have to make him understand I have no interest in him."

I nod. "Of course," I say. "Well, good luck."

"Thanks, I'll probably need it," she says. Then, realizing what she just said, she stammers. "I mean, well, you know men . . . OK, I'll see you around."

She turns and walks off. My eyes linger on her longer than they should.

Then, I retire to the sacristy, take my vestments off, and prepare for my second major meeting of the day.

***

The Myer Estate was once on the outskirts of Myerton when built in the 1800s. Since then, the town had grown around it, but a large expanse of grounds and a stone wall separate the estate from the surrounding homes. The metal gates open as I drive up. I suppose someone is watching my arrival on a camera somewhere. The driveway curves through a tree-lined lawn leading to the entrance.

The Myer home is a sprawling example of pre-Civil War Greek Revival architecture, added on repeatedly through the years as the family's wealth and influence grew. Two stories with two one-story wings on either side, the house is a whitewashed stone and brick edifice that looks like its builders meant for it to stand as long as the mountains surrounding it. But time has taken its toll. Ivy snakes up its walls, with scaffolding showing the house is undergoing some restoration. The worn roof shows evidence of work being done on it. In the bright July sun, the whole place looks vaguely ominous. In the dark, I imagine it looks like something out of Edgar Allan Poe or Stephen King.

I seriously doubt any monsters ever inhabited the house. The Myer family has been known through the decades for their philanthropy and generosity in the town, and throughout the tri-state area, for generations. More than one hospital wing and college building has the name 'Myer' attached to it. It is hardly a family known for evil.

I park my car and walk up. Before I can ring the doorbell, Rebecca Myer opens the door. I wear my clericals with a black suit coat, appropriate, I thought, for lunch with the Myers family. Rebecca herself is much more casually clad, in tight yoga pants and an oversized t-shirt tied at the waist. She wears no makeup and has gathered her shoulder-length hair in a single ponytail. Had I not known better, I would have thought Rachel Watson was standing before me.

"Welcome, Father Greer," she says, appearing genuinely happy to see me. "Come in. Pardon the mess."

I walk into what had once been an elegant entryway, with a wide staircase going up to a landing on the second floor. I can see where a chandelier once hung, there was now only the chain dangling from the ceiling. A paint-splattered drop cloth covers the floor, and ladders are on either side.

"We're renovating the old place," she explains. "Win wanted to restore the house to the way it was when his great-grandfather was here."

"It seems like an extensive project."

"It is," she says, her smile fading a bit. "It's taken a lot more time and a lot more money than he thought it would. But still, it makes him happy. And the house is historically important. Did you know it was the first house in Myerton wired with electricity? Thomas Edison himself came to oversee the project. This was before the town had a power plant, so Edison constructed a small one on the property. There's a photograph, and the building is still there, on the edge of the woods behind the house." She leads me into a side room, a large living room with several comfortable looking couches and armchairs, one wall lined with bookshelves, the other with photographs, with windows overlooking the front lawn.

"Here it is." She points to an old photograph on the wall. There's the famous inventor himself, standing next to an otherwise nondescript building with a wire coming out of the roof. Next to Edison stands a man, slightly taller, with a moustache and wearing round rimmed glasses.

"That's Win's great-grandfather," Rebecca says, pointing to the other man in the picture.

"I see," I say as I walk along the wall of photographs. Most of them are family pictures, a few are of the house or other houses that I assume were owned by the Myers over the years. There are also photos of various buildings, the Myer name prominent on them; these must be the results of the family philanthropy. Interspersed are more personal photos, family gatherings, funerals, and weddings. Near the end, I see color photos of a more recent wedding. I stop at one photo. Rebecca is in a white wedding dress, long veil, holding a bouquet of pink flowers. She's standing next to a man wearing an Army dress uniform who could have been the twin of the man in the picture standing next to Edison. That man has to be Win Myer. There's little doubt he's a Myer. On either side are bridesmaids and groomsmen—the party numbers twelve, six of each. Standing next to Rebecca is her maid of honor, Win's best man is to his left. I look at the faces of the bridesmaids; they, along with Rebecca, are smiling, showing the joy typically associated with the day.

At the end of the line of young women is Rachel. She's staring straight ahead at the camera. Her face is expressionless.

Another photograph next to it shows the family, the Watsons, with the radiant bride and groom. I recognize Ms. Watson, beaming with pride at the marriage of one of her daughters. A man who must be Rachel and Rebecca's father is there, smiling like a man not used to smiling, looking uncomfortable in his tuxedo. And there's Rachel, with the same expression—or lack of expression.

I am about to ask why Rachel looks so unhappy when Win Myer walks into the room. He's not too changed from the picture. Slightly taller than me, muscular, his sandy blond hair beginning to thin, a man in his early thirties who looks like he's carrying the burdens of a man in his late fifties.

"Sorry, I was taking a phone call," he says. He appears agitated.

"I didn't hear the phone ring," Rebecca comments.

"The call was to my cell phone, not the main phone," he responds, a little abruptly. "More problems from those tree-huggers about the Point Arthur project."

"Oh, why can't they see that you're on their side?" She turns to me. "Win's been trying to move Myer Holdings into clean energy projects. He wants to construct a wind farm just north of town to provide electricity to most of the surrounding area."

"But some environmentalists," Win continues, "want the project stopped. Something about disrupting patterns of bird migration. We've told them all the studies we've commissioned show any disruption will be minimal. Anyway," he smiles, "nice to meet you, Father Greer."

It's cool inside the house, but I see beads of sweat on his forehead. The phone call must have upset him.

"I'll see to lunch," Rebecca says. "It will still be a few minutes. Win, why don't you show Father to your office."

Win nods as she leaves. "Father," Myer turns to me. "Would you like a drink? I have a well-stocked liquor cabinet," he says as he walks out of the room. I follow him into another room, much more masculine, with shelves lined with books. His home office, I assume, from the desk piled with file folders and other papers. He walks up to his liquor cabinet and pulls out two glasses. He uncorks the crystal decanter and pours an amber liquid. "Want one, Father?" he asks me.

"No, thank you," I say. "I don't really drink, but I'll take a cola if you have one."

He gives me a slightly disdainful look, but he smiles and says, "Of course, Father." He reaches into the mini fridge and pulls out a can. He pours the cola over some ice and walks over, handing me the glass.

"Please," Myer says, showing two chairs. We sit and he leans back, nursing his drink.

"I appreciate you coming over," Myer says.

"Thank you for inviting me," I say. "Lovely room. This is quite a house. Rebecca says you're restoring it."

"Yes, this is my passion project. Getting the family estate back up to snuff. Like it was in great-grandfather's day, back when the Myer name meant something around here."

"Well, I still think it does," I say. "Your family name is on the town, on the college, which I still believe you're on the board of trustees for."

"And a still significant source of donations," Myer adds. "But as the overall percentage, not nearly what it was in the past."

"Where did you get the idea to restore the home?"

"Oh, that was Marjorie's idea."

"Marjorie?"

"Rebecca's mother, Marjorie. Yes, she wanted her daughter to live here after our marriage. You see, Father, the old place had gotten so run-down that we had decided to get another place in the new development on the other side of town—it's really too big for just two people—but Marjorie had her heart set on seeing us live here. So she persuaded me to restore the estate." He sipped his drink. "It's been a haul, and I've spent quite a bit of money, but we're pleased."

"And you're living here during the renovation? That doesn't sound too convenient."

Myer shrugged. "It is what it is. But I didn't have you come here to talk about the house." He puts his drink on the table beside his chair. "What are we going to do about this situation with Father McCoy and Rachel?"

"As I told you on the phone, Mr. Myer—"

"Win," he says. "Call me Win."

I say, "As I told you on the phone, Win, I'm looking into the allegations and will recommend to the Archbishop the appropriate course of action, depending on what I determine."

"And what have you determined?"

I pause before answering, "I will not share that with you. I'm still looking into it." I could not tell him what I had found out, what Rachel had told me, and I needed to talk to Father Leonard again.

"I see," he replies. He sits back in the leather armchair. "So tell me, Father," he says, "What will it take?"

"I don't understand?"

"Oh really, Father Greer. You know what I'm saying. But I'll be a little more explicit. You know my family has been a member of Saint Clare's for generations. I was baptized there and, even though the family's not really been religious, over the years we've donated to the parish. You know, my great-great grandfather oversaw the reconstruction of the church after the original building burned in the 1850s. It's a place of historical importance, you know, one of the oldest in this part of Maryland, one of the few surviving examples of Ionic-style churches."

"I'm aware of both the church's history and your family's relationship with it."

"It's a relationship I've been glad to continue," Win goes on. "You know, Rebecca grew up in Saint Clare's, that's where we were married, so she still has a lot of affection for the place. I've made several sizable donations over the years. Mostly anonymous, mind you." He sipped his drink. "I've been by the church many times and know that the church needs repair. The roof, for example, needs replacing. On a structure that old and that big, that will add up to some money. It would take you years of bingo and rummage sales to raise the amount needed. Now I," he touches his chest, "could write you a check for the full amount today. You'd have no worries."

"I see," I say quietly.

"I think King Henry IV of France said, 'Paris is worth a Mass.' Don't you think a new roof for Saint Clare's is worth one priest? I mean, don't the needs of the many outweigh the needs of the few?"

I smile. "Or the one?"

Win returns my smile and toasts me with his glass. "Very good, Father Greer. Not that many people these days would get the reference."

I fold my hands in front of me. "Can I ask why you're so interested in this? Why are you so eager to see Father McCoy transferred out of Saint Clare's?"

"Ah," he says. He stands and goes to pour himself another drink. "I understand why you would wonder about that. A big part of it is because she's my sister-in-law. I have a great deal of affection for her, always have. She's like the little sister I've never had. That's one reason I agreed to spy on them when Marjorie asked me. But truth be told, Father, there's more to it than that." He sits back down, the ice clinking in his glass as he slowly twirls his drink. "I suppose I feel guilty."

"Guilty?" I say.

"Yes, for my role in this whole thing," Win says, "The fact of the matter is, Father Greer, that I'm responsible for getting Rachel the job."

"I was aware you met with Father McCoy and gave the Church a sizable donation. So it was to persuade him to give Rachel the parish secretary's job?"

"Yes," he replies. "I didn't persuade, really, I just pointed out how qualified Rachel was, given her education and background. And considering she wanted to become a nun."

"I didn't think the family supported that?"

"Oh," he waves his hand, "no, we don't, not at all. But Rachel wanted the job, so I thought—"

"Wait," I interrupt. "Did Rachel ask you to talk to Father Leonard?"

"Ask me? She practically begged me. It was a couple of months after she had moved back to Myerton to take a program manager's job at one of the tech firms outside town. She called me one day saying Saint Clare's was looking for a new parish secretary and asked me to talk to Father Leonard about giving her the job."

"Did she say why she wanted the job?"

"Oh, she said something about wanting more time to pray, to attend daily Mass. I pointed out it'd be a huge pay cut for her, but she said she had more than enough savings to make up for any shortfall. She told me it wouldn't be for very long, anyway."

"What do you think she meant by that?"

He shrugs. "I guess because she'd be entering the convent soon." I saw a touch of sadness enter his eyes.

"So you met with Father Leonard," I say. "And did you mention how much money you'd given in the past?"

"Well," he smiles sheepishly, "I'm afraid I may have alluded to it. Until I mentioned the donation, Father Leonard was very reluctant to say he'd even interview Rachel. I got the impression that he really didn't want her to have the position."

I found that interesting, considering the warmth Father Leonard expressed about Rachel in our first meeting. "I'm sure he appreciated your generosity," I say. "But I doubt he gave Rachel the job because of it."

Win shrugs. "Perhaps, perhaps not. But I feel I contributed to whatever happened and I want to fix it."

"Well," I say, "I can't tell you everything, but let me put your mind at ease. I've found no evidence that Father Leonard abused his position to take advantage of Rachel." I told the strict truth. But not the whole truth.

"I hope he didn't," Win says, his face darkening. "Every time I think about the possibility of that sweet, innocent girl being taken advantage of, I just get so . . . so . . . " He stops and clears his throat. "Anyway, Father, about Father Leonard . . . "

I put my hand up. "I understand your concern, Win, I really do. I can imagine being in your position. But my duty here is to report to the Archbishop whatever I find, good or bad. I won't be persuaded to bend my report towards any particular recommendation."

Win smiles and opens his arms. "You can't blame a guy for trying, Father. No hard feelings, I hope?"

"Not on my part," I say.

"Good, good. I guess I'll just have to trust your integrity." He stands. "Shall we meet Rebecca? I'm sure lunch is ready by now."

***

After a very fine and convivial lunch, I say I have another appointment that afternoon. Win thanks me for coming and says he has some business calls to make. Rebecca walks me to the door.

"Thank you for coming," Rebecca says. "I hope Win didn't press you too much about Father McCoy."

"He was direct about it," I say. "I understand where he's coming from. He cares about your sister very much."

She gives a short laugh. "Oh yes, Win cares about Rachel, that's for sure." At my raised eyebrows, she shakes her head. "Never mind, Father. It's nothing. Thanks for coming."

Seven

"Sounds like you had a pleasant visit," Anna says. "Phew, it's a hot one today!"

We're walking up the hill at the cemetery towards the old oak tree that shades Joan's grave. Anna is carrying a vase; I'm carrying a bunch of peppermint carnations, Joan's favorite flower. The sky is a clear blue, and the sun is beaming down on us, baking us in the still air. I'm glad I changed out of my clericals into shorts and a polo shirt before making the trek.

"Oh, it was. Very nice. Lunch was delicious, and both of them were very pleasant. I'm just trying to get my mind around Win Myer's interest in all of this. I'm not sure Rebecca likes it too much."

"He really must care about Rachel."

"He cares about something, I'm just not sure what. What do you know about their background?"

She stops and turns to me. "Now, Tom, why would you think I'd know anything? I've never even really met them."

"Because, Anna, I know you gather information the way a squirrel gathers nuts for the winter."

"You make me sound like an old gossip," she huffs.

"You're not old, and a gossip talks. You just listen. At least that's what Joan always told me." We get to the grave. Anna leans over and puts the vase down, allowing me to place the flowers inside. She takes a bottle of water out of her bag and pours the contents in. We stand quietly for a few minutes, looking at the marble headstone gleaming in the light. I pull out my prayer book and begin reciting the prayers for visiting a graveside. At the end, we cross ourselves. I bend over and kiss the headstone and say, "I love you, Joan." Anna gently strokes the stone.

Walking back to the car, Anna says, "I don't know that much about the families, other than what everyone knows about the Myers."

"Win Myer is an only child, I take it?"

She nods. "Yes, a later-life one, apparently. Both of his parents are dead; he inherited the entire Myer family business when he was in his mid-twenties. He and Rebecca were high school sweethearts from what I understand."

"He went to school here in Myerton? He didn't go to a fancy prep school in Baltimore or D.C.?"

Anna shakes her head. "Apparently not. He attended Myerton High School. Regular big man on campus, football starter, academic all-star, graduated valedictorian. I think he was in ROTC in college because I heard he served in Afghanistan for a while. He married Rebecca before going overseas. Then his parents died, he left the Army, moved back home, and took over the family businesses."

"Are the Watsons a wealthy family?"

"Hardly," she says. "But from what I understand, Majorie Watson really advocated the two getting married. But it wasn't that hard, as I say, since they had dated in high school."

"Any idea why he'd take such an interest in this situation?"

She shrugs. "Rebecca loves her sister. I guess he's just concerned on his sister's behalf."

I shake my head. "It just seems odd to me. Rebecca and her mother are both concerned, but there's something about Win Myer's interest that strikes me as different." I pause. "He admitted asking Father Leonard to give Rachel the job."

"Well, that explains things, but why did he do that?"

"According to him, Rachel begged him to talk to Father Leonard on her behalf."

She stopped and looked at me. "Really?" Anna thinks for a minute. "There really was no need; she was qualified. She must have wanted the job a lot."

I nod my head. "I accept her explanation why she wanted the job."

"Do I hear a but?"

"But," I continue, "why did she want so desperately to work here that she'd have her very wealthy and successful brother-in-law take time out of his busy schedule to intercede on her behalf? And why would he do it?" I shake my head.

"Tom," Anna says warily. "What are you doing?"

I look at her. "What do you mean?"

"It sounds like you're looking for a complicated explanation when a simple one will do. What do they call it, Occam's Razor?"

I laugh. "Sorry, you're right. I'm overthinking things. It's probably just as everyone has said," I say to her.

But inside, I'm thinking there's something off.

"Well, anyway," I continue, "I need to talk to Father Leonard."

"I'm surprised he's not back by now," Anna comments.

I hesitate. "He's probably just getting some peace and quiet at Our Lady of the Mount. I wasn't expecting him until tomorrow, anyway."

Anna nods. "That's good. If there's one thing that young man needs, it's peace and quiet."

"I just need him to come back so I can put this whole matter to bed," I say before I can think.

"Rather unfortunate choice of words, isn't it?"

I sigh and wipe my sweaty brow. "It's the heat. Anyway, the sooner Father Leonard gets back here, the sooner I can resolve this situation."

We get to the car. Before opening the door, I look at Anna. "What do you think the hardest part of being a priest is?"

Anna looks at me, thinking. "Toddlers rushing the altar during the consecration?"

I laugh. "Believe it or not, that's not at the top of the list." I pause. "It's loneliness."

"What do you mean?" Anna says, getting into the car.

"I mean, it's a very lonely job. After a hard day, I come back to the Rectory and there's no one there to greet me, no one to ask me how my day was, no one who seems happy to see me." I pause. "I guess for me that's been the biggest adjustment. I know what it's like, more than most other priests, to have that."

She pats my hand. "Maybe you should get a dog."

I look at her and chuckle. "No, thank you. I don't like dogs."

Anna looks at me. "What prompted this?"

"Oh, I don't know, just thinking. If Father Leonard and Rachel got too close, too close for a priest, I think I understand how it could happen." I look at her. "Not that it would be right. But, understandable." I sigh and start the car.

"Well, in this case, I think you're on safe ground. If there's one priest I know who would never break his vows, it's Father Leonard McCoy."

***

Loud ringing jars me out of a deep sleep. The time on my phone says it's 11:30 p.m. It's not my cell phone ringing, but the Rectory phone by my bed. I fumble for the receiver.

"Saint Clare's Parish," I yawn, "Father—"

"Father Tom!" says a breathless voice on the other end. It's Father Leonard. "Father Tom! I . . . I . . . oh, Holy Mother of God . . . oh, my dear Jesus . . ."

"Leonard, Leonard!" I say into the phone, fully awake now. "What's wrong, where are you?"

"I'm, I'm here . . . oh, Tom, it's horrible. Something terrible has happened. Oh, Saint Michael, pray for me!"

"Where are you?"

"Where am I? Where am I?" I hear only breathing on the other end of the phone. "I'm, I'm at her townhouse. Oh, dear Jesus!"

"Whose townhouse? Rachel Watson's?"

"Yes, yes! Please hurry? Oh, my Lord!" I hear the phone drop to the floor. He's dissolved into hysterical sobs.

"Leonard! Leonard!" I hang the phone up and throw on my clothes. I'm halfway down the stairs when I realize I have no idea where Rachel Watson lives. I dash into the office. After a five-minute search, I find her address. She's about ten minutes from the Rectory.

I sprint to my car and peel out of the Rectory driveway. I make the ten-minute trip in less than seven owing to the lack of traffic at that time of day. Father Leonard's car is parked outside the address, a small townhouse in a row of townhouses of recent construction. There is no one around.

I walk up to the door and am about to knock when I hear a sound coming from inside. Putting my ear to the door, I hear muffled sobs. The door is not completely shut and opens as I lean against it and step inside.

It's dark in Rachel's home, the only light coming from streetlights filtered by drawn shades. I follow the sound of Father Leonard's crying down the short entry hallway. The way the townhouse is constructed, the main living room area is up a flight of steps. I walk softly up the steps, Father Leonard's sobs getting louder and louder.

I reach the top of the stairs. I see two indistinct forms in the dim light. My hand searches along the wall for a light switch. Finding what I'm looking for, I flick the lights on. They illuminate the room.

What I see chills me to the bone.

Father Leonard is sitting on the floor, his arms wrapped around his legs in a fetal position, his head down, his body wracked with sobs.

Laying on the floor beside him is the lifeless body of Rachel Watson.

Eight

I stand frozen in place, transfixed by the sight. The only sounds in the room are Father Leonard's sobs. Outside I can hear the cacophony of a summer night, crickets chirping along with the other nocturnal creatures.

I move slowly towards Rachel. She's lying on her back, arms down by her side, her lifeless eyes staring into space. Blood has soaked the carpet. Tentatively, I touch the red blot. It's already dried. She's been dead for some time.

I pull out my prayer book and begin to say the necessary prayers over her. After a few minutes, I make the sign of the cross. Then, I go to check on Father Leonard. He's stopped crying, but now he's staring into the distance.

I kneel beside him. "Leonard," I touch his shoulder and whisper his name. He does not respond, doesn't blink. "Leonard," I say louder, shaking him gently. He still doesn't respond.

As I stand and reach in my pocket for my phone, a glint of light catches my sight. It's a kitchen knife, about six inches long, covered in blood. It's on the floor, about a foot from Father Leonard.

I dial 911 and tell them what's happened. They say they'll send the police and an ambulance.

"There's no hurry on the ambulance," I say softly. "It's already too late."

When I finish talking to 911, I make another call.

"Detective Parr," I hear Helen yawn. "Someone had better be dead."

If the sight before me wasn't so horrific, I would laugh. I forgot that Helen wakes up with a disposition somewhere between Godzilla rampaging through Tokyo and a grizzly bear poked with a stick.

"Someone is, Helen, otherwise I wouldn't call you at this hour," I say gravely.

"Tom? What the hell!" she says. "Why are you calling me at . . . do you know what time it is? What is it? Did you say someone's dead?"

"Yes," I say, and describe the situation briefly.

"What's the address?" I hear her writing Rachel's address down. "You've called 911? I'll be there in about twenty minutes. Touch nothing, Tom. And don't move Father Leonard until someone gets there."

I look at the pathetic man, still curled up in a ball. "That'll be no problem. I doubt I could get him to move if the house was on fire."

While I wait, I take the time to look around Rachel's home, being careful not to disturb anything. She is—was—an impeccable housekeeper. There is a place for everything, and everything is in its place. Her place bears no evidence of a violent act having taken place a short while ago. Except, of course, for the dead body and pool of blood.

I walk into the living room. Again, the room is clean, with not a thing out of place. An empty vase sits in the middle of a simple wood coffee table, the table itself flanked by a sofa and a loveseat, with an armchair opposite. There are pictures on the wall, a couple of mountain scenes. There are several photographs. Two are copies of the photos from Rebecca's wedding. Others are of a younger Rachel, obviously in college, with groups of other young women at different parties. Unlike the wedding photographs, she is smiling, even laughing.

I walk from the living room to the kitchen. There is a knife block on the counter, one knife missing. I shudder. Whoever killed her did so with one of her own knives.

Handwritten notes cover the refrigerator. To do lists, the beginnings of a grocery list, a reminder of a doctor's appointment from two weeks before. I study the grocery list. Bread, eggs, milk, assorted fresh vegetables, nothing out of the ordinary.

"Police," I hear from downstairs. "We're coming up. Keep your hands where we can see them." I slowly walk out of the kitchen with my hands out so they're easily seen.

"I'm unarmed," I call. "I'm Father Tom Greer from Saint Clare's Parish. I called 911."

"Father Tom?" a familiar voice says. In a minute, Dan Conway, his sidearm in his hand, comes up the staircase. "It's okay," he calls down the stairs. Holstering his weapons, he approaches me.

"Are you all right, Father?" he asks. Behind him, I see other officers followed by two paramedics. One walks to Rachel, kneels down, and checks for a pulse. "She's gone," she says.

Dan looks at Father Leonard. "Is he hurt?"

I shake my head. "I don't know. He hasn't said a word to me since I got here."

To the paramedics, Dan says, "Check him out."

The other paramedic squats in front of Father Leonard. He says, "Sir, sir, can you hear me? Are you injured?" Father Leonard says nothing. The paramedic checks his eyes with a penlight. "Pupils are equal and reactive. You say he has said nothing?"

"Not since I got here," I answer.

"Julie, help me get him up." The paramedics each take an arm and help Father Leonard to his feet. It's only when Leonard stands that I see he's not wearing his clericals. Instead, he's wearing a white polo shirt and khaki trousers.

The shirt is covered in blood. As are his hands.

***

Red and blue lights flash in the darkness. The normal 3:00 a.m. summer stillness is pierced by the sounds of movement, calls across the parking lot, and uniformed police officers scurrying about, wrapping the area around Rachel Watson's townhouse in yellow crime scene tape. Some of her neighbors, awakened by the commotion, have gathered on the sidewalk. Others stand in their doorways. A few peek out of their windows. All want a glimpse of what's going on. A steady murmur joins the chirping of crickets and the light squeaks of bats flying through the moonlit sky.

I'm sitting next to Father Leonard in the open door of the ambulance. A blanket's around his shoulders. He stares straight ahead into the distance. I see his lips moving, but cannot tell what he's saying. Praying, I suppose.

Close to thirty minutes after I called her, Helen arrives. She looks in my direction before going into the townhouse. The murmur of the crowd dies down. I look up. The technicians from the medical examiner's office are wheeling out a gurney carrying a black bag. I know the bag contains Rachel Watson. Helen is coming out behind it, then walks past it to where I am sitting.

"Do you want to give her last rites before they take her?" she asks.

"I said the prayers before y'all arrived," I reply.

Helen looks at Father Leonard. "How's he doing?"

I shake my head. "I don't know. He hasn't said a word since I got here."

"What was he doing here, Tom?"

I tell her about the phone call, about coming to Rachel's townhouse, and describe the scene that greeted me when I arrived. Helen notes that down in her notebook.

"But what was he doing in her place at 11:30 p.m.?" she says, pointing to Leonard.

"I don't know, he didn't tell me on the phone," I say, telling Helen the exact truth.

Helen fixes me with a look. "Hmm," she says. "Why do I feel there's something you're not telling me?"

"Helen," I say slowly. "I can't tell you some things. But I'm telling you the truth when I say Leonard did not tell me why he was in Rachel Watson's apartment."

She taps her notebook with her pen. "Are we going to go through this again, Tom? If you have information pertinent to this, you need to tell me." She pauses. "Unless—oh, hell!" she yells, causing people to stop and look in her direction. "Get back to work, nothing to see here," she hollers at the officers and technicians, who quickly get back to work.

"He confessed to you, didn't he?" she said, pointing to Leonard.

"No," I shake my head vigorously. "No, Helen, he hasn't told me anything. That, I can assure you."

"But there is something, isn't there?" She looks to that coroner's van as they're loading Rachel. Helen turns back to me. "Her?"

"You know I can't answer that" I say.

"Detective Parr," one of the paramedics interrupts us, "you wanted to know about Father McCoy's condition?"

"Yes," Helen says. Pointing with her pen she says, "Is that blood his?"

"He has no wounds, there's not a mark on him. There doesn't seem to be anything physically wrong with him."

"So why's he like this?"

The paramedic looks at Leonard and shrugs. "Shock, pure and simple. We should take him to the hospital, just to have him checked out."

"Fine," Helen says. Looking at me, she asks, "I assume you'll ride with him?"

"If that's all right?" I say to the paramedic, who nods. The other paramedic joins us, and the two help Leonard into the ambulance. I'm about to climb in when Helen touches me on the shoulder.

"Listen," she whispers. "I understand, Tom. But if you know something, even if it implicates him, I need to know."

I sigh and nod. "I'll tell you what I can, I promise."

The paramedic closes the doors behind me. I sit on a metal box and look out the window to see Helen watching us as we drive off.

**

At Myerton General, the paramedics take Leonard into the Emergency Room, where the doctor examines him. The young priest has no other injuries.

"So there's nothing physical that could cause this?" I say, pointing to Leonard. He's still said nothing, still stares straight ahead except for the occasional blink.

The doctor says, "No, there's nothing physically wrong with him. I'd say this is psychological, a severe emotional shock." She writes something on her tablet. "I will admit him for 24 hours of observation and ask the psychiatrist to have a look." She leaves to put the order in for a room.

When she leaves, a young uniformed officer comes into the room with a paper bag. "Father, we're supposed to get his clothes. They're evidence."

"He's in no condition to help with that," I say. "I must help if that's all right."

He nods and hands me a pair of gloves. Carefully, we remove Leonard's blood-soaked shirt and place it in the bag. He's wearing a brown scapular of Our Lady of Mount Carmel, a sign of his devotion to Mary; it's become stiff with blood. His chest has blood on it. I guess the nurses will wash him later. Next, his shoes and socks, followed by his pants and underwear. Trying to maintain as much of his dignity as possible, the officer and I put a hospital gown around him. During the entire process Leonard says nothing, but responds when we ask him to move.

The officer closes the bag and seals it with red evidence tape. Nodding at me, he leaves, acknowledging the other officer who is now standing outside the examination room.

It's about an hour before they move Leonard to a room. Once there, the nurse fluffs his pillows and tucks him in, Leonard as compliant as a small child. She leaves, then comes back with a tray containing a syringe.

"The doctor ordered a sedative to help him sleep," she explains. I look out the window. The sun is rising over the mountains, the entire sky an orange glow. She jabs Leonard with the needle, and in a few minutes, his eyes close and I hear him snoring quietly.

I sit, watching him sleep, and wonder what I will do next.

Nine

A hand on my shoulder and a familiar whiff of vanilla cause me to open my eyes and sit up. I don't realize where I am for a moment. Then, as the fog lifts, I look around and see the hospital bed containing a still-sleeping Father Leonard. Sun is streaming through the windows. And Helen is looking down at me, holding two cups of coffee.

"Here," she says, handing me one cup. "I thought you could use this."

"Thanks," I say, taking the cup and sipping the coffee. Sweet, strong, and creamy. I close my eyes and feel myself reviving.

"What time is it?" I ask.

"A little after 8:00 a.m.," she says. "I came over after we wrapped up at the scene."

"Find anything?" I ask as I drink.

"Lots of blood. And the murder weapon," she says. "A kitchen knife, from the knife block in her kitchen. Whoever killed her didn't plan it, used what was easily at hand."

I nod. "I saw it on the floor."

"Also," she says, then takes a drink of her coffee, "no signs of forced entry, so whoever it was she let them in." She pauses and looks at me. "Like she knew her killer."

"Not necessarily," I point out. "Her killer could have picked the lock on her door, or maybe she left the door unlocked."

"You're saying a robbery gone wrong?" Helen says. "That's a theory, I suppose. We'll check with her family to see if anything was taken. But I don't think so."

"Why?"

"Three reasons," she holds up a finger. "One, whoever killed her used a knife from her kitchen, which means the killer didn't bring it. Also, for a robber, a knife is a very clumsy weapon to use in the dark. Two, the place is clean. Not just clean—immaculate, like she just finished cleaning it before her murder. And three, it looks like she was expecting someone."

"How can you tell?"

"The two packed suitcases in her bedroom."

I open my mouth to speak. I hadn't gone into her bedroom.

"Was she taking a trip?"

I pause for a moment. "Well," I say slowly, "I may have heard something. Ask her family."

"Wasn't she the parish secretary? She'd have to let you know."

"Well, I'm not—"

"No," Helen says slowly, "but you're at Saint Clare's with some thin excuse about giving him," she points to Father Leonard, still sleeping, "a break. But both you and I know it's something to do with him and the victim."

I nod my head. "I need to speak to the Archbishop before I can say any more."

"Is Father Leonard in some kind of trouble?"

"Honestly, I don't know. He may be. Some things I learned I cannot tell you." Nodding to Leonard. "You'll have to ask him yourself."

Helen nods and looks at Father Leonard. "The nurse told me he's still sedated. Did he say anything to you?"

I shake my head. "He hasn't said a word since he called me, and I told you everything about that."

"So no idea why he was in her townhouse?"

"I didn't even know he was back in Myerton. He had gone to the monastery for a personal retreat." I pause, struggling with what I know. But I can't keep it from her, not this, because I'm concerned about how it looks. "I called the monastery and spoke to Brother Martin. I told him I needed to speak to Father Leonard. He called me back later, saying that one of the other Brothers had seen him leave. He had let no one know where he was going." I pause. "He didn't answer his phone when I tried to call him."

She's been making notes in her notebook. "So the first time you heard from him since—when, Friday?—was when he called you late last night."

"That's right."

At that moment, my phone buzzes. I grab it out of my pocket. It's Anna.

"Good morning," I say, trying to sound as nonchalant as possible.

"What's happened, Tom?" Anna asks.

"What do you mean?"

"What I mean is, one, why is there no priest here to say the 8:00 a.m. Mass?"

I sit up and look at the clock on the wall. It's 8:15 a.m..

"Oh, gosh, Anna, I'm—"

"And two, why are there reporters crawling all over Saint Clare's?"

I look at Helen. "Reporters?"

"Yes, at least three news trucks from Frederick and Baltimore. Nate Rodriguez is here too—wait, he's coming this way. Hold on." Through the phone, I can hear murmuring as Anna speaks with Nate. The next voice I hear is not Anna's, but Nate's.

"Father Tom," he says excitedly, "did you discover Rachel Watson's body? Was Father McCoy found standing over her? Can I get a statement?"

"No, Nate, you cannot get a statement from me," I say firmly. "Now give the phone back to Mrs. Luckgold, please."

"But Father—."

"Now, Nate," I say as Helen rolls her eyes. I give her a questioning look and she mouths, "Pain in the neck."

"Tom," Anna says, "Rachel's dead?"

"Yes, that's true. I'll explain when I get there." I hang up and say to Helen, "There's a circus going on at the Church. I'd better get over there." I look at Father Leonard, who's still sound asleep, then at her.

"I won't question him without you," she says, reading my mind. "But I need to know the background to this, Tom. I need to know exactly what prompted His Eminence to send you here."

"I'll get the Archbishop's okay, I promise. But I'm sure it has nothing to do with this."

But in fact, I'm not at all sure.

***

A circus is an orderly affair compared to what greets me when I arrive at Saint Clare's.

Six news vans, two from Baltimore, one from Frederick, a couple from D.C., and one from a Pennsylvania station have all converged on Myerton like moths drawn to a flame. Reporters are dispersed along the sidewalk in front of the parish grounds, each speaking into their microphones while cameramen transmit their images back to their studios live, providing viewers with their morning mayhem to go with their shredded wheat or avocado toast. Other reporters, probably representing newspapers, mill around with their recorders and notepads.

Among them I see Nate, who has both a camera and a notebook. I wonder again what he's doing there. Last I heard, he was selling the documentary he made about Joan's murder to some online company out of New York, but I don't know if it ever aired. The monastery has Internet, but allows no streaming.

As I pull into the driveway, the gaggle of reporters spot me and run in my direction. The TV reporters all turn and move their cameras towards the Rectory. I'm surrounded by men and women shouting questions and shoving recorders in my face as I try to get out of the car. Nate shoves his way through and pushes the crowd back.

"Let Father Tom get out of his car," he yells, "I'm sure he'll talk to us as soon as he gets out of the car." Everyone moves back enough to allow me to get the door open. I get out and start walking towards the Rectory. The gaggle follows, shouting questions.

"A comment, Father Greer?"

"We understand that the victim was the parish secretary, is that true?"

"Is Father McCoy a suspect?"

"Does the Archdiocese have a statement?"

At the door to the Rectory, I turn a motion for quiet. "I understand you have a job to do," I say. "All I ask is that you keep in mind this is a place of worship, so please be respectful of the property and the people who come here to pray. Please do not ask them questions."

"Is Father McCoy a suspect?"

"You must ask the police about that."

"Is it true you found him sitting beside Rachel Watson's body?"

I look at the reporter who asked the last question. "I have no further comment at this time." I turn to go into the Rectory as the gaggle continues to shout questions at me. Anna closes the door behind me.

With a look of concern she asks, "Are you okay?"

I run a hand through my hair. "About as well as can be expected, I guess. I need a shower and some coffee."

She hands me a cup. "Here, I poured this when I saw you drive up. Do you want me to call the police, to get them off the grounds?"

I look out the window and shake my head. "No, they're back on the sidewalk, and as long as they don't harass any of the parishioners, we'll leave them alone."

"They probably know you don't like reporters," Anna says with a smile, "and don't want their equipment broken."

I forced the last reporter I dealt with off church property and broke her camera. She later wound up dead, but that had nothing to do with me.

"So it's true. Rachel's been murdered."

I walk into the living room with my coffee and plop into an armchair. I lean my head back. "Yes, it's true."

"How's Father Leonard involved?"

"I don't know."

"But you found him sitting next to the body, didn't you?"

I recount the phone call from the hysterical prelate and what I found when I got to her apartment.

"He hasn't said a word to anyone. Doctors say he's in shock. They have him sedated right now."

"And he didn't tell you why he was over there?"

I shake my head. "No. Maybe when he wakes up."

I hear a knock come from the kitchen. Anna and I look at each other.

"I'll go see, maybe it's a parishioner," Anna says getting up. She goes into the kitchen and returns a minute later. "It's Nate," she says with a sigh.

"Just let him in," I say. "By the way, what's he doing now?"

"I think I heard he started a news vlog, focusing on crime and investigations." Anna goes back into the kitchen and returns a minute later, Nate Rodriguez in tow, complete with the familiar frantic excitement.

"Father Tom, thanks for talking to me."

"No, Nate, I'm not talking to you, I just let you in because I want to ask you something."

"Okay, sure, anything."

"How did you find out I found the body?"

Nate shrugs. "The reporter who asked you the question. She's pretty well established with sources, even in Myerton. Probably has a source in the police department or the State Attorney's office."

It really doesn't matter how they found out. The news would have gotten out, eventually. The problem is, I have not had the chance to speak with the Archbishop. He is the one person in Maryland who needs to know the most, and would not appreciate learning the news secondhand.

I excuse myself and go to the office. Picking up the phone, I dial the Archdiocese.

The Archbishop's secretary puts me through right away.

"Hello, Father Tom, I was going to call you later," he says. "Bring me up to speed. What have you found out so far?"

He hasn't heard yet, I think. *Good.*

"Something's come up, Your Eminence," I say slowly. "Something you need to know before you hear about it from someone else."

Silence. "What?" the Archbishop says gravely.

"Rachel Watson. She's been murdered."

I hear nothing but breathing coming from the other end of the phone. "How horrible, just horrible. She was young, wasn't she? Terrible for her family, to lose someone like that, though I suppose you would know better than most, Father."

"Yes," I mumble.

"What was it, a robbery?"

I take a deep breath. "The police don't know yet, but there's more."

He says nothing for a moment, then whispers, "Holy Mother of God. Don't tell me, Tom."

I spend the next fifteen minutes recounting the events of the last twenty-four hours. About Father Leonard's mysterious departure from the monastery. About his frantic call to me. About what I found when I arrived at Rachel Watson's apartment. About Father Leonard's condition.

"As far as I know," I conclude, "he's still asleep."

"And you say he's said nothing since you found him."

"The last time he's spoken a word was on the phone to me."

The Archbishop sighs. "Do you think the police see him as a suspect?"

"I'm not sure. Detective Parr—"

"Is she leading the investigation?" the Archbishop asks.

"She's the lead detective in Myerton—actually, I believe she's the only detective in Myerton—so of course she'd head the investigation."

"She's the one you worked with a few months ago, isn't she?"

"Yes."

"Do you have a good relationship with her?"

I pause before answering. Should I tell him everything, that the reason I know Detective Parr is because I once loved her and was engaged to marry her? Or should I keep that quiet for now. After all, it's not really relevant.

Is it?

"Father Tom? Are you still there?" Archbishop Knowland asks over the phone.

"Yes, yes, I'm still here," I say. "We have a good relationship, yes."

"Didn't you say she attends Saint Clare's?"

"Yes. And to anticipate your next question, she has heard the rumors about Father Leonard and Rachel Watson."

The Archbishop sighs. "Well, she was bound to find out sooner or later. I assume she figured out why you're there?"

"I said nothing to her, and she doesn't know the specifics. But she surmised that my being here has something to do with Father McCoy. She is a detective. An excellent one."

""Do you think she'll give Father Leonard a fair shake?"

"One thing I can assure you about Helen," I say, "is that she's a woman of integrity and strong convictions. She'll follow the evidence no matter where it goes."

He takes a deep breath. "I cannot ask for anything more than that. Tell her I appreciate her work, and that she can expect full cooperation from the Church." He pauses. "Do you think Father Leonard has anything to do with this young woman's murder?"

"No, sir, I really don't."

"So what was he doing over at her apartment at that time of night?"

"I don't know. I won't know until I talk to him." I pause. "The police will talk to him."

"You make sure you're there when Detective Parr questions him. In the meantime, I will contact the lawyers, see what I should do at this point." He pauses a moment. "I'm putting Father Leonard on administrative leave. Tom, you're in charge of Saint Clare's until this whole matter is cleared up."

"I understand, sir." I was about to hang up when the Archbishop says, "What did you find out? About the reason I sent you there in the first place? Was there any truth to the original allegation?"

I think for a moment. Before I can answer, the Archbishop says, 'No, never mind. Forget I asked. It's better if I don't know. God bless."

I hang up the phone and lean in my office chair. There's a painting of Saint John Vianney, the patron saint of priests, on the wall.

"Dear Saint John Vianney," I mutter, "please pray for Father Leonard." Then, "And for me. I need all the help I can get."

Ten

I've just finished saying Noon Mass when Helen calls.

"What are you doing this afternoon?" she asks.

"What did you have in mind? Lunch? I have a hankering for a chilled tomato bisque. I hear The Bistro serves a good one."

"Nothing so enjoyable, though it sounds tempting," she laughs. "I was wondering if you could be there when I talk to the Watsons."

I stop. With all my concerns over Father Leonard, I had completely forgotten about the Watsons. They had lost a daughter, violently, unexpectedly. They were in shock, grieving, possibly despondent.

I knew their feelings all too well. I should go, offer my condolences, give them some spiritual comfort.

"I'm not sure they would enjoy seeing me," I say. "The one time I've talked to Rachel's mother didn't go so well."

"When did you meet her—wait, don't answer that," Helen says. "It's the thing you can't tell me unless the Archbishop gives you permission, isn't it?" She pauses. "Well, did he?"

"He told me to tell you the Archdiocese would cooperate in any way possible"

"So you can tell me?"

"Yes," I say. "I'll get you the document, but I was sent here in response to an anonymous letter that alleged inappropriate behavior on Father Leonard's part with Rachel Watson. You should also know I've learned that it was Rachel's mother, Marjorie Watson, who sent the letter. I cannot tell you anything else I learned."

Helen takes a deep breath. "Whoa," she says. "That's motive, you know?"

"Now, Helen—"

"What else did the Archbishop say?"

"He's appointed me to the parish and placed Father Leonard on administrative leave."

"That shouldn't surprise you, Tom," she says. "The parish can't have a murder suspect saying Mass now, can they?"

"So he is a suspect," I say.

"Of course he's a suspect, the person who finds the body is always the first suspect."

"By that measure," I comment, "I should be a suspect."

"Technically, you didn't find the body, you found Father Leonard with the body, so unless you did it and you staged the scene to frame him, then no, you're not a suspect. You're not that clever."

"I don't know whether or not to be insulted," I say. I put my phone on speaker and continue removing my Mass vestments. "But I'm still not sure my being there is the best idea."

Helen didn't speak for a minute. Then she sighs. "Look, truth is—I want you there. It would help me out. The part of this job I've never been good at is—well, is the first interview with the victim's family. I always send a uniformed officer to do the initial notification, putting it off as much as possible. It brings back too many memories of when someone came and told me John was dead. Honestly, doing it scares me."

"I'm surprised to hear you say that," I say. "When we were together, nothing scared you."

"Well, that was a long time ago," she says quietly. After a pause, she says, "So, anyway, how about it?"

"Okay, Helen, for you, I'll do it. But don't be surprised if they aren't too happy to see me."

"I'll have my gun, I'll protect you," she chuckles. "We'll see you there."

"We?"

"Yeah, I guess I should tell you. Brian will be there, too."

I furrow my brow. "Why is the State Attorney going to be there?"

"You know this is an election year, right?"

"I guess I knew that, but what—"

"You've heard that money is the mother's milk of politics?"

"Yes, but—"

"Well, Winthrop Myer IV is the cow," Helen says. "He's a big donor to Brian's campaign, so Brian thinks it's important that he takes a direct interest in the investigation."

"This isn't going to be a problem for you, is it?"

She's quiet for a moment. "Why would it be?"

"Frankly, your past relationship—"

"Is in the past, Tom," she says firmly. "I made it as clear as I could to him over lunch that I had no interest in him. We're both professionals." She pauses. "Will his being there be a problem for you?"

"Why would it be a problem for me?" I say.

She sighs. "It wouldn't, I guess. Just meet us at the Myer Mansion at 2:00 p.m. I'll text you the address."

"No bother, I already have it."

"Oh?"

"Yes, I was over there yesterday afternoon for lunch. Win Myer invited me to discuss . . . some issues."

"I see," Helen says. "So, how was lunch?"

"Good," I reply. "Rebecca is a gracious host. Win, well . . . he seems like a good guy. But he's slick. I don't think he's used to being told no."

Helen says nothing. "I'll see you at 2:00 p.m.," she finally says before hanging up.

I'm suddenly aware of how tired I am. I've had little sleep in the last 24 hours, only about four hours. It has already been a long day, and it is about to get a lot longer.

***

I pull up to the front entrance of the Myer Mansion. Helen and Brian Dohrmann are already there, standing by a car I take to be his. Unlike Helen's rather sensible sedan, Dohrmann's is a burgundy Dodge Charger, complete with a racing stripe down the side.

"Mid-life crisis," I mutter under my breath. Out of jealousy, to be honest. It is one fantastic car.

You're not just jealous of the car, are you? the lover says. *You're jealous because of HER.*

You have no reason to be jealous of either, the priest says.

While the priest and the lover begin to argue—again—I pull in behind the Charger. Dohrmann turns to Helen when he sees me and says something to her. He doesn't look pleased. Helen shakes her head and walks towards me as I get out of the car.

"Father Tom," she says with a smile, "Thanks for coming."

"Of course, Helen, glad to do it. I don't believe we've met, have we?" I say, turning to the unhappy-looking man next to her. Extending my hand, I say, "Father Tom Greer."

There's a brief flash of recognition when he looks at me—why, I don't know—but he grasps my hand and says, "Brian Dorhmann, Father Greer."

"Father Tom, please," I say with a smile.

He doesn't smile, but says, "Fine. Brian, then. I know about you through your wife's case, of course, and your corrected statement. I could have prosecuted you, you realize that, don't you?"

I struggle to retain my smile as I say, "And I really appreciate you showing me mercy."

"Oh, mercy had nothing to do with it. Detective Parr made an impassioned plea on your behalf." He grins. "Helen and I are . . . friends. Isn't that right, Helen?"

Helen glowers at him. "We have a very good working relationship, Brian," she says with a pleasant enough smile, but a tone that says 'go to hell'.

"I hope Detective Parr did not inconvenience you?"

"Helen, inconvenience me? It's never an inconvenience. I had nothing else to do this afternoon. Besides," I say pointing at the collar I'm wearing, "consoling the grieving comes with the territory."

"Hmm," he says before turning to Helen. "Shall we?" he says and begins walking toward the front door.

Helen looks at me. "Sorry about that," she mutters.

"Did I run over his dog or something?" I whisper.

"I really don't know what his problem with you is," Helen says, "other than the fact that you're a priest."

"He doesn't like priests?"

"Doesn't like religion, doesn't believe in God—take your pick."

This perplexes me. "Why did you go out with him?"

She opens her mouth to answer, then shakes her head. "Never mind."

Dohrmann rings the doorbell. I expect Win Myer or Rebecca Myer to answer. Instead, it's a pudgy, balding man who looks to be in his early fifties. He's about six inches shorter than I am, which makes him about the State Attorney's height. His eyes are red from crying. I recognize him from the wedding picture. He's Rachel's father.

"Hello," Dohrmann says, "I'm Brian Dohrmann with the State Attorney's Office, and this is Detective Parr of the Myerton Police." I see Mr. Watson look over Brian's shoulder at me. Leaning between Brian and Helen, I say, "I'm Father Tom Greer of Saint Clare's Parish."

"Yes," he growls, "I know who you are. You're responsible for all this." He looks at Dohrmann and Helen. "Ed Watson, I am—I was Rachel's daddy," he says, dabbing his eyes with his handkerchief.

"I'm so sorry for your loss," Helen says, "but we need to ask some questions. May we come in?"

"Questions . . . yes, yes, come in," he says, stepping aside to let us in. "Everyone is in the living room this way," Mr. Watson says. We follow him.

The room is brimming with grief. Majorie Watson is sitting on a couch, appearing stoic, staring out a window. Next to her, Rebecca sits patting her mother's hand and wiping her own tears. Thrown down in an armchair, Win Myer is staring at a point in the distance and nursing a drink.

"You!" he says, standing up when he sees me. "How dare you show your face here! This is your fault!"

Ed Watson steps between Win and me. "Now, son, just take it easy," he says, trying to calm Myer down.

"Take it easy? Take it easy!" he mutters. "He's responsible for the death of your daughter, and you're telling me to take it easy?"

"Win, please," Rebecca says. "That's enough."

"Now don't criticize Win like that," Marjorie Watson whispers.

"But Mama, Father Greer is a guest—"

"An unwelcome one," she says.

"Hear that?" Win says. "You're not welcome here. Please leave. Now!"

"Win," Rebecca says, "Stop."

"Rebecca," Majorie says, "I told you—"

Laying her hand on Marjorie's shoulder, Rebecca says gently, "Mama, this is my house. Father Greer came here to offer his respects. He's our priest. He'll stay." Turning to Win, she says less gently, "sit down."

Win looks about to say something. Instead, he goes back to his chair and returns to his drink.

Rebecca walks over to us. "I apologize, Father Greer," she says, "we're all in shock." Turning to Helen and Dohrmann, she introduces herself and motions for them to sit. I go over to one bookcase and lean against it, arms crossed, perusing the contents out of the corner of my eye.

"I want to say, first, Win," Dohrmann says, "that you have my word that we will find the person who committed this heinous crime."

"Oh, I already know who did it," Win says. Draining his glass, he stands up, "What I don't understand," he says, pointing to Helen with the glass, "is why you haven't arrested him yet?"

"Arrested who, Mr. Myer?" Helen asks as she takes out her notebook.

"Who?" Win says incredulously. "Father Leonard McCoy. The priest who was forcing himself on her."

Helen and Brian look at me. I close my eyes. So much for that.

"He knows all about it," Marjorie says, pointing to me. "Did nothing about it, tried to cover it up just like they always do, like they did with those perverts who molested those little boys."

"Mama, Rachel denied anything happened," Rebecca says.

Helen interjects, "I think we need to get to the reason we're here."

"Exactly," Marjorie Watson says. "Why are you here instead of arresting Father McCoy?"

Helen is about to say something when Dohrmann places his hand on her arm, which she discreetly pulls away. "These are routine questions in any investigation, Mrs. Watson," he says. "I assure you that as soon as we have evidence pointing to a suspect, we'll make an arrest. And I assure you that as soon as he can talk, we will interview Father McCoy."

A vague look of irritation passes across Helen's face. I'm forced to suppress a smile. She always hated it when someone spoke for her.

"We understand," Ed Watson says. "Let's let the Detective ask her questions so she can get on her way."

"Thank you," Helen says. "Now, when did anyone last see Rachel alive?"

There's a pause before Marjorie says, "The last I saw of Rachel, she was running out of the Rectory after our meeting with Father Greer."

"We'll get to that later," Helen says. "So that was Friday afternoon?"

"Yes," Marjorie Watson says softly. "Rachel was upset by the whole scene, she ran out of the place, and I didn't see her again." She stares out the window. "Oh, my baby girl," she whispers.

"The scene didn't upset her, Mama," Rebecca says to her mother. "You upset her."

"How did I upset her?"

"Oh, I don't know? How about continuing to disparage her desire to become a nun? Detective Parr," Rebecca says to Helen, "my mother is right. The last time we saw Rachel was that afternoon during our meeting with Father Greer. She got quite upset, and left. She had driven her own car; I had driven Mama."

"I see," Helen says, "so that was the last time you saw or spoke to her?"

"Yes," Marjorie says.

"No," Rebecca replies.

Everyone looks at Rebecca. "You spoke to your sister between Friday afternoon and the time of her murder?" Helen asks.

"Well, not exactly spoke," Rebecca says. "I received an email from her on Sunday morning."

"I didn't receive any email," Marjorie says.

"No, mother, I'm sure you didn't. You wouldn't have liked what it said, anyway."

"What did it say," Dohrmann says, ignoring Helen's look.

"She wrote that she had decided after a lot of prayer and thought to enter the convent. She was going to leave Monday morning," Rebecca said. "She said she loved me, that she would probably never see me again, but she wanted me to know that she would always pray for me and all of us and that she'd hope to see us all together in heaven someday."

"When did she send it?" Helen asks.

"I must double check, but I think it was sometime Saturday night," Rebecca replies.

"But you didn't see her or speak to her otherwise?"

"No, not at all." I can't see her face, but I saw her wipe away a tear from her cheek.

"Did she have any enemies?"

"Enemies? Of course not," Win says. "Rachel was the kindest, gentlest creature you'd ever want to meet. She was just, just such a wonderful person. I can't believe . . ." Overcome with emotion, he stops talking. Rebecca looks to one side.

"So you can't think of anyone who would want to do her harm?" Dohrmann asks.

"Other than that priest," Ed Watson says, "not a soul."

"Wait," Rebecca says. "There was someone at her old job she was afraid of. I think that's one reason she left and took the job at the parish."

Win looks at Rebecca and snaps his fingers. "That's right, she mentioned that to me. He was giving her a hard time, always trying to get her to go out with him."

Rebecca looks at Win. "When did she talk to you about this?" she asks with an even tone.

He looks at his drink. "When she asked me to talk to Father McCoy about hiring her as parish secretary."

"Win!" Marjorie says, "You got her the job at the parish? Why would you do that?"

Win sighs. "Sorry, Marjorie, looking back I shouldn't have, obviously, but she wanted the job, and she asked me to help her."

"And you could never say no to Rachel, could you?" Rebecca says, her sarcasm mixed with a tinge of bitterness.

"Now, Rebecca—"

"If I might ask," Helen interrupts, eager to get the interview back on track, "did she ever mention his name?"

The family thinks. Finally, Rebecca says, "Oh, I'm so bad with names. Richard? Robert? Roger? I really can't remember."

"Don't waste your time with him," Marjorie Watson says, "when you found the murderer next to her body."

Helen makes a note, then asks, "Mrs. Watson, you didn't receive an email from your daughter?"

"No, but then I don't really do email," she says. "But she hasn't sent me a letter, at least that I've received yet."

"She asked me to tell you myself," Rebecca says.

"What about you, Mr. Myer?" Helen says.

"Me? An email from Rachel? No, I don't think so."

Rebecca looks at her husband, a puzzled expression on her face. "Are you sure? I could swear she emailed both of us."

"Really?" Win says. "You know how busy I've been with this whole environmental impact issue. Detective," he says to Helen, "I could have received the email, but I didn't read it if I did." He shakes his head. "But I don't see why you're asking all these questions. We've already told you who you should arrest. I don't know why you don't do it!"

"We have not even spoken to Father McCoy yet," Helen says.

"Well, you need to get up and go do your job then," Marjorie says.

"Father McCoy," I say, "has been in no condition to talk since that night. He's probably still under sedation."

As soon as the words leave my mouth, I know I've overstepped. Helen looks exasperated. Dohrmann looks irritated.

"What Father Greer says is true," Helen says. "Father McCoy is in the hospital under sedation. As soon as the doctors clear him, I will interview him and get his statement."

"And then you'll arrest him," Win says.

"Win, we'll make an arrest as soon as we have evidence that points to a suspect," Dohrmann says. "Detective Parr is still early in her investigation."

Win points at Dohrmann and says, "You just remember which side your bread is buttered on. I've spent a lot of money on your campaign. I expect to get a good return on my investment. I don't want you caving to pressure from the Church."

"I assure you, Mr. Myer, there will be no pressure," I say. "If—if—Detective Parr determines that she has enough evidence to arrest Father McCoy for murdering Rachel, the Church will not stand in her way." I say that, hoping that it was true—for Helen's sake as much as for the sake of the Church.

"And even if it did," Dohrmann adds, "it wouldn't work. I'm only interested in justice."

Win nods. "Good. I'm glad we understand each other."

While Helen asks a few more questions and waits for Rebecca to return with a hard copy of the email from Rachel, I wander around the room, looking at the titles on the shelves and the wall of photographs. Again, I see the photographs from Rebecca and Win Myer's wedding showing a dour Rachel. Why did she look like that? Was she upset that her twin sister was marrying before she was? Did she resent the attention she was getting from her mother, who seemed to prefer one daughter over the other? Was this the reason she had decided on religious life, to escape her family?

I look more closely at one photograph. Rachel was unhappy in this one. But she wasn't the only one who looked out of place. Usually, the two people you can count on being the happiest in a wedding picture are the bride and the groom. And Rebecca was the very stereotype of the radiant bride, her face beaming with joy, and her eyes sparkling.

Win was something else. He was smiling, but it wasn't a joyful smile. Not like I was in my wedding picture with Joan. That was the happiest day of my life, before my ordination, and you could tell from my face in our picture.

Win looked dissatisfied. An odd look for a man on his wedding day.

"When were you two married?" I ask him.

"What?"

"You and Rebecca, when were you two married?"

"We married right before I went to Afghanistan," Win says.

"You were in the Army?"

Win nods and walks up to a picture on the wall. The photograph shows Win in camo fatigues among a group of other men, similarly dressed, in a rocky area. "Special Forces," he says, pointing to a photograph. "One tour in Afghanistan. I had to leave the Army when my parents died. They were both sick for a long time. They couldn't even attend the wedding."

"Win and Rebecca were high school sweethearts," Marjorie interjects with a smile. "Inseparable. Isn't that right, Rebecca?"

Rebecca smiles. "Yes, Mama, that's right. We dated in high school, beginning in my junior year. He took ROTC and went into the Army right after college."

I notice Rebecca. Her smile is strained, as if the memory is tinged with pain.

"You two went to the same high school?" I turn to Win. "I'm surprised your parents didn't send you to a fancy prep school."

"My parents loved this town," he replies. "They saw themselves as the caretakers of the Myer family heritage here. They wanted me to be the same. So, I went to Myerton High School. Just like any other teen boy."

"Hardly like any other teen boy, Win," Marjorie says with pride. "Captain of the football team, class president, valedictorian." She looks at me. "Rebecca was very fortunate Win picked her."

"Oh, Mama," Rebecca says. "I'm not a piece of fruit, for crying out loud!"

"I don't see what these questions have to do with Rachel's death, Father?"

"Oh, they don't," I say, smiling. "I just have a curiosity about people. Occupational hazard, you see."

"Well, Brian," Win says, turning away from me. "Do you have anything else for us?"

"No, not today," Helen says as they stand. "I'll be in touch if I have any more questions." She turns to Rebecca. "You have that email?"

"Here you go, Detective," she says, handing her a single sheet of paper.

Helen studies it. "Mr. Myer," she says, "is this your email address?"

Win takes the paper from Helen and studies it. "Yes, that's my work address. If she sent it there, I wouldn't have seen it, not on a Sunday. It's probably in my inbox right now; obviously I haven't gone through my emails today."

"Of course," Helen says, taking the paper.

We say our goodbyes and follow Win out of the room. Rebecca says, "Oh, when can we have Rachel's body?"

Helen stops and says, "It will be after the post-mortem, which will be in a couple of days. We'll notify you."

"Thank you. Father," Rebecca says to me, "can you help with the arrangements?"

Marjorie interjects, "Why him?"

Rebecca turns to her. "Because Father Greer is our priest, and Rachel would have wanted a funeral Mass." To me she says, "Can you?"

"I'll be honored to," I say. "I'll come over in a few days to discuss the arrangements."

Win Myer shows us out. As we're walking to our cars, Helen's phone rings.

"Hello? Yes, yes. Good. Okay, thanks." Helen hangs up her phone. "Father McCoy is awake. I'm going to talk to him. I assume you want to be there, Father?"

"I would like to, if that's okay. But can't it wait, Detective? I mean, he's been through quite a shock."

Dohrmann starts to speak when Helen says, "Yes, that's fine, but he's your responsibility. Bring him to the police station tomorrow morning at 10:30 a.m. I have quite a few questions for him."

"Believe me, I have questions for him too," I say. "Are you going to look into that man Rachel mentioned was harassing her?"

"I will, Tom."

I nod and turn towards my car.

"Wait a minute, Father," Dohrmann says. "I have a question for you." Placing his hands on his hips, he says, "What were they talking about in there?"

I hesitate before saying, "There was an anonymous complaint received by the Archbishop about Father McCoy last week."

"What were the allegations?" Dohrmann presses.

"The kind you'd imagine," I say, "that Father McCoy was engaged in inappropriate behavior with the parish secretary."

"Rachel Watson."

I nod. "The Archbishop sent me here to talk to Father McCoy and Rachel, to find out if the allegations were true."

"What did you find out?" he asks.

I pause before answering, "I can tell you I found out that Marjorie Watson sent the anonymous complaint , that Win Myer was spying on Father McCoy and Rachel, and that the letter contains insinuations with no explicit events recounted."

"But are the allegations true?" Helen asks.

I look at her. "That, I can't tell you."

"Why," Dohrmann says, "because you don't know if they're true or not?"

"No, Brian. He knows," Helen says, "but he can't tell us. Can you?"

"I can tell you that there was no force or coercion on Father McCoy's part. He didn't threaten Rachel or commit any criminal acts."

"But you can't say exactly what you found. Because of the seal, right, Tom?"

"The seal?" Dohrmann asks.

"The seal of confession, Brian."

He rolls his eyes. "Oh, not this!" he says. "A woman is dead. Murdered."

"I know. But anything anyone tells me in confession, I must keep private."

"But she's dead!"

"That doesn't matter," I say. "Church law is very clear. I cannot violate the seal for any reason."

Dohrmann looks at me incredulously, then at Helen. "Well? What are you going to do?"

"What would you like me to do, Brian?"

"What—" he says pointing at me. "He has material evidence in a murder case that he's withholding. I want to know what he knows."

"He already said—"

"I don't care what he said," he says. "I want that information."

Helen lifts her chin. "But Brian, he's right. I don't like it as a police officer. But as a Catholic . . ." She trails off and looks at me. "If a priest held my deepest darkest secrets, I'd want to know that they were safe."

Dohrmann looks at her incredulously. "Even if it means protecting a murderer."

"We can find the information some other way," Helen says firmly. She crosses her arms. "Or don't you think I'm a good enough detective?"

He opens his mouth to speak, looks back at me, then says to Helen, "Of course I think so." He sighs. "Fine, fine. Okay." He walks to his car and stops in front of me. Pointing his finger at me, he says, "But I promise you Father, I will drag you into the Grand Jury myself if it comes to that. And if you don't answer my questions, I'll throw your butt in jail."

"I'll bring my pillow," I say with a smile. Out of the corner of my eye, I see Helen roll her eyes.

"You smile now, Father," he scowls. "We'll see how you're smiling after a few days in jail." He then turns to walk to the car.

Helen shakes her head. "He's serious, Tom, he'll do it."

"I'm serious too. You know that," I say. "But thank you for backing me up."

She hesitates before saying, "You know my beliefs as a Catholic. But the detective part of me still thinks you need to tell me."

"I understand that," I say. "Look, you're right, you're a good detective. You'll figure it out without me breaking the seal." I stare at her. "Just remember there are two people involved here."

She looks at me and nods. "I'll see you tomorrow, with Father Leonard." She gets in her car and drives off, leaving me standing in the Myer driveway.

I'm about to get in my own car when I look back towards the house. Win Myer's in the window, looking at me..

***

"Well, Father Leonard," the doctor says, looking at her tablet, "there's nothing physically wrong with you. All our tests are normal."

"Then why can't I remember anything?" Father Leonard asks. He's sitting up on the edge of his hospital bed, dressed in a green polo and khaki shorts with tennis shoes.

"I'd say it's psychological trauma, the shock. The brain will block out something that's that traumatic; it's a defense mechanism."

"Do you think he'll remember?" I ask.

"Maybe with time, treatment might help."

"How much time?" Father Leonard asks, clearly worried.

"There's no way to know, Father," the doctor says. "It may be days, it could be months, even years." She smiles and pats his arm. "Now you go home, take it easy for a few days."

"I'll see that he rests. Thank you doctor," I say.

She nods and leaves the room. "Rest," Father Leonard says. "Rest. How can I rest?" He puts his head in his hands.

I pat his back. "It will be okay, Leonard."

"How?" he says, looking at me, stricken. "How is it going to be okay?"

"It will be," I say again.

"I don't see how."

I sigh. "Let's just get you back to the Rectory."

He stands up and takes a step forward. He turns to look at me.

"Was it horrible?" he whispers. "I mean, Rachel."

I pat him on the shoulder and nod.

"Do you think she suffered?"

I answer the question as honestly as I can. "If she did," I say, "she's not suffering anymore."

"No, no, I suppose not," he mutters. "Poor Rachel, my poor, dear Rachel," he adds quietly, a tear snaking its way down his cheek.

My poor dear Rachel.

"Let's go, Leonard. You need to sleep," I say.

"When I get back to Saint Clare's," he says as we walk out of his room, "I will go into the church, spend some time in front of the Tabernacle praying for her soul."

"I'll join you," I say.

"I'd prefer to be alone," he says, stopping in the hallway. I turn to look at him. "I prefer to be alone," he repeats.

I nod. "Of course."

We continue walking. He sighs and says, "I suppose I must talk to the Archbishop."

"Eventually, but not right now."

"And I must get back on top of the parish. I suppose you'll be leaving now."

I stop. Looking at him, I say, "No, no. I'm staying for the time being."

"There's no reason for you to," Father Leonard says. "She's dead. The allegations don't matter now."

It's odd that he would say that, I think. *Very odd.*

"Leonard," I say, "I've already talked to the Archbishop. He's put me in charge of Saint Clare's temporarily. You're on leave until this whole matter is cleared up."

He looks at me, blankly.

He really does not understand what's going on.

"Don't you understand? I found you sitting next to a murdered woman, your clothes covered in blood—not your own, so probably hers. You say you have no memory of what happened. You are linked to the woman. You were her boss. You admit giving her spiritual counsel. And there is an allegation of inappropriate conduct against you." I pause. "Now do you see?"

He looks at me blankly, then I see his face fall. "I see," he sighs. "Well, it's what I deserve. I've lost everything, and now I'm a murder suspect." He closes his eyes and drops his head, muttering something I can barely hear.

"God is punishing me."

Eleven

Something wakes me. Sounds coming from Father Leonard's room. I look at the time. 2:00 am.

As I come to consciousness, I hear slaps, muffled utterances, one after another. I get out of bed and pull on my robe. I walk to Father Leonard's room and knock softly on the door. I can hear the sounds more clearly now. Firm slaps, rhythmic, repeated. Father Leonard is muttering softly to himself. I catch one or two of the words when his voice rises with a slap.

Then I realize what he's doing.

I place my hand on the doorknob, then remove it. He wants his privacy, and I don't want to violate it, not for this. This is too personal. But I want to make sure he's all right. I lightly grip the doorknob and quietly turn until I hear the latch slip. Slowly, I push open the door and peer inside.

What I see confirms what I hear. A shirtless Father Leonard, back to the door, firmly scourging himself, praying the Miserere, David's psalm of penance.

Repeatedly, he brings the seven-cord rope whip down on his back, the three knots tied into the ends of each cord leaving a discernible red mark. A couple look like they're bleeding, but I see no other signs of injury. I quietly exhale, unaware until that second I had been holding my breath. From personal experience, the discipline doesn't draw blood, sensationalistic movies notwithstanding.

Normally, at least, it doesn't draw blood.

On one occasion, in my early days at Our Lady of the Mount, it had. Father Abbot gently but firmly explained to me its proper use, its purpose. Penance, not punishment. Mortification, not mortality.

I stand watching Father Leonard for a minute, then quietly close the door.

***

I say nothing to Father Leonard about the night's events when he sits down for breakfast. Anna is here, having come for 8:00 Mass, then gone into the Rectory kitchen to prepare food. Before Mass, I only had coffee, observing the Eucharistic fast, so by 9:00, when I sit in front of the scrambled eggs, bacon, toast, orange juice, and coffee, I'm hungry. I normally don't eat a lot for breakfast, but we have a long day ahead and I will need my strength.

Father Leonard comes into the kitchen and sits. Anna smiles and places a plate in front of him. He looks dully at the food.

"No, thank you, Anna," Father Leonard says, pushing the plate away from him. "I won't be eating today. Just coffee, black, please."

"You will need your strength, Leonard," I say. "You have a long day ahead, answering Detective Parr's questions."

"Tom's right, Father," Anna says, pushing the plate back to him. "Just eat some."

"Really, no, thank you, I'm fine," the young priest whispers.

"At least have some—"

"I said no thank you!" Father Leonard yells at Anna. Shocked, Anna takes a jump back. Collecting herself, she picks up the plate and takes it to the counter. She grabs a coffee mug, pours a cup, and returns to the table, placing it in front of the priest with a clunk, sloshing some contents on the table. Fixing him with a glare, she turns and leaves the kitchen.

I look at Father Leonard quietly. He slumps. "I'll go apologize. I shouldn't have raised my voice." He moves to get up.

"No, no, sit," I say, touching his arm. "Anna will be fine. You can apologize later."

He nods and looks at his coffee. He shifts uncomfortably in his chair, gently rubbing his right thigh. I look down and see the impression of a braid under his pants leg.

Father Leonard is wearing a cilice, a spiked metal braid, around his thigh.

The discipline, the cilice, and fasting, I think. *You're piling on the penances.*

"How are you feeling?" I say.

Father Leonard sighs. "I don't know, honestly. Numb."

I pick up my coffee cup. "How did you sleep?"

"I didn't," he says. "I tossed and turned. At one point I went into the Church and prayed before the Tabernacle."

"I didn't hear you leave."

"No, well, I think you were snoring," he mumbles. His eyes widen. "Not that you snore, Father. I mean, I'm sure—"

I chuckle. "It's all right, Leonard." I know I snore. Joan would sometimes describe me as a car without a muffler, though I don't think I'm that loud. In seminary, I kept having a succession of roommates, so maybe she was right.

"Are you ready for this morning?"

"I've never been questioned by the police before," he says. "What do you think they'll ask me?"

"They'll probably start with why you were at Rachel's apartment in the middle of the night," I say. Looking at him, I ask, "Why *were* you there, Leonard?"

He looks at me, then stares straight ahead.

"Leonard," I press. "Why were you at Rachel's apartment?"

He says nothing. I slump back in my chair and shake my head.

This is going to be a long day, I think

***

At the police station later that morning, Helen is getting irritable.

"Tom," she says to me in the break room around the corner from the interrogation room, "him not talking only makes him look guilty."

"I know that, but it's his right not to talk to you. You know that."

"Yes, yes, I know, but he hasn't asked for a lawyer yet."

I look towards the interrogation room. "Honestly, I'm not sure he will."

She looks perplexed. "Why?"

I shake my head. "He feels guilty about something. I have a good idea about what, but he has said nothing to me either."

"So," she says slowly, "you haven't heard his confession?"

"No, he hasn't asked me to hear it." I trace the rim of my coffee cup. "He needs to. He knows that. But he's taking his punishment on himself for what he did. Whatever that was."

"But you said you have a good idea what he feels guilty about?"

"Only part of it," I say. "But there's something else. He left Our Lady of the Mount without telling anyone. He didn't contact anyone after he left, and the next I hear from him he's in Rachel's apartment." I shake my head. "There's something else here, and only he knows what it is."

"Well," Helen says, putting her cup down on the counter, "he needs to say something."

We're about to leave when Brian Dohrmann walks into the room. "Well, Hel—what's he doing here?" he points to me.

"Good morning, Brian," I say with a smile. "I'm here with Father Leonard. Offering moral support."

"Huh," he says. "Sure you're not looking out for the Church's interests?"

"As far as I can tell, there is no threat to the Church's interests."

"Well," he says with a dismissive wave of his hand, "I'm not here to argue with you, Father. What has he said, Helen?"

Crossing her arms, she says, "Nothing."

Dohrmann says, "What do you mean, nothing?"

"I mean other than 'Good Morning, Detective', and 'I'd rather not say, Detective', and 'I remember nothing until I saw her body', and crying," Helen explains, "he hasn't answered my questions."

"Has he asked for a lawyer?"

"No," I interject. "And before you ask, the Archdiocese hasn't contacted one on his behalf."

Dohrmann looks at me, then back at Helen. "Have you pressed him?"

Putting her hands on her hips, she says, "Are you questioning how I do my job, Brian? Because I don't care who you are, or what our relationship was, I won't take that crap from anyone."

He puts his hands up. "I'm not questioning how you do your job, Helen. But maybe you're just a little too close to this."

"Why? Because I'm a Catholic?"

"Well, it might cause you to go softer on him because he's a priest."

Helen glares at him. I place my hand over my mouth to suppress a smile. The last time I saw that look, she almost had me arrested.

"Okay, fine," she says slowly. "If you think you can get him to talk, be my guest."

"All right, let's go." He turns and walks out of the break room. Helen looks at me and, seeing the smile on my face, spits out, "What?"

"Oh, nothing, nothing," I say, still smiling.

We leave the break room and meet Dohrmann outside the door. "No, not him," he says, pointing at me.

"He won't say anything, Brian." Helen says.

"I don't care, I don't want anyone on Father McCoy's side in there."

Helen sighs. I say, "It's all right."

"You can watch through the two-way mirror in here," Helen says, showing me a room next to the interrogation room. I enter the room and close the door behind me. There's a large window into the next room; from many TV cop shows, I know the other side is a mirror. I also know that because last year, I spent time where Father McCoy is sitting now.

He's slumped in his chair, leaning forward, resting his head on his hands in a rough attitude of prayer. He doesn't even look up when the door opens.

Dohrmann and Helen enter the room and take their seats opposite Father Leonard. He looks up.

"Hello," Father Leonard says.

"Father McCoy," Brian begins, "I'm Brian Dohrmann. I'm the State Attorney for this county. Do you know what that means?"

He nods. "I know who you are, Mr. Dohrmann. I recognize you from the campaign signs around town."

"So you know I'll be prosecuting the person who killed Rachel Watson."

"Yes, I guess that's true."

"Now I'm here because I understand you haven't been answering Detective Parr's questions. That you refuse to answer her questions."

He nods. "Yes, I have not answered her questions about why I was at Rachel's apartment that night."

"Why is that?"

He drops his eyes. "Because I believe it's my right as a citizen not to answer questions. Am I correct?"

"Well, yes, yes, that's true."

"Besides, my being there has nothing to do with her death."

Dohrmann sits back. Helen says, "How can you be sure?"

Father Leonard looks at Helen. "Because I know why I was there," he whispers.

"Why don't you tell us, Father," Helen says softly.

Father Leonard shakes his head. "No."

"Listen, Father—" Dohrmann snaps.

"Father Leonard," Helen says, interrupting. Dohrmann glares at her and slumps back his chair. She continues, "Let's start somewhere else, can we?"

"Okay," Father Leonard says.

Helen pulls out her notebook. "You were at Our Lady of the Mount Monastery from Thursday afternoon onward, is that correct?"

He nods. "I had gone there on a private retreat at the suggestion of Father Greer. I needed time to pray and meditate."

"On anything in particular?" Helen asks.

Father Leonard looks at his hands. "Yes, but I'd . . . "

"That's okay, Father, you don't have to tell us. I'm just trying to get a timeline right now. When did you leave the monastery?"

Helen already knows the answer to that question, because I told her.

"Saturday afternoon," Father Leonard answers.

"Who did you tell you were leaving?"

Another question she knows the answer to.

Father Leonard looks to one side before answering. "I told the extern—I'm sorry, the brother who serves as the Monastery's contact with visitors."

"And what is his name?"

"Brother Martin."

Brother Martin had told me Father Leonard had left without telling anyone. "Why did you lie, Leonard?" I mutter to myself. What is worse, Helen knows he's lying.

"So you left the monastery Saturday afternoon. Where did you go?"

"I don't remember," Father Leonard answers. "Nowhere in particular. I drove around the mountains. I think I stopped for dinner."

"Where did you sleep that night?"

"I didn't," he replies. "At least I don't think I did."

"What did you do the next day, Sunday?"

He hesitates. "I found a Mass and attended. I don't remember the name of the parish, or where it was. It was somewhere south of Frederick, could have been in West Virginia."

Helen sits back. "Aren't you required to say Mass at least once on a Sunday?"

He nods. "I didn't that day. Something I must go to confession for."

"Why didn't you stay at the Monastery, say Mass on Sunday morning, then leave afterwards?"

He shakes his head. "I needed time to think."

"I thought you went to the Monastery to think and pray?"

"I did," he says. "It didn't help. I thought a change of scenery . . ."

Helen looks at him. "Did it?"

He nods slowly. "Yes, at least I thought so."

"So what happened Sunday afternoon after the Mass?"

"I drove to an overlook off of 270, south of Frederick. I sat in my car and stared out, I said a Rosary." He hesitates before going on. "I guess you'll find this out anyway, checking her cell phone records. You do that, don't you? That's what they do on TV."

"Yes, we've requested her records," Helen answers. "Did you call Rachel Watson?"

Father Leonard nods.

"About what time?"

"I honestly don't remember. I can check my phone," he reaches into his coat pocket and pulls it out. A moment later he says, "I called her at 4:30 p.m."

"What did you two talk about?"

I look at Father Leonard. He's struggling with something. I think I know what it is. But I can't say anything.

"Father Leonard?" Helen presses.

"No, no, I'm sorry," Father Leonard says, practically crying. "No, I can't tell you, it doesn't matter, anyway."

Dohrmann leans to Helen, "I've had enough of this. Father McCoy, if—"

A knock at the door interrupts him. Helen says, "Come in?" A young uniformed officer comes in and whispers something in her ear. Helen looks at me, then whispers something to Dohrmann. He throws his hands up and utters an expletive.

The officer opens the door and in walks an African-American woman in her late thirties, dressed in a purple business suit. She looks vaguely familiar.

"Good afternoon, Detective Parr, Brian," she says with a smile.

"What are you doing here, Angela?" Brian says, unhappy to see her.

"The Archdiocese has hired me to represent Father McCoy," she replies. "Father McCoy, don't say another word." Turning to Detective Parr, she says, "Detective, is my client under arrest?"

"No, no, he's down here under his own volition," Helen says.

"Then if you will excuse us, I think we're finished here," the lawyer says. "Come on Father, let's get you back to your church where we can have a nice long talk."

Father Leonard looks thoroughly confused, but does as he's told. His lawyer opens the door and gently guides him out. She's about to leave when Dohrmann steps forward.

"What kind of stunt is this, Angela? What kind of game are you playing?"

"Game, Brian? This is no game," she says with a smile. "I'm looking out for the best interests of my client. Just as you are yours."

"My client is the people of the State of Maryland."

"Brian, you and I both know that your client is Winthrop Myer," she says. "If this were any other case, you wouldn't be here." Angela looks at Helen. "Have a nice day, Detective." She leaves the room, leaving Helen and Dohrmann alone.

He dashes from the interrogation room and the next thing I know, the door to where I am flies open. "So the Archdiocese has hired no lawyers, have they?" Dohrmann yells. "I should have known. You're circling the wagons!"

"Brian, please calm down," Helen says.

"Brian, I knew nothing about this," I say. "When I spoke to the Archbishop—"

"Oh, don't waste my time," he says before flying out of the room, slamming the door.

Helen looks at me with her hands on her hips. "Well, Tom?"

"Helen, I promise you, I don't know who that woman is, and I had no idea the Archdiocese retained her."

Helen exhales. "Okay, Tom." She shakes her head. "This will get bad."

"Why? Who is this Angela?"

"Who is Angela? Angela Jenkins. She's a local defense attorney."

"Okay, but why is Brian so upset?"

Helen looks at me. "You really don't know. Oh, why would you, you've only been back in Myerton a few days. You know, Brian is running for re-election as State Attorney, right?"

I shrug. "Yeah."

"Well, Angela Jenkins is his opponent."

Twelve

"I'm on your side, Father Leonard, I really am," an exasperated Angela Jenkins says, "but I can't help you unless you're honest with me."

"I didn't ask for your help," Father Leonard mutters. "I don't want your help. No one can help me."

She sits back and sighs. We're in my office; she is in the chair next to Father Leonard, I'm behind the desk. We've been at it for an hour. In that entire time, Father Leonard has added almost nothing to his statement at the police station. This, despite repeated assurances from his lawyer that it's necessary for his defense.

Jenkins shakes her head and looks at the legal pad propped on her lap. "Okay, let's go over this again," she says. "You called Rachel Watson at 4:30 p.m."

He nods.

"So where were you when you called?"

"The overlook off of I-270, just south of Frederick, I already told you that."

"Why did you call her?"

He sat quietly and looked at his hands. "I told her I wanted to see her."

"Okay, okay, that's good, now we're getting somewhere. Why did you want to see her?"

"No," he jerks his head up. "No."

Jenkins looks up from her pad. "Father Leonard—"

Shaking his head vigorously, he says, "No, I can't tell you. I won't tell you. Not you, not them, not anybody."

"Leonard," I say gently, "she needs to know."

"No, she doesn't," he says sharply.

"We'll get back to that later," she says. "So what time did you arrive at the apartment?"

"I got there about 7:00 p.m., I think. I don't remember."

"She let you into the apartment?"

He looks off for a moment. He shakes his head. "No," he whispers. "I knocked and rang the doorbell, but there was no answer. I remember knocking and calling her name. I tried the doorknob, and the door was unlocked, so I let myself in."

I think to myself, *he's remembering a lot all of a sudden.*

"So what happened next?"

He hesitates. "I remember stepping inside her apartment. The curtains were closed, so it was dim in the apartment, no lights were on, which I thought was odd. I think I called out for her." He shudders, clears his throat, shakes his head. "Then I felt a presence."

"There was someone else there?" I ask.

"No, not some*one*," Father Leonard says, "some*thing*. A presence. Out of the darkness behind me." I see tears coming from his eyes. "Suddenly, I felt like I was suffocating. Everything went dark. The next thing I know, I'm laying on the floor next to—" He doesn't finish, but collapses in sobs.

Jenkins puts her pen down and reaches out to rub his shoulder. "It's okay, Father, it's okay. That's enough for now." She looks at me and motions with her head to step out of the office with her.

In the hallway, she says to me, "I need more from him. I can't give him an adequate defense unless he explains why he was there."

"I've asked him, and he won't tell me. If he did, maybe I could get him to tell you."

"I also need to know the exact nature of the relationship with Rachel Watson," she says.

"He insists they were just friends," I say.

Jenkins looks at me. "But you know differently, don't you, Father?"

I really need to work on my poker face, I think. To Jenkins, I say, "Anything I know beyond what Father Leonard has said, or Rachel Watson told me, is privileged."

She nods. "I understand. The initial allegation to the Archdiocese was vague and seems innocuous. I'm surprised the Archbishop bothered to send you here."

I had not told her about that. "How did you find that out?"

"The Archbishop told me on the phone when he retained me," she said. "He sent me a copy of the accusation and gave me some information about my client." She looks into the office at Father Leonard, his head bowed in prayer again. "Born in Wisconsin, parents both dead, attended all-boys Catholic high school there, attended seminary here in Maryland, ordained about three years ago." She looks at me, "He's young to have his own parish, isn't he?"

"Under normal circumstances, yes," I say, "but our Archdiocese, like almost every other one in the country, has a shortage of priests. When circumstances demanded that Saint Clare's have a new priest, the Archbishop assigned Father Leonard."

Jenkins nods and crosses her arms. "Well, if he will not cooperate with me, there isn't a lot I can do for him. Do you think he'll listen to you?"

"I can try, but he hasn't been willing to talk to me yet. I'll give it another shot."

"Thanks." She pauses. "Can I ask you a question, Father?"

"You can ask," I say.

"Were they having a sexual relationship? Father Leonard and Rachel Watson?"

I stare at her, saying nothing.

She looks at me and shakes her head. "You can't say, can you? Well, I'll just have to hope he tells me."

"Can I ask you a question?" I ask.

Jenkins smiles and replies, "You can ask."

"Why did you take this case?"

"In the interest of justice, everyone has the right of legal counsel."

"Yes, yes, I know, but what's your real reason?"

"The real reason? People cannot fool you, can they, Father?"

"Not all the time," I say slowly. "Well?"

"The real reason, besides the reason I just gave you—which I really believe in, otherwise I wouldn't be a criminal defense attorney—is because I don't want to see him railroaded for political reasons."

"By your opponent in the upcoming election for State Attorney, right?"

She nods. "The town is a lot larger, and they're not as in control as they used to be, but the Myer family still has a lot of power in this area. You know he's Brian Dohrmann's biggest contributor, right?"

I nod.

"With money comes influence," Jenkins says. "Oh, I'm not saying Brian will deliberately frame the person Win Myer wants him to for the murder, he has more integrity than that, but he's a human being, and human beings are not always motivated by their better angels. But you would know that better than I would."

"So you think Dohrmann may shape a case to please Win Myer?"

"Please Win Myer, to look tough on crime, even let voters know he will not be intimidated by the Catholic Church, which as you know doesn't have the best reputation in the world right now."

"Well, I don't know about Dohrmann," I say, "But Detective Parr is a woman of integrity. I trust her to do the right thing."

"From everything I've heard around town, I agree with you. Look," Jenkins says, looking at her watch, "I have a meeting with another client." Pointing to Father Leonard, she says, "See if you can get him to talk to me. I'll be in touch."

She goes back into my office to retrieve her briefcase. "Father Leonard," she says, placing her hand gently on his shoulder. He jumps and looks at her, startled.

"I have another client I need to meet with," she says. "I will speak to you later."

"Speak to me later," he repeats. "Got it. Speak to me later."

After she leaves, Father Leonard looks at me. "If it's all the same to you," he says, standing, "I think I'll go on to bed."

I look at the time. "It's only 6:00 p.m."

He shrugs and sticks his hands in his pockets.

"Don't you want something to eat? Anna can get you some soup if you'd—"

"Thank you Father, but I'm not hungry," he says as he starts out of the room.

"Leonard, wait," I stop him, placing my hand on his shoulder. He turns to look at me.

"I want to help you. Your lawyer wants to help you. The only way we can do that is if you talk. Now if you don't want to start by talking to her, I can hear your confession, and by that, I don't mean your confession to the crime, I mean why you were at Rachel's apartment to begin with, and frankly what your relationship with her was." I pause and look in his eyes.

I see a flicker, just a flicker of relief. I sense his shoulder relaxing beneath my hand. He opens his mouth.

Then, he snaps it shut, the tension in his shoulder returns.

He shakes his head. "I don't want help," he mumbles. "No one can help me."

"Leonard," I shout, "for heaven's sake, do you know what kind of trouble you're in?"

With pitiful eyes, he looks at me and answers, "It's what I deserve." With that, he leaves my office and walks upstairs to his room.

A while later, I walk past the closed door and hear the slaps of the discipline against Father Leonard's bare back.

***

Breakfast the next day comprises a cheddar cheese, ham, and mushroom omelet, hash browns, coffee, and orange juice. The smells coming from the kitchen hit me when I enter the Rectory after 8:00 am Mass. Anna had slipped out after communion. I now know where she went.

"Anna," I say, sitting down before the plate she placed on the kitchen table, "you really don't need to keep doing this."

"I enjoy doing it," she says, wiping her hands dry. "Besides, it's not like I have a lot going on."

I take a bite of omelet and chew thoughtfully. Anna pours herself a cup of coffee and sits down. "Father Leonard still asleep?"

I nod as I chew. Swallowing, I wash the breakfast down with some orange juice. "His door was still closed when I went into the church."

"How is he doing?"

I shake my head. "Not good. The poor man is suffering. Problem is, he won't talk. Not to me, not to the police."

"That probably doesn't bother his lawyer," Anna comments, "though I can't imagine Brian Dohrmann is happy with his opponent as Father Leonard's attorney."

I look at her, surprised. She smiles. "I hear things, you know."

"What do you know about Angela Jenkins?"

She sits back. "Not too much," she says. "She's not native to Myerton, I think she's from Philadelphia originally. I'm not sure how she wound up here, but she's been an attorney in town for about five years, mainly criminal work, but she's also done more community advocacy work. You know, pro-environmental work and the like." She snaps her fingers. "Come to think of it, I think she's the lawyer for the group working against Myer Holdings' wind farm."

I raise my eyebrows. "Really? That's very interesting. Why is she running for State Attorney?"

Anna shakes her head. "I guess she wants the job, probably as a stepping stone to something bigger, State Delegate or State Senator. She'd be the first African-American elected to county office. That'd get her a lot of attention."

"I just hope she's not looking at Leonard as one of those stones she's stepping on."

"From what I've heard, she is a talented lawyer with a lot of integrity. I don't think she'd let her ambition affect her defense."

Behind me, I hear shuffling. I turn to see a bedraggled Father Leonard trudge into the kitchen. He pulls out one chair at the kitchen table and drops into it.

I look at him, opening my mouth to speak, when Anna says gently, "Father, can I get you something to eat?"

Father Leonard slowly shakes his head. "No, thank you, Anna."

"Leonard," I say, "you need to eat something. You had no dinner last night."

"Tom's right," Anna says. 'How about toast and coffee, something light?"

"Fine," he says, "fine. Toast and coffee, thank you."

Anna pours him a cup and sets it in front of him. Father Leonard stares at it blankly. I look at him as I finish my breakfast. Standing, I motion to Anna. We walk to the doorway to the kitchen.

"Can you stay and keep an eye on him? I'll be in my office."

"You go work, we'll be fine," Anna says reassuringly.a

In my office, I'm just sitting down when the rectory phone rings.

"Good morning, Father Tom," Rebecca Myer says, "I hope I'm not interrupting you."

"Not at all, Mrs. Myer," I say. "What can I do for you?"

"Well, I was wondering if I could talk to you about the funeral arrangements for Rachel," she answers.

"Absolutely," I say. I pull my appointment calendar to me and flip through the pages. It's a pro-forma flip. I know the pages are blank. "Any day this week would be fine."

"Could we make it early this afternoon?"

"Of course," I say. "I'll come out to your house—"

"I'd like to meet with you at Saint Clare's," she interrupts. "Not here. It will just be me."

"Oh? Your mother—"

"My mother isn't interested in the funeral arrangements," she says carefully. "She's letting me handle all of that. I just want to make sure we do what Rachel would have wanted."

"I understand," I say. "Is 1:30 pm a good time?"

"That will be fine," she answers. "1:30 p.m. I'll meet you there."

As soon as I hang up, my cell phone rings. *It's going to be one of those days, I'm afraid,* I say to myself. I look at the number.

It's Helen.

"Did I catch you in the middle of saving a soul?" she says.

"Not currently, soul saving isn't on my schedule for another hour. Shouldn't you be catching a bike thief?"

"That's not until this afternoon," she says, "This morning I have 'call ex-fiancés who became priests' on my calendar."

"Oh, well, I guess it's a good thing I'm free. What's up?"

She hesitates before saying, "How's Father Leonard this morning?"

Now it's my turn to hesitate. "Should I be talking to you about him? He has a lawyer now."

"Angela Jenkins is his lawyer, not your lawyer. I can't talk to him directly, but there's nothing to keep me from talking to you about him. Besides, I'm just asking how he's doing. You know, he is my parish priest."

"Okay, you're right." I sigh. "Not well at all."

"Has he talked to you?"

"Yes, but I know no more about why he was there than you do."

"Well," Helen says slowly, "I may be able to answer that."

"How?"

"Gladys Finklestein—my computer genius, remember?—was able to access Rachel Watson's phone and retrieve her text messages and call log. We don't have a report from the cell phone company about her other calls for the past month, yet. We won't be getting that for several days, but we do have a record of a call from Father Leonard's number to Rachel Watson at about 4:30 p.m."

"We already know about that," I say.

"The call," she continues, "lasted twenty minutes."

"What?" I say, unable to conceal my surprise. "He didn't tell us what they talked about, nor did he mention how long the call was."

"Considering the thirty text messages he sent her from about 1:00 p.m. onward, he probably called to keep her from leaving."

I almost drop my phone. "Thirty text messages? He mentioned nothing about texting her."

"From the messages, I'm not surprised."

"Well," I press, "what do they say?"

"I'd rather not tell you over the phone."

"You want me to come down to the station?"

She says nothing for a minute. "Tom, I shouldn't even be talking to you about this, much less showing you. But I thought you should know."

"Are you going to share these with his attorney?"

"Oh, yes, we're obligated to," Helen says. "I thought you should know for other reasons."

I let that sink in. "Okay."

"But not the station," she says. "How about lunch?"

"I don't think I will have time today, I've got noon mass and I'm meeting with Rebecca Myer to discuss funeral arrangements. Any idea when the body will be released?"

"I'm traveling to Baltimore tomorrow to meet with the state medical examiner; I'll know more then."

"Mind if I tag along? I've got to go by the Archdiocesan Office, anyway." That is a lie, but a small one. I just want to be there when the medical examiner tells Helen what they found.

"Sure, I'd enjoy the company," Helen says. "Anyway, why don't you come by my apartment later this afternoon? I'll show you the text messages. Unless you're scared to?"

"Why would I be scared?"

"I don't know. A priest, alone in a single woman's apartment. After everything with Father Leonard—"

"I think I can trust myself," I chuckle. "And you."

Helen says nothing for a moment. "Yes, Father Tom," she says, "you can trust me."

.

Thirteen

I stand with Rebecca Myer at the front of the church. She's looking around with slight wonder at the vaulted ceiling, the carved traditional marble altar holding the tabernacle behind the modern altar, six candles and a crucifix arranged along the front edge facing the congregation. To the left, a statue of the Virgin Mary; to the right, one of Saint Joseph holding the child Jesusa,; each statue with red votive candles flickering in the dim light. Stained glass windows down either side of the church cast a kaleidoscope of color, each window a scene from Jesus's life except for the one closest to the entrance to the sanctuary. That one portrays Saint Clare and is opposite the statue of the saint, with more votive candles arranged in front.

"You've been inside Saint Clare's before, of course," I say.

Still looking up, she nods her head. "Oh, yes, many times. The last time, I think, was my wedding. I may have been here at Christmas a couple of times since. I just forgot how breathtaking it is," she whispers. "So peaceful. I can't believe something so beautiful was built when the town was so small."

I smile and join her. "It was the Irish laborers' way of honoring the God who had helped them survive the potato famine and the passage across the Atlantic to Baltimore," I say. "Their pennies, and larger contributions from the townspeople, many of whom were themselves Catholic—Maryland was at the time one of the most Catholic states in the country—and many who were not." I look at her. "Your husband's great-great-grandfather, who was himself a devout Catholic, gave a large sum from what I understand."

"You can really feel a presence here," Rebecca whispers. "It's not like anything I've experienced anywhere else." She looks at me. "Is that God?"

I smile and nod. Turning towards the tabernacle, I say, "Remember, the Church teaches that God the Son, Jesus, is present in every tabernacle in every physical church around the world in the Eucharist. So yes, I would say the presence you feel is God."

"Mama brought Rachel and I when we were younger, but I'm not sure she really believes anything," Rebecca says. "She is a very practical woman, which makes her cold to many people. She taught Rachel and me that material things were important, the most important things in life. I guess that came from her growing up poor; from what she told me, her family didn't have much at all when she was little. She married Daddy, who's been successful in his business, so we've always been comfortable, but she wanted more for Rachel and me."

"More than Rachel becoming a nun?"

Rebecca laughs. "By the time Rachel told us that, we had stopped being surprised by her. Mama was never particularly close to Rachel, but after that . . . things were never the same."

She sighs. "I'll admit, Father Tom, I loved my sister but never really understood her in the last few years." She pauses. "We were twins, shared a womb for nine months, and were born only ten minutes apart—I'm the oldest, for what that's worth—but we were very different people."

"You look alike."

"On the outside, in many ways, we were the same," Rebecca says. "Inside, we were different. Rachel was smart but not particularly pretty, I'm pretty but not particularly smart—oh, I don't mean that as vain, it's what we'd tell each other."

"You grew up together, but I gather Rachel went away to high school?"

Rebecca nods. "We started out together at Myerton High. Right before our sophomore year, Mama decided that Rachel should go away for the rest of high school to a boarding school."

"Why did she do that?"

"She said it was because it would be better academically for Rachel. But there was another reason." She turns away from me to look at the altar.

"Where did she go?"

Rebecca laughs. "Well there, Father, is where, it gets funny. My 'Christmas and Easter' mother decided that the only place for Rebecca was an all-girls Catholic preparatory school in Wisconsin."

I raise my eyebrows. "Why in the world?"

Rebecca shakes her head. "Mama's said it was the worst decision she ever made, but at the time she went on and on about how prominent all the girls who went there were, how strong it was academically, how from there, Rachel could write her ticket into any Ivy League school she wanted."

"She didn't go to an Ivy League school, did she?"

"No. She wanted to come home, go to Myer. Mama wanted her to apply to a big-name school out of state. Instead, she went to Emmitsburg. We should have realized something was going on, but Rachel did a good job convincing Mama and Daddy that the only reason was because it had an excellent business school and she had won a scholarship—both of which were true." She sighs. "But the day of her graduation, she announced to us she was thinking about becoming a nun."

"And you all had no idea?"

"No, none. Mama was furious, ranted and raved during the entire dinner after graduation. Daddy said nothing—he usually says nothing. I was confused. Hurt that she hadn't told me. We had been close before she went away to school, despite our distinct personalities. I thought she could tell me anything. I guess she didn't feel the same way."

"Maybe she was afraid you'd tell your parents, or try to dissuade her."

Her laugh echoes off the walls. "Oh Father, you couldn't dissuade Rachel of anything once her mind was made up. And I wouldn't have tried. After I got over my hurt, I realized how I really felt."

"How did you feel?"

Rebecca looks at me, then the tabernacle. "Proud. And envious." She sighs quietly.

"She didn't enter religious life immediately, though. She went to work in Baltimore if I remember correctly."

Rebecca nods. "Yes, she worked there for a few years, then moved back here to take the job she had before becoming parish secretary at Saint Clare's."

"You became close again after she moved back to Myerton."

"Yes, yes, we did," she whispers.

We stand together quietly for a minute, then I say, "Win has seemed pretty upset by everything that's happened."

Rebecca's expression darkens. "Win's always been . . . protective of Rachel. He was that way in high school. They went out once or twice before Rachel went away."

"And you started dating him after your sister left?"

"Oh, Father, I had no interest in Win while he was dating my sister," Rebecca says. "But after Rachel left, Mama got it into her head that nothing would do except Win Myer and I would get together." She pauses. "And Mama usually gets what she wants."

"Except with Rachel."

"Yes, except with Rachel. Her announcing she was quitting her job to work at Saint Clare's because she wanted to become a nun was the last straw."

"Had she told you she was still considering it?"

"Yes, she had told me she was still thinking about it. I knew about her going to a convent near Emmitsburg for weekend retreats. We kept that from Mama. But it came as a surprise to me when she told Mama and Daddy. Mama was so upset. That meeting in your office was the first time in months they had even spoken."

"So you knew she was thinking about becoming a nun, but her email the day of her murder still surprised you?"

"The last I had heard, she was having second thoughts, that maybe she wasn't called to be a nun, that maybe God wanted something else from her. I remember her being confused for the last couple of months, distracted even, but excited at the same time."

"When did that start?"

"Shortly after she moved back to Myerton. I was glad to have her back. I had been lonely without her." She pauses. "Win's away a lot on business, and when he's home, he works a lot." She turns away, looking like she was contemplating the scene of the miracle of the Wedding at Cana, where Jesus turned water into wine.

"And after that, she began to express doubts?"

"Yes, like I say, she seemed confused, but also happy. It was very strange. I kept meaning to ask her about it. Then I received that email and I supposed whatever doubts she had were gone." She shakes her head. "Now, I guess I'll never know," she whispers.

I look down at her and place my hand on her shoulder. "Maybe someday."

She gives a sharp laugh. "Not likely, Father. I'm not winding up in the same place Rachel is, I'm afraid."

"You know, you can do something about that."

She looks up at me. "Maybe someday, Father. But for today," she continues, "tell me about my sister's funeral. Have you done many?"

"Actually," I say, "Rachel's will be my first."

"But you know how to do it, right? It's part of your training, isn't it? And you've been to other Catholic funerals?"

Slowly I turn to look towards the altar, focusing on the spot where the casket would lay.

"Only one," I whisper, "and I don't remember much."

***

In almost twenty years, I have forgotten that Helen is a terrible housekeeper. Her apartment is small, made smaller by the clutter scattered throughout the place. Almost every surface is covered with papers, books, and clothes, clean and dirty. I have no desire to go into the kitchen; I remember what a disaster it always was.

"Try to find yourself a seat," Helen says when she lets me in. "I haven't had time to clean."

"In the past year?" I say. She turns and gives me a look. "Sorry," I say with a grin.

"Hmm. You want something to drink? I have water and . . . maybe just water."

"I'm fine, thanks."

I pick up a stack of folders from a chair. Holding it in my hands, I look at Helen.

"Just put it anywhere," she says with a wave of her hand. "I'm going to change into something more comfortable." At my look, she laughs and says. "T-shirt and shorts, Tom, that's all I meant." She leaves the room with me still holding the folders.

Against the wall, there is a table that she apparently uses as a desk, so I place the folders on it. Over the desk is a large cork board, its surface covered with newspaper clippings and photographs, along with notes in her indecipherable handwriting. All have to do with a series of shootings in D.C. a few years ago. A couple of the articles have photographs of Helen, described as the lead detective.

Among the piles of folders and papers on the table is a framed portrait of a man. I pick it up and examine it closely. He's handsome, with curly brown hair and a winning smile. Dressed in a tuxedo, it must have been taken on his wedding day.

"Okay, that's better . . ." I hear Helen behind me, her voice trailing off. I turn to see her. She's not looking at me, but at the framed picture in my hand.

I hold it up. "John?"

She nods slowly, walking towards me.

"He looks like a nice guy," I say.

She swallows and smiles slightly. "He was," she says quietly. She takes the picture from me and looks at it, stroking it lightly with her finger. "This was taken on our wedding day. I loved him. I still do."

I nod. "I understand."

Helen looks at me. "I know," she says.

We stand looking at each for a few minutes in silence. Part of me wants to say something, but I'm not sure what. Another part of me wants to put my arms around her to comfort her obvious grief.

But another part of me—a big part—feels jealous of this man who had something I didn't—now, never will.

"Well," Helen says finally. "You didn't come over here for this. Here are the text messages between Father Leonard and Rachel." She walks to her bag and pulls out a folder. "You can take these, they're copies."

I take the folder. "Why are you giving them to me?"

She sighs. "Because I think you should know, for reasons other than the crime."

"What do they say?"

"Look for yourself."

I sit down in the chair I cleared and open the folder. Helen shoves a stack of laundry off the couch and sits opposite me. I read. The more I read, the more disturbed I become.

We sit in silence for the next several minutes. I reach the last of the text messages, the one where Father Leonard says, *I'm going to call you. Please answer*, and close the folder. I sit with the folder on my lap, leaning my head against the back of the chair, with my eyes closed.

Oh, Leonard, I muse. *What were you thinking?*

"Well?" Helen asks.

I look at her. "I admit it doesn't look good, but it doesn't mean he killed her."

"Perhaps not," she replies. "But it shows someone desperate, obsessed with seeing her, or at least talking to her. Her responses are those of a woman not too interested in either until the last couple."

"But he talked to her, he went over. She must have agreed to see him."

"Or, she told him not to come over, and he went to her place, anyway."

"There's no evidence of that!"

"Hey," she says, holding her hands up, "don't get mad at me. You're the one with the wayward priest. I'm just telling you how I see the texts, and how Brian will see them."

I plop them down on another stack of folders sitting on the coffee table. "Only if he's already decided Leonard's the murderer."

Helen hesitates. "He hasn't, but he definitely has decided that Father Leonard is the prime suspect."

I look at her. "What about you?"

"Me? It's still too early. We don't have the evidence reports back, and I haven't seen the post-mortem." She looks at me. "I'm just following the evidence, Tom. That's all I ever do."

I shake my head. "Well, what about that guy from her office?"

"Him? I'm looking into him." She stands and goes to her desk. Plucking a folder off a precarious pile, she opens it. "Name's Richard Strump. Turns out Rachel filed a police report on him for stalking her back in February. He was parked outside of her townhouse for hours. Officers arrived and told him to move along. He gave them some trouble, and he wound up in the county jail for the weekend." She looks up. "Apparently it wasn't the first time he's done something similar. According to the notes here, their company HR department had numerous harassment complaints filed against him. He kept his job—how, I don't know—but the arrest was jus,t too much. They let him go not long after."

"Well, there you go," I say. "She was responsible for him losing his job. Sounds like a motive to me?"

"Tom, they fired him in February. There are no other reports of harassment or stalking. You're saying he kept this anger against Rachel inside for months, then decided to kill her?"

"Revenge is a dish best served cold," I say.

"Don't quote Khan to me, Tom," she says.

"Okay, but are you going to look into him?"

"Yes, yes, I will. But it's not on the top of my list."

Later I'm in my car, thinking about Helen's last comment.

She's very busy, being the only detective in Myerton.

Maybe she could use some help.

Fourteen

"Hey, are you awake?"

I'm staring out the window of Helen's car as we travel I-70 towards Baltimore. Her voice startles me.

"Huh, what?" I say and turn to her.

She glances at me before returning to the road. "I asked if you were awake."

"Yeah, yeah, I'm awake," I say, stretching. "I've been awake the whole time."

"You haven't said a word since we left Myerton," Helen says.

"Sorry," I say, reaching for the to-go cup of coffee in her cup holder. We had stopped by The Perfect Cup on our way out of town. "I have a lot on my mind."

"Trying to figure out what to tell the Archbishop about Father Leonard when you see him, huh? What are you going to tell him?"

I shift in my seat, kicking aside the fast food wrappers covering the floorboard of her sedan. "I haven't decided yet. I haven't decided what it means."

"I would think it would be obvious," she says. "'Let me talk to you, I have a question to ask you.' 'I can't live the rest of my life without you, Rachel.' 'Please don't leave me again.' 'I want you Rachel, I'll give everything up for you.'" She pauses. "Except for coming out and saying, 'I'm leaving the priesthood to marry you,' it's clear what his intention was in going to Rachel's apartment."

"But he hasn't said that was why he was there," I say. "Okay, I'll grant you, he wanted to talk to her. He wanted to talk to her desperately. She had told her sister and her brother-in-law she was entering the convent. She was leaving the next morning."

"That's what she told Father Leonard, too," she says. At my glance she says, "We found an email to Father Leonard on her computer."

"We don't know that he saw it."

"You're ignoring the texts," she says with exasperation. "She said, 'Didn't you get my email? I've decided. It's for the best, Leonard.' He answered, 'You can't leave.'"

I sigh and nod. "I guess you're right. But none of that adds up to Leonard being guilty of her murder. In fact, it works against that theory."

"Angela Jenkins will argue that." She hesitates, then says, "Brian, however, is ready to have him arrested and charged."

"What?"

She nods. "He thinks the texts establish enough to have him arrested and charged with manslaughter, at least. I've persuaded him to wait until we get the autopsy report and other

339

forensics back, but he's determined." She shakes her head. "No, Tom, I don't know why. I have to say, though, Father Leonard sure looks guilty."

"But you know him," I say. "He's too scared of his own shadow to murder anyone."

"Maybe plan to murder someone, but in the heat of the moment, overcome with desperation, who knows?"

"But what about someone else? What about Richard Strump? Have you asked him where he was at the time of her murder?"

"There's no evidence there was anyone else in the apartment."

"But Leonard—" I stop myself, realizing I was about to tell Helen what he had told me and his lawyer.

"But Leonard what?" she asks.

I hesitate. "I'm not sure I should tell you. It's something he said to me and his lawyer."

"Listen, Tom, I stuck my neck out showing you those texts. You owe me. What did Father Leonard say?"

I sigh and tell her Leonard's account of going into the dark apartment, feeling a presence, feeling suffocated, then waking up next to Rachel's body hours later.

Helen drives along contemplating what I just said. After a few minutes she says, "'A presence?' He said 'a presence?'"

"That's how he described it, a presence that suffocated him and caused him to black out. Maybe Strump killed her. Then when Leonard came in, Strump knocked him out?"

She shrugs. "Or Leonard could have blacked out after killing her, or he's lying about the whole thing." At my look, she says, "I'm saying what Brian will try to argue, Tom."

"What do you think?"

She shakes her head. "I just follow the evidence, Tom."

"And what does the evidence tell you?"

She thinks for a moment. "I don't have enough yet, but honestly," she sighs, "I don't think it looks good for him."

"But Helen—"

"Tom, I promise you, I will look into Strump, but for right now I think we should change the subject, don't you?" she says, cutting off further conversation.

"Okay, maybe we should." I look at her. Then I settle back in the seat.

We drive along, the silence thick between us.

***

The Archbishop leans back in his chair, his hands folded on his chest, and looks up at the ceiling of his office. I had spent thirty minutes or thereabouts telling him what I found out—or at least what I could. I couldn't share Rachel's confession, even with the Archbishop. But I told him about the text messages.

Finally, he speaks. "So Father McCoy broke his vow of celibacy."

I nod. "I believe there is evidence that he did."

"Am I right in saying there are things you cannot tell me?"

"Yes, Your Eminence."

He nods. "And you are right, you have no choice." He pauses and looks at me. "Father McCoy has not confessed?"

I shake my head. "Not as far as I know. He has said nothing to me about any of this. But he feels guilty. Inordinately so."

"His use of the discipline and cilice shows he's handling his own penance," the Archbishop says. "He has to know how spiritually dangerous it is to undergo those penances without proper direction."

"I don't think he cares," I say. "Frankly, I'm afraid of what he might do next."

He looks at me. "Do you think he might hurt himself?"

"With his state of mind, I wouldn't discount it."

The Archbishop sighs. "You must get him to talk to you, Tom, so you can counsel him. Before something worse happens."

"I'll try, sir."

He leans forward. "What about the investigation? How is Detective Parr handling things? Any problems?"

"As I told you, she's a professional. She's following the evidence." I pause. "The State Attorney is putting together his case against Father Leonard already. He doesn't want to wait for all the evidence."

"What's he like?"

I choose my words carefully. "He has personal reasons to act," I say. I explain to him about the election, about the political relationship between him and the Myer family.

"It also doesn't help that the attorney you retained for Father Leonard is his opponent in the upcoming election," I conclude.

The Archbishop grimaces. "Okay, I did not know that when I contacted her. Our lawyers gave me her name as a good defense attorney with no biases against the church. Her father was a Baptist preacher, apparently, so she's not hostile to the faith."

"She seems to be a talented lawyer, and I'm sure she'll represent Father Leonard well, but she has her own interests in the case besides merely seeing that justice is done."

"Everyone has ulterior motives, Father Tom, even priests," he says. "As long as her motives don't undermine Father McCoy having the best defense possible, I don't care what they are. I'm trusting you to keep an eye on her. If you think she isn't giving him the best defense possible, let me know."

"Be sure that I will."

"Good, good. Now," he says, "what to do with Father McCoy? Assuming he's not found guilty and sent to prison for murder." He sits back and drums his fingers on the desk. "He will need to spend time in penance and prayer."

"He'll need rest," I point out. "He's going through hell right now."

"A hell of his own making," the Archbishop says. "He must go through counseling, to see if he can return to his vows. But that means that Saint Clare's will be without a priest again."

We sit in silence for a long time. The question implicit in the Archbishops' statement floats between us.

Finally, I nod. "Yes, your Eminence."

The Archbishop smiles. "Good, good. We won't do anything until after this is over. In the meantime, I'll let Father Abbot know your return to the monastery is delayed indefinitely. Don't worry, I'll help him find another priest to serve the monastery."

I stand. "Thank you. I'm glad. I owe the Brothers a lot."

***

The Office of the Chief Medical Examiner is in a modern-looking building on West Baltimore Street in Baltimore. Unlike many jurisdictions around the country, they perform all autopsies in suspicious deaths in the state in one location. It's here that they transported Rachel Watson's body. Helen and I are here to see her, for me to arrange for her transport back to Myerton for her funeral, and Helen to receive the report of the forensic pathologist to confirm the cause of death.

"You were in there a while," Helen had said when I walked out of the Archbishop's office. She had waited for me in her car, eating a bacon, egg, and cheese croissant sandwich and washing it down with an iced coffee. She handed me a chicken biscuit when I got in the car.

"We had a lot to talk about," I had said.

Now we are standing in one of the examination rooms of the Medical Examiner's office. It's pretty much as portrayed in many TV police dramas, tile and stainless steel. The exam table, where the autopsies are performed, resembles the table in an operating room. Only here, the purpose is to find the truth instead of to heal. A body on the table is covered with a sheet.

The door opens, and a woman dressed in scrubs walks in. "Detective Parr?" she asks.

"Yes?"

"Hi, I'm Dr. Kashyap. I performed the post-mortem on Ms. Watson." She looks at me with confusion.

"I'm Father Tom Greer," I explain. "The family asked me to see to her release and return to Myerton."

"Ah," she says, nodding. "Do you want to wait outside while I go over the results with Detective Parr?"

"He can stay," Helen says before I can respond. "You're not squeamish, are you, Father?"

"No, no," I say with more certainty than I feel.

"Okay, suit yourself," Dr. Kashyap says. She walks to the table and pulls the sheet down, exposing Rachel Watson's lifeless body from the head to her waist. Modesty demands that I avert my eyes. There is no gore, just a carefully stitched y-incision across her upper torso and a thin slit in her stomach.

Opening the folder in her hands, she recites, "Watson, Rachel, white female, age 28, etc., etc." She proceeds with the time of the autopsy, the weight and condition of her organs, all very clinical.

Helen interrupts. "Do you have an approximate time of death?"

Referring to her notes, she says, "Between the stomach contents and the liver temperature taken at the scene, I estimate sometime between 6:00 pm and 8:00 pm Sunday night."

"Cause of death?" Helen asks.

"The victim had one wound," the doctor says. She points to the one in her stomach. "A sharp object entered the upper abdomen, penetrated the liver, and nicked the inferior vena cava. This is the cause of death. She exsanguinated because of a stab wound."

"Murder weapon?"

"A sharp knife like a kitchen knife."

That matches what they found near the body. Near Father Leonard.

"The sad thing is, they could have saved her," the doctor comments. At our looks, she explained, "The inferior vena cava has rather low pressure. Unless a stab wound is right into the inferior vena cava, any blood loss is relatively slow. Based on the wound, she could have lived for a half-hour, maybe forty-five minutes after being stabbed." She looks at Rachel. "If she had gotten to the hospital in time, it's likely she and her baby would have survived."

Helen and I look at the doctor. "What?" Helen asks.

"Her baby," the doctor repeats. "When she was murdered, Rachel Watson was about eight weeks pregnant."

Fifteen

"Okay," Helen says, "let's go over this again, Father McCoy."

We're sitting in the interrogation room at the Myerton Police station. Helen is across the table from Father McCoy and Angela Jenkins. I'm in a chair off to the side. She let me sit in as long as I was quiet. We have been here for about an hour, Helen asking questions, Father McCoy giving brief answers when he answered at all, his lawyer making notes on her legal pad and occasionally interjecting.

"My client," Jenkins is saying, "has already answered your questions, Detective. I don't see why you keep going over the same ground."

"Because, Ms. Jenkins, your client isn't telling the truth," Helen says.

"And you know that how?"

Helen hadn't mentioned the text messages up to this point. I notice her take a file folder from the bottom of the stack in front of her. She opens it and takes out a small stack of stapled pages.

"Because of these," she says, handing the papers to Father Leonard. He doesn't take them, but stares at a point behind Helen, staring at his reflection in the mirror. From where I'm sitting, I see his face. Anguish, pain, guilt—all etched in his expression.

"What's this?" Jenkins says, taking the papers and flipping through them.

"These are text messages your client sent the victim the afternoon before her murder," Helen says. "He sent dozens of messages and talked to her on the phone for about twenty minutes."

"He's already told you he talked to her," she said, tossing the papers on the table. "He told you he went to the apartment where he was attacked, was rendered unconscious, and woke up next to the body of the victim. He doesn't deny that. I'm wondering why you're still questioning my client when you should look for the person who was there before he was."

"We're looking into it, I assure you," Helen says, "but I want to know why he sent these messages."

"She was leaving," Father Leonard blurts, almost a whisper, his eyes still fixed on the mirror. "She told me she was leaving. I got an email saying she was leaving, I didn't get it right away, I didn't get access to my email until that afternoon."

"Father McCoy, don't—" Jenkins says, touching his arm.

"I tried to call," Leonard continues, ignoring her counsel. "She wouldn't answer. So I texted, and I said . . . well, you see what I said."

"What did you say to her on the phone?"

"I just wanted to see her, to talk to her, to have a chance to . . ." Father Leonard trails off.

"To have a chance to what?" Helen presses.

"To persuade her to, to ask her to . . ." Father Leonard slumps in his chair, staring at his folded hands, but says nothing else.

"If you have nothing else, Detective," Jenkins says, gathering her papers, "unless you will charge my client, then I think we're done here."

"Not quite, Ms. Jenkins, there is just one more thing," Helen says. She glances at me out of the corner of her eye. I lean forward slightly.

She takes another folder from the bottom of the stack and opens it in front of her. Quietly, she asks. "Father, did Rachel tell you she was pregnant?"

The question explodes in the room. Jenkins' eyes get big, and she jerks her head to look at Father Leonard. Father Leonard sits bolt upright, the anguish and pain replaced by shock and surprise.

"What? What? Pregnant? With a baby?" Father McCoy sputters, his voice raised. "What are you talking about? She said nothing to me about—I mean she mentioned nothing—I didn't know, I swear I didn't know."

"Father McCoy, please—" Jenkins says through gritted teeth, trying to get her client to shut up.

"She didn't tell you she was pregnant?"

"No, no, not a word! Oh, my Lord. Oh, my dear Lord! Oh, Blessed Mother!" he cries, slumps back in his chair with his hands over his face, and sobs. I stand up and move towards him. I kneel beside him and put an arm around his shoulders. He leans to me, still sobbing.

I look at Helen. She looks impassive, every inch the professional. "Detective," I say, "do you have everything you need right now? I think he's had enough, don't you?"

Helen nods slowly. "I think you're right. Father McCoy, you're free to go." She turns to Jenkins. "I'll want him back for more questions."

Jenkins nods. "You'd better be looking into his story, the person who was there in the apartment, the real killer, instead of targeting my client."

"I assure you we're looking at all possibilities," Helen says standing up. She looks at me and motions with her head.

I pat Father Leonard's shoulder. "I'll be with you in a few minutes, then we'll go back to the Rectory and get you something to eat." I stand and follow Helen into the hallway.

"Tom, you know how this looks, don't you?" she says.

"Oh, come on, Helen," I say, "you saw his reaction. He didn't know she was pregnant."

"He could be lying, you know. That could be an act for your benefit." Helen pauses. "Do you think she knew?"

"At eight weeks?" The times Joan was pregnant, she always knew by then. Unfortunately, soon after came miscarriages. Except for the last one.

"Yes," I say finally, "I think she would have known. Have you checked with her doctor?"

She shakes her head. "Not yet. I'll get the information and contact them as soon as possible." She crosses her arms and looked at me. "Wouldn't her being pregnant put the kibosh on her plans to enter the convent?"

I purse my lips and raise my eyebrows. "I hadn't thought of that. It would have, most definitely, at least put a wrench into the plans."

"I mean, she wouldn't have been planning to have an abortion, would she?"

"No, I don't see Rachel, from what I know about her, taking that route. Committing a mortal sin."

"But hadn't she already? Fornication is a mortal sin, after all."

I sigh. "And one sin often leads to another. So I admit it might be a possibility. More likely, though, she would have had the baby and put it up for adoption."

"But she couldn't do that in the convent, could she?"

I shake my head. "No, I don't believe convents come equipped with birthing rooms and midwives. She was up to something," I pause. "Maybe a call to the Mother Superior of the convent is in order."

"I'll take care of it," Helen says.

"Let me do that," I say. "It might be easier coming from me. They may not be very willing to talk to you." At her look, I say, "I promise I'll tell you what I find out. But I'll tell his lawyer as well."

She nods. "Fair enough."

At that moment, the door to the viewing room swings open and a very irritated Brian Dohrmann walks out.

"I've been in there waiting for you, Helen," he says. "What kept you?" He looks at me. "Oh, I see."

"I was just talking to Father Tom," Helen says.

"Hmm," Dohrmann says with scepticism. "Well? Why haven't you arrested him?"

"Because I'm not prepared to do that yet," she replies. "The forensic evidence is not back yet, we just got the post-mortem yesterday—"

"Yes, I heard of your little trip to Baltimore," he says, eyeing me with suspicion.

"I was there to arrange for Rachel's return to Myerton, on behalf of the family," I volunteer. "That's the only reason."

"Are you sure? That's the only reason? Or are you spying on the investigation?"

"Spying?" I laugh. "Brian, spying for who?"

"Are you serious? Do you think I'm an idiot?"

"Which question do you want me to answer first?" I say with a smile. Helen rolls her eyes.

Dohrmann opens his mouth, then shuts it quickly. He takes a deep breath. Turning to Helen, he says, "I just don't understand what you're waiting for?"

"Evidence," Helen says. "Probable cause. You know, a legal basis for an arrest?"

"I think you have enough, Helen. You have him finally admitting he came to the apartment to talk to her. You have those texts showing him desperately trying to contact the victim in the hours before her murder. You have the accusations against him. You have the fact that she was pregnant. It's clear to me, even if it isn't to you."

Helen's face hardens. Her eyes take on a dark hue, one I remember too well.

"He said he didn't know she was pregnant," I say, "and I'm not sure what you think all this adds up to."

"You wouldn't," Dohrmann spits. "So let me draw it out for you. Either he screwed her or he didn't, maybe she consented, maybe she was coerced. But it looks like he did. He wanted to see her, to talk to her about keeping quiet about his little indiscretion so it wouldn't ruin his career in the Church. Then she tells him he's pregnant, he's the father. He kills her to keep her quiet. Motive, means, opportunity."

"Very good, Brian," I say with a tight smile. "You should sell that story to Lifetime."

Dohrmann clenches his fists and makes a motion to me. I draw myself up. Helen steps between us and puts a hand on Brian's chest.

"Stop," she says. "Ignore him. Father Tom has a sarcastic streak. Don't let him goad you."

"You need to do your job," Dohrmann says to her. "I want you to arrest Father McCoy now! Now are you going to do it, or do I need to call the chief?"

The hand on his chest becomes a jabbing finger. "Listen," she shouts, causing two people in the hallway behind Dohrmann to stop and walk back in the direction they came from. "I don't care who you are! I don't care if you are the President of the United States! I don't care how many dates we've been on! You will never tell me how to do my job! And you will never threaten me again! Do we understand each other?"

Dohrmann looks shell-shocked. It is obvious he has never experienced Helen in full attack mode. I should sympathize with the poor man.

But I don't.

They stare at each other for a few minutes, not speaking. Father Leonard and Jenkins come out of the interrogation room. They stop and look at us standing in the hallway. From the look on Jenkins's face, it's clear that she heard at least part of Helen's explosion.

"If you will excuse me," I say to the two combatants, "I'm going to take Father Leonard back to the Rectory."

"Fine," Helen says, looking at Dohrmann.

"Fine," Dohrmann says, looking at Helen.

We're almost to the door of the police station when I hear footsteps approaching behind us.

"Wait one moment." We turn to see Helen and Dohrmann approaching us. She is holding a folder, looking serious. He has a look of triumph.

"What is it, Detective?" Jenkins asks.

Opening the folder, Helen says. "We just got the forensics report. The blood on your client's shirt matches Rachel Watson's."

"Well, that's not surprising; my client had no wounds on him."

"But he's never explained how he got her blood on his shirt," Dohrmann says.

"There's more," Helen continues. "The fingerprints on the murder weapon match Father McCoy's. There were no other prints on the knife. Just his." She closes the folder.

She inhales. "Father Leonard McCoy," she intones, "I'm placing you under arrest for the murder of Rachel Watson."

***

I burst through the door of the Rectory. I had left the police station as soon as they had taken Father Leonard into custody. He had said nothing as they led him away, not protesting his innocence, just a look of resignation on his face.

"It will be all right, Leonard," I said as they walked him down the hall.

"No," he mumbled, "it won't. It hasn't been all right for a while."

"Can I bring you anything?"

He stopped and looked at me. "My breviary and rosary, can you get those? They're on the table by my bed."

I looked at Helen, who nodded. "He can have them."

Anna hears me and emerges from the living room. "What is it, Tom?" she says at my frantic look. "What's wrong?"

"They've arrested Leonard," I say, "and I've got—"

"What do you mean, they've arrested Father Leonard?" Anna demands. "Why did they arrest him?"

"I don't have the time to explain, Anna," I say as I bound up the stairs to Leonard's room.

"But, Tom!" Anna shouts behind me.

"I'll explain later," I shout back. "Right now I've got to get something and get back to the jail."

I go into Father Leonard's room. The bed is unmade, and looks like someone had been tossing and turning in the night. He hadn't slept well. On the bed is the corded flagellum. The police have probably already discovered the cilice. No doubt Helen will ask about that, and no doubt Dohrmann will see that as evidence of guilt.

His breviary is on the nightstand. When I reach to pick it up, it slips out of my fingers and falls to the floor, face down, the pages splayed open. I pick it up by the spine. Several pieces of paper fall to the floor. Two are prayer cards, one of Saint John Vianney, the other of the Blessed Virgin. I pick them and the third card, which fell face down, off the floor. I stick the two cards back in the breviary and turn the other over. I stop and peer at it.

It's not a prayer card. It's a small, wallet-size photograph, the type typically part of school photo packets. This isn't a school photo, showing an awkwardly smiling adolescent Leonard McCoy. He's in the picture, but it was taken at a school dance. Leonard's dressed in a gray tuxedo, bow tie, and white starched shirt, his red hair bright in the faded color photograph. Standing next to him is a young girl, about sixteen or seventeen, wearing a pale green prom dress, her left arm bedecked with a wrist corsage. Her hair is up, yet still looks soft. She has the same look on her face as Leonard, one a mix of adolescent awkwardness and unbridled joy. It's the happiest moment of the happiest day of their young lives.

I look more closely at the girl. She's slightly pudgier in the photo, but there's no mistake.

I close my eyes and shake my head.

"Oh, Leonard," I whisper.

Sixteen

It's after normal visiting hours by the time I get back to the station. I called Helen on the way, letting her know I was on my way to see Father Leonard. She told me she would let the guards know I had permission to see him for a few minutes. I didn't tell her what I had just learned. I wanted to talk to Father Leonard first. He had to tell me the story himself, but what I knew explained so much.

The guard escorts me to the visiting room. After about ten minutes, the door opens, and the guard escorts Father Leonard in. He's not handcuffed or shackled, and he's still wearing the same clothes he had on.

Except he has no belt, and his shoes are missing the laces.

He sits in the chair in front of me, looking desolate. He sees the breviary on the table in front of me and I notice his eyes brighten.

"You brought it," he whispers. "Thank you." He reaches for it and pulls it across the table, clutching it to his chest. It's precious to him, that much is obvious.

Or rather, what's inside is.

"How are you doing? Are they treating you okay?"

"As well as can be expected, I suppose," he says, slumping against the back of the chair.

I look at him for a few minutes, saying nothing. He sits in silence, staring at a spot on the table.

"Is there anything you'd like to talk about?" I finally ask.

He raises his eyes to look at me. Slowly, he shakes his head. "No," he whispers.

"Leonard," I say gently, "I can't help you if you don't talk to me."

"My lawyer says not to talk to anyone."

"About the case," I say. "I'm not asking about the case. I'm asking if there is anything you need to tell me, anything you want to talk to me about, anything I need to know so I can help you."

"No one can help me," he mutters. "No one. I don't want help."

"Leonard—"

He cuts me off by standing up. "Thank you for the breviary," he says as the guard opens the door, having seen him move through the small window. "But I think I should go back to my cell." He turns around to walk to the door. He opens the breviary as he takes a couple of steps, then stops. The guard prods him forward, but Leonard stands in the room, his back to me, flipping through the pages.

I pull the small photograph out of my coat pocket. "Are you looking for this?" I say, placing it face-up in the middle of the table. Leonard turns and sees it. His shoulders slump, his head drops.

"Can you leave us for a little while longer?" I say to the guard. He looks at me, then at the pathetic figure standing before him, and nods. He walks out of the room and closes the door. Father Leonard and I are left alone in the cold grey room, the young priest standing motionless.

"Sit down, Leonard," I say. He does, still looking down, still slumping, the very expression of defeat. I slide the photograph towards him. For the first time in a while, he smiles and picks it up.

"That was a glorious night," he whispers. "She was so beautiful. The prettiest girl there."

"So that is Rachel Watson," I say. It's a statement, not a question, since I already know the answer.

Father Leonard nods. "Yes, that's Rachel. It was my school's dance—they didn't call it a prom, but that's what it was, our senior prom."

"Why don't you start at the beginning," I say.

He looks at me. "The beginning? That seems like a long time ago." He sighs and puts the photo down. Looking at the wall, he goes on, "It was my mother's idea, going to that school."

"The boys' school in Wisconsin."

He nods. "She always wanted me to be a priest, from the day I was born. I don't remember a time when she didn't say, 'Leonard, you will be a priest when you grow up.' She called me her Samuel, her offering to God." He smiled ruefully. "She loved Star Trek and the Lord. She may have named me after the doctor on the Enterprise, but there was no other career on offer. Apparently, I had been a difficult pregnancy, after years of her not being able to carry a child to term. So, she told me, one day she was kneeling in her parish church before the Tabernacle and she said if God would allow her to have a child, she would offer that child to his service." He opened his hands. "So my fate was sealed even before I was born."

"But you can't enter the priesthood because someone wants you to," I say. "It's a sacred calling; you have to receive it yourself."

"And I did," he replies. "The older I got, the more certain I became that I was to become a priest, just like my mother said. I loved the church—it was the only place I ever felt comfortable." He looks at me. "I was an awkward child. I didn't have many friends, I wasn't any good at sports. I'd rather spend my time in my room reading or praying than spending time with other people." He shakes his head. "I guess being alone wasn't good training for a parish priest."

"Relating to people is a necessary part of the job," I say.

"That's been the hardest part, the people," he says. "Anyway, I went to parochial school, served at the altar as soon as I could, spent every hour I wasn't at home or at school in the Church. It became my second home. My sanctuary." He swallows. "More so after my mother got sick."

I look at him. "What happened?" I ask quietly.

"Cancer," he says. "They diagnosed her when I was twelve. She fought it for two years, with multiple rounds of chemotherapy and radiation. But she lost." A tear flows down his cheeks. "On her deathbed, she made me promise I would follow God's call to the priesthood. So I did." He looks at the table. "I was fourteen."

"How did you wind up at the boarding school?"

"That had been arranged before my mother died," he says. "My father, well, he took her illness hard, drank—he was never violent, just sad. They both agreed I would go away to high school after she died, and from there, enter seminary. The high school was particularly for young men discerning the priesthood, almost like a minor seminary."

He sits back. "I wanted to go to the school. I was so hopeful. An entire school of boys like myself, committed to serving the Lord, looking forward to studying for the priesthood. I thought it would be round after round of study, prayer, spiritual discussions, everything I didn't have growing up."

I look at him. "It didn't work out that way, though."

"Things were no different," he says. "The boys, they were just like the ones I knew at home. Maybe even worse. There were still cliques they excluded me from, sports I couldn't play. They still teased me. They were all obsessed with girls and sex—two things I knew little to nothing about. Except for the ones obsessed with the other boys, there were more than a few there. So I wound up being more alone than I had been. I had no family, no friends, no one."

"So how did you meet Rachel?"

He brightens at her name. "Rachel," he repeats. "She was attending the all-girls school about five miles away. Monthly, the two schools would have socials, dances, get-togethers, carefully monitored, of course. Even though theoretically we were all on our way to seminary, the teachers thought it important that we be exposed to the opposite sex. The thinking was, I guess, that if we had calls to the priesthood, we'd have to know how to interact with women in our parishes, and if we weren't, we'd need to know how to talk to girls to get a wife later."

"Rachel was one of the girls, right?"

"Oh, yes," he says. "I still remember. It was a spring dance or something, Lent was over and it was Easter season, so the girls had decorated their gym in spring colors—you know, yellow and greens. It looked very bright and cheerful when we walked in. The dance was a required activity, so I had no choice but to go even though it was the last thing I wanted to do. So I sat in a chair in a corner while everyone else talked, laughed, and got to know each other."

He pauses, then his expression brightens. "Then I saw her. She was sitting on the other side of the gym, looking as miserable as I felt. She was slumped in the chair and her arms were crossed. She didn't want to be there and didn't want anyone to talk to her. I felt an immediate kinship with her. I must have spent half an hour summoning up the courage to walk across the room to talk to her, but finally that's what I did." He stopped and looked at the picture. "Maybe I shouldn't have. Maybe none of this would have happened."

"What happened next?" I press.

"I walked across the room and sat down next to her. I didn't know what to do next. I had spent so much time focusing on walking up to her, I didn't think about what I'd do once I had done that. So I just sat there like an idiot for a long time. Every so often, I'd turn to face her and open my mouth to say something, but nothing would come out. So I'd stay quiet. Finally, Rachel turned to me and said, 'If you're going to sit there, either say something or go get me a glass of punch.' She startled me, she had spoken so directly. But I got up and got her a glass of punch. After that, we started talking. By the end of the night, we were talking and laughing. It was the best night of my life up to that time."

He sits back in his chair and folds his arms across his chest. With a slight smile, he says, "After that, we'd spend time together at each dance. At some point, the teachers of both schools turned the monthly get-togethers into opportunities to teach ballroom dancing. So they taught us the waltz and other dances, along with manners and etiquette."

"Because you all needed to know how to get on in eighteenth-century Vienna," I quip. Father Leonard stares at me blankly. "Sorry, go on."

"She was my dance partner. We were actually not too bad, although we were both awkward and not in the least athletic. It didn't matter to either of us. I just enjoyed being with her, holding her close, I still remember what her hair smelled like. Neither of us had much experience dating, and we weren't dating."

"That went on for the next couple of years. We'd see each other at least once a month, and when the two schools had group field trips, we'd pair up. We were both still shy. I couldn't even hold her hand in public, only when we danced." He looks at me. "But I was soon in love with her. I didn't know it. But I was." He sighs. "Which just made things complicated."

"You know, Leonard, you weren't a priest yet," I point out. "You could have done some more serious discernment, talked to your spiritual director. Maybe—"

"No, that wasn't an option," he cries, shaking his head vigorously. "I couldn't disappoint my mother that way. I had promised her on her deathbed. No, I was still determined to become a priest. But Rachel, my feelings for her, confused me."

"Tell me about the photo," I say.

"It's exactly what it looks like. It was the last dance, one that honored the graduating seniors. Rachel and I both knew after that night, we wouldn't see each other again. She had another year at her school, and I—I was entering the seminary. Even though she was Catholic, she didn't fully understand. I think she felt the same way about me as I did about her. That night, that last night we spent together, oh, Tom, I've carried that memory with me for years. Just like I've carried that photograph. So I'd remember the last time I was truly happy." He stops and drops his head.

I look at him in silence for a few minutes. Finally, I said quietly, "Then she showed up at Saint Clare's."

His head jerks up, his eyes flashing. "I couldn't believe it when I saw her," he declares. "I mean, I hadn't seen her in so long, and I wasn't sure at first if it really was her, but there she was, sitting in the third row to the right of the altar. I was beginning my homily when I spotted her. I stopped in mid-sentence. I know everyone must have thought I was having a stroke or something. I don't remember the rest of that mass, I don't know how I got through my homily, and I'm not a hundred percent sure to this day that I didn't forget part of the prayers."

"After Mass, I hurried to the front of the church and scanned every face as people filed out, looking for her, not wanting to miss her. Part of me felt like a fool, but most of me was just so excited to see her again. Finally, I saw her. She was standing off beside one of the columns, waiting for the crowd to thin out. After what seemed like an eternity, we were left alone on the portico. We just stood there, looking at each other. Finally, we walked toward each other. We stopped about a foot from each other, neither of us knowing what to say. She spoke first. She said, 'Hi.' That's all she said. We stood there for the next thirty minutes talking. That's when I found out she had moved back to Myerton to take a job, and she was discerning a call to religious life. I told her how wonderful it was to see her, how happy I was about her consideration of a call."

Father Leonard stops and looks at his hands, which he rubs together. "She asked me to have lunch with her. That's brought me back to reality. I couldn't... I couldn't find myself in a situation like that. As strong as I felt, I kept thinking about what my mother would say. So I said no, that it was probably best if we just kept our relationship as pastor and parishioner." He takes a deep breath. "That's when it started."

"What started?" I ask.

Father Leonard spreads his hands. "She kept contacting me," he says. "She was there every Sunday, and sometimes during the week. Sitting on the front row, right where I could see her every time. She'd talk to me after mass, each time asking if I wanted to get lunch, dinner, coffee—each time, I said no. At one point, she asked me, 'What are you afraid of, Leonard?'"

"What were you afraid of?"

With plaintive eyes, he says, "Her. My feelings for her. Seeing her awakened inside me the memories of what it was like in high school, the feelings I had for her, that I had suppressed for so long."

"Leonard," I say, "you have a picture of her in your breviary. It doesn't seem to me you were suppressing your feelings."

He shrugs. "It was just a happy memory I didn't want to lose completely. So yes, I'd look at her picture every day. But it was safe. She was gone. I thought I'd never see her again."

"But you knew where she was from," I point out. "Didn't it occur to you when you were assigned here that you might run into her."

"I didn't think about it."

I look at him. I don't believe him.

"But," Father Leonard goes on, "I could take it, as long as I only saw her once or twice a week." He slumps in his chair. "Then we advertised for a parish secretary,"

"And she applied for the job."

"I just about had a stroke when her resume arrived at the Rectory," Leonard exclaims. "I was tempted to throw it away, but Anna had brought it to me, so she would have known. Besides Fern (last name), she was the only other applicant for the job. That's one reason I begged Anna to stay on."

He sits up in his chair. "I decided before the interview not to hire Rachel. The other applicant would be perfectly acceptable, I decided. It was better than the alternative." He sighs. "Then Winthrop Myer paid me a visit. He made it very clear to me that unless I hired Rachel, he would make no more donations to the parish. I know how sizable his donations are."

"He gave you a substantial one that day. What did you tell him?"

"I agreed to give Rachel the job," he says. "I couldn't stand up to him. I didn't want the parish to lose out because of my own weaknesses. It's not like she wasn't qualified."

"No," I admit. "Rachel's business training made her perfect for the position, if overqualified."

"I have to admit, it was great at first, seeing her every day. I tried to keep things professional. But quickly, I let my guard down. We'd work, she'd attend the noon mass, we'd pray the Rosary and Evening Prayer together before she went home. And we'd talk. We'd talk about the past, we'd talk about the Scriptures, about spiritual topics." He inhaled. "We'd discuss her call to religious life."

"Did you try to discourage her?"

He looks at his hands. He's twisting his fingers together quicker now. "Not actively. I don't think so. I don't know now. I think maybe at first, but then I saw how genuine her interest was." He shook his head. "I wasn't about to oppose God's call, no matter how much I may have wanted to."

I lean forward and place my hand on his. "What happened at the Memorial Day picnic?"

He closes his eyes and sighs. "That's when things fell apart. Things were so chaotic, so noisy, with all the children. I needed to get away, go somewhere quiet for a little while. So I walked off from everyone else. Rachel saw me and followed. She found me under a tree. She sat on the grass next to me. We sat quietly for a few minutes, when she turned to me and asked, 'Do you remember how to waltz, Leonard?' The next thing I knew, I was holding her, and we were waltzing. She was humming, we were moving together, and suddenly we were in high school again."

He clenches his eyes shut. "I don't know how it happened, but suddenly I kissed her. Just a quick kiss—we had never kissed before then, and honestly, I'd kissed no one before. She looked shocked, but not as shocked as I was. I began to apologize when she threw her arms around my neck and started kissing me. We stood there, kissing for what seemed like forever. She broke first. We stood there, our arms around each other, just looking into each other's eyes. Then I heard a rustling behind me and Miriam Conway calling my name. We quickly separated, but I could tell she had seen something. She told me it was time to bless the food. We walked back to the rest of the crowd and avoided each other the rest of the afternoon."

Father Leonard sits back in his chair and looks at a point behind me. "That night I was sitting in the rectory when she walked in. I stood, and we just looked at each other. Then . . ." He shook his head. "God help me, Tom, I broke my vows for the first time that night."

I nod. He is confirming what Rachel told me in the confessional. "That wasn't the only time, was it?" I say.

"I tried, Tom, I really tried!" he cries. "I even fired Rachel, told her we couldn't see each other again, but I couldn't stop thinking about her. I couldn't pray. I couldn't sleep."

"What about her call to religious life? What was she saying about that?"

"She was still determined to become a nun. After each time, we'd swear it wouldn't happen again, that we both needed to repent and go to confession, renewing our calls. And we'd do fine. But it happened twice after Memorial Day."

"Weren't you concerned that someone would see you, that they'd find out what was going on?"

He shakes his head. "I didn't care. It was only after the visit that I got worried."

I'm confused. "Visit? Who did you get a visit from?"

"Her brother-in-law."

I stare at him, amazed. "Winthrop Myer paid you a visit."

"He stopped by the Rectory, barged right in. He grabbed me by the shirt and pushed me against the wall. He said if I didn't stay away from Rachel, if I didn't keep my filthy priest hands off of her, he'd beat the crap out of me—he didn't say crap—and he called me all sorts of foul names. He called me a filthy pervert who shouldn't even look at someone as precious as Rachel."

"He must have seen you go into her apartment."

"Apparently, he did. You told me Mrs. Watson had asked him to spy on Rachel, right? He must have seen me go in one night and stay for a long time."

Win Myer had said nothing about visiting Father Leonard at the Rectory to confront him about Rachel.

"Well, after that I was more determined than ever to stay away from Rachel, to renew my commitment to my vow of celibacy, and recommit to my life as a priest." He slumps in his chair. "But so much had happened, and I couldn't stop thinking about her. So I began to think . . . ."

"You were reconsidering your priesthood, weren't you?"

He nods. "Yes. By the time the Archbishop received that letter, I was in turmoil. I was only going through the motions during Mass, during my prayers. I could barely eat or sleep. When the accusations were made, I panicked."

"You denied everything."

"Yes, I denied everything. I rationalized that I wasn't lying, that I never forced her to do anything. She was willing. More than willing." He stops talking and goes back to staring at his hands.

I lean forward and rest my chin on my hands. "Tell me about the day of her murder."

He sighs. "You already know."

"Why don't you tell me in your own words."

He swallows. "Okay, okay. You already know I left the monastery without telling anyone. I needed to get away. Believe it or not, I couldn't think there. I needed to decide once and for all what I was going to do. So I left and drove. I stopped for the night at a cheap motel near Thurmont, tried to get some sleep, but I couldn't. I left there about 9:00 a.m. the next morning and began driving again."

"When did you get her email?"

He shakes his head. "I don't remember exactly. I just remember getting it. I remember reading it. I remember screaming. I was going to lose her again."

"Her email told you she had decided to enter the convent," I say.

"The moment I read her email, I decided." He shuts his eyes tight. I say nothing.

"I decided," he whispers, "I decided that if I couldn't have her and remain a priest, then I could no longer be a priest." Then he was silent. The sentence hung in the air between us.

"You started texting her. You wanted to talk to her," I say.

"I had to tell her what I decided. I was going to ask . . . to ask her to marry me."

"What was your plan?"

"That we'd leave. That we'd just leave, that we'd find someone to marry us, that I'd so broken my vows that there would be no question of my being laicized."

"It's not automatic, you know," I point out. "It wouldn't have happened overnight."

"I didn't care about being a priest anymore," he shouts. "I didn't want to serve God, I didn't want to say Mass. I just wanted to be with her."

I sigh and look at her. "So what happened?"

"You know from the texts. She wouldn't see me at first, saying that she was determined to go away, that she had to go away."

I held up my hand. "Wait, what did she say?"

Father Leonard looks at me. "She said she had to go away."

She had to go away. I remember. That was exactly what she said in the texts. She hadn't mentioned the convent in the texts, only in the emails.

"She didn't mention the convent?" I mutter to myself.

"I became frantic," Father Leonard continues. "I sat in that overlook for hours, trying to get her to call me. Finally, she did."

"You talked to her for twenty minutes according to the call records."

"I had to persuade her not to leave. I told her I had decided that I loved her, that I wanted her to go away with me, to become my wife. She was confused, uncertain, said things were more complicated now, that she had something to tell me, but she wouldn't do it over the phone. She asked me to come to her place." He exhales slowly. "You know the rest."

We sit in silence for a few moments. Finally, I say, "She was going to tell you she was pregnant."

He nods. "I suppose she was. That must have been what she was getting at. That would have just made me more determined, knowing she was carrying my child. I wouldn't have let her leave me, take my child. I would have done anything to make sure that didn't happen."

I sit and think about what he has told me. On the one hand, it answers a lot of questions. About how Rachel became parish secretary in the first place. How their relationship blossomed so quickly into a sexual one. It never made sense to me that Leonard would break his vows with a woman he had known only a couple of months. But now, it makes sense. It was still wrong, but it has logic. Rachel just wasn't a woman; she was the woman Leonard had loved for years, the woman whose photograph he kept tucked in his breviary, the thing a priest keeps closest to him, looks at multiple times a day.

But there are other questions. Rachel was pregnant, so what about her call? Why mention going to the convent in the email but not in her texts? Was it just a shorthand she reverted to in answering Leonard, or was it something more? Was she really going to the convent? Or was she going somewhere else? Did anyone else know? Almost as important, why had Win Myer not mentioned his confrontation with Leonard at the Rectory?

"What should I do?" Leonard finally asks me.

"You know one thing you should do," I say, "need to do. We'll get to that in a minute. The other thing—you need to tell your lawyer. She'll tell you what you need to say to the police."

He nods. "I'll talk to her tomorrow. Can you be here?"

"Yes, I'll make the time." I sit back and look at him. "So are you ready now?" I ask.

He nods. "Yes Father, please."

Smiling, I take my prayer book and the small purple scapular from my pocket. I kiss it and place it over my shoulders. I look at Father Leonard across the table.

I say, "Let us begin this sacrament of God's mercy . . ."

Seventeen

A week later, I'm standing by the graveside of Rachel Watson, watching as they slowly lower her casket in the ground.

Standing with me are the members of her family. Her father stands with his arm around his wife. Mrs. Watson wears a black dress and is standing looking down at the casket. She's been dry-eyed the entire day, sitting stoically through the funeral mass and saying nothing during the graveside service. Mr. Watson stands quietly, every so often wiping a tear away. Rebecca, also in black, stands with her husband, a white handkerchief clasped in her hand, every so often wiping tears from her eyes. Her grief is in stark contrast to her mother's self-control. Win Myer looks desolate, a man bereft but using every ounce of strength to keep from showing it.

I say the final prayers and close my book. The Watsons and Win Myer turn and begin walking away. Rebecca stands by herself near the grave. I walk up to her and stand quietly. She's looking into the hole where her sister now lies. We stand like that for a few minutes.

"She's happy now, right, Father?" Rebecca says finally.

I nod. "Yes, I would say so. So would the Church."

"So she's in Heaven right now?"

I shrug. "Honestly, she's more likely in Purgatory. Most souls spend time in purgatory before entering heaven. The Church teaches that only the purest souls go straight to Heaven after they die."

"And in Purgatory, what is she doing?"

"She's being purified from the sins she committed on this earth, during this life. She's also probably praying for those she left behind. I can imagine she's praying for her killer."

Rebecca looks at me questioningly. "All the resentments and anger, they pale compared to what she's seeing now," I explain. "The souls in Purgatory are happy even though they are not in Heaven yet, because they can see where they are going."

"And Hell?" she asks. "What's there?"

"Eternal separation and punishment."

"Do you really believe that?"

I turn to look at her. "If I didn't believe in it all, I wouldn't be much use to anybody as a priest."

She nods, then walks away. I walk beside her towards the cars. The Watsons and Win Myer are standing by Myer's vehicle, waiting for Rebecca. My car is parked nearby.

"Are you coming to the house? That's where everyone is, for the after-funeral reception."

"I wasn't invited," I say. Looking at Win Myer, whose eyes are fixed on me, I say, "I'm not sure I'll be welcome."

"I'm inviting you. I want you there. Rachel would want you there. And as for Win . . ." She pauses. "As for Win, I'll make sure he's on his best behavior."

"He's taken your sister's death hard," I observe.

"Yes," she says coolly. "He has."

"Were they always close?"

"At one time, in high school. You know they dated before she went away."

"I remember you mentioning that. And then you two started dating?"

"That was mama's idea," she says. "She wanted me to marry Winthrop Myer from the time he first showed any interest."

"Interest in you, after Rachel left?"

She shakes her head. "Oh, no. Interest in her."

I stopped. "I don't understand."

Rachel smiled slightly. "Mama never thought much of Rachel and Win together, opposed them going out. She worked really hard to break them up, not that there was much to break up, really; they only went out a couple of times. That's one reason that they sent Rachel away to school, to get her away from Win."

"Did they see him as a bad influence or something?"

"No, I really don't know. Considering how she worked to push the two of us together, it couldn't be that. I've sometimes thought Mama didn't think Rachel was good enough for Winthrop Myer."

"And you were," I say.

She shrugs slightly. "I suppose. Anyway, Mama put us together and Win went along with it."

"But you two are married, so obviously he loves you."

"Really, Father, you think so?" She shakes her head. "I've always wondered. Win's always been so protective of Rachel, I've wondered . . ." She continues walking to the car.

I stand among the graves, watching her. Jealousy? Was she jealous of her sister, of the way Win felt about her? From Father Leonard's account of Win Myer's little visit to him, her husband had some powerful feelings about his sister-in-law. Was he just protective, like a brother? Or did Rebecca think there was more?

I feel the vibration of my phone in my pocket. It's Helen.

"Am I interrupting anything?" she asks.

"No, just finishing up Rachel Watson's funeral."

"Oh, I forgot that it was today. How did it go?"

"As well as funerals go, I guess. What's up?"

"I thought I'd let you know Brian is presenting Father McCoy's case to the grand jury tomorrow."

"No surprise about that," I say. "He's been wanting to do that since the day of the murder."

"What you need to know, Tom, is that he's asking the grand jury to indict him on first-degree murder."

I'm stunned. "What? On what basis? He believes Leonard went to Rachel's apartment intending to murder her?"

"Yes," she sighs. "I've tried pointing out to him that the evidence doesn't support any kind of planning, that everything points to a crime of passion, but he's got it fixed in his mind. He will argue that Father Leonard saw Rachel as a threat to his priesthood, that he killed her to cover up his behavior. That he knew she was pregnant and was afraid everyone would know what he did."

"It's not known that she was pregnant, is it?"

"No, we've kept that part out of the news so far, but it's only a matter of time before that little detail becomes public knowledge. I didn't even mention it to the family."

"Well, I have said nothing either. But Helen, Leonard claims he didn't know about the baby."

"What can I say, Tom, Brian will tell the grand jury he's lying."

"Does he really think the evidence supports first-degree murder? That he can get the grand jury to indict on that charge?"

"You've heard the cliche, a prosecutor can get a grand jury to indict a ham sandwich? Brian's good. He'll get the indictment, if for no other reason than to force Angela Jenkins into a plea deal."

"But Leonard's innocent, Helen."

"He may not be guilty, Tom, but he's hardly innocent in this. His statement proves that."

"But that's an issue for the Church to deal with," I say. "He broke his vow, perhaps the most serious vow a priest takes. It needs to be dealt with. But it doesn't make him a murderer."

"Perhaps, Tom," she replies.

I'm silent for a moment. "You think he's guilty, don't you?"

I hear her sigh. "Of premeditated murder, no, I really don't. But I think he killed her. All the evidence points to him."

"But there was someone else in the apartment before Leonard got there."

"We found no evidence of anyone in the apartment other than Father Leonard and Rachel."

"Have you even bothered to interview Richard Strump?"

She hesitates.

"You haven't, have you?" I say. "But Leonard said—"

"I know, he talked about a presence, about being suffocated, about passing out, then waking up hours later," she continued. "But I'm telling you, there's nothing to support that story. He made it up. Or is still confused or something. No Tom, what we have doesn't support his story." She pauses. "Besides, there is no one out there with a motive. Father Leonard's the only one. That's what Brian will tell the grand jury."

"Except Richard Strump. I don't understand why you haven't interviewed him."

"Because nothing points to anyone else, Tom!" she shouts into the phone. "I'm sorry, but the only one the evidence points to is Father Leonard McCoy. You may not like it, but that's the truth!"

We tell each other goodbye and I hang up. The Myers and the Watsons have driven off, leaving me alone at the cemetery. I look up the hill to my right and see the large maple tree shading a single headstone from the hot July sun.

Before I go to the Myers', there's a visit I need to make.

***

I arrive at the Myer Estate an hour later. Rebecca Myer greets me at the door.

"Thanks for coming, Father," she says as she closes the door behind me.

"Sorry I took so long, I had a stop to make first."

"Parish emergency?" she asks.

"No, I just had to see someone," I say.

She shows me into the dining room, where the table is spread with a variety of food. Fruit bowls, vegetable platters, a variety of cold cuts, and breads. I grab a plate and make myself a sandwich. I get a glass of water and go to find a quiet place to sit down for a few minutes.

The crowd is conversing quietly in small groups. In one of the armchairs sits Marjorie Watson. Edmund sits next to her on a folding chair. I walk up to the Watsons.

"Can I get you anything?" I ask.

"You've already done enough," Edmund Watson says, standing. He walks away.

"What are you doing here?" Marjorie Watson asks.

"Rebecca was good enough to invite me," I explain.

"Oh," she says. "I see. Well, that's okay, then." She sits back in her chair. Looking me in the eye, she says, "I suppose you're expecting to be paid?"

"Rebecca's handling the details," I say. I indicate the chair her husband vacated. She shrugs indifferently. I sit, balancing the plate on my lap.

"Your daughter's done an outstanding job keeping things together," I say.

"She's a wonderful daughter, a good wife to Win," Marjorie comments with a smile. "Always has been. She and Win are a great match. Best decision she ever made was to marry Winthrop

Myer. I mean, just look around," she says, motioning at the surroundings. "She'd never have all of this otherwise."

"She told me that Rachel and Win dated in high school?" I ask, looking at her reaction.

She sits up and looks at me. "She told you that, did she? Well, it's true Win took Rachel out a couple of times, a school dance and one party at the country club. But it was never going to go anywhere."

"Oh, why is that?"

"Because Rachel, well, was Rachel," she says. "She just would never make a wife for Winthrop Myer. Someone else, maybe, but not him."

"Why not? I only met her twice, but Rachel seemed like a very nice, pleasant, intelligent young lady."

"Oh, she was all those things," she says, a slight smile playing on her lips. "But she had her head in the clouds, not an ounce of practicality about her. You know, Father, Win wanted to keep dating her, but Rachel—for reasons I will never understand—she turned him down. I asked her why, and she told me he wasn't what she was looking for." She looked around her. "Can you imagine? Unfortunately, poor Win couldn't let her go. I tried talking to him, but he still had his heart set on Rachel. Eventually, I made my decision."

"What decision was that?"

"To send Rachel away so that Win would forget about her, so he would give Rebecca a chance."

I look at her. So Rebecca's belief was true. The primary reason Rachel went away to high school was to get her away from Winthrop Myer.

"I wanted Win to fall for Rebecca," Marjorie continues. "Rebecca would make a good wife for Win, he just needed to see it. And he did, he did. It took a while, but," she waves her hand again, "he did."

We sit quietly for a moment as a tear falls down her cheek. "Tell me, Father," she whispers. "Did I do something wrong?"

I shake my head. "It's not for me to say. Do you think you did?"

Marjorie sighs. "I didn't think so at the time. For a long time, I convinced myself it was best for everyone. But Rachel came back from school changed. She always had a touch of melancholy about her, but she was sadder. The day of Rebecca's wedding, I found her crying in a closet. She didn't tell me why. I thought she had convinced herself that she'd never find a husband, that she'd be alone forever. Then she got this idea about becoming a nun." She shakes her head.

"How did she seem after that?"

Marjorie thinks for a moment. "She seemed happier, I'd say."

I smile. "That's because she had found someone she'd be with forever."

She looks at me uncomprehendingly. My plate's empty now, so I excuse myself to find a place to put it. I wander back into the dining room and place it on a small table along with others. Walking back to the main room, I pass the open door to Win Myers office. I peek inside.

Myer is sitting behind his desk, his head back, looking up at the ceiling, a drink in his hands. He's whispering something repeatedly. He's not seen me, so I take a step into the doorway and lean forward, straining to hear.

I can barely make it out, but he's repeating one word.

"Rachel. Rachel. Rachel."

Eighteen

The headline in the Myerton Gazette is straight and to the point.

PRIEST INDICTED FOR MURDER

The article states what I already know, that the county grand jury returned an indictment against Father Leonard McCoy, former priest of Saint Clare's Catholic Church in Myerton, for first-degree murder in the death of Rachel Watson. The reporter had called the previous day asking for a statement. I gave her none, having learned my lesson about talking to the press. The Archdiocese had no comment. Angela Jenkins was quoted in the paper, saying, "My client is being railroaded by an ambitious prosecutor who cares more about satisfying the wealthy and privileged than justice." The paper quotes Brian Dohrmann saying, "The grand jury heard the evidence, and I'm looking forward to getting justice for Rachel Watson."

I put the paper down when Anna places the plate containing a cheese omelet, bacon, and buttered wheat toast in front of me. She sets a jar of strawberry preserves on the table, then sits down with her coffee.

"I guess what they say about prosecutors is true," I comment.

"That they can get a grand jury to indict a ham sandwich? If Brian Dohrmann can persuade a grand jury that Father Leonard McCoy is a cold-blooded killer, then I hope I'm never ticketed for jaywalking. He'll give me the chair," Anna says as she drinks her coffee. "Well, what are you going to do about this?"

"I'll pray for him and the situation, but I know of nothing else I can do."

"Do you think he's guilty?"

I pick up a triangle of toast and slather on a spoonful of the strawberry preserves. I take a bite and chew while I consider her question.

"Well?" she presses.

I swallow. "I've tried to decide if I believe he's guilty. And I'll tell you, Anna, despite all the evidence, I still don't think he did it." I sigh. "But if I were on that jury and knew nothing else about him except what the State Attorney was telling me, the evidence he was showing me, I'd think he was guilty. Not first-degree murder, but that he was guilty of something."

"But he's not done anything he's been accused of, right?"

At my hesitation, Anna says, "Unless he is guilty of something. What?"

Since it was all going to come out soon anyway, I saw no reason not to tell her. So I told her what I could. About Father Leonard and Rachel, about their relationship, and about Rachel's pregnancy. As I tell the story, Anna looks more and more shocked and surprised.

"So that's everything, and I'd appreciate it if you keep it to yourself. It's going to all come out soon enough, but I'd like it to stay quiet for a while."

She nods and drinks her coffee. Anna sits quietly, looking out the window, processing the story I just told her.

"It doesn't add up to murder," she says. "If he loved her—and from what you've told me he did—he'd have no reason to kill her."

"According to Helen, the State Attorney is working on the theory that he used her, that she confronted him with the baby and demanded he take care of her, and he killed her to cover up evidence of his sin. So as not to damage his priesthood."

"Brian Dohrmann is an idiot," she says. "And to think I was going to vote for him. I must look at Father Leonard's lawyer more closely."

"I don't think he's an idiot," I say. "I think he wants a conviction so he can present it to the voters. You know, not afraid to stand up to a powerful institution like the Catholic Church."

"But afraid to say no to Winthrop Myer," she says, standing up and taking my plate and her cup to the sink.

Winthrop Myer. I think about him, sitting in his office at the house the day of Rachel Watson's funeral. Alone, in the dark, with a drink. Repeating her name over and over again. I remember Father Leonard's account of his meeting with Win Myer, how the man roughed the young priest up. I remember what Rebecca said about Win and Rachel dating in school, and what Marjorie Watson said about why she sent Rachel away.

For such an unassuming person, Rachel Watson had been the center of so many machinations, so many emotions, when she was alive. She was the one her mother wanted out of the way; she was the one who lost out to her sister; she was the one who had a brother-in-law with a deep interest in her; she was the one who led a young priest to break his vows and give up his calling. And, in death, she was the one who that same priest was accused of murdering.

The murder is connected to the relationships she had, as most murders are. I just don't know how.

"What are you going to do?" Anna says.

"Again, Anna, I don't know there's anything I can do."

As I say that, I think about Father Leonard's story of that night, the story the police discounted, about there being a presence in Rachel's apartment, about being suffocated and passing out, and waking up next to her dead body, his shirt covered in blood. The story the authorities discounted as a lie.

But the police had found no evidence of another person. The only evidence they found pointed to Father Leonard as being the only one at the apartment.

There was no forced entry, so Rachel was expecting someone. She let in the person who killed her. It was someone she knew. Father Leonard fell in that category. But so did several other people. Her sister, her mother, her brother-in-law, her father. But no one had said anything about being in her apartment that day. Had anyone seen anyone other than Leonard enter her apartment?

But why kill Rachel Watson at all? Who benefited?

There is only one person who benefited from her death. And he is sitting in jail at that moment.

I shake my head. There are so many questions about this murder, but the one thing I keep running into is that the person least likely to have committed this murder is the one who benefited the most.

Except he isn't the only one who had a motive. There was one other person, someone Helen hasn't bothered to interview. Richard Strump.

Something else bothers me. The day of her murder, Rachel Watson had sent Leonard, her sister, and her brother-in-law emails saying she had decided to go ahead and enter the convent. But she knew she was pregnant and couldn't enter the convent. Her bags were packed, so she was going somewhere. Leonard had told her he wanted them to run away together, so she was ready to go. But she was leaving Myerton before they even talked.

"So where was she going?" I say.

"What?" Anna says, startled.

"Sorry, I was just thinking out loud."

Had Rachel said anything to the Mother Superior at the convent? Had anyone asked her?

"Didn't you say Nate Rodriguez has that vlog now?"

"What? Yes, why?"

"I think I'll call him." To her quizzical look, I say. "There are just too many questions. I need to find some answers. Maybe Nate can help."

***

Nate must have broken the land-speed record getting to the Rectory, arriving about half an hour after I called him.

"I'm glad you called," he says as he quickly sets his recording equipment up. "I want to do a podcast on Father Leonard, but wanted to wait until after the trial. Then you called, and well, here I am."

"Thanks for coming so quickly, Nate." I pause and look at him as he finishes setting the microphones up to record. "We need to talk first."

"Sure, sure, okay," he says, sitting in a chair across from my desk, perched on the edge, expectantly.

"I don't believe Father Leonard is guilty," I say. "I have no evidence, but there are a lot of holes in the state's case. I need your help to look into this."

"Just call me Watson," he says with a grin, bouncing up and down in the chair like an excited toddler.

"We need to keep this quiet. We don't want to step on any toes."

His smile slowly fades. "So no interview."

"No interview, not yet. I need you to use your journalism skills to look into some things."

He sighs. "Okay, I'll be glad to help."

I take a sticky note and a pen. As I write, I say, "Rachel had a problem with one of her former co-workers harassing and stalking her. His name's Richard Strump. I need you to look into him." I hand him the sticky note.

"Richard Strump," he says. "You say he used to work with Rachel?"

"Apparently, he was arrested outside her townhouse back in February. He was fired a few weeks later for that and, apparently, harassing other women on the job."

"I can get a copy of the arrest report—they are public record," he says. "I'll find out where he lives."

"See if you can talk to him. And be careful."

Nate grins. "You know me, Father."

Yes, that's what worries me, I think.

"I also think you should interview Rachel Watson's neighbors, ask them if they saw or heard anything that night."

"Don't you think the police already questioned them?"

"Oh, I'm sure they did. But maybe they've remembered something since then."

"Okay, what else?"

"That's all for now, Nate," I say.

He nods. "I'll get right on it." He smiles sheepishly. "You know Father Tom, since I'm here, and I set everything up..."

I return the smile, but shake my head. "No, Nate, not now. If you'll excuse me." I stand and leave my office. I find Anna in the parish secretary's office, reorganizing the filing system.

"Anna," I say. "I have nothing on my schedule this afternoon after the Noon mass, do I?"

She stops and looks at the calendar on her desk. "No, you're clear all afternoon."

I nod. "Good. I've got a little trip out of town to make. I'll be back later tonight, so don't bother with dinner. I'll get something on the road."

"Where are you going?" she asks as I walk out of her office.

"To find out where Rachel Watson was going."

Nineteen

The young nun shows me into the small room. It's simply appointed, a couple of pictures of saints and the current pope on the wall, a statue of Our Lady in the corner. Two armchairs are in the center of the room, across from each other. The convent is semi-cloistered, so they allow visitors on a limited basis. I will not have to speak to the Mother Superior through a grill, but in this room set aside for the reception of visitors.

"Have a seat, Father," she says. "I'll go fetch Mother Evangeline."

I sit in one chair and look around for a few minutes. After only a short time, the door opens and the young nun returns, this time accompanied by an older nun clad in the traditional habit. She's physically imposing, about my height. I can tell nothing about her hair color, covered as it is. Her face is firm, but not intimidating. Her eyes are clear and focused, but soft and kind. She gives the impression of someone who has a great responsibility, but also one who is capable of great compassion.

"Bring us some lemonade, Sister, if you would please," she says to the young sister. She gives a slight bow and leaves the room. Mother Evangeline smiles as she approaches me.

"Father Greer," she says, inclining her head. "It is a pleasure to meet you."

"Thank you for meeting me on such short notice," I say. Mother Evangeline moves to her chair and sits. I resume my position across from her.

"I am still saddened by the news," she says. "The convent will pray the office of the dead for her soul. So sad, so tragic. And you say a young priest stands accused of her murder?"

"He's been arrested and indicted for the crime," I say. "I do not believe he did it."

"In my experience," she says grimly, "anyone is capable of anything, given sufficient motivation."

I consider what she says. "What can you tell me about Rachel Watson?"

She folds her hands and sits back in the chair. "I met Rachel a few years ago. She was working at a firm in Baltimore and came here for a women's retreat weekend. At the end of the weekend, she asked to speak to me. She said she had received a call from God that weekend to enter the religious life."

"What was your reaction?"

"I was pleased but wary." At my glance, she explains, "More young women than you would imagine come here for a weekend, find the experience attractive, and decide they're being called to this life. It's so different from the one they're living in the world. Most are in careers, have boyfriends, the like. Here, we are apart from the world. It attracts many who are tired, tired of what they experience out there. But it's fleeting. Many come, but few stay."

"What did you tell her?"

"I explained that we could lead her through discernment, but it was a long process before she could enter the convent as a postulant. There would be opportunities for discernment weekends, for spiritual direction, and I would have to work with her parish priest. She was attending a parish in Baltimore, so I got in touch with the priest. We went on from there." She stops and looks up as the young nun places a tray with a pitcher of lemonade and two glasses on the table between us, then watches as she leaves and closes the door.

She pours two glasses and takes one. "She attended each discernment weekend—we have them once a quarter—and she was the only one who did so consistently." She smiles. "I took that as a good sign, that she really had a call, that she was serious about discernment." She takes a sip and smacks her lips. "So good, so good," she mutters.

"Did she tell you she had decided to join?"

She shook her head. "No, as serious as she was, she kept putting off the decision. Then she moved back to her hometown. I took that as a sign she was getting things ready to make a move. She attended the Advent retreat here and told me she needed to get some things in order but she would get in touch after the first of the year about entering in the spring." She sat back. "But winter and spring came and went, and I heard nothing else from her."

"What did you think?"

"That she had changed her mind, like so many young women. I thought it most likely that she had met a young man and decided that she was called to the vocation of marriage instead of the religious life."

I think about what she says. That corresponds with her reuniting with Father Leonard and becoming the parish secretary.

"Then," she says, putting the now empty glass on the table, "one day, she called. She apologized for not getting in touch sooner, but explained that she had a crisis of faith, a reason to doubt her vocation. She assured me she was ready to enter the postulancy as soon as she settled her affairs at home." She looks at her hands. "There was something about her voice, her tone, which told me that her decision was a hasty one."

"What do you mean?" I ask.

"Father Tom, when you've been here as long as I have, you can tell just from talking to a young woman why she's contemplating this life. For some, a smaller percentage than I'd like, it's a genuine desire to follow God, to spend the rest of their lives in prayer and service. For most, they see it as an escape, a way of avoiding the pain in their own lives instead of dealing with it in the world head-on. It's not a bad motivation, mind you, but it's not the best." She sighs. "What part is a genuine call from God, and what part is avoidance, only the Lord knows."

The Mother Superior's words resonate with me. So much of what she says is familiar to me, to my circumstances, to the reasons I became a priest. I've struggled with the same question. Was I called? Or was I just avoiding pain? Was I doing that now?

"And Rachel?"

"Rachel, I sensed it was more the latter. I supposed there had been a nasty breakup with a young man; that was the usual reason."

"What are some other reasons you've seen?"

"Oh, there's a variety," she says with a smile. "Believe it or not, often it's a way to rebel against parents. It's funny, when I first entered the convent, so many young women rebelled by leaving the religious life and the Church of their childhood altogether. Now it's like they see the best way of rebelling against their parents is by embracing this life, and the stricter the life, the better. Ironic, isn't it? But then the Church has always been unfashionable and rebellious."

A desire to rebel. Against her parents, especially her mother, who had done so much to control her life. Was that the primary reason Rachel wanted to become a nun?

"When was this conversation?"

She looks to her side, as if trying to remember. "Let's see, I think it was just after Memorial Day."

Now it made sense. Memorial Day. The day of the picnic, and the beginning of everything.

"I thought everything was settled, or at least we began to prepare for her. I didn't hear from her again until two weeks before her death."

"She called you again?"

"Oh no, Father," she shakes her head. "She showed up here unannounced."

I lean forward. "Really? What happened?"

"It was just after Vespers when someone started ringing the doorbell. Not just once, but repeatedly. One sister went to answer and Rachel rushed in. She was hysterical, frankly sobbing, begging to see me. I'm surprised she had made it all the way here from Myerton without having an accident. I didn't see how she could have driven herself in that circumstance."

She stops and pours herself another glass of lemonade. I beg off when she offers me the pitcher. She sits back with her glass, tracing the rim with her finger.

"We finally got her calmed down," the Mother Superior continues, "gave her a good stiff brandy—we keep it for medicinal purposes, Father," she explains at my look of surprise. "After the brandy and some time, she could speak to me about why she was there. Since she had no suitcase, I knew it wasn't to stay."

"What did she tell you?" I ask, but already know the answer.

"Everything that you already know," she replies with a smile. "That she had begun a sexual relationship with the priest at Saint Clare's and had found out she was pregnant."

She put her glass down. "That changed everything. She couldn't enter the postulancy in that condition; as wonderful as children are, it's just not what we're equipped for. She knew that, said she still wanted to enter after the baby was born, and explained that she was planning on placing the child for adoption." She pauses. "I asked her if she had told the father. She said she hadn't, that she had no intention of doing so. That she was making plans to leave, take a job somewhere and have the baby quietly, then come back here and enter the postulancy. I had another suggestion."

"Which was?"

"Our order has a home for young unwed mothers in Virginia," she says. "It's one of the few in the country, though more are opening every year. I told her I could get her a place there, she could be cared for and the baby born there, and we would help coordinate the adoption. It would take a couple of weeks to arrange. She agreed to that. After we prayed together, I sent her on her way. She seemed more at peace."

"What did you say to her about telling Father McCoy?"

She gets a grim expression on her face. "I firmly advised her to tell the young man, that he had a right to know, if for no other reason than to understand the seriousness of his sin. But she was adamant that he not know; she said it would destroy him, that he was too good a priest to do that to." She shakes her head. "Though I have serious doubts about his goodness."

"It is a complicated situation," I say. "Father McCoy is a good man who made a serious mistake. But it wasn't done in haste. It was a culmination."

"Oh? In what way?"

I explain about their prior relationship, about Father Leonard's continued love for Rachel through the years of seminary and his early priesthood. She nods.

"I see. I did not know that." She sighs. "Attachments of the heart are the hardest to give up when you enter this life." A wistful expression passes over her face. "Yes, very hard," she whispers.

"As it turns out, it wasn't necessary," she says. "So sad, such a loss."

"I'm not sure what you mean?"

She looks at me. "The miscarriage. She called me a few days before her murder and told me she had lost the baby, and that after she recovered, she'd be at the convent to begin her postulancy."

I'm stunned. Before I can say anything, the convent bell tolls. The mother superior looks up. "Ah, that would be None," she says as she stands. I look at the time. It is just before 3:00 p.m.

"Would you care to join us before you leave, Father?"

I nod. "Yes, I would be happy to."

I follow Mother Superior from the room. My mind reels from what she just told me. A miscarriage? That was impossible. She was still pregnant at the time of her death; the autopsy showed that.

As I walk with Mother Superior to the chapel, a thought occurs to me, one that causes my blood to run cold.

"No," I whisper. "Not that."

"Excuse me, Father," Mother Superior asks.

"Sorry, I have one more question," I say quickly. She stops and turns. "You said she seemed like she was in no condition to drive. Did anyone see her leave?"

"I'd have to ask the sister who showed her out—oh, wait, here she is. Sister Dymphna," she stops a middle-aged nun. "You were with Rachel Watson when she left after her visit a couple of weeks ago, correct?"

"Yes, Mother Superior," she answers quietly.

"Did you see her walk to her car?"

"Yes. It was late at night and there's not a lot of light outside."

"Was anyone in the car with her?" I ask.

She looks at me, then the Mother Superior. The older woman nods, then the nun answers, "It was dark so I couldn't see very well." She stops to think, "Wait, that's odd."

"What sister?" Mother Superior asks.

"When Rachel got in the car, she got in on the passenger side."

"The passenger side, not the driver's side? Are you sure?" I ask.

She thinks for a moment, then nods her head. "Yes, quite sure. She got in her car on the passenger side."

***

I'm on my way back to Myerton, processing what I learned at the convent, when my phone rings. It's Nate.

"Hello?" I say.

"Father Tom," he whispers. "I found something. You need to come quick."

"Where are you? Why are you whispering?"

"Where am I? I'm outside Strump's house. You need to get here. I think I found out who killed Rachel Watson."

"I'll be there as soon as I can," I say before hanging up. I press the accelerator and look at the needle on my speedometer going past 75.

Twenty

"There was no one home," Nate whispers, "so I talked to his neighbors. That's when I found out."

We're sitting in his car, a mid-1990s Honda that has seen better days. The upholstery is worn, the paint has faded, and one of the back doors is held closed by a length of rope. Across the street is a small brick bungalow with a chain-link fence.

"You keep saying that," I say. "What did you find out?"

"His next-door neighbor," he points to a similar brick bungalow, "told me Strump is really quiet, doesn't talk to many people. Never had a problem until the other day."

"What happened the other day?"

"The fire."

I sigh. "What fire?"

"The one in the barrel in his backyard," Nate says. "He set it and then left. The neighbor was worried the fire would get out of control—you know we haven't had a lot of rain, and it's been hot, things are dry—so he doused the flames with his garden hose."

I shake my head. "Lots of people have burn barrels. It's not unusual."

"The neighbor said it was," Nate replies. "He'd never seen Strump do it before. So I got curious. What was he burning? So I looked."

"You went in his backyard? That's trespassing, Nate."

"But I found something. Come see it."

I look in his earnest and excited eyes. Then I look across the street. "Okay," I say against my better judgement. "But we need to do it quickly, before he comes back."

"He's been gone for hours," Nate says. "He must be out of town."

We sneak across the street and slowly open the gate. It squeaks on the rusting hinges. We pause and listen. Hearing no one, we walk into Strump's yard.

"It's around this way," Nate whispers. He pulls out his phone and uses the flashlight to illuminate our path. I follow him as we tip-toe through the grass around to the back of the house.

"There," he shows with his light. About twenty yards from the house is a metal barrel.

We walk to it and Nate shines his light inside.

"See? See?" he whispers excitedly.

I roll my eyes. "Nate, really? This is what you called me for?"

"What?" he says.

I shake my head and look down. The barrel is filled with porn magazines.

"You don't think this means something?"

"All this means," I whisper, "is that he was trying to get rid of his porn collection."

"But who pays money for porn magazines anymore when you can get it for free online?" Nate responds. I look at him. "Not that I would know, Father, I mean I've heard, not that I—"

"Calm down, Nate," I say, holding my hand up to stop him. I look down again and sigh. Then something catches my eye.

"Get me a stick or something," I whisper to Nate. Nate goes off and returns with a short garden trowel.

"Here," he says. "It's the only thing I could find."

"Shine your light right here," I say. With the trowel, I gently lift the charred magazine on top.

"Let me see your light," I say to Nate. Taking his light, I look at what's underneath. It's a photograph, printed out on photo paper from a color printer. The fire has singed the edges, and the water-stained part of the image, but I have no trouble making out who it is.

It's a photograph of Rachel Watson, outside of her apartment.

"Police, don't move!" Nate and I look at each other. A neighbor must have seen us and called the police.

"Raise your hands and turn, slowly," says the authoritative voice. We turn into the glare of flashlights. Squinting, I make out a figure pointing the light with one hand and a gun with another. Standing next to the one figure is another figure, also pointing a gun at us.

"We're not armed," I say.

"Father Tom?" My panic subsides as I recognize the voice.

"It's me, Dan," I say.

"Father Tom," Dan Conway says. "It's okay, Casey, I know him." Both officers holster their weapons and walk forward.

"We had a report of prowlers," Dan explains. "What are you two—hello Nate, how's your Uncle?—doing back here."

"Looking for evidence," Nate blurts.

"What?"

"He's right, Dan. We found something Detective Parr needs to see," I say, pointing at the barrel.

Dan shines his flashlight into the barrel. He whistles, then says, "Casey, get Detective Parr. Tell her she needs to get here ASAP with a crime scene team."

***

"Trespassing, Tom!" Helen shouts, three feet from me. Her fury flows over me like a hot wind from a raging wildfire. I did not expect her to be so angry. I thought when she arrived outside

Strump's house that she'd take one look at what Nate and I found and she'd be—well, maybe not pleased, maybe not grateful, but certainly not furious.

But I took one look when she got out of her car and knew I was in for it. The resounding slam of her car door put the exclamation point on that.

"Trespassing," she repeats, "if not harassment."

Nate says, "He asked me to do it, Detective! It wasn't my idea!"

"You be quiet," she points to Nate. "I'm yelling at him now. I'll get to you." She turns back to me and opens her mouth to continue.

"Listen, Helen," I say, "I asked for Nate's help to look into Strump, to see if we could find anything that might tie him to Rachel's murder. Which we did. Aren't you even going to look?"

"And have a charge of an illegal search? No way, Tom. I already told you—"

"I know what you told me!" I shout. "I'm trying to help a good man who made a serious mistake avoid being tried for a crime he didn't commit! If you had been doing your job in the first place, interviewing Strump, instead of kowtowing to your ex-boyfriend, I wouldn't be standing here right now!"

She's staring at me, her mouth open, a fire growing in her eyes. I know I've gone too far, but I can't stop.

"Do you think I wanted to do this? Do you think I enjoy playing detective? Believe it or not, I don't! Not one little bit! I just want a quiet life, serving God's people as a priest, like every other man who wears the collar!" I take a deep breath. "But if justice demands I sneak around in the dark like Jessica Fletcher in a cassock, then I'll do it!"

I stop talking. I'm suddenly aware that the eyes of the other officers are on us. Helen's eyes have lost their fire, replaced by astonishment. I cannot remember a time in our past when I ever spoke to her this way.

"You're not wearing a cassock, Father," Nate mutters to me.

"Shut up, Nate!" Helen and I say in unison. We are staring at each other, like two opponents across a dueling field, each waiting for the other one to fire first.

Dan slinks up to us. "Excuse me, Detective Parr?"

"What is it, Officer Conway!" Helen snaps.

"Um, I think the owner of the house just got here."

Helen and I look at Dan, who is pointing past us. We turn to see an unassuming, rather portly man with thinning black hair, walking up the sidewalk from where he parked his green sedan.

"Officers," he says when he gets to us. He regards Nate and I with confusion.

"Richard Strump?" Helen asks.

"Yes," he says. He's fidgeting with his keys, shifting from one foot to another. "Is there a problem?"

"We found out what you were burning in your backyard," Nate blurts out.

"What?" he says, with panic in his voice. "What—what were you doing in my backyard?"

"Be quiet, Nate!" I hiss.

"These Officers found Father Greer and Mr. Rodriguez in your backyard," Helen explains. "Do you want to press charges for trespassing?"

"Press charge—no, no, that's okay. It's fine. No charges. Thank you." He moves to open his gate.

"One moment, Mr. Strump," Helen says. "Do you mind if I ask you a couple of questions?"

"Questions?" he asks nervously. "What questions?"

"Did you kill Rachel Watson?" Nate asks.

I grab Nate by the arm. "Come on, Nate, let's go!" I step towards my car when I hear Dan yell, "Hey! Hey!" I turn to see that Strump is running down the sidewalk. Not so much running, more plodding like an overweight Ewok. Dan takes off after him and has no trouble catching him. He brings Strump back to us.

"Do you want me to take him in?" Dan asks Helen.

"Why did you run, Mr. Strump?" Helen demands.

The portly man is wheezing. "I—I—whew, shouldn't have done that. I'm sorry." Strump bends over and grabs his knees. "Let me catch my breath."

"Why did you run?"

He looks up at Helen. "Why? I panicked."

"Obviously." She crosses her arms and looks down at the little man. "Would you care to tell me why?"

He stands up and sighs. "We better go inside." Strump looks at me. "Can the Father come?"

Helen looks at me. "If you'd like."

Helen, Strump, and I walk through the gate, leaving Nate and the other officers on the sidewalk. Stump unlocks the door and shows us inside.

"Pardon the mess," he says as we walk into the living room. It's only marginally cleaner than Helen's apartment. We find places to sit.

"After I heard about Rachel Watson," he begins, "I was expecting a visit."

"Why is that, Mr. Strump?"

"Because of my arrest," he says, looking at his hands. "Because of my stalking Rachel."

Helen reaches in her bag and pulls out her notebook and a pen. "That was back in February?"

He nods. "February 24," he whispers. "I'll always remember that date."

"Why is that, Mr. Strump?" I ask. I expect a non-verbal rebuke from Helen, but one does not come.

Strump looks down. "Because that's when I hit rock bottom," he whispers.

"You were fired from your job soon afterward," Helen continues, "because of your arrest?"

"That—and the other things," he says, still not looking at us. "There were several women at work that I—well, I mistreated them. I did things. Shameful things."

"Did you stalk them too, Richard?"

He nods. "But that was the only time I got caught."

"I bet that made you angry," Helen says. Strump looks up. "At Rachel. I mean, she had you arrested. She was responsible for you losing your job. That would have made anyone angry."

"I won't lie to you, Detective, Father, I was. Very angry. At her, at myself. For a couple of months, I didn't even leave the house. I did nothing to find another job." He exhales. "Then one day, I woke up and looked at my life. And faced the truth about myself. That's when the anger just vanished."

"What happened?" I ask.

"I admitted to myself that I had a problem," he says. "With women. With sex." He looks at his hands. "With porn."

"Ah," I say. "That's what you were burning."

"Yes," he responds. "I had gotten rid of my cable and had a friend put a blocker on my internet—he's the only one who has the password and gets a report every day about my internet usage—but I still had my collection of magazines." He swallows. "And the photographs I took."

"Photographs of Rachel," Helen says.

"Yes, Rachel, and other women. Mostly clothed. Some not." He pauses again, wipes a tear away.

"This is all very interesting, Mr. Strump," Helen says. "But I have to ask, where were you the night of Rachel Watson's murder?"

He puts his hand in his shirt pocket, takes a small disk out and tosses it on the coffee table in front of us.

I pick it up. "It's a sobriety chip," I say.

Strump nods. "Sex Addicts Anonymous. I got that Sunday. Three months of sexual sobriety." He looks at Helen. "The night of Rachel Watson's murder, Detective, I was at a meeting. I have about two dozen people who can tell you I was there from about 6:00 to 9:00 that night."

Twenty-One

"Are you satisfied now?"

We're standing at the end of the walkway leading to Strump's house. I look back at where we just left.

"You will check on his alibi, right?"

Helen puts her hands on her hips. "Of course I will, Tom. I mean, unless you'd like to do it for me? Hey, I have an idea, you do that and I'll say Mass this Sunday. How does that sound?"

"Listen, Helen, I—"

"No, you listen, Tom." She points her finger at me. "You have got to stop playing detective. One of these days, you will get hurt. You almost did last time."

"All I was doing—"

"I know what you were doing," she says. Her expression softens. "I know you were only trying to help Father Leonard, to find someone else—anyone else—who killed Rachel Watson." She touches my arm. "You need to face the fact that he did it."

I shake my head. "No, Helen, I can't believe that. He's not capable of murder. He loved her."

"People kill people they love all the time."

"He couldn't have done it."

"The evidence says otherwise."

"The evidence is wrong."

She sighs. "No, it's not, Tom," she says quietly. "The evidence points to him. It's the simplest explanation. Occam's Razor, remember? You taught me about that years ago."

I look at her.

"Anyway, just leave the detective work to me from now on, okay? I'm not always going to be there to get you out of a jam."

***

"Father Tom," Rebecca Myer says, "what a surprise."

It's the next afternoon. "I hope I'm not coming at an inconvenient time," I say as I step into the foyer of the Myer home. "And I apologize for not calling first, but I was out on my sick calls and was passing when I thought I'd stop in and see how you were doing."

She closes the door and stands with her arms crossed. "Fine, I suppose," she says. "It's still hard to believe, even though it's been, what, two weeks? It seems like only yesterday we got a visit from the police telling us that Rachel . . . " She trails off as tears well up. I hand her my handkerchief.

"Thank you," she says as she dabs her eyes. "Sorry about this."

"Not at all," I say.

"Grief is so strange, so unpredictable. I'll be going along with my day, and suddenly I'll see something small, or hear a snippet of music, and it all comes rushing back. Do you understand what I mean, Father?"

I nod. I'm intimately familiar with grief.

"Anyway, come in and sit down. Can I get you something?"

"No, I'm fine," I say as we enter the sitting room. Taking one of the armchairs, she perches on the edge of the sofa near me. "Is your husband home?"

"No, he's out of town on business for a couple of days. Continued problems with the wind farm project."

"And how is he doing?"

She sits back and looks out the window. "He thought a lot of Rachel," she says carefully, "cared about her a great deal. He's taken it hard. Harder than I remember him taking his parent's death."

I look at Rebecca. She is carefully choosing her words, and her voice is even. Her face betrays irritation.

"I must tell you, Rebecca, that I have a reason for coming here besides checking on you."

She smiles. "The whole 'just passing by' didn't seem likely, considering how far from a major road we are."

I return the smile. "I have a question."

"I hope I can answer. What is it, Father?"

I look her in the eye. "Did you drive Rachel to the convent one night about two weeks ago?"

Her smile disappears. She gets up from the couch and moves to the window. She stares out, not answering.

"You did, didn't you?"

She nods. "She was hysterical. I couldn't let her drive herself."

"Did she tell you why?"

"You mean, did she tell me she was pregnant with Father Leonard's child?" she says, spinning around. "Yes, yes, she told me. She told me everything that afternoon."

She paces. "She showed up unannounced, crying. Win was here, and knowing how he is about her, I took her through the house as quickly as I could to the back porch. I got her calmed down enough to tell me. She hadn't been feeling well for a couple of weeks, and her period was late. She went to the doctor, not having the courage to try a home pregnancy test, apparently. She got the news there. From what she told me, she ran out of the office as soon as the doctor said the words." She stopped and looked at Father Tom. "I was furious when she told me, not at her, but at him. I thought everything you hear about priests preying on members of their parish was true. That's what I was angry about."

"But she told you the story, didn't she?"

She gave a short laugh. "Oh, yes, as soon as I called him a bastard, she told me everything. About how they had met years earlier, but nothing happened. How she started attending Saint Clare's and was stunned to see him come in to do the service. About how they reconnected, how she took the parish secretary's job just to be near him." She paused. "She even told me about their first time." She shook her head and sat down. "I would have thought as educated as she was, she would have taken precautions, but I don't think it was something they planned."

"No, not from what I understand," I say.

Rebecca shoots me a glance. "I take it Father Leonard told you his side of the story."

I look at her, not indicating anything. "Oh, you can't tell me, can you," she says. Putting up her hands, she says, "Okay, I understand." She sits back on the couch.

"Why did she want to go to the convent that night?"

Rebecca shrugs. "I'm not sure. She just said she needed to go somewhere, that she'd be back the next day, probably. I could see she was in no condition to drive herself—I'm surprised she made it here from the doctor's office—and I knew Win had a meeting at the country club that evening so he wouldn't miss me. So I told him that Rachel and I were going out that evening and we'd be back later, then I drove her in my car. I didn't even know where we were going. I thought, honestly, she wanted me to take her to a clinic, you know . . . to take care of the problem." She looks down at her hands. "I'm ashamed for thinking that, but it crossed my mind."

"Did you suggest the possibility to her?"

"Oh, no," she shakes her head. "We had had more than one discussion about that, and I knew what her position was. I should have known that wouldn't be a possibility, but given the circumstances, I thought she might have decided to just get rid of the child."

"So I was a little surprised when we stopped at the convent. I had never been there before. She asked me to wait for her in the car while she went to talk to somebody. She practically ran to the front door, rang the bell several times before someone let her in. She was in there about an hour before she came out. I have to tell you, Father. The change was astounding. She was . . . calm, at peace, even happy."

"She told you what she and the Mother Superior had discussed."

"It seemed like an ideal solution. Go off to have the baby, put it up for adoption, then return and enter the convent—that frankly, I still didn't understand, but she was my sister and I loved her, still love her." A tear runs down her cheek. "So we drove back here, she got in her car, and went home."

"Did you tell anybody?"

"Absolutely not!" she exclaims. "Not Mama, not Win. She swore me to secrecy. We hatched a plan. It would take her a couple of weeks to get things arranged, but I would drive her to the maternity home when all the arrangements were made, under the guise of my going to a spa for a few days." She paused. "I was supposed to pick her up Monday morning."

"And the email about her entering the convent she sent you and Win?"

She smiles. "Clever, eh? That was the cover story. It would tamp down questions. And it was true, in a way. The maternity home is run by the order she's entering, and she would enter the convent after the baby was born."

I sit back and think about what she just said. "She called Mother Superior a couple of days before her death and told her she had miscarried. That was a lie. What was she going to do, Rebecca?"

Slowly, she says, "She called me on Wednesday, the Wednesday before her murder. She told me she had changed her mind about having the baby, that she didn't want to go through all that only to give the baby up. That she had to enter the convent as quickly as possible." She hesitates before saying. "She had made an appointment at a clinic in Hagerstown for Monday afternoon."

I close my eyes. To deal with the consequences of one sin, she decided to commit another. Something that happened too often.

"Did she tell you why she decided to have an abortion?" I ask.

Rebecca shakes her head. "No, and I didn't ask. I figured it was her decision. She was old enough, you know. So we made a slight change to our plans. I'd pick her up Monday morning, drive her to Hagerstown, she'd have the abortion, then we'd check in to a hotel for her to rest for a couple of days. Then I'd take her to the convent." She sniffles. "That's the last time I heard from her."

We sit in silence in the room. I hear movement behind me. "I thought I heard voices," Win Myer says jovially. "Rebecca, who—oh! What is he doing here?"

I stand and turn around, smiling. Win Myer is not.

"Hello, Win," I say. "I just came to—"

"He came to see how we were doing," Rebecca interjects. "Isn't that nice of Father Tom? I didn't expect you back so soon. How was your trip?"

"How are we doing? A damn sight better now that that monster will be when he gets what he deserves," he says, ignoring Rebecca's question. "I can't even believe you'd have the gall to show up here."

"I came," I say, my smile disappearing, "to see how you two were doing. Rachel was Rebecca's sister, and from what I understand, you cared deeply about her. Her death has been hard for both of you."

"What would you know about that?" he spits. "How would you possibly know about the pain of losing someone so precious, someone you cherished, someone—what Rebecca?"

I turn to see Rebecca shaking her head and motioning slightly at me. She must have heard my story.

"Win, stop," Rebecca says. "Father Tom—"

"He needs to understand the pain Father McCoy caused! You and your mother!" he cries. What he means, though, is apparent. He's referring to his own pain. Rebecca's face betrays her thoughts. She knows.

"Just let me know when he's gone," Win says, spinning around and stomping from the room. I turn back to Rebecca, who's watched him leave.

"Sorry about that, Father," Rebecca says. "He's taken Rachel's death hard."

"Well, you told me they were close."

"No, that's not true. They weren't close, at least Rachel wasn't close to Win. It's all Win."

"I'm not sure I follow."

"Oh, Win cared a lot more for Rachel than Rachel cared about him, in the last few years anyway," Rebecca explains. "I think our marriage upset her. I know she was upset the day of our wedding. After that, she kept her distance. Win, however . . ."

"You think he still loved her," I say.

"Think? I know he still loved her," she says. "He still loves her. Maybe not more than he loves me, though sometimes I wonder. I'd see it on his face every time he looked at her. I got used to it. But I trusted my sister."

I think how hard it would be to get used to someone I loved loving someone else more than me. The pain would have gotten unbearable. I look at Rebecca.

"And you didn't resent Rachel? Not even a little?"

"No, not at all."

"I'm sorry, Rebecca, but I find that a little hard to believe," I say.

"Why? It was Win, not her. She felt nothing about him anymore."

"But she was here," I say. "You'd be reminded every time you saw her that your husband loved her more than he loved you."

"No, I don't think—"

Pressing on, I continue, "No one would blame you if after a while you came to resent your sister's very presence." I pause. "And wanted to see her gone."

She looks at me, her mouth open, a protest dying on her lips. "What are you saying, Father Greer?" she asks coolly.

"Saying? Nothing. Just making an observation."

"I see," she whispers. She stands and walks toward the entrance to the room. "Thank you for stopping by Father, but I have things to do before dinner." She walks to the front door and opens it.

I stand in the foyer looking at her. "I'm sorry if I upset you," I say.

"Have a good evening, Father," Rebecca says. I incline my head and walk out.

Once in my car, I think for a moment before leaving. Then I get out and walk back to the house. An irritated Rebecca answers my knock.

"What is it, Father?" she says with exasperation.

"I just want to be clear," I say. "You didn't tell anyone about Rachel's pregnancy? Not your mother?"

"No, she made me swear not to."

"And you've said nothing to Win about it?"

"Win? Are you kidding? He would have gone crazy if I had told him. I can see him killing Father McCoy with his bare hands if he knew. You know, maybe I should have told Win. Then maybe my sister would still be alive!" She slams the door in my face.

On the drive back to Saint Clare's, I think about what I've learned that day. Rebecca had driven Rachel to the convent two weeks before her murder after finding out she was pregnant. At the convent, Rachel arranged with the Mother Superior to go to the Order's maternity home to have the baby and give it up for adoption. She had sworn her sister to secrecy, and Rebecca told me she had told no one. There were arrangements for Rebecca to drive Rachel to the home the Monday after her murder.. Then Rachel calls Rebecca to say the plan has changed, that she decided to have an abortion. Rebecca calls the Mother Superior and makes up a story about having a miscarriage, that she'd be at the convent the following week. Rebecca had no idea why Rachel changed her mind about carrying the baby to term. I couldn't figure that one out either. It was a secret that Rachel took with her.

"But was that the only secret?" I say out loud. Was there another? I had assumed—everybody had assumed—that Rachel's baby was Father Leonard's. But what if it wasn't?

I pull over. Rachel confessed to me about Father Leonard. But she hadn't mentioned the baby. She was already planning to have an abortion and didn't mention that. What else hadn't she told me?

And if Father Leonard wasn't the father of her baby, who was? There is one other possibility. Winthrop Myer.

I shake my head. Rebecca said that Rachel had been careful to keep her distance from Win. But that wasn't entirely true. Rachel felt comfortable enough with Win to get him to persuade Father Leonard to hire her as church secretary. What if they were a lot closer than Rebecca knew?

Or what if Rebecca suspected they were closer? Despite her protests, she had to resent her sister because of her husband's affection for her. It would have only been natural.

It is also a motive for murder.

I turn that thought over in my head. Rebecca could have killed her sister in a fit of passion, the jealousy and resentment she felt finally boiling over. Maybe she thought she and Win were going away together. Maybe she didn't believe that the baby was Father Leonard's, that the entire story was a cover. Maybe she became convinced that the baby was Win's, the product of an affair they had?

As much sense as it made, there were problems. Rebecca Myer is a slight, thin woman, a good four or five inches shorter than Father Leonard. I couldn't see how she could have subdued the bigger man, rendered him unconscious, and then staged the crime scene to frame the young priest.

"You're grasping at straws, Tom," I say, "that's what Helen will say."

I ponder all of this before dialing Helen's number.

"Tom," she says, "what's up?"

"Listen, I've learned some things you need to know. Things you need to look into. Things that bring Father Leonard's guilt into question."

"Damn it, Tom, really, you've got to stop playing detective!"

"I'm not playing detective," I protest. "I had questions, and I got some answers. I want you to follow up, since you're the professional."

"Well, what is it?"

"We've both been assuming that Father Leonard was the father of Rachel's baby."

She pauses. I can hear her thinking. "You're thinking maybe someone else?"

"Did they do a DNA test on the baby?"

"I assume they can, if they haven't," Helen replies. "We took DNA from Father Leonard at booking. Its standard procedure." She pauses. "All right, Tom, I'll ask them to run a DNA comparison to see if Father Leonard is the father or not. But it's all going to be moot in a few days, anyway."

"What do you mean?"

"I mean," Helen says, "that Brian and Angela Jenkins are talking about a plea deal for Father Leonard."

"A plea—but Jenkins has seemed so confident."

"Apparently, she's not as confident as you think she is. Nothing's settled yet, but in a few days Father Leonard's likely to plead guilty to the murder of Rachel Watson."

Twenty-Two

"It's the best deal under the circumstances, Father Leonard," Angela Jenkins says. "This way you won't spend the rest of your life in prison."

"Just the next twenty-five years," I say. "You'll be an old man by the time you get out."

"He'll be in his mid-fifties," Angela retorts. "That's not much older than you and I are. Besides, he'll be eligible for parole way before then, and I think it's a pretty good bet that he'll get out of prison after only a few years."

"Yeah, years he shouldn't have to spend, anyway."

"Look, Father," she says to me. "I don't know what you want me to do."

"I want you to defend an innocent man," I exclaim. "It's your job, isn't it?"

"It's my job to give my client the best defense possible, to represent his interest as well as I can," she jabs the table with her finger. "That's what I'm doing."

"You think you'll lose," I say.

She draws herself up before saying, "The state's evidence is damning. I think a jury would have a hard time finding reasonable doubt given the physical evidence and his own statements."

"I don't see how a reasonable jury will take his statements as a confession of guilt."

She opens up a folder on her desk. "The state will call Anna Luckgold to the stand. According to this, she told Detective Parr that a few days before Rachel Watson's death, he arrived back at the Rectory in an extremely agitated state after a visit to a parishioner."

I nodded. "Yes, I remember. That parishioner said something that rattled Father Leonard."

"'She asked me if I was still screwing that young secretary of mine,'" Jenkins read. She looked at me and Father Leonard, who stared at his hands. "Does that ring a bell?"

I sigh. "Yes, that's what he said, she said."

"Which prompted Father Leonard to say," Angela continues, "'She's ruined me, she's ruined me.'"

I look at Father Leonard, who still sits in his chair saying nothing.

"That combined with the fact that we now know he was intimate with Watson, that she was carrying his baby, gives him motive, according to the state. That Father Leonard here plotted her death as a way of covering up his behavior."

"It was consensual," I say, "Father Leonard didn't force himself on Rachel."

"We only have his word on that," she replies.

"She spoke to her sister."

"The state will say it's hearsay."

"We don't know for sure that Leonard was the father, anyway," I point out.

At that statement, Leonard jerks his head up. "What?"

"I know the police have requested a DNA comparison to confirm paternity," Jenkins says, "but it doesn't really matter if he's the father or not."

"What are you talking about, Tom? What is all this?" Leonard says, his voice frantic.

Jenkins pats the arm of her client. "Just calm down, Father." Leonard looks at her, then slumps back in his chair.

"It matters, Ms. Jenkins, because it gives other people motive," I say.

"There is no evidence of anyone else being in the apartment."

"You're afraid of the effect of losing on your chances in the election," I say, pointing at her for emphasis.

"Now look, Father," she says, slapping the table and standing up, leaning across the table, and glaring at me. "If I thought for a second we had a chance in hell of winning at trial, I'd do it. This has nothing to do with the election. This is not about me personally. This is about keeping him from spending the rest of his life in Jessup."

"But he's innocent," I plead.

"Oh, come on, Father! The innocent wind up in prison all the time! What makes him special is that he is one, a priest, and two, a white man. And plenty of the latter are innocent and behind bars."

"Stop, please, just stop," Father Leonard whispers. We almost don't hear him over our own argument. Both of us look at him.

He raises his head to look at us, an expression of resignation on his face. "I'll plead. I don't care." He closes his eyes and shakes his head. "It's what I deserve, after all I've done."

I sit down and grip his shoulder. "You didn't kill her, Leonard. Yes, you sinned. You broke your vows. But we can fix all that. You have got to stop punishing yourself."

"That's easy for you to say," he yells. His eyes have a dark expression, one I've never seen before in Father Leonard McCoy. "I carry this with me every day. I cannot get everything I've done, how I've betrayed the Church, God, my mother, out of my mind. And how do we know I didn't kill her? The fingerprints on the knife are mine. Maybe I blacked out after killing her and don't remember."

"Oh, Leonard, don't be ridiculous," I say. "You said—"

"I remember what I said, Tom. A presence. Being suffocated. Blacking out. Waking up next to her dead body, covered in her blood." He gasps. "The police say no one else was there. I probably imagined it all." He shakes his head. "There's just no sense in fighting it." He looks at his lawyer. "Tell them I'll take the plea. Let's get this over with."

Angela looks at me, then back at Leonard. "Okay, Father," she says, gathering up her papers. "I'll get in touch with the State Attorney. It will take a few days, and a court appearance. You must make a statement."

"Fine, fine, I'll say whatever they want me to say," he replies.

She leaves Leonard and I alone in the room. I look at him for several minutes. Finally, I say, "Leonard, I don't—"

"Tom, please," he says, looking at me with tears in his eyes. "Say nothing. It's done. It's my penance. Like she says, I won't be in prison for the rest of my life. When I get out, maybe then . . ." He returns to looking at his hands.

I look at him for a few more minutes, then stand. I pat his shoulder, then leave the pitiful figure alone in the gray room.

**

I'm alone in the Church, the only light coming through the stained glass windows, the votive candles burning in front of the shrines to Mary, Joseph, and Saint Clare, and the presence candle burning in front of the tabernacle. I've been kneeling on the bottom step below the altar since I returned from the meeting with Leonard and Angela Jenkins.

I look up at the cross, bearing the image of the suffering savior. God became man, perfect, sinless, who became sin for the entire world. Guiltless, allowing himself to be beaten, ridiculed, spit upon, and nailed to the rough wood for the guilty. A willing victim of the greatest injustice in all man's tortured history.

I close my eyes and think of Leonard, a man far from guiltless, far from sinless, who is about to plead guilty to a crime I know he didn't commit. And why? To punish himself for the sins he committed.

I shake my head. I pray for guidance.

An opening door disturbs the quiet of the church. Footsteps resound on the marble floors. I look up to see Winthrop Myer approaching.

"Your housekeeper said you'd be here," he says as he stops by me. I stand up.

I smile. "Anna's not my housekeeper, not officially anyway. She's my mother-in-law."

"Oh, I see," Win says. "That's why I came here. After you left, Rebecca told me about—well, I am embarrassed and angry with myself for what I said. I'm not a man who can admit easily when he's wrong, so it's taken me a few days to summon up the courage to come here. I apologize for what I said to you, Father Tom."

"It's all right, Win, no harm done."

"Thank you." He looks around. "I haven't been in Saint Clare's since the day of my wedding. It's beautiful here. Quiet. Peaceful."

"That's why I was here. I needed some peace."

"And then I showed up to disturb it," Win says. "I just wanted to come by and apologize. I'll let you get back to your prayers." He turns and walks away.

"Could you have been the father?" I ask.

He stops, but does not turn around.

I take a step towards him. "Could you have been the father of Rachel's baby?"

He spins around. I expect an angry retort. Instead, I am face to face with a man in agony. Tears are already streaming down his face.

"I don't know, Father," he croaks. "I don't know."

Win Myer collapses on the pew beside him, his body racked with sobs. I sit down beside him, my arm around him, holding him as he cries. He's saying things I can't understand.

We sit like that for a while. Finally, his sobs subside. He takes a deep breath. "Sorry, Father," he whispers, wiping the remaining tears away with his hand.

"It's okay," I say. "Do you want to tell me what happened?"

He's staring at the altar. "I haven't been to confession in—well, decades. I guess it's long past time." He turns to look at me. "How did you know?"

"I didn't," I say. "But you seem like a man who's been carrying an enormous burden of guilt for something more than just getting Rachel the job here."

"Yes," he says. He slowly shakes his head. "I am so ashamed. I've been ashamed of myself ever since it happened. You know I dated Rachel a bit in high school, before she left to go to that boarding school, before Rebecca and I got together."

"Rebecca and Marjorie told me that."

"I really liked Rachel in high school," he says. "I mean, she was just so different from the other girls. I was a Myer, the Big Man on Campus. Everyone treated me like I was something special. The girls—all the girls wanted to date me because I was a Myer and I had money, an expensive car, the whole works."

"But not Rachel."

He shakes his head. "Rachel saw me for who I really was and liked me for it. She didn't care about the money or the car. She just enjoyed being with me." He sighs. "It was so nice."

"Then she left and Marjorie put you and Rebecca together," I say.

"Yes. My mother wasn't much of a mother, but Marjorie—well, she really seemed to care for me. But for whatever reason, she didn't want me and Rachel together. So she sent her away. I was so upset when she left, but then I started dating Rebecca with Marjorie's encouragement." He closes his eyes. "Since they were twins, it was almost like I was still with Rachel. Sometimes I'd just imagine that Rebecca was Rachel. I remember one time I called Rebecca 'Rachel,' without thinking." He pauses. "She didn't like that very much."

"The day of the wedding, Rachel looked upset. Do you know why?"

"Yes," Win says. "I hadn't seen her very much over the years, just when she was at home for Christmas. But I still thought about her a lot. The day of our wedding, I saw her. And . . . and she was there, looking so beautiful in her bridesmaid's dress. I don't know what came over me, Father. I just started blabbering about how I still had feelings for her, that I felt about her in a way I didn't feel about her sister, that she only had to say the word and I'd ditch Rebecca and be hers."

"What was her reaction?"

"She was horrified, upset that I would say anything. She told me she would never betray her sister that way, that if I didn't want to marry Rebecca, it was up to me, but she'd have no part of it." He took a deep breath. "I was devastated. I decided to break it off with Rebecca, that I couldn't go through with our marriage, not feeling the way I did. So I went to Marjorie and told her. She . . . she talked sense into me. I pulled myself together and went through with it."

"So you just suppressed your feelings for Rachel?" I say.

"Yes," he says. "Or at least I tried. I think Rebecca suspected over the years how I really felt, but I did the best job I could to be a loving husband to her. I owed it to her. And Marjorie. Besides, Rachel was living in Baltimore and then there was that thing about her becoming a nun, so it wasn't too hard."

"But she moved back to Myerton. Didn't that make things more difficult for you?"

"She stayed away from us mostly, only seeing Rebecca at family occasions and alone. I never saw her alone until the day she came by to ask me to help her get the job at Saint Clare's." He smiled. "It was my first mistake."

"When did your second mistake happen?"

He takes another deep breath. "Memorial Day, that night," he whispers. "She came over here, visibly upset. She wanted to talk to Rebecca, but she was out of town on a girls' trip for a few days. I took her into my study and poured her a drink to steady her nerves." He pauses. "Rachel was a light-weight with alcohol. She told me what happened with Father Leonard."

"How did that make you feel?"

"Jealous, angry," he says. "That priest had something I never had, Rachel in his arms, in his bed. I—I couldn't stand it."

I look at him. "You raped her," I whisper.

"She was drunk!" he cries. "Practically passed out. She—she didn't resist."

"She was in no condition to," I say bitterly. "You committed a crime, Win, not just a sin."

"I loathed myself after it was over. I had imagined it so many times. It was nothing like I wanted it to be." He's crying again. "When she woke up the next morning and remembered what happened, she started screaming at me, yelling that she hated me, that she never wanted to lay eyes on me again. I begged her not to say anything, that it would destroy Rebecca and her Mama, pleading with her to keep it quiet."

"She agreed to do that?" I'm a little incredulous.

He nods. "Yes, she promised not to say anything. She just told me to stay away from her." He pauses. "And that's what I did. I never saw her alone again."

He bends over and puts his head in his hands. I consider what he just said to me.

"Do you think Rebecca suspected anything?"

"No," he says. "At least she never let on."

"Did you know Rachel was pregnant?"

"I overheard her telling Rebecca." He slumps and looks at me. "I was furious. I went to the Rectory, thinking I'd beat Father Leonard to death. But I just threatened him."

"The baby? Could you have been the father?"

He sighs. "It could have been mine. I don't know. Rebecca and I haven't had the best of luck having children ourselves. Turns out I'm the problem. Low motility." He shrugs. "The doctors said it would still be possible, just difficult."

I sigh and shake my head. "Win, did you get concerned that Rachel might tell someone?"

He sits up and looks at me. "If you're asking me did I kill her, no, Father, I didn't. I couldn't have." He paused. "I'm not even sure now how I can go on in a world without Rachel."

Twenty-Three

"I'm assigning you permanently to Saint Clare's, Father Tom."

The statement from the Archbishop delivered over the phone does not surprise me. After I told him about Father Leonard's plan to take a plea deal, it was inevitable.

"Yes, Archbishop."

"Have you seen him recently? How is he doing?"

"I haven't spoken to him in a couple of days," I say. "When I last saw him, he was . . . pitiful is the only word I can say."

"He sounds like a man guilty of something," he says.

"Oh, he's guilty of many things," I agree. "But not murder."

He pauses before saying. "Perhaps, perhaps."

"No, sir," I say, "no, he did not kill Rachel Watson."

"Your loyalty does you credit, Father, but I'd say on balance, if I were on a jury hearing the case . . ."

I sigh. "As I explained to you, he's pleading guilty so he won't spend the rest of his life in prison. But he's also doing it to continue performing penance."

"You've heard his confession," the Archbishop says. "Gave him his penance."

"Yes to both, Your Eminence," I say. "But he's not able to forgive himself, no matter how much absolution he's received."

The Archbishop sighs. "How unfortunate, how sad," he says. "Nothing he's done is unforgivable."

"Only by himself, sir," I say. "In doing what he's doing, he's allowing the actual killer to escape justice. If he won't help himself, I will."

"You're a good man, Father Tom," the Archbishop says. "As a priest, you can be a pain in my backside. But you're a good man."

"Thank you sir, I appreciate that."

I hang up and Anna walks into the office with a sandwich and a cola. "You haven't had lunch yet. I thought you'd be hungry."

"Thanks," I say, accepting the plate and glass. I take a bite and chew.

"So you're here permanently," she says, sitting across from the desk.

I nod and swallow. "Yes, at least as long as the Archbishop wants me here."

Anna looks at me. "Are you okay with this?"

"I don't really have a choice."

"You know what I mean," she says, leaning forward.

I nod. "Yes, I know." I sigh and take another bite of my sandwich. Swallowing, I say. "I'm tired. I've avoided this place long enough. God wants me here. So, I guess you all are stuck with me."

Anna smiles. "Well, I for one am glad."

"Thanks." I pause and look at her. "I need you to do something for me," I say slowly.

"Anything, if I can."

"Would you consider becoming my parish secretary and housekeeper?"

"I thought I already was," she exclaims. "I'll do it. I'll even move in here."

"You don't need to do that. I mean, you'll have to sell your house."

"I've been needing to downsize for years, I just haven't had a good excuse. But I'll keep the house, probably rent it out. There are always visiting professors or new hires at Myer College looking for places to live, and Myerton isn't flush with rental properties. Unless you don't want me?"

I laugh. "I'd appreciate the company."

She pauses. "Well, since I'm parish secretary, Miriam Conway still wants to have a nativity pageant."

I laugh. "Did she put you up to this?"

"No, absolutely not," she says. "I just think it would be a good idea. It'll get the parish a lot of positive attention which, frankly, after the last year we could use."

She's right. Saint Clare's has been the focus of two major criminal investigations since last summer.

"And," Anna continues, "it will give you a lot of goodwill among the young mothers who, let me be honest, carry a lot of weight in the parish. You'll want them on your side."

I nod. "I'll call Miriam as soon as I can."

At that moment, my phone rings. "It's Helen," I say.

Anna says, "I suspect you have a few things to talk about." She stands up and leaves my office, shutting the door behind her. I look at the closed door, wondering how much she's figured out about Helen and me.

I answer the call. "Did I catch you at a bad time?" Helen asks on the other end. "I know how busy you probably are."

"No, I was just talking to Anna about a few things."

"Have you eaten? I thought we could grab a bite."

I look at the remnants of the sandwich. "Ack, you caught me just as I finished. How about coffee?"

"The Perfect Cup? Sure, sounds good to me." Helen pauses. "I have something to discuss with you."

***

The young waitress brings us our order at the table along the sidewalk, me an iced coffee in recognition of the time of year, Helen a chicken salad on croissant with a sweet tea.

"I hope you don't mind," she says before tucking into the sandwich. "I haven't eaten since breakfast," she explains with a mouthful of food.

"No, I ate earlier," I say. "Busy?"

She nods before swallowing, washing the sandwich down with a gulp of tea. "A couple of cases. No murders, thankfully. You know, this was a quiet town before you came back. Since then, two murders. All associated with Saint Clare's."

I laugh. "Are you saying I'm responsible?"

She smiles. "If I were a more suspicious person, I'd have to wonder. But it's just a coincidence. Probably."

"Well, you'll have more opportunities to find out." At her look I say, "I've been assigned to Saint Clare's permanently, or as permanent as any assignment in the Church is, as long as the Archbishop wants me here."

She sits back. "So you're staying this time? No monastery?"

I shake my head. "No, no monastery. I will be a parish priest here."

Helen cocks her head to one side. "How do you feel about that?"

"Anna asked me the same question." I sit quietly for a moment. "Contented. Satisfied that this is where I belong. Where God wants me to be."

We look at each other across the table for a minute, our eyes fixed on each other. A breeze carries the faint scent of vanilla from her hair across the table, tickling my nose, triggering memories of past moments together. I see the sun shining off her raven-black hair, which brings out the azure blue of her eyes. They're deep pools. I remember a time when I could lose myself in those eyes.

Suddenly, Helen turns her attention back to her sandwich. I sit back and say, "So what did you want to talk to me about?"

She swallows her food, takes another drink of tea, wipes her mouth with her napkin. Helen folds it carefully, then absentmindedly twists it in her hands. "I have something to tell you. And something to ask you."

"Okay. What is it?"

She clears her throat and looks me in the eye. "Do you ever miss it?"

This is not what I was expecting. "Do I miss what?"

"It," she says without explanation. "You know, the thing as a priest you can't have, or at least shouldn't have."

At my quizzical look, she says, "Oh, come on, Tom, you know what I'm talking about."

I smile slightly and say, "Helen, I don't understand what you're getting at."

"Oh, you, you're just being difficult," she says with exasperation. Leaning across the table, she says with a low voice. "Sex. Intimacy. You know." She sits back to wait for my answer.

"What prompted this?" I ask.

She shrugs. "Father Leonard. Rachel. The whole situation. Two people who knew each other years ago, finding each other again. It's clear Father Leonard carried the memory of Rachel and his feelings with him for years. They meet again, and one thing leads to another." She pauses. "For both of them, it was new. But you know what it's like to be intimate with another person. You were married to Joan. I was married to John. Before them, while we never—well, we were intimate in other ways. I just want to know if you miss it at all?"

I smile slightly. "Do I miss physical intimacy? No, not really. Sometimes, though, I miss the other."

At her questioning look, I explain, "Just having someone to come home to, to talk to, to share experiences with. That's the real sacrifice of celibacy, at least it is for me. The physical part. You can take a cold shower, pray a rosary, do many things when you're tempted. But there's nothing you can do when loneliness comes." I sigh. "And being a priest can be very, very lonely."

Helen smiles. "I thought you like being alone?"

I look up. "Now that I'm alone most of the time," I say, "not so much."

"So you get tempted?"

"I am still a man, Helen. That didn't change the day they ordained me."

She looks at me and whispers, "Do I tempt you, Tom?"

I look at her. The silence is heavy between us for a moment. I clear my throat. "Honestly?" I say quietly. "Do you really want to know?"

She stares at me for a moment, obviously struggling between two possible answers to my question, then nods.

I take a deep breath. "Sometimes, when the sun hits your hair just right or I allow myself more than a brief glance at what you're wearing or we're talking and I can see your eyes—I remember us together. Am I tempted? In a way. Not to break my vows, but to allow myself to get closer than I should. Again, the loneliness is the worst part of this job."

Helen nods. "I understand that."

"So," I say, "what about you? Do I tempt you?"

Helen takes a sudden interest in her iced tea, Avoiding my gaze, she says, "That's why I asked to see you. To tell you—" She straightens her shoulders and looks at me. "To tell you I can't do this anymore."

"Do what anymore?" I ask, feeling my stomach knot up.

She waves her arm between us. "This. Whatever this is."

"We're just friends, Helen. There hasn't been anything even remotely—"

"I know that," she says quietly. "That's what makes it so hard for me."

I look at her and shake my head. "I—what are you saying, Helen?"

She sighs. "For years, I didn't miss it. John's death and my grief, my missing him pushed out any thoughts or desires. But over time, you remember what it was like—sex, yes, but everything else you were talking about too." She looks at her plate. "I'm still hungry."

Helen signals the waitress and orders a cinnamon roll. I ask for a chocolate doughnut.

"Last year, after you came back," she continues, "the feelings of loneliness got stronger. I remembered what our life together was like. Oh, it wasn't perfect, and the way it ended was awful, but we had a lot of good times." She looked at me. "Here you were, suddenly back in my life. But you were . . ."

"I was unavailable" I say.

She nods. "I thought the fact that you were a priest would deter me. It wasn't like I would try seducing you away from the Church, get you to break your vows. I know you too well. But I found myself thinking about you more and more. And the more I thought about you, the more unhappy I got."

"Why are you unhappy?"

Helen gets a slight smile. "I'm an only child, remember? When they find out, people always ask me if I got whatever I wanted. I said yes, but only because I'm very picky about what I want. But when I want something, nothing else will satisfy me. Do you see what I'm saying?"

I'm at a loss. "No, I really don't."

"Tom," she says with exasperation, "I'm unhappy because I can't have you. Because there can never be an us. Because that's what I realize I want. Us." She pauses as she wipes a tear from her eye. "And that's something that can never be."

I sit in front of this woman I used to love—am I really thinking in the past tense—who's just admitted that she wants me. "Helen—I—I—I don't know what to say."

She takes a deep breath. "There's nothing you can say. You're a priest. We both know what that means. But I—I can't do it anymore."

I just look at her as she says, "I was already thinking about what to do, but I wasn't certain you'd be staying. Now that I know, my mind's made up."

"What are you going to do?" I ask quietly. But in my heart, I know the answer.

"Tom, I'm leaving Myerton. I've received a job offer from the police department in a town about the size of Myerton near where I grew up in Nebraska. My aunt and uncle are still alive, but they're getting on in years, so—"

"Helen," I say quickly, "look, you don't have to leave. We can stop spending time together—I mean, you want me to stop playing detective anyway. No more lunches or coffees together. I'll only see you at Mass, or you can go back to attending Mass in Frostburg. You don't have to uproot your entire life just because of me."

"But I'm not, my dear Tom," Helen whispers. "I'm doing it for me. Because—because I'm scared what might happen if I stay."

We lapse into an uncomfortable silence. My mind is turning, the lover and priest arguing loudly.

You know this is best, Tom, for both of you, the priest says.

You can't lose her again, Tom, the lover says.

I clear my throat and say, "Helen, I—"

"Oh, good, there you are." I turn to see an excited Nate Rodriguez bouncing up the sidewalk towards us. Excited is Nate's natural state, so it doesn't surprise me, but today he seems particularly exuberant.

"Hi, Nate, what is it?"

With a grin from ear to ear, he stops next to us. "I did it, Father Tom. I really did it."

"What d'you do now, Nate?" Helen asks, a weary tone in her voice.

Looking at her, he says triumphantly, "I found a witness."

"A witness? You found someone?" I ask.

As he nods vigorously, still grinning, Helen says, "Wait, what? Tom, you asked Nate to find a witness to Rachel Watson's murder? Skulking around Richard Strump's backyard wasn't enough for you?"

"I had to do something, Helen, you had—"

"Great, just great. Thanks a lot."

"Let's just hear him out, Helen. Nate, what did you find?"

"Like I just said. A witness. The next-door neighbor. Actually, not right next door. His place is a few doors down from Rachel Watson's townhouse. But he has a clear view of her place. I was there. You can see the front of her place real clear. The crime scene tape is kind of falling off, Detective."

Helen is about to say something when I put my hand up. "A neighbor, you say?"

"Uh-huh."

"We interviewed the entire neighborhood already, Nate," Helen says. "No one saw anything."

"But you didn't interview the guy I found."

"How do you know that?" I ask.

"Because," Nate says triumphantly. "He left town the night of the murder and just got back two days ago."

Helen's mouth drops open. "Damn," she whispers as she gets up and grabs her tote bag. "Nate—well, I guess I have to say good work. Send me the name and address to the Father's phone."

"Right," Nate says, pulling his phone out of his messenger bag.

"What?" I say, surprised by the sudden turn of events. "Why my phone?"

She looks at me, a slight smile appearing on her face. "You are coming with me, aren't you?"

Twenty-Four

"Look, I already told the nervous kid," says the voice from under the 1973 Ford Mustang, "I know nothing about that girl's murder. I didn't even know anything about it until I got back from my business trip two days ago. Darn oil plug rusted." The man scoots out from under the car, his face and hands covered with grease spots and dirt.

"Mr. Walkin," Helen says. "Any information you can give will help."

"You may help keep an innocent man from going to prison," I say.

"Huh, you talking about that young priest? I heard he got the girl knocked up. Priests shouldn't do that, you know?"

"Please, sir, can you tell us what you saw that night?" Helen gets out her notepad.

Walkin stands up and walks over to his tool bench. We're standing in his garage, the Mustang on jack stands, the air hot and heavy with the smell of motor oil mingled with sweat. It's almost overpowering. A trickle of sweat rolls down my spine. Black clericals are not what you really want to be wearing in the summer, and it's not even that hot today.

"Look, all I know is what I told the kid."

"Well, tell me now."

Walkin looks at Helen. "Listen, I was in a hurry that night, so I only caught glimpses of stuff. And the only reason I noticed was because it was so strange."

"What was strange?" I ask. Helen shoots me her standard 'be quiet' look.

"The people," he explains. "Rachel was a quiet girl, I guess I should say young woman, she was closer to thirty, I guess. She didn't get visitors. She'd come and go, we'd exchange good mornings or afternoons or evenings when we'd see each other. But she kept to herself. And like I say, she didn't have visitors."

"That night was different?"

"Yeah. I was in a hurry to get packed and get out of town. I was taking a red-eye out of Dulles to Seattle. I was going to leave earlier, but stuff came up. It takes a couple of hours to get there, you know, and my flight was leaving at 11:00, so I was cutting it close. So I was throwing things in the car, running in and out of the house. I remember looking toward her place when I saw someone go inside."

"Go inside? Did they knock or just let themselves in?" Helen asks.

"I didn't see her knock, but she could have."

"Her?" I say. "It was a woman. Are you sure?" Helen glares at me again.

"Yeah, I'm sure. I may be older, but I can still tell a man from a woman, even though that's difficult these days."

"Can you describe her?"

"A woman, she was wearing a dress, I don't remember the color. Could have been blue. Or red. Maybe yellow."

"How tall was she?"

Walkin thinks. "About your height. She was a little thinner, not as chunky as you."

I stifle a snort. Helen's jaw clinches.

"Did you see her leave?"

He shakes his head. "No. She could have, I guess, I was in and out, she could have left when I was inside."

"Did she drive herself? Did someone drive her?" Helen asks.

He shrugs. "Didn't notice. Like I say, I was trying to get packed. I didn't notice anything else until the guy showed up."

Helen and I look at each other. "What guy?"

"Tall guy. Even at a distance, with these eyes, I could see his red hair. But that's not what got my attention." Pointing to the entrance to the parking area, he says, "He must have taken that turn at about twenty. You could hear his tires squeal. He sped in here into a parking space and jumped out of the car practically before the car stopped moving. Not even sure he turned the engine off."

"And you're sure he had red hair," Helen asks.

"Yeah, I'm sure. Bright red hair. Almost didn't look real. But you couldn't miss it."

"Did you see him leave?"

"Like I told ya, I didn't see anything else. After he went inside—"

"Did he knock?" I ask, ignoring Helen's eye roll.

"Knock? Maybe. Yeah, I think he did. He knocked and rang the doorbell, like he couldn't wait to get inside." He paused. "You know, I think I'd seen him there before, coming out. One morning."

Helen and I look at each other. "How long ago was that?"

"Maybe a month, maybe more. Don't really remember."

Helen makes notes in her notebook. "So he knocked and rang the doorbell?"

"Yeah, then the door opened and he went inside."

"Did you see someone let him in?"

"No, didn't see that."

"About what time was all this," Helen asks.

"Let's see," he thinks. "I finished loading the car and pulled out not long after that so, maybe 7:00?"

"7:00? Are you sure?" I ask with excitement.

"6:45, 7, 7:15 no later than that."

"And you didn't see anyone leave after the man went inside? And no one else went into the townhouse?"

"Like I say, not while I was here."

Helen thanks Walkin, who grabs a socket wrench and scoots back under the car. We walk out of the garage. I turn to Helen and say, "Did you hear—"

"Shush, Tom, let's wait until we get in the car," she says with a hushed tone.

We get in her car and she lays her head back on the headrest, hands gripping the steering wheel, her eyes closed.

"An eyewitness we missed," she says. "I can't believe it."

I say nothing for a moment. Finally, she sits up and starts the car to let the air conditioner cool the stuffy interior.

"Did you hear what he said? He says someone got to Rachel's townhouse before Father Leonard did. A woman."

"A woman. So he was telling the truth." She sighs. "Two murder cases in a row and I get it wrong. What am I doing in this job, anyway?"

I put my hand on her shoulder. She jerks her head to look at it, and I remove it quickly. "Listen, you said it yourself. You had the physical evidence. It pointed to Leonard." I pause. "And you were under pressure from Brian."

"I'm a professional, Tom," she snaps. "I don't allow outside pressure to keep me from doing my job. No, I let myself ignore any other possibility once the forensics came in. Father Leonard killed that girl to hide his sin, I thought. That made the most sense." She stops. "Maybe I was blinded by my feelings. I think I still have problems with the Church, the way they've done things, because of John's experience."

I nod, remembering her late husband's abuse at the hands of his priest as a young person. "Understandable. So do I."

She stares out the window in silence for a few minutes. "This case just stirred everything back up, colored my judgment."

"You did a good job, from what I could see, standing up to Brian's rush to charge Father Leonard."

"I did it because I didn't want Brian to think he could run over me because of our past relationship," she says, turning back to me. "I ignored my gut, my sense that despite everything, some things didn't make sense. I didn't follow up on the initial interviews, I didn't recheck the neighborhood. If I had—"

"Walkin got back just a few days ago," I point out. "You could have still missed him."

"Why are you doing this, Tom?"

I smile. "Undeserved guilt is something I know a little about. I don't want to see you beat yourself up."

She looks at me, then nods. "Okay, so we have a witness that brings the entire case against Father Leonard into question. We have an unknown woman entering Rachel Watson's apartment before Father Leonard. How long before did he say?"

"I don't think he did. So it could have been an hour, it could have been fifteen minutes."

"But she was still there when Father Leonard arrived, which means there was someone in the apartment we missed." She closes her eyes. "And what description do we have? A woman, about my height, wearing a dress. That only describes, say, almost every woman in the area."

I turn from Helen and look out the window. "What is it?" she asks.

"It also describes one woman I can think of," I say. "And she also had a motive, the most ancient motive of all."

"And that is?"

I look at Helen. "Jealousy."

***

The lights are on at the Myer house when we arrive.

"Now, listen," Helen says before we get out of her car. "Don't say anything, Tom."

"I won't say a word," I raise my hand to swear.

"That's what you always say. I can interrogate a suspect without your help, you know? I've been doing this job for a long time."

"I know all that," I say. "So, is she a suspect?"

"You're the reason we're here, Tom! What do you think?"

I didn't want to think what I had been thinking. But there was only one woman I could think of who had motive to murder Rachel Watson, whose appearance at her door wouldn't surprise her.

A few moments after Helen knocks, Win Myer opens the door. "Detective," he says pleasantly to Helen. Looking at me with a slight scowl, he says, "Father."

"I hope we're not interrupting," Helen says. "May we come in?"

"Well, we're just finishing up dinner, about to have coffee and dessert in the library. Would you care to join us?"

"That's very gracious of you," Helen says, "but we don't want to trouble you." I look at Helen, but she stills me with a glance out of the corner of her eye.

"No trouble, it's just family. Rebecca, myself, her mom and dad." He shows us into the library. I walk to the wall with the photographs, looking again at their wedding pictures. There is Rachel, looking dour. Win, his smile patently fake. But this time, I look at Rebecca.

Her smile is genuine. Happy, a joyful bride on her wedding day. The happiest day of her life.

"Detective," I hear Edmund Watson say. "I don't see why you're here. You arrested the guy who murdered Rachel. What point is there in your showing up and interrupting our evening?"

"Some new information has come to light," Helen says. "New information that could cast some doubt on things."

"What? Are you saying that the priest is innocent?" Marjorie Watson asks.

"I'm saying, Ms. Watson, that the information needs to be investigated, just to make sure there hasn't been a miscarriage of justice."

"What information is that?" Win Myer asks. He's entered the room with a drink in his hand.

Helen turns to face him. "Information that places someone in addition to Father McCoy at Rachel's townhouse at the time of the murder." She turns, walks up to Rebecca Myer, and looks down at her. Rebecca looks up at Helen, a look of surprise on her face.

"What? So Father McCoy was telling the truth?"

"We'll get to that in a minute, Ms. Myer." Helen takes out her notebook. "But first, did you tell Father Greer you were to meet Rachel at her apartment on Monday morning?"

Rebecca looks at me. I avoid her gaze. I had tread very close to the line of what I could tell Helen. But I only told her enough. Helen had filled in the rest, or at least the rest to complete the basic picture.

"Yes, I was supposed to meet Rachel on Monday morning."

"Oh, what are you talking about, Rebecca?" Marjorie asks impatiently.

"I was supposed to meet Rachel at her apartment and drive her somewhere," Rebecca says to her mother.

"What? You told me you were going to a spa," Win says.

"That was a cover story to explain where I was going."

"And where were you going, Ms. Myer?" Helen asks, her pen poised above her notebook.

She hesitates before saying, "I was going to drive her to Hagerstown. To an abortion clinic."

Helen sits down in a chair. "I see."

"I know. I lied to you," Rebecca says. "It didn't seem a big deal, that it had nothing to do with her murder. The email? It was all part of the cover."

"So she really wasn't leaving to go to the convent?" Helen says. "You and she were going to Hagerstown so she could have an abortion."

Rebecca nods. "From there, I would take her to the convent after she rested for a few days."

"She had told you," Helen says, "that Father McCoy was the father."

"Yes, who else could it have been?" Rebecca asks.

I look over at Win, who has become white as a sheet.

Helen looks at her for a moment. "Tell me, Ms. Myer," she continues. "What was your relationship with your sister like?"

"My relationship with Rachel?" Rebecca asks, confused.

"Really, Detective, why all these questions? Get to the point!" Win Myer says, his speech a little slurred since he's downing his second or third drink of the night.

"I will in a moment, Mr. Myer," Helen says over her shoulder. "Please don't interrupt."

During this, I'm scanning the wall of photographs. I settle on the one of Win in Afghanistan. Next to it is the group photo of his platoon, a smiling Win Myer standing on the end.

"Well, Rebecca," Helen asks quietly.

"I loved my sister—love my sister, detective," Rebecca says. "She was my best friend, despite our differences. Even after she said she wanted to become a nun, I didn't understand it, but," shooting a glance at her mother, "I didn't reject her."

"I didn't reject her," Marjorie protests. "I shared my opinion with her, that it made little sense for a well-brought up, educated woman. She rejected me."

"Anyway," Helen says, "there were no problems between you two?"

"Only the usual between siblings," she replies.

Helen makes a note in her book, then appears to read something. Looking back up, she says, "Didn't Rachel and your husband date in high school."

Rebecca is about to answer when Win says, "That was only a couple of times. After she went away, Rebecca and I started dating then fell in love. We're married, you know."

"But you've always had a lot of affection for Rachel, haven't you?" Helen asks. I have said nothing to Helen about my conversation with Win. She drew her own conclusions from the little I said.

"Not that it's any of your business, but yes. I've always looked at Rachel as the sister I never had. I've felt, well, like a brother. Protective."

"Oh, that's a bunch of crap and you know it," Rebecca suddenly screams at Win. "Brother! Only if you had incest in mind!"

"Really, Rebecca, calm yourself," Marjorie says.

"Oh, shut up, Mama! Just shut up! I'm just so sick of you and him and your little scheming! You got him involved with this whole thing, getting him to spy on Rachel and Father McCoy!"

"That was only after Win came to me with his concerns," Marjorie says. "I agreed with them and he volunteered."

"You have him wrapped around your little finger," Rebecca continues, in full heat now. "And you're wrapped around his. Seems like everyone is tied to everyone else in this family except me!"

She stands up and strides toward Win. "And you! Don't give me that big brother crap! You never got over her! She was the one you always wanted, not me! The only reason you dated me was because of her!" she points to Marjorie. "God, the only reason you married me was so you could call her Mama and stay close to Rachel!"

Helen and I are looking at this spectacle when Helen says, "Would you care to elaborate on that, Ms. Myer?"

She turns to Helen and takes a few deep breaths. "We started dating in high school after they sent Rachel away to boarding school," she begins. "Mama pushed it. After Rachel left, Win would come over to the house, began spending a lot of time with us." She paused. "I thought at first that he wanted to spend time with me. But he always seemed happiest around Mama. And over time, I came to realize he wanted me for two reasons. One, because of Mama. And two, so he'd always be close to Rachel, even if only as a brother-in-law." She looked at Win. "That must have made it easier to stand me, huh, since we were twins and I looked like her."

"Now, Rebecca, don't be—" Win says.

"Don't. You. Dare. Call. Me. Ridiculous," Rebecca says firmly. "You really think I've been fooled all this time? The only reason I never said anything was because I was certain Rachel would never betray me by having an affair with you. Even though I knew you'd jump at the chance if she ever gave you the slightest hint of interest."

"Were you certain, Ms. Myer?" Helen asks.

Rebecca turns, a questioning look on her face. "I'm not sure what—"

"Did it ever cross your mind that Rachel's baby might not be Father McCoy's after all?"

Rebecca glances at me, no doubt remembering a similar question from me.

"She told me it was his baby," Rebecca says, walking back towards Helen.

"But did you believe her? Or did you, deep down, worry that it might be your husband's?"

"No," she shakes her head.

"You were already jealous," Helen presses. "Did you think your worst fears had been realized, that your sister and your husband—"

"No, no, not at all! I trusted Rachel!"

"But maybe she betrayed that trust," Helen continues. "Maybe that drove you to do something about it?"

Rebecca stares at Helen, her mouth open, shocked.

Helen stands up and looks Rebecca in the face. "We found a new witness, who saw someone matching your general description entering Rachel's apartment before Father McCoy arrived. Before her murder." She looks at Rebecca, letting the force of her words settle in. "What do you say about that?"

"I wasn't there," Rebecca whispers. "It wasn't me."

"If it wasn't you, Ms. Myer, then who could it have been?"

Helen's question floats in the room's silence. I look at the family, torn by their own emotions. I wait for something to rip the tension.

"It was me," Marjorie Watson says. She stands up and looks at Helen.

"It was me, Detective. I was there. I killed my daughter. I framed the Father."

Twenty-Five

The next few minutes are chaotic. Helen stands, looking confused. Rebecca Myer screams and collapses on the couch in tears. Edmund Watson stands next to his wife, talking in her ear, saying, "What are you talking about, Marjorie? What in the world are you talking about? What nonsense is this?" Marjorie Watson for her part stands stock still, staring into space, her jawline firm.

"Well," Helen whispers to me when she walks to where I am standing. "This is a fine mess."

"What are you going to do now?"

"Do? Do? I'm going to listen to what she has to say," Helen says. "Either she's covering for the daughter or she's telling the truth. We can check to see if Rebecca has an alibi. In the meantime, Tom, let me do my job. And keep your mouth shut. Just sit over there, will you please?" She indicates an armchair in the corner. I nod and go sit down.

By the time Helen returns to the family, things have calmed down somewhat. Edmund's sitting down, still looking confused. Win has taken a seat, slumping either from intoxication or resignation. Rebecca is sitting on the couch, her hands folded in her lap, her head down, her shoulders moving slightly, showing she's still crying.

"Have a seat, Mrs. Watson," Helen says, indicating a chair. Marjorie sits on the edge of the chair, stiff, head held high.

"You can ask your questions," Marjorie says, "But I've already confessed. I did it."

"One thing at a time, Mrs. Watson," Helen says, turning to a fresh page in her notebook. "So why don't you tell me what happened?"

She pauses a moment before speaking. "I got a call from Win about 3:00," she begins. "He was upset. He told me about the email, about Rachel's plan to enter the convent. He knew she hadn't told me, but he thought I should know. And he was right. I'm her mother. I should know these things."

Turning to Win Myer, Helen says, "You said you hadn't read the email."

Win avoids her look, taking another sip of his drink.

Turning back to Marjorie, Helen asks, "What did you do?"

"At first, nothing," Marjorie says. "I just stewed. I was angry that she hadn't told me." She pauses. "The more I thought about it that afternoon, the more upset I got. The more determined to put a stop to it before she ruined her life. So I went over there."

"Did she know you were coming?" Helen asks.

Marjorie shakes her head. "We hadn't spoken since the meeting with Father Greer."

413

"The meeting where you admitted sending the anonymous letter to the Archbishop," I say from the corner.

"Father Greer," Helen says, looking at me. "Please do not interrupt again or you will have to leave."

I hold up my hands. "Sorry, Detective. I won't say a word."

Helen glares at me, then turns to Marjorie. "Is what Father Greer says true?"

"Oh, yes, I sent the letter."

"Did you witness everything you described in the letter?" Helen asks.

"Why is that important?"

"I just want to get a complete picture," Helen replies. "Did you see what you described in the letter?"

"Well, no, not in so many words," she says hesitantly.

"Where did you get the information?"

"Well . . . well from Win mostly," she says. Helen turns to look at Win Myer, slumped in the chair.

"And how did he come into possession of it?"

"He grew suspicious of Father McCoy after Rachel started working at the parish," Marjorie replies. "He told me he felt guilty about getting her the job. He began looking into things, just to make sure nothing bad was going on. Then he found out about their carrying on at the Memorial Day picnic."

I look at the two of them. Win is looking down at his drink.

"So the day of her murder," Helen continues, "you went over there to—"

"To talk some sense into my daughter, or try one last time," Marjorie says. "I showed up and knocked. She answered right away. I could tell she was expecting someone else."

She was. Rachel had opened the door expecting Father Leonard. But instead, it was her mother.

"How did she react to seeing you?"

"As soon as she saw it was me, she got all angry. She demanded to know what I was doing there. I told her it was to talk her out of throwing her life away. She asked me what business it was of mine. I told her it was because I was her mother. She laughed at me, saying it had been years since I had acted like a mother to her. She was just mean and spiteful, ungrateful for everything I had given her."

"You had treated her badly for years, Mama," Rebecca says. "What did you expect?"

"I did not mistreat her! Was I firm? Yes. She had no idea what was best for her." She shakes her head. "I tried to talk some sense into her. I told her she'd be throwing her life away if she went to that place. I said, if you want to be religious, fine, but you can do it in a quiet, respectful way, a way that won't make people think there's something wrong with you. I mean, you see what I mean, detective?"

She exhales. "Then she told me she wasn't going into the convent right away. I was happy, relieved. For a minute."

"Then she told you why," Helen says.

"I can't believe she had done something so stupid, getting pregnant, something only a lower-class piece of trash would do these days, with all the birth control that's available. Isn't sex considered a sin, Father? I guess they just ignored that one. Then she told me she was going to have an abortion."

She sighs. "I thought I had a chance. I told her she couldn't go into a convent, not having done that. That she needed to forget about it, come to her senses."

Marjorie's tone strikes me as odd. She is describing a very emotional scene in an almost emotionless way.

"Then she went crazy," she continues. "She ran into the kitchen and grabbed a knife. She ran at me with it, screaming at me to get out, to leave her alone."

"Were you scared?"

"No, not really. Surprised more than anything else. I told her to put the knife down. She lunged. I moved out of the way and grabbed her arm, trying to get the knife away from her. We struggled. Suddenly, she cried out. We both looked down. There was blood coming from her stomach. She'd been stabbed in the struggle."

Helen has stopped writing at this point. "She stabbed herself," she repeats. "In the belly."

"Yes, in the stomach. I let go of the knife. She slid to the floor, then fell over. She was dead."

That couldn't have been true, I think.

"Did you try to help her, or call for help?" Helen asks.

"I was going to call someone," Marjorie says, "when there was a knock at the door, then the doorbell."

"Father McCoy."

Marjorie nods. "He was outside. I looked at Rachel, then realized the opportunity."

"Opportunity?"

She exhales. "To pay him back for what he did to her."

I sit up and open my mouth, about to say something. Helen turns to look at me. I slump back in my seat, closing my mouth.

"You framed Father McCoy for murder because he had gotten your daughter pregnant? Is that what you're telling us?"

Marjorie nods. "Yes, that's what I'm saying."

Helen shakes her head and sighs. "What happened next?"

"I grabbed something off the coffee table, something heavy, I think it was a vase or something, I don't remember. I heard him open the door, and he called her name as he walked up the stairs. It was dark in the living room, so he couldn't see me. When he got to the top of the stairs, I snuck up behind him and cracked him across the head with the vase. Fortunately, it didn't break, but he went down hard. He was still alive but knocked out. I grabbed him and dragged him near Rachel's body. I smeared some blood on his clothes, then took the knife and wiped the handle clean, fingerprints, you know. I placed the knife in his hand to make sure the handle would show his prints, then tossed it on the floor between him and Rachel. Then, I wiped down any surface I might have touched. I wiped the vase clean, placed it back on the coffee table. Then I got out the vacuum cleaner and vacuumed the whole place. I took the bag with me when I left. Later, I burned it in the grill out back. Along with the clothes I was wearing. They had Rachel's blood on them."

"What did you do then?" Helen asks quietly.

"Detective, what do you think I did? I went home. I snuck in the back way and stripped my clothes off in the laundry room. I had just done laundry so there was a housedress I could throw on. I bundled my clothes and put them at the bottom of the hamper. I was going to wash them, but it occurred to me that the blood might not come out. So I burned them as soon as I got an opportunity."

Helen finishes writing. She looks at Marjorie Watson for several minutes. Win's eyes are closed. I can't tell if he is asleep or thinking. Edmund looks dull. Rebecca is staring out the window, resting her chin on her balled-up fists.

"That's my story, Detective Parr," Marjorie says. "That's my confession. I killed Rachel. I framed Father McCoy. There, you have it. Arrest me."

Helen stands up and takes her phone out of her purse. "This is Detective Parr," she says when someone answers. "Send a car out to the Myer home. We're taking someone into custody. Call the chief and let him know I need to see him as soon as possible." She pauses, then adds, "Call the State Attorney. He should be in the office today." She hangs up her phone and says, "Ms. Watson, you must come down to the station to make a formal statement. But right now I'm arresting you for obstruction."

"What?" she says. "But I killed Rachel. I told you that."

"You say you were there when she died," Helen says. "Your story points to a tragic accident. But you deliberately set about to frame an innocent man and send him to prison for the rest of his life for murder. It was cold, it was calculating, and it hindered my investigation. I may not charge you with murder or anything else in Rachel's death, but I sure as hell will see you go to prison for that!" She grabs her bag and pushes past the woman, heading to the entrance to the room. There, she turns. "Coming, Father?" she yells.

Quickly, I get up and trot to catch up with her. She's outside in the driveway by the time I do so, standing with her hands on her hips, looking into the sky, a stream of muttered profanities flowing freely from her lips. I stand warily to one side while she does this.

Finally, she stops and turns to me. "Have you ever heard of anything like that in your life?"

"Honestly, no," I say. 'What she said—what everyone said—was just remarkable."

"Bat-crap crazy if you ask me. I mean, I feel sorry for Rachel and Rebecca, with a mother and father like that. And Win, he's no prize, I'm surprised Rebecca's put up with it for all these years."

"Probably her mother's influence," I say. "Though it's clear that Rebecca is her favorite." I point back at the house. "Do you think it's a good idea to leave Marjorie Watson alone?"

"What's she going to do? High-tail it out the back door, scamper across the tennis courts, vault over the property wall? She gave up her story freely. She almost seemed proud of herself. Proud. And the story she told about how Rachel died?" She shakes her head. "I've had serial killers express more emotion when they described killing their victims. Cold. Absolutely cold."

I nod. "Yes. She confessed freely." I turn and look at the house.

"What is it, Tom?" Helen asks wearily.

"What do you mean?" I say, turning back to her.

"I mean, there's something. What is it? Just tell me. I'm too tired to pull it out of you."

I furrow my brow and approach her. "Didn't that whole scene strike you as . . . odd?"

"The bunch of them are odd," Helen exclaims. "The story is odd, a mother coolly describing the death of her daughter practically in her arms, then how she framed a priest—a priest, for heaven's sake!"

"But her account, what she said happened, the way she said it. There is something about it that doesn't sit right with me."

"Oh, for goodness' sake, Tom."

"For example," I press. "She said her daughter pulled a knife on her and was killed in the struggle. But that would have been completely out of character for Rachel."

"People do strange things when they're angry," she replies.

"She describes a struggle with the murder weapon. Wouldn't that usually leave both of them cut? Were any cuts or wounds on Marjorie's hands? Did the medical examiner find any on Rachel's hands?"

"Tom, please—"

"And," I point at the house, "she says she cracked Father Leonard across the skull with a vase, and that she knocked him out."

"Okay?"

"Marjorie Watson is a good foot shorter than Father Leonard," I say. "Also, a heavy object like she described would have left a big bump, maybe even a gash. But the doctors found nothing." I pause. "And then there's—"

"No, stop," Helen says, raising her hand. "Just stop. Tom, I don't know what you want. We have someone saying they framed Father Leonard. That alone sets him free."

"But her confession doesn't fit all the facts, Helen." I shake my head. "No, there's something wrong with this whole thing."

"Dammit Tom! Stop playing Father Brown and listen to me. You said you never believed that Father Leonard killed Rachel Watson. Well, we've just had someone exonerate Father Leonard. Maybe it doesn't fit the evidence perfectly, but it's enough to call the entire case against him into question. Maybe Rachel died exactly as Marjorie Watson says, maybe she didn't. But I know this. I have a confession to obstruction, and I have a confession to at least an accidental death, at most a negligent homicide. I'll take the win. You should too, you know. Another innocent man walks free, Tom, thanks to you."

Her phone rings. She digs through her bag and pulls it out. Looking at the number, she sighs. "And now I have to tell the State Attorney he will have to go into court and move to quash an indictment." She shakes her head, then answers. "Brian, sorry to bother you, but there's something you need to know." She walks off to where I cannot hear her.

I'm left standing alone by her car in the driveway. A few minutes later, a police car pulls in. Dan Conway gets out, nods his head at me, then walks toward Helen. Helen hangs up, says something to Dan, and they walk together to the house. A few minutes later they emerge, Marjorie Watson walking between the two of them. Edmund follows behind them, telling his wife he will call their lawyer, not to say anything else, while Marjorie tells him to keep quiet. Rebecca stands in the doorway, watching the police taking the woman responsible for her sister's death away, a look of confusion and disbelief on her face.

Someone is missing. I look around. Finally, I see Win. Instead of standing behind his wife, comforting her as I would expect a husband to—as I would have in the same circumstance—he's by himself in the library, looking at the scene through the window.

He catches sight of me, then turns quickly away.

Dan helps Marjorie Watson into the back of his car, then closes the door. He drives off. Helen walks up to me.

"I need to go to the station, but I can drop you off at the Rectory first."

"Thanks." I look back at the house. "Give me a minute," I say, and walk to Rebecca.

"Are you okay?" I ask.

She stares past me for a moment. Then she looks at me. "I don't know," she whispers. "I really don't know." Tears flow, then sobs. She collapses against my chest, painful wails torn from the depths of her soul floating into the early summer evening.

I say a quick prayer and pat her head. Through the open doorway I can see Win Myer. At my glance, he turns and walks off.

Twenty-Six

After a few minutes of sobbing, Rebecca calms down enough to give me the name of a friend we can call to come over to be with her. I have no confidence she'll get any support or comfort from her husband. The woman arrives about fifteen minutes after I call, then Helen and I leave.

"Brian wasn't happy?" I say to her as we drive.

"He wasn't unhappy," Helen says. "He accepted the facts. That we had got it wrong."

She drives along in silence. We continue that way until we get to the Rectory.

"Thanks for the lift," I say.

"I couldn't have you walk home in the dark, now could I? I'll let you know when Father Leonard's hearing will be."

I watch her drive off, then walk into the Rectory and head into the living room. I collapse on the couch, then lean over so I'm laying on it. I close my eyes. I could fall asleep right here.

"Tom? Is that you?" I open my eyes and sit up. "Where have you been, Tom?" Anna says. "You've been gone for hours. You were having coffee with Helen, and then I expected you back."

"Things happened," I say, wiping my hand across my face. "I could use a drink."

"I'll get you a coke."

"Put some rum in it, will you," I say. She stops and looks at me. I never drink anything harder than beer. Unless under stress. And today, I'm under stress.

"You'll understand when I explain what's happened."

I'm astonished that Anna sits through the entire story without saying a word, almost without moving. She looks for all the world like a little girl sitting around a campfire listening to a ghost story.

"So, they will release Father Leonard in a few days," I finish. I've drunk the rum and coke and I'm feeling relaxed. Not drunk, just relaxed.

Anna shakes her head and sighs. "No wonder you started drinking," she mutters. "That's some story Marjorie told."

I nod. "It is some story, all right."

Anna's eyes narrow. "You don't believe it, do you?"

"Not all of it, no," I say. "The part about Marjorie framing Father McCoy? Yeah, that I believe. She's calculating enough to do that. She schemed to have her favored daughter marry into the richest family in town, she plotted to get her other daughter out of the way. I'm sure she did all that she said, smearing Leonard with Rachel's blood, wiping the fingerprints, even vacuuming the apartment to remove any traces of evidence. All that I can see her doing." I stop talking.

"But the other part of her story?" Anna asks,

"It's too, I don't know, too something," I say, my exhausted mind groping for the right word. "Some parts just don't make sense to me."

Anna rests her chin on her hands. "What does Helen think?"

"Helen's just thankful that an innocent man's not going to prison," I say. "She believes Marjorie is telling the truth. I don't think she believes some details of the story, but the whole—yeah, she buys it."

"Then why don't you? She's the detective, not you. Solving crimes, catching criminals, that's her job." Anna stands up. "Maybe you should stop thinking about this, just be thankful Father Leonard's been exonerated. Let the police worry about the other. You need to settle down."

"Well, I'm not going anywhere," I say with a sweep of my arms.

"That's not what I'm talking about," she replies as she takes a step forward. "I mean Helen. Neither of you has said anything, but I'm no fool. Maybe someday you'll feel comfortable enough to tell me y'all's story, I know there's one, and I'm dying to hear it. I will not go crazy and scream at you if you tell me, no matter what it is."

I look at her. "You're right. I'm sorry. I'll tell you about Helen, but not tonight. I'm too tired."

"I've waited this long," she says. "But whatever feelings you have for Helen, you need to deal with them and put them away. Father Leonard's situation should be warning enough for you."

I nod and sigh. "Right again, Anna. But it's not going to be a problem. She's leaving Myerton."

"What? Where is she going?"

"Nebraska. A police department in a town near where she grew up."

"When is she leaving?"

I shake my head. "I don't know."

Anna looks at me, stunned by the news. Her face softens, she leans over and gives me a kiss on the cheek. "I'm sorry, son," she says, then leaves me alone.

I look at the fireplace. "So am I, Anna," I whisper. "So am I."

***

It's about 2:30 a.m. in the morning when I wake up with a start. A dream. Another dream about the night of Joan's murder. Finding her killer and unburdening myself of the guilt I'd carried for ten years hadn't stopped the dreams entirely. But this one differed from all the others.

In every other dream, it had been Joan laying dead in my arms, just as it had been the night of the murder. In every other dream, Randy Earl had stood over me, pointing the gun at my head.

Tonight, Helen lay dead in my arms. Tonight, a shadowy figure pointed the gun to my head. I woke up when it pulled the trigger.

I swing my legs over the edge of the bed and run my hand through my hair, making a note that I'm in desperate need for a haircut. I haven't had one since going to the monastery. I realize I'm hungry, remembering I hadn't had dinner the evening before. So much had happened, I forgot to eat.

I pull on my robe and go down to the kitchen. In the fridge, I find half a cold roasted chicken. I take the whole platter, get a glass of water, and walk into the sitting room where the television is. I click it on and flip through the four hundred channels. Finally, I come across an old war movie, black and white. Spies behind enemy lines, trying to break into Nazi headquarters or something like that. I tear off a chicken leg and eat.

Father Leonard's getting out of jail. He's not going to prison. He didn't murder Rachel Watson. But there's still everything else he did. All of that will have to be dealt with. An idea comes to me, one that would solve several problems at the same time. I must call the Archbishop in the morning to tell him they will release Father Leonard and to run my idea past him.

Then there's Helen. She didn't say it in so many words, but she's leaving because she still has feelings for me. After all these years, my coming back awakened something in her. She wants there to be an "us." And that's something I can never give her.

But what are my feelings for her? I shake my head and take another bite of chicken. Any feelings I have for Helen don't matter.

On screen, a group of paratroopers is sneaking through the woods outside of some Nazi headquarters. I don't know why they're there. Either to kidnap someone, kill someone, steal something, or blow something up. In a war movie, the options to explain a group sneaking through the woods at night are limited.

My mind wanders to Marjorie Watson. The methodical way she framed Father Leonard. The depths of evil to which human beings can descend will never cease to amaze me. All for vengeance. All because—

I stop chewing. Why did she go to such lengths to frame Leonard? Simple vengeance for his relationship with her daughter? Did she care that much, did it enrage her so much that she would even vacuum Rachel's apartment to remove any trace of herself? Her presence in the apartment could be explained well enough. She was Rachel's mother. It would have made sense that she would be there. And according to her account, Rachel's death was a tragic accident, brought about by her own actions. Why cover up what wasn't even murder to begin with?

But what if it wasn't just vengeance? What if it wasn't really an accident? Her entire story bothered me. It just made little sense to me.

What if she wasn't covering up for herself?

What if she was trying to protect someone?

On screen, the paratroopers stop at the edge of the woods, and time the guards as they patrol back and forth across the entrance to the facility.

If she was trying to protect someone else, then her entire story was a lie. Or at least the part about how Rachel died. But who would she go to such lengths to protect?

One paratrooper is sneaking up behind a guard, who has stopped walking and has his back to the woods. Why is his back turned? He wouldn't do that in real life. Any threat would come from the woods, not the building. I shake my head. I'm trying to make fiction logical. Real life never is. Why should fiction?

I tear off some breast meat from the carcass. As I chew, I turn the question over in my mind. Who would Marjorie care about that much, to create an entire story that implicated her in not one but two crimes?

The paratrooper has stopped about two feet behind the guard, who is still standing with his back to the woods. Either the guard is deaf, or the big paratrooper has the deft footing of a ballet dancer, because the guard doesn't hear the threat coming out of the dark.

It would have to be someone with a motive to murder Rachel. That was a very limited list. One, Father Leonard, was already eliminated thanks to Marjorie's story. It's ironic that it happened that way; she helped the man she wanted so badly to frame.

The paratrooper moves forward slightly.

Rebecca was jealous of her sister. Jealous of her husband's feelings for her sister. Was she fearful that Rachel's baby was Win's, that she had proof of her worst fears coming true? Was Marjorie trying to protect her daughter, keep her from being arrested on suspicion of murder?

Finally, the paratrooper leaps, grabs the hapless German guard around the neck. The guard struggles, unable to cry out because of the muscular arm constricting his windpipe. I expect the paratrooper to pull out his knife, to finish the soldier off. Instead, he keeps his grip. Gradually, the guard stops struggling, loses consciousness. The paratrooper gently lowers him to the ground, then cuts the wire fencing around the facility.

I pick up my glass and bring it to my lips.

Then I stop. I sit on the edge of the couch.

Someone out of the darkness, suffocating someone to unconsciousness.

I stand up and start pacing. Father Leonard insisted there was a presence in the townhouse when he arrived. Marjorie says she was there. She says she came up behind him and clocked him on the back of the head with a heavy vase. But Leonard said he was suffocated unconscious. From behind. By the unknown presence.

One thing I know. Marjorie Watson is physically incapable of doing that. She's too short, for one. For another, she doesn't have the strength to do it.

So who would be tall enough and strong enough to grab him around the neck and hold him as he struggled long enough to render him unconscious?

And who would know how to do that without killing him?

I look at the screen. The paratroopers are following their leader through the wire.

Someone would have to have training in how to subdue someone quickly and quietly.

Someone like a Green Beret.

I dash up the stairs to my room and grab my phone off the nightstand. I find Helen's number. I'm about the press dial when I stop.

It's 2:30 a.m. in the morning. Do I really want to wake her up over a hunch? I sit on the edge of the bed looking at the phone. I send a quick text, then get up and get dressed.

***

I question my sanity as I sit outside the Myer house. It's 3:30 am, and the place is dark.

"So what's your plan now, Tom?" I say to myself. "Brilliant idea, coming here in the middle of the night. What did you think you would do?"

I have no idea. When I left the Rectory I had a vague idea of confronting Win Myer with my suspicions, to try to get him to admit to the murder of Rachel Watson. The more I drove, however, the more I realized what a crazy idea that was on several levels.

First, I have no evidence. Second, if Win Myer is a murderer, then he's shown he has no problem killing. Third, no one knows where I am. My text to Helen was short and to the point, but "I know who did it ... call me" would give her no idea where to look if I go missing.

In all, not one of my more brilliant ideas.

But here I am, sitting in my fifteen-year-old car outside the Myer house, which looks much more foreboding in the dark than it does in the daylight. Which is saying a lot, because it looks very foreboding in the daylight.

A line from a Star Trek episode comes to mind. "We are committed," Captain Kirk said, which prompted Scotty to ask, "Aye, but to what?"

"To what indeed, Scotty?" I ask myself out loud.

I square my shoulders and cross myself. "Saint Michael the Archangel," I mutter, "defend us fools in battle . . ." Which is not exactly how the prayer goes, I know, but under the circumstances, I need the prince of the heavenly host to know exactly who he needs to defend tonight.

I take a deep breath and get out of the car. I walk up to the door.

Instead of knocking or ringing the doorbell, I try the doorknob. It turns. I push the door open slowly, trying to keep it from squeaking on the hinges.

I stand in the open doorway, peering into the darkened interior. Dark except for a light coming from under a closed door.

The door to Win Myer's office.

I stand there for a few minutes not knowing what to do. Then, I do the dumbest thing possible.

I enter a dark, creepy house in the middle of the night. At this point, I can hear Saint Michael throw down his sword and shield and say, "That's it, I can't help this stupid priest."

Anyone who has seen any number of horror films knows that the number one rule is you never enter a dark and creepy house. It's the rule that uncounted teenagers break in every movie. It's how they wind up as corpses.

And here I am, walking unannounced and uninvited into the house of someone I believe is a murderer.

I tip-toe across the polished wood floor of the entrance, trying my best not to make a sound, alert for the sound of anyone in the room with me. I don't hear anyone, so I continue toward Win Myer's office. I don't hear anyone inside.

I get to the door and reach for the handle. I hesitate, then grip it. I turn the knob and slowly push the door open. I look inside.

The office is empty.

I take two steps away from the room. But I can't go any further. Something is blocking my escape.

A presence in the dark.

The next moment, a powerful arm grabs me around the neck. I grab at the arm, clawing at it, trying to extricate myself from its grasp. I kick, my shoes contacting shins.

"Shh, quiet, quiet," a voice whispers in my ear. I smell alcohol. "Don't struggle. Don't struggle. Struggling will only make it worse."

The light coming from the office gets dimmer and dimmer. Darkness begins to envelope me. I hear a voice say, "It will be all right, Tom."

I recognize the voice.

I whisper, "Joan."

Then blackness.

***

Light is streaming through the windows when I wake up. My entire body is sore. I cough, my throat hurts. I rub it to bring it some relief. I probably have a bruised neck, I think.

I look around, unsure where I am at first. Some kind of brick building, the windows dusted over with age and neglect. The entire place is dusty, covered in cobwebs. I hear the scurrying of tiny feet behind a rusted piece of equipment, looking for all the world like an old steam engine or turbine. The large flywheel is connected by a now-rotted belt to a smaller piece of equipment, from which wires run to the wall.

I slowly get to my feet. I'm unsteady and my head hurts. I stagger to the window and look out.

Across a grassy expanse, I see the rear of the Myer house. I seem to be on the edge of the woods. I turn to look at the equipment in the room with me.

The power house. I'm in the power house, the one that Thomas Edison himself built.

Win Myer. He must have brought me here after knocking me out. Put me in a place where I wouldn't be found for a while, knowing it would be hours before I woke up. Giving him enough time.

But time to do what? I rub the back of my neck, running the possibilities through my mind.

Time to turn himself in, to keep his mother-in-law from being punished for his crimes? No, he would have spoken up during Marjorie's confession if he had any real idea of taking responsibility for what he did. Time to leave Myerton, to run where the law might not find him? He has enough money to do that. But why run if no one suspected him? There is no evidence—I have no evidence, just a hunch. There is no one who knew the whole truth who could accuse him. Or would accuse him. Marjorie knows the truth, and she will go to prison to protect her son-in-law. Father Leonard couldn't identify him. Rachel Watson is dead.

Everyone who can accuse Win Myer of murder is dead, couldn't or wouldn't.

I stop my pacing. I'm wrong. There is one person who knows the truth. One person who can accuse him.

Win Myer.

"Oh, no," I whisper. "Dear Lord, no, not that."

I'm still a little unsteady as I make my way to the door. The hinges have rusted, so it's a little difficult to pull open. I manage to do so, and squint as the light pours in.

I plod across the huge back lawn, making my way with uncertain steps up the slight slope towards the house. It's hot, and I'm soon sweating under the exertion.

I stop about halfway and bend over to catch my breath. From the direction of the house, I hear someone calling my name.

I look up. It's Helen.

I knew she'd find me.

Focusing on her, I continue my slow trek up the hill. She sees my struggle and hurries down the grass towards me. I topple over when she grabs me.

"I've got you, come on, let's get you inside." To a nearby officer, she yells, "Get the paramedics, now!"

"How did you know where to find me?" I gasp.

"I didn't know you were here, not until I saw your car in the driveway," she says. We get to the patio and she takes me inside. The cool air hits me, reviving me some. She helps me to a chair.

"What do you mean, you didn't know I was here?"

"Tom, you sent me a text message at 2:30 this morning that only said. 'I know who did it... call me.' How was I going to figure out where you were from that? I mean, it's not like you said, 'I'm going over to the Myer house where I may be killed.'"

"You didn't ping my cell phone?"

"Frankly, I was about to have Gladys do just that—you have really got to stop confronting murderers on your own, Tom. I'm not always going to be here to save you."

"You didn't this time," I say, rubbing the back of my neck.

She ignores my comment. "Like I said, when Anna called me to say you missed 8:00 Mass—why don't you just stop doing it, I think you miss most of the time—and you weren't in the Rectory, I knew you had done something stupid. I was going to try to locate you when we got a call from Rebecca Myer."

I stop and look at Helen. "Win Myer's dead, isn't he?"

Helen nods. "She found him in his office. He shot himself in the head. She didn't hear the gunshot. It's a big house and their room is on the far end from his office." She pauses. "He left a note. Not so much a note as an essay. It's five pages long."

"What did he say? Did he confess?"

Just then the paramedics come. Helen stands by, concerned, while they check me out. Blood pressure, respiration, ask me to follow their finger with my eyes, check for any injuries.

"How is he?" Helen asks.

"He looks okay, blood pressure, respiration, O2 levels, heart rate all look normal," one medic says. "But we should take him to the hospital to have him checked out."

Helen's about to respond when I say, "I'm not going anywhere, not right now."

She looks at me but, noticing my determination, says, "Fine, Tom. Fine." To the paramedics she says, "Just wait outside." They gather their equipment and leave us alone.

"What did the note say?"

"It would be easier to tell you what the note didn't say," she said. "Like I say, it goes on for five pages. Some of it reads like he was drunk; it rambles, and the handwriting is almost illegible. But the gist of it is he went over to Rachel's a little after 6:00 p.m.. He said he wanted to try one last time to talk her out of going to the convent. According to the note, he had been stalking her off and on since she got back to Myerton. He's been obsessed with her since high school. The note goes on about how much he loved her, how he always loved her." Helen sighs. "The whole thing is a weird combination of creepy and pitiful."

"So he went over to Rachel's."

"She told him she wasn't going to the convent," Helen continues. "She told Myer that Father Leonard was on his way, that they were going to run away together. He was leaving the priesthood, and they were going to marry and raise their child together."

"But she wasn't going to do that," I say.

"I know," Helen says. "But that's what he said in the note. He broke down, apparently, and told her how much he loved her, how he had always loved her, and begged her not to go. He told her if she stayed, he'd divorce Rebecca so they could be together, he'd be the child's father. According to note, she rejected the idea, said she could never do that to her sister, and besides any feelings she once had were gone. She loved Leonard and wanted to be with him." Helen paused. "He said he decided that if he couldn't have her, then no one could, though he also said he didn't mean to kill her."

"He stabbed her in the stomach to kill the baby," I said.

"He said that's all he wanted to do. He said he didn't mean to kill her."

I shake my head, imagining the scene. The look of shock on Rachel's face, a desperate and desolate Win Myer watching as she sinks to the floor, blood pouring from her belly.

"Where does Marjorie Watson come into this?"

"He says he called her," Helen says. "He didn't know what to do, so he called Marjorie. She got there around 6:45 p.m. and was helping him figure out what to do when Father Leonard arrived. He rendered Father Leonard unconscious, then framed him the way Marjorie claims. Myer said he forced her to help him."

"Why did he kill himself?" I ask. "Guilt?" I think of our conversation in the church, and his last words to me.

"The note doesn't give a reason," Helen says. "After the rambling confession, it just stops. Like I say, it looks like he had been drinking. There's an empty scotch bottle and glass next to him, along with the gun in his hand."

She puts her hands on her hips. "Now, will you go to the hospital?"

I shake my head and try to stand up. I reach out to Helen for help. "Where's Rebecca Watson? I should go see her."

"Why?"

"Because it's my job, Helen!" I exclaim. "I'm a priest! She's hurting. Her sister is dead, her mother confessed to a crime, her husband just killed himself after confessing to murder, and her father doesn't seem like he knows what planet he's on half the time. She needs someone, and right now I'm the one who's here. She needs comfort. You have demanded that I let you do your job.

Now I'm demanding you let me do mine. Now, are you going to help me up and tell me where she is?"

Helen opens her mouth to say something, then shakes her head. "Fine, Tom," she says as she helps me to my feet. "You've gotten more stubborn the older you've gotten. You can talk to her for a few minutes, but then you're going to the hospital."

The surrounding room tilts a little as I get to my feet. I'm still unsteady and it takes a minute for me to get my footing. I nod and say, "All right. Might be a good idea."

"She's in the living room," Helen says as we walk down the corridor from the entrance to the patio. On the way to the living room, we pass Win Myer's office. The door is open. Crime scene technicians are taking photographs, noting the position of everything in the room. Win's body hasn't been moved yet.

"Wait," I say to Helen. "Take me to him."

"Tom," Helen sighs.

"My job, Helen. Please."

She helps me into the room. Helen signals to the technicians to stop what they are doing. I make it the last few steps to his desk on my own.

He's slumped across the desk, the gun in his right hand. The empty scotch bottle and glass sit in mute testimony to the pain he was trying to numb, to the courage he was trying to summon, to take the last desperate step of taking his own life. There's a pencil cup to his left, spilled over at some point.

I shake my head. I say a prayer for his soul and make the sign of the cross over his lifeless body. I sway a little. Helen is at my side to keep me from keeling over or touching anything in the crime scene.

"Come on," she whispers. "There's nothing else you can do."

I nod. Win Myer is beyond anyone's help now.

We get to the living room. Rebecca Myer is sitting on the sofa, looking out the window, her hair disheveled, wearing a bathrobe and slippers.

I step into the room. "Rebecca," I say quietly. She doesn't acknowledge me.

"May I sit with you for a few minutes?" I ask. At first, there's no response. Then a slight nod.

I walk across the library and sit down. Her hair is damp, and I'm hit with a familiar smell. Vanilla.

For several minutes, she doesn't speak. Through the open door, I can hear the movement and the murmur of the police and the crime scene techs as they go about their job.

"I'm sorry," Rebecca whispers. "I'm sorry Win hurt you."

"I'll be fine," I tell her. "No permanent damage done."

"I'm surprised he didn't kill you. He's killed before, you know. First in Afghanistan in the Army. He used to tell me when he was drunk. He'd cry over it, cry like a baby. I'd cradle him in my arms." She takes a ragged breath. "He'd only ever let me touch him when he was drunk."

I listen quietly to her, touching her shoulder.

"He killed my sister," she gasps, tears returning. "He killed her because he couldn't have her, because she wouldn't have him. I always knew, I always knew, Father. I was right, you know."

"I'm so sorry."

"I always knew he wanted Rachel. But I knew Rachel would never betray me." She pauses. "Maybe if she had betrayed me, Rachel would still be alive. I'd be alone, devastated, angry with her, and never be able to forgive her. But she'd still be alive."

"You mustn't think that way."

"And Mama," she went on. "She tried to protect Win by confessing to the crime."

"Looks to me like she confessed to protect you," I say quietly, stroking her shoulder, trying to comfort her.

"No, no, I know her. She was concerned Detective Parr would get to Win. She couldn't have that, not her golden child. If it was just me, I might be in jail. She'd have let me go."

"I've seen her with you, she favored you. She sent Rachel away so you could have Win instead of Rachel."

Rebecca shakes her head. "She favored me because I was with Win." She gives a short laugh. "She couldn't have him herself. Maybe I should have worried about her instead of Rachel. Given half a chance, Mama would have slept with Win, I know."

She sighs. She goes back to staring out the window. "He killed my sister. He wanted her. And he killed her."

"He wanted Rachel instead of you," I whisper. "That's why you killed him, isn't it?"

Rebecca turns to me. "How do you know?"

"For one, your hair is wet. You told the police you came downstairs and saw the body, then called them. Shooting him at such close range would have made a mess. You had to take a shower to clean up. Am I right?"

She nods. "Anything else?"

"The gun. It's in his right hand. Win's left-handed, isn't he?"

She gives a short laugh. "Yes. I can't believe I forgot that. I guess in the shock."

"Why don't you tell me what happened?"

"A confession, Father?"

"An unburdening."

She looks at me, then nods. "I woke up, and he still wasn't in bed. The sun was coming up, so I went downstairs to look for him. I found him in his office. He had passed out drunk, I saw the empty bottle and the glass from the doorway. I went to wake him up, help him upstairs to finish sleeping it off—it wouldn't have been the first time. It was only when I got to the desk that I saw the gun. And the note."

"You read it."

"The entire thing. It was like, like every fear I had set in black and white. It was all there, his confession to murdering Rachel mixed in with his declarations of love for her, saying he had always loved her, always wanted her." She pauses. "It was all there. I had proof that what I had always suspected was true. And to top it all off, he had killed her."

I say nothing, just a prayer in my mind for this poor woman.

"He said in the note he couldn't live with himself, that he wanted to die," she continues. "So he had every intention of killing himself. I guess he passed out drunk before he could pull the trigger. The gun looked like it had fallen out of his hand when he slumped over."

"Out of his left hand," I say.

With a tight smile, she says. "Yes, out of his left hand. I remember little of what happened next. I think I just stood there looking at him, stood there for a long time. I thought what a pitiful excuse of a man he was, what a coward, to kill an innocent woman, to allow Mama to lie for him instead of taking responsibility, to lie to me for years, saying he loved me when he didn't."

"You got angry."

"I did, Father Greer. The more I looked at him, the angrier I got. Finally, I decided that if he wanted to kill himself, I'd help him. I picked the gun up off the desk and put the barrel to his head. But I couldn't pull the trigger. God help me, I couldn't do it. I mean, even after everything, even if he didn't love me, I still loved him. I thought once he sobered up, I'd get him to turn himself in, and somehow we'd get through everything."

She shudders. "I had just moved the gun away when he stirred. I leaned over and shook him slightly. 'Win,' I whispered in his ear." She closed her eyes. "He said . . . " She cries again.

"He said Rachel," I finish quietly.

She nods and collapses against me, sobbing. I hold her for a long time, her body wracked with sobs. Finally, I see Helen standing in the doorway. I look at her, then back at Rebecca. She's calmer, sobs replaced by quiet tears rolling down her cheek.

"I need to go, Rebecca. But I think you know what you need to do," I say to her. She looks at me, then nods slowly.

I get to my feet. I'm steadier now, the room not tilting as much. I make my way across the room to Helen.

"What did she say?" she asks as I pass her.

I stop and look back at the figure on the sofa. She's looking out the window again.

"She'll tell you," I whisper. "I can't, remember?"

Twenty-Seven

The crowd of reporters shouts questions as Father Leonard and Angela Jenkins walk out of the courthouse. I'm standing a short distance away, watching the spectacle unfold.

"Father, how does it feel to be free?"

"What are your feelings about Win Myer?"

"Are you going to stay in the priesthood?"

"Where are you going after this?"

"People, people, please," Jenkins says, motioning to the crowd to quiet down. The shouts give way to murmurs, which finally give way to silence. "Father McCoy is extremely pleased that the State Attorney moved to quash the indictment and the judge accepted it. Neither gentleman had much choice given that the actual perpetrator of this horrendous crime gave a full confession in writing before his own death."

Reporters ask questions again, but Jenkins goes on. "It's a good day for justice, it's a good day for the people of Myerton. But it's a reminder of the great responsibility officers of the court have to look at the evidence without prejudice, without trying to put their thumbs on the scale of justice to benefit the rich and powerful at the expense of the weak. That's what Brian Dohrmann did in this case. Fortunately, thanks to the hard work and the personal integrity of a few people, a miscarriage of justice was averted. Now let me get the good Father back to his parish where he can rest. Thank you."

Jenkins takes Father Leonard, looking as confused as ever, by the arm and forces her way through the press of reporters. They haven't seen me yet, and since I'm partially hidden behind a tree, I'm certain no one will see me.

"Hiding from someone?" I jump. Helen has snuck up behind me.

"Just the baying hounds of the press," I say.

"What? You want to deny the representatives of the fourth estate a chance to ask you questions?" she says with a smile.

"In a word, yes," I say.

"Don't blame you," Helen says. Her eyes follow Jenkins and Father Leonard to the attorney's car. "What will happen to him?"

"Father Leonard," I say, "has some work to do."

"What do you mean?"

"Prayer, thought, he needs to decide if he wants to stay a priest or not. You don't think that's work? Trust me, it's work."

"He's not staying here, so where is he going?"

"I've talked to the Archbishop about that," I say. "I suggested he spend several months at Our Lady of the Mount. It's perfect. They need a priest to provide the sacraments, Leonard needs a place where he can pray and heal." I pause. "The monastery is the perfect place for that."

Helen is looking at Angela Jenkins as she gets into her car. "Leave it to her to turn it into a political speech," she mutters. "Brian'll hit the roof when he sees it."

"How is he doing?"

She shrugs. "I don't know. I haven't seen him today."

The crowd of reporters having dispersed, we emerge from my hiding place and walk towards the sidewalk.

"What are you thinking about?" Helen asks.

"Swords."

She stops. I turn to her. "You know how Scripture describes the Word of God?"

"Ah, wait, don't tell me—"

"As sharper than a two-edged sword. Soldiers used a two-edged sword in battle. Do you know why the sword had two-edges?"

She shakes her head. "It can cut if swung down or if brought up," I explain. "Either way, it can kill."

"And you were thinking about swords because?"

"I was thinking about how love is like a two-edged sword. It has such power to bring people together. It brings hope. It brings life into the world. It's wonderful. It's one of the three theological virtues. God is love. The entire Church rests on Love. Love has so much power for good." I shake my head. "It also has so much power for evil."

At Helen's questioning look, I go on. "Look at all that's happened. Father Leonard loved Rachel. The love he felt led him into sin, into breaking his vow of celibacy. Rachel loved Leonard. Her love led her to question her call to the religious life. Win Myer loved Rachel, a love which was perverted into obsession, which is why he killed her. Marjorie Watson loved her son-in-law, which led her to dispose of one daughter and betray another. Rebecca Watson loved Win, but couldn't live with him not loving her, so she killed him. So love can create. It can also destroy."

Helen sighs. "You always were the life of the party, you know that?"

I laugh. "It's just the musings of a cynical priest, Helen."

Looking at her watch, she says. "I'm hungry. How about lunch?"

Just then her phone rings. Helen rolls her eyes and fishes the phone out of her bag.

"Yes, Dan, what is it?" She listens. "Well, it took them long enough, but why . . . What!" Helen's eyes get big. "Say that again? You're sure of the time?" She listens as Dan Conway tells her something. She looks at me. "Contact the bank. I want the surveillance footage yesterday." She listens and smiles. "Good job, Dan, you've earned your pay for the week. We'll be right there." She hangs up.

"Come on, Tom, we have a problem," Helen says over her shoulder as she strides off.

I trot to catch up with her. "Wait, what's going on, Helen?"

She turns around. "We finally got Rachel Watson's bank records. It's standard practice in any investigation, but it took the bank a long time to get them together. Apparently, they just changed computer systems and they've had problems." She inhales. "She made an ATM withdrawal from the branch near her townhouse at 6:42 p.m. on the night of her murder. So the person Walkin saw entering Rachel's townhouse was Rachel."

I look at her, wide-eyed. "But that means she couldn't have been in her apartment when Marjorie Watson says she got there. She couldn't have been in there when Win Myer says he killed her."

"And," Helen says slowly, "no one else entered the townhouse before Father Leonard."

I'm feeling sick to my stomach. "Oh, my dear Lord," I whisper.

Helen nods. "Yes Tom. I'm sorry, but you've been wrong all along."

Twenty-Eight

"I was taking a nap in my cell," Marjorie Watson says. "I don't know why you'd drag me out to ask me more questions. I confessed days ago. You have Win's note. You've already released Father Leonard."

"We've had some additional evidence," Helen says. "This shouldn't take too long if you're honest with us now."

"Why is he even here?" she points to me. "The last thing I need is a priest."

"Never mind why he's here," Helen replies. "I have two things to show you." She opens the folder in her hands.

"This," Helen says as she lays a piece of paper on the table in front of Marjorie, "is a listing of all Rebecca's financial transactions in the last week of her life." She points to a line at the bottom of the page. "This is the last one. An ATM withdrawal for $600. We assume that was to pay for the abortion in Hagerstown."

Marjorie shrugs. "So?"

"Look," Helen says. Marjorie leans forward to read where Helen's finger has stopped. She squints, then looks up at us with surprise.

"But, but, that's—" she sputters.

I nod. "Yes. The last withdrawal she ever made was at 6:42 p.m. on the night of her murder. Around the same time you claim you arrived at her townhouse. And after the time Win Myer claimed in his suicide note that he killed her."

She's wide-eyed, her mouth slightly open as Helen places a photograph in front of her. "This is from the ATM surveillance camera. It's Rachel. Look at the time stamp." She sits back and crosses her arms.

Marjorie picks up the photograph. Still looking at it, she sits back in her chair, tears beginning to well up. "She didn't do it," she whispers.

I lean forward. "You thought Rebecca had killed her sister, didn't you?"

Biting her lip, she nods. "The detective seemed so sure," she whispers. She shakes her head as the tears flow down her cheek. "I couldn't, I couldn't see her go to prison. I'd already lost one daughter."

"So you made up the entire story," Helen says, "because you wanted to draw attention away from Rebecca."

"Yes," she says.

"You'd confess to a crime you didn't commit, go to prison?" I say.

"You're not a mother, Father Tom," she says. "Despite what Rebecca and Rachel thought, I love my daughters. I'd do anything for them. I've done everything for them. Oh, I know how I come across. I'm not a snuggly mommy type, I never was. I wanted my girls to be strong and independent, but I wanted them to be secure. When Rachel showed no interest in Win Myer in high school, I put Rebecca and him together. Sending Rachel away may have been a mistake, but I did it out of love." She sighs. "I know it makes little sense, but that's all I've ever done."

"Out of his love for you, Win confessed in his suicide note. He was covering for you. He knew you were trying to take suspicion off Rebecca. Plus, he felt guilty over . . . other things," I say.

"Did you go to Rachel's townhouse that night?" Helen asks.

She shakes her head. "No. At the time of her murder, I was home. I don't remember what I was doing. Edmund was out with some colleagues of his. So I have no alibi."

Helen shakes her head. Pointing to the picture, she says. "Rachel provided you with an alibi." She stands up. "I must talk to the State Attorney, but you'll be free in a few days. You should call your lawyer. I'll arrange for that."

We start at the door when Marjorie asks, "So Father Leonard killed my daughter?" She fixes me with a glare. "So, you are responsible, Father Greer, for Rachel's death. If you had just listened to me, she might be alive today."

I glance at her but say nothing. Helen opens the door and we step into the hallway. Helen tells the officer to take Marjorie back to her cell.

We walk together down the hallway to her office. She drops into her desk chair and places her head on her arms.

"Where's Father Leonard right now?" she asks.

"He's probably at the Rectory," I say.

She looks weary when she sits up. Grabbing the receiver of her desk phone, she presses some buttons. "This is Detective Parr," she says to the person who answers. "Send a car to the Saint Clare's Rectory and get Father Leonard." She pauses. "I don't care what they tell him, just bring him here!" She slams the receiver down and looks at me. "What?"

I'm looking to one side, staring at a spot on the wall. "Huh? Oh, I was just thinking. You were right. And as much as it pains me to say it, Brian was right. Leonard did it. He fooled me." I pause. "Apparently, I'm a very gullible person."

Helen smiles. "You think the best of people, that's one reason I fell in love with you."

I look at her. "I've become more cynical. I should have clung to that this time. Then I might have seen through Leonard's deceptions."

"Excuse me, Chief." I turn to see Gladys Finklestein in Helen's doorway. "This just came in for you." She rolls in and hands an envelope to Helen.

"Thanks, Gladys," Helen says.

"No problem, Chief," Gladys replies. Turning to me she smiles. "Hi, Father Tom," she says, slightly breathlessly.

"Hello, Gladys," I reply. "How are you doing?"

"Me? Oh, I am much better now. It's been a while since I've seen you."

"You haven't been at Mass, I've noticed."

She actually bats her eyelashes and plays with a strand of her blue hair. "So, you've missed me?" she asks. "Because I've sure missed you."

"Gladys!" Helen says.

The young woman jumps. "Huh? Oh, yeah. OK. I'll just go back to my office." She starts to the door and turns around slightly. With a coquettish grin, she purrs, "Bye, Father."

Looking after her as she leaves, I say, "You weren't kidding about her."

Helen doesn't answer me. Instead, she says, "These are the results of the DNA test on Rachel's baby. It's definite. Father Leonard was the father."

Before I can answer, her phone rings. "Yes?" she answers. Looking at me, she says. "What do you mean there's no one at the Rectory?"

I pull my phone out and dial Anna. After a few rings, she answers. "Hello," she says. In the background I hear other people and the pinging of cash registers.

"Anna, where's Father Leonard?"

"Father Leonard? Why are you asking? You know where he is."

"What do you mean?"

"When he got back to the rectory, he told me you told him to go to Our Lady of the Mount immediately. He packed his things and left about half an hour after he got back. I've been wondering where you've been."

I look at Helen. "Thanks, Anna." I hang up.

"He's gone," I say, "But I know where he is."

Twenty-Nine

Helen calls the state police and asks them to go to Our Lady of the Mount to detain Father Leonard.

"I want to talk to him," I say.

"Tom, this is a police matter. Besides, what makes you think he'll say anything to you now? He's either not spoken or lied this whole time."

"Because he's carrying a tremendous burden," I say. "He has to be getting tired. He needs to tell someone. Besides, I need to know why."

"He can tell me when I arrest him."

"That's not what I mean."

We look at each other. "If you hear his confession," Helen says slowly, "you won't be able to tell me what he said."

I nod. "That's true. I'll try to get him to agree to confess to you for his crimes, but there are no guarantees." I pause. "But he's at the end of his rope. Otherwise, he wouldn't have left Saint Clare's so abruptly."

"I don't know, Tom," Helen shakes her head. "I'd rather you spoke to him after I took him into custody and interviewed him."

"You've interviewed him before," I point out, "and you got very little. And none of the truth. So you won't be any further behind than you were."

Helen sighs, then nods. "Okay, when we take him into custody, I'll allow you fifteen minutes. After that, I'm taking over. Sound good?"

I nod. "Sounds great."

"It's not like I need his confirmation of what we already know," Helen says. "The physical evidence really points to him. Brian got an indictment once. He'll get another one. It would just be easier all around if he confessed."

"Easier for Brian, don't you mean?"

"Don't start Tom, not now. For me, too. I mean, I'm the one who followed your word. That it was Rebecca the neighbor saw go into Rachel's townhouse. I'm the one who bought Marjorie Watson's story. And then there was Win's note."

I nod. "But I so wanted to believe Leonard was innocent. He just doesn't seem like the type to murder someone."

"Take it from me, Tom," Helen says, patting my arm. "Most murderers are like that. They're not perpetually mean. They look perfectly normal on the outside, and most of the time, they are. But something pushes them into thinking they have no other choice but to take a human life."

"People always have a choice."

She shrugs. "Maybe they just can't see it. Or maybe they see the choice as an impossible one."

***

I consider what Helen said to me as we drive to the monastery. It's dark by the time we turn off the main road onto the long gravel drive. Outside of Brother Martin's cabin are two Maryland State Police cars, their occupants speaking to Brother Martin by the light of the headlights.

Helen parks and gets out. I fumble with my seatbelt and follow her.

"Troopers," she says. "What's going on?"

A Latina trooper says, "Detective, the suspect was not in his cabin. This gentleman," she indicates the elderly monk, "refuses to let us into the main building."

Looking at me, Brother Martin says. "I've explained to these officers, it's the great silence. We cannot disturb the brothers."

"It's important, Brother Martin," I say. "We need to find Father Leonard. Do you have any idea where he is?"

He shakes his head. "No. He got here right after Vespers and asked for the same retreat cabin he had last time. I hadn't been expecting him and explained that the cabin hadn't been cleaned after the last retreatant. He insisted it was no problem. He practically demanded the cabin." Brother Martin looked grim. "Such a different man than last time. I should have known something was wrong. But I knew he had been under a strain, so I ignored my concerns."

"And that's the last you saw him?"

"Yes," Brother Martin replies.

"We need to find him, Brother Martin," Helen says. "Can you please let us search inside the building?"

"I'm sorry Detective," he shakes his head. "We cannot break the great silence. Besides, I strongly doubt he's there."

"Why is that?" Helen asks.

"Because they lock the door from the inside, and I'm the only one outside with a key."

Helen and I look at Brother Martin. "Since when did the brothers begin locking the door?" I ask.

"Right after you left this last time, we had an intruder in the middle of the night. Got to the chapel and tried to take off with the candlesticks. Fortunately, Brother Bartholemew heard him and subdued the man."

I smile. Brother Bartholemew is a former defensive tackle for the Baltimore Ravens.

"Brother Bartholemew," Brother Martin explains to Helen, "suffers from insomnia."

"So if he's not in the main building," Helen says, looking around, "where is he?"

"We were just about to call in a search team with dogs, get a helicopter with infrared and night vision," says the other State Trooper.

While they're talking, I'm looking in a familiar direction.

"That won't be necessary," I say quietly. "I think I know where he is."

***

I'm right.

Father Leonard is on his knees before the statue of Our Lady in the Grotto. The moonlight brightly illuminates the statues of both Mary and Saint Bernadette. I can make out Leonard on the ground between Bernadette and the statue. He's muttering loud enough so I can hear him. He's saying the sorrowful mysteries of the Rosary.

I try to tiptoe up to him, but I step on and break a small branch. Father Leonard jumps up with a cry, spinning around.

"Who—who's there," he stammers. "The police? Have you come for me? I didn't mean to do it!"

I approach carefully, not wanting to spook the already fragile Father. "It's me, Leonard," I say.

"Oh," Father Leonard says with a sigh of relief. "Father Tom. I thought—"

Walking closer, I say, "You're right, Leonard. The police are here. They know what you did, Leonard. They know you murdered Rachel."

Father Leonard's mood changes. He advances toward me, his fists clenched. In a moment, he's transformed from a pitiful lamb to a raging bull, his breathing heavy. He turns and stomps off a few feet. "Stupid girl," he mutters. "Just like my mother warned me about."

"What did your mother warn you about?"

He spins around, extending his hands. "Women, Father Tom! Surely you understand what they're like!"

I shake my head and sit down on one of the rough-hewn benches stretched before the Grotto. "Why don't you tell me? What did your mother tell you about them?"

He paces like a caged animal, stricken, wounded, looking for an escape. Only instead of running, Father Leonard is looking for something else. Understanding.

"She warned me, she warned me all about them," he says. "How they were sent by Satan to tempt me, to distract me from my calling. 'The devil has the power to take on a pleasing shape,' she'd say, every time a girl showed any interest in me. I had a friend in kindergarten. She had pigtails and green eyes. I can't remember her name, but she was my only friend. One day, my mother came to pick me up from school. I walked up to her holding my friend's hand and said she was my girlfriend." He paused and shuddered. "I was smiling until I saw the look on my mother's face. She yanked me away from my friend and practically threw me in the car." He looked down at his feet. "When she got me home, she used one of my father's belts on me. She yelled at me the whole time, saying the devil sent all girls to take me away from my calling, that I needed to stay away from them."

"My God," I whisper.

"She kept me home after that," Father Leonard says. He stops his pacing and looks at me. "She was right. That's what women are for us, aren't they? Tempting us, testing us constantly, wanting to take us from serving the Lord to serving their fleshly needs."

"She didn't keep you home the entire time, did she? You went to Mass, you saw girls your own age there?"

"I stayed away from them," Father Leonard says. "After Mass, we'd go straight to the car and go home. I'd spend the rest of the day meditating on the mass readings or studying." He brightens up. "I taught myself Greek and Latin that way. It's amazing what you can do when you're not distracted."

"But surely you were friends with boys? She couldn't object to that?"

"Oh, she said they were just as bad, worse. She said they'd either try to show me indecent pictures of girls to tempt me to defile myself, or they were little perverts who'd try to turn me into a pervert." He sighed. "Besides, it's not like anyone wanted to play with me, anyway. I was the weird boy with the science-fiction name and the strange mother. So they stayed away from me."

"I don't understand, Leonard," I say. "If she was so concerned, so protective, why did she want you sent away to a boarding school for high school?"

He smiles and sits down opposite me. "She thought it would be okay. She was concerned that after she died, there would be no one to protect me—my father really didn't care, you see. Besides, a rather strict and traditional order ran the school, and since it was all boys, she told me it would keep me free from temptations. She was wrong."

"That's when you met Rachel."

"Yes," his face brightens for a moment, then darkens. "Every time I saw her, every dance, I just felt the temptation so strongly. I'd go back to my room and do penance. I kept thinking I had disappointed my mother."

I look at Father Leonard. "You were afraid of disappointing your dead mother by seeing Rachel?"

"I knew she was already disappointed," he whines. "I knew she could see everything I was doing. I'd hear her voice, her warning voice, in my head every day. I even felt the marks on my back from years ago. I had been so careful, but I found myself drawn to Rachel. I—I couldn't help myself."

"You were young, Leonard," I say. "You're still young. This life we have, it's hard, it's a discipline. It's not for everyone. Maybe you were finding…"

"No, no, don't say it!" He cries, shaking his head vigorously. "No, I'm a priest. I was always meant to be a priest. My mother told me she promised God I would be a priest."

Father Leonard plops down on the bench in front of me. In the dim light, I can see his shoulders sagging. He's defeated, exhausted. But there is still more he needs to say.

"So you graduated high school, went away to Seminary," I say quietly. "You kept Rachel's photograph."

"I wanted to forget about her," he whispers. "But I couldn't. She … she had a hold on me. Every time I looked at her picture, I'd feel happy." He drops his head. "Then I'd hear my mother's voice telling me to tear the picture up. But I couldn't. I knew that disappointed her."

"The day of her murder," I say, "Did you really plan on asking her to marry you? Did you really plan on leaving the priesthood?"

"Yes!" he screams. "Yes! I was content to stay a priest until I got her email saying she was going away. I saw that, and I realized I didn't want her to go. The only way I could think to get her to stay was … to give up everything for her." He pauses. "To disappoint my mother for her."

I put my hand on his shoulder. "So you went to her apartment, told her what you had planned, and asked her to marry you. What happened?"

He stands up with a jerk, his fists clenching. "She said no," Leonard says through gritted teeth. "After everything I had done, after everything I was prepared to do, she said no, she was going to the convent. We needed to forget about each other, I needed to renew my call." He's breathing heavily. "I—I just couldn't believe it. After everything. I thought she was different. But my mother was right. Satan had used Rachel to pull me away from God."

"Did she tell you she was pregnant?"

Even in the dim light, I can see the rage in his eyes. "That made it worse! Not only was she a tool of Satan, she was going to murder an innocent."

"You couldn't let it happen, could you?"

"No!" The pitiful expression is gone, replaced with a maniacal one. "No, I couldn't let her do that to an innocent child. I had to deliver her soul from hell before she could condemn herself. Don't you see, Father? I saved her from committing a grave sin!"

I look him steadily in the eyes. "You stabbed her."

"Yes! Yes! I had to! She left me no choice!"

"But she didn't die right away."

He shakes his head. "No. She lay on the floor gasping, looking at me with her eyes wide. I held her, stroked her hair, told her it would be all right, that she had a chance to repent of her sins. I said the prayers for the dying and gave her absolution. I had just made the sign of the cross when she breathed her last."

"Then you sat with her dead body for hours," I whisper. "You concocted a story, then called me, pretended not to remember anything, said a presence suffocated you in her townhouse?"

He nodded. "I think I knew it wouldn't work. I knew God was punishing me for turning my back on Him and on my calling. I deserved to go to prison." Then he smiled. "Then when Marjorie, then Win, confessed to her murder—even to framing me—I could see it all. God was showing his approval. He had forgiven me for everything, allowing me a second chance."

I shake my head. "No, Leonard. We found out that Rachel got to her townhouse just before you did. That the only person who could have killed her was you. Besides, you just confessed to the crime."

"Only to you, only to you," he says. "And you can't tell anyone!"

"He may not be able to," Helen says as she walks into the clearing from the woods. "But I can. Father Leonard McCoy, you're under arrest for the murder of Rachel Watson."

He jumps up as she approaches. "But you eavesdropped on my confession to Father Tom!" he cries. "You can't say anything either! You'll be excommunicated!"

"But I wasn't hearing your confession, Leonard," I say slowly.

Father Leonard looks down at me, wild-eyed. "What? Yes, you did! You asked me—"

I shake my head. "No, I said nothing about hearing your confession."

"He's right, Father Leonard. We have the entire conversation on tape."

Father Leonard looks at her, then at me, then collapses onto the bench. He turns and looks up at the statue of Our Lady bathed in the moonlight. He lowers his head and sobs.

Epilogue

The headline of the Myerton Gazette says it all.

Saint Clare's Priest Arrested, Charged with Murder

I don't read the article, since I already know what it says. Much of it is just a summary of the press conference at the Police Station earlier that morning, and quotes pulled from the statement of State Attorney Brian Dohrmann. That contained a defense of the state's original case against Father Leonard, criticism of the defense attorney, and what I thought was a gratuitous slap at the Catholic Church.

Anna comes into the office with a cup of coffee. "Did you read it?" I say as I take the mug from her.

"I read it," she says, sitting down. "I still can't believe it."

I shake my head. "Neither can I. I can't believe I was so wrong."

"It's not your fault, Tom."

"He had me completely fooled. I really thought he was innocent, I believed his entire story."

"He had us all fooled. No one I know thought he was guilty."

"I was so quick to judge the Myers and the Watsons. I just knew one of them had something to do with it."

"From what you've told me, Marjorie Watson thought so, too."

I shake my head. "But the only member of the family guilty of murder was Rebecca. Because of her jealousy."

Anna sits back. "What will happen to her?"

"I don't know," I reply. "I guess she'll be indicted for murder. I understand Angela Jenkins has signed on as her defense attorney."

She raises her eyebrows. "I guess her disdain for the Myer family has its limits."

I shrug. "My calendar is clear today, isn't it?"

Anna nods her head. "You had two meetings today. I rescheduled them for next week. I figured you'd be busy."

"Thanks. I want to go see Father Leonard, spend some time with him."

"How was he when you left?"

I consider her question. "Calm. Surprisingly so. I heard his confession—for real, this time—and granted him absolution."

Anna cocks her head to one side. "You almost crossed a line with him at the monastery, didn't you?"

I grimace. "I got right on the line. But he never asked me to hear his confession then, he just started talking. I used, shall we say, prudential judgement? But I will take it up with my confessor when I see him."

"Well, speaking of confessions," Anna says, sitting back. "You've still never told me the story about you and Helen."

I smile and place the now empty coffee mug on my desk. "All right, all right," I say. "The fact of the matter is that years ago, Helen and I—"

My phone rings. "Speak of the devil," I say when I see the number. Answering, I say, "Hi, I was just talking about you."

"Tom," Helen says, a solemn tone in her voice. "You need to come down to the jail."

The blood drains from my face. "What's wrong, Helen?"

"It's Father Leonard," she says. "A guard found him in his cell." She pauses. "He's dead, Tom. He hanged himself with torn strips of his shirt."

I hang up the phone without saying a word. Anna looks at me with concern. "Tom? What is it?"

I look at her. I've lost the ability to speak. Without a word, I get up and walk out of my office, Anna calling after me. I walk from the Rectory to the church.

The church is quiet, the morning sun streaming through the stained glass, the votive candles flickering. I cross to the center of the sanctuary and kneel on the bottom step. I look up at the tabernacle. Tears form in my eyes.

Taking my rosary, I pray for the souls of the dead.

The Redemptive Return

The Father Tom Mysteries, Book 3

Prologue

Burying the dead is a corporal act of mercy.

No one is more in need of mercy than a murderer and a suicide.

A priest who is both needs mercy the most.

I'm standing under the blazing July sun next to the grave of Father Leonard McCoy, priest of the Roman Catholic Church and confessed murderer. Only child of Meredith and Benjamin McCoy, deceased. Born October 22, 1990; died July 21, 2020, by his own hand using a rope fashioned from his shirt in a cell in the Myer County Jail.

About two hundred yards away, slightly shaded by a large maple, is another grave. There lies Rachel Watson, murdered at the hands of Father Leonard McCoy.Born March 24, 1992; died July 10, 2020. With her is buried her eight-week-old unborn child, fathered by Father Leonard.

Before this July, in my six years as a priest, I had never performed a single funeral.

In a matter of weeks, I performed three.

The first, Rachel Watson, I did before a packed Saint Clare's parish. If not every member, almost every member was there to pray for the soul of this poor woman.

The second, Winthrop Myer III, Rachel's brother-in-law, killed by a jealous wife, was even better attended as befitting one of the pioneer families of Western Maryland. Dignitaries from across the state, Washington, DC, Virginia, West Virginia, and Pennsylvania attended. The Governor sent his condolences. There was even a message from the White House.

Father Leonard's mourners number two. One is Anna Luckgold, my late wife's mother and more of a mother to me than my own. The other is Helen Parr, the woman I once loved and whose heart I once broke, the detective who brought my wife's killer to justice, and who maintained Father Leonard's guilt in the face of my stubborn insistence on his innocence.

The other parishioners of Saint Clare's, who this broken man shepherded for over six months, could not find it in themselves to pray for the soul of one of Our Lord's lost sheep.

As I finish the final prayers at the graveside, Portia's words from *The Merchant of Venice* pop into my head.

The quality of mercy is not strained.
It droppeth as the gentle rain from heaven
Upon the place beneath. It is twice blest:
It blesseth him that gives and him that takes.

For Father Leonard, mercy was almost non-existent.

I make the sign of the cross over Father Leonard and the duet of mourners. I'm baking in the sun. Underneath my layers of vestments, my body is dripping with perspiration. I'm fairly certain I'm beginning to sunburn. Now would be the time to leave.

Instead, I just stand where I am, my hands clutching my copy of the Rite of Christian Burial, staring down at the casket.

You could have prevented this.

You should have prevented this.

Now, three people are dead because of you.

A hand on my shoulder and the scent of vanilla tells me I'm no longer alone.

Reading my thoughts, Helen whispers, "Tom, this wasn't your fault. None of what happened was."

She's been saying the same thing to me for days now. My eyes remain fixed on the casket.

"I know, Helen," I whisper.

"Do you?"

I glance at her out of the corner of my eye. Concern is etched into every tiny line and every small corner of her face. Her eyes, their deep azure blue usually vibrant, are sad.

Of course they're sad. It's a funeral.

Only the sadness, I suspect, is not for Father Leonard.

"Let's go," she says quietly, gently pulling on my arm.

"No," I say, pulling my arm away. "You go on. I'll talk to you later. I need to see Joan first."

"I can go with you."

I shake my head. "I want to be alone."

"I'm not sure—"

"Helen, please!" I snap. I close my eyes. "Sorry," I whisper.

Wordlessly, she pats my shoulder and walks away. I take one last look at the grave and turn in the direction of Joan's.

She's buried up a slight hill, underneath a large, expansive oak tree. Even under the shade, the heat is almost unbearable. I'm certain to die of heatstroke before I get back to the Rectory.

I don't care.

I stand in front of the place where my wife is buried. The woman who died in my arms fifteen years ago, murdered by a bullet fired by her emotionally disturbed ex-husband. An ex-husband I knew nothing about before last October.

Like Rachel Watson's, her funeral was well-attended, with scores of mourners lining the pews to pay their last respects and pray for her soul.

But then, she wasn't a murderer who died by his own hand. In that, she was very different from Father Leonard.

In one respect, however, Joan was very much like both Father Leonard and Rachel Watson.

I couldn't save her, either.

My knees weaken and I collapse on the grass in front of her headstone, whether from the heat or the emotions piling on me, I don't know.

I stare at her name etched in the marble, just above the words, "Loving wife and daughter."

I cover my face with my hands and bend so my forehead is touching the ground.

One

Given a choice between nightmares and insomnia, I'll take insomnia every night.

I may be tired in the morning, but at least I'm not shaking.

Checking my phone for the umpteenth time tonight, I see that only ten minutes have passed since I checked it last.

3:10 a.m..

I went to bed at 10:00 p.m., exhausted again,

I haven't slept a wink, again.

It's been this way since July. Since the new nightmares began.

I wouldn't have had nightmares if I had listened to Helen in the first place.

Of course, a lot of things would have been different if I had listened to Helen in the first place.

For one, Father Leonard might still be alive .

***

"Tom, you really shouldn't go in there."

Helen had looked at me, imploring me to listen to her just this once, to stop being so stubborn and just take her word for it.

I arrived at the jail about 30 minutes after she called. I should have been there sooner but I had made a short detour, a perhaps selfish but at the same time necessary one, to the Blessed Sacrament to say a Rosary, seeking solace for myself before I could offer it to him.

Five decades of the Rosary usually takes no more than twenty minutes from beginning to end.

That night, I barely got through one before I quit.

That was the last Rosary I had tried to pray for the last six months.

But then, there are a lot of things I haven't done in the last six months.

"Helen," I had said. "I need to. I need to see him. I . . . I . . . I need to give him Last Rites."

She had shaken her head. "You don't want to see this," she had said, gently. "You really don't. He hasn't been moved yet. He's still as he was found."

"I've seen dead bodies before."

"Have you ever seen a body after a hanging? It's not pretty."

I had looked at her. "Helen, I know what you're trying to do. I appreciate your concern. But please, let me do my job."

Helen hesitated before nodding. "OK. I'll take you."

She had escorted me from the small office she had taken over temporarily to Father Leonard's cell. They isolated him from the other inmates, partly because of the assumption that if a Catholic priest was in jail, he was a child molester, and would be an instant target of the other inmates. His cell was a small room with a slit window cut in the door. It was no wonder he wasn't found in time to save his life.

"Open the door," Helen had told the officer stationed outside the cell.

As soon as the door opened, the first thing I noticed was not the sight.

It was the smell.

I had looked at Helen. "He soiled himself," she had explained, quietly. "It's typical."

I stepped into the room. Father Leonard's limp body was hanging from the rail of the top bunk. He was shirtless except for a t-shirt. His arms dangled at his sides, his fists tightly clenched together.

It's only when I got closer that I saw the scratches around his neck, blood from them staining the makeshift noose.

"You changed your mind," I whispered. "You tried to free yourself."

I closed my eyes and said a quick prayer of thanksgiving.

The rest was anticlimactic. I had said the necessary prayers and left the scene to Helen and her technicians.

As I walked past her, she stopped me with a hand on my shoulder.

"Don't blame yourself," Helen had whispered to me. "There is nothing you could have done to prevent this."

I had said nothing in response, but gave her a terse nod before leaving.

That night I had the first nightmare.

***

I was in his cell. All went exactly as it had been in real life.

Except when I made the sign of the cross over Leonard's body, his head jerked up. His arm, no longer lifeless, came up and his hand clasped me around the throat.

"This is on you!" he hissed. "This is your fault. Everything that happened is your fault."

I managed to break away and staggered backwards. I bumped into something. Turning, I found myself face to face with Rachel Watson.

"Your fault! Your fault!" she screamed.

Panicking, I turned to run to the door. In my way was Win Myer, pointing a condemning finger at me.

"You didn't listen. You didn't listen. You didn't listen," he repeats.
I managed to get around him.
It's when I got to the door that I heard the cries of an infant.

***

The buzzing of my phone jars me awake. I must have dozed off finally.

I pick up the phone. Area Code 850. The Florida Panhandle.

My sister is calling me from Bellamy. At almost 4:00 a.m..

"This can't be good," I mutter. I answer and yawn, "Hello?"

"Tommy!" says a woman's voice through the static and drops of a poor cell phone signal.

"Sonya?" I say. "What is it? Has something happened to Mom?"

"Oh, Tommy, I need your help," my sister says. I hear what I think is the sound of leaves crunching. She sounds panicked and out of breath.

"What is it this time?" I ask with little sympathy. "Another dealer after you to pay up?"

"No, no, nothing like that, I promise," she says. "Oh, God! They're getting closer!"

"Where are you?" I say. "What's going on? Who's after you?"

"You need to help me, Tommy! I can't trust anyone else and I don't want Mom to get hurt!"

"What the hell are you talking about? Who'd hurt Mom?"

There's no sound for a minute, just Sonya's labored breathing. "I don't have much time," she whispers.

"What was that? Sonya, you need to speak up. I can barely hear you."

"Listen carefully, Tommy, please! You need to come home. You can help stop them. You can help the girls. You need to help Chrystal."

"Girls," I say, thoroughly confused. "What girls? Who's Chrystal? Are you drunk or high again?"

"Remember that—." The signal drops so I miss what she said.

"What, Sonya? Remember what?" I shout into the phone.

"—-Look there. Everything you need is there." Sonya falls silent. Through the phone I hear what sound like distant voices and the crunching of leaves.

"Tommy," she whispers. "They're almost here. I'm sorry for everything. You're going to find out things about me. I know I was wrong to do them. I tried to do the right thing in the end. You've gotta know that. I love you."

"Sonya! Who's—." That's as far as I get before the line goes dead.

I stare at my phone. I consider calling back, trying to get Sonya on the phone.

My sister was scared about something, so scared she called me, her older brother who's spoken to her only a handful of times in the last five years.

But why call me in the first place, when I'm 900 miles away?

And how do I know this isn't one of her drug and alcohol-fueled delusions?

I consider just letting it go, just chalking it up to that. I should just forget about it, and go downstairs, and finally tackle that pile of paperwork Anna's been after me about.

But the niggling feeling in the back of my mind won't stop.

I scroll through my contacts and find the only other person in Bellamy I speak to besides Mom.

"Hello?" a gruff and groggy voice answers.

"Gus? It's Tom. Sorry to wake you."

"Tom? What's wrong?" Gus yawns. "Is it Aunt Nola?"

"No, no, Mom's fine so far as I know." I pause for a moment. "I got a really weird call from Sonya."

"Sonya? When's the last time you spoke to her?"

I think and try to remember. "Probably the last time was when Mom was in the hospital with her ingrown toenail. A few months ago."

"Well, why was she calling you?"

"That's just it, she didn't really say. She sounded like she was running through the woods, kept talking about 'they' were coming after her, that she needed my help and couldn't trust anybody."

Gus is quiet for a minute. "Did she say anything else?" he asks.

"No, no, not really. It wasn't the best connection so I couldn't hear everything."

"Huh." Gus says. "Well, I wouldn't worry about it too much. You know Sonya. Probably all in her mind. Got into some bad stuff, you know? I arrested some kid at the high school peddling magic mushrooms. Maybe she got some of those."

"Yeah," I sigh. "It's probably that. Sorry to wake you Gus."

"Right," Gus says.

After I hang up, I sit on the bed for a minute. In spite of everything I know about Sonya, in spite of what Gus said, I have a red alert going off in the back of my mind.

I check the time. 4:30 a.m.. No reason to try and sleep. I might as well get up.

I stand and stretch. "Ooh, errg, uhm," I say as I feel my joints loosen and I hear the popping and creaking of my arthritis. Every morning is another reminder that I'm not 25 anymore.

I sigh. "No," I whisper. "If I were 25, I wouldn't be alone."

Moving shadows through the window catch my attention. I walk over and pull the sheer curtains back so I can see clearly.

"Damn," I whisper.

It's snowing.

Again.

Two

"I don't know how much more she can take, Father."

I'm standing in Saint Clare's attic, directly over the altar. I'm wearing a heavy coat, a scarf and matching ski hat crocheted by Anna, leather gloves, and fur-lined boots.

My teeth are still chattering.

I look where Rob MacMillan, parishioner and general contractor, points. Even I, whose knowledge of construction wouldn't even allow me to build a birdhouse, can see what he's talking about.

After three days of heavy, wet snow, Saint Clare's roof is sagging, the trusses clearly straining to support the 150-year-old slate roof that's covered by approximately five feet of snow dumped by a storm two days ago.

"So, it might collapse?" I ask.

"No, Father," Rob says as he types something on his tablet. "There's no might about it. It's going to collapse. Frankly, I'm surprised it hasn't already. These trusses are the originals. You can see in a couple of places where they've been shored up over the years, but they're rotting. It can barely support the weight of the slate alone. But a cubic foot of snow weighs about 20 pounds, and it's five feet deep over the whole roof. I could do the math for you—"

"That's okay, Rob," I say. "Can you fix it?"

He sighs. "At this point the only thing I can do, Father, is replace everything—the trusses, the roof, the slate tile. That's a lot of area to cover. It's not going to be cheap."

"I'm not worried about the money," I say, shaking my head. Which is only partly true. Win Myer had left a sizable monetary donation to the Church in his will, in addition to the Myer Estate house and grounds—which I'm still not sure what to do with. The money should be enough to pay for the roof.

"Well," I say, "when can you start?"

"I can start as soon as the snow melts and we have about a week to ten days of clear weather," Rob says. "I'll throw all my guys on the job to get it done as quickly as possible, but it will still take a while."

He pauses and looks back at the trusses. "I just hope we don't have any more snow before it melts. If we do, Father, I just hope you aren't standing at the altar when it gives way."

***

454

We make our way out of the attic after Rob promises to send me an estimate for my approval. The parish council already authorized the work, so I can go ahead without consulting them first. I watch him walk to his truck, then stare up at the roof.

White snow rises upward, meeting the sky. The sky itself is blue, not a cloud floating by. The sun is already doing its work; water drips from the snow-laden branches in the church yard, sounding like a spring shower. There's melting on the roof as well, for water drips from the roof and I hear the sound of water moving through the downspouts.

"Lord," I whisper. "Please don't let me get any more bad news today."

"Morning, Father!" I turn to see Alice, our letter carrier, making her way through the snow.

"Alice, you're early today!" I say as I step towards her.

"Had to get an early start," she says. Alice stops and looks through her bag, pulling out a large bundle of letters held together by a rubber band. "With all the snow the last couple of days, we couldn't get out to deliver. That neither rain nor snow stuff is a bunch of crap, not with six feet of snow. So we have to make up for it." She hands me the bundle. "Hope it's nothing you've been waiting for."

"No, I haven't been waiting for anything to come," I say, weighing the bundle in my hands. "Probably just bills and junk mail."

She shrugs. "That and packages are about it anymore. No one sends letters. It's all email."

"I don't think people write much by hand anymore," I comment. "Not anything important, anyway."

Alice tells me to have a good day and trudges off through the snow back to her mail truck. I go inside the toasty-warm Rectory, where I'm greeted with the smell of frying bacon and the sound of dishes clattering in the kitchen.

Anna's fixing me breakfast, like she does every morning. She used to leave 8:00 a.m. Mass right after Communion so it would be ready for me when I got back to the Rectory. But since there is no 8:00 a.m. Mass anymore, she just arrives at 8:30.

Sometimes, I'm already at my desk.

Much of the time, I'm still in bed.

"Anna?" I call.

"In here, Tom." I go into the kitchen and sit at the table, placing the stack of mail beside me.

"So what's the verdict?" Anna asks from the counter.

"The patient is on life support," I say as I unbundle and begin to go through the stack of envelopes, circulars, and catalogs. Most, as I suspected, are bills, the remainder junk mail.

Anna places a plate of scrambled eggs, bacon, and whole wheat toast in front of me and sets a glass of orange juice alongside.

"Thanks," I mutter. I pick up my fork and dig into the offerings, eating silently for a while.

"Tom," Anna says, finally, "I hate to keep nagging you, but there are several things that we really need to talk about. We have to go over the year-end financials, for one thing. The Parish Council wants to meet with you. You haven't sat down with them for months, and there are several pressing issues—"

I dismiss that statement with a wave of my hand. "Just tell them I'm busy."

"Why would I lie to them?"

I stop in mid chew and look at Anna, leaning against the counter with her arms crossed, a look of disapproval on her face.

I swallow my mouthful of food. "You have something to say, Anna?" I ask, evenly.

"Oh, a lot of things," she says. "But let's start with—"

At that moment, the doorbell rings.

"I wonder who that could be," Anna says, walking to the door.

"It's okay, Anna," I say, scrambling to my feet. "I'll get it."

She turns to look at me. "Oh," she says. "I see. Why don't you just give her her own key, Tom? It's almost like she lives here anyway."

I glare at Anna. "Can you please handle any phone calls," I say, "so I'm not disturbed?"

"Oh, of course," Anna says, a trace of sarcasm in her voice. "Wouldn't want you being disturbed during your meeting."

Without another word, I leave the kitchen to get the door. I love Anna, and I'm lucky to have her as my secretary. But lately she's been getting under my skin in a major way when I talk about *her*.

Especially when I talk about her.

By the time I'm at the door, butterflies flutter in my stomach. My heart beats a little faster. I take a deep breath and open the door.

I smile when I see her.

Helen Parr is waiting for me.

Three

Before we know it, it's almost 11:30 a.m. I don't know where the time went.

Lately, it always seems to stop when I'm with Helen.

"Wow, look at the time," I say, standing up.

Helen stands and puts her bag over her shoulder. "Sorry to keep you so long, Tom. I only meant to stop by for a few minutes."

"Hey," I laugh. "No need to apologize. Today's my day off, so I have no other meetings or calls to make. I was going to go over parish administration stuff that Anna's been after me about, but I'd much rather talk to you."

Helen smiles, "And I'd much rather be here talking to you than where I was supposed to be."

"Oh, where was that? The Medical Examiner's Office in Baltimore?"

"No. No place that pleasant. I had a meeting over at the courthouse. With Brian."

I can't help but notice the tone she uses in saying his name. It is one a person might use when mentioning something unpleasant.

Like hemorrhoids.

I know any relationship they had ended a long time ago—even before I returned to Myerton. Still, I can't help the surge of jealousy that I experience when she mentions being with him. "You had a meeting with Brian?" I say as calmly as possible.

She looks at me, maybe detecting the tone in my voice. "Yes," she says evenly. "We were supposed to go over evidence in a trial that's coming up. I'll have to call and apologize." She pauses a moment. "You know, I am Chief Detective. Brian is State Attorney. And, thanks to the voters of Myer County, he will be for the next four years."

She says this to me, but it's almost like she's repeating it to herself.

"Though now that Dan's been made a detective," she adds, "it won't be me Brian works with every time there's a case."

"How is Dan?" I ask. After his work on Father Leonard's case, Chief Lowden had made Dan Conway a detective, working directly under Helen.

"Oh, he's great," she replies. "I appreciate the second pair of hands. I've had my eye on him for a while, but I was a little taken aback when the Chief didn't consult me before promoting him, but apparently Dan said if the promotion wasn't forthcoming, he'd quit."

"That doesn't sound like Dan," I say.

"I thought it was odd, too, so I asked him about it. He mumbled something about needing to be at home more." She shrugs.

She looks at the time again. "Now, I really need to get going," she says. Smiling, she adds, "I really enjoy our talks, Tom."

"Well, we can keep talking," I say, looking at the time. "How about lunch at The Bistro?"

"Ooh, sounds tempting," Helen says. "I'm starving. But I need to get back to the office. I'll probably just grab a sandwich at my desk with Gladys."

"Sounds like fun."

"Not as much as you think."

"How is Gladys? I haven't seen her in a while."

"Still pinning for her forbidden love," Helen says sarcastically. "She asks me about you every Monday, wanting to know how you looked on Sunday."

"She could see me herself," I say, "if she came back to Mass."

Helen sighs and shakes her head. "I know. I've actually mentioned it. But whenever I do, she seems to—I don't know, it's like she closes in on herself."

"Any idea why?"

She hesitates. "Some, but as her supervisor it's really none of my business."

Helen turns to leave. "Oh," she says, digging through her bag, "I almost forgot the reason I'm here in the first place." She produces a black wallet and hands it to me. "It finally came in."

I open it and find a gold police badge that looks exactly like Helen's, but instead of "Detective" mine says "Police Chaplain." The ID card with my picture, complete with an awkward smile and Roman collar, says the same thing.

"The one you'll wear at crime scenes comes on a chain," she says as I stroke the badge with my thumb. "I'll get that to you. Though maybe I should just bring it with me the next time one of the kids finds a dead body behind the Rectory."

I look at her. "What do you mean, 'the next time'? There've been no bodies found behind the Rectory."

Helen grins, her deep azure blue eyes twinkling. "I figure it's just a matter of time."

Our eyes lock. Her grin slowly disappears.

I look back down at the badge. "I still don't see how you persuaded the Chief to do this."

"Oh, it wasn't that difficult," she says, adjusting the bag on her shoulder. "I pointed out that I found you valuable in meeting with family members, plus you could see to the spiritual needs of the department. And since you've been at the crime scenes of the last two murders in Myerton, we should just make you an official part of the force."

I cock an eyebrow. "And that persuaded him."

"No," she smiles. "What persuaded him was that I told him you'd do it for free."

We laugh as she turns to go.

"Wait, Helen, before you go," I say, "I have something for you, too."

She turns back. I reach into my pocket and pull out a blue velvet box.

Helen's eyes widen. "What's that, Tom?" she whispers.

"I wanted to give it to you for Christmas," I say as I present the box to her. "It didn't get here in time."

Helen stares at the box laying in the palm of my hand. She doesn't reach for it at first, then she tentatively takes it.

"What's wrong?" I ask.

"Huh? Oh, nothing, nothing," she replies. Not taking her eyes off the box in her hand, she says, "I'm just thinking about the last time you gave me a blue velvet box."

I remember. That time, the box contained a gold ring topped with an azure blue sapphire. I had to go to half a dozen jewelers to find one that matched her eyes. When I found one, I got my first credit card.

I finally finished paying it off two years after I left her.

"I was just looking at the ring the other day," Helen continues.

"You still have it?" I'm a little surprised.

She looks at me. "You let me keep it, remember?"

"Oh, I remember, it only seemed right. I just didn't think—"

"It was too pretty to get rid of. I keep it in my memento box. Along with the rings John gave me."

We stand looking at each other in uncomfortable silence. Finally, I say, "Don't you think you'd better open it? I assure you, it's not a ring."

Helen laughs, that laugh so like her and so unlike Joan's. "No," she says as she opens the box, "I didn't think—"

She gasps. Her eyes are huge as she looks at the object nestled on white satin.

"Tom!" she whispers.

I smile. "You like it?"

"Do I like it? I . . . I love it! It's absolutely exquisite! But you . . . you really shouldn't have! I mean, I didn't get you anything nearly this nice."

"Oh, that's not true," I say. Her present to me hangs on the wall behind her. An oil painting of Jesus, The Divine Mercy, as He appeared to Saint Faustina. It's unlike any other image I've ever seen. When she gave it to me outside the rectory after the disastrous Living Nativity, it took my breath away.

"Helen," I had said. "It's—this is fantastic."

"You like it?" she had said with a smile.

"I love it! Where'd you find it?"

"The Painted Lotus," she had answered. "Bethany Grabell painted it. I went in there to check out some harassment complaints she had filed and saw this. I just had to get it for you."

"I didn't know she could do work like this," I muttered as I looked at the painting. It was impressionistic, full of bright colors and vibrant brush strokes. But it was unmistakably Jesus, one full of energy and power.

I step closer to Helen. "You've been my protector two times in the past year," I say to her. "I thought I'd return the favor."

"But this—this is too much," she whispers. Her eyes are huge and sparkling like a little girl's on Christmas morning when seeing a new bicycle.

"Don't you think you should put it on?"

Helen reaches into the box. "I'm almost afraid to," she says as she draws out the delicate gold chain. Dangling from the chain is a small round pendant with the figure of a winged angel with a sword killing a dragon. The inscription on the front says, "St. Michael, protect us."

"It's beautiful," she says.

"He's the patron saint of police officers," I say. "Look on the back."

She looks at me quizzically, then turns the medal over. Inscribed there is "TJG to HMP, Christmas, 2020."

"I didn't want you to forget who gave it to you," I say nonchalantly.

"There's little chance of that," she mutters, looking at the medal as it sways on the chain, the light reflecting from it's gold surface.

Something on the front of the medal catches her eye. She brings it closer for a better look. Her head snaps up.

"Tom!" she says with astonishment. "This is 18 karat gold! This must have cost you a fortune!"

I dismiss the statement with a wave of my hand. "Are you going to appraise it or put it on?"

She laughs and begins to try to work the clasp. Her hands are shaking.

"Here," I say, taking the chain from her trembling fingers, "why don't I do that for you."

She turns her back to me, scooping up her shoulder-length black hair so I can see the back of her neck. My eyes linger on it for a moment while my shaking fingers try to work the clasp.

"Tom?" Helen asks. "Everything okay back there?"

"Huh—oh, yeah, everything's fine. This clasp—it's kind of small. Wait, got it!" I put the thin gold chain around her neck. The clasp is not just small, it's very delicate. I get closer to her so I can see.

Instantly, I'm enveloped by the heady smell of vanilla from her hair. I inhale deeply, and the scent unlocks memories of long ago.

I shake my head. *What is wrong with you, Tom! Get it together*! my inner priest says.

It's nothing more than a pleasant memory, my inner lover replies.

Don't lie to yourself, Tom, the priest says.

"Just a sec," I say, "almost—okay, good, done." I step back as Helen drops her hair and shakes it out.

Turning around, she smiles and asks, "How does it look?"

I look at the small gold circle against the creamy skin just below her neck, dangling in the V caused by the top button of her blouse being undone.

"Beautiful," I whisper.

We stand looking at each other for a minute.

"Ahem." I look over Helen's shoulder. Anna is standing in the doorway with her arms crossed. She doesn't look happy.

Four

"Ah, Anna," I say quickly. Helen stifles a schoolgirl's giggle and turns around.

"Am I interrupting?" Anna asks.

"No, no, we're finished," I say.

"Tom was just giving me a belated Christmas present," Helen says.

"Was he now?" Anna says with raised eyebrows.

"It's a Saint Michael's medal," I explain.

Helen steps to Anna so she can see. Anna peers at it. "It's beautiful," she says. "Tom, you have an urgent call to return."

"An emergency?"

"It sounded that way to me. Good thing I was here to get the phone."

I look at Anna. She's upset, almost angry.

But her implication is right. I hadn't heard the Rectory phone, and I had turned my cell phone off and left it in my office.

Helen looks at the two of us. "I need to get back to the station. I'll see you later, Tom." Helen steps past Anna. "Have a good day, Anna," she says on her way out.

"You, too, Helen," Anna says. Her eyes follow Helen into the doorway. The front door closes, then she turns to me.

"What's the number?" I say, walking towards my office.

"Never mind that right now," Anna says. She steps into the living room, sits on the couch, and folds her hands. "We need to have a talk, Tom."

"Okay," I say, sitting in the recliner and folding my hands on my lap. "What do you want to talk about, Anna?"

She takes a deep breath. "What are you doing, Tom?"

I sit up, trying to look neutral. "I don't know what you're talking about."

"Don't give me that, Tom," Anna says. "You know exactly what I'm talking about. That medal. That 18 karat gold medal." She waves her hand at me. "Oh, don't give me that look. I've seen enough jewelry in my life to tell quality at a glance."

She leans forward. "An expensive Christmas present. For Helen. Your ex-fiance." Taking a deep breath, she adds, "The woman I sometimes suspect you're still in love with."

"It wasn't that expensive," I mutter, ignoring her last statement.

"For a banker or a business executive, maybe. But for a priest? Don't forget, I know exactly how much the parish pays you. And I have some idea how much that cost you. A thousand? Twelve hundred?"

I look at my folded hands. "I got it on sale."

"So, what? Nine hundred?"

I don't answer. It's true, I'm not paid much as a priest. But I don't have many expenses. My car is over ten years old. My clothes are all the same color. Groceries for one aren't that much. My savings are pretty good.

Though buying Helen's gift did take half of what I had.

"Why'd you give it to her?" Anna asks.

I shrug, trying to look relaxed. "I wanted to give her something to show how much I appreciate her as a friend. I thought, given her profession—"

"Oh, the Saint Michael medal was a great idea. But you can get a stainless steel one for twenty, thirty dollars. You didn't have to give her one like that. What, did you get it engraved, too?" She sees the look on my face and rolls her eyes. "Oh, Tom. What are you doing?"

"Nothing, Anna, nothing."

She shakes her head. "Don't give me nothing, Tom. It's just the latest thing."

I'm confused. "What are you talking about?"

"I'm talking about the fact that you haven't been the same since the summer. Since Father Leonard's suicide, you've been—this way."

"What way?"

"Tom, do I have to spell it out?"

"I'm afraid you're going to have to," I say, sitting back with my palms on the arms of my chair. "I really don't understand what you mean. I've been just fine."

"No, you haven't Tom," Anna blurts. "You haven't been fine for months. You've been depressed, grumpy, short-tempered, not focused on your work. You stopped saying the 8:00 a.m. Mass—"

I dismiss that with a wave of my hand. "I missed most of them anyway."

"You don't attend most parish functions. You barely stay five minutes outside after Mass to greet people, then spend an hour hiding out in the sacristy, often talking to Helen. Not to mention all the other times when it's just you and Helen together, either here or around town."

"What is all this? Are you spying on me, or something?"

"Oh, no, Tom. It's not spying when it's something everyone can see."

A chill goes down my spine. "What do you mean?" I say slowly.

Anna closes her eyes and sighs. "I mean, Tom, I'm not the only one who's noticed how much time you're spending together." She looks down, then adds. "People say you're both acting like Father Leonard and Rachel did."

"Now, wait just a damn minute—"

"Don't take that tone with me, Thomas Jude Greer!" Anna says, waving an admonishing finger at me. "I'm just telling you what people are saying. The fact that it's gotten a lot more frequent since she decided not to take that job in Nebraska has quite a few tongues wagging."

"I had nothing to do with that."

"Are you sure? Has she ever told you why she turned it down?"

I look at the ceiling. "She told me she decided she didn't want to move back to Nebraska. That was it. What else would there be? And why should I care what a bunch of old gossipy women have to say?" I exclaim.

"It's not just the old gossipy women, as you call them," Anna replies. "It's the young moms too. You know, the ones who haven't quite forgiven you for the near disaster at the Living Nativity?"

"Now, that alpaca escaping was not my fault. Besides, it attacked me first."

"Maybe. But you made quite a spectacle of yourself when it happened. Screaming and yelling at the children, not to mention your language. Apparently little Catherine Conway's been having nightmares about you. Dan and Miriam have to practically drag her into the Church every Sunday morning. She's under the impression that you're really a child-eating monster."

I slump back. I remember. It was not my finest hour.

"Of course," Anna continues, "what Miriam claims she saw doesn't help matters."

"Oh? And what is she saying?"

"She says she saw Helen hug and kiss you, in front of the Rectory, after the pageant was over, as the snow started falling," Anna says, "in her words, 'just like when Matthew asked Lady Mary to marry him on Downton Abbey.'"

Beads of sweat burst forth on my brow. Miriam Conway. That sweet-looking mother of four has proven to be quite the gossip. She threw the gasoline on the Father Leonard situation that turned a small fire into a raging inferno.

"That—ahem—it was nothing like that," I stammer. "It was just a peck. She was just wishing me a Merry Christmas."

"A handshake wouldn't have done?" Anna asks. Before I can answer, she says. "Tom, I'm not saying anything inappropriate is going on between you and Helen. But the appearances, what people are seeing, are suggestive. Especially after Father Leonard and Rachel."

"I don't care what it looks like! People are free to believe what they want." I take a deep breath. "We're just friends. That's all."

"Isn't that what Father Leonard said?"

"I'm not Leonard!" I shout, slamming my fist on the chair arm. Anna jumps.

"Then," she says calmly, "there's your anger."

"Well, how do you expect me to be, when you're insinuating—"

Anna shakes her head. "I'm not talking about this, Tom. I'm talking about your homily. The one people are still talking about."

"I don't know what you mean," I say.

"That homily on forgiveness you gave back in September."

"Why? What was wrong with it?"

"What was wrong—okay, maybe you don't remember."

"I thought it was pretty good, one of my best."

Anna starts counting off on her fingers, "First, it was forty-five minutes long. Second, you threw more fire and brimstone at the congregation than God threw at Sodom and Gomorrah. And third, you banged the pulpit so hard you broke it."

I'm exasperated. "What's your point, Anna?"

"My point, son," she says gently, "is I'm worried about you. All of this is so strangely familiar. I've seen you like this one other time. Right before you left."

"This is nothing like that," I say, dismissing the statement with a wave of my hand. "I'm fine. A little tired, maybe. Worried about the roof, certainly. But fine."

"No, Tom, you're—"

"And frankly, Anna, who I choose as a friend, or who I choose to give a gift to, or what that gift is, is really none of your or anyone else's business!" I say sharply.

Anna stiffens. "I see. Well, I guess I'll just go to the kitchen and start your lunch."

I glare at her. "Who was the phone call from?" I ask firmly.

Anna looks at me. "Your mother. At least she said she was your mother when she asked to speak to Tommy."

I wince. Only my mother and my sister still called me Tommy.

"Do you need the number?"

"No," I sigh. "I have it."

Without a word, Anna turns on her heels and walks out. I slump and shake my head. I'll apologize later. But I've got to get this over with.

I walk to my office and grab my phone. Scrolling through the contacts, I stop on the three-letter palindrome that, even at forty-five years old, causes my stomach to twist in knots.

Mom.

I dial the number. She picks up on the second ring. "Tommy?" Mom asks. She sounds like she's been crying.

"Mom? What is it?"

"Oh Tommy, you need to come home. Please, you just need to come home!"

"Mom, I can't. I'm just—"

"No, Tommy. It's Sonya."

I knew it. It had been a while, but only Sonya could make Mom this upset. "What's she gotten herself into now?"

I hear heavy breathing on the other end. "She's—she's missing, Tommy. She hasn't been home in three days."

Five

At Mom's words, my stomach twists in knots.

Three days.

Since the day of Sonya's phone call.

"Have you tried her friends?" I ask.

"I've tried all her friends I know of—you know, I don't know all of them. I tried her job, but they say she hasn't been to work in a few days. Said she had called in sick. I said that couldn't be, because I was her Mom and I knew she wasn't sick."

"Wait, Mom," I say. "Her job? What job?" The last I heard, Sonya was unemployed, like she has been most of her life.

Most employers aren't too eager to hire an addict, even an ex-addict like Sonya claimed to be.

"Oh, Tommy, I know I told you," Mom says. "You just didn't listen. You never listen. Sometimes when you're on the phone it seems like I'm just talking to the air."

That may have something to do with the fact that about halfway through a conversation with Mom, I lay the phone down and start doing something else.

"She's worked at The Belvedere for a few years," Mom continues.

"What's The Belvedere?" I ask.

"You know, Tommy, either you don't listen or you're in the early stages of dementia," Mom says. "I know I told you. The Belvedere is that exclusive restaurant on the other side of town. Charlie Lumpkin's place."

"Okay," I say slowly. "They say she called in sick?"

"Yes," Mom says. "Oh, Tommy! I just know something's happened to my baby! You need to come home!"

"Mom, what exactly do you expect me to do?"

"Do? Why, look for her!"

I roll my eyes. "Mom," I say slowly. "Why don't you just call Gus? He's the Sheriff, after all. It's his job to find her."

"I've called Gus," Mom whines. "He's been all 'Aunt Nola' this and 'Aunt Nola' that. Saying it's probably nothing. That she's off on a bender, or maybe with a man. I asked him to organize one of those searches like you see on TV, but he says he has no place to start."

My mind begins to turn. "Okay, Mom," I say slowly. "Let me talk to Gus. I'll see if I can get something done for you."

"Oh, Tommy," Mom sobs. "Thank you. You really are a good son. Even if you did abandon me all those years ago."

I sigh, but instead of pointing out that I went to college instead of "abandoning her," I say, "I'll let you know what I find out."

Hanging up, I think about what Mom just told me.

Mom hasn't seen Sonya for three days.

Three days ago, Sonya called me in the middle of the night, scared and panicked.

I sit in my desk chair and stare at the wall, trying to figure out what it means. If it means anything at all.

Sonya's my younger sister, and when we were kids, I felt protective of her, especially after Dad's death. But Sonya didn't want protection. She never wanted me to take care of her. Instead, she turned to drugs and alcohol. The last twenty years have been a continuous cycle of addiction, rock-bottom, and recovery. She was constantly in and out of rehab, and came very close on several occasions to being put in jail for a range of offences ranging from drugs to prostitution. It never surprised me when she got herself in trouble. It was no more than she deserved, after everything she did to Mom and me after Dad's death.

But something about this feels different. Something feels wrong.

I told Mom I'd speak to Gus. I dial his number.

"Tom," Gus says gruffly, "if you're calling to badger me about Sonya—"

"Wait a minute, Gus," I say. "I just told Mom I'd call to talk to you about—"

"I know what she asked you to call about," Gus snaps. "Sonya. She's been calling me every couple of hours for the last three days, asking if we've found her. I've tried to explain to her that there's no evidence of foul play, and with that, I'm not going to deploy resources I don't have to search for a missing person who may not actually be missing! Especially when I don't have a place to start!"

"But Gus," I say calmly. "Mom's worried, you know how she can be. Can't you just, you know, look for Sonya a little? Just to placate Mom?"

"The voters didn't elect me County Sheriff to placate Nola Greer!" Gus yells. Then, quietly he adds, "Look, Tom, I didn't want to tell your Mama this; hell, I don't even want to tell you. But Sonya's been keeping some pretty nasty company lately. I did some asking around, and it seems that she told a couple of people that she had met a new guy, someone she said was rich and wanted to take her on a little vacation, somewhere off the coast, if you know what I mean."

I let that sink in. If she had gone away with this guy, outside the United States, it was probably . . .

"Drugs?" I ask.

"I can't be sure, Tom, but it sounds like that's where this guy made most of his money."

I sigh, the breath leaving my body with a mixture of anger and grief.

"I gotcha, Gus," I say, "Thanks for letting me know. I'll deal with Mom."

"I appreciate that, Tom, because I really don't have time for this today. There's an entire cattle truck of dead cows turned over on the Old Bellamy Road, and I've got to get out there to coordinate the round-up, or cleanup as the case may be."

"Again, Gus?"

"I'll call you if I hear anything about Sonya," he says right before he hangs up.

I look at the silent phone in my hand. Gus is almost certainly right. Sonya's probably fine, her call the other night notwithstanding.

But that red alert in my mind won't stop.

Then, looking at my phone, something dawns on me.

"You need a place to start, old buddy?" I say. "Maybe I can help with that."

Six

I probably shouldn't have walked all the way from Saint Clare's to the police station. By car, it's not that far. But I still haven't dug my car out from the last roof-endangering snow storm, so walking was my only option. Wearing multiple layers of clothing, including a heavy wool overcoat and a knitted scarf Anna gave me for Christmas, by the time I get to the station my body is covered in sweat. I'm ok walking that far in regular weather conditions, but having to trudge through snow and slush has worn me out and left me gasping for air.

So by the time I'm at her office, I don't so much open as fall against her door, flinging it open. I grasp the door frame to keep from face planting on her floor.

Panting, I growl, "Helen, I need you!"

Helen jumps out of her chair, half-eaten sandwich in her hand, her eyes as big as saucers. She's with a young woman in a wheelchair, her hair colored light blue. The young woman looks at me, then back at Helen.

She slaps the desk with her hand. "See? I told you it would happen like this one day, Chief!"

"Shut up, Gladys," Helen says. "Tom?"

"Water," I gasp. "Please!"

Helen hurries to me and grabs me by the arm. "Did you run here from the church?" she asks as she sits me in a chair next to Gladys Finklestein, the department's computer expert.

I shake my head. "Walked," I rasp. "Really need to get more exercise. Phew."

"Here," Helen says, handing me a bottle of water. I unscrew the cap and gulp it down thankfully.

"Oh, that's better," I say. "Thanks." I look to my left to find Gladys staring at me, her mouth slightly opened, her face flushed.

"Good to see you again, Gladys."

"H . . . H . . . Oh!" That's all that she can manage.

I look at Helen. She shakes her head and rolls her eyes. "Is everything okay?" she says to me, sitting down.

I shake my head. "I don't know. It's my sister."

"Sonya?" Helen says.

"Do you have a brother?" Gladys asks breathlessly, a glazed look in her eyes.

"No, just a sister," I say to her.

"Oh," she says. "That's too bad."

"Gladys!" Helen snaps.

The young lady jumps a bit. "Sorry, Mom," she says, a sheepish grin on her face.

"Hmm," Helen responds. To me, she asks, "What's wrong with Sonya?"

I explain about the late night phone call from Sonya. About Mom's phone call. About my rather frustrating talk with Gus.

"So I don't know what to think," I conclude. "I mean, you know how Sonya is."

"I remember," Helen nods. "I didn't know you were still in contact with her."

I sigh. "Not really. Every now and then she'll call, usually when something's wrong with Mom. Her call the other night was the first time I'd talked to her in months."

Helen is rocking back and forth in her chair. "What worries you about this, Tom?"

I shake my head. "I don't know. It began with the call, something about how she sounded . . ."

"You think she's in real trouble this time," Helen finishes.

"Yes," I nod. "I do."

She smiles and leans forward. Propping her chin on her hand, she asks. "What can I do?"

"Well," I say slowly, taking my phone out. "She was outdoors, so I know it's a cell phone. I thought, maybe, you know, you could do that thing you did to find me those times?"

Helen chuckles. "Okay, sure. Gladys?"

"No problem, Chief. What's the number?"

I hand her my phone. She looks at it for a second. "Okay," she says as she wheels herself out of the office. "Sit tight. I'll be back."

"Don't you need to write the number down?" I ask.

Gladys stops and turns slightly. "Why would I need to do that?" She turns back and rolls out of the office.

I turn back to Helen with a questioning look on my face. "She has an eidetic memory," she explains. "Never writes anything down."

"Ahh," I say, nodding. "So, that's in addition to having a 186 IQ, being a graduate of MIT with a Masters at 20, being an overall computer wizard, and having excellent taste in men."

Helen rolls her eyes. "I should never have told you about her crush on you and calling you Hot Priest. It's gone to your head."

"Do I detect a hint of jealousy, Detective Parr?" I say with a grin.

She shrugs. "What is there to be jealous of? First, she's young enough to be your daughter. And second, I know what—or, I should say, Who—has your heart."

My grin vanishes. I look at Helen across the desk, the same thoughts flitting through my head earlier when I was putting the St. Michael's medal on.

"At least that's the way it should be," I say in a low voice.

Her cheeks redden. The atmosphere in her office has changed, suddenly becoming charged with words best left unspoken.

"What?" she whispers.

"Okay, I've got it!" Gladys says as she wheels back into Helen's office. We jump, startled out of . . . whatever the hell that was.

Gladys glides to a stop to the left of Helen's desk. She's about to say more, but instead looks at Helen and I. "Okay, ah, would you like me to leave?"

"What? No, no, everything's fine," Helen says quickly. "What have you got?"

"Well, the phone's not active, and hasn't been for 72 hours," Gladys says, picking up the tablet on her lap and placing it between Helen and I, "but I was able to access its last known location."

She swipes and pulls up a map of what I recognize as Bellamy County. Gladys slides her fingers across the screen to zoom in.

"The phone your sister called on, Father Greer," Gladys says, "was somewhere in here."

She points to a circle that encompasses a large subdivision along with surrounding wooded areas.

"How much area is that, Gladys?" Helen asks.

"It's about a half-mile radius," she answers.

"You couldn't get any closer?" I ask.

Gladys shakes her head. "There are not a lot of cell phone towers in the area."

No, indeed, I think. There's not a lot of anything in that part of Bellamy.

At least, not anything good.

Seven

"What do we do now?" I ask Helen.

"What do you mean?"

"I mean, how do we find her?"

"'*We*' don't do anything, Tom. You pass this information onto the Bellamy County Sheriff and they do something."

"Look, Helen," I say. "The Sheriff of Bellamy County is an old friend of mine, and he is convinced that she's run off with some sort of drug lord turned sugar daddy. He's not going to do anything."

Helen looks at me for a moment with a peculiar mix of pity and . . . something else . . . affection . . . impatience . . . I'm too distracted to tell. Then she puts on her cop face and says calmly, but firmly, "Tom, given Sonya's background, that doesn't seem out of the question."

"I know, I know, but I just don't think she'd do this to Mom"

Helen looks at me questioningly and opens her mouth to say something but I keep going.

"I know, I know. She's never been too considerate in the past. But the last few years, she has seemed to care more about Mom's feelings, maybe not enough to change her behavior but enough to make up a lie to keep her from worrying while she was out of town."

"OK, Tom, let's go with that. Where do you think she is?"

"I don't know. You're the cop."

"Yes, here in Myerton, and once in DC, but never in Bellamy. I don't know how things work down there."

"Well, then, what do you think I ought to do?"

"I think you should stay put and let this thing play out."

"But what about the phone call?"

"What about it? Maybe Sonya and the sugar daddy had an argument and patched it up and now are somewhere where they don't want to be disturbed."

"OK, OK, you're probably right."

And I meant that, when I said it. I truly believed she was right.

But that didn't mean Mom would.

***

"Tommmmyyyyyyy," she cries into the phone when I try to tell her what Gus and Helen had said, "She's just not like that anymore! You need to come home! If you don't have the time or inclination to do that, I'll just go looking for her myself. Diana said she'd go with me."

I groan inside. Diana is my mother's oldest and dearest friend. She's also on oxygen some of the time and booze much of the time.

I clutch my phone tighter and close my eyes. "Mom," I say calmly. "That's not a good idea."

"Well, what choice do I have, if you won't help me?"

"Mom, Gus told me—"

"And I'm your mother, and I'm telling you Sonya wouldn't do that, not now. I need your help this once. I never ask you for anything, Tommy! Can't you do this little thing for me?"

I sigh into the phone. "Mom, it's not that simple. I've got responsibilities here. I can't just drop them and fly down there to go on a wild goose chase trying to find Sonya when she's probably not missing to begin with!"

"It's always like this with you, Tommy," Mom whines some more. "Everyone and everything matters more than Sonya and me. Helen mattered more. Joan mattered more. Now it's the Church. Don't you think that Jesus would want you to help your mother in her time of need?"

"Mom," I plead, "please, just try to understand—"

"Okay, Tommy, you just stay there in your church, with your huge responsibilities and everyone calling you Father," Mom says bitterly. "But if something happens to Sonya, it'll be your fault."

Those last two words jab me in the heart

Your fault.

I close my eyes and take a deep breath. Gus was my best friend growing up—well, one of my two best friends, technically, but Gus was always the one I could rely on. He's the County Sheriff. If he says Sonya's run off with a sugar daddy-cum-drug lord, I have no reason to doubt him.

My Mom is, well, my Mom. She's always been very good at making me feel guilty. At the same time, she's always had a blind spot when it comes to Sonya. In Mom's eyes, there was nothing really wrong with Sonya. She wasn't an addict, she had chronic pain. She wasn't an alcoholic, she just liked to drink. She didn't have multiple stints in rehab, she went away for rests. She didn't steal money, she borrowed it and would pay it back eventually. For those reasons, I have every reason to doubt what she's saying.

Then there's Helen, who told me to leave it to the County Sheriff. I've learned the hard way not to listen to her at my peril.

Finally, there's Sonya.

Or I should say, the Sonyas, because in my mind there are more than one.

There's Little Sister Sonya, the one with whom I used to tromp through the woods around our house on adventures, the one with whom I had to bathe in tomato juice when we got too close to a skunk when I was six and she was four, the one who swam in the lake in the woods with my friends and me during the summer, the one I protected from the boys when she was a precocious 11-year-old and I was 13, the one who I guess deep down inside, I still want to believe is there and who I want to protect.

There's Addict Sonya, who started hanging out with the wrong crowd after our Dad's death, the one who first came home drunk at 3:00 a.m. when she was 14, the one I caught stealing from Mom's supply of Xanax at 16, the one Mom would call me about every other week it seemed like while I was at college, the one who drained Mom's bank account and left her scraping by paycheck to paycheck, unable to stop working until forced to by time and her health.

These two Sonyas battled in my mind over the years, with Addict Sonya winning again and again.

The questions I need to answer are simple.

First, which Sonya called me the other night?

Second, what should I do in the face of Gus and Helen's advice?

And third, do I want to add Sonya to the cast of my nightmares?

I realize that the only question that matters is the third. And I immediately know the answer. No.

Eight

"Ladies and gentleman," says the voice over the loudspeaker. "We're waiting for a couple of more passengers, and then we'll be ready to pull away from the gate and begin our trip today to Tallahassee, where currently it's a sunny seventy-five degrees. Even with this slight delay, we're still good for an on-time arrival at 11:50 a.m."

I put my headphones on and look out the window. Snow is still in piles near the terminal, a reminder that the temperature has not risen above the mid-thirties in a week. At the very least, Bellamy's going to be warmer.

I lay my head back and close my eyes. I've been up since 5:00 a.m., left by 6:00 a.m. for the two-hour-drive to Dulles International Airport to allow the requisite two hours before my scheduled flight time of 10:00 a.m. But even though Dulles is usually a busy airport, on this midweek morning it didn't take long to go through security. I was at the gate by 8:30 a.m. I spent the hour before boarding reading email, checking Twitter, and praying Morning Prayer—though I didn't finish.

That happens a lot lately, when I bother opening my Breviary app at all.

After I told Mom I'd come, I made a reservation for the next flight to Tallahassee—the major airport closest to Bellamy. It is the one I'm sitting on now.

Then, I made two phone calls.

***

The first was to the Archbishop.

"Do I understand you to say, Father," the Archbishop had intoned, "that you do not know how long you'll be gone?"

"Unfortunately, Your Eminence, that's true. With my mother being a widow and there being no other siblings, I believe I need to stay either until we find out what happened to my sister, or until she's satisfied that Sonya's fine wherever she is."

"Hmmm," he had said. "This doesn't come at the best time, Tom. We're not exactly flush with spare priests right now. And I'm going to be in Rome for a couple of weeks." He pauses for a moment, the sound of his fingers drumming on his desk coming through the phone. "Well, I can send Father Herbert. He's nearing retirement anyway. I think they can spare him."

I thanked the Archbishop and was about to hang up when he said, "You do expect to be back in time for Ash Wednesday, don't you Tom?"

"I see no reason not to," I said. "That's three weeks away, and I can't see myself staying in Bellamy that long."

Oh, hell, no!

My second call after the Archbishop was Helen.

***

Frankly, I didn't expect Helen's reaction to my news.

"What the hell are you thinking, Tom?" she exploded.

"I really don't know," I chuckled.

"This isn't funny! Damn, I should have known you'd do something like this!"

"Something like what?" I had asked firmly.

"Go off half-cocked and decide to play Father Brown again," she said. "Fly down there to Bellamy to placate your bat-crap crazy mother!"

"Look, Helen," I snapped. "She's my sister and she's in trouble. I need to go do something."

"Why now, Tom? You haven't cared about her for years!"

"Because I don't think I can take someone else dying because I did nothing!" I yelled into my phone.

Helen was quiet. 'Tom," she said gently. "Father Leonard wasn't your fault."

Ignoring the comment, I say, "I'm really only going down there to placate Mom. I'll talk to Gus, pass on the information Gladys came up with, and let him investigate if he chooses to. If he doesn't, I'll go through the motions enough to satisfy Mom and fly back. A week, tops."

She sighed. "Just . . . just be careful, Tom. If anything has happened to Sonya, it sounds like it's because she's gotten involved with some pretty rough characters."

Something in her tone struck me. "You're scared."

"Damn right I am scared!" she said. "I don't want anything to happen to you. I . . . I . . . I've gotten used to having you around."

I chuckled. "Oh, Helen. I appreciate your concern. But it's Bellamy. And as much as I don't like the place, nothing bad ever happens there."

***

I hadn't told Helen the truth.

Plenty of bad things happened in Bellamy.

Which is why I was dreading the trip.

Which is why I hadn't visited the town in years.

Some days all you can do is listen to Adele on repeat. Which is what I'm doing as I wait for the plane to take off. My head is back, my eyes are closed, and I'm relaxing to her soothing, bluesy vocals.

I sense someone come into the row and plop a large bag in the empty seat next to me. *It must be the late passenger.* But I don't move to look to see who it is. I could care less. I'm not interested in conversation. I just want to be left alone.

But whoever it is taps me on the shoulder. I continue to pretend to be asleep. Certainly, whoever it is can't be that rude.

Then, they tap me more forcefully.

I'm a second from ripping my headphones off and giving this person a piece of my mind when something tickles my nostrils.

Vanilla.

My eyes pop open.

Helen's standing over me with her hands on her hips, looking decidedly pissed off. In the seat next to me is a large black duffle bag.

"Helen?" I say, betraying my confusion.

"Are you just going to sit there, or are you going to help me get this thing into the overhead bin?"

My mouth is open to ask another question—mainly, what the hell she's doing here—when the flight attendant stops by.

"Excuse me," he says politely. "But we're going to be pulling away from the gate in a minute. You and your husband need to get that bag in the overhead bin."

"We're just discussing that," Helen says. Turning to me, she says with a wicked smile, "Well, honey?"

I jump up, nearly hitting my head on the low ceiling formed by the overhead bins. "Ah . . . yes, dear."

The flight attendant leaves. Helen steps back to let me get to the bag and hoist it into the bin.

I pull on the handles of the bag.

It doesn't move an inch.

"What do you have in this thing?" I whisper.

She shrugs. "Just a few things Gladys thought we might need."

"What? Bricks?"

"Stop whining. I checked the really heavy stuff along with my gun."

I snap my head up. Before I can say anything, she says, "Come on, let's get this stowed before they decide to make us walk the plank—or the wing, whatever."

Between the two of us, we manage to wrestle the bag into the overhead compartment and shut the door just as the flight attendant starts making his way back to us. Seeing our compliance, he just smiles and goes to give the traditional pre-flight "in case of emergency" talk.

Leaning across the seat between us, I whisper, "What are you doing here?"

"What the hell do you think, Tom? I'm going to help you find your sister."

"I kind of figured that," I say. "I mean, why did you decide to come?"

"Oh, there were several reasons. First, I'm a cop. Even though he's your friend, the Sheriff isn't going to listen to you in the same way he would a fellow LEO. I can at least run interference for you and keep him from throwing you in jail."

"Gus isn't going to do that."

"Tom, do we really need to review the number of times in the last year I almost tossed you in a cell?" Helen asks. When I don't answer, she says, "Didn't think so. Second, whether we're working with Gus or, as I suspect will be the case, without him, I've got all the stuff I brought with me that'll at least make it a little bit easier to find her. Third, I know what being in Bellamy does to you. I remember from the last time I was there. I can help you handle all that."

Helen drops her eyes and folds her hands. She hesitates.

"Is there something else?" I ask.

She looks at me, takes a deep breath, and nods. "I've gotten used to having you in my life again," she whispers. "I couldn't stand it if anything happened to you. I couldn't stand knowing . . . that . . . that . . . you got hurt or worse because I wasn't there."

A tear snakes down her cheek. She sniffles and wipes it with her hand. "No," she rasps. "I couldn't handle that."

I lay against the seat and smile. A little strand of hair has fallen across her face. Without thinking, I reach out and brush it back behind her ear. She's startled by the gesture and jumps, but then settles back and smiles, returning my look.

We sit quietly through the flight attendant droning on about emergency exits and what to do in the unlikely event of a water landing. Finally, Helen pulls herself up straight.

"So," she says. "That's why I'm here."

"And, I am really glad you are."

She nods. "Good. Frankly, I'm just glad to get out of the snow for a while. It will be like a vacation."

I snort. "Helen, I guarantee you this trip will be many things, but a vacation won't be one of them."

Nine

"Why do you get to drive?"

Helen looks at me from the driver's seat. "Two reasons. One, I made the reservation before I left Myerton. Two, you drive like an old woman and I'd like to get to Bellamy sometime before nightfall."

I cross my arms and look out the window. I feel her hand rub my shoulder.

"If you smile, I'll get you a cookie."

"I don't want a cookie."

She pauses. "Milkshake?"

I look at her over my shoulder. "Chocolate?"

"Any flavor you want, sweetie."

My heart flutters. She hasn't called me sweetie in twenty years.

I catch the look in her eye. From that, and the flush in her cheeks, I can tell she didn't mean to.

"I mean, ahem," she shifts uncomfortably in her seat and grips the steering wheel. "Chocolate's fine, if that's what you want. Just stop pouting."

I sit up in my seat like an adult. "Okay," I say. "You can drive. The stretch from Tallahassee to Bellamy is terrible anyway. Mile after flat mile of nothing but asphalt, pine forest, and dead armadillos."

Helen laughs. "So, what do you want to do, anyway?"

I take a deep breath. "Well, there's what I want to do and what I should do. What I want to do is head straight to the Sheriff's Department and show Gus the location information on that phone Sonya used to call you. But then," I sigh, "there's what I should do."

"What's that?"

I turn to Helen. "Stop by Mom's house first." I slump in my seat and shake my head.

"It's your home, Tom," Helen says quietly.

"No," I whisper, shaking my head. My jaw clenches as I feel tears well up in my eyes. "It hasn't been my home for a very long time."

Not since the day Dad died.

I take a deep breath and try to pull myself together. As I do, Helen's mention of home causes a question to pop into my head.

"Helen," I say, "where are you staying? There aren't really any hotels in Bellamy—there's that old motel north of town, but no one goes there to sleep."

"Oh, that," she says. "I thought, maybe, your mom would let me stay?"

I'm slightly surprised. "I mean, I guess so," I say. "We can do it like last time."

She laughs, "So, I'll take your room, and you sleep in the den downstairs."

"Sounds like a plan." I look out the window at the passing countryside. "Thanks for coming," I say quietly. "I'm really glad you're here with me."

"Tom," she says, "there's no place I'd rather be."

***

Tallahassee is only an hour or so from Bellamy, so it wasn't too long until we were on the dirt and gravel road leading to Mom's house.

My eye spots the old Live Oak tree, Spanish Moss hanging down like icicles do in Myerton. I take a deep breath.

"We're here," I whisper.

Helen slows down to take the turn off the road onto the drive.

Out the front window I see my childhood home. The old two-story cracker farmhouse, shaded by another Spanish Moss-covered Live Oak. The yard where I used to play. The swing set, a Christmas present one year, now rusted, the chains and seats long gone. The outbuilding where the lawnmower used to be. An old water pump that was out of use by the time I was born. The screened porch where, on a summer evening, Dad and I used to sit while he read me stories, opening up the world of wonders contained between the covers of books he used to bring home to me or ones I'd pick up on our weekly trips to the County Library. I'd later sit on the swing and read to myself, trying to shut out what was going on inside.

Sometimes, the porch wasn't far enough.

"Tom?" I turn to Helen. I don't know how long we've been parked.

She smiles and takes my hand. "It's okay," she whispers. "I'm here."

I give it a slight squeeze, then let go and get out of the car.

It's then that I see the Bellamy County Sheriff's Department vehicle parked nearby.

"Oh, no!" I whisper and begin running to the house. Helen runs behind me.

I take the steps to the porch in one bound, flinging open the screen door. It bangs against the mesh and wood enclosure. Without losing my stride, I throw myself against the front door and dash into the familiar old living room.

Mom's sitting on the couch, her head in her hands, sobbing. Next to her sits a large man, a good six inches taller and fifty pounds heavier than me, wearing a Sheriff's uniform, his arm wrapped around her.

My old friend, Gus Slidell, looks up at me. He has tears in his eyes.

In an instant, I know the truth.

I'm too late.

Again.

Ten

I ask Gus to take me to Sonya, so I can at least give her last rites. He tells me that they've already transported the body to Tallahassee for the autopsy, but he had called the priest from Saint Philip's, our family parish. He had come and prayed over Sonya's lifeless body.

I nod, comforted by the fact that at least she'd had that.

Even if I hadn't gotten here in time to do it.

After Gus leaves, Helen puts Mom to bed. While she's attending to her, I'm sitting on the couch. I find the Breviary app on my phone and open it to the Prayers for the Dead. I begin praying the Litany of the Saints.

"Lord, Have Mercy," I read

Behind me, Helen responds quietly, "Lord, Have Mercy."

I pause and turn to look at her. She smiles. "Your Mom's asleep," she whispers. "I think she was exhausted from crying."

"Thank you," I say. I scoot over on the couch. "Join me?"

She hesitates for a second before nodding and walking around the couch. We sit close together to see the screen.

"Christ, have Mercy," I continue.

"Christ, have Mercy," Helen says.

"Lord, have Mercy."

"Lord, have Mercy."

Back and forth, back and forth, first me, then her, we read the ancient prayer to the saints. With my words, I inhale, breathing deeply of the heady scent of vanilla that is my incense right now. I exhale as Helen responds to me, our words matching the steady cadence of my speech and her response to me.

"Saint Peter and Saint Paul."

"Pray for her."

"Lord, be merciful."

"Lord, save your people."

"From all evil."

"Lord, save your people."

Tears begin to fall from my eyes, hitting the screen of my phone. It's getting difficult to read, and I'm getting too choked up to speak.

Helen reaches for my phone, her hand brushing mine. I look at her questioningly.

"Let me read for you," she whispers.

I smile and give it to her, closing my eyes and leaning my head against the back of the couch.

"Bring Sonya to eternal life, first promised to her in baptism," Helen says.

"Lord, hear our prayer," I respond.

"Raise Sonya on the last day, for she has eaten the Bread of Life."

"Lord, hear our prayer."

We go on like that through the rest of the prayer. I'm listening to Helen's voice, soothing and melodic as she reads. I'm still sad, but as I hear her, I know that somehow things are going to be okay.

Because she's with me.

"Christ, hear us."

"Christ, hear us."

"Lord Jesus, hear our prayer."

"Lord Jesus, hear our prayer."

I sit up and look at Helen. "I'll finish up," I say, holding my hand out for my phone. She smiles and hands it to me.

"God of mercy," I say, "hear our prayers and be merciful to your daughter Sonya, whom you have called from this life. Welcome her into the company of your saints, in the kingdom of light and peace. We ask this through Christ our Lord."

Together, with one voice, Helen and I say, "Amen."

I place my phone on the couch beside me, and look at Helen. Her expression is one of sympathy, care, concern.

I clear my throat. "Thank you," I whisper.

Helen wraps her arms around me. I rest my head on her shoulder.

Then, the tears start.

Then the sobs.

Then the howls.

My whole body is shaking. I'm clinging to Helen for dear life. She's patting my back, stroking my hair, saying words of comfort in my ear.

The harder I cry, the harder she hugs me. I grip her like a drowning man holding onto the last plank of a sunken ship.

Because that's what is happening to me.

I know I'm not just crying for Sonya.

I'm crying for Leonard.

I'm crying for Rachel.

I'm crying for Win.

I'm crying for Joan.

I'm crying for all those I could have saved—should have saved—but couldn't either because of my own cowardice or stubbornness.

If I had only come down to Bellamy instead of waiting. I could have saved her.

Instead, I listened to Gus and Helen.

And now, Sonya's dead.

I pull away from Helen and look at her. "I shouldn't have listened to you!" I rasp.

She looks confused. "What?"

"You told me to wait!" I spit. "Gus told me to wait! If I hadn't waited—"

Helen takes me firmly by the shoulders. "Look at me, Tom," she says. "You couldn't have saved her."

"How do you know that!" I cry. "You can't possibly know that!"

"Tom, I asked Gus. According to the ME, she's been dead for about four days." Helen pauses. "Sweetie, she probably died not long after she talked to you."

I stare at her dumbly. I close my eyes and sigh. "Sorry," I say. "You're right. There's nothing I could have done." I look at the ceiling. "There's nothing I can do for her now."

Helen takes a deep breath, and slowly lets it out. "Well, maybe there is," she says.

I look at her. "What?"

She bites her lower lip. "I asked Gus where her body was found. A cleaning person found her in a dumpster behind one of the big-box stores out by the interstate. Gus says it's a place that's frequented by addicts looking to score illegal Oxy. He thinks that Sonya went there to score and got into a fight with one of the dealers, who killed her and dumped the body. I will tell you, Tom, her car was found in the parking lot."

I look at Helen, then stand up and walk to the mantle. I fiddle with the bric-a-brac, then turn.

"But I know where that is," I say. "That's miles from where Gladys says Sonya was when she called me."

Helen nods. "That's right, Tom. So the question is, where was she really killed, who killed her, and why?"

She gets up and walks to me. "You may not have been able to save her," she whispers, "but maybe you can help catch her killer."

Eleven

"I'm getting more," Helen says. "Do you want anything else?"

She's standing over me holding a heavy-duty paper dinner plate. Not fifteen minutes earlier, she had sat next to me with that same plate laden with slices of spiral-cut ham, a heaping serving of hash-brown casserole, a generous serving of broccoli casserole, two deviled eggs, and two homemade rolls.

"No, thanks," I say. "Are you still hungry?"

She looks down at me, her eyebrows narrowing. She places one hand on her hip and cocks her head to one side. "You got a problem with that?" she says, her voice lowered to a slightly threatening alto.

I look at her. Helen always had a healthy appetite that contributed to her full-figured hourglass shape. Twenty years later, her figure is still perfect.

Today, the curve-hugging black dress she's wearing reminds me of that.

"No," I say with a smile. "Not at all."

She smiles and turns to walk over to the food-laden dining table. "Hey," I say. Helen turns back to me. "Do me a favor? Can you just leave off the deviled eggs?"

She snorts. "Still don't like them?"

"Can't stand them," I say. "They smell like farts and wet gym socks to me."

Helen pouts. "Ooh, poor baby," she mocks. "Such a delicate nose."

There's something about the way she says that, along with the pout, that causes me to blush. Helen must notice, because she gets a serious look on her face and then turns her attention back to the food.

I shouldn't. I know I shouldn't. But I allow my eyes to linger on her while she's going around the table, examining each dish with a careful eye that until that moment I thought she reserved for crime scenes.

Yes, that black dress really . . .

A firm hand clasped on my shoulder thankfully brings me back to reality. I look up and see Gus towering over me. I haven't seen him since the day they found Sonya's body. His face is still filled with sorrow.

"Hey," he says.

"Hey," I respond.

"Mind if I join you?" he asks, indicating the armchair next to where I am on the couch. I nod and he sits.

"Thanks for expediting Sonya's autopsy," I say. "I know Mom appreciated it."

"It was the least I could do for Aunt Nola," Gus sighs. "I'm surprised she was cremated. I didn't think you people did that."

"No," I smile slightly. "It's not encouraged, but it is allowed. It was less expensive, and I don't think Mom could have gone through the Funeral Mass with Sonya's casket there. She can't sit on Mom's mantle, though. Before I leave, we'll place her in the vault of cremated remains at the cemetery next to Dad."

"I noticed you were up there doing all the stuff with the other priest," Gus says. "Why didn't you do it all yourself?"

"Mom said she wanted her parish priest to do Sonya's funeral," I say. "I thought he did a good job, considering he'd never met Sonya until after she was dead."

I had thanked Father Sanchez for giving Sonya Last Rites. "Father, that's what we're called to do, isn't it?" he had said with a big smile.

I had nodded in agreement, but inside, the condemning voices said, *You couldn't even do that for her. What kind of priest are you?"*

"I'm surprised to see Helen with you," Gus says. "What's going on between you two?"

I shrug. "It's like I've told you before in my calls and emails. We've become friends again since we reunited."

"Friends, huh?" Gus grins. "You sure that's all there is?"

I point to my Roman collar. "This means there can't be anything else, just as sure as if I had a wedding ring on my finger."

Gus' grin slowly vanishes. "Don't you get lonely? I mean, I'm not married, you know, but I know how I get. I can do something about it, though. How do you stand it?"

I swallow the lump that's in my throat. "It's . . . it's just an occupational hazard," I say with a brave face. "You get used to it."

Gus nods. "Look, I didn't come over here to talk about this. I just want to say again how sorry I am about Sonya. She . . . she was a special person, you know?"

I don't know how to respond to that. I'd hardly call Sonya a special person. A recovering addict, maybe, but not a special person.

I shake off my unmerciful thoughts about my dead sister. "I remember she had a crush on you as a kid," I manage a smile. "Drove us crazy. She always popped up when we were trying to play Risk."

Gus laughs. "Yeah." His smile slowly disappears. "Darn near broke my heart when she became an addict. That Oxy—it's from the devil, Tom, and you know I don't believe in any of that. I get one or two ODs a week."

"You told Helen she was found behind the Valu-Mart out near the interstate?" I ask.

"That's right, that's right," Gus affirms with a nod. "Shot. Tossed in a dumpster like trash. Damn dealers. We've got a couple of suspects. They're like rats, though. They run into their holes when the police show up."

"But Mom's told me Sonya's been clean for several years now," I say. "That near-OD got her attention, apparently."

Gus shrugs. "It did for a while." He leans forward and lowers his voice. "Listen, Tom," he whispers. "I don't intend on telling your mama this. But Sonya's apparently been using again for a couple of years."

I sit back and sigh. "I thought it had to be something like that. I've never really believed she'd stopped. So many times before, Sonya would swear she'd quit, but it was all a lie."

"Yeah," Gus says. "She was good at that."

"But there is one thing I don't get," I say.

"What are you two talking about in such hushed tones?" Helen asks. I look at her as she settles in next to me.

"Sonya," I explain to her.

"What don't you get, buddy?" Gus asks me.

"I just don't understand what she was doing in Bellamy," I say. "You told me she'd left the country with some drug dealer or something like that."

I'm looking at Gus when I finish. He's staring at me with absolutely no expression on his face. As kids, Gus was really good at this; we'd have staring contests, which he always won, because he could keep his face absolutely still, showing not the slightest trace of emotion.

That is, unless . . .

Then, I see it. The subtle downward curl of the corners of his mouth.

Damn!

"That's what an informant told me," Gus says. "I haven't been able to locate her to press her on this."

"Didn't you try to confirm the information?" Helen asks around a mouthful of dinner roll.

Gus shrugs. "It didn't seem necessary. I mean, I wasn't looking to arrest Sonya. She wasn't under any kind of investigation. I was just doing it informally, as a favor to Aunt Nola." He looks at his watch. "Sorry, buddy, I've gotta go. Listen, how long are you going to be in town?"

"I really don't know that yet, sport," I say, looking at him firmly.

Gus's jaw tightens. He got my message.

"Well," he smiles. "Maybe the three of us can grab lunch before you leave."

"Maybe," I say, returning the smile. "But I'm sure we'll be seeing quite a bit of each other, Gus."

The smile disappears. I see him swallow. He looks at me, then Helen. Without saying another word, he leaves.

I follow him with my eyes as he walks out the front door. "So, what do you think?" I ask Helen.

"About what Gus said?" Helen says. "His explanation makes sense. Informants aren't always good sources. They report rumors as fact, or make stuff up. I hated dealing with them in D.C."

"Yes," I nod. "His explanation makes perfect sense. There's just one problem."

"What's that, Tom?"

I turn to look at Helen.

"He's lying."

Twelve

Helen blinks at my statement. "How do—?"

"Tom?" I turn to see a distinguished looking man about my age walking towards me. On his arm is a voluptuous redhead, about fifteen years younger than he is, not so much walking as strutting through Mom's living room as the crowd parts to let her pass. Her dress is black, but a little too revealing for a funeral. She's wearing a black cloche hat with a black ribbon wrapped around the crown. As she gets closer, I'm hit with the scent of magnolia blossoms and rose petals.

I notice something else too. She has a small rose tattoo on her left—

I feel a slap on my shoulder. I start and turn to Helen. Leaning forward, she whispers. "Eyes up, Father. Oh, and here's a napkin for that bit of drool."

I take the napkin and flash an awkward smile, which disappears as soon as I see her expression.

She's pissed.

"I thought that was you," the older man says when they reach us.

"Charlie Lumpkin," I say, standing up and shaking his hand. "How long's it been?"

"Almost ten years," he says. "I last saw you when you came to town right before you entered seminary."

"So," the younger woman says with a combination of purr and growl. "You're Sonya's priest-brother?"

"That's what Mom always told me," I grin. There's something about this woman with Charlie, something about the combination of red hair and emerald green eyes, combined with the scent of magnolia and rose, that's slightly hypnotic.

"Ahem," Helen says as she taps my shoulder. I turn to look at her. She's crossed her arms and has an eyebrow cocked as if to say, "Really, Tom?"

"Oh," I say nervously, "where are my manners? Charlie Lumpkin and—I'm sorry, I didn't get your name."

"I'm Rose," she says, her voice as smooth as velvet. "Rose Lumpkin. Charlie's wife."

"Ah, okay, ah, Charlie, Rose, this is Helen Parr, my . . . friend."

"Wait, Helen?" Charlie says. "I thought you looked familiar. I met you when he brought you to meet Aunt Nola after y'all got engaged."

While Helen is nodding, Rose says. "Wait, engaged? You were engaged to this handsome man?"

Helen's eyes darken. "Yes," she says evenly, "for almost two years."

"And he left you to become a priest?" Rose pauses and looks Helen up and down, then shrugs. "Oh well, I guess some just can't—"

"Oh, no, no," I say quickly. "Nothing like that. I became a priest after my wife died."

"Oh," Rose says, placing her hand on her ample bosom. "How tragic." Looking at Helen, "So he left you for another woman, then, is that it?"

I see Helen's jaw clench and her hands tighten into fists. All I can think is that it's a very good thing she's not armed.

But her gun is upstairs in her luggage.

"Rose," Charlie says quickly, handing her car keys. "We're leaving soon anyway. Why don't you go wait for me in the car?"

"Okay, baby," she purrs. Rose leans in and gives his earlobe a little lick. "Don't keep me waiting," she whispers. Turning back to us, she says. "Nice meeting both of you."

"Nice meeting you, Rose," I say pleasantly.

"Hmmm," Helen says.

After she walks off, Charlie turns to us with an embarrassed grin. "Sorry about her," he says. "Rose doesn't have much of a filter."

"Apparently," Helen mutters.

"You know, Sonya worked for us," he adds.

"Worked for you?" I say, furrowing my brow. "Mom said she worked at an inn and restaurant on the other side of Bellamy. The Belvedere, I think it's called."

Charlie nods. "That's right, old pal. The Belvedere. That's my place. Well, mine and Rose's."

"Really? I thought you had a medical practice in Tallahassee?" I say.

"I did. I gave it up when I married Rose. She had a nine-figure inheritance after her last husband died. I'd always wanted to open something like The Belvedere." He shrugs. "Much less of a hassle than running a medical practice these days. Much more lucrative, too. We attract a pretty exclusive clientele."

"To Bellamy County?" I ask. "It's rather off the beaten path for that, isn't it."

"Hey, you'd be surprised, Tom." he shrugs. "Plenty of people want to get away somewhere they can't be found, away from prying eyes, to indulge in the different activities we have to offer. Hey, you and Helen should come have dinner with Rose and me at the restaurant as our guest. It was named the best in Florida last year, and our chef's considered one of the best in the entire Southeast."

I look at Helen, who has a look I can only describe as dubious, then back to Charlie. 'Okay, we'll try it before we have to leave."

"Just out of curiosity," Helen says, "what did Sonya do there anyway?"

"Oh, she was our Director of Guest Experiences," Charlie says. "Fancy name for head concierge. She made sure our guests' needs were taken care of, if they had a special request she'd see it was fulfilled, whatever activities they wanted were scheduled. You know, that sort of thing."

"Really?" I say. "And you hired Sonya for that? I mean, Charlie, she'd never done anything like that before."

"Hey, what can I say?" Charlie shrugs. "She was a natural."

"Nola said she tried to contact her at work the day she disappeared," Helen says. "She was told Sonya called in sick that day?"

Charlie puts his hands up. "I don't really deal with the day-to-day, you know. We've got staff for that, so I don't know anything about that. But listen, Rose is in the car, so I'd really better be going. Tell your Mom how sorry I am about Sonya. I'll call you about dinner, Tom."

I watch Charlie go off. I cross my arms and stroke my chin.

"What is it, Tom?" Helen asks.

"I don't know," I murmur. "Did anything strike you about our conversation with Charlie and Rose?"

"What struck me about *Rose*," Helen says, "was how she started coming on to you the moment she walked up here."

"Coming on to me?" I ask.

"Mm-hm," Helen nods. "And you were just eating it up."

"Oh, I was not, Helen, don't be ridiculous."

"Really? Do you normally drool when beautiful women walk in the room?"

I fix her with a serious look. "I've been known to," I say quietly.

Helen's cheeks color and she looks away. "So, ah, um," she stammers. "Ah, what about them?"

"They hired Sonya to work at their exclusive inn, or restaurant, or whatever, as a concierge? Helen, have you ever heard me say anything that would lead you to believe Sonya could do something like that? And why would they place an addict—okay, recovering addict—in a position of such responsibility?"

She shrugs. "To be fair, Tom, you don't really know what your sister was like the last few years. You weren't in close contact with her."

I sigh. "You're right about that," I say. "But there's something going on here that doesn't feel right."

She gets a bemused look on her face. "Are you saying your gut is telling you something?"

"Hey, I learned from you to trust it." I put my hands on my hips. "There's that call. There's Charlie and his wife employing Sonya. There's Sonya's body being found miles from where Gladys says she called me. And there's the fact that Gus lied to me."

"Yeah, I was going to ask you about that," Helen says with her arms crossed. "How do you know?"

"When we were kids, I could always tell when Gus was lying. It took me a few years to figure it out, but right before he started to tell a lie, the corners of his mouth turned down. That's what happened right before he told me that he had gotten that story about Sonya running off with a sugar daddy-cum-drug lord from an informant of his."

"So what are you thinking?"

I shake my head. "That I'm being lied to about what happened to my sister. And Helen, I'm sick to death of being lied to."

Thirteen

The last of the mourners leave about 4:30 p.m. I'm helping Helen with the kitchen cleanup. In the distance, the sky's darkening as a line of clouds get closer, going from bright and sunny to a dull grey. The wind is picking up, what was a gentle breeze blowing harder ahead of the approaching front.

Mom's sitting in her armchair in the living room. She hasn't moved from that spot since the last person said their goodbyes, nor has she said more than ten words to me today.

Ordinarily, I'd count that a blessing.

Today, I find it ominous.

"Do you think your Mom's all right?" Helen whispers as she hands me a serving dish to dry.

"I don't know," I whisper. "I haven't asked her."

"Well, go in there and talk to her," Helen says. "You're her son. You're all she has left."

"Great," I say, rolling my eyes. "Something else she can criticize me for."

"Tom!"

"What? It's true. It's not like Mom's had a lot of good things to say about me in the last few years. Not since I told her I was entering the priesthood."

"I've always wondered about that," Helen says, handing me a glass. "Why was she against you becoming a priest?"

"She never really said," I say, drying and putting the glass in the cabinet. "She didn't like me going so far away to college. She wanted me to go to Florida State so I could be near home. But after Dad died, and everything began to happen with Sonya, all I wanted to do was to get as far as a scholarship and three summers worth of savings could take me. And that was Maryland."

I put down my towel and lean against the counter so I'm facing Helen. We met in Maryland, and wouldn't have if I'd gone to school an hour from home. She's still wearing her black dress, but she has an apron on over it. Her black hair that usually flows in soft curls over her shoulders is put up in a ponytail. One little tendril flows over her cheek. Her eyes are a smokey blue, picking up the grey light from the approaching storm. Her lips, I dare not look at.

There's a distant flash of lighting and a rumble of thunder. I move my attention back to the counter.

"Charlie," Helen says quickly, returning to the plate she was washing.

"Yes, what about him?"

"Was he a friend, too, like Gus?"

"A friend, yes, but not like Gus. Gus was—is, I guess—my best friend. Charlie's the son of Mom's friend Diana, you know, the one with the oxygen tank and hip flask at the funeral. We played together a lot when we were kids. Gus, Charlie, and I would wander all over those woods, much of the time with Sonya trailing behind us."

"What do you mean, not like Gus?"

I lean on the counter. "It's hard to explain. Gus was older, but not that much older than me, so we were pretty much equals, and as I say, he's my best friend. Charlie, he was a couple years younger, and since our mothers were so close it sometimes seemed like we were brothers, if you get my meaning."

"I'm an only child, remember," Helen says, handing me a bowl to dry. "I don't get the whole sibling thing."

"Well, Charlie and I were close, because we were together so often," I furrow my brow. "But there was always something, a tension between us. I'd call it a rivalry, but I don't know what we'd be rivals about. Charlie was handsome, gregarious, outgoing, charming—basically, everything I wasn't. Still, there was an undercurrent of . . . I don't know, sometimes I got the feeling Charlie resented my very existence."

"That's odd," Helen says, handing me a deviled egg plate. I wrinkle my nose as I take it.

"We were kids," I say as I dry the plate. "That's all it was. Is this the last one?"

Helen pulls the stopper out of the sink, allowing the dish water to drain. "Yeah, that's it." Drying her hands, she says, "Let's go see your mother."

I follow her out of the kitchen. Mom's still sitting in her chair, staring at a spot on the wall.

"Mrs. Greer," Helen says quietly. "Everything's cleaned up."

Mom nods.

"Is there anything I can do, Mom?"

"Huh!" she says. "I think you've done enough, don't you?"

"Ma'am?" I ask.

"Doesn't matter," she says, shifting in her chair to look at me. "So you and Helen will be leaving tomorrow, I assume?"

I shake my head, "No, Mom. We're staying at least a few more days."

"Why?"

"Why? Well, for one thing, I need to make sure you're going to be okay now that Sonya's gone."

"And why should you give a damn about that now," Mom shouts, "when you haven't for almost thirty years?!"

My mouth falls open. "Mom, I . . . "

She points a bony finger at me. "You know this is your fault, don't you? All of it. None of it would have happened if you'd just done what I asked you to."

"Mrs. Greer," Helen says, "According to Gus, Sonya was already dead—"

"I'm not talking about this! I'm talking about everything! You weren't here, Tommy! You galavanted off to Maryland, you never came home to visit, you just left me here to handle all your sister's problems, didn't think for one minute about me while you were up there having fun, living your life, meeting her," she shoots a finger at Helen.

"You leave her out of this Mom!" I yell.

"You could have gone to FSU, but no, you just wanted to leave me! Leave us!"

"I had a scholarship!"

"You had one to FSU that would have paid for everything, and you turned it down! The only reason you did that was because you just wanted to get away."

"Dammit, Mom!"

"And you betrayed me, you betrayed Sonya. Just like you betrayed your Dad."

I feel like I've been punched in the stomach. "No. No," I say, shaking my head vigorously. "D—Don't, Mom, please!"

"You had to go to that Quiz Bowl practice, didn't you? If you hadn't, you could have been here to save him. You knew CPR. You could have called an ambulance. You could have done something. He might still be alive today if it weren't for your selfishness!"

My heart falls into the pit of my stomach. My mouth is cotton. Tears well up in my eyes. "M—M—Mo—Mom, it . . . he . . . I . . ."

"You know he relied on you, Tommy," Mom's saying. "You know how much he needed you. And you let him down. Because of your own selfish need to do what you want. You've always been this way. I'm surprised Helen stood you as long as she did. But maybe you weren't like that with her, huh?"

My mouth is moving but I'm making no sound.

"What kind of priest are you, anyway? Priest. Hah! You know what I thought when I saw you assisting Father during the Mass today? I thought about how selfish and self-centered you were to be up there, putting on an act for everyone, like you actually cared about Sonya, like you cared about God, like you cared about anyone but yourself!"

I'm becoming disoriented. It feels like a hand is squeezing my heart. I'm struggling for air.

I've got to get out.

I spin around and dash through the door, across the porch, and push open the screen door. Leaping down the steps, I hear the screen door slam shut behind me with a "crack".

There's a rumble of thunder in the distance from the black clouds approaching. The sky looks ominous. When the storm comes, it's going to come fast and hard.

I break into a run and head to the woods. Even though it's been a long time, I can see the path. There's only one place I want to be.

And I need to get there right now.

Fourteen

"Tom! Tom!" Helen calls after me as I walk. I don't turn. I just keep my eyes fixed on the woods.

Gus, Charlie, and I cut the path ourselves when I was twelve years old. It's overgrown, but still passable. I rush past the treeline onto the path. As I walk, branches and thorns brush my pants; I'm fortunate I'm wearing long pants and my clerical shirt, otherwise my arms and legs would be a bloody mess by the time I get to where I'm going.

I don't even stop to consider that it probably fell down a long time ago. But I don't care. I have a primal urge to run to the place where I went when home got too much.

A branch scrapes me on the forehead. A moment later I feel a trickle of blood flowing down my face. I keep running.

The thunder is closer, lightning is beginning to flash, and the first drops of rain are splashing on the leaves on their way down to the ground. First one, then another, strikes my head. It's January, so it's not the warm rain of a summer thunderstorm. It's cold, the product of a front crossing the narrow peninsula, heralding a coming drop in temperature in its wake.

In Myerton, it'd be snowing. Here, it's an ice-cold drenching rain.

I quicken my pace as the drops fall faster. Ahead, I see the old cabin. It's weathered, but my sanctuary is still standing after thirty years.

By the time I reach the cabin and open the door, my shirt is drenched. It's cool and clammy against my skin. I'm beginning to shiver.

I don't care.

The interior smells damp, but otherwise it's dry. The bench I used to spend hours sitting on, reading or just enjoying the peace and quiet, is still here. I scan quickly for snakes, but see none. Wet and exhausted from my trek, I drop to my knees in front of the bench and lay my head down.

Water drips from my hair. My hands grip the bench. I shut my eyes, trying to force Mom's words from my mind. I clench my teeth to stifle the screams I feel coming from inside. Through my shut eyelids, my tears flow.

Desperate for something to hold onto, to keep from descending further into a pit I may not be able to get out of, I dig in my pocket for my Rosary. Propping myself up on my elbows into a kneeling position, I make the sign of the cross and clutch the crucifix tightly in my hand. The edges of the cross dig into my flesh.

I open my mouth to begin the Apostles Creed, and nothing comes out.

My mind is blank.

I have forgotten the prayers.

I sit on the floor, clutching my beads for a moment, my mind searching for the words. But they are gone.

What good is a priest who can't remember prayers that a seven-year-old memorizes before their First Communion?

Then the words come in a rush, as if released from behind a dam.

"Ibelieveingodthefatheralmightymakerofheavenandearth . . ."

My heart is racing, my breathing heavy. I can't control the rush of words.

"Ourfatherwhoartinheavenhallowedbethyname."

I feel like I'm drowning in words I no longer understand, in words I no longer believe.

Why am I even on my knees trying to pray? Do I really believe in it anymore? Do I really believe *any* of it anymore?

"Hailmaryfullofgracethelordiswiththee."

When did it happen? When did it die? When did I stop loving it?

Was it when Leonard died?

Did I ever really love it, or have I been fooling myself all these years?

"Hailmaryfullofgracethelordiswiththee."

Was Mom right? Was it all my fault? Would Sonya still be alive if I hadn't gone so far away? Would it have really been so bad to stay here?

"Hailmaryfullofgracethelordiswiththee."

A sudden rush of cool air, bringing with it just a hint of vanilla, tells me I'm no longer alone.

Helen's here.

In my darkness, a light comes on.

I see everything clearly now.

I hear the soft click of the low pumps she wore to the funeral on the wood floor.

"Glorybetothefatherandtothesonandtotheholyspirit. . ."

She's kneeling next to me, so close.

So very, very close . . .

"As it was in the beginning," she whispers, "Is now and ever shall be, world without end, Amen."

"Thefirstsorrowfulmysterytheagonyinthegarden."

"The First Sorrowful Mystery, the Agony in the Garden."

"Ourfatherwhoartinheaven—

"—Hallowed be thy name, thy Kingdom come, thy will be done—"

"—onearthasitisinheaven—giveus—thisdayour—dailybread—"

"—and forgive us our tresspasses, as we forgive those who trespass against us—"

Before I can say the next part, she reaches over and turns my head to face her.

Looking steadily in my eyes, Helen whispers, "And lead us not into temptation, but deliver us from evil. Amen."

She's waiting for me to begin the next prayer, the first of the ten for that mystery. The mystery of Jesus' suffering, when the torments he was going to undergo in the next eighteen hours unfolded before him. When He knelt alone in the Garden of Gethsemane, begging, pleading with his Father.

"Father, if you are willing, take this cup away from me."

The next prayer is on my lips. I only have to say the first word, "Hail."

Instead, I whisper, "Helen."

Her breath catches. She hears the tone in my voice.

I let my Rosary fall through my fingers, clattering on the wood floor between us.

I place my now-free hand under her chin and gently tilt her head as I bring mine down and press my lips to hers.

They're just as I remember them. Still as soft. Still as sweet.

Helen stiffens in surprise, but only for a second. She slowly melts into my kiss.

I move my hands onto her shoulders. Gently, I push her away just enough to see her eyes. They're half-closed, but even so I can see they reflect my desire for her.

Her lips move. In a faint whisper, she breathes, "Tom."

I pull her to me and cover her mouth with mine.

I'm so very tired of words.

She stiffens again, then relaxes against me. Our arms encircle each other, pulling us closer as our mouths devour each other. I'm losing myself in a twenty-year-old memory, of holding her like this, of kissing her like this.

The Priest in my head is screaming, *You shouldn't be doing this!*

But it's drowned out by my own long-buried passions.

I sense the storm outside lightening up. The rain is beginning to taper off. The thunder sounds more distant and less frequent.

Inside the cabin is a different story. Here, my all-consuming desire for the woman in my arms is washing away all of my grief, all of my self-loathing, all of my anger, all of my bitterness, all of my loneliness.

There's no Leonard.

There's no parish.

There's no vow of celibacy.

There's only Helen.

And I want her.

Here.

Now.

My hands want to move from her back, but I leave them where they are. Helen's have moved from my back to my front. She slips one hand inside my shirt, her fingers gently stroking my chest. Her other hand joins the one, and she unfastens a button. She spreads the cloth open and trails her fingers upward, searching for the top button.

She reaches the tab of my Roman collar, and freezes.

Helen pushes me away, breaking our kiss. She looks at me, confusion written all over her face, her breathing heavy from our exertions.

"What are we doing, Tom?" she whispers.

"It doesn't matter," I say, shaking my head and moving in to try to kiss her again.

"What do you mean, it doesn't matter?" she says, holding me just outside the reach of her lips. "Of course it matters!"

"No, it doesn't!" I say frantically. "Here, it doesn't! We're all alone! No one can see us!"

"Tom, you know someone can see us," she says firmly.

"I don't care anymore!" I scream. "So what? Is He even there? I sure as hell haven't seen Him lately!"

"Tom!"

"Don't you see, Helen? I don't care! I don't dare care! Look where caring got Leonard. He tried to do the right thing, he denied himself, and it drove him mad. He ended up a murderer, a suicide, maybe even in hell for all we know. If he'd just done what he wanted, taken the woman he loved and ran away from rules laid down by a bunch of grumpy old men hundreds of years ago, he'd be alive now. He'd be happy!"

"Would he, Tom? Would he really?" Helen stops and takes a deep breath. "You don't know that. He might have drowned under the shame of his own misdeeds. He might have realized that having Rachel was not such a great thing as wanting her. It happens that way more often than you think."

"But it wouldn't happen to us." I say. "We'd be great together. Just think about it. We could leave Myerton, move somewhere where nobody knows us, and live the way we really want to."

"The way we really want to, Tom? What makes you think that's what I want?"

Her words drive all the air out of the room and all the passion out of my mind.

"What do you mean? You love me, and I love you." She gives me a look. "Oh, come on, great detective! You haven't picked up on that? You think I hang out with you in the sacristy because it takes that long to hang up my robes. I love you. I'm in love with you, and you are in love with me."

The look on her face is a red-hot icicle, burning and freezing my heart at the same time.

"Wait a minute," I say, slowly. "You do love me, don't you? I mean you're always up for lunch together. You followed me here, not just to Bellamy but here, to where I was when I needed you most."

"Yes. I did all those things. Because I do love you." Helen says quietly.

"See?" I feel I'm desperately trying to win a debate with her, just marshalling all the points in my favor to prove my point. "You . . . you kissed me back. You were unbuttoning my shirt. You want me!"

"Of course I want you! I wanted us to keep going! I was as lost in the moment as you were!" Her voice changes, taking on the tone she uses when she interviews a witness. "But Tom, think. What did I do next?"

"Well, I mean, I guess you suddenly lost interest."

She laughs at that. A throaty, bitter laugh.

"Oh no, my darling, I can assure you I haven't lost interest."

"Then, what?" I ask, now thoroughly confused.

"I stopped, Tom. I stopped myself. Because I love you."

I stare at her, rolling the words over in my mind. "But . . . But, that makes no sense."

"Doesn't it? Would someone who loves you take advantage of you when you're so vulnerable? Fulfill my own longings at the expense of your soul?" She shakes her head. "No, Tom. I love you more now than I ever have. Enough to stop. Enough to consider more than just what I want. More than just what you want."

"Helen, what is there to consider? This is our chance to start again. To get back what we lost all those years ago."

"What *we* lost?" Helen shakes her head vigorously. "Tom, *we* didn't lose anything. *You* snatched it from me, because you wanted something else more than me. And you do now. You're just too hurt and too scared to see it."

"Is that what this is about?" I get up off the floor and stomp off a couple of paces. Turning around, hands on my hips, I shout, "Some sort of revenge, a nasty payback for my leaving you? Really, Helen! I would have hoped you'd have moved past that by now."

Helen stands up and stomps across the floor, getting right in my face.

"Oh, don't flatter yourself!" she shouts. "You know as well as I do that we both moved on! I loved John and you loved Joan! Neither of them was some sort of second prize!"

Helen takes a step back and drops her voice to a pleading whisper, "We loved them, truly and uniquely, differently and the same as the way we once loved each other."

"The way we could love each other again," I whisper.

"No, Tom," Helen says, shaking her head. "Because you moved on again, and you belong to someone else now just as surely as when you once belonged to Joan. What kind of woman, what kind of person would I be if I ever tried to take advantage of you during a rough spot in your marriage?"

"But this is not just a rough spot!" I scream. "Don't you see? I don't *want* to be a priest anymore. I am sick and tired of having people depend on me and letting them down. And it's not just about Leonard. I'm letting everyone down. Old people avoid me, young people gossip about me, little children are terrified of me. Hell, even that alpaca ran away from me!"

"I thought you said that wasn't your fault?"

"Oh, c'mon Helen! When you're a priest, everything that goes wrong in your parish is your fault. God gets the glory for what goes well, you get the blame for what goes badly. Have you ever considered what it is like to be under that level of scrutiny all the time?"

Helen laughs and waves her hand playfully, "Hey, cop here, remember?"

"Yes, you're a cop, but at the end of the day you can go home and take off your gun and everything else if you want to and find comfort in someone's arms. I can never do that."

"No, Tom, you can't." Helen lowers her eyes. "And because you can't, I can't either. I believe in both of us enough to believe that we both can live with that, just as we have been before now."

I shake my head. "No, Helen, not now. The genie, as they say, is out of the bottle. There's no putting it back."

"Then Tom, we'll just have to do what Alladin did and make the genie serve us."

"And how exactly do you propose to do that?" I ask ruefully.

"I don't know my love, but I believe in us, and God, enough to believe that we can."

"And if I don't believe in God right now?"

She smiles and her eyes are soft with an inner light that I'm not sure I've ever seen before.

"Then I'll believe enough for both of us until you can believe for yourself again."

Fifteen

I let the hot water wash over me as I try to make sense of everything.

After the words we exchanged in the cabin, we walked together in silence back to the house. We nodded good night to each other before going to bed.

I did have two things to be thankful for. First, the day left me so emotionally and physically exhausted that I slipped into unconsciousness soon after my head hit the pillow.

Second, my sleep was dreamless.

Now awake, I'm forced to confront the question we only touched on last night at the cabin. *What do we do now?*

The words we spoke to each other last night can't be taken back. Neither of us can deny the truth of what we said.

We love each other.

And I don't want to be a priest anymore. At least, I don't think I do.

I can't figure out what I'm going to say to Helen. I mean, what do you say to a woman after you've declared your love for her and said you were willing to abandon God to be with her? There are really no good options.

But standing in the shower as the temperature changes from hot to warm on its way to cold, I realize there really is only one thing I can say right now.

Nothing.

Talking further about everything right now is not going to fix it. What happened yesterday was a long time coming, and working out what it means for us is going to take a lot of thought.

But for now, we have more pressing matters.

Namely, what really happened to Sonya?

***

The smell of crispy bacon hits me as I walk down the stairs. My growling stomach reminds me that I never ate dinner, and I didn't eat much after the funeral.

"Mom?" I call.

"It's just me, Tom," Helen calls.

I stop on the stairs. I wasn't prepared to face her so soon.

I take a deep breath and square my shoulders. I plaster a fake smile on my face and walk down the rest of the way.

"Good mor—" My greeting fails on my lips as I see Helen, seated at the table, looking as beautiful and as desirable as yesterday in the cabin. In front of her is spread a veritable feast. Scrambled eggs, sausage, bacon, and stacks of fluffy, golden-brown pancakes.

Helen swallows a mouthful of food and looks at me. "Good morning," she says with a smile.

"Did . . . did Mom cook all of this?" I say, slightly amazed.

"No. I did."

I snap my head up. "But . . . but you can't cook!"

Which was true twenty years ago. No, Helen had many fine qualities. Cooking ability was not one of them. Oh, she learned to make great tomato bisque and grilled cheese. She made lasagna the night I proposed that I'm sure would have been fine if we hadn't gotten distracted and remembered it only when the smoke detector went off. But every other attempt while we were together ranged from barely edible to a disaster. Bless her heart, she just couldn't cook. Which is why we either ate out or I cooked.

I remember the last time—the only time—she made me pancakes, she proudly set before me a plate with these black misshapen round things. Only a blind man could have mistaken them for pancakes. I gave eating them a valiant try, but I just couldn't. This resulted in Helen locking herself in the bathroom and crying for an hour.

"Ah, no," Helen says with a bemused smile. "I couldn't cook. I learned to cook when I was in law school. I lived in a basement apartment in the home of a widow. When she found out I couldn't cook—there was an incident involving my attempt to make peanut butter cookies and the fire department—she set about teaching me. I found out I actually like doing it. I just don't get many opportunities."

"It just looks incredible," I say as I sit down. Soon my place is heaped with the delicious offerings and I begin eating with relish.

We eat in silence for a while. I'm trying to figure out how to begin. I mean, I know what I have to say. I just don't know how to bring it up.

Fortunately, I don't have to.

"Tom," Helen says, putting her fork down. "I think we need to talk for a minute."

I nod while I'm swallowing. "I know," I say.

Taking a deep breath, Helen begins, "Look, we need to face a few things. For one, everything we said to each other in the cabin is a hundred percent true. We love each other. You're having a severe crisis of faith right now, and I'm not about to take advantage of that. We need to work through a way forward that works for everyone—you, me, and God."

"I was thinking the same thing in the shower," I say. "But I realized, it's going to take time."

Helen nods. "Yes, it is. You're hurting right now and struggling with your vocation. But I don't really believe you want to leave, and I certainly don't want to be the reason you do. So, what we do going forward is something we're going to need to figure out."

"And we're not going to do that today," I say. "We have something more pressing."

"That's right," Helen says. "Lord willing, we have the rest of our lives to work through what together looks like for us. But we only have days to find out who killed Sonya and why."

"OK, so where do we start?" I ask Helen, thankful to have a chance to change the subject.

"I'm so glad you asked," she replies with a smile, "for a lot of reasons."

We both laugh. Any remaining tension I feel is washed away as I hear that wonderful, throaty laugh of hers. A glance from her tells me she's thinking the same thing I am.

We may be in for some rocky times, but we both want things to work out.

Whatever that looks like.

"There's one thing that's been bothering me," Helen continues. "We know that Sonya had a cell phone with her when she called you on what was most likely the night she was killed. The question is, where is that phone now?"

"You'd know better than I would," I answer. "Don't they keep stuff like that locked up in some evidence case or something?"

"Normally, yes, but I heard your mother ask Gus if he had Sonya's phone. It seems they had taken some pictures together when they went to something in Tallahassee and your mother wanted to try to get them. But Gus said they didn't find a phone on her."

"Hmm. That's weird."

"My thoughts exactly."

"She sounded like she was running when she called," I say. "Maybe she dropped it after we hung up?"

"If so, we need to go look for it."

***

An hour later, Helen and I are standing in the middle of the woods behind a new subdivision. I look at her, feeling a bit hopeless.

"So" I ask for the second time that day, "where do we start?"

Helen's expression mirrors my own. Gladys was only able to narrow down the phone's location to a square half-mile.

The rest would be up to us.

"Tom," Helen says after a minute, "I need you to think. Did you hear anything in the background of that call that might help narrow down where she was?"

"Not really," I reply, searching my mind. "She was running, out of breath."

"Did you hear anything like a car or a train whistle or even a bike bell?"

I shake my head.

"OK, then," Helen says, looking around. "We'll have to do a grid search. We'll start here and walk in opposite directions for 100 steps. Then we each take two steps to the right and search back, using this tree to keep us straight. As we return, we each go another 100 steps past the tree and turn to the right again. Got it?"

"I guess, but isn't this going to take a long time?"

"Do you have a better idea?"

"We could just stay here and say a prayer to St. Anthony," I grin.

"What?" she asks, looking annoyed.

"You know," I say, but Helen looks even more confused. "The patron saint of lost objects."

I say the old prayer. "St. Anthony, St. Anthony, please come around. Something is lost and needs to be found."

"That's great, Tom," Helen says, patting me on the shoulder condescendingly. "Why don't you stay here and pray and I'll execute the search by myself."

I grin at her, holding my hands up in surrender. "OK, OK, I'll do both." With that, I head off as instructed, my eyes on the ground and my voice lifted with more enthusiasm than I have felt recently for any form of prayer.

I pray as I walk, using the cadence to count my steps. I was about to turn and head back for the tree when someone calls out, "You two looking for something?"

Looking up, I see a man in his early 30s, wearing jeans and a plaid flannel shirt, approaching us. I don't think Helen sees or hears him, intent as she is on her search.

"As a matter of fact, we are," I answer.

"Care to tell me what it is?" he asks.

"Sure. It's a hot pink smartphone in a clear case with a nick on the corner nearest the camera."

When we told Mom that morning what we were doing, she had insisted on giving us a detailed description of the phone before we left. Not that I thought the woods would be strewn with them.

But I guess you never know.

"I got it right here," the stranger says, pulling it from his pocket and handing it to me.

"This is amazing!" I cry. "Where did you find it?"

"Right over there," he said, waving his arm to his left. "Good thing it has that waterproof case. We've had some nasty weather over the last few days."

By this time, Helen has joined us and is examining the phone. Looking at our new friend, she asks, "Any way you can show us exactly where you found this?"

" 'Fraid not," he replies, "that was several days ago and that storm last night did a number on these woods. There are limbs down everywhere and even I'm turned around."

"That's OK," she says, "we're just glad to have it back."

"I figured the real owners would be around sometime to look for it. It was obvious those other guys were just out to score a free phone."

"What other guys?" I ask.

"Oh, these big Neanderthals out here Friday with their metal detectors. I come through every day about this time to pick wild mushrooms for, umm, medicinal purposes, and I rarely see anyone else. So these guys stood out. They didn't look like the types to have a hot pink phone but I asked them anyway if they were looking for something. I guess it could have belonged to one of their daughters or girlfriends or something. Anyway, one of the guys says, 'a phone' and when I asked what kind, he got nasty and said 'none of your business' so I got out of here."

"Well, thanks so much for keeping it for me. I'd like to give you some sort of reward," Helen says, reaching for her wallet.

"Not necessary at all. It's my pleasure. You'd be surprised how often I come across stuff people have lost out here and I say to myself, 'Hang on to that, Anthony, somebody will be looking for it someday.'"

I see Helen's jaw drop as I put out my hand to him and say, "Thanks so much, Anthony. I really appreciate you coming around."

Sixteen

For once, I get to drive. After all, I know the way home.

Helen is quiet in the passenger seat next to me, contemplating the phone in her hands. She turns it over and over.

"What's wrong?" I say.

"I'm trying to figure out what we're going to do with this," she answers, holding up the phone.

"I'd think it'd be pretty simple," I say, swerving slightly to give a family of possums plenty of room. "We charge the phone, turn it on, and see what we can find out."

"Tom," she sighs. "When are you going to realize things are rarely that simple?"

I smile ruefully and shoot her a quick glance. "I've learned a lot about that on this trip."

Helen gives a bitter laugh. "Okay, point taken. But I'm talking about police work. We've got two problems. First, we'll have her contacts and text messages, and that'll give us a lot, but we'll need some way of checking the phone numbers. Second, and this is the biggest problem, is getting into the phone in the first place."

"Oh," I nod. "I see what you mean."

"If Sonya was like, oh, I don't know, everybody else on the planet, her phone's locked with some kind of password. And since this is a newer model, it's probably biometric."

"So, fingerprint, retina scan, facial recognition," I shake my head. "Considering she's dead and her body cremated . . . "

"Eww, Tom," Helen says, appalled. "We don't do things like that. That's just the sick minds of Hollywood. No, there are ways around it."

"So, do that."

"Oh, I wouldn't even try, Tom. These things are designed to delete everything if you guess the wrong password too many times or use the wrong fingerprint or something."

"What would you do with it back home?"

She chuckles. "That's easy. Gladys. She'd have this thing open in less than five minutes."

"Why don't you send it to her?"

"Oh, all sorts of reasons, the biggest one being that since this is evidence in a homicide, we shouldn't even have it. We should turn it over to Gus."

I shake my head. "Helen, I don't think—"

"No, I agree, we can only trust him so far. So we're going to keep it for now. But it has to stay with us. Shipping it to her risks all sorts of chain of custody problems down the road when this comes to trial."

I look at her. "OK," I say gravely, then turn back to the road.

After a moment, I say, "So you need Gladys? Why not just ask her to fly down?"

"What?" Helen says, sounding astonished I'd suggest such a thing. "I can't ask her to do that!"

"Why not?" I shrug. "You're her boss, right?"

"Yeah, but this isn't an official investigation," Helen points out. "I can't order her to do anything. We could both get in trouble."

"What about all that stuff she sent with you? Won't that get her into trouble?"

"Huh! Knowing Gladys, everything mysteriously vanished from inventory and will miraculously reappear when we get back."

"Just call her and see if she can come," I say. Waggling my eyebrows, I add, "You can tell her I'd consider it a personal favor."

"Oh, you are impossible, you know that?" she says as she pulls out her phone and dials Gladys.

"So I've been told."

A moment later the car is filled with the sound of an alto chipmunk saying, "Ahoy, Chief!"

"Gladys, I have you on speaker. Father Tom's here with me."

"Oh, he is?" she says, her voice suddenly low and throaty. "Hi there, Father," she purrs.

"Hi, Gladys, how are you?"

"Oh, I'm much better now," she sighs.

"Gladys!" Helen says sharply, shooting me a side glance. "Listen. We've got a situation down here and we need your particular set of skills. I'll grant you administrative leave so you don't have to use any of yours."

Gladys laughs. "Chief, I have plenty of leave, since I never take any. I'll be glad to fly down to help you and Hot—Father Greer."

I smile. "Gladys, why don't you just call me Tom?"

There's the sound of heavy breathing for a moment, which is soon replaced by giggling. "Tom," Gladys says. "Hee, hee, hee. Tom. Okay, Tom."

"Pull yourself together Gladys, and tell me how soon you can get here?"

"Ah, wellllll, I've got a little problem," Gladys says, slowly.

"Is everything all right? You're not sick, are you?" Helen says with concern.

Gladys sighs. "No, Mom, nothing like that. It's just, I can't come down for four days because . . . I have a, ah . . . visitor."

"Oh?" Helen looks confused. "You didn't mention that before I left."

"It was kind of sudden," she says. "An old friend from MIT. He just got a position at Myer College beginning in March, so he came down to get the lay of the land. I've been showing him around and we've been catching up."

"Well, that's nice, Gladys," I say. "What's the position?"

For some reason, she hesitates. "Ah, well, you see, he was just named Myer's new president."

Helen and I look at each other, our jaws dropping at this piece of news. "Gladys, just how old is he?" Helen asks.

"Oh, Mom! Just calm down. He's not much older than you are."

"How much older is not much older?" Helen asks, firmly.

"Well, to give you some idea, he was one of my first professors when I started MIT and he was . . . forty?"

"Forty!" Helen yells. "Do you mean that when you were sixteen, you were dating a forty-year-old man!"

"Oh, no, Mom! No! Eew! Richard's not some perv. We didn't get together until I was eighteen."

"So you started dating him when you were eighteen?"

Another long pause. "I guess you could call it dating. We'd usually go to dinner or something first."

From the look on Helen's face, I decide an intervention is in order.

"Gladys," I say. "Are you telling us you're, ahem, with a man old enough to be your father?"

She pauses. "Yes," she says quietly.

"Why?"

She sighs. "Because . . . because sometimes I just get tired of being alone. I know it's not a good idea, Father Tom. Even I know that. But . . ." She sniffles.

"It's OK, sweetie, it's OK," Helen says quietly. "But don't you think it'd be better if he stayed somewhere else?"

She takes a deep breath. "Yeah, Mom. I think you're right. I'll do that. I promise." She pauses. "Thank you, Mom. Thank you, Father." She pauses here and says, "That sounds a little formal. What if I just call you Dad?"

I look at Helen and smile, "Gladys, that's fine if you want to. But listen, we really need your help," I say. "Something only you can do. I'd take it as a personal favor if you could get down here as soon as your . . . friend leaves."

"Oh, Dad," Gladys says, still sniffling. "I'd do just about anything for you. I'll fly out the day he leaves. He's flying out of Dulles, so I'll just hop a ride with him."

"Fine, Gladys, fine," I say. Thank you!"

"No probs, Dad!" Gladys says. "Mom? We good?"

Helen sighs. "Of course, dear. See you in a few days."

The call ends, and we drive a few miles in silence.

All of a sudden, Helen slaps the armrest. "Forty-eight!" she shouts. "He's forty-eight, Tom!"

"Now, Helen . . ."

"Don't you 'now Helen' me! Gladys is sleeping with a forty-eight year old man!"

"And," I say, "she says she's stopping. We talked to her; she listened. And that's all we can do."

Helen exhales and nods. "I guess you're right." She looks at me and smiles. "She called you Dad."

"I heard," I say. "It felt good."

"People call you Father all the time."

"I know," I whisper. "It's just that it's been a long time since anyone's said it to me with such . . . gratitude."

We fall into an uneasy silence, the subject of my crisis of faith having raised its ugly head again.

Right then, I decide a subject change is in order.

"Are you hungry? How about some cobbler? There's this great place downtown."

She smiles and says, "Sounds good."

***

The Courthouse Diner on Main Street has been a Bellamy institution for almost seventy-five years. Overlooking the old Bellamy County Courthouse square, the diner was opened by a couple of friends returning from Europe after World War II. For several decades, it was one of the few restaurants in the area.

Among my few happy memories of childhood were the Saturday afternoons, twice a month, when Dad would take me to the library. I'd check out an armload of books, mostly history but some fiction. Dad would have a book or two, usually one of the mystery novels he loved to read—-he's the one who introduced me to Father Brown, Hercule Poirot, and Lord Peter Whimsey. We'd stop by the diner on our way home. Dad would order a cup of coffee and a peach cobbler with vanilla ice cream and two spoons. For me, he'd order a soda, the only time I would drink a soda since Mom didn't buy them for the house. The waitress liked me, so she'd always serve it to me with a cherry in it. Dad and I would sit and eat our cobbler, talking about the books I picked out and other stuff.

The last time we were here was a week before he died.

We're at a booth by the window. We each have a peach cobbler with vanilla ice cream. After having eaten about half, Helen seems calmer and less likely to decide to hunt down the new President of Myer College like a dog when she gets home.

"So we have Sonya's cell phone," I begin. "We can't do anything with it until Gladys gets here. Maybe we should go over what else we know?"

Helen puts her fork down and takes a sip of coffee. "Good idea. So what do we know?"

"Well, for one," I say, "we know that Gus is lying about something."

"Which means that we can't trust him fully," she sighs. "Damn. That's going to make this really hard."

"Why? You're a good detective. You've got those care packages Gladys put together for you. What do we need Gus for?"

"Information, for one," Helen says. "We'll need a copy of the autopsy report. We'll need any witness statements he has. Also, there's the little matter of my not having any jurisdiction here. No one has to talk to me. Frankly, I could get in a lot of trouble."

"Look, I don't want that to happen, so if you want to . . ."

"Oh, no, Tom," Helen shakes her head. "I'm in. I was in this thing as soon as I decided to come."

I smile. "Thank you. So how are we going to get a copy of the autopsy?"

"I've gotta think about that one," Helen says. "For now, let's just stick with what we know."

"That's not much," I say.

"No, but it's something. So?"

"So." I stare at my coffee cup, tracing the rim with my finger. "We know that Sonya called me in the middle of the night. She sounded like she was running in the woods, trying to hide from someone. Later, her body was found in a dumpster behind the big-box stores near the interstate. She'd been shot." I take a drink of coffee. "That's it."

"No," Helen says slowly. "That's not quite everything. You're forgetting what she said to you on the phone."

"Oh, right!" I search my memory for the contents of our conversation. "She said she needed my help. She said I could help stop them. That I could help the girls. She mentioned a name . . . Chrystal, that was it."

"Which begs the question, who are they and who are these girls she was talking about?"

I nod. "She also told me to remember something, but the call dropped a few seconds and I didn't catch what I was supposed to remember."

"We'll need to figure that out," Helen says.

I slump in the chair and sigh. "So, where do we start?"

"Wellll," Helen says, "you're not going to like this. But we need to find out more about Sonya, especially the last few days of her life."

I see the expression on Helen's face and sigh. "Oh, no. Do we really have to?"

"I'm afraid so," she says. She reaches across the table and pats my arm reassuringly. "We need to talk to your mother."

Seventeen

"But I don't know anything, Tommy," Mom says, wringing her hands and shaking her head.

Fortunately, by the time we got home, Mom was already in bed. So I had a twelve-hour reprieve from what I knew was going to be a difficult conversation at best.

I just had no idea how difficult it would be.

"I know it seems that way, Mrs. Greer," Helen says reassuringly. "But you actually knew Sonya better than anyone else. Why don't you start by telling us about her job? She was working at The Belvedere. When did that start?"

"Oh, let me think," Mom says. She looks at a spot on the wall, then continues, "It was about the time Diana had her lung removed. I remember because she wanted Sonya to take care of her while she recovered. You know how crazy Diana was about Sonya. Well, anyway, Sonya stayed with her for about two weeks and Charlie was in and out the whole time, checking on his mom like good sons do."

Her subtle point is not lost on me.

"Well, anyway, he had married that Rose, and you know, Diana has never liked her. Seems she has quite a checkered past. Been married a bunch of times and started dating Charlie before her last one was even cold. Now don't tell Diana I told you that. You know she thinks the sun rises and sets in Charlie, but then, he is a good son."

Again, not lost on me.

"And you know, Rose actually has a rose tattoo right on her . . ."

"Mom!" I nearly yell. Then, getting control, I continue in a more composed manner. "You were saying about Charlie and Sonya?"

"Charlie was so impressed with Sonya's work for his mother that he insisted she come work for him. And, I might add, he paid her extremely well."

"Oh, really," I say sarcastically. "You know this because she finally started paying you back all the money she stole from you through the years?"

"Tommy, why do you always have to be so nasty about your sister? You know, she told me one time that it was your attitude that drove her to drugs in the first place."

Okay, that's IT!

I jump to my feet, screaming, "My attitude! My attitude! So trying to get her sobered up overnight so she wouldn't miss school the next day drove her to drugs? Following her around in Gus' car while she drove yours to try to score drove her to drugs? Hauling her to rehab every single time I came home drove her to drugs? Yeah, it all makes sense now. I should have taken a page out of her book and done what I damn well pleased all my life and then everything would be OK!"

I storm out of the room, slamming the screen door behind me, and head straight for the rental car. Helen's right behind me.

I turn and extend my hand. "Give me the keys, Helen!" I growl.

"I'm not going to do that, Tom."

"Oh, yes, you are!" I say, taking a step toward her.

"Tom, stop!" she says in her best cop voice. "Stop now!"

I stop for just a moment before turning on my heels and marching up the drive toward the highway. Helen trots along behind me, asking me where I'm going. I don't answer, I just keep walking. In a moment, I realize I don't hear her steps behind me.

I keep walking until I get to the road and then remember that I'm not in Myerton anymore. There are no sidewalks out here, just poorly mowed edges. I pause for a minute and then turn toward town. I take a few steps before the first truck comes by, a big one that nearly blows me into the ditch. I pull myself together and make another few yards before the log truck rolls past, its cargo reminding me of childhood stories of people decapitated for following too close. By the time the chicken truck covers me with a light dusting of feathers and lord only knows what else, I'm ready to head back home and call a cab.

By the time I've walked back to the house, my temper's cooled, replaced by embarrassment. I'm almost forty-six years old, and I let my seventy-year-old mother goad me about my sister.

Again.

I'm looking at my feet as I walk, trying to figure out how I'm going to apologize to Helen and Mom. When I get near the house, I look up and stop.

Helen's sitting on the steps, her knees pulled up, She's resting her chin on her hand. She's not angry. She looks more bemused.

"Did you enjoy your little walk?" she quips.

"Why didn't you come after me?" I ask.

"Well, I started to, then I remembered how far we were from town," she says. "And considering how winded you were after a ten-minute walk from Saint Clare's to my office, I had a feeling you'd be back soon."

I smile ruefully, then drop on the step next to her and put my head in my hands.

"I'm sorry, Helen," I say, shaking my head.

She reaches around and pats me on the back. "Hey, it's okay. But you know, you've gotta stop letting her goad you. You're a grown-ass man, not a little boy anymore. You just need to let what she says roll off your back."

I sit up and look towards the road. "Do you think Sonya really blamed me?" I whisper.

"Does it matter?"

I shrug. "Not anymore, I guess." I wipe my face with my hand. "I should go back inside, apologize to Mom, pick up where we left off."

I stand up and extend Helen a hand to help her up. She grabs it and I pull—a little too hard, as it turns out. She winds up standing about three inches from me, her hand on my chest to steady herself.

We look into each other's eyes, then I hear a small voice in my head.

What profit is there for one to gain the whole world and forfeit his soul?

Even if it's the world I see in the eyes of the woman I love?

I pull away and close my eyes. Taking a deep breath and letting it out, I feel Helen's hand drop from my chest. When I open my eyes, I see Helen. Her jaw is fixed, determined. Her eyes reveal desire, disappointment, resolve.

"You okay?" she whispers.

I shake my head, slowly. "No. Are you okay?"

Helen shakes her head. "No. But I will be. And so will you."

I nod. "Well," I say, "let's talk to Mom some more. Standing out here isn't going to get us any closer to Sonya's killer."

When we return to the living room, Mom's still in her chair. She's twisted several tissues into bits that are scattered at her feet.

Walking to her, I bend down to hug her. "Sorry, Mom. I shouldn't have yelled like that."

"No, you shouldn't have, Tommy," she whimpers. "My baby was murdered—murdered!—and you're treating me this way. I'd have expected that being a priest would have made you less self-centered. But, I guess not."

I'm trying to decide how to react—do I take what Mom said with good grace or do I squeeze harder until I hear a rib crack—when Helen comes to my rescue.

"It's a hard time for everyone, Nola ," Helen says. "Tom's upset too, you know."

I stand up. "Yes, Mom," I whisper. "Sonya and I weren't close the last several years, but she was still my sister."

Mom nods, a benevolent smile on her face and pats my arm with her wrinkled hand. "I understand, Tommy. Must have been your guilt speaking. Probably a lot for you to handle."

Reflexively, my jaw clenches, as do my hands. Swallowing, I manage to say very calmly, "Yes, Mom."

I walk back to the couch and plop down next to Helen. She gives me a reassuring pat on my leg, then says to Mom, "Okay, before Tommy lost his temper—." She must feel me bristle at her comment, because she shoots me a sideward glance and subtly shakes her head.

"Before Tommy lost his temper," Helen repeats, "you had just mentioned that Charlie paid Sonya well?"

"Oh, very well!" Mom exclaims. "I mean, Charlie even advanced her money to buy a whole new wardrobe. She came back from Tallahassee with scads of the prettiest and most stylish outfits you could imagine. But, then, Sonya always had a nice figure and could wear clothes very well."

She pauses and looks at Helen. "I'd been meaning to tell you," Mom says to her, "how pretty you still look for a woman your age."

"Why, thank you, Nola," Helen grins.

Now, there's one thing about Mom. She's developed the back-handed compliment to an art-form. I'm steeling myself for what comes next. I just hope she doesn't say anything about—

"I mean, considering how much weight you've gained since I last saw you," Mom adds.

I can testify from personal experience that it's very hard to get under Helen's skin. She loves nothing more than a good argument. It's the one thing I could never get used to when we were together, hating conflict the way I do. There was almost no topic that was off limits, from the sublime to the ridiculous. We once had a four-hour debate over who had the most women fall for them in Star Trek, Kirk or Spock. When faced with incontrovertible evidence that I was right (Spock, hands down), she resorted to unfair tactics to win.

And, boy. Win, she did.

The one topic that was off-limits, however, was her weight.

As I'm sitting next to her, Mom's words having sucked all the oxygen out of the room, I can feel Helen stiffen and sense the boiling anger welling up from within.

I decide a change of subject is needed. Fast.

"Did Sonya buy anything else?" I ask. I can hear Helen grinding her teeth, and the reassuring hand on my arm has become a claw digging into my flesh.

"Oh, yes," Mom says. "And to answer your earlier question, Tommy, she did pay back the money she borrowed."

I manage not to point out that Sonya 'borrowed' from Mom's purse on a regular basis, not to mention the hundreds if not thousands she conned out of her.

"Well, that was good," Helen manages to say.

"Oh, she was so generous with me," Mom continues. "She bought so many new things for the house, including a new mattress for me. She even bought us new cars. Sonya's was a cute English one, you know, the ones that look like jelly beans."

At Helen's look, I whisper, "A Mini Cooper."

"It must be at the Sheriff's Department," Helen whispers.

"Mom," I say, "do you know how much Sonya was paid?"

"Oh, I don't know, Tommy. Probably a lot more than both you and Helen, given the type of people her work put her in contact with."

Helen and I look at each other. "Mom," I say slowly, "did you ever meet these people?"

"Well," she says, "in a manner of speaking. She took me to dinner there for my birthday. All sorts of people stopped by to say hello to her. They all looked rich, lawyers, doctors, businessmen, you know. I recognized at least one Congressman or Senator. And you know, I could swear one of the men looked exactly like a member of the royal family."

"What sort of restaurant was it?" Helen asks.

"Very swanky. More of a date night place than a family joint. Most of the people there were couples out for a night on the town, though there were a few groups of two or three women, I guess what they call a Ladies Night now. But the sweetest thing was the dads there with their daughters, you know, like a special 'dad and daughter' time. They were fussing over them and treating them like they were so grown up. It was precious."

She sighed. "I just wish your dad had done things like that with Sonya. It would have meant so much to her."

Something is bothering me about this, but I can't quite put my finger on it as Mom prattles on.

"Of course I'm way too old to be watching men but the women were just so beautiful, so stylish. And so cosmopolitan. Some were very exotic, looking like they were from South America. Others had very white skin and spoke with the most beautiful accents, though they didn't really speak English well at all."

"And you say they were young?" Helen asks. Out of the corner of my eye, I see concern spreading over her face.

"Oh, yes. I mean, not all of them. The wives were a little younger than their husbands, but their daughters were, I'd say, late teens."

I ask, "What did they say to Sonya?"

"They thanked her for arranging everything. Sonya asked if they were pleased with her choices for them. You know, she just wanted to make sure people were satisfied and had a good time."

I jumped up from the couch. "You know what I could use? A cup of coffee. Mom, you want some?"

"Well, that would be—"

"Good. Helen," I say, turning to her, "can you help me?" I start walking to the kitchen as Helen scrambles to her feet behind me.

"I've got low fat creamer, Helen," Mom calls after us.

Helen stops and turns on Mom. I grab her by the arm and drag her into the kitchen. I quickly close the shutters to the pass-through and drag her as far away from the door as I can, so there's no possibility of Mom overhearing us.

I turn to her and whisper, "What did that sound like to you?"

"Probably exactly the same as it sounded to you," Helen whispers back.

"Wealthy men, beautiful women, some young, foreign, don't speak English very well," I say. "I mean, it can't be anything else, can it?"

"I can't think of anything else, Tom," Helen sighs. "It sounds for all the world like your sister was some sort of madam."

Eighteen

Instead of making coffee, Helen and I tell Mom we're going into Bellamy for lunch. We have a lot to discuss.

I'm in my room changing clothes when Helen calls, "Tom, I need you in the bedroom, now!"

I freeze for a minute, then shoot out of my room like a bullet out of a gun.

Fortunately, I have my pants on.

But I forgot my shirt.

I fling open the door to find Helen standing at the open closet, holding an emerald-green cocktail dress.

When I abruptly enter the room, she jumps a little. When she sees me, her eyes widen and she sucks in a breath. "Ah, did . . . did you forget something, Tom?"

I look down. "I'll go pull a shirt on," I say, turning to leave.

"No, no, no need to do that." She takes a deep breath and lets it out slowly. "I found this in your sister's closet."

I cross my arms and cock my head to one side. "A little fancy for lunch, don't you think?"

"I wasn't going to wear it, Tom." She looks at it again. "Anyway, your mother would be quick to point out it's too small for me. No, this is a designer original from Paris. Probably not more than ten dresses in the world like it. And I found it in your sister's closet in a little armpit town in Florida. Care to guess how much this dress might be?"

"I don't know. $300?"

She shakes her head. "Add a zero and you might be close."

"Holy crap!" I exclaim. "Are you sure?"

"I'm no expert," she says. "But in D.C., we worked a joint operation with Customs to stop a gang smuggling designer knock-offs from China and passing them off as the real thing. I had to study what the real dresses looked like to detect the fakes. And from the looks of it, your sister's closet is stuffed with the real thing. I've got a pretty good idea what real dresses like this cost."

I walk to the closet and stand next to her. "How much do you think's in here?" I ask Helen.

"We're probably looking at around $100,000 worth of outfits here."

"My gosh," I whisper in amazement. "How much was she getting paid?"

"Well, if she was doing what we suspect, we may not be able to find out," Helen says. "But we can have Gladys look into her finances."

"Okay, you call Gladys. I'll finish getting dressed."

***

"Man, it's crowded," Helen says, surveying the diner "You want to go somewhere else?"

I shrug. "There's really nowhere else, unless you want to go to one of the chains by the interstate."

A group gets up from a booth near the window and we grab it. After a few minutes, a harried waitress comes and starts quickly clearing the table.

"I'm sorry about this, hon," the young woman says to us. Her name tag says Zoey. "I'll get to y'all as quick as I can. It's just me working today."

Sliding easily back into my small town Southern roots, I am compelled to make the comment into a conversation. "Someone call in sick?" I ask.

"Sick?" she says with a disgusted tone. "Jennifer just didn't show up, again. Won't even bother to pick up the dang phone. I told Rick, 'Look, this is the third day she just didn't bother. You need to hire somebody else.' But you know how it is," she adds, looking at Helen, "He's waiting for her to turn up again with her sexy little walk and tight skirts, just like he always does."

Helen looks stunned while I want to ask if Rick is related to Mr. Brent who owns the place and, if so, how's his wife. She had some kind of weird skin disease last I heard. But it's crowded and I don't want to be a pest.

Zoey carries off the dirty dishes and returns a moment later, wipes the table with a damp cloth, and hands us a couple of menus, promising to return in a few minutes to take our orders.

I spy the cheeseburger platter and decide that's what I want. I close my menu and look across at Helen. "Find something you like?"

"Well, ahem, after what your Mom said, I probably ought to order the chef's salad," she says. "But since I could care less, I'm getting the chicken fried steak."

She closes the menu and looks across the table at me. "Do you think I've gotten fatter, Tom?"

I sit back in the booth. "Why would you ask me that, Helen?"

Helen shrugs. "Listen, I know what I look like. I know how big I am. You remember the number of diets I was on when we were together. It was almost as bad when I was married to John. I had to work my ass off, literally, to meet the physical requirements for the Academy. I struggled when I was in D.C. to keep my weight under the maximum. One of the things I decided when I moved to Myerton was that I wasn't going to care anymore. I'd do my best, but I was going to eat the food I wanted to eat and wear the clothes I wanted to wear. For the first time in years, I was actually satisfied with how I looked."

"And one remark from my bat-crap crazy Mom blew that up?" I say.

She sighs. "It just made me realize I'm not twenty-two anymore and . . ."

"Let me stop you right there, Helen Parr. This is something we really don't need to be talking about. But since you brought it up, let me put your mind at ease about something so we can move on. I don't love you because you're fat. I don't love you in spite of the fact that you're fat. I don't love you because, other than Joan, you're the most beautiful woman I ever met. I don't love you because even over twenty years later, the sight of you makes my heart skip a beat, something that hasn't happened since Joan died. I love you, Helen, because you're you, and I don't see that ever changing."

Helen smiles, a tear rolling down her cheek. "Dammit, Tom," she whispers, wiping the tear with a napkin. "You say stuff like that, and it makes our situation that much harder."

"Then we'd better move on to something else, like ordering our food and figuring out where Sonya got all her money."

Zoey comes and takes our order. No sooner has she left our table when Helen's phone buzzes.

"It's Gladys," Helen says. Answering and putting her on video chat, she says. "Hi, Gladys. You're here with Tom and me."

"Oh," she breathes. "Hi, Tom."

"Morning, Gladys," I say. "How are you?"

"Me?" she squeaks. "Oh, I couldn't be better."

"That was quick, Gladys," Helen says, looking at me.

"That's because there wasn't a lot to find, Chief," Gladys says. We hear the clattering of a keyboard.

"What do you mean, Gladys?"

"Well, I did find records of her being employed by a company, CRL Holdings, Limited. It's an offshore company registered in the Cayman Islands. I located records of her salary, taxes withheld, even payments to a 401K and health insurance."

"Okay? Her mother said she was paid a good salary."

"But that's just the problem, Chief," Gladys says. "She wasn't. Her salary was less than $30,000, and after all the deductions, she actually took home less than $25,000 a year."

"What about bank accounts, credit cards?"

"She does have a small bank account in the First National Bank of Bellamy, but there hasn't been a lot of activity in there for a couple of years. Including, and this is really strange, no deposits."

Helen and I look at each other. "Does she have another bank account?"

"There's none listed on her credit report. Which brings up the really weird thing. Her credit score."

"What's weird about it?" Helen asks.

"She doesn't have one," Gladys says.

"What do you mean, she doesn't have one?" I exclaim.

"I mean, Tom, your sister had no credit. Not a single credit card or loan."

"Gladys, are you sure about all of this?" Helen asks. "I mean, she has a closet full of designer clothes and she bought two cars in the last year."

She shrugs. "I don't know how she did it, but I'll tell you one thing for sure. There's no way she could have afforded anything like you describe on her salary."

"At least," I say quietly. "Not her official salary."

Helen nods. "Paid under the table? It fits with what we suspect."

"Did you mention a car?" Gladys says. "I've got records for two registered in her name."

"Can you figure out where she bought them?"

"Just a sec," she says. "Let me enter the VIN numbers—got it. There was a 2019 Mini Cooper purchased in October 2019 from Henderson Imports in Tallahassee, Florida, and a 2020 Acura a few months later."

"But there's nothing about her financing them?"

"No, Tom." Gladys says my name like she's trying to summon a dead aunt at a seance. "Not even a record of a check clearing."

"So how did she pay for them?" I ask Helen.

"Frankly, Tom, there's no way of knowing without questioning someone at the dealership."

"Which you can't do," I add, "Without jurisdiction."

"Well, yes and no."

"What do you mean?"

"I mean, Tom dear, that it's about time you test drove a new car."

"But Helen, I don't need a new . . ." She looks at me as what she's thinking hits me. "Right," I nod, getting it.

And what better place to patronize than one recommended by my dear sister?

Nineteen

We get to the dealership about 3:00 p.m., a little late in the day, but Helen assures me it is better to try to catch suspects off guard when they're tired, even better if they happened to have had a heavy lunch. We arrive, having gotten our story figured out on the way.

I am no sooner out of the car than a tall, thin man with a shock of black hair that stands on end in the cold is at my side. Extending his hand, he says, "Danny Carter, nice to meet you. How can I help you fine folks today?"

I hesitate, being uncomfortable with a lie, even one we've rehearsed and I feel is necessary. Fortunately, Helen takes the lead.

"Hi, Danny. I'm Helen Greer and my husband Tom and I have just packed our one and only daughter, little Ruby, off to college. Best of all, she got a scholarship so we have all the money we've saved for her education just eating a hole in our pockets. So I said to Tom, 'Honey, why don't we live a little. Let's treat ourselves to a new car.' So we sent my car off with Ruby this morning and rented something to get us here and we are ready to buy."

For just a minute, I thought I saw tears of joy well up in Danny's eyes.

"Ma'am," he said, "You have come to the right place. Now a lot of scoundrels out there would take advantage of what you just shared with me but I am not one of those men. No, ma'am. Here at Henderson, we are committed to seeing every customer get the best deal we can offer them. It's like Granddaddy Henderson always said, 'Folks are folks.'"

From the look on her face, I could tell this threw Helen off her stride. She was about to blow her role as a folksy down-home wife by asking some stupid question like what he meant by that, so I jumped in.

"That's exactly what my sister, Sonya, said. She bought not one but two cars here last year."

"Sonya? You mean Sonya Greer?"

Now even I am taken back by this level of familiarity and say, "I have to admit, I am impressed that you remember her that well."

"Those deals are not easy to forget. Just out of curiosity, will we be handling your transaction the same way?"

I hesitate, not knowing what he means but Helen jumps in with, "Yes, absolutely."

I think his smile is going to break his face as he asks, "What kind of car did y'all have in mind?"

Helen speaks up. "Something sporty, maybe a convertible."

Catching her excitement, I add, "Yeah. In red"

"Well, let's step into the showroom. I think I have just the thing for you."

Fifteen minutes later, we are flying down Interstate 10 at speeds that drive all thoughts of Helen out of my mind.

It would be better if I was driving.

But then, the experience definitely reminds me of my need for God.

Messing with the radio, she lands on this loud, thrumming music that I recognize from the 80s. Grinning from ear to ear, she shouts, "I remember this. It was from a TV show set in Hawaii. The star was a real hunk and I used to rush home from school every day to catch the reruns. Oh man, that guy was gorgeous. What was his name?"

"Tom," Danny shouts from the back seat.

"Yeah?" I shout back, barely able to hear him over the music.

"No, I was talking to her."

"Sorry," Helen says. "I thought you said Tom."

"I did."

"Then what?" I asked, beginning to get irritated.

"You need to slow down," Danny insists.

"Tell her," I say, "She's the one driving."

At this, Helen shoots me a dirty look and drives the accelerator into the ground. "Don't worry," she insists, "I know what I'm doing. Now, if I could just remember that guy's name."

"Tom," Danny shouts again. "Thomas . . . " The wind catches the rest of his words, but I've had enough.

"Helen," I say, "please slow down. The song is over now, you've had some fun, and this guy has started using my full name."

"OK," she says, pouting. "Have it your way. But you know I am trained to handle speed."

"Lady," Danny chimes in, finally catching his breath as Helen approaches the right side of the speed limit, "the guy on the TV show you're talking about, his name was Tom. He wore flowered shirts and drove a red Ferrari, though rarely like you have this Corvette." Then, plastering a smile on his face, he adds, "So, do we have a deal?"

I look at Helen and she glances at me. For a moment, I am struck by how lovely she is with her hair tousled by the wind. A Roman goddess, just out of the reach of a man trapped in a Roman collar.

That thought stops me. I'm not trapped, and it's not fair to claim I am. I could walk away from the priesthood tomorrow, but to what end? For Helen? Would a man who quit so easily even deserve her?

I am completely lost, both mentally and spiritually, in these thoughts as we pull back into the dealership.

We climb out of the car and Danny asks a second time, "So, are you ready to seal the deal?"

"That depends," I say, coming back to reality with a thud. "Will you give us the same deal you gave Sonya?"

"Well, now, I really shouldn't, what with her buying two cars and you only wanting one, but hell, why not. Just bring the money on into my office and we'll lock the door and count it out like last time."

I guess we both look confused because he adds, "Is that a problem? I mean, we can't really have that kind of cash just stacked up there on the counter. Last time, she insisted that we count it behind closed doors."

Helen catches on quicker than I do. "Sure," she says. "Tom, remember, Sonya explained this to us when she recommended this place. We just need to go to the car and get the money."

I just stare at her and say, "right," through a dumb fog.

"You two bring that same powderpuff blue duffle bag?" Danny asks with a grin.

"No," Helen replies quickly, "Ours is black."

Trying to say something intelligent and failing miserably, I add, "I usually wear black."

"OK, Tom," Helen says, grabbing my arm, "let's not make Danny here wait." Then, turning to him she adds, "We'll be right back."

Helen walks me to our car, looking discreetly over her shoulder at Danny. "Okay," she finally says, "he's gone inside. Let's get out of here."

We scurry the last ten yards or so to the car, Helen climbing in and cranking the engine before I even open the door. For a split second, I was worried she'd start driving away before I was even inside. Fortunately, I'm in my seat with the door closed before she guns the engine and speeds out of the dealership.

"'I usually wear black?'" she says mockingly as she heads to the Interstate. "What the hell, Tom?"

"I beg your pardon, Danica Patrick!" I shout. "I was still recovering from my near-death experience. I can't believe I'm letting you drive now!"

"Oh, stop being such a baby!" she yells.

"I'm not being a baby!" I snap. "Now, pull in up here," I add, pointing to a Sprockets drive-in. "Why?"

"I need a milkshake to calm my nerves."

Helen pauses. "Actually, a snack does sound good after all that."

***

"Do you really think that's a good idea, Tom?"

I look at Helen, who's looking at my food.

More specifically, the footlong chili dog I'm about to consume, washed down by a chocolate milkshake.

"Hey," I say, "if I can survive your driving . . ."

She playfully slaps me on the shoulder before returning to her cheese-covered tater-tots. "Okay," she says as she chews, "well, that was something."

I nod. "Seems like we're on the right track, thinking Sonya was into something sketchy."

"Sketchy? Tom, listen, she bought two cars with a duffle bag full of cash. Only big-time drug dealers do that."

"So what are you thinking? That Sonya's some kind of drug-lord?"

"No," she shakes her head. "From what you've told me about her, I don't think she's capable of that. But she could be involved with someone who is."

"Well, Gus did tell me that story about her being involved with a drug lord."

"You said he was lying."

"When you think about it," I shrug, "many lies are built on some sort of foundation of truth. Based on what we know, Sonya was in all likelihood involved in something criminal."

"Don't forget," Helen adds, "according to what your Mom said, she's probably involved with prostitution, maybe a touch of human trafficking."

I sigh. "And considering where they were when Mom saw all this, whatever's going on is centered on The Belvedere. And Charlie's probably involved."

"I don't think we can jump to that conclusion yet, Tom," Helen says, sipping her soda. "Sonya could have been doing all of that without Charlie's knowledge. He told you he's not hands-on there."

"Should we go talk to him?"

Helen pops another tot in her mouth and chews as she considers my question. "No," she said. "Not yet anyway. There's a lot more we need to find out."

"Right," I say, polishing off my chili dog. "It's almost 5:00 p.m. and I'm tired. Can we put a pin in the detective work today?"

Helen stretches. "Sounds like a great idea. We need to head back. But before we go, I need to make a stop at an electronics store."

I look quizzically at her. "What do you need from an electronics store?"

She looks at me and smiles. "Sweetie, you snore. And that wall between your room and mine is really thin."

"I do not snore. At least Joan never mentioned it."

"Tom," she says gently, "Joan's been gone for ten years. Things change over time. Our bodies change. A lot of wives complain that their husbands start snoring when they reach middle age."

Without thinking, I ask, "Did John start snoring?"

Seeing the look in her eyes, I immediately regret the question.

"No, he didn't," she says wistfully, "but then again, he never had the chance to."

And Joan never had the chance to complain about me.

Twenty

Helen bought noise-canceling headphones. Apparently, I snore *really* loudly.

I have no clue, of course, sleeping alone as I do.

The irony of the situation occurs to me as I lay awake staring at the ceiling of my old room, when I hear Helen roll over and start snoring herself.

I check the time. It's a little after 2:30 a.m.. Apparently, insomnia is featured tonight on the menu of Tom's Sleep Problems. Well, it is better than the alternative.

We got back from Tallahassee about 6:00 p.m.. We were still hungry, so we grabbed some food left over from the funeral and curled up together on the couch—okay, we didn't curl up *together*, I was on one end, and Helen was on the other end—in the family room to watch something. After arguing for about half-an-hour over what to watch, we'd agreed on *Casablanca*, a movie we'd never seen all the way through.

At least not together.

We didn't see it all the way through this time, either. About half-way through, I made Helen turn it off.

"Why?" she'd asked.

"Don't you remember?" I had said. "We never got past this part."

"Oh, sweetie, of course I remember," she had smiled. "But that doesn't matter now."

I had sighed. "It shouldn't," I had said, closing my eyes. "But it does to me."

Our eyes lock and she understands what I mean. She quickly looks away as I stand and head upstairs to my room, not even pausing long enough to say goodnight. I pause in the hall as I hear her going around the house turning out the lights, locking the doors.

I should have done that, I think, ashamed of my own cowardice in the face of temptation. But then I hear her coming up the stairs and I retreat into my room, shutting the door with as much finality as I can muster.

It is precious little.

I've laid in my bed for hours now, unable to sleep, unable to still the thoughts that tumble through my mind like water over the rocks in a rapids. I'm trying to make sense of everything that's happened in the last forty-eight hours, of everything I've learned about myself and about Sonya.

About myself, I've learned how very far away from God I've grown.

About Sonya, that she was into some pretty serious stuff that may have gotten her killed.

There's nothing I can do about the latter, I realize. Helen and I have a lot of work before we can even speculate on the connection.

But laying in the dark, I realize there's something I can do about the former. Something I should have done from the beginning.

I reach for my phone, and get on my knees.

It doesn't take long for me to find what I'm looking for in my Breviary app. Psalm 51. David's prayer of repentance.

"Have mercy on me, God, in your kindness," I mutter. "In your compassion, blot out my offence. Oh, wash me more and more from my guilt and cleanse me from my sin."

I stop at the last word. Sin. I re-read the first words of the Psalm.

Where was God's mercy for Leonard in his final moments? If I really believe that God is all-powerful, then how do I reconcile that with the fact that He could have stopped Leonard from killing himself? The Church still teaches that suicide, like any form of murder, is a Mortal Sin. Would an all powerful and merciful God really permit one of his children to go to Hell?

But I also remember the scratches. He did change his mind in those last moments. I want to believe he did. I want to believe I would. But I also don't want to let myself get so far away that it comes to that.

My mind continues to wonder. Where was God's mercy during those first years after our Dad died, when Sonya descended into a pit of addiction and crime, a pit she apparently never fully left, and the place that may have set the stage for her death?

Where's God been as my desire for Helen has grown over the last few months? Would an all powerful and merciful God really have allowed one of his priests to fall in love with someone they could never have?

And is it a sin for me to love her? How could love ever be a sin? God the Father is love; Christ is love incarnate; one of the gifts of the Holy Spirit is love. Given all that, how can I be sinning if I love Helen?

I shake my head. I know all the answers to my questions. I learned them in seminary. They're in the Catechism. God is all powerful, but He endowed us with the freedom to choose the good. Sin is choosing evil instead. When we sin, we separate ourselves from God. The God that gave us the freedom to choose in the first place. Because, as the knight told Indiana Jones, we chose poorly. Then we need to repent, go to confession, express contrition, and receive absolution.

Then, cleansed of mortal sin, we get to do it all over again.

Blah, blah, blah.

I remember it all. It once made sense to me. After my despair and grief over Joan's death drove me lower than I had ever been before or since, it was my rediscovered faith that saw me through. It was God's hand that brought me to Our Lady of the Mount, to the Lourdes Grotto where I believed I received my call to the priesthood. I studied the teachings, I learned the rites,

I practiced the liturgy. The joy I felt the day of my ordination was every bit as overwhelming as that I felt on my wedding day.

Now, that joy is gone. Nothing makes sense to me, I'm not sure I believe in it anymore. Not in God. Not in the Church. They say that the first is a father, the second a mother. The former makes the rules, the latter enforces them.

So, what does that make me? Their child? If so, are they abusive, trying capriciously to keep me from having what I want? Or is the problem with me? Am I a child reaching for a beautiful, hypnotic, but deadly poisonous snake?

This is the question of the centuries. "Hath God not said?" And I realize I am not going to answer it tonight.

Exhausted from trying, I decide to do something I know I shouldn't.

I go to my bedroom door and open it, intending to turn left toward the bathroom. But once in the hallway, I find myself turning right, toward Helen's room next door.

I tell myself that I'm just going to talk to her, check on her, make sure she's all right. I promise myself I'll do nothing more than that. I knock softly. There's no answer. "Helen," I whisper. No answer. I knock a little harder, wanting her to wake up so that—

What? I can make sure she's OK, or that she can tell me I am? That there is a future out there worth having? That we will figure something out together? That if I've lost my faith in God, I can still believe in her?

She still doesn't answer and I stare down at the door knob, willing myself to walk away even as my hand clutches the cool old metal and I start to turn it.

But it doesn't budge. I close my eyes. Apparently, Helen knows me better than I know myself. I stand frozen in time, scenes from movies swirling in my head, of men kicking doors down and striding through to grab the women they love. I then remember something I heard my Baptist grandmother say time and again.

"Tommy," she said, holding my soft, little-boy hands in her rough, work-hardened ones, "Always remember that Jesus is a gentleman. He'll knock on your heart but he'll never bust in."

"In persona Christi." In the person of Christ. That's what the Church says I am as a priest. And in that moment, God grants me the grace to be that one more time, and walk away from Helen's door.

I go into the bathroom, where the other day I noticed Mom had a bottle of prescription sleeping pills. I open the bottle and take out two, reminding myself with grave determination to take no more. I swallow them and head back to my room.

That's when I hear sounds from downstairs.

Broken glass. The turn of a knob. The slow squeak of hinges. Feet plodding on the carpet.

Someone's breaking in.

My first instinct is to get Helen. She's a cop, she brought her gun with her. She'll be able to handle the situation. But with those headphones on, I'd have to bang on the door to wake her. The sound would alert the robbers, either causing them to run or motivate them to stop the sound of the noise.

I decide the best course of action is to call 911. I hurry back towards my room to grab my phone when I notice something.

The footsteps are getting closer to the staircase. And they're shining their flashlights on the upstairs landing.

The movement stops. I walk very quietly towards the edge of the stairs. They're speaking.

"The boss say where it was?"

"Probably her upstairs bedroom, the first on the left after the staircase."

"They weren't more specific than that? Shit, this will take all night."

"Hey! You want to tell 'em we couldn't do it?"

"You kidding? The boss is bat-shit about this. We don't dare go back without it."

"Then let's go. Keep your voice down."

They begin to walk up the stairs. I hurry to my bedroom to get out of their sight.

Whatever they're here for, it's in Sonya's room.

The room Helen's sleeping in.

With that realization, I settle on the third option.

I need to handle this myself.

I quickly scan my room looking for something—anything—as a weapon. But there's nothing. Not even an old baseball bat.

Makes me wish I'd played baseball as a kid.

I'm trying to think about what I can do. I know they're here, but they don't know I'm here. I have the element of surprise.

Then I realize what I can do.

I can surprise them, maybe throw them off guard, frighten them enough to scare them off.

Beyond that, I have no plan.

"Dammit," one of them whispers. "It's locked."

They're at Helen's room. I'm out of time.

I fling open my door and grope for the light switch. Finding it, I flood the hallway with light, revealing the intruders.

"Hey!" I yell at the top of my lungs. Then, I suck in a deep breath.

There are two of them, which I already knew.

And they're big. Really big. Like, Dwayne Johnson big.

They're also surprised. But instead of running away, they stand there, looking at me.

Which leads me to realize something else, something I hadn't figured on.

They're not wearing masks. Which means I know what they look like.

I guess the same thought occurs to them, because the next thing I know they're advancing on me down the hallway with grunts and growls. Before I can get back to the relative safety of my room—though I doubt a one-inch-thick bedroom door would have stopped them—they grab me.

At this point, I realize I've had enough. I yell at the top of my lungs, "Let go of me, you bastards!" I start swinging my fists wildly. I manage to connect with someone's nose, because one of them lets go and starts howling. But the other one has a firm grip on me. He draws back and socks me in the jaw. I drop to the floor like a rag doll. I shake my head and try to get up, but the one I hit—at least, I think it's him—gives me a hard kick in the stomach, knocking the breath out of me. He follows that up by a hard—and I mean *very* hard—-kick in the groin. The pain is excruciating, shooting through me and causing me to see stars. I reflectively curl into a fetal position to protect myself from anymore kicks down there. Then, I feel a hard kick to the back of my head.

Then, darkness.

***

I feel grass against my left cheek and the sun on my right. Birds are chirping, and I hear the sound of a gentle breeze blowing through trees.

I open my eyes. Green grass. What looks like stumps in rows.

I sit up and look around.

I'm in the Lourdes Grotto at Our Lady of the Mount.

The Blessed Mother is looking down on me, a gentle, loving smile on her face, as she appeared before Saint Bernadette over one hundred fifty years ago. Her statue glistens in the Sun as it usually does, but as I look at it, I'm not sure if it is reflecting the Sun's light or if the light's radiating from it.

Behind me I hear the rustling of leaves. I stand up, keeping my eyes on the statue of Mary.

More rustling. I'm no longer alone.

Slowly I turn. I see. I smile.

At the edge of the wood is a young woman, her chestnut brown hair flowing over her shoulders. The white dress she wears has a powder blue ribbon around the waist.

She looks just like she did on our wedding day.

Our eyes meet. She smiles.

I whisper her name.

"Joan."

Twenty-One

"You can't stay here, Tom."

Joan and I are sitting on the front bench under the watchful eye of Mary, our only companion aside from the statue of Saint Bernadette frozen in rapture and adoration at the appearance of the Immaculate Conception. Even the birds have left us alone.

"That's what you told me the last time," I say.

"It's even more true now," she says.

I know she's not real—that none of this is real. But her hand feels warm on mine. She smells the way she did when she was alive, all honeysuckle and lavender.

"You don't know what it's been like for me."

"Oh, my dear, I do," she smiles. "I know all about what you've been going through. I've seen everything."

I know what the Church believes—that those in heaven and in purgatory know what's happening on earth. But I'm ashamed that Joan's seen me.

"It's okay, Tom," she says, reading my thoughts. "You can be forgiven for all of that. God will forgive you. You don't need to be ashamed, and you don't need my forgiveness."

"It's just been so hard. I feel completely lost."

"But you're not lost. He hasn't abandoned you, He's stayed with you through all of this. You've just not felt him because of your own pain."

I sigh. "I don't even know why I'm still in Myerton. I mean, I found your killer. That's the only reason I can think of why God sent me there in the first place. I'm not doing anyone any good by staying."

Joan laughs, that clear tinkling bell of a laugh she had in life. "Oh, Tom! Do you think the only reason God sent you back to Myerton was to find my killer? That could have happened without you."

I look at her, uncomprehending. "What other reason could there be?"

She smiles at me, taking my hand in hers. "You know. Look in your heart. You know."

I'm quiet, barely breathing, looking in Joan's eyes. I'm trying to figure out what she means.

Then, it comes to me. Of course. It's the only thing possible.

"Helen?" I whisper.

Joan smiles. "Yes. Helen."

"But . . . but why? I don't understand?"

"Don't you?"

I look into her eyes. "I love her, Joan."

"I know," she says.

"But I can't love her and stay a priest."

"That would seem to be a problem," she nods.

I pause, hesitant to ask the next question. "Does God still want me to be a priest?"

She sighs. "I'm afraid you're going to have to find that out for yourself. Just like you did the first time."

"But," I protest, "you told me to become a priest when you came to me."

She shakes her head. "No, my darling. I told you God didn't want you to stay here. You decided that meant you had a call to the priesthood."

I'm astonished. All these years, I remembered her telling me God wanted me to become a priest, to serve him that way for the rest of my life.

But she's right. She never said that.

"So, have . . . have I been wrong all these years? About being called to the priesthood? About everything?"

Joan smiles. "Sorry, Tom. That's another thing you're going to have to decide."

"But I don't want to decide," I say like a petulant child.

At that, Joan gets a severe look on her face. "You have no choice," she says with authority. "Remember, He doesn't force us to do anything. He gave us the freedom to choose the good. He gave us the responsibility to decide. If you stay a priest, it will be because you decide to. If you decide to leave, however, be very clear on why. Do not do it for her, Tom. Don't put her in that position. That's the surest way to turn love into resentment."

Joan stands up. She looks down at me, a smile on her face once again.

"But when you're trying to decide, just make sure you're asking the right question."

Looking up at her, I ask, "The right question?"

"Yes," she nods. "It's not, 'Do I stay a priest?' The question is, 'Who do I love more?'"

God, or Helen.

A seemingly impossible choice.

"I'll pray for you, Tom, and for Helen," Joan says. "I like her. I think we would have been friends. She's good for you."

"Joan," I say. "Do you know what I decide?"

She shakes her head. "No, my darling. But He does."

From the woods, I hear a little girl's voice. "Mama? Mama?"

I look in the direction of the voice, then at Joan. She smiles and nods.

"I want to go see her," I whisper.

"You will, someday," she says.

Joan turns and begins to walk back to the woods.

"Wait! Don't leave yet!"

She turns and walks back to me. She takes me by the shoulders, steps up, and kisses me.

"I love you, Tom. But it's time for us to go."

"Tom!"

I look around. I hear other voices. Women's voices. They sound worried.

"Tom! Please wake up! Come back to me!"

I grimace as pain begins to shoot through my body.

Joan and the Grotto are fading from my sight. "Go to her, Tom. She needs you. You need her."

The voices get louder. They sound worried. Someone's been hurt. Someone they love.

"But—"

"Go, Tom!" Joan says, in a commanding voice, as she vanishes from my sight along with the Grotto.

I'm left in darkness. There's nothing.

Then someone says my name.

I turn, and walk toward the voice . . .

Twenty-Two

The next thing I hear is a squeaky voice whisper, "You're right, Mom, he is cute when he's asleep."

"Joan?" I whisper as my eyes flutter open. I see a face smiling down at me. Out of focus, but I can see raven black hair.

"I told you I wouldn't always be around to make sure you didn't get hurt," Helen quips.

My vision clears. I smile weakly.

"I thought I could scare them off," I croak.

"You should have woken me up," she says. "I do have my gun, you know."

"I didn't think you'd hear me because of the headphones, because when I—" I stop myself before I can finish the sentence, before I reveal my shameful secret to her.

I try to sit up. Pain shoots through me. I grunt.

"That's enough of that," Helen says as she helps me lay back down. "You lay still."

"God, okay, I admit, that was stupid," I say.

"Tom, you scared the hell out of me when I saw you crumpled on the floor like that," she says. "I got out there just as one of them was about to kick you in the head again. As it was, they still pushed me out of the way, even though I had my gun. They ran down the stairs and out of the house. Fortunately, I think I clipped one of them, judging from the howl I heard."

"You shot at them?" I say incredulously.

"I managed to squeeze off a couple of rounds," Helen says. "My aim wasn't too good, I was still shaky from finding you. Fortunately, one of the bullets missed Nola and hit the wall."

I sit up and quickly fall back on the bed in agony. "You almost shot Mom!"

"Oh, it missed her by a mile," Helen says. "She made a big deal out of nothing."

"I wish you'd had let the guy kick me in the head again."

"She's fine, she's fine," Helen says. "I told her you'd patch the drywall and replace the glass in the front door."

My mouth falls open. "But . . . but . . ."

I'm cut off when a sharp pain radiates from my groin. "How badly am I hurt?"

"Doctor says it could have been a lot worse. You don't have any broken ribs. No internal injuries. No skull fracture, but you do have a pretty serious concussion. And, you have other injuries . . ." Helen blushes and looks the other way as I hear a slight squeak of rubber wheels on the floor next to me. I turn my head slightly to see Gladys sitting in her wheelchair right at eye level with me.

I'm confused and blurt out, "I thought you couldn't get here for a while?"

She pats my hand softly and says, "Hey, as soon as Mom told me what happened, I was on the first plane out." She looks around and adds ruefully, "I know what it's like to wake up in a hospital."

I shift again, trying to get comfortable. Some of what happened comes back to me and I desperately want to see certain damage for myself. But I'm not about to look right now.

I am trying to figure out an excuse to get them to leave when the door to my room flies open.

"Oh, Tommy!" Mom's anguished voice bursts into the room.

"By the way," Helen whispers. "Your Mom's here."

"Thanks for the warning," I whisper back.

Helen makes way for Mom. She flies to my hospital bed and lands on me a little too hard, wrapping me in a hug that sends pain shooting through me.

"Oh, Tommy," Mom says, "I've been so worried. But it's going to be okay."

I return the hug. "I'm fine, Mom."

She stops hugging and looks at me. "I just spoke to the insurance company, and I'm completely covered for the damage after you pay the deductible!"

I open my mouth to speak, but words fail me. Helen rolls her eyes. Just then, a nurse comes in.

"Ah, Mr. Greer," she says with a thick West-Indian accent, "you're awake. How do you feel?"

"OK, I guess." I say weakly.

"Well, it's a miracle you're doing as well as you are, Mr. Greer," she says as she checks my IVs and looks at the monitor leads. "A nasty concussion, some pretty bad bruises, the swelling in your groin, of course, but no broken bones, no internal injuries." She turns to Helen, Mom, and Gladys, "I have to do a few things. Why don't you ladies get some coffee? You look like you could use a break."

Helen nods and looks at me. "We'll be back in a little while."

"I'll still be here," I quip.

"Don't worry, Tommy," Mom says as Helen and Gladys lead her out. "I'll be fine!"

I wave as they leave. The nurse puts the blood pressure cuff on my arm and presses a button on the monitor. As it inflates, she says, "Your wife's been worried about you, Mr. Greer."

I look at her. "My wife?"

"Uh-huh," she says as she watches the numbers on the screen climb. "She hasn't left your side since you came in. Raised quite a ruckus when we tried to get her to leave. You've got quite a woman there."

Still looking at the screen she raises her eyebrows. "That's very odd," she mutters.

"What is it?" I ask.

"Your blood pressure's high," she says. "Funny. It's been normal the entire time."

Twenty-Three

About a half-an-hour later, after the nurse had left and I'd had a chance to survey the damage down below, Helen returns with two cups of coffee and a bag. Thankfully, Mom's not with her.

"I persuaded her to go home," she says in response to my look. "I had Gladys take her."

I sigh. "That was a true act of mercy," I say as she hands me one of the coffees. I take a sip. It's hot, sweet, and creamy.

"That really hits the spot," I say, shifting on the bed to get comfortable. "Thank you, Mrs. Greer."

Helen's cup stops at her lips. She smiles sheepishly, saying, "Oh, the nurse told you that, huh?" She shrugs. "It was the only way they would let me stay. Fortunately, they didn't ask for my identification. I guess they didn't want to push a hysterical wife."

"You were hysterical?"

"I won't lie, Tom, I wasn't the picture of calm," she says, taking a sip of her coffee. "You're not upset, are you?"

"Not at all, but I am curious as to why you didn't just say you were my sister."

"Actually, maybe that would have been better. The only thing is, that would put your mom in charge. She would be the one your doctors would be talking to about your, um, injuries. But hey, as you're always reminding me, confession is good for the soul. Let me just call that nurse right now and confess my lie."

She reaches for the call button with a mischievous look on her face as I try to grab her hand and stop her.

"No!" I insist. "I am wrong, you are right. Please, please, remain my wife, at least until this is all over. I'm glad it was you I saw when I woke up. I don't know what I would have done if it was Mom six inches from my face." I shudder a little bit.

She laughs and sits in the chair by my bed. Placing the bag on the small table, she opens it and pulls out a cinnamon roll. Tearing off a piece, she pops it in her mouth. "Mmm-mmm, that's good," she says.

"Did you bring me something?" I say, smiling.

She stops mid-chew. Finishing, she swallows. "Um, I did get two, but I didn't think . . ."

I laugh. "It's okay, I'm just messing with you."

"Ahem." Helen blushes. Gus is standing in the doorway, his sheriff's hat in my hand.

"I can come back later, if you two want to finish, uhm, talking?"

I grin. "Jackass!"

"That's what it says on my business card," he says, returning my grin. He gives Helen a hug, then shakes my hand.

"You look a lot better than when they wheeled you in here," Gus says. "We were worried about you."

"So I hear," I say, glancing at Helen.

"Your guardian angel or whatever you call it was working overtime on that one."

"I looked that bad?"

"Bad? Oh, yeah, Tom."

I lay my head on my pillow. "They broke into Mom's home, Gus. Tried to get into Sonya's room, where Helen was sleeping."

"That's what it looks like to me," Gus says. "Can you tell me what you remember?"

I close my eyes.

"I was just coming out of the bathroom when I heard the glass breaking. I went back into my bedroom to get my phone and call 911. That's when I heard them coming upstairs. They were talking about getting something out of Sonya's bedroom. I knew I had a couple of minutes, because Helen had locked the door."

Out of the corner of my eye, I see Helen jerk her head up and look at me. Anger mixed with confusion replaces concern on her face.

"Why didn't you call me?" Gus asks.

"You wouldn't have gotten there in time," I say weakly. "They would have been long gone, and who knows what they would have done in the meantime."

Gus nods. "Still, pretty stupid of you to take on two huge guys like that. Can you give a description of them?"

"They were, I'd say, late twenties to early thirties. About six-three, around 280 or so. Muscular, they wore all black like something out of the movies. Clean shaven. Can't remember eye color."

"Those are pretty detailed descriptions, Tom," Gus said hesitantly. "Are you sure about them? I mean, they knocked you around pretty good."

"Gus, I'm a priest who's terrible with names," I smile. "I've become very good at remembering faces. Sorry I can't give you anything else."

"You've given me plenty. I'll run their descriptions to see if I can get any hits. Guys like that should stick out like a sore thumb around here."

I nod. "Oh, there's one other thing," I say. "Someone sent them there."

"Oh?" Gus' jaw tightens at that, and the 'Oh' comes out with a little uncertainty.

"Yeah," I say, fixing my old friend with a stare. "They kept referring to 'the boss,' and how 'the boss' was bat-shit crazy to get whatever they were looking for."

"Really?" Gus says, looking more nervous now.

"Uh-huh," I say, still staring at him. "Didn't say a name. But from just the way they talked it was pretty clear they were scared of the boss. Strange, don't you think, Gus? Big guys like that, scared?"

"Well," Gus says nervously. "You know. People. There's, ah, all kinds."

"Yeah," I smile. "I guess. But there's one other thing that bothers me. They knew exactly which room was Sonya's. Now, only someone who'd been in Mom's house before would have known that, don't you think?"

"Look Tom," Gus says, "these guys sound like pros. They may have gotten into the house and cased it any number of ways. You know how scatterbrained your Mom is."

He turns to Helen. "Did you bring your gun with you?"

I start at the question. Helen nods. "It's back at Nola's," she says, "along with my ID. But I don't have a carry permit for Florida, and my jurisdiction—"

"Consider yourself deputized," Gus says. "It'll save me from posting a deputy on the door."

"Gus, I don't think it's necessary—"

"Tom, those guys tried to kill you, probably because you could identify them," Gus says. "They may try to finish the job."

The gravity of his words sink in.

Gus says goodbye and shuts the door of the room. Once we're alone, Helen turns her gaze on me.

"How are you feeling?" she asks.

"Not too bad." I say. "Tired, but OK."

"Do you feel up to a couple more questions?"

"Sure," I say, assuming that she wants more of a description of my attackers.

But instead of her cop voice, the next words I hear are all woman.

"Tom," she says with just the slightest hint of accusation, "how did you know my door was locked?"

I lay there for a second, trying to think of a lie. Unfortunately, it seems that my commitment to honesty remains stronger than my commitment to chastity. Still, maybe I can come up with something sort of true.

"Tom," she asks again, gently, "did you try to open my door last night?"

I know I'm caught, and worse than that, I know I don't want to lie about this. Looking into her azure blue eyes I confess, "Yes, Helen, I did."

"I see," she says, and then more firmly, "To what end, Tom? What was your plan?"

"You want the truth?" I ask.

"That would be my preference, yes."

"I don't know. I might have been satisfied to hear your voice. I told myself that that was all I wanted. And maybe it would have been. But we'll never know now."

She sighs and looks down at her hands, studying them, as if the answer to her questions are on them. Then, with her head still lowered, she says.

"Before we go any further, I have one more question."

"What?"

"Tom," she whispers, "the doctor told me you had a significant amount of prescription sleeping pills in your system. Not a lethal amount, by any means, but more than would typically be prescribed. Were they yours?"

"No," I say, not meeting her eyes. "They're Mom's. I had seen them in the medicine cabinet earlier."

"And did you take them because of me?"

I hear the pain and fear in her voice and realize what she is asking.

"No, Helen, absolutely not!" I assure her. She raises her head but turns it away from me, staring instead out the window.

"Look at me," I command with more force than I feel up to.

She turns and I see tears streaming down her face. I reach out my hand and she takes it, pulling it to her face and clutching it to her cheek, so that I feel her tears on my fingertips.

"Helen, I was tired of thinking about Sonya and God and you. Yes, I did try your door and no, I don't know what I would have done if it had been open. But I took the pills to sleep, nothing more"

"But the dose? Why so much?

"Listen, Mom is a small woman. I figured it would take more to put me out. That's all. It was all then and it's all now."

She lets go with one hand and begins wiping her eyes with the corner of the sheet, even as she's still clutching my hand to her face.

"It's just . . . I was so afraid . . . afraid I'd driven you to something terrible. And that it was all my fault."

"Your fault? How could it be? I'm the one who started everything."

"In the cabin, yes." Helen takes a deep breath and lets it out slowly. "But I'm the one who got on the plane, knowing how I felt about you. Deep down, I knew I was going not just to help you but to be with you. I couldn't stand the idea of not seeing you for three weeks or worse, something happening to you."

She looks down, unable to face me anymore. "I was acting like a love-sick teenager, Tom. I tried on everything in my closet when I was packing. I wanted to feel beautiful, to be attractive to you.

"I knew it was wrong. I knew as soon as I got on the plane. And then, after the cabin, when I realized what I had driven you to, I thought about leaving the next day. But I hesitated over breakfast and then, after we talked to your mother and I realized what might be going on, and that Gus was either too blind or too corrupt to see it, I felt I needed to stay.

"So I willed myself to behave, even after what you said on the porch. I didn't even wear make-up when we went to the dealership, and barely even brushed my hair. I thought I could put you off by really looking my worst."

Then, rubbing her tired eyes and running her fingers through the tangled thicket her hair had become overnight, she adds, "Is it working?"

Looking into her sleepless eyes that watched me all night, and seeing her mess of unkempt hair that was still so black it reminds me of a chilly, starless sky, I smile sadly and reply, "Not so much."

Tears well up in her eyes again. "Then I have to go!" she says, her voice choked with emotion. "I'll fly back to Myerton tomorrow and by the time you get home, I'll be gone! I was prepared to do it last summer when I got the offer from Nebraska. After everything happened with Father Leonard, I asked them if I could delay making the move. I was still going to go, for all the reasons I told you. But as time went on, and we spent more of it together, I—I—I realized I didn't want to go anywhere you weren't. That, Tom, is why I turned down the offer. Since then, I've had some calls from a good-sized town in Montana. Their mayor, some guy named Bart Ovisaries, wants me to come out and interview for a job as their Chief of Police. It'll be more money and a better position. It will just be better for both of us if I take the job."

I panic. "No, Helen, no," I plead. "You can't do that!"

"I can and I must, Tom!" she cries. "I can't keep doing this to you and I can't take much more of what it's doing to me!"

She starts sobbing again and looks ready to collapse. Surprising myself, I say a quick prayer, not asking for help for myself this time, but for her.

And the answer suddenly appears, clear as day.

"Helen," I say, very calmly. "When did you last sleep?"

"I'm fine, Tom, I was able to doze a little in the chair."

"That's not what the nurse said. She said every time she came in to check on me you were wide awake, watching me."

"Still, I'm sure I drifted off some time."

"All the same, by my calculations you haven't slept in more than 24 hours. You're exhausted and not thinking straight. Go to Mom's house and get some rest. Give me a chance to get out of here and get my head cleared of the drugs and we'll talk, really talk this time. How about that?"

"OK, I could use some sleep but that doesn't mean—"

I've already buzzed the nurse, who appears before Helen can finish her sentence.

"Nurse Williams, could you please help my wife call an Uber and make sure she gets out to the front of the hospital. She is overtired and I am concerned for her safety."

"Certainly, Mr. Greer," she says with a twinkle in her eye, "I need to stay on the floor but I'm sure security will be glad to escort her." She takes Helen by the arm firmly as she protests and says pleasantly, "You come with me, dearie, and we'll get you all situated. I'll call you myself later and give you a report on our patient here." Then, calling over her shoulder she adds, "Oh, and Mr. Greer, I'll check on you when I come back to make sure you don't need a shot of something to help you rest."

I recognize a warning when I hear one and close my eyes, planning to fake sleep, only to have the physical and emotional exhaustion of what I've been through make it all too real.

As I drift off I think, *I need to talk to Helen as soon as I get home.*

Then, another thought jars me.

Someone broke into Mom's house looking for something that's in Sonya's room.

They didn't find it.

They could come back.

Twenty-Four

I wake up in a dark room and for a minute, forget where I am. One move to reach for my phone reminds me not only that I'm in the hospital, but also why.

I get my phone and pull up the screen to find out it's 4:00 a.m. in the morning. I remember one time I was up this early was when the Archbishop sent me on a short retreat to Our Lady of the Mount after Leonard's suicide. The bell had woken me then, calling me to begin my day by praising God. I knew the brothers were silently rising and leaving their cells, softly chanting. I remembered how I had so often joined them joyfully during my time with them before I left for seminary.

That day, however, I rolled over, covered my head with my pillow, and went back to sleep.

Not this time. I may not be a priest next week but I am today, and it's time to say Morning Prayer. Gritting my teeth, I pull up my Breviary app and begin by making the sign of the Cross and saying, "Lord, come to my assistance."

For the first time in months, I give it my all. It's better, but something is missing. Something separates me from God like a layer of barnacles on my soul.

I am just finishing when the nurse comes in.

This one is young, maybe about 12 in my mind but probably more like in her mid-20s. She takes my vitals, asks about my pain level, looks at everything, and then asks if I need anything. I hesitate and then say, "Yes. I need a priest. Do you have one on staff?"

"The clergymen in town rotate hospital duty. I can send whoever's here up."

"No," I emphasize, "I need a Catholic priest." She looks confused so I add, "I need to confess some stuff." This gets her attention and she scrambles off with promises to get back to me "real soon."

She proves as good as her word and returns in a few minutes, saying cheerfully, "You're in luck. Father Marsh is on duty today. I just spoke with him and he's on his way." Then, with a look of serious concern on her face, she whispers, "I'm sure whatever you've done, it can't be that bad." I thank her and send her on her way.

I open my Confession app and begin the Examination of Conscience, getting only halfway through before Father Marsh knocks on the door.

"Mr. Greer," he says with a slight accent. "I am Father Marsh. How can I be of help?"

I look into the smiling gentle face of this man of God, taking in his ebony-colored skin and his ivory teeth and for a moment, my heart leaves me. His looks and his accent make it clear that he is from Africa. Every Catholic knows African priests make the very best confessors—but only if you are serious about changing. Something about the harshness of their homelands and

547

upbringing, I suppose, gives them an amazing ability to ferret out any efforts on the penitent's part to justify themselves.

Fortunately, I quickly realize that this is exactly what I need and without hesitation, I say, "I need you to hear my confession, Father."

He pulls a chair up close to my bed, unrolls and dons the purple stole of his office—our office, I have to remind myself—and clears his throat.

"Let us begin this Sacrament of God's mercy in the name of the Father, and of the Son, and of the Holy Spirit."

"Bless me Father, for I have sinned. It has been four months since my last confession," I say in a low voice. "Father, you need to know I am a priest."

"Then you know how this goes," he chuckles. He pauses before saying, "You sound troubled, my brother."

"I am," I whisper.

Again, silence. "You are doubting your calling."

I swallow. "Yes."

"You're older. How many years have you been ordained? "

"Almost eight. I became a priest after my wife died."

"Ah, I see," he says.

He sits quietly, waiting for me to begin. That's what we're taught in seminary. This is the time for us to listen as the penitent lists their sins. Most lists are relatively simple. I yelled at my kids, got angry with my wife, a coworker irritated me. Occasionally, you'll have a big one. Pornography, masturbation, something else sexual. But usually it's pretty standard stuff. I have yet to have someone confess to murder.

Come to think of it, yes, I have.

So there's a way this goes that every Catholic grows up knowing. In and out in under ten minutes.

My problem is I don't even know where to begin.

As if reading my thoughts, the Father says, "Why don't you start with what finally brought you to this point today?"

I chuckle. "This will take a while."

He laughs. "I have no place else to be, brother."

I took a deep breath. "To understand why I'm here, I need to start with Helen."

For the next half-hour, I tell this fellow priest my story, trying to hit the things most relevant to why I was there. Joan. Meeting Helen again. Becoming aware of our mutual attraction. Leonard. My growing uncertainty about my calling. My growing feelings for Helen. Sonya's death and my inability or unwillingness to forgive her for the past. The cabin. Trying her doorknob.

"For these and all my other sins, Father, I am very sorry."

He sits quietly for a moment, stone-faced.

He's probably trying to figure out how long a thousand Hail Marys will take.

Then, Father March does something unexpected.

He smiles.

"Oh, my brother," he says, his voice filled with compassion. "The Lord has blessed you with many great crosses, hasn't he?"

"Blessed?"

"Yes. Oh, I know the pain is terrible, and yes, you have fallen into sins which you are right to repent of and seek God's mercy for. But you are a man who is truly blessed. You have known love in all its forms. You have known the love of a wife. You know the love of Christ, His Church, and the Blessed Mother. And you know the love of this woman you speak of with such affection."

"But I can't love her," I whisper. "I do so much. But I know I can't."

"Why? Why can't you?"

I'm taken aback, not only by the question but by the vehemence with which he asked it.

"Because . . . because . . . we're prohibited. Our vows—"

"No! No! NO!" he shouts. "Father, you are misunderstanding our vows." He takes a deep breath. "What are the vows in question?"

Really? We're going to play twenty questions? "Celibacy. And chastity is included in that."

"And what do those vows prohibit?"

Apparently, we are going to play twenty questions. "We can't marry. We need to remain sexually pure, so no sexual acts with another person, no masturbation, nothing like that."

"That's right," he says. "We cannot marry. We cannot engage in acts of sexual intimacy. Both are grave sins for us." He pauses. "What is not on the list?"

I'm not sure what he means for a moment. I go over what I just said in my mind. I review the little the Catechism says about priestly celibacy. I go over the discussions in my seminary classes in as great a detail as I can remember.

Then, I know.

"Love," I whisper.

He smiles. "Exactly. The Church does not prohibit us loving another. It can no more do that than prohibit us from breathing."

"But," I say, "we're taught that celibacy, not taking a wife, having a family, allows us to serve with an undivided heart."

"True," he says. "Because we do not have the cares and concerns of a husband and father, we can devote our attention to our parishes. But I believe there are many kinds of divided hearts. Right now, yours is divided against itself. You're struggling with the feelings of love you have for this woman. You're struggling over what it means for your calling. This struggle is causing you immense pain. It's in this struggle that your physical desires—which you have to a greater degree than most other priests, because you've enjoyed the pleasures of the marital bed—are coming to the surface. To make your pain go away."

"It's not working, though," I say derisively.

"It usually doesn't. A husband experiences sexual attraction to a woman not his wife. It causes him pain, pain exacerbated perhaps because of marital strife. He thinks that acting on his attraction will make the pain go away. So he commits adultery. And instead of going away, the pain increases."

I sigh. "So what do I do?"

"You can start by accepting that you love this woman," he says. "Then, you need to see that loving this woman does not in and of itself put you in conflict with our Lord. It's only if this love is expressed outside the boundaries established for us by the Church that it does."

"I just . . . I so much want her to be in my life. That can't happen if I remain a priest."

"Tell me," he asks quietly. "What do you miss most in a wife?"

I don't even need to think about that. "Companionship. A confidant. Someone to share my day with, my thoughts, my fears. Someone who understands me, and accepts me for who I am, warts and all."

"Not the sex?"

I chuckle. "Most of the time, no."

"Father," he says. "You can have everything you miss in a wife with this woman and still remain a priest. You cannot be sexually intimate, true. But you can be spiritually close, emotionally supported, and supportive. If you can accept that, and figure out how to do that, and if she is willing to be like a wife to you in every way except name and act, then you can and should love this woman."

"And if I can't?"

He doesn't answer for a moment. "If you cannot, or she cannot," he says slowly, "then you'll have a choice to make. Which relationship will you end?"

I sit quietly. Father Marsh, a man I just met, has summed up my struggle in one sentence. But he's also given me hope that it doesn't have to be either-or.

Which is exactly what Helen was trying to tell me in the cabin.

"Now, as to your sister and your inability to forgive her," he says.

Okay, now he's going to lower the boom.

"Lack of forgiveness is a grave sin, Father. Perhaps graver than the sexual sins you've already confessed. It's not easy to forgive someone who has wronged us. This is why our Lord commands it. But as a priest, you are a vessel of God's mercy. In the confessional. If you were in my place, what would you tell a penitent?"

"That's easy," I sigh. "That they needed to forgive, and ask forgiveness for how they wronged the other person."

"I see my job is half done," he chuckles. "You know what you do. My suggestion is to do something for your sister. I don't mean say Masses for her or pray for her soul—though of course you should do that. Think of something you can do now to help you try to see your sister in a different light. Try to see her as a hurt and suffering child of God, instead of just someone who hurt you and with whom you are angry. Try to think of something that will help you see her world through her eyes. Can you think of something?"

I don't even have to think. I know what it should be.

"Yes," I whisper. "I know what I need to do."

Father Marsh orders me to say one rosary for Helen and another one for Sonya as my penances. These are pretty severe but he assures me, "You need the practice." He gives me absolution and shakes my hand, assuring me of his continued prayers.

He turns to leave, then says, "Oh, one more thing, Father. This is not a penance, for you cannot complete it now, but you need to speak to your bishop when you get home. He needs to know of your struggles so that he can help you."

I nod. I knew I was going to have to do that. "I will. I had already planned on having a talk with him."

"Good, good," he says with a smile. "May God bless you, my brother. I will leave you with Our Lady."

Lighter than I've felt in months, I grasp the beads and begin.

Twenty-Five

When I finish the required decades, I continue praying, delighting once again in Our Lady and her Son. I am doing so when I hear a knock on the door.

"Come in," I call. In response, a sheepish-looking Helen peeks around the door.

I smile and wave to her to come in. She eases through the door, looks me over quickly, then says, "You look better."

"So do you," I reply without thinking. But she does. She's obviously still tired but she looks like she's better prepared to face the day. Her hair's brushed, and she has a touch of lipstick. She has color back in her cheeks.

"Have they said anything about when they might let you out?" she asks.

"No," I reply. "I haven't seen the doctor this morning." I pause, considering if I should tell her. "I have seen a priest, however."

"Oh?" she replies with raised eyebrows.

I nod. "He heard my confession. All of it. Everything." I look at my hands and feel a tear come. "I'm sorry, Helen."

She sighs. "Oh, Tom."

I hold up a hand. "Please. I need to finish. I didn't realize until yesterday how my feelings, my acting on those feelings, affects you. I've been so focused on my own pain—how much it hurts to love you and not be able to have you—that I didn't see how much pain you're in. I should have, and I'm sorry."

"Tom," she whispers. "There's no need for you to apologize. I've made my choices with full knowledge of the reality of the situation. I've chosen to fall in love with a priest. I could have stopped myself from doing it at any time. I could have stayed away from you. I could have left Myerton. But I didn't want that. Because . . . because what we have is so special to me . . ."

"It's special to me, too," I say. "And I was satisfied. But my feelings for you got wrapped up in this conflict inside me. When that happened, I was no longer satisfied just having you as my friend, my companion, my confidant. I wanted . . . more."

Helen nods, a rueful smile on her face. "That, I understand."

I take a deep breath. "Helen," I say. "I love you. But you're not my first love. The Church is. I don't know if ultimately God wants me to stay a priest or not. But you said it yourself. I'm married. I can't just leave when things get hard."

She closes her eyes and nods. "That's the last thing I want, for you to leave the priesthood for me. It's been so difficult to see the change in you at Mass these last few months."

"I'm curious about what you mean?" I say.

"Remember what Gladys told you after she saw you celebrate Mass? She described it as passionate. She told you she felt like she was watching the tenderest act of love she'd ever seen. The loving and gentle way you held the Eucharist when you presented it to us turned her insides to jelly."

"Hmm, not sure I've ever had that effect on a woman." I grin.

A little smile plays on her lips. "Aside from the fact that that's not true, I assure you, she was right. I've been to a lot of Masses, Tom, and I saw it. You loved what you were doing. It was like you were joined with the liturgy body and soul."

Grasping my hand a little harder, she leans closer to look at me. "I haven't seen that in months. Not since Father Leonard. You've lost your love for it, Tom. You don't look at the Eucharist the way you did. The gleam you had in your eye every time you celebrated Mass is gone."

She lowers her eyes. "I only see it," Helen whispers, "when you look at me. And Tom, I love you too, but I will not be the other woman. I'll be your friend. I'll be your companion. I'll be your confidant. I'll take care of you when you're hurt. Hell, when it's called for, I'll rescue you from bad guys. But I will not be the one you cheat on the God I love with. He deserves better than that."

I nod slowly. "You're right. I can't promise I'm not going to stumble. But I'm committed to trying everything possible to repair my relationship with God."

"And while you do that, darling," she says, smiling, "I'll be praying for you, and supporting you, and doing everything I can to help you. But Tom, and it hurts me to say this, I was serious about leaving Myerton. And I will, if that's what it takes for you to remain a priest."

"I understand what you're saying. But I want to tell you something. If I decide to leave the priesthood, it won't be for you. It'll be because God tells me to."

I take her hand and squeeze it in mine. We both exhale, and I can feel the tension in the room disappear.

I take another deep breath. "OK, now that that's out of the way, we've got more urgent issues. It hit me right after you left. They didn't find whatever they were looking for, so they're bound to be back. You've got to get back home to protect Mom."

"Don't worry about that," she insists, more relieved than concerned. "She's staying with your Aunt Diana until we get home. And," she adds before I can ask, "Gus has someone watching the house 24/7."

"OK, then." I ease back against the pillows, thankful to have some things off my mind.

"But there's something else, Tom. Gladys got into Sonya's phone last night and there was an unsent text message to you. All it said was, "Look under my Nutcracker." There was no punctuation at the end so she might have meant to write more but then again she might not have. I turned that bedroom inside out and did not find anything remotely related to anything

J. R. MATHIS AND SUSAN MATHIS

Nutcracker. I stopped by Diana's on my way here and asked your mom about it and she insisted that Sonya had never shown any interest in Nutcrackers of any kind."

"She's right," I say. "I mean, I guess we must have heard the music at Christmas but beyond that, I can't remember any significance about the word."

"OK," Helen says, her best cop face on. "What else could it mean? Did anyone in the area put up Nutcracker decorations?"

I shake my head, "Not that I can think of, but Helen, I've been gone a long time. And, Christmas has been over for a while."

"Then let's go in a different direction. Could it be a nickname for someone?"

I smile ruefully, "Well, there's at least one guy running around out there that I would call that."

Helen blushes and says with a smile, "So it was some sort of warning that you failed to heed?"

"If so," I reply, "I promise I'll never make that mistake again."

We both laugh and it feels good. I realize that this is what I want, what I love more than the way she smells or the softness of her lips or, yes, even her mysterious body. I want *her*, her throaty laughter, her sharp mind, her sparkling eyes. If I could just have this . . . it might be enough.

Before I can consider this further, there's a knock at the door and the doctor strides in, very businesslike.

"Well Mr. Greer, you look like you're feeling better," he says. "The nurse tells me you were able to pass urine. That's a good sign. Let's just take a look at everything."

He passes his light over my eyes briefly and rotates my shoulder slightly, making me wince. "I'm sorry," he says, "I know it's sore but there is no serious damage." Then, without warning, he pulls back the blankets and lifts my gown. As he does, Helen closes her eyes like a 13-year-old at a horror movie. I don't know whether to be flattered or horrified. She stands there like that until the doctor pulls the blanket back in place with a resounding snap. Then I watch with amusement as she opens first one eye and then the other, just to make sure everything is covered up.

The doctor makes a few notes and then turns to me.

"As I told your wife," he says, "the MRI we did last night did not indicate any permanent damage to your genitals, though your testicles could continue to swell for a few more days. Your penis is also badly bruised as you might have noticed when you urinated."

Noticed? I almost cried.

"So, no sexual activity for at least two weeks. I understand you're here from out of town and will probably be home by then. Just check in with your regular physician and let them give you the go-ahead for intercourse before you try anything."

My regular physician is an elderly Dominican who spent most of his career as a medical missionary to the Congo. I doubt any sort of "go-ahead for intercourse" will be forthcoming.

I realize with horror that he's still talking. "You two may need to try some different positions the first few times. I'll have the nurse attach an illustrated fact sheet to your discharge orders."

By this time, I am reaching in vain for my morphine drip. Helen has turned bright red before going completely white.

"So, if you have no questions, I'll put in your discharge papers."

"No, I have no questions," I say as fast as I can.

"Now what about you, Mrs. Greer? Injuries like these can be very traumatic for the partner, too."

Sounding not unlike Peewee Herman with his throat in a vice, Helen squeaks, "No, I have no questions. Not a one. None at all."

"Good. Well, I hope that you enjoy a speedy recovery Mr. Greer and are back to normal soon."

He turns to leave but stops at the door. "Oh, one more thing."

I hear Helen mutter, "Oh please God, no." I want to pull the blanket over my head, but instead say in the best voice I can summon, "Yes, doctor."

"You're going to want some sort of loose pants to wear home. I know you're travelling so I can ask the nurse to outfit you with some scrubs."

"That will be fine, doctor. Thank you."

He leaves and Helen collapses into her chair, bent over with her face in her hands. I realize I'm very hot under these blankets but wouldn't dare think of removing even one of them.

Finally, after a few minutes I say, "That really is weird about the Nutcracker."

Looking relieved, Helen chimes in, "Yes, it is."

Twenty-Six

We get back to Mom's house a few hours later to find Gladys making herself at home in the den. I mean, really at home. She has equipment set up on nearly every surface and a Hello Kitty sleeping bag on the couch. Thankfully, Mom agreed to stay one more night at Aunt Diana's.

Though I had to pay a high price for persuading her.

"Well, if you're sure, Tommy. I mean, I guess it's OK, since that little crippled girl can act as a chaperone. Of course, it's not like you could get into trouble with what's happened to you down there and all. I guess it's a good thing you're not going to want children or anything. You know, maybe God knew this was going to happen and that's why he let you become a priest."

I am way too tired and sore to have this conversation, so I just say, "Yes, Mom, that must be it."

Gladys and I are sitting in the den, me in my Dad's old recliner, the most comfortable chair in the house, and her on the couch. We're talking again about the Nutcracker but coming up with nothing while Helen is upstairs changing clothes.

She comes down in comfy-looking sweatpants and a T-Shirt, carrying a coffee mug and looking perplexed.

"What's up?" I ask.

"Someone's been in my bedroom," Helen says.

"What do you mean?"

"This morning, I was still feeling pretty rough so I made myself a cup of coffee first thing and then carried it back upstairs to finish while I got dressed. I realized I didn't have a coaster so I set it on a napkin I had in my purse. I know I did this because I remember thinking that I certainly didn't want to take a chance with damaging anything of your mother's, especially with food."

"I get that. But what's your point?"

"The mug was on the dresser but the napkin was on the floor."

"Are you sure you didn't drop it yourself?"

"Positive. I was obsessed with protecting that Ikea-era antique."

"Hmmm. So you think the bad guys came back while we were gone?"

"Well, that's just the thing. Gus assured me he had people watching the house. In fact, he was here when I got home and someone else was on guard when I left."

"Then no one could have gotten in," I say, thoroughly confused.

While we are talking, Gladys is uncharacteristically silent. Still fiddling with some connections, she suddenly says, "Unless it was one of the cops who broke in."

Helen and I look at Gladys, who is still working.

"But why would any one of them do that?" I ask.

Gladys stops what she's doing and looks at me. "Maybe to try to find what your attackers couldn't."

"But that would mean . . ." I begin.

"That Gus is either involved in this or knows who is," Helen finishes.

I slump back in my seat, suddenly exhausted. My side and shoulder feel sore and tender and, well, other things are even worse. But there is so much to figure out. I pull myself together and ask, "So, where do we go from here?"

"We've got to find this Nutcracker," Gladys declares. "Could it be a business or a restaurant?"

"Not that I can think of," I say.

"Let me do a search," she adds, tapping away on her keyboard.

Then Helen chimes in, "Someone needs to question Gus and try to see what he's hiding, someone he'll trust."

"That would be me," I say, speaking through what feels like a thin fog.

"Yes," Helen agrees.

"I'll go ahead and give him a call now. Maybe he can stop by tonight."

I turn my head to the table where my cell phone is and the light from the lamp hits my eyes, causing an explosion of pain in my head. I close my eyes and try to feel for the cell phone but accidentally knock it off the table. I try to reach over the side to get it but my shoulder just won't let me.

I'm about to try again when I hear Helen call my name. I turn slowly, waiting for my head to stop spinning. That's when I see it.

Helen is looking at me in a way that I have never seen before, something between affection and scrutiny playing across her face. Then she turns to Gladys and says, "Gladys, I'm going to take Tom upstairs now and put him to bed."

Gladys looks like she is about to giggle but something in Helen's tone stops her.

"We'll talk more about this when I get back," Helen finishes.

I want to protest but my heart is just not in it. Helen steps quickly to the chair and bending beside me, throws the latch that propels it forward. But instead of letting it land with the "thwack" it normally would, she controls its move back into an upright position. Then she takes my cell phone and puts it in her pocket before extending her hand to me to help me up.

"This isn't necessary," I start to protest, determined to stand on my own, but as I sway a little and she steadies me, I realize it is.

"Come on, Tom," she says with a smile. "Yield to the logic of the situation."

I do and she guides me upstairs, her left hand under my elbow, her right in the small of my back. As we leave the room, I swear I hear Gladys sigh and sniffle a little behind us.

I pause at the bathroom door and Helen takes the hint. She opens it and then pulls it shut, not closing it completely. I want to tell her that it's not necessary but I'm not 100 percent sure it's not, especially given what happened last time I went.

Fortunately, this time is better and we're soon down the hall in my room. Before she can say anything, I say casually, "These scrubs are so comfortable, I think I'll just sleep in them."

"That's a good idea," she replies, saving us both significant embarrassment. Then she pulls back the covers from my unmade bed and helps me settle in.

I hate myself for this but I relish her taking care of me. It feels better than anything has felt in a long time.

Maybe the priest was right. Maybe this can work.

Looking around my room, she realizes my meds are still downstairs and insists on going down to get them. I brace myself for a fight when she comes back.

She comes into the room with my bag, a pleasant smile, and a big glass of water. She places it on my nightstand, then retrieves a prescription bottle containing five Oxycontin tablets.

"Helen," I say softly in the hopes that my head won't split open, "I don't need those, just some Tylenol."

She eyes me warily and says, "Why not?"

"You of all people should know, after Sonya. I'm not going to take a chance getting hooked."

"Tom," she begins.

I cut her off, speaking through gritted teeth, "No. A little suffering is good for the soul. I can offer it up. I'll be fine."

"But it's not necessary, Tom," Helen says. "You're not your sister. Besides, it's only five pills.

"That's what it was when Sonya got hooked."

"Yes, but that was a long time ago. They didn't know then what we know now."

"Maybe, but it's not worth taking a chance. Now, are you going to bring me the Tylenol, or do I have to get it myself."

"No, I'll get it for you, if you're sure that's what you want."

"I'm sure."

She returns with two white pills, which she hands me with only a slight look of disapproval. I wash them down with the water she hands me and she gets up to leave. She stops at the doors and turns, saying casually, "I'm leaving this door and my door open so just call out if you need anything."

I almost protest, but then realize I've been disagreeable enough so I just thank her and say goodnight.

Twenty-Seven

I sleep pretty well, only getting up once to top off my meds. I pick up my cell phone to say Morning Prayer, deciding that kneeling is not a good idea but sitting in a chair is doable. Having successfully finished my prayers without collapsing, I decide to make my way to the shower. That goes so well that I conclude it is safe for me to make my way downstairs. I try not to be upset that no one has bothered to start breakfast, though there is the distinct smell of coffee in the air.

I get to the door of the den and hear the sound of typing coming from the other side. I knock softly, not wanting to startle Gladys. She opens the door, pressing one finger to her lips and then pointing over her shoulder. Behind her, a sleeping Helen is stretched out on the Hello Kitty sleeping bag. Gladys motions me out the door and softly closes it behind her. Then she turns to me and says, "Good morning, Dad."

"Good morning, Gladys," I reply as we make our way into the kitchen. "Why is Helen asleep on the couch?"

Grinning, Gladys says, "She fell asleep there about four and I didn't want to wake her."

"Well, where did you sleep, then?" I ask, looking around for signs of blankets or pillows or something.

"Me? Oh, I'll catch some winks later. I kinda got caught up in everything and lost track of time. Anyway, what about some breakfast?"

"Sounds good to me. I think Mom has some cereal around here."

I find a box of acceptable-looking granola and a couple of bowls. Pouring the cereal and milk for Gladys, I ask, "Find anything last night?"

Taking the bowl, she plunges in a spoon and eagerly eats. "Um," she says around a mouthful of granola, "we searched every combination of Nutcracker we could think of, and came up with nothing. There's nothing in the area where your sister could hide something in that was even remotely associated with Nutcracker."

I chew and swallow. "That took you all night to figure out?"

"No," she says before shoving another spoonful of granola in her mouth and chewing. "Chief asked me to pull some information on the Sheriff."

I put my spoon down. "Gus?"

"Um-hum," Gladys answers.

I pause. Do I really want to know what she found out about my best friend?

"Ah, Tom," Gladys says, "Chief asked me not to tell you myself. She wants to do it."

"How bad is it?"

Gladys drops her eyes. "I'm sorry, Dad. I know he's your friend."

I shake my head. "That's a long time ago."

We eat in silence for a moment. "Gladys," I say, "may I ask you something?"

She nods. "You may have noticed, I don't have much of a filter."

I chuckle. "Why do you call Helen Mom?"

"The same reason I've started calling you Dad," she answers.

At my confusion, Gladys smiles. "You know I lost my parents when I was eight years old."

"A hit-and-run accident, right?"

She swallows and nods. "My grandparents were fantastic people and I loved them so much—still do. They did the best job they could with me, but I'm not sure anyone's really prepared to raise a kid like me. They tried really hard to make up for the loss of my parents. But . . ." She sniffles and wipes a tear from her eye.

"It's not the same," I whisper.

She looks at me. "When?"

"I was 12 when my Dad died."

"But you still have your Mom."

I smile ruefully. "That, Gladys, is a complicated situation."

"Mom told me not to be surprised about anything she says," Gladys laughs. "But, still, she's your Mom and you still have her."

She wipes a tear. "So when I started MIT, I was one of the youngest students on campus. I kind of stuck out like a sore thumb—I mean, there weren't any other sixteen-year-olds in wheelchairs in an introduction to forensic science class, or any other for that matter. I was really alone for the first time, and I wanted to be more than just the child genius in a wheelchair. I wanted . . . I wanted people to notice *me*."

I smile. "The wild hair, the clothes. That's when it started."

She sighs. "Yes, that and . . ."

"Ah! I see," I nod.

"Do you know how ridiculously easy it is for a young woman to get a man to notice her if she just acts a certain way or talks a certain way? I mean, being a man, I guess you would. I never thought of myself as pretty, I guess because of the chair, but all of a sudden I started having men pay attention to me. Most of them were my own age, or close to it anyway." She stops and lowers her head so she's looking at her hands.

"But you weren't interested in them," I say quietly. "You were interested in someone older."

She nods. "Do you want to know why I started with him?" she says in a barely audible whisper.

By him, I know she means the incoming President of Myer College. "Was it because somehow he reminded you of your father?"

Gladys nods, then starts sobbing, her shoulders shaking as she cries. I manage to kneel on the floor so I'm eye level with her, and wrap my arms around her to comfort her. She grabs hold of me tightly, squeezing me so hard I'm soon reminded that not only my groin was kicked. But I don't wince. I don't pull away.

After a few minutes, her sobs begin to subside. "I . . . I just wanted someone to care about me, to treat me like a daughter. I missed Mom and Dad so much, I just wanted . . . to be taken care of."

"But Gladys," I say, "you have to know, those men, they . . ."

"I know, I know, Father. But I didn't care. At least I could pretend. And they were really sweet to me, the male professors I . . . and the one female professor . . . I guess I should be ashamed, and part of me is—was then—but at the time, I just didn't care. I was happy. At least, I thought I was. The pain wasn't as great when I was with them. And that's all that mattered to me then."

"Oh, Gladys," is all I can think of to say.

"Long answer to a short question, I know," she manages a smile. "It started about three months after the Chief hired me. She's probably told you I practically live with my computers. I mean, I have an apartment not far from the department, but I don't like being there—too quiet. I was working late, and I guess I fell asleep at my work station. Chief found me and took me to her office—she has a couch. She got me out of the chair and laid me on the couch, covering me with a blanket she had there for some reason—I think she sleeps there sometimes, Tom—and tucked me in. I remember just as I drifted off, I said, 'Good night, Mom.' Now, like I say, I was falling asleep, but I have this memory of a kiss on my forehead and someone whispering, 'Good night, sweetie.' And she's let me call her Mom ever sense—not at the office, but when we're out or she's talking to me less like a boss."

She sighs. "Tom, I'll admit, because I'm not embarrassed by it now, I did develop a huge crush on you the first day I saw you, and I nicknamed you Hot Priest, and I went all squishy inside when you'd speak to me. But the other day, when you talked to me about Richard . . . well, it was the first time in a very long time that a man had talked to me like they really cared about me as a person, like . . . a Dad." She looks at me. "Do you mind? Can I call you Dad sometimes?"

I laugh. "Gladys, I have people calling me Father every moment of the day practically. Of course you can call me Dad." I feel a lump in my throat. "If my wife had lived, and we had a daughter, I'd like to think she would have grown to be as special a young woman as you."

She reaches out to hug me, and I pat her on the back. "Now, daughter," I say, "finish your breakfast. We've got work to do."

Gladys is tilting the bowl to her mouth to drink the rest of the milk when Helen stumbles in.

She looks much worse than I feel. Her hair is tousled and she's surveying us through squinted eyes. "Coffee," she demands.

I point her to the pot and she grunts. I can't help but to smile. Even when we were together, Helen woke up like a cross between Godzilla about to rampage through Tokyo and a grizzly bear awoken early from a winter's sleep. It took at least one cup of coffee for her to become civil.

Sometimes, more than one cup.

Helen pours a cup—she's taking it black today, never a good sign. She plops down in a chair and rests her chin on her hands.

"You okay?" I ask.

"Huh," she grunts. "What's your mom got in that sofa, nails?"

I shrug. "You never know with her."

She stretches, and even from where I'm sitting I can hear the popping of her joints. "God! What a night."

"Gladys has filled me in on everything, including the fact that you fell asleep on the couch about," I look at the time, "five hours ago."

She shakes her head. "Wild goose chase," she mumbles. "I think your sister was screwing with you, all that Nutcracker crap."

I look at Gladys. "Let's leave Mom alone with her coffee for a few minutes. You can show me anything you found."

"Don't tell him, Gladys!" Helen commands. "I'll . . . I'll handle that."

Gladys looks at me, then her. "It's okay," I whisper. We leave Helen alone with her coffee. Soon after, I hear her walk up the stairs.

Helen joins us in the den about twenty minutes later, looking much more human. She's showered, her hair brushed, and she's wearing a soft-looking sweater and a denim skirt—she's always preferred skirts to pants.

"Feel better?" I say.

"Yeah, much, thanks," Helen says sheepishly, "Gladys, I sorta drooled on your Hello Kitty sleeping bag. I'll throw it in the wash as soon as I get some more caffeine in my system."

"That's not necessary, Mom," Gladys says.

"No, I insist. I'm sure there's some blankets around here that you can use if you need a nap." The way Helen says that, it's clear she means it as an order rather than a suggestion.

The words seem to break through her adrenaline, because Gladys yawns and says, "If you're sure, I might take you up on that." Turning to me, she asks, "Dad, which way to the linen closet?"

"There's a narrow door under the staircase just around the corner," I say, "I'll get them."

"No, I will," says Helen before I can move, "You're still recovering."

She returns quickly with a stack of sheets and a worn bedspread covered in lines of musical notes. She starts toward the couch when Gladys cuts her off, taking them from her.

"I can make my own bed, thank you, Mom," she says. We leave her, closing the door behind us.

We're sitting at the table not five minutes later. I have just poured Helen a bowl of cereal when Gladys yells, "Hey guys, come in here!"

We both move as quickly as our various states of infirmity will allow into the den. Gladys is staring at the blanket covering the couch.

She looks up at me and asks, "Tom, what do you know about this blanket?"

"Huh?" I reply, confused by the question. "Not much, I mean, I think Mom got it for Sonya back when she was taking piano lessons. She thought it would encourage her. It didn't really, Sonya still wouldn't practice, but she did love this blanket. As far as I know, it's been on her bed ever since. I have no idea why it isn't now."

"Oh, I know, Tom," Helen says. "You mother made the comment to me that she had taken Sonya's favorite blanket off the bed because she felt like it wasn't nice enough for company. But Gladys" she asks, turning her attention back to her blue-haired assistant, "what is this about?"

"Chief," Gladys says proudly, "these notes are the notes for the Nutcracker Suite."

Twenty-Eight

Ten minutes later, Helen and I are upstairs in her room. Helen is on the floor, looking under Sonya's bed with a flashlight.

"I tell you, Tom, there's nothing here except a number of dust bunnies." She gets back to her feet and sits down on the bed. "The blanket is woven or I'd insist we cut it apart and look inside. This bed is solid wood, with nowhere to hide anything."

"OK," I say, "let's think. Sonya's message said to look under the Nutcracker. If she meant this blanket, it was on her bed at the time she wrote that so maybe something to do with the mattress?"

"I guess it's worth a try," Helen agrees, beginning to strip the sheets off the bed.

All we find underneath is a fresh white mattress.

"Well, that's a bust," Helen says.

I nod while staring at the flat surface. Something's not right about this, but I can't quite place my finger on it.

Then it hits me.

"Helen," I say, pointing at the mattress, "this is not Sonya's. Mom bought new mattresses about 30 years ago and never replaced them. Sonya's had flowers on it. So, are you sure that's the actual mattress?"

She puts her hands on her hips and scrutinizes the mattress. She gets on her knees by the bed and examines the surface closely, tilting her head to get a better angle.

"Wait a minute," she mutters. She runs her hand over the smooth, fitted surface. Scrambling back to her feet, she says, "This looks like some sort of cover you'd put on a new mattress to keep it clean."

Helen starts running her hand along the underside, muttering, "If I'm right, then there should be—got it!" She looks up triumphantly and says, "There's a zipper."

With that, she grasps the tab she found and begins unzipping the cover. After wrestling with it for about five minutes, she gets it off, revealing Sonya's old, flowered mattress, just like I expected.

What I didn't expect was the long piece of silver duct tape running right down the middle.

I reach for the tape when Helen grabs my arm and pulls me back.. "Tom," she says, "stop what you're doing right now and go downstairs. Ask Gladys to give you the crime scene kit and bring it back up to me."

"But why, this is no—" I stop when I see the look in her eyes. She's all cop now.

"Will do," I say over my shoulder as I head downstairs.

It takes me longer than it normally would for me to get down and back up the stairs. I'm still pretty sore, true, but I also had to first tell Gladys what we found. She then made me wait for her to outfit me with a pair of glasses that have a camera built into the frames. I was not surprised that she was able to quickly pair the camera with her cell phone, but I was a bit taken aback that she was carrying them in a pink glasses case in her purse.

I wondered why she had them in her purse but was afraid to ask.

Back upstairs, I hand the kit to Helen and then step back as Gladys instructed me. Standing in the fully open doorway, I have a perfect view of the mattress and am able to both record and transmit to Gladys everything that happens next.

Helen turns and faces me. "This is Detective Helen Parr, Myerton Police Department, badge number 865. It is Monday, February 8, at 9:35 a.m.. We are in Sonya Greer's bedroom in the home of Nola Greer, 14562 Old Bellamy Road, Bellamy, Florida. I am about to commence a search of her room for evidence in her homicide, specifically what may be hidden in this mattress."

I pan the room and focus on the mattress. Helen moves around to the other side. "As you can see," she says, "there is an approximately three-foot long strip of duct tape down the middle of the bed. Tom," she looks at me, "are you feeling okay? Do we need to stop?"

"No, I'm fine, keep going," I say with more certainty than I actually feel. I'm actually getting more and more queasy as time goes on, a feeling brought on not so much by my injuries as the dread at what Helen's about to find.

As I watch and transmit to Gladys, she dusts the duct tape for prints. "Tom," Helen says to me, "can you get a good shot of this? Gladys, run these prints for me, please." I stand as still as my rapidly beating heart will let me, to give Gladys the pictures she needs.

"Okay, I'm going to remove the tape now and place it in an evidence bag." She slowly pulls the tape away from the mattress, bends it so the sticky sides are together, and drops it in the plastic evidence bag. She seals it and places her initials on it before handing it to me to place on the bedside table.

"I'm now going to separate the cut in the mattress to see what if anything it contains." She carefully does just that. I'm standing by the bed, so I can't immediately see what she sees.

She sucks in a breath. "Oh, shit!" she whispers. Looking at me, she says, "Tom, come here."

I get closer to the bed and bend over so my palms are supporting me—not the most comfortable position, frankly—and look inside the opening.

"Dammit, Sonya," I say. "What were you into!"

Inside Sonya's mattress are stacks of fifty-dollar bills, all bound together with rubber bands. We've found out how she bought the cars and the designer dresses.

"I'm seeing stacks of fifties, looks like it fills much of the mattress," Helen is saying, back in her professional cop mode.

"Is this what those guys were looking for?" I say, weakly.

Something has caught her attention. Grabbing her flashlight, she shines it into the opening and reaches in, pulling out a manila envelope.

"No, if I had to guess," she says, holding it up so I can see the front. "They were looking for this."

On the front, in Sonya's precise handwriting, is one word.

Tommy.

***

It takes Helen about twenty minutes of work before she pulls the last of the stacks of bills out, all placed carefully next to the opening on the bed. All told, there are about fifty bundles, totaling who knows how much.

She pulls the last bundle out of the mattress and holds it up to me. It is at this point that I suddenly need to sit down.

Helen sees me wobbling, and scurries to the other side of the bed just in time to help me ease into the wicker chair by Sonya's bed. My head is spinning as I try to process what I have just witnessed. Helen leaves the room for just a moment and returns with a glass of water.

I gulp it down under her watchful eye. "Helen," I gasp, "What the hell does this mean?"

"Beyond the fact that your sister had a lot of money hidden in her mattress?" Helen shakes her head. "I have no idea, Tom. But as soon as you feel up to being left alone, I need to take this money downstairs so Gladys and I can count it." Picking up the envelope, she says, "I also need to open this."

"Why don't you open it now?"

"Uh-uh," she says. "Chain of custody. I need to have Gladys as a witness."

"You can do it here, I have the camera, Gladys can see it."

"No, Tom. It'd be—"

"Dammit, Helen!" I yell, on the verge of tears. "I need to know what Sonya left for me! I need to know what the hell she was killed over!"

With that outburst, I can't hold my emotions in check any longer. I collapse in the chair, my head in my hands. The tears come hard and hot. The physical pain from my injuries is now matched by an emotional pain, the pain of knowing that my sister was into something that got her killed.

And I hadn't been able to stop it.

Helen crouches in front of me and clasps my wrists in her hands. "Tom," she says gently, "you need to rest."

"No, no. I'm fine," I say with more enthusiasm than I feel.

"No, you're not, but you will be in a little bit. The doctor warned me that you might be dizzy from time to time for a few days and when that happened, you needed rest. Now, do you feel like walking to your bedroom?"

"I'd rather go downstairs with you."

"I know, sweetie." she says, running her fingers through my hair in a vain attempt to straighten it out. "But you need to stay up here, not just because you need the rest, but because I need to focus on this right now, and I can't do my job if I'm worried about you."

Once again, her logic is unassailable. I nod and she begins to help me up. Pain shoots through me, and I almost collapse back into the chair.

"I think I need more Tylenol now."

"Of course, baby," she whispers. "I'll bring it to you."

As she did last night, she tucks me into bed. Leaving for a moment, she brings me two white caplets and a glass of water. "Open wide," she says, and pops them in my mouth.

I lay back on the pillow and snuggle down. "Thank you, Helen, for nursing me."

She smiles. "Tom, I may not be able to be in your bed when you're well, but nothing can stop me from being by it when you're sick." Then, she bends down and kisses me lightly on the forehead—a kiss, not of a lover, not even of a wife, but of a . . . I'm not even sure of the word. But whatever it is, that's the way she kissed me.

"I'll leave the door open," she says walking out of the room. "Yell if you need me."

I see her leave, then carefully roll over on my side and snuggle down under the covers.

Soon, I drift off, the touch of her lips on my forehead still present.

Twenty-Nine

I wake up feeling refreshed and not in as much pain. As my eyes focus, I see my room is dim, as if it's late in the day but not quite twilight.

My back is to my window, but there's enough light coming in to cast the shadow of another person on the wall.

I roll over and start to say, "Hello, sweetie—", then I stop.

It's not Helen.

It's Mom.

"Feeling better, Tommy?" she says in that nasally voice of hers.

"I was," I mutter. "What are you doing here?"

She huffs. "Well, isn't that just gratitude for you," Mom says. "Here I am, an old woman, just wanting to take care of her son, and he asks, 'what am I doing here?'" She begins to sniffle. "I was just checking on my little boy, that's all. You're all I have left, Tommy. Can't I just help take care of you?"

I nod. "Of course Mom, I'm sorry. I'm still pretty sore."

"And I guess your . . . injury is probably worrying you too, isn't it? I mean, even though it doesn't get regular use, you're still a man, and—"

"Mom! Please, I don't want to talk to you about this! I don't want to talk to anybody about this! Where's Helen?" I ask.

"Huh. Helen," she says with a slight sneer. "She and that crippled girl—"

"—her name is Gladys, and you can't call her crippled, Mom!—"

"—are locked in that den. Kicked me out, Helen did! Kicked me out of my own house! I mean, all I did was ask a few reasonable questions and wanted to sit there while they counted my money."

I put my hand up. "Wait a minute," I say. "Did . . . did you know about the money in Sonya's mattress?"

She looks at me like I've just said the Earth is flat and the moon is made of green cheese.

"Of course I knew, Tommy. Why wouldn't I? It's my house, after all. Besides, Sonya said it was mine."

"Mom," I say, "when did she tell you about the money?"

"Oh, I don't know, maybe a week before she was . . ." Mom doesn't finish the sentence but instead dissolves into a flurry of sniffles.

"Did you see how much money Helen pulled out of there?"

"Yes I did, Tommy, and I have to tell you, I'm not happy with her about that. Sonya made it very clear that was my money, and then to have Helen come in here and take it. I almost called Gus."

I stiffen. "You didn't?"

"Well, I tried, but that crip—I mean, Gladys did something to my phone so I couldn't call out."

I cannot suppress the smile and think, *that's my girl!*.

"Mom, you saw how much it was? The stacks of fifties bound by rubber bands. How exactly do you think Sonya got that?"

She shrugs. "Oh, I guess she saved it from her salary?"

And with that, I've had enough.

"Dammit, Mom!" I shout. "She had thousands—maybe tens of thousands—of dollars stuffed in her mattress! She only brought home $25,000 a year! There is no way in hell she could have ever saved that much?"

"Well, it was probably tips from those men I told you about."

"Tips? Really, Mom? Were they tipping her a thousand dollars at a time?"

"Oh, Tommy, I don't know how much wealthy men like that—"

"There is no possible way you, a grown woman who went to college and everything, can be this stupid, Mom! No one deals in cash anymore! Why would she have kept it in her mattress! And don't tell me about your Great-Uncle Nesbit who didn't trust banks because during the crash after the Florida land boom, his Daddy lost all his savings! The only people who deal with thousands and thousands of dollars in cash are criminals!"

"Now I will not have you talking about your sister that way," Mom says, shaking a bony finger at me. "Your sister was no criminal—"

"Mom! For . . . mmmfff . . . sake! She was an addict! She drank, took pills, stole from you! She was arrested for possession a couple of times and at least once for prostitution that I'm aware of—and the only reason I know that is because Gus called me right after it happened since we ALL know you weren't about to tell me anything like that about your PRECIOUS Sonya."

"She was precious," Mom wimpers. "She was a good girl, Tommy. She took care of me, better than you did."

"She wasn't Mother Theresa, for . . . arghs . . . sake! She used you! She used everybody she came in contact with. And as far as my not taking care of you, you didn't want to have anything to do with me after Dad died!"

"Your father's death was your fault, Tommy!" Mom screams.

If she had slapped me across the face with a bag of pennies, she couldn't have hurt me more. I just look at her, this woman who I call Mom but who hates me so much. I'm too stunned to say anything. I'm too stunned to cry.

Mom just broke something I'm not sure can be fixed.

"Tom?" I turn from Mom. Helen's standing in the doorway, her arms crossed, concern etched in every corner of her face. Concern changes to anger when she sees the pain, the hurt, the anguish that I know is cut into mine.

She strides into the room. Gripping the footboard of my bed, she looks at Mom. "Nola," she says in her firmest don't-mess-with-me cop voice, "I think you need to leave. Tom needs to rest."

"But, but," she whimpers. "The things he said to me . . ."

"Nola," she says quietly. "You will leave this room right now. If you don't, I'm fully prepared to carry you physically out of here."

"But this is my house!" she whines.

"Yes, it is," Helen replies, her voice even, her eyes cold.

Mom looks at me, then Helen. "Well, okay," she says, standing up and walking to the door. "I'll go see if Gladys would like a sandwich."

"She's fine, Nola," Helen says firmly.

Mom looks back at her, then leaves. Helen carefully closes the door, and walks over to sit on the bed.

"Are you okay?" she says, stroking my cheek and looking in my eyes.

"I . . . I don't know, really," I say. "I . . . I guess so."

"We could hear it downstairs through the closed door. You two were really loud."

I nod. "I thought, I guess, if I yelled loud enough that she'd understand. But I don't think she wants to. I think she wants to continue living in this fantasy world about Sonya."

Helen nods. "Did I hear right? Did she know about the money?"

"All this time we've been trying to figure out what Nutcracker was, how Sonya paid cash for two cars, what those goons who almost killed me were looking for, she knew. Sonya told her about a week before she died."

"A week?" Helen repeats. She stares out the window. "Huh, so she knew they were on to her," she mutters.

"What Helen? Who are you talking about? What'd y'all find—"

"Shush, Tom," she whispers, placing a finger against my lips. "I'll tell you. But you need to eat something. It's after four o'clock. You've been asleep for six hours. I'll go bring you something."

Helen gets up, but before she can go, I grab her arm. She turns back to me.

"Do you know why yet, Helen?"

Helen looks grim, and shakes her head. "Not yet. But I do know some things. Things you need to know. But first, you need food."

Thirty

About twenty minutes later, Helen walks into the room carrying a tray holding a steaming bowl, two plates, and two cans of diet soda. "Here," she says, placing the tray on my lap and grabbing one of the plates and one of the cans. "Eat."

I look at her offering. A steaming bowl of fragrant tomato bisque and a grilled cheese sandwich.

"You haven't made this for me in a long time," I whisper.

"It was the first thing I learned to cook, remember?" Helen says.

"Mom had all the ingredients?"

"Not quite. She had bread and American cheese, and butter, of course. The soup is a combination of jarred garlic and herb pasta sauce and some half-and-half. Turned out pretty good, I think. There's not much in her kitchen."

"Mom's not much of a cook," I say, plunging my spoon into the creamy-red concoction. It's warm, slightly sweet, and familiar.

"Delicious," I say with a smile.

Helen returns the smile as she chews a bite of her sandwich. "Do you know the first time I had tomato bisque and grilled cheese in, I don't know, twenty years?" I shake my head, and Helen says, "At lunch at The Bistro with Gladys, the first time I ever saw you say Mass."

"I remember that," I say, swallowing a bit of the grilled cheese. I first noticed Gladys. She stood out, sitting in her wheelchair on the front row, wearing a yellow pillbox hat, yellow dress with a short jacket, a lace scarf over her head, and white elbow length gloves. In all, she looked like she had raided Jackie Kennedy's closet. "I was surprised to see you there."

"I saw the look on your face, Tom. You weren't surprised, you were shocked."

"Well, you had practically thrown me out of your office a few days earlier, so . . ." I take a spoonful of soup and swallow. I take a bite of my sandwich. "What were you saying about lunch with Gladys and tomato bisque?"

"Oh, that," she looks down at her plate. "I spilled some of it on my dress because of something Gladys said."

"What did she say?"

She lowers her eyes and blushes. "Not important right now. Finish your soup before it gets cold."

We sit in silence for the next few minutes, the only sounds in the room are the chewing of our grilled cheeses, the clink of the spoon on the bottom of the soup bowl, the gurgle of soda as we tilt the cans to drink. It's a nice, companionable silence, one I haven't experienced for a while.

When you eat alone most of the time, silence isn't a companion.

I finish the last of the sandwich and spoon the last of the soup in my mouth. "That hit the spot," I say. "Thanks."

"Feeling up to some news?" Helen asks.

I nod. "I suppose I'd better hear what you found out."

Helen takes a deep breath. "Okay, well, the first thing you should know is that Gladys and I counted the money—your Mom raised a fuss, as she told you, but I got her out of there. The total that I pulled from your sister's mattress is over $150,000."

My mouth drops open and I feel my eyes bug out. "$150,000?"

"Uh-huh," Helen nods. "We're going to have to get one of those currency counters to make sure, but Gladys says it's right."

I shake my head, "Damn."

"Damn is about right," she says. "So now we need to figure out why she had that much money in the first place."

"Yes," I say. "What was in the envelope?"

"Ah," Helen smiles. "The envelope, now that's the most important thing we found. It contained two things. A flash drive and an unmarked keycard—I have no idea the significance of that. Gladys is seeing if she can hack into the security system of The Belvedere and try to find out what it goes to."

"Isn't that illegal?" I ask, my brow furrowed.

"Oh, extremely," Helen says with a smile. "But Gladys has, well, special skills. She can get in and get out without anyone ever finding out."

I shake my head and smile. "She's a remarkable young woman. What about the flash drive?"

"Now that is the most interesting part. There were about twenty files or so that Sonya says look like they were downloaded by someone—presumably your sister—from The Belvedere's servers."

"What are the files?"

Helen shakes her head. "We don't know. They're all encrypted. Gladys is confident she can crack them, but it's going to take time. She's working on the largest file first, thinking that must be the most important."

"How much time?" I say. "Hours? Days? Weeks?"

"Sorry, honey," Helen says, "she doesn't know."

I plop back against my pillows. Through clenched teeth, I say, "Dammit, we're running out of time! We can't stay here forever!"

"We need to be patient, Tom," Helen says.

"Patient? Patient? We've been patient! Where has it gotten us? Nowhere. How much longer, Helen, are we just going to lay around and wait for something to happen?"

She says nothing for a moment, then softly, she asks, "Are you talking about this, or . . . something else?"

I look at her and smile. "This, I assure you," I say. "I'm content with where we are with us. I'm just frustrated. I'm tired of being infirm. I need to do something. And don't tell me I am doing something by resting, Helen. We've got to get more. We've got to be a little more aggressive."

"Tom," she sighs. "You may be right. But if we're aggressive too soon, or in the wrong way, someone else will get hurt."

I nod. "Tell me about Gus," I say. "Gladys told me you found out something about him, but wouldn't tell me what."

"I asked her not to, because I thought it would be easier coming from me." Helen comes and sits on the edge of the bed and takes my hand. She looks in my eyes, her lips formed into a thin smile.

"Gladys has a friend from MIT who's a special agent in the FBI Field Office in Jacksonville." At my look, she chuckles, "He's 28 and gay, I asked her. So anyway, the FBI and the Florida Department of Law Enforcement have a joint task force investigating public corruption in North Florida and the Panhandle." She pauses.

"Gus is one of the targets," I say.

Helen nods. "He's into some bad things, it looks like. Bribery, money laundering. According to Gladys' friend, he has a couple of offshore bank accounts with hundreds of thousands of dollars."

"Better than a mattress, I guess," I mutter.

"Well, we really don't know that." Helen smiles.

"So, who's paying him?" I ask.

"That, they don't know," Helen says. "These payments come through a variety of shell corporations that are so tangled up, they can't get where the money comes from in the first place. Their theory is that the money's coming from a variety of people and criminal enterprises, many overseas."

"But Gus is just a county sheriff in a small county," I say, confused. "It's hardly Chicago in the 1920s."

"Well, something bad's going on here. We know that. And Gus is somehow involved."

I just notice that Helen hasn't looked me in the eye the entire time. "There's something else, isn't there?"

Helen looks at me, a pained look on her face. "Tom, Gladys' friend said they didn't have enough evidence for an arrest, just one source who says he heard something."

"What is it, Helen?"

She sighs. "Tom, there are rumors that Gus is involved in a couple of mysterious disappearances. Possibly murders."

My mouth drops open. "What?"

"The agent claims that their source says Gus was used by someone in the area to take care of problems. Who or what they are, the source was vague on. But, yes, Tom. That's it."

I stare at Helen in disbelief. The part about Gus being a crooked sheriff is unbelievable enough. When we were growing up, he was one of the most honest kids I knew. Charlie would climb a tree to tell a lie, but Gus was honest to a fault. To my knowledge, he never took anything that wasn't his, and in spite of his size, he never hurt another living soul. Now, Helen is telling me that Gus—that Gus, the Gus I grew up with—is not only crooked, but is also suspected of being a hit man of some kind.

And if he killed someone . . .

I throw the covers off and sit up quickly. Too quickly, as it turns out, because the sudden movement causes my head to spin and I'm soon laying back on the bed.

"Whoa, Tom," Helen says, helping me back on the pillows. "That's enough of that."

"I need to see him, Helen!" I say, my teeth clenched in a mixture of anger and pain. "I need to look the son-of-a-bitch in the eye and ask him if he killed my sister!"

"You're still in no shape to go anywhere, Tom," Helen points out. "The doctor says you need to take it easy for a couple of days."

I plop back against the pillow and stare at the ceiling. "I don't think we have that long."

"What do you mean?"

"I don't know," I say. "It's just a feeling. It looks like whatever Sonya's involved in is connected with The Belvedere, right? She's been working there a couple of years, probably helping set up escorts, or whatever they call them, with the guests. She happily took cash under the table and socked it away in her mattress, using it to buy cars, clothes, everything. Does that sound right?"

Helen nods. "Yeah, sounds good to me."

"But all of a sudden, something changes. Was Gladys able to figure out when she downloaded those files from The Belvedere's computers?"

"According to her, they were downloaded about a week before she died."

"And Mom told me," I say, nodding, "that Sonya told her about the money a week before she was killed."

Helen and I look at each other. "She was getting her affairs in order," Helen says. "She knew they were onto her, or at least she was afraid they might be."

"She found out that the people she worked for—let's face it, Charlie Lumpkin and his wife, Rose—were into something, or were getting into something, that was so bad she wanted nothing to do with it. In fact, she wanted to stop them." I pause to let that sink in. "She died trying to do the right thing," I mutter, "for the first time in her life."

"And she called her big brother," Helen says, placing her hand on mine, "because she trusted that you'd do the right thing."

I close my eyes. "Dammit," I say as the first tear falls, "you'd think I'd be dried up by now, all the tears I've cried this week."

Helen reaches out to my face, and catches the tear with her thumb. She's about to pull away when I grab her wrist. I close my eyes and rub the back of her hand against my cheek.

After a moment, I let it go. Helen pulls her hand away and puts it in her lap.

I take a deep breath. "I need to talk to Gus," I whisper, "I'll call and tell him I want to talk to him here. I want him to look me in the eye and tell me he didn't kill my sister."

Thirty-One

"Tom, this is probably the worst idea you've had since telling Miriam she could have live animals at the Nativity."

I look at Helen as I strain to get my shoes on. "Well," I smile ruefully, "at least there won't be an alpaca trying to kill me."

"Yeah, I've been meaning to ask you about that," Helen says. Her arms are crossed and there's a mix of concern and irritation on her face. "I know I'm hardly the theological expert you are, but I don't remember ever seeing an alpaca in the Nativity scene at my Grandma's house."

"There probably wasn't, since there were no alpacas in Bethlehem or anywhere else in the Near East. But Miriam insisted, since the animal people offered it."

"But why an alpaca?"

I shrug, remembering instantly why that's still not a really good idea. "Simple. The camel had another engagement."

She rolls her eyes. "You priests really have your own set of troubles, don't you?"

I sit up and look at her. "You have no idea," I mutter.

Helen blushes and looks away. "Why won't you listen to me?"

"Because in this instance, I know what I'm doing."

"Do you? Are you thinking this thing through at all?"

I take a deep breath. "I spent all night thinking this thing through. This is the best way."

Helen shakes her head. "I just don't see why you don't meet him here."

"I need him somewhere quiet, somewhere he'll be relaxed. There's a better chance he'll let his guard down."

Plus, I don't want her anywhere around if I decide to do something drastic.

"Do you even feel up to walking to the cabin?"

I sigh. "I'm fine, Helen," I say with determination. In fact, I'm far from fine. I'm still sore. And if I move too fast, I still get dizzy from the concussion. But if I say any of this to Helen, she'll stop me.

And I need to do this. Alone.

I look at her and see the expression on her face. "You're scared."

"Scared! Scared!" she shouts. "I'm not scared! I'm terrified! Tom, you have no idea what went through my head when I found you unconscious outside my room. I spent every moment by your hospital bed, pleading with God to let you wake up. When Gladys got there, she tried to get me to leave, but I wasn't about to leave you until you woke up. I don't know what I would have done if . . . if I'd lost you then. I don't know what I'll do if something happens to you now."

She dissolves into tears and I put my arms around her. She buries her head in my chest, her shoulders heaving with sobs. I pat and stroke her hair, whispering words of comfort and reassurance.

"I love you so much, Tom," she says through muffled sobs. "I don't know what God means for us, but I at least want to have the chance to find out."

"I do, too," I whisper, "But Helen, I have to do this."

She pulls away from me, wipes her face with her hand, and pulls herself together. "Okay, Tom," she says, "But since you want to do this alone, you'll do it my way."

"Fair enough." As she turns to leave, I say quietly, "Let me take your gun."

She turns sharply. "Tom? What the hell?"

"Look," I say, acting as nonchalant as possible. "You said it. We're going to be alone. If something happens—"

"Have you ever fired a gun?" Helen asks.

I think. "Hmm, maybe when I was in high school? I took a class in gun safety. It was the only PE credit I could get without getting sweaty."

"Oh, Tom, that is such a bad idea."

"Look, Helen," I say sharply. "I'm not a child. Just let me have your gun."

She glares at me. "Fine," she spits and stomps out of my room.

I take a deep breath and let it out.

She bought it.

She'd never have given in if she suspected what I have in mind.

A minute later, she returns with a small revolver. "What's this?" I ask.

"My backup weapon," she says. "I used to wear it in an ankle holster—but, since I wear skirts that don't always go down to my ankles, I wear it a little higher up."

I raise my eyebrows. "How high up?" I say with a mischievous smile.

"Well, Father, you'll never find out."

"Alas, no," I sigh. "So, where's my holster?"

"You'll be wearing a jacket, right? Just carry it in your pocket. And for heaven's sake, Tom, don't shoot yourself."

"Trust me, Helen," I mutter. "I'm not planning on shooting anyone."

Which is technically not a lie.

I follow her out of my room. "So, Helen, I'm curious," I say. "In addition to your regular weapon and your backup, do you carry anything else?"

"I carry a knife sometimes," she says. Turning, she puts up a finger, "And no, you may not ask me where I keep it."

I try unsuccessfully to suppress a smile as we walk downstairs. Gladys is waiting for us, the pink glasses case in her lap.

"Dad," Gladys says, "I wish you'd listen to Mom on this."

"Gladys, don't you start. I'll be fine."

"Well, here," she says, handing me the case.

"No, Gladys," I say, "I don't need that, and besides, Gus knows I don't wear glasses."

"Okay, Dad," she sighs. She hands me a smaller case. "At least wear this so we know what's going on."

I open it. It looks like a tiny hearing aid with an almost microscopic antenna.

"Huh," I say, "just like in the movies."

"They occasionally get it right," Helen says. "I'm going to have to insist on this. If you don't, I'll shoot you in the leg to keep from going."

I nod. "Okay, okay, no need to resort to violence, officer." I put it in my ear, my fingers finding the tiny switch that turns it on. "I think I've got it on."

"We'll test it when you get outside," Gladys says, wheeling herself towards the den. She stops and turns around, then comes back to me. She hugs me around my waist. "Please be careful," she says. "I'd hate to lose another . . ." She sniffles and backs up. Looking up at me, I can see her eyes misty with tears. "Mom can be there in a flash, remember that." She turns around and goes back to the office.

I look at the time. "He'll be there soon."

"How's he going to get there?"

"There's a back way that not a lot of people know about. A lake that borders a little dirt road that leads back to the main road. Gus knows it. We used to swim there as kids during the summer."

Helen nods. "Do you think he knows why you want to talk to him?"

"Probably," I nod. "I'm sure telling him I wanted to meet at the cabin gave him some idea."

We stand there, not looking at each other for a few minutes. Finally, Helen looks at me.

"You need to get going," she says, her voice cracking slightly.

"Right." I look in her eyes, those deep pools of azure blue that are so easy for me to lose myself in. That I did lose myself in.

Unbidden, the memory of the last time I—we—were in the cabin comes to mind. I'm overwhelmed by the urge to do what I did then. To hell with Gus. To hell with finding Sonya's killer. I just want . . .

I shake my head to clear the memories. They vanish as I mentally pray the Our Father.

Thy will be done, on Earth as it is in Heaven.

No matter how much it hurts.

"I'll be back," I say with a slight smile. I turn and grasp the doorknob. I pull the door open and am about to step through the threshold.

"Tom," Helen says. I turn just enough to look at her.

"Come back to me, please," she whispers.

I pause a moment, then say, "No matter what happens," I whisper, "I'll always be with you."

Turning quickly before what remains of my determination leaves me, I stride onto the porch and begin to walk towards the woods.

Thirty-Two

"You still hear me, Dad?"

I adjust the volume a little. "Hear you just fine, Gladys."

"He's late," Helen says in my ear.

"Gus was never on time for anything," I say. "He was born two weeks late, 12 pounds 13 ounces."

"Ow!" Gladys exclaims.

"Look," Helen interjects, "I say give him another five minutes, then bag it."

"Trust me," I say. "He'll be here. He wants to be here."

There's a pause. "What do you mean, Tom?" Helen says slowly in her best cop voice.

"I told him I have something he wants," I say, "and if he wants it, he'd better talk to me."

"What the hell, Tom!" I wince as Helen screams at me through the earpiece. "Why'd you do that?!"

"It's okay, Mom," Gladys says.

"What!" Helen exclaims.

"Gladys, I told you . . ." I say.

"I can't have you two fighting," Gladys says, "not when—"

The sound of leaves rustling outside the cabin gets my attention. "Quiet," I whisper. "He's coming."

A minute later, the door opens and Gus enters. He's wearing civilian clothes, jeans, and a plaid shirt with a jacket and a ball cap.

I don't see his gun.

"Tom," he says with a grin. "You look better than when I last saw you."

"Thanks," I say. "I'm feeling better. But, you don't mind if I sit during our talk, do you?"

"Naw, of course not, old buddy," he says. Looking around the cabin, he chuckles. "I guess I'll stand. Boy, this place brings back memories."

"I remember when we found it that summer, you, me . . . Charlie." I say the last deliberately, and Gus winces at the mention of the name.

"Yeah," I continue, "we spent a lot of time together here as kids, chewing the fat, playing Risk." I chuckle. "Arguing The Original Series versus The Next Generation."

"You and Charlie almost came to blows over that one," Gus laughs.

"Well, I spent most of the time trying to keep you two from killing each other," I point out.

Gus shrugs. "Well, he was an ass most of the time then. Still is, frankly. People don't change, Tom."

I look at him. "Sometimes they do, old friend," I say quietly.

He looks around, not meeting my eyes for a minute. "Well, I guess you did, huh?"

"Yeah, yeah, I guess you could say I did, becoming a priest. But you know, Gus, I've been thinking about that a lot lately. Really, I'm not that different. For one thing," I say evenly, "I'd never betray an old friend."

Gus jerks, and I see a bit of fear enter his eyes. "Look, Tom," he says slowly, "I came here because you're an old friend. You need to stop this before—"

"Before what, Gus? Before someone else gets killed? Are you going to use that old movie line on me?"

"Tom, please," Gus says, a little frantic. "You don't know what you're up against. You . . . you have no idea!"

"Well, why don't you just tell me, old friend?" I spit.

"Tom," Gus pleads. "Stop, just stop. Just walk away. You and Helen and that blue-haired girl in the wheelchair get on the next flight back home and forget about all this."

"I have a name, you know," Gladys mutters.

"Forget about all this?" I yell. "You expect me to just walk away before I find out who killed Sonya."

"Yes! Yes!" Gus shouts, "That's exactly what I mean, Tom! I don't want them to do to you what they did to Sonya!"

I take a deep breath. In my ear, I hear Helen whisper, "Oh, shit."

"Did you kill her? Did they have you take care of a loose end for them?" I whisper.

"What?" Gus says. He shakes his head frantically. "Oh, no. Oh, no, no, no. I swear to you on Mama's grave that I didn't—"

I reach in my pocket and pull out Helen's gun. Pointing it at Gus, I say through gritted teeth, "Answer the damn question!"

Gus puts his hands up. "Okay, old buddy. Just . . . just calm down and put the gun away."

"Crap!" Gladys says. "Did you give him a gun?'

"He asked for one," Helen says, frantic. "Tom, Tom, there's something I need to tell you—"

"Tell me Gus, or I swear I'll shoot you. Did you kill Sonya!"

"No! NO! I didn't! I couldn't have!"

"But you know who did it?"

He shakes his head. "No, no, I don't know who exactly." Breathing heavily, he adds. "I'll tell you what I can, just put the gun down."

"You might as well, Tom," Helen sighs. "I took the bullets out."

My eyes get as big as saucers at this news. "Okay," controlling my nerves as much as I can, "I'll put it away. You tell me what I want to know, and I'll give you what you came for."

"Dammit, Tom!" Helen yells.

"Mom, I told you, it's okay," Gladys says.

"Talk, Gus," I say.

Gus sighs and looks at his feet. "They pay me to keep my mouth shut and keep the state and the feds from digging around."

"Who, Charlie?"

Gus nods. "Yes," he says. "He came to me a few years ago, right after he opened The Belvedere. Said he was attracting a bunch of high-profile people who wanted their privacy guaranteed. Asked me—"

"Paid you—"

"Paid me to basically keep hands off of his place."

"What all is he into, Gus? Prostitution and what else?"

He shakes his head. "I don't know. That all started when he married Rose."

"Rose?" I say.

"I'm on it, Dad," Gladys says, clicking keys.

"Yeah, Rose," Gus sighs. "She got her claws in Charlie, persuaded him to get involved in all sorts of stuff."

"What stuff?"

"I swear, I don't know, Tom," Gus says. "They pay me not to ask questions."

"They pay you quite a bit, don't they?" I say.

He nods. "A whole lot more than the county does." He stops. "But you already know that, don't you?"

I pull a USB drive out of my pocket and show it to Gus. "Here it is, old friend. Everything that the Feds and the State have on you. Every bank account, every record of payment. They have enough to put you away for a long time."

"Tom," Helen says in my ear, "what are you doing?"

"But they haven't done it yet," Gus says.

"No, they haven't," I nod. "But they could arrest you as soon as you leave here. In fact, they're waiting for us to call."

"Dammit, Tom!" Helen says.

"Mom, he knows what he's doing," Gladys says.

"Gladys, he never knows what he's doing!"

"Is that what this was? A trap? You hold me at gunpoint and get me to confess to receiving bribes? That's not fair, Tom!"

"You misunderstand, Gus," I shake my head. "I'm not here to have you arrested. I'm not interested in what's on this USB drive. I'm more interested in your soul."

585 THE RELUCTANT RECTOR: THE FATHER TOM MYSTERIES BOOKS 1-3

"Oh," Helen whispers.

"What?" Gladys says.

"Shush, Gladys," Helen answers. "Let him do his job."

"My soul?" Gus scoffs. "Do you forget who you're talking to? Mama spent years trying to pray me to Jesus. It never took. What makes you think you can do any better?"

"Because I'm looking at my old friend," I say quietly, "and see someone who's caught in a web he didn't make. Who was a good, decent man once. Who wouldn't hurt a fly. Who couldn't stand to see anyone hurt. Who became a cop because he had a sense of justice."

"Justice? Tom, there's no justice. Do you know how many people like them I arrested in Jacksonville? Oh, I had all the evidence to put them away, but they had the lawyers and the money to walk over and over and over again. Instead, I'd put away the people who worked for them, who did their dirty work, who had never had a chance because of the part of the city they were born in or because of the color of their skin. I arrested a mother of three who'd been in an accident and injured her spine, who got so hooked on Oxy that she eventually started using heroin, then started dealing in it. The people who made the Oxy? The people who sold it? The doctors who prescribed it? Did I arrest them? No. Because they had the money. You get to think about it enough, you really begin to wonder whose side you're on."

"So, what? If you can't beat them, join them?"

"Something like that."

"But Gus," I say. "It doesn't have to be that way."

"What do you want me to do, Tom? Just spit it out."

I get to my feet and walk to him. I put my hand on his shoulder. "Help us. Help us stop them. Tell us how we can find out what they're up to. Help me get justice for Sonya."

"Tom," he says, "Not with these people. You're never going to get it. They've got powerful people under their thumb. It's hopeless."

"That's what the apostles thought when they crucified Jesus," I point out. "Look what happened."

"But this time," Gus says, "nothing you do is going to bring Sonya back to life."

Thirty-Three

As soon as Gus leaves, I drop to my knees. My head is hurting again, and I know I'll never make it to the house on my own.

"Helen," I gasp.

"She's on her way already, Dad," Gladys says.

"Thanks," I say, trying to catch my breath. I'm on my hands and knees, which is good, because when the wave of nausea hits and I throw up breakfast, it doesn't get on my clothes.

I'm about to heave again when the door opens and Helen kneels on the floor next to me. She puts an arm around me and her hand on my neck.

"It's okay, sweetie," she whispers.

I cough, then manage to say, "Little bit different than the last time we were here, huh?"

"Uhhhh, guys? What does that mean?" Gladys says in my ear.

"Nothing, Gladys," Helen says, "nothing. Turn it off please."

"But I—"

"Now, Gladys!" Helen commands.

Gladys huffs. "Yes, Chief."

My stomach now emptied of its contents, my breathing more regular, I ease back on the floor and look up at Helen. "No bullets," I say. "Really?"

"I wasn't about to give you a loaded gun," she says. "What did you think you were doing?"

"You said it to Gladys," I gasp. "My job. I had to try, Helen."

"I know," she says. "So, what's the next step?"

"Oh, damn," I say, smiling. "I thought you'd know."

"Right now," Helen says, "it's to get you back to the house so you can rest a while." Standing up, she extends a hand. "Come on, Tom."

I look at the proffered hand and shake my head. "I can't stand yet, Helen," I say. "I don't think I can make it even with your help."

"Well," she says, "if you can't walk . . ."

Next thing I know, she's run back to the house and brought back Gladys' wheelchair. Soon, I'm bouncing along the path as she pushes me.

"You know," I chuckle, "a guy could get used to this."

She swats me on my shoulder and says, "Behave, Father!"

I start laughing, "Sorry, Detective!"

She starts laughing as well. I hear Gladys call, "What's so funny?"

"Nothing, Gladys," Helen laughs.

"Nothing at all!" I add.

We get to the porch and Helen helps me out of the chair. I'm able to stand on my own two feet, and manage the steps holding onto the doorframe. Inside, I make a beeline for the den, collapsing into Dad's recliner—a little too hard for my still tender groin's liking. Helen comes in and pulls the lever to put the footrest out. She moves Gladys back into her chair. Having done that, she leaves, returning a few minutes later with a glass of ice water.

"Thanks. Okay," I pant, "I admit. Maybe not my best plan."

"Maybe not, but we did learn a lot," Helen says.

I'm about to say something when a sharp pain shoots through me. "Helen," I croak, "Meds. Quick."

"Will you take the Oxycontin now?" she asks, a pleading tone in her voice.

I nod. "Okay, okay, I give. Help me lean this back."

She comes over and assists as I lean the recliner back into an almost horizontal position. "I'll be right back, sweetie," Helen says and leaves.

I'm staring at the ceiling when I notice Gladys eye level with me. "She really loves you a lot, you know that, right?" she says with a more serious tone than I've ever heard from her.

"I know," I sigh.

She cocks her head to one side. "You feel the same way about her, don't you?"

"You are a very perceptive young lady, Gladys."

She looks contemplative for a second. "I . . . I don't understand," she says. "If you love each other, then why don't you two just . . . you know?"

"Because Gladys," I say with a smile. "I'm already married. And Helen's too honorable a woman."

She's about to ask another question when Helen comes in, stopping just inside the doorway. "You two look like you're in a deep conversation," she says.

"Just talking about the Church," I say.

"Yeah," Gladys says, a little distant as she goes back to her workstation. "The Church."

Helen looks at Gladys, then back at me. "Is that for me?" I ask.

"Yes," she says. She has one caplet. "Here," she says as I open my mouth and she pops it in, handing me the water to wash it down with. She takes the glass out and returns a moment later with a blanket. She throws it over me and adjusts it.

Having tucked me in, Helen leans over to whisper, "Rest for a while. You've done your part today."

Through half-closed eyes I see her smile. I return it and nod.

Soon, the combination of weariness and the medication sends me into a deep and dreamless sleep.

***

The first sound I hear upon regaining consciousness is the tapping of keys.

The second sound is a confused voice saying, "So, after he kissed you, and you kissed him back, you pushed him away? Why would you do that?"

Stretching, I say, "Because, Gladys, she's an honorable woman."

The talking and the tapping both stop.

At that, Helen soon scurries into my field of vision. "How are you feeling?"

"Other than a little groggy, fine. I could use some coffee."

"I'll get you some. You're gonna want to be wide awake for what we found."

I sit the recliner up, noticing my pain is much more tolerable than earlier. Gladys looks at me with a sheepish grin.

"So," I say, smiling ruefully, "she told you about the cabin."

"I kept after her," she says. "I finally wore her down. So, why'd you kiss her?"

"Oh, Gladys," I say, looking at my hands. "There's no simple answer to that."

"You did it because you love her," Gladys says. "Seems pretty simple to me."

"No, see, there's where you're wrong. I've loved Helen for a long time now, and never kissed her—thought about it, yes, along with other things I shouldn't have—but never did it. I kissed her that day in the cabin because . . . because I was lonely, and hurt, and broken, and angry with God, and confused, and all sorts of things that have nothing to do with love. It was need, not love, that made me kiss her."

"So," Gladys says, "if you had the opportunity again, you wouldn't kiss her?"

I'm not sure how to answer her, because I don't know the answer. Same circumstances, but with a clearer mind? Would I do what I did in the cabin during the storm? Knowing everything I know?

Fortunately, I don't have to answer, because at that moment Helen comes back with my cup of coffee.

"Thanks," I say, "I needed that."

"Did you tell him?" Helen asks Gladys.

"No," she answers, tapping the keyboard. "I was asking him if he'd kiss you again."

I cough as the coffee goes down the wrong way. Helen looks at me. I say, "What did y'all find while I was asleep?"

Helen sighs with relief and smiles, grateful for the subject change. "Gladys was finally able to crack a couple of the files. The largest one and one of the smaller ones."

I step to Gladys' workstation and bend over to look at the screen over her shoulder. Helen pulls a chair for me to sit in. She sits on the other side of Gladys.

"Okay, both files are lists of names and other information," Gladys begins. "This one," she clicks with her mouse, "is a long list of names, dates, and these codes over here."

I scan the names, stopping at one. "Wait a minute," I mutter. "I recognize that one. That . . . that's the Lieutenant Governor. And he," pointing to another name down the screen, "he's a prominent Evangelical."

"There are hundreds of names, mostly men," Helen says. "A few women, a number of couples."

Name after name scrolls past. Politicians, business executives, heads of charitable organizations, all prominent men and women in their fields.

All in this file that Sonya stole from The Belvedere.

"Wait, stop, Gladys!" I say as a name leaps from the screen. I lean in closer to make sure I'm seeing it clearly. "Can you make this larger?"

"Who is it, Tom," Helen says?

"Just a minute, I want to be sure." Gladys zooms in on the name.

I look, then fall back in my chair and close my eyes.

"Oh, dammit," I whisper.

"What is it," Helen says, looking at the name. "Who is he?"

"That, Helen," I say, pointing at the name, "is none other than the official Papal representative to the United Nations."

Helen jerks her head to look at me, then back to the screen. "Are you sure, Tom?"

"Oh, I'm sure, all right," I nod. "He visited the Archdiocese a couple of years ago. I gave him a tour of the Archives. I spent a week practicing his name so I'd not mispronounce it."

"But what is a Vatican official doing on a list of names from an establishment outside a small town in rural Florida?"

"Think about it, Chief," Gladys says. "Most of these names are highly prominent people, all at the top of their fields. If they want to indulge in various activities, Bellamy is the right place to do it."

"Far from the media spotlight, low population, local law enforcement under tight control," Helen says. "Okay, it makes sense."

"But what are we looking at?" I ask, as Gladys continues to scroll down.

"It's what in the old days they would have called a madam's little black book," Helen says. "Welcome to the digital age."

I'm looking at the screen as name after name after name scroll past, some I recognize, others I don't. "Wait, Gladys," I say. "What are these codes? Each name has them."

"I'm not sure," Gladys says. "I've never seen them before."

Helen peers at them. "I do," she says. "I've seen a system like this in other human trafficking cases I've worked. The codes represent the 'John's' preferences in a girl, what they like to do. I don't know what the letters mean in this case, but these two—these two I know exactly what they are."

I see what Helen's pointing at. "18+, U18," I say, then sit back, "18+, that must mean over 18, right? So this person—oh, wonderful, he's the president of Save the Seas—prefers a girl over 18."

"And this one right below," Helen says quietly, "the one with U18—"

"Under 18," I whisper. "Oh, Sweet Mother of God!"

"There are a lot, Chief," Gladys says. "I'd say almost half."

"Dammit," Helen says. "Underage girls. The Belvedere trafficks in underage girls."

Only you can save the girls. You need to save Chrystal. Now Sonya's words come back to me.

"She knew," I whisper.

"Tom," Helen says gently. "More than that. Sonya was involved."

"But she changed her mind," I say, frantically. "She got all this information. It's what got her killed. She called me to finish the job."

"Tom, yes, that's what it looks like," Helen says, "but her hands weren't clean in this. I agree, something turned her against it. But still, she was involved for a long time."

"Okay, what was it that changed her mind?"

"I think I know," Gladys whispers. "Look, the names here in the smaller file I cracked. Look at the code."

Next to about a dozen names are the codes. In the string of codes is a new one.

U16.

"Oh, dear Lord," I whisper. "That was it."

"They're looking to bring in younger girls," Helen says.

Thirty-Four

"Any idea where they're getting them from?" Helen asks.

I'm still trying to process the stunning news I just received.

Sonya was involved with Charlie and Rose Lumpkin in prostitution and human trafficking.

The trafficking included young girls.

Charlies and Rose were looking to bring in even younger girls for their clients.

Somehow, this got Sonya killed.

Gladys is saying something to Helen, part of which I hear through the fog of my own thoughts. "It's probably here," Gladys says, "But I've only cracked the encryption on these two files. It's going to take time. I'm doing what I can, but I don't have the computing power I'd have back home."

"Okay," Helen says crisply. "We'll just have to go with what we have."

"What did you find out about Rose Lumpkin?" I ask.

Helen sees the weariness and confusion in my face. "Tom," she says quietly, "are you up to anymore of this? You should rest."

"I've been resting, Helen!" I snap. "I've rested enough."

"You're still recovering, Tom!" Helen bites back.

"I don't have the luxury of just laying around here, doing nothing," I yell. "Time's running out. There's something horrifying going on in my hometown—I know it's a little craphole place in the middle of the armpit of the nuttiest state in the union, but it's still where I grew up and I'm a little fond of it—and there's nobody but us to stop it!"

"Us? Stop it?" Helen says, incredulous. "What do you mean by stopping it? This isn't trying to find one killer, Tom. This is a well-organized group of criminals, probably with ties across the country, possibly internationally as well. We can't stop them ourselves."

"What do you want to do, Helen?"

"What we should have done when we found all that money," Helen snaps. "Call state law enforcement. Contact the FBI Field Office in Jacksonville. Give them what we have. Let them handle it. That's what I'd do in Myerton."

"But we're not in Myerton," I point out.

"No, we're here, where I have no authority and no backup."

"Ah, hello," Gladys says, looking up from her keyboard.

"You know what I mean," Helen says to her. "Look, Tom, when it was trying to find your sister, it was different. When we found out your sister was dead, trying to find her killer was something I thought you needed to do for closure. But first you had the crap beaten out of you.

591

Then we find out that Gus is on the take. Now, this," she says, pointing at the screen. "This is too big for us to handle!"

"I'm telling you I have to do this, Helen," I say. "Sonya asked me to do it!"

"Why, Tom?! Why now! Why after all these years are you finally interested in doing anything your sister asked you to do? Because she's dead? You paid no attention to her when she was alive!"

"I know that!" I scream. "Don't you think I know that! Don't you think that the guilt is eating me alive, on top of the guilt I already carry?"

"Stop it!" Gladys screams. Helen and I stop and look at her. She turns to face us, tears streaking her face.

"Stop fighting! Just stop fighting with each other!" she begs as she cries. "Mom, Dad, please! Whatever this is that I'm seeing right now, you both know it has nothing to do with Dad's sister, or prostitution, or a dirty cop, or anything. This is all about the two of you. I don't understand it. I may never understand it. But . . . but you've got to put it aside for those girls. Mom, Dad's right. We have to help them. There's not that much time left."

"What do you mean, sweetie?" Helen asks, softer now than she was a moment ago.

"While you two were fighting," Gladys says, wiping her face with her hand, "I got another file open. I wasn't sure what I was looking at first, but then I realized what it was. It's a shopping list."

Gladys turns back to her monitor. "See," she says. "It's a list of names like the other one we saw and their preferences for girls. I wasn't sure why there were the dollar amounts on the one list and not on the other. Then I realized there was only one thing it could be."

We're both staring at the screen, then it dawns on me. "Bids," I mutter.

"Oh, no, Tom," Helen whispers. "I think you're right."

"It looks like The Belvedere is looking to branch out," Gladys says quietly. "Not just providing girls by the hour."

"They're going to sell these girls to those men," I whisper.

Helen whispers a string of profanity that I know she reserves for only the most stressful situations. "You said we don't have much time?"

Gladys points at the screen. "We don't know exactly where the girls are coming from," she says. "But see this notation here? 'LA pickup 2/16 12:00 p.m.' That's only four days from today."

"So they're bringing these girls in four days from now," Helen says. "'LA. What is that, Los Angeles?"

"Louisiana," I say. "LA is the postal abbreviation for Louisiana. You can get to New Orleans from here in about six hours, so at most a seven-hour trip, fourteen hours round-trip. It's a lot easier to get this number of people from Louisiana than from clear across the country."

Helen taps her chin, then sighs. "Okay, okay, I concede," she says. "We're going to have to handle this ourselves. But we're going to let that friend of yours, Gladys, know what we have planned, when we figure out what that is."

"It'd be nice to know who we're up against," I say.

"I was about to tell you that when you two started arguing," Gladys says over her shoulder.

"We were not arguing," Helen says.

"We were having a discussion," I add.

Gladys chuckles. "You two are such an old married couple," she mutters.

We're about to protest when Gladys says, "Okay. So The Belvedere is in an old plantation house on the other side of the county.

"The Bellamy Plantation?" I ask. "But that old place was falling down when I was a kid. I can't believe it's still standing."

With a tap of a couple of keys, Gladys brings up a website. "Does that look like it?" she says, pointing to a picture of a beautiful white-columned mansion that looks like it was plucked from a still of *Gone With the Wind*.

I lean closer to look at it. "Wow," I say. "It could be. It's certainly the right size, and the general design looks right."

"It was purchased several years ago by CL Holdings," Gladys says. "CL Holdings is owned by your old friend, Tom."

"Charlie Lumpkin," I nod. "Makes sense. When we were teenagers, the three of us used to ride out there and explore the old place. I found it creepy, but Charlie loved the place."

"Where did he get the money to buy it and do this to it?" Helen asks.

"Here's where it gets interesting," Gladys says, tapping more keys. "So Charlie Lumpkin worked on restoring the plantation, telling people he was going to turn it into an exclusive Inn and Restaurant. I've got articles from newspapers and magazines about him doing it. Problem is, he ran out of money before the project was half-finished." A click of her mouse brings up an article headlined, "Bellamy's Tara Gone with the Wind?", with a picture of a scaffolded plantation home.

"About this time, Charlie divorced his first wife and remarried." Gladys clicks on another tab and brings up a picture of a beautiful, voluptuous red-head.

"Rose," I say.

Gladys nods, "Yes. Rose. At least that's the name she's going by now."

"What do you mean?" Helen asks.

"When Rose married Charlie Lumpkin, her previous husband had died six months earlier. Her previous husband was Thomas Hamilton," Gladys clicks and brings up a photograph of a slightly younger Rose with a man who looks to be in his early nineties.

"Aahhh," Helen and I say at the same time.

"When he died, he left her a very wealthy woman," Gladys says.

"So," I interject. "Charlie married Rose, and Rose gave him the money to open The Belvedere."

"Rose bought him out. Because it's privately held, there's not a lot of information publicly available, but CL Holdings became CRL Holdings about a month after they married. Best I can tell, Rose owns 95 percent of the company."

"That jibes with what Gus said about Rose being in control of Charlie," Helen says. "Gladys, you said Rose Lumpkin is the name she goes by now. What did you mean?"

"What I mean, Mom, is before she was Rose Lumpkin and Rose Hamilton, she was this woman."

With a click, Gladys brings up a black and white police mugshot of Rose, about ten years younger but definitely Rose. Her lips are curled into a sneer, her chin is held up in defiance.

"Nina Wainwright," Helen reads. "An alias?"

"No, it looks like this is her real name," Gladys says. "She had dozens of aliases over the years, but the record matches this name to a birth certificate for a Nina Ann Wainwright."

Peering over her shoulder to look at the record sheet, "Arrested for . . . of course," she mutters.

"Prostitution, Helen?" I ask.

"In this case, yes."

Gladys says, "She's got dozens arrests for prostitution going back almost two decades. There are more than a few arrests for running an escort agency and a couple of federal arrests for sex trafficking across state lines. That's not including arrests for assault and a couple for attempted murder." Gladys whistles. "This gal's one stone-cold bitch."

"How much time did she serve in prison?" I ask.

"Best I can tell? She's not spent a day in prison."

"But how is that possible, with that number of arrests?" Helen says.

I look at her. "It's like Gus said. Besides, the names in her black book? Prominent men and women? They wouldn't have wanted to cross Rose lest their secret life be exposed."

I look at the mug shot. I see the sneer, the contempt Rose has for the world. In the eyes, however, I see something else.

Fear. Shame. Sadness.

"Where did she come from, Gladys?" I say quietly.

"Her arrest record goes back to when she's eighteen, then stops."

"Makes sense," Helen says. "Juvenile records are sealed; they wouldn't be in the system."

"But is it likely that she started all this when she turned eighteen?" I ask.

"If she started in prostitution before she was eighteen," Helen says, "I have a hard time seeing her as someone who'd want to bring young girls into that."

"But Mom," Gladys says quietly. "I think Dad's right. There's no arrest record, but I found a missing person's report for a Nina Wainwright. Her parents reported her as a runaway."

Gladys brings up a photo of a young girl, obviously a school photo, her mouth in a broad grin, her eyes sparking with the innocence and wonder of youth.

"She was seventeen when she ran away," Gladys says.

"That poor, poor woman," I mutter.

"Tom," Helen says. "That woman is in all likelihood responsible for your sister's death. She's responsible for ruining the lives of dozens if not hundreds of girls over the years. She's managed to evade justice for a decade at least. She doesn't deserve your pity."

"Helen, don't misunderstand me," I say. "She's an evil woman. It's not pity I feel. It's sorrow, sorrow that this vibrant young girl," I point to the screen, "became this broken young woman," I say as I take the mouse from Gladys and bring up the picture. I stare at her, then look at Helen.

"She's as much a victim as the girls Sonya wants me to save are."

"She's a victimizer, Tom," Helen says.

"Yes," I nod, "she is. But that's the way sin works. One person's soul gets broken, they break another's soul, and so on and so on. What starts with one infects hundreds, thousands."

"Sounds like a pandemic," Gladys remarks.

"Sin is similar to a virus. Just as virulent. Just as deadly. And there's only one cure."

"What's that," she asks.

I smile and look at Helen. "God's mercy."

We're silent for a few moments, then I say, "Helen, what do we do next?"

She takes a deep breath and lets it out slowly. "There's only one thing we can do, I think. But it's dangerous."

"What is it?"

Helen looks at the picture of Rose on the computer screen and crosses her arms.

"We need to go into the lion's den."

Thirty-Five

"Tom, we have a problem," Helen calls from her bedroom.

I have just laid down on my bed and gotten comfortable, trying to ride out the last hour before I can take more pain relief. "Can we talk about it here?" I shout back. She marches into my room, a look of aggravation tinged with embarrassment on her face.

"I looked up The Belvedere online and they say jackets are required," she declares without preamble.

"Oh, is that all?" I reply. "No problem. I've got my suit and I probably have an old dress shirt in the back of the closet that still fits. We're good."

The look of embarrassment leaves her face, allowing aggravation to take over completely.

"I'm not talking about you, Tom," she huffs. "I'm talking about me. If you have to wear a jacket, that means I have to have a dinner dress, and I didn't bring one with me, mainly because I don't own one."

"Oh," I reply. "Well, maybe Sonya—"

"Tom Greer!" she shouts. "There is no way in hell your sister has anything in her closet that would remotely fit me."

I'm trying to think of an appropriate response that won't make her even more aggravated with me. Fortunately, Gladys yells gleefully, "Shopping trip!"

Helen grimaces but then calls back down. "I guess that's the only thing to do. I'll be down in a minute."

"Are you going all the way to Tallahassee?"

"There's no time," she sighs. "I saw a little boutique near the diner the other day. Hopefully they have something appropriate in my size."

"Hey," I smile. "This is the South. Your size is nearer the norm."

I think it's a complement. Instead of saying thank you, she just scowls at me. "I hope you're right, or this little date is over before it starts." She stops when she realizes what she said. We just stand there in an awkward silence.

Fortunately, Gladys says, "Mom, if you want to, you can just stay here and I'll pick up something for you."

Helen's look of horror at the thought of an unsupervised Gladys picking out a dress for her almost causes me to laugh. "I'll be right there," she yells before beating a hasty retreat.

I open my phone to check my email while calling out in my most 1950s sounding voice, "You girls have fun. I'll be right here when you get back."

***

And I was, sound asleep apparently, when Helen hung a new white shirt and a red satin tie on my doorknob with a note, "Gladys says this will look great on you." I sigh contentedly before making my way to the bathroom to get a shower.

Not only is the door closed but it's locked. I knock and say sheepishly, "You going to be much longer?"

If my voice was that of a lamb, Helen's is that of a lion, "Yes," she roars, startling me. "I am damn well going to be longer! You can take your shower downstairs!"

"But Helen," I say mildly, "I need my shaving gear and a towel."

The lion sounds angry now as she growls, "Look by the stairs!" And there it is, in a neat pile, everything I brought with me from Myerton, as well as the X-Files towel I got for my birthday during my first year in college.

Gathering my gear with what's left of my dignity, I duck back into my room for my suit before going downstairs, only to find Gladys ensconced in that bathroom. Thankfully I only need a shower or I might have to resort to doing something off the porch that once got me spanked.

Resigned to my fate, I wait for Gladys to emerge which, thankfully, is not that long. I prefer in these situations not to make eye contact or in any way acknowledge what is going on but apparently Gladys was raised with a different set of values.

"All yours!" she calls cheerfully as she rolls past me. "And by the way, you need to buy your Mom some new air freshener. That stuff smells worse than what it's supposed to be covering up."

"Thank you, Gladys," I say, trying not to blush. "I'll check into that."

Thankfully, I'm able to get my shower and get dressed in the bathroom, in spite of the fact that it is smaller than most closets. My body does not thank me for the contortions this takes but I come out with my pants and shirt on, finding my coat and tie still waiting for me where I left them. Knowing Gladys' love for inappropriate humor, I am thankful for this and slip them on quickly before she remembers her hidden stash of itching powder.

I am standing in front of our old hall tree mirror tying my tie when I hear someone on the stairs. I turn and gasp in astonishment.

It's Helen, coming down the stairs in a red dress that catches her just above the knee, red high heels, and red lipstick.

I open my mouth and then close it again, and then open it again only to have Helen interrupt me with, "Not a word, Tom Greer, not a word."

"But Helen," I say.

"Gladys talked me into this," she huffs as she continues down the stairs. "I don't know how. I mean, it didn't look so short in the store." She reaches the floor and bends over a little, trying to make the dress cover her knees.

I avert my eyes quickly and say, "Helen, your legs are fine. Please, please stop trying to cover them up."

"Oh, that sounds just like something a man would say!" she says irritably.

"Only a man trying very hard to not look at your cleavage."

At this, Helen brings her hand to her chest and stands up so quickly she nearly falls off her heels. I reach out to keep her from toppling over. When I do, I catch a whiff of vanilla.

For just a moment, one moment, my inner lover says, *we are alone in the world and no one will know if I linger over her curves for one minute more. That red dress, it's the color of a fresh, ripe apple.*

Right, my inner priest reminds me. *You wouldn't be the first man to fall prey to an apple.*

Sighing, I step back, only to bump into Gladys. With a big, goofy grin, she asks, "So, Dad, what'd ya think?"

"Gladys," I say, not taking my eyes off of Helen, "Your Mom is the most beautiful woman in the world, and the dress very nearly does her great beauty justice."

Helen's face colors and she demands, "That's it, both of you stop that right now or I'm going to march right back upstairs and change into that black dress I bought for the funeral."

"No, don't do that," Gladys and I cry in unison.

"I'll behave, I promise," Gladys adds.

"Me, too," I say with more conviction than I feel.

Determined to get us back on track, I look at my watch and say, "We'd better get going if we want to make that reservation."

"Okay, guys, here you go," Gladys says. She hands me the pink case with the spy glasses, as well as the tiny transmitter. She hands Helen another tiny transmitter.

"Hand me your phones," Gladys says. At our looks, she explains, "I'm giving you burner phones. The transmitters are synced to them so the signal will reach this far."

We obey. She hands us our new phones. "Okay. I'll be able to hear everything and see everything."

"You have the Highway Patrol on speed-dial if things go sideways." Helen says.

"And Jeremy," she answers. "He's waiting with the FBI tactical response unit at the Patrol barracks."

I look at Helen. "Do you think there will be any trouble?"

"Better to prepare, Tom." She takes a deep breath and says. "Okay, I think we're ready. How do I look?"

I hesitate, trying to pick words that are accurate but not expressive of thoughts I really shouldn't be entertaining.

Finally, after an eternity, I say the only thing I can say, because it's the truth.

"You look lovely tonight, Helen," I say softly.

Helen lowers her eyes and clears her throat. When she looks back at me, I can see the red in her cheeks. "Well, th—thank you, Tom," she stammers. "You . . . you look very handsome."

We stare at each other for a second, then Helen says, "OK, let's get started."

"Just one more thing," Gladys cries. "I want to get a picture of the two of you."

"Gladys," I begin, "I don't think—"

"I have the keys," she says, waving them triumphantly, "and no one's getting them until I get my picture."

"Oh, all right," Helen says, "but make it quick."

We stand together in front of the door like two cousins going to their senior prom together.

"C'mon guys," Gladys complains, "Try standing in the same zip code. Tom, will the Vatican police rush in if you put your arm around her shoulders?"

I often pose with my arm around people's shoulders, even women. At wakes, after baptisms, on Christmas and Easter. People love having their pictures taken with their priest. So it is very easy for me to slip my arm around Helen, and even easier to draw her close to me.

"That's more like it," Gladys grins. "Say cheeseburger pizza."

As we obey her instructions, I am taken back to the only other time anyone ever said that to us. We were at Maryland and some guy was doing a Valentine's Day spread on love. We were walking across campus hand in hand, basking in the glow of our recent engagement. He asked us a few questions and then asked us to pose for a picture. Full of pure joy, we did so, capturing forever a time when the sun always shone but it was never hot.

I snap back to reality when I hear Gladys say, "You can let go of her now, Tom, unless of course you don't want to."

"Oh, of course he wants to," Helen insists, ducking from under my arm.

I worry that my concussion has suddenly worsened, but I quickly pull myself together and say with as much dignity as I can muster, "Yeah, we need to get going."

A few minutes later, we are heading down the road toward The Belvedere when our phones ding. Helen is driving because I'm not allowed to for another week, and so I check my messages.

Gladys sent the picture. I smile.

Pure joy indeed.

Thirty-Six

Less than an hour later, we are seated at an elegant little side table in one of the nicest restaurants that I have ever been in. The exterior may be a restored plantation home, but inside the entire main floor is a modern-looking restaurant. There's a continual chatter and clink of silverware against plates, mixed in with the dance music coming from the live orchestra. The light is, I'd say, medium, allowing Gladys to see everything clearly. Everyone is dressed the same way Helen and I are, so we more or less fit in.

But I immediately notice that, while most of the men are my age or older, the vast majority of the women are younger than Helen.

Much, *much* younger than Helen.

The waiter hands us our menus, and asks for our drink order—water for both of us—then leaves us to make our selections. One glance down at the menu causes me to shudder because of the prices. After some discussion, we agree that the best thing all around is to go with the prix fixe menu, without alcohol. I decide that if the waiter gets snippy about it, I'm going to tell him that I have a head injury and Helen is my 20-year-old daughter who suffers from a weird aging disease. Fortunately, this is not necessary, thanks no doubt to the emphasis in modern society on tolerance, and the fact that they have probably had more than one Baptist bigwig dine here.

The meal is good, but not nearly as good as the opportunities to people-watch.

Helen swallows a bite of what the chef calls *légumes d'été,* but I am pretty certain are bits of zucchini and yellow squash, before saying softly, "Don't look now, but isn't that Senator Benson? The one who ran for Vice President last year?"

I wait until she gives me the all clear and glance out of the corner of my eye, avoiding turning my head as much as I can. "Uh-huh, that's him," I say, "but that's not his wife."

"How can you be sure?"

"I met both of them at a family values dinner in Baltimore last year. I was invited to give the invocation."

"Maybe it's his daughter," Helen continues.

"Nope," I insist. "No one in the family is Asian."

We eat in silence for a few minutes before someone else catches my eye.

"Helen," I say, pointing with my hand flat on the table, "I'm pretty sure that guy over there is the president of the One Earth Federation. Weren't you on his guard detail last time he came to speak at Myer?"

"Yeah," she says, "and according to his background info, he and his wife have been happily married for 20 years and have one son."

"Well, honey, if that's his wife, you need to go arrest him for child marriage."

Even in the midst of a potentially dangerous situation, we manage to laugh at that. "Oooh, Tom," Helen says with a grin, "this is fun! It's like being on a stakeout but with better food. See anyone else?"

"Not from here, but then it's hard to see most of the room."

"I gotta tell you guys," Gladys says, "I'm not seeing much here. Can you, you know, get up and move around, get me some other angles?"

"And what exactly do you propose we do?" Helen says.

"Well, there is a band," Gladys says. "And a dance floor."

I pause for a moment, contemplating Gladys' suggestion. At the moment, the band is playing a pretty jazzy number, and I remember Helen liked to dance. It might be fun to get out and move a little.

At the same time, I know that I will happily grab any excuse to hold her in my arms, and I know that is not a good thing.

But then I remember. I am trying to gather information about Sonya's murder, and that should trump everything else.

"Gladys, I think that's a great idea. Helen, would you care to dance?" I ask. "It will give us an excuse to move around the room and give Gladys a better look at what's going on."

She smiles and says, "It's been a while, but I'm game if you are."

Gladys squeals and claps her hands. I wince, but Helen either didn't hear her or is used to her prodigy's enthusiasm about, well, everything.

I take her chair and we make our way to the dance floor as I run over the steps of the rumba in my mind. It's going to be fine, I tell myself. We'll be close, but not too close. Just close enough.

But as we get to the edge of the floor, the song finishes and the band begins to play *Hallelujah*, by Leonard Cohen.

What are the chances?

I pause, not certain what to do. I'm about to suggest we sit this one out when I see her waiting for me on the dance floor.

As the song begins, I take Helen into my arms.

> *Now, I've heard there was a secret chord*
> *That David played, and it pleased the Lord*
> *But you don't really care for music, do you?*
> *It goes like this, the fourth, the fifth*
> *The minor fall, the major lift*
> *The baffled king composing Hallelujah*
> *Hallelujah*

Hallelujah
Hallelujah
Hallelujah

I know that I'm holding her too tight.

I know that we're seeing nothing.

I don't care.

At this moment, I am one with King David. One with the man who had it all and threw it away for the love of a woman. I stand with David on that balcony, watching Bathsheba bathe.

I want to rush back in time and ask him, "Was it worth it? You lost your infant son, your grown son, so very much."

But I know exactly what David would say at that moment, there on the balcony. "What son? What kingdom? There's nothing but her right now."

Your faith was strong but you needed proof
You saw her bathing on the roof
Her beauty and the moonlight overthrew ya
She tied you to a kitchen chair
She broke your throne, and she cut your hair
And from your lips she drew the Hallelujah
Hallelujah
Hallelujah
Hallelujah
Hallelujah

"Yeah, David, what about that?" I say to the King. "Her son, your son with her, was the wisest man in history. But what you two did that night laid the groundwork for something that would tear your people apart and establish a sense of separation and bitterness that plagues mankind today. Knowing that, didn't you regret it? I mean, that's a lot of pain for a lot of people just so you could have the woman you wanted."

David looks at me again and says, "Find your own answers. I made my peace with God more than 3,000 years ago. Now it's your turn."

You say I took the name in vain
I don't even know the name
But if I did, well really, what's it to you?
There's a blaze of light in every word
It doesn't matter which you heard
The holy or the broken Hallelujah
Hallelujah

Hallelujah
Hallelujah
Hallelujah

"Helen," I whisper. "Oh, Helen."

I hear a tiny gasp in my ear from Gladys, but she makes no other acknowledgment of hearing me.

Why can't we stay like this? Here, on this dance floor, with you in my arms, forever? I don't need to sleep with you. I don't need to take you and show you off and call you my wife, as much as I would love to. I just need to hold you here, to be with you, our bodies entwined.

I did my best, it wasn't much
I couldn't feel, so I tried to touch
I've told the truth, I didn't come to fool you
And even though it all went wrong
I'll stand before the Lord of Song
With nothing on my tongue but Hallelujah
Hallelujah
Hallelujah
Hallelujah

My best. Is this really my best? My best for me, my best for you? No, I know it's not. And so, my darling, before it all goes wrong, I'll stop. Today, I'll choose to stop, to do without, for your sake and mine, but most of all so that someday, when we both stand before the Lord of Song, we can ultimately shed our all too mortal limitations and sing the eternal Hallelujah.

The music ends and I guide Helen back to the table. I feel I am leading the most precious woman on earth, for that is what she is to me. I pull out her chair and seat her, getting one last whiff of vanilla.

I am at the same time angry and grateful at being called to make such a great sacrifice of loving her and yet never fully knowing what we might have been together.

She looks at me quizzically for a minute and pauses as if waiting for me to say something. When I don't, she lowers her eyes to her hands and says briskly, "So did you see anything?"

I'm still trapped in a fog. I'm a man finally making it to the surface after nearly drowning. I know that I must look dumb, for that is how I feel at the moment, struck dumb by what I've just experienced.

"I didn't get too much," Gladys says quietly. "The, ah, angle was . . . not good. I couldn't really hear over the music."

I pull myself together as best I can and reply, "Not much. How about you?"

"That's the thing, Tom," she replies, "other than the fact that we are obviously one of a very few traditionally-aged couples here, I didn't really notice anything that unusual. I'm beginning to suspect that we are on a bit of a wild goose chase."

"But the list?" I say. "The codes? What about those?"

"I'm not saying there's nothing going on, and this place is somehow involved," Helen says, "I'm just saying there's nothing here that indicates there's human trafficking going on."

"What about all the young women with older men?"

"They're men. Men tend to prefer women who are young and pretty. And young women sometimes like older men. Gladys should have taught you that," she smiles.

"She is right about that, Tom," Gladys says.

"Okay," I sigh, "I'll concede. Whatever's going on, we're not going to find anything sitting here. You're right. A wild goose chase."

At that moment, the waiter appears with our bill. I glance down at the white slip of paper so carefully concealed in its leather cover.

"A very expensive goose chase," I add.

Helen chuckles and reaches for her purse. "Let me get this, Tom."

"No, Helen," I protest, picking up the folder. "I'll get this. The only reason we're here is because of my sister. It's only right."

"Hey," she leans forward—oh, why does she have to keep doing that?—and whispers, "as a member of your parish I know how much you make so I know that I make a lot more. I've got this."

With that, she snatches the folder out of my hand and drops it in her lap.

As much as I would love an excuse to wrestle her to the ground and take it from her, I remember that we are not supposed to draw undue attention to ourselves. I say simply, "Well, if you're sure."

"I'm sure." Helen takes her bag and begins to unload the contents onto the table. As always, I am both impressed and confused by the sheer amount of stuff she carries around with her. Within seconds, there are half a dozen tiny items discreetly piled on the table, everything from lipsticks to the weird key card thing we found in my sister's mattress.

Fortunately, Helen finds her wallet and pulls out her credit card before the waiter returns. In fact, except for the key card, she has most of the stuff tucked back in when he arrives.

Making eye contact and smiling, she is about to hand him her credit card when he reaches down and takes the check off the table, along with the key card.

Without missing a beat he says very pleasantly, "Very good. Someone will be right with you," and disappears.

Helen and I freeze, staring at each other with a "what the . . ." look on our faces. In our ears, Gladys sputters, "What the actual . . . guys, what the hell was that?"

Helen speaks first. "Maybe we're about to learn something after all."

Thirty-Seven

Before I can reply, a beautiful and very smartly dressed young woman comes to our table and hands me a small slip of paper, saying, "Your receipt, sir." I look at it and gasp.

Not only has the price of our meal been marked up by more than 100 percent, but Helen left an extremely generous tip.

"I'm seeing it, Dad," Gladys says in my ear. "Whatever happens next, just make sure I can see everything and describe what I can't."

I'm about to question the woman about what exactly this was paying for when she says, "Please follow me."

At this point, Helen catches my eye and I get the message: shut up and go along with this.

I get her chair and we are on our way across the dance floor and through the other tables to a different door than the one we came in. The door opens to a covered walkway.

Knowing that Gladys is both seeing and listening to everything, Helen casually narrates our little trip while I move my head so Gladys can see what we're seeing.

"You know," Helen says, "I really wish you people would get this back walkway closed in. I know that it's supposed to look like the old walk from the plantation to the kitchen behind the house but it could use a makeover."

Our escort laughs softly and politely but says nothing. We're approaching a large, nondescript concrete block building of much more recent construction than the restored plantation home, obviously painted to blend in with the tall azalea bushes that surround it. Light streams from all of the high, short, and obviously opaque windows but I can hear no sound from inside.

Stopping at a door marked *Maintenance,* our guide inserts the key card into the lock and taps in a few numbers.

Wanting to show Helen that I can narrate, too, I comment, "I've always wondered why this door is labeled maintenance?"

At this, our guide laughs again and says brightly, "Because it's where we store all our best equipment."

Opening the door, she gives a knowing wink. "I hope you two have an enjoyable night."

As we step inside, I am immediately aware of two things.

First, our escort was not lying about the building housing their best equipment.

Second, she was not referring to tractors and mowers.

The room we enter is as brightly lit as the restaurant was subdued. To my right are about a dozen gambling tables, each crowded with men and women happily throwing dice, dealing cards, and spinning the roulette wheel. It's like something from a 1960s Rat Pack movie, except that there are both scantily clad women and men serving drinks and hanging over the arms of the patrons.

The situation to my right is different—disturbingly so. There, rows of tables and chairs surround a stage featuring several very scantily clad women pole dancing while the patrons, mostly men but a few women, watch the performance hungrily. Their salacious looks must be similar to Herod's as he watched Salome dancing for him and his guests.

One dancer in particular catches my eye. I can't help but notice as she rotates around her pole that while her face and body are that of any older teenager, her eyes have the careworn look of someone twice that old. I sigh for her and all the others like her who feel their only worth lies in how men—and even some women, apparently—view their bodies as objects. I even grieve for those watching, blissfully unaware of the harm they're doing to their souls.

Helen chooses that moment to take my arm and snuggle close to me. "C'mon baby," she says with a little purr, "let's get a drink."

This startles me and I turn back to her. She's slipped into the role that's expected of her in our surroundings. I realize that our lives may very well depend on what we do—what I do—next.

Getting into the spirit of things, I reply, "Sure, doll." Taking shameless advantage of the opportunity, I guide her to the bar with my hand on the small of her back.

We sit down and I order a ginger ale while Helen opts for a Rum and Coke. Before the bartender can go fix our drinks, she leans forward to catch the young man's eye.

Conspiratorially, she asks, "Is there somewhere private my husband and I could enjoy our drinks?"

"Of course, madam," he replies with a grin, apparently used to hearing the question. "Is there anyone in particular that you would like to serve you this evening?"

"As a matter of fact there is," she says, almost purring. "Is Chrystal working?"

"Let me check," he says, glancing at his tablet. "Why, yes she is. She just finished with her previous customer and needs a little time to freshen up. Do you mind waiting, say about fifteen minutes?"

"Oh, no, not at all," Helen says brightly, "I'm sure we can find something to do to pass the time while we wait."

"Very good," he says, tapping the screen. "Will you be wanting her for a couple of hours, or for the entire evening?"

I blanch, but Helen says in a husky tone, "Oh, the entire evening, of course." Leaning closer, she says in a low voice, "It's my husband's birthday."

I take that as my cue to leer suggestively, though I feel less Hugh Grant and more Hugh Laurie at the moment—hell, I don't even feel up to Hugh Laurie.

I lean on the bar next to Helen and wrap my arm around her, pulling her closer to me, getting hit with the full force of vanilla for the second time that evening. In as suave a voice as I can muster, I say, "My wife promised me a special treat tonight."

I know I'm acting, but the words still make me sick to my stomach. I don't know how Helen does it.

She passes our bartender a twenty dollar bill, and he glances toward the stage, whispering, "Room twenty, third door down on the left."

Helen grabs my hand firmly and says in a voice she usually saves for mentions of cheesecake, "C'mon, honey, I've been looking forward to this all week."

***

A few minutes later we find ourselves in the most lavishly decorated bedroom I have ever seen.

There are mirrors on every wall. Several baskets of what I will only describe as "toys" are scattered around the room. I am both amused and gratified to see each is in a sealed plastic bag and labeled, "Sanitized for your Safety." In the middle of the room is a four-poster bed with curtains.

I approach the bed with a mixture of curiosity and fear. There are more baskets on the bedside table, these filled with a variety of lotions and other liquids whose purposes I dare not contemplate. I pick one up and find to my horror that it's labelled Vanilla Vice. Before I can stop myself I sniff it and am carried away in my mind to a place I have no business being.

Helen picks that moment to creep up behind me and say playfully, "Find something you like?"

I drop the bottle like a hot coal and croak out, "No, not at all." Then I turn and look up, leaning over the bed slightly to catch my reflection and Helen's in the mirror over the bed.

Well, buddy, you better add lying to your list of sins today.

Fortunately for both of us, Helen is completely on the job now and says calmly, "Gladys, you getting all this?"

"Mostly," she says, adding, "Do you want me to make any special notes about the Vanilla Vice bottle Tom was looking at when you walked up?"

I blush to my hairline as Helen says firmly, "No, Gladys, that will not be necessary."

"Okey-dokey, then," she says with a giggle. "Tom, I need you to walk around the room and take a careful look at everything. Remember, I can only record what you see."

Wondering again why I got stuck wearing the camera glasses, I walk slowly around the room. This means I spend most of my time looking at myself—and often Helen—in the mirrors.

Okay, actually, it isn't that bad of an assignment.

I'm continuing my circuit when there's a knock at the door.

I jump, but Helen is ready for it. Looking at me, she whispers, "Don't forget. She's got to talk to you so we can get this on film."

"Helen," I say nervously, "are you sure I'm the right person for this?"

"Tom," she says, looking in my eyes, "you are the only person in this room trained to try to save this girl's soul. That's what we're going to have to do if we have any hope of saving her life."

Thirty-Eight

With her words ringing in my ears, I watch Helen open the door a little and let Chrystal in. She sticks her head out long enough to make sure there's no one in the hall before closing the door.

Chrystal sets down the tray of drinks and sidles up to me. "Hey, sugar," she purrs. "I hear it's your birthday. So, what are you in the mood for?"

Before I can answer, Helen says firmly, "Answers."

Chrystal starts at this. She begins moving toward the door but Helen stops her, saying, "Don't worry, honey, you're not in any trouble. Sonya sent us."

At the sound of Sonya's name, tears well up in Chrystal's eyes and she collapses onto the bed.

"Oh, I'm so glad," she says. "Is she okay? I've been so worried since she disappeared. They don't let us watch the news or read the papers or anything. Is she here with you now?"

Helen catches my eye, letting me know that it's my turn now.

Pulling the bench at the end of the bed around so I can face her, I take Chrystal's hands in my own and ask gently, "How long have you known Sonya?"

She replies, seemingly puzzled, "Since I got here." I wait, and she adds, "back in June."

"Hold steady, Tom," Gladys says in my ear. "I want to get a clear picture to try to run facial recognition for missing persons."

"And where were you before then?" Helen asks.

"At Saint Magdalene's, where we all were," Chrystal answers

"What do you mean, 'where you all were'?" I repeat.

"Well, not everyone here, maybe, but everyone I know."

I am now thoroughly confused. "Chrystal, can you start from the beginning? How did you get to this Saint Magdalene's?"

With that, she bows her head, tears spilling down her cheeks.

"It's not all my fault," she whispers, "Jerry didn't have any right to treat me that way. It's his fault I had to leave home"

"Who's Jerry?" Helen asks.

"Mom's boyfriend, at least he was then. Who knows who she's dating now."

"So what about Jerry?" I say, gently. I sense we're getting into some very sensitive territory for Chrystal, and I don't want to spook her.

She takes a deep breath. "He moved in with us last spring," Chrystal begins. "It must have been right after Easter because he bought me this huge stuffed bunny, I mean huge, like as big as I am."

Considering this child's no more than five-foot-four, that's still one big bunny.

"Yeah, okay, he bought you a bunny," Helen says, a little too impatiently. I look at her and shake my head slightly. She looks apologetic and nods.

"I thought it was kinda sweet at the time, you know," Chrystal continues, "like he was trying to impress me. He was always really nice to me, and Mom liked that about him."

Her face goes white now, and she looks away. I've seen this look before in the videos that were required viewing in seminary, the ones prescribed by the Archdiocese in their attempt to reverse decades of deception and cover-up.

I have a sick feeling I know where this is going.

"But he didn't stay nice, did he?" Helen asks, more gently than before. She sits on the bench next to me. I scoot over to give her room.

Chrystal sighs. "I guess it depends on what you mean by nice. Jerry said he had a great way for me to make some money. Said he had friends that liked stuffed animals and that they would pay me for pictures of me holding mine. So we started out with me sitting on the couch with that big rabbit, kissing him on the cheek and stuff like that. Then, Jerry told me the men liked the pictures and that they wanted to see more of me. He started giving me presents he said were from his friends, mainly jewelry but other stuff. Jerry would always take pictures of me wearing them, he said to show his friends that I like them and all."

Chrystal pauses and bows her head again, twisting her hands in her lap. "But I knew something was wrong," she says, "when they started sending me clothes, especially things I couldn't wear in public."

I am feeling sick to my stomach and am afraid I am about to throw up. Helen notices this and says camly, "Chrystal, my friend Tom here was in an accident a few days ago and isn't feeling well. Do you mind if he takes his ginger ale in the spa room while you and I keep talking?"

"Oh sure, that's fine," she says, surprisingly comfortable with both of us.

I jump at the chance to leave and head straight for the bathroom. There, I am both relieved and horrified to find a huge tub with a long tile bench running down the middle. I wet a washcloth and try to calm down.

Of course, I know that stuff like this goes on. We're trained in seminary to not flinch in the confessional, no matter what we hear. But this kind of sin is as far from Saint Claire's as we are from the moon.

By the time Helen knocks on the door, I've collected myself. She slips inside and asks, "You all right?" I'm ashamed that she is worried about me in the face of what she's been listening to.

"I'm fine," I say, "How's it going out there?"

"It's going well." Helen pauses, then looks at me and puts her hand on my shoulder. "But Tom, there's something you need to hear, and it's really bad."

"Worse than I walked out on?" I cry in a whisper.

"In some ways no, but in other ways yes."

Before I can ask her anything else, she heads back into the bedroom.

"Chrystal," she says gently, "do you mind telling Tom what you just told me, about Saint Magdalene's?"

"Yeah, well," she says, "I only had enough money to get a bus ticket to New Orleans. I'd always wanted to visit there and, I don't know, I heard that they were always hiring waitresses and stuff, so it'd be really easy to get a job. When I got off the bus, there was a priest there at the station. I mean he looked like a priest, you know, had the collar and everything like on TV and in the movies. Anyway, he came up to me and said I looked lost. I tried to bluff but he seemed to see right through me. He asked if he could buy me a sandwich and I was really hungry and I figured since he was a priest and all, it would be OK. So we sat and ate at the diner next to the bus station and I told him about Jerry and why I left. He told me that what Jerry had done was terrible and that I had made the right choice. He asked me how old I was and when I told him fifteen, he congratulated me on being so brave for someone so young."

"Chrystal," I say, "I need to step out for a minute. Can you give me a couple of minutes?"

She nods while Helen looks at me, a little concerned. I beat a hasty retreat to the bathroom and close the door.

"Gladys," I whisper. "Please tell me you're getting all this."

"I am, Dad," she says quietly. "Every word."

"You're recording too, right?"

"Of course."

"When she's done telling this part of the story," I say, "I need you to send a copy to Walter Knowland, the Archbishop of Baltimore. I'll send you the email address. Do a cover email, explaining who you are and what's attached. Tell him I'll call him when I can."

"Sure, Dad," Gladys says.

"It's important that he gets it directly," I emphasize. "I don't want anyone else getting this before he does."

Gladys laughs. "Oh, you just leave it to me."

I return to the room. "I'm sorry, you were saying, Chrystal?"

"So, yeah, we were eating, and everything was fine. He told me that it wasn't safe for me on the streets and that he headed up a home for girls like me who had run away. He said that there were sisters there, you know, nuns, who took care of them and that they went to school and learned to be secretaries and then he helped them get jobs in businesses around the city.

"I couldn't believe it when he told me this," Chrystal smiles. "It was like a miracle. So I was thrilled when he took me there.

"The house was out in the country, further from New Orleans than I thought it would be. We got there right around dark. I remember the sun was setting when we pulled up. An older woman came out the door to meet us. She was dressed kinda like my grandma does but except she had this big cross around her neck. She said she was Sister Margaret and that she was glad I was there."

"So what was it like at this place, Saint Magdalene's?" I ask, praying that Gladys is getting everything clearly.

"It was wonderful. There were nine other girls there, mostly around my age. Sister Margaret and the other nun, Sister Agnes, they cooked for us and let us watch movies and even bought us makeup and new clothes, and not the cheap kind of clothes that come from Valu-mart. These were really nice and very fancy, like the models wear in the magazines."

Now she pauses and catches a glimpse of herself in the mirror. "Yeah, this is the last dress they bought me."

I'm suddenly overwhelmed. Why would a group of nuns buy a teenage girl the short, sequined cocktail dress she's wearing now?

Still trying to figure out what's going on, I ask, "If you were so happy there, why did you leave?"

Chrystal snorts at this and shoots me a dirty look. "Because I got a job. Here. Doing what you and your wife here and everybody else are very happy to pay me to do."

"Wait a minute," I start to say, "We're not . . .", but Helen stops me.

"Remember, Chrystal, we talked about this," she says. "That's not why Tom and I are here. We're here to help you. Tom is Sonya's brother, and she called us to come and get you and the other girls out."

I ask again, "How did you end up here?"

She sighs as if speaking to a stupid child. "Sonya hired me to come here," Chrystal says. "She said that The Belvedere needed waitresses and her boss had sent her to Saint Magdalene's because they had girls here who had been trained for that. She drove up one day in a big van and spent the day interviewing us. The Sisters assured us that they had worked with The Belvedere in the past and that they would give us good jobs.

"We were so excited. Sonya spent the night in the guest room and we all packed our pretty clothes and make-up and hair stuff. The nuns had spent a lot of time teaching us how to look pretty. They said we would get better jobs if we were nice and looked good.

"We left with Sonya the next morning, all hugs with the Sisters and promises to write. As we were pulling out of the driveway, I saw another van coming in. Father Jerry was driving and it was just full of the prettiest little Asian girls I'd ever seen. I thought, 'Well, isn't that nice. They even help girls from other countries,' though I did wonder how so many of them ended up here at the same time."

"So, Chrystal," Helen asks gently, obviously knowing where this is going, "what happened next?"

"We got to The Belvedere that night. It was late but I could see the house. It looked like something out of a romantic movie. I thought, 'This is the start of my latest adventure,' or something sappy like that.

"I was a little disappointed when we drove past the house, but I thought, 'Oh yeah, Chrystal. You're not going to live in the restaurant. Duh.' We pulled around to the back of this building and Sonya stopped the van."

Chrystal stops and takes a deep breath. With a shudder, she says, "And that's when I saw her for the first time. The woman who would ruin not just my dream but what was left of my life."

"Who was that, Chrystal?" Helen presses, "We need a name."

Taking a deep breath, Chrystal blurts out, "Rose."

Just then the door flies open. Rose walks in, with Charlie right behind her. The two goons who beat me up slide into the room behind them and close the door.

"Oh, crap!" I hear Gladys say in my ear.

Rose stands in front of us, her arms crossed. She looks at Helen and me, a malevolent grin spreading across her face.

"Did someone mention my name?"

Thirty-Nine

"Mom, Dad, just stay calm," Gladys is whispering in our ears. "I just need a little time."

"My, my," Rose says, smiling with the same malevolence she entered the room with, "aren't you two all dressed up for a night of fun?" Her eyes narrow when she looks at Chrystal. With a flick of her head, she signals one of her goons—I decide to call him Goon 1—and he grabs Chrystal by the arm and pulls her off the bed.

"Hey! Don't you—" I start to say, only to be cut off by Goon 1 backhanding me. I fall to the floor, stars floating in my eyes, the metallic taste of blood in my mouth.

Charlie walks over and pulls me to my feet. "You should have listened to Gus, old buddy," he says to me. "You just should have listened."

"Yes, Father," Rose says with a sneer. "You should have listened and left town while you still had the chance. Charlie told me how smart and determined you were as a kid." She shrugs. "I guess you're not really all that smart."

She turns to Chrystal, held tightly by the arm by Goon 1. She grabs her face and pulls her forward. "Stupid girl!" she hisses. "Couldn't keep that tongue of yours from wagging, eh? Lucky for you you're so popular, or I'd make sure you'd never be able to use it again." To Goon 1, Rose says, "Take her back with the others."

Chrystal doesn't even attempt to struggle as she's led from the room. At the door, she glances back at me. Her eyes are filled with sorrow and hopelessness.

When the door closes, Rose turns to us. "You know," she says, beginning to pace, "I'm tired of Greers sticking their noses into my business and trying to upset my plans."

Helen looks at her. "Oh, Rose," she says, "I'm not a Greer."

"Maybe not," Rose smiles, "But you were going to be once, a long time ago, weren't you Helen?"

At her surprised look, Rose says, "Oh, Gus told me all about you both, at least what he knew, which considering what a hick he is was actually quite impressive. The rest, well, the Internet is a wonderful thing." She leans in closer to Helen. "What is it? Still lonely from the death of your husband—what was his name, John?—after all these years? So sad the way he died. I bet that just makes you feel so awfully lonely sometimes." She whispers in Helen's ear, "Is that why you're trying so hard to fuck this priest?"

Helen's face reddens with fury and she tries to grab Rose. Goon 2 steps forward and pulls a large silver pistol from a shoulder holster concealed under his jacket and points it at Helen's head.

I gently take Helen's arm and pull her away from Rose. She sees the action and smiles. "Oh," she mocks. "How sweet!"

"What are you going to do with us, Rose?" I say. "What do you want?"

"Father, it should be obvious what I want, but I'll spell it out for that blue-haired child who no doubt is watching this right now."

"I have a name, you know," Gladys mutters.

Looking into the camera glasses, Rose says, "You have what's mine. You may have made copies, I have no real way of knowing, but that's okay. I just want the real drive. You have two hours—"

"God," Gladys says, "Why do the bad guys always give the good guys so much time?"

"—to give the drive to Gus; he'll be stopping by for it. Otherwise, you'll never see your friends here again."

"Oh, bitch," Gladys says slowly, "you have no idea who you're up against."

"Remember—two hours." Rose ends by yanking the glasses off my face and stomping on them with her heel. She put her hand out. "Earpiece and cell phone, please, Father."

I take the tiny transmitter out of my ear and place it along with my phone in her outstretched palm. She hands them to Goon 2. Turning to Helen, she says, "Same with you, Detective." Helen complies.

"Getting the real drive's not going to help, you know," I say. "You were right. We have copies, and they've been sent to the FBI. They know all about your operation."

"Maybe," she nods. "But it'll be useless to them once we've scrubbed our computers here. They won't find the originals, and any lawyer I can hire—and I can hire the best—can say they were doctored or faked by a man distraught over the death of his sister."

Charlie sidles up to his wife. "Rose, honey," he says, very much the milquetoast, "can't you just let them go? I mean, we're leaving here anyway, and—"

"Charlie," Rose says, pinching the bridge of her nose and closing her eyes. "You leave this to me. Go and do . . . whatever it is you do."

He looks like he's about to protest, then thinks better of it. With one last apologetic look to me, he leaves the four of us.

"Your old friend talks too much, Father. But I guess there's no harm in telling you. Unlike in the movies, you're not going to get out of here at the last minute and foil my evil scheme," she says, the same mocking smile on her face.

"You're leaving Bellamy?" Helen says.

"Oh, yes," Rose nods. "This place has been lucrative—sin always is, you know, the more taboo the better—but there's not much room for expansion. Even here, it's too in view. No, I've got a place all picked out. Big, quiet, secluded, one only the most determined—and the wealthiest—can get to.

"I'm sure you know, Detective," Rose says, pacing again, "all about sex tourism. Men and women will pay thousands of dollars to travel overseas to different countries to indulge in whatever . . . activities they desire. Well, I think some of that money should be spent here, in the good old USA."

"So, that's your way of making America great again?" I say.

Rose laughs. "Oh, Father, that's funny. Really funny. But in a way, yes. A resort in the Alaskan wilderness, far from prying eyes, where I can offer people willing to pay top dollar anything they desire—including things that would curl that little collar of yours."

She stands in front of us. "What? No, 'you'll never get away with this'? Huh. I'm disappointed. Father, if you still pray, you'd better pray I get what I want. Tick-tock."

With a final sneer, Rose turns to leave. She's at the door when I speak.

"Why did you kill Sonya?" I ask.

Rose turns to us, revealing cold, steel grey eyes, devoid of emotion.

"She got in my way," she says calmly. "I don't like people who get in my way."

Forty

"So, Helen, you're the expert here. What happens next?"

Since Rose took our phones and I don't have my watch, I don't really know how much time has passed. My best guess is she left us about thirty minutes ago. Helen and I haven't said a word since she left. I've been pacing around, finding myself increasingly disquieted by all the mirrors and their multiple views of Helen sitting on the bed.

For her part, Helen's been contemplating her hands in her lap, as if staring at them will give her an answer to a question she'd rather not ask me.

"Well, Gladys probably already called the state troopers and the FBI," Helen says. "They know where we are—maybe not right now, but they know we're at The Belvedere. Hopefully, they'll get here before Rose's deadline is up."

"And if they don't?"

Helen sighs and then pauses, thinking through what she wants to say next. She stands and walks over to me, her azure blue eyes filled with sorrow.

"Tom," she says after a moment, "Rose is no church secretary."

"Obviously, but what do you mean by that?"

"I mean," she says, looking me in the eye and taking my hands, "that they've already killed at least once. They can do it again. I don't think Rose has any intention of letting us live, even if she gets what she wants. Otherwise she wouldn't have told us her plans."

I clutch her hands and look down at the gold medal dangling just below her neck. An angelic warrior slaying a dragon with a double-edged sword.

Helen and I have no weapons to fight with.

Except one.

"St. Michael, the Archangel," I begin, "defend us in battle."

Her voice joins mine, "Be our protection against the wickedness and snares of the devil."

Our voices rise together with a surprising level of anger. "May God rebuke him, we humbly pray."

I hear Helen's voice falter. That only makes mine stronger, and with a conviction I haven't felt since the day of Leonard's suicide, I say, "and do thou, O Prince of the Heavenly host, by the power of God . . ."

Helen recovers and looks at me with a grateful smile. Together we say, ". . . cast into hell Satan and all the evil spirits who prowl about the world seeking the ruin of souls."

With one voice, we say, "Amen."

As we release our hands to make the sign of the Cross, I look her in the eye. With a conviction that comes from somewhere outside myself, I say to Helen, "It's going to be all right."

Trying to lighten the mood, I laugh and say, "I'm really glad that I made it to confession, though."

Helen's laugh seems to catch in her throat. She turns her head so I can't see her face.

"Tom," she saids softly, "um, what happens if someone dies without having confessed a bunch of stuff?"

"Well," I say, caught between wanting to give comfort and needing to be honest, "it would depend on the 'stuff.' Are we talking about mortal sin?"

"Probably," Helen says. "Maybe. It could be, but under the circumstances—I'm not sure?"

"What do you mean, you're not sure?"

She takes a deep breath, still not looking at me. "What if you've slept with a man you're not married to?"

"But we haven't—" I start to say.

Then I remember.

Brian.

Trying to control the anger and jealousy boiling inside me, I say, "You—you slept with Brian?"

She bites her lip and nods. "I know I should have told you—"

"Hey," I say, waving my hands. "You didn't need to tell me anything. I mean, we're not in a relationship or anything."

"Tom, please, I need to explain—"

"No, you don't," I say. Straightening my shoulders, I say, "Haven't you already confessed this?"

"It happened not long after you left," Helen says instead of answering my question.

"Helen, really, you don't—"

"I didn't tell you in our emails, but—but I was lonely for you. I missed you. I thought I'd never see you again. So, one day, Brian invited me to dinner. I accepted, because I was tired of being alone every night. But I had no intention of sleeping with him."

Calmly, with a grace that can only come from God, I ask, "So, how did it happen?"

"You know me," she smiles sheepishly. "Even though I'm a big woman, I've never been able to hold my alcohol. Well, he ordered wine, and I drank. And drank. And drank some more. I don't remember anything after some point that evening, but the next thing I know, I'm waking up in Brian's apartment. In his bed."

We're quiet for a moment. In a flash, my jealousy is gone, replaced by a furious rage directed at one Brian Dohrmann.

"So, you were drunk," I say quietly. "Is it possible he put something in your drink?"

"I've thought about that, actually. I remember going to the ladies room, so he could have slipped something in my wine then."

I clench my fists. "That bastard," I whisper.

"Tom, whatever Brian did, the fact of the matter is I let my guard down. I was trying to drown my sorrow over you, and things got out of hand. I have no one but myself to blame."

"But you were drunk," I say gently. "A person can't commit a mortal sin if they did something without full knowledge and will. Sounds to me like both were impared that night."

She nods and sighs. "Well, you're right about that. I wouldn't have slept with Brian under any other circumstances."

"What I don't understand is why you haven't talked to someone about this, who could explain that to you."

"I did. To Father Leonard. In the confessional." Helen's look of disgust tells me everything I need to know.

"He treated it like it was no big deal, didn't he?" I say quietly.

"He didn't laugh it off, but at the end he didn't say anything about it. So he absolved me, but I still have this guilt."

I take a deep breath. "Helen, at best your sin was venal. Between the alcohol and the possibility that Brian slipped you something, what happened doesn't fall into the category of mortal sin."

Helen smiles. "That does make me feel better. But I've avoided going to confession at all since that time with Father Leonard. And after you got back—I just couldn't. Not to you. I was going to find another church where no one knew me and confess to the priest there. I just haven't yet."

I take a deep breath and let it out slowly. The impact of what she just told me hits me harder than Rose's goons ever could.

Helen didn't feel she could come to me for the sacrament of confession because of my feelings for her. And because of that—because of me—her soul's in danger at our hour of peril as much as her body is.

More clearly than ever before—perhaps really for the first time—I see the depths of my sins. I realize once again how much my feelings for Helen have betrayed her. All this time, she's been a penitent with no priest to hear her confession.

We both sit there in silence as the seconds tick away in my head. I know what I need to do, what I can do, what only I can do. I have been so focused on what I can't have that I have forgotten what I do have.

One of those things is the ability to give Helen one last, amazing gift.

I get up slowly and take her by the hand. She asks no questions as I lead her to the door to the bathroom. I open it into the room so it makes a screen between us. I kneel on my side, because I want to be with her in what could be our last minutes together.

I retrieve my purple stole, the one I always keep rolled up in my pocket for times like this. It is both a sign of my office and a fence that divides us at this moment and for all time. I kiss it, thankful for it even as it causes me pain. It is not just a fence but also a door, a door to God that I can open for her now.

I feel her kneel against the door. I say with a voice that starts out as a weak croak but quickly gains strength, "Let us come together before the throne of God's mercy in the name of the Father, and of the Son, and of the Holy Spirit."

At this moment, I'm no longer Tom Greer. I'm no longer the man who loves the woman behind the door. It's not my ears that are about to hear Helen pour out her darkest secrets. I am, as the Church teaches, in the place of Christ, and it's He who will hear what this penitent soul has to say.

"Bless me, Father, for I have sinned," Helen begins quietly. "It has been ten months since my last confession. In that time I have cursed, a lot, and have taken the name of the Lord in vain, a lot. I have been angry, a lot, and have sometimes been rougher on a suspect than I ought to be."

She pauses briefly, then says with a rush, "And I slept with a man I'm not married to. It was just once, and I was drunk. But I'm not making any excuses for my behavior."

I sit quietly for a moment and then ask, "Is there anything else?"

There is silence on the other side of the door for several moments. Then, she whispers, her voice tinged with sorrow and shame, "Father, I have fallen in love with my priest and have tried on numerous occasions to make him fall in love with me. In doing so, I have lied to him, and have even neglected my job in order to spend more time with him."

I am surprised to hear my heart beating as she says this, not because of my attraction to her but because of my repugnance at my own culpability in her sin. As I kneel, seeking God's wisdom for the proper words of comfort to speak to her, Helen says with a soft exhale, "For these and all my other sins I am truly sorry."

Suddenly, I hear a voice that is so obviously not my own come out of my mouth. "God is so glad that you have made a good confession. He is here with you now, and will continue to be. He has allowed you a hard burden of loving a man you can never make a life with. But He has, and will continue, to give you the grace to bear it. For your penance, say three Our Fathers, offering up your suffering for those who have sinned against you in this life. Now, say an Act of Contrition."

Though I know that Helen knows the Act of Contrition, I nonetheless lead her in saying, "O my God, I am heartily sorry for having offended Thee, and I detest all my sins because of thy just punishments, but most of all because they offend Thee, my God, who art all good and deserving of all my love."

Together, with voices grim with determination, we conclude, "I firmly resolve with the help of Thy grace to sin no more and to avoid the near occasion of sin. Amen."

Now it's my turn to speak. I say with more joy in my heart than I've felt in months, "God, the Father of mercies, through the death and resurrection of his Son has reconciled the world to himself and sent the Holy Spirit among us for the forgiveness of sins; through the ministry of the Church may God give you pardon and peace, and I absolve you from your sins in the name of the Father, and of the Son, and of the Holy Ghost. Amen."

I rise from my place and walk around to her side of the door, helping her up and taking her in my arms, not in any way that is remotely "a near occasion of sin," but as a shepherd holding a found lamb.

We stay that way for what at the same time seems a moment and an eternity. Then, the door opens and Rose reappears with her goons.

"Oh," she says slyly, "did I interrupt something?"

I turn to her, my arm still around Helen's shoulders, and say calmly, "Nothing you'd understand."

Forty-One

Apparently, Rose is not amused by my remarks.

She looks at Goon 2 and nods toward me. In one motion, he grabs and slams me against the wall, holding my head so my face is pressed against the mirrored surface. I'm just thankful the glass doesn't break and cut me.

The wind's knocked out of me, and I'm quickly reminded this same goon kicked the crap out of me not a week ago. Behind me, I hear Helen's protest, then her struggle against Goon 1 who was obviously directed to hold her still.

Rose looks at me with contempt. "Oh, Father. Or maybe you prefer to be called Daddy, hmmm? I understand a lot more than you think I do."

She leans in closer. "I know all about you priests," she hisses. "I've known quite a few in my time, and none of them were interested in my soul. To them, I was just a piece of ass. You know, most of them were the worst perverts of all. So yeah, I understand all about men like you, Father."

Rose grabs a fistful of my hair and yanks my head back, forcing me to look at her. "Without that collar," she spits, "you're just like any other man, worse than most because at least they make an honest living. They're not hypocrites who threaten people with hellfire just for wanting to have a little fun."

Screaming through clenched teeth, she slams my head into the glass. Helen screams, "No!" My vision blurs and my knees weaken. I slide down to the floor against the glass. A warm, liquidy feeling on my forehead tells me that this time, the mirror did break.

I don't think I'm hurt badly. But on top of my other injuries, I'm not in the best shape.

Through the fog, I hear Helen say, "Enough of the theatrics, Rose. What's your plan for us?"

Blood is trickling down the side of my head as I lean against the glass, fighting against the growing nausea, struggling to focus as the room spins around me. My breathing is ragged. I'm struggling to hold on to consciousness.

But it's a battle I'm losing.

As I feel myself slipping into darkness, I hear Joan's voice.

She needs you, Tom.

But what help can I be to Helen, like this? I've no way to fight for her. No way to protect her. I'm weak. I'm in pain. I can't even stand up. If I try, they'll kill me.

Again, Joan's voice comes from the enveloping darkness.

She needs you, Tom.

Then I realize what Joan's telling me.

Someone in this room needs me, needs what only I can offer.

But it's not Helen.

"What happened?" I manage to ask.

Rose stops speaking and says to me, "What? Did you say something?"

I force myself to look at her. She's staring at me, and through the haziness, I think I see a crack of uncertainty.

Clearing my throat, I say a little more loudly, "What happened to you?"

"I don't know what you mean," Rose says haughtily. To Goon 2, she says, "Shut him up."

Goon 2 is about to slam my head with the butt of his gun when I say, "What happened, Nina?"

"Stop!" Rose commands Goon 2. Her eyes are huge, and the crack of uncertainty I saw earlier widens.

My vision is clearing, so I can see more of the room now. Helen is behind Rose, staring at me, visibly worried about what I'm doing.

If I could talk to her, I'd tell her what she's told me on numerous occasions.

I'm doing my job. But it's more than a job.

It's my life.

"What did you say?" Rose says quietly.

"Nina," I say. "That's your name, isn't it? Nina."

A bitter smile plays on her lips, but her eyes appear to soften, the cold steel grey giving over to a blue-greenish tint. "Nina," she says. "No one's called me that in years."

"Tell me, Nina," I say. "What happened? You weren't always like this. I've seen your high school picture. You were a beautiful young lady with a bright future."

She rolls her eyes and shakes her head. "Oh, Father, Father, Father. I know all the tricks men like you use. You manipulate people's emotions to get what you want."

"I don't want anything, Nina—"

"Rose!" she screams and takes a step toward me.

"Nina," I say calmly. "I don't want anything from you. I want to help you."

"You just don't want to die," she laughs.

"I don't want to, you're right," I say. "But I'm ready to die. Before I do, I want to help you."

She crosses her arms. Her shoulders are square, her spine rigid. She narrows her eyes and the sneer widens on her lips.

"I know what you're thinking, Father," she snarls, "somebody must have hurt me, some priest abused me, my daddy touched me, my parents got divorced and neither one wanted me. Because that's what people like you always think about people like me. That only someone completely damaged and broken would allow themselves to be used in all sorts of ways for money."

She lets out a nasty, ironic laugh. "Sorry to burst your bubble, Father. You're wrong about me. I'm not damaged at all, not broken in the least. I've done everything I've done because I wanted to. It's as simple as that."

"But there had to be a reason you chose all this, Nina."

She shrugs. "I actually had what you people would consider an ideal family. Grew up in a warm, happy parish with five older brothers. I was the only girl so I always had new clothes, even though my brothers had to wear hand-me-downs. We all went to Catholic school, my mom volunteered there, and my dad showed up to every game we played. He paid me plenty of attention and said that I was special because I was the only girl among so many boys. He told me how they'd hoped and prayed for me and how happy they were with me. They really offered me what they and their friends believed was a perfect life."

"So," I say, not able to help myself, "what happened?"

"Nothing. Nothing at all. I just didn't want what they were offering. My clothes were new but never as fashionable as the other girls in the neighborhood. The older they got, the shorter their skirts and shorts got, while mine stayed the same. The shorter the skirts, the more attention they got from the boys. Me? I was like the Ugly Duckling among a bunch of beautiful swans. Mom said it was better for me to focus my attention on my mind and personality and not worry about drawing attention to my body. I mean, what the hell was that about?

"And then, there was the Miss Tuscaloosa Pageant circuit. My friend who lived next door participated every year. I'd watch her walk out to her car in high heels, make-up, big, teased, curly hair, even when she was in elementary school. I begged Mom and Dad to let me participate but they just said that girls shouldn't use their bodies to get ahead in life.

"Man, were they wrong. You know what I bought myself with my 17th birthday money? A cell phone. One that I could use to call who I wanted to, when I wanted to. That's when I learned about how much money a pretty girl could earn and how easy it could be. Not long after, I left home, went to New Orleans, and found a job as a dancer. That was the beginning.

"I'll admit, it was hard at first, but I soon got the hang of it. From dancing I went to posting photos on the Internet, then webcam shows. Finally I hooked up with a guy, Andy, who handled the camera work for me in return for, well, you know. I didn't start turning tricks until then, and by that time I had a bit of a following online, so I could be picky. Andy acted as a sort of bouncer for me. In return for a piece of what I earned, he'd stay outside the door and make sure no one hurt me—unless, of course, they paid extra.

"Andy and I finally got married, though of course it didn't last. For some reason, he thought we had enough money and that I ought to quit the business. But I was just getting started. I got rid of him almost as quickly as I did his baby. Then it was on to the next guy, and the next. I'd take them for what I could, marry them if they insisted, and then move on.

"All the time, I was building towards this. I started with a couple of girls, then made the right connections to get more. All I needed was the money, the right front man, and the perfect location. The money was easy enough—my last husband was old and rich and everyone believed he died of a heart attack. He had no children, so everything came to me."

"And then, you met Charlie," I say.

"Ah, Charlie was perfect. Typical man. Loved being seen around with a pretty young thing. He had this place started, but needed money. I provided that. And the vision for what you see here. I wanted to build a place where wealthy men and women could indulge their deepest, darkest fantasies."

She smiles. "And that's what I've done," she says. "All those men taught me an important lesson. The best thing I had was a young, sexy, nubile body, and I learned to use it extremely well. And that's what I'm teaching those girls. That if they want to get anywhere, if they want to get where I am, they've got to use the only asset they have."

"But Nina—"

"Don't call me that!" Rose screams. "Nina's dead!"

I shake my head and begin to stand up. "No, she's not," I say. I'm unsteady on my feet—either I'm swaying or the room is swaying, I can't tell. Helen steps toward me, but she's stopped by Goon 1.

"Nina's not dead," I say, staggering a little toward the woman, who was once a little girl, standing in front of me. "That's who you are."

"No," she shakes her head. "Nina was weak!"

"Nina was a girl," I say, "whose parents loved her very much, who couldn't see that all they wanted to do was teach her that she was a person, not an object."

I stop a foot from her, steadier now, a strength not my own keeping me on my feet. "That's what you've taught these girls, that they're just objects to be used."

"No!" Rose declares. "I've empowered them! I've freed them to become what I am!"

"You've enslaved them to other people's lusts."

"Your sister helped me, Greer," she says. "Sonya brought these girls here, did to them what I told her to do."

"But at some point, she stopped, didn't she?"

Rose—Nina—scoffs. "Suddenly, after two years of getting girls here, training them, setting them up with clients, she got a conscience. Started saying maybe we shouldn't have younger girls. I told her that was where the money was—the younger they were, the more men were willing to pay."

"She found out about your plans to expand to selling girls."

"Yes. Oh, she threw a huge fit, and threatened to go to the authorities with what she knew." Rose shakes her head. "I never thought she'd do it. I mean, her hands had as much dirt on them as anyone."

I look her in the eye. "And then you found out she stole the files."

"Those files could ruin me!" Rose screams. "I had to get them back! To do what I wanted to do, there had to be no trace!"

"So, what happened, Rose?"

She shrugs. "I decided she needed to be persuaded. I sent Jake and Brent," she says, nodding at Goon 1 and Goon 2, "to get her, bring her here so she could be persuaded to return what she stole. But Dumb and Dumber here didn't engage the child locks in the back. She got out and ran into the woods."

I don't need to know anymore. Having escaped, she ran in the dark through the woods. Knowing they'd get her eventually, she called the only person she really trusted to do the right thing.

Her big brother.

But they caught her. Maybe she fought back, maybe it was an accident, I'll never know. But they shot and killed her. Then, they took her body and threw it in a dumpster like so much trash.

"Those men were wrong," I'm saying. "All those people have been wrong. You're not an object. You're a person. You have dignity. The girls—they're people who have dignity."

Rose rolls her eyes at this. "Next you're going to tell me that God loves me, and he's merciful, and all I need to do is confess my sins, and I'll be forgiven, blah blah blah."

I smile. "Well, yes, actually. I was going to say something like that to you."

Rose laughs in my face. "No, Father. No. See, I know the truth. There's no God. There's no Heaven. There's no Hell. Sin? Just made up to keep people from having a good time, to make people ashamed. Actually, I guess I should thank you for that last part. The more ashamed they are of their chosen sin, the more they're willing to pay for it. So no, Father. I'll pass."

She turns her back on me and walks to the door. "What if you're wrong?"

Rose turns around and shrugs. "I'll deal with that when it happens, which is going to be a long time yet." She looks at her watch. "Oh, dear," she mutters. "On the other hand, it looks like time's almost up for you and your little girlfriend here."

She walks to the door. "Jake, Brent, make sure you get rid of their bodies really well. No trace this time, understand?"

Rose is reaching for the door when it flies open. Charlie rushes in, clutching a tablet. He's as white as a sheet.

"Rose!" he says, his voice dripping with panic. "We've got a problem."

"Oh, what is it?" Rose says irritably.

"We started to scrub the files from the computers here and transfer everything offshore when we were locked out!"

"What do you mean, locked out?"

"I mean exactly that," Charlie says, his voice rising. "Every file, every program, every system we have is completely frozen. All the security systems are offline. We can't make change for a five-dollar bill at the bar!"

"Well, that's what we pay that tech geek for!" Rose roars. 'Tell him to fix it. Now!"

"He's tried. He says the person who did this is a genius. He's never seen anything like it before. All that comes up on the screens is this," Charlie says, handing the tablet to her.

Rose grabs it from his hands and looks at the display. Her eyes get huge and her face becomes red with rage. She marches up to me and shoves the tablet under my nose.

I take it from her and look at the screen.

And I start laughing.

I turn and hand the tablet to Helen. After a second, she starts laughing, too.

The tablet displays one word, neatly done in the 18th century script one might see on a treasure map.

Ahoy!

Forty-Two

Rose doesn't find the situation as funny as Helen and I do. She turns on Charlie and screams, "You tell that pencil-neck little shit computer expert you hired to fix this!"

Charlie scurries out of the room to follow Rose's order. Having dispatched him, Rose turns on us. I'm standing next to Helen—actually, by this time, Helen is holding me up.

She opens her mouth to say something when there's a rumble somewhere nearby. Rose and her goons look in the direction of the noise.

Helen whispers to me, "I think the cavalry's coming."

"Go see what that is," Rose says. The goons head for the door, but she says, "Wait, one of you give me your gun."

Goon 1 hands his pistol over to her and they quickly exit. Rose turns to us, pointing the pistol at our heads.

"Nice try, Father, trying to get me to feel sorry for what I've done, ask God to forgive me. But you miscalculated. You assume I feel sorry for everything I've done. I don't. In fact, I don't think I've done anything wrong at all."

"You had Sonya killed," I say.

"Mmm, okay, that may have been wrong, who's to say? I mean, without God—who doesn't exist—anything is possible, right? We're just animals, rutting, fighting, clawing each other to get ahead. Sonya tried to stop me. I needed to get rid of her. Simple."

She looks at me steadily over the barrel of the gun. "Now, the only question I have is, who do I kill first? You, Father?"

I look her in the eye, my chin up. "Just get it over with," I say quietly. "I'm ready to die. My conscience is clear. If you kill me, I know where I'll go. I'll be with my wife, my daughter. I'll be happy."

"Aw, how sweet," Rose says, a mocking smile on her face. Turning to Helen she says, "I bet that makes you really feel good, to have your boyfriend talk about his dead wife like that."

She steps to my side and puts her arm through mine. "Thanks to Tom," she says, "my conscience is clear, too, and I have every hope that if I die, I'll be with my husband."

She shakes her head. "My, my, such nobility of spirit," she chuckles, "I guess the only question I have to answer is, who do I want to see miserable before I kill them?"

Rose looks back and forth between us. She settles on me, and smiles. "You know, Father, killing you right away would be too easy. I think I want to see you suffer a little first. So," she points the gun at Helen, "you get to watch her die."

I'm staring at Rose, a protest on my lips, then I look at Helen. Her eyes are closed, as if she's prepared for the bullet to slice into her body, and for whatever comes after.

She's at peace, because I was able to serve her one last time as her priest. Not her husband, not her lover, but as an instrument of God's mercy.

And I realize in that second, that's how much I love her.

"Would you like to say anything to her, Father, before she dies?"

I look at Rose steadily. "She knows everything," I whisper.

At that moment, there's a large explosion somewhere in the building. Small arms and automatic weapons fire erupts along with cries, screams, and shouted commands. Rose turns to the door. With her distracted, I lunge for the gun and manage to knock it out of her grasp. She roars with anger as she scurries across the floor to retrieve it.

I grab Helen by the arm and drag her with me into the bathroom, pulling the door closed behind us.

"Bathtub!" Helen yells. We climb into the large circular tub, crouching as low as we can. Outside, Rose is pounding on the door and trying the lock. We hear small bursts and pings as she tries to shoot the lock off.

Suddenly, she stops shooting as there's the sound of boots and commands. "Put it down! Put the gun down!" Two shots answer. A fusillade of automatic weapons fire responds, bursting through the wood door and sending a shower of splinters and dust over us.

Then, it stops. No more gunfire.

Muffled voices yelling, "clear," "clear," "suspect down, get the paramedics," are all we hear. Then, there's a pounding on the door and a familiar voice.

"Mom! Dad! You okay?"

We look at each other, smiling but not surprised that somehow, someway, Gladys is here.

"Fine! We're both fine!" Helen calls. I climb out of the tub, then offer Helen my hand. When she steps out, her foot catches on the edge of the tub and she stumbles. I grab her to keep her from falling, and she winds up against me, my arms holding her tight.

We stare into each other's eyes. Our heartbeats, so rapid already because of the terrifying experience we just had, speed up. The red in Helen's cheeks must match mine, judging by how hot they are right now.

"You know how much I want to right now, don't you?" I say breathlessly.

She swallows and nods. "As much as I want you to," she whispers.

We stand like that for what seems like an eternity, when there's a knock at the door. "Ah, guys? Want us to come back later?"

We smile and start to laugh. But we don't let go of each other. After a minute more, Helen clears her throat. "We'd better go before they decide to break the door down."

I grin. "Yeah, we better not keep our daughter waiting."

We separate and walk to the door, me guiding Helen with my hand in the small of her back, and push it open. We're both looking down, expecting to see Gladys in her wheelchair, and are startled when we see not a petite blue-haired young woman but find ourselves staring at a massive stomach and chest covered in a dark green Sheriff's uniform.

"Up here, guys!" We look up and see Gladys grinning down at us, being carried piggy-back by Gus.

Our mouths fall open. "Gladys? Gus? What the—?" I manage to say.

"I was able to persuade Gus to help," Gladys says with a grin.

"Huh! Persuade nothin'!" Gus says. "Threatened to tank my credit score, have me put on every terrorist watch list, even cancel my cable subscription."

"So that's the only reason you did it?" I say, smiling at the big man.

"No," Gus says. "No. I guess you could say I finally saw the light."

I open my mouth to say something when movement behind Gus catches my attention.

Three paramedics are working frantically on Rose, lying motionless on the floor.

"Excuse me," I mutter and step around Gus, putting my purple stole on as I walk.

I stand off from the two men and one woman working on her, trying to stop bleeding from three holes I can see in her chest. She's on oxygen, and an IV's already started.

"Stay with us, come on just stay with us!" the woman yells at Rose.

One of the men says to another, "We've gotta get this bleeding under control. Shit! She's losing a lot."

"Pardon me," I say. They ignore me, so I shout, "Hey! Excuse me, please!" and try to push my way past.

The nearest paramedic looks at me and holds his hands up.

"Hey, you need to—" he begins to yell and then sees the purple stole.

"I'm a priest," I explain. "I need to give her last rites. Please, I won't get in the way."

He looks at his colleagues, then back to me. "Yeah, Father, okay, but just a minute."

He moves and I kneel on the floor next to Rose. I bend down close to her ear so she can hear me. The paramedics are working to save her life.

I have only a minute to try to save her soul.

"Rose," I say in her ear. There's no response. "Rose," I say again.

There's a slight movement and a faint grunt. I see her eyes flutter open. She notices me. Her face is devoid of emotion, the eyes almost lifeless.

"Rose," I say to her, looking directly in her eyes so she can see my lips, "You may not have much time left. Please, Rose, for the sake of your soul, let me hear your confession."

She makes a light motion with her head, which I interpret as a signal to come closer. I turn my head so she's speaking in my ear.

In a barely audible whisper, she says, "Go to hell."

Forty-Three

"I think all that aggravated your concussion, Father Greer," the woman paramedic, named Liz, says after checking me out at the ambulance.

"I'd like to take you to the hospital to have them look at you," she adds.

"I'm fi—" I start to say.

"He'll go," Helen says, looking at me firmly with her arms crossed. "Right, Tom?"

I smile sheepishly. "Whatever you say, dear."

Looking slightly confused, Liz asks Helen, "Are you family? His . . . sister?"

Before Helen can speak, I quickly say, "No, my wife."

Helen suppresses a smile while giving me a dirty look—I don't know why, she started this thing we do of lying to health care professionals—but nods. "Yes, what he said."

"Oh!" Liz looks at both of us, her mouth open, "okay then. Ah, well, Ms. Greer, would you like to ride?"

"I'll drive and meet you at the hospital, Tom," she says. "Our car is here," she explains to Liz.

"I'll go with him!" Gladys yells as she comes to a stop right in front of the hapless paramedic.

"And you are?" Liz asks.

"That's our daughter," I quip before Helen can speak.

Liz looks over her shoulder at me, then at Helen, then at Gladys—who grins and gives her a little wave—then back at me.

I shrug. "We're an odd little family," I smile sheepishly.

"Uh-huh, okay, well, ahem," Liz says, contemplating her clipboard. "Just, ah, ju—just let me check with my colleagues and we'll be off." She scurries off, shaking her head and looking back over her shoulder.

Gladys says, "What's her problem?" She hands us back our cell phones.

"It's been a stressful night," I say.

"Gladys, I am curious about one thing," Helen says. "We told you to call the Florida Highway Patrol and the FBI."

"Uh-huh, I did. They were here."

"But from what I could see, FHP led the assault."

"Yeah."

"But how did that happen?"

Gladys shrugs. "It's like my Uncle Fred used to say—if you want something done right, call a State Trooper."

"Well, you did great, Gladys. Thank you." I hesitate a moment, then add, "Could you leave Mom and me alone for a bit?"

Gladys looks at both of us, then nods. "Sure. I need to go check on my minions anyway."

As she heads back to the building, I turn to Helen. "Her minions?"

"The FBI computer forensics team out of Quantico," she explains. "Apparently, they've never seen ransomware like Gladys'. She's the only one who can unfreeze the files. So, Myerton is lending Gladys to the FBI Field Office for a few extra days."

"Has she said anything about what they found on The Belvedere's computers?"

Helen smiles and rubs my back. "She says it looks like this thing goes far beyond just here and Louisiana. Rose was part of an international human trafficking operation, spanning about a dozen countries and hundreds, maybe thousands of young girls."

I shake my head. "My God," I whisper. "So many young souls."

"And you saved them, Tom. Just like Sonya knew you would."

I'm watching a group of girls who look to range from 15 to 25; they're in various states of dress and undress, being attended to by people from local churches handing out blankets and hot drinks.

"What's going to happen to them?" I say, nodding toward the group.

"It depends," Helen says. "The adults will no doubt be charged with prostitution, but since many of them were probably coerced, it's unlikely they'll actually serve any time."

"And the young girls?"

"They'll try to reunite them with their families, those that want them. The rest, well," Helen sighs and shakes her head.

I'm about to ask another question when Gus walks up.

"Hey, old buddy," he says.

"Gus, I—"

He cuts me off with a wave of his hand. "Don't mention it. I'm just glad I came to my senses when I did." He looks at his feet. "I was really beginning to hate myself, doing what I was doing. I know Mama's not proud of me."

"She is now," I say. "What's going to happen to you?"

"Oh, I've already given the county commission my resignation," he says. "I have a lot to answer for, I know. But don't you worry about me, Tom. I'm going to be all right. I know enough about Charlie and his operation here to put him in Raiford for the rest of his life."

He looks over at some men in Florida Department of Law Enforcement jackets. "I think they're here for me," Gus indicates with his head. "I'll be seeing you. Good luck, Tom."

I take his proffered hand. "I'll include you in my prayers, Gus. God will forgive you, if you let him."

"Yeah. Yeah." Tipping his hat at Helen, he walks to the waiting officers.

"That's another one," Helen says.

"Another what?" I ask.

"Why, Tom," she smiles. "Another soul you've saved tonight."

"I'm just an instrument Helen," I say, shaking my head. "It's God who does the saving."

"I know that, darling," Helen says, slipping her arm under mine. "But if you weren't here, if you weren't here as a priest, all those souls would still be in danger."

She looks down. "Mine included," she whispers. "Thank you. I . . . I know that it couldn't have been easy to hear my confession."

Do I tell her the truth? Do I tell her it just about tore me up inside? Do I tell her about the weight of guilt I felt knowing that she had come so close to oblivion because of my failure as her priest, because of my desire for her as a woman?

No. All that is true. But what I tell her is more important.

"Helen," I say, looking her in the eye. "You weren't confessing your sins to Tom Greer, the man who loves you more than anyone else on this earth. You were confessing your sins to your priest who, in those moments, was Jesus for you. And as soon as you confessed those sins, and I spoke those ancient words of the Church, Jesus took those sins and removed them as far as the east is from the west. He doesn't remember them, or hold them against you. And I want you to hear me, Helen, because it's important you understand this. I don't either. It's done. It's over."

With those last words, Helen breaks down and begins sobbing. She leans her head on my shoulder and I place my arm around her, comforting her as a shepherd should.

As a pastor must.

After a few minutes, her crying stops and she wipes her eyes. "Well," she sniffles. "We did what we came to do. We found out what happened to Sonya."

"And more," I say. "So much more."

"Yes," Helen says. "I guess we can't avoid it anymore."

I shake my head. "No. We need to talk about everything. About us, and what it means for my priesthood. About my priesthood, and what it means for us. Helen, so much has changed here. Things can't be the same when we get back to Myerton."

"I know," she says. "We need to figure out what 'us' looks like."

"And," I take a deep breath. "We can't do that on our own. We need guidance. And there's only one person who can do that."

Just then, my phone rings. I dig it out of my pocket. When I see the caller id, I turn the phone so Helen can see it. She chuckles and shakes her head.

Answering the phone, I say, "Good evening, Your Eminence. I was just about to call you."

Forty-Four

I am not surprised when the Archbishop calls.

I am surprised that it includes a dinner invitation for the evening we return to Maryland.

For both myself *and* Helen.

"Just a small gathering at the residence," he says, "you, Detective Parr, myself, and Father Wayne, just to show my congratulations for what you did down there."

"Your Eminence, it really isn't necessary," I reply.

"Oh, I think it is," he says. "You both put yourselves in mortal danger to save those young women. That's to be commended. The press is already asking questions about you. I expect there's going to be some news stories in the days ahead about this."

He pauses. "Tom," he says, more seriously this time, "I forwarded the information you sent to the Archdiocese of New Orleans. They're going to work with the authorities down there to break up this Saint Magdalene's. You'll be pleased to know that so far, they've found no connection between it and the Archdiocese or any other official Church body. The priest the girl mentioned does not appear in the records of any diocese in the United States. But this is going to be looked into by the highest authorities here and in Rome, and I promise you one thing. There will be no cover-up. No more sweeping problems under the rug. We need to shine a bright light on corruption and bring it out in the open."

I take that as my cue. "As I said, Your Eminence, I was planning on calling you. I have something I need to discuss with you, and I want to do it face to face."

"Well, that's fine, Tom," he replies. "But may I ask what it's about?"

"No, Your Eminence," I say. "I, ah, need some more time to figure out what I'm going to say to you.

***

Part of figuring out involves talking with Helen about, well, everything. About our love for each other. About our mutual desire that I stay in the priesthood. About our mutual desire to stay in each other's lives. About our mutual love for God and his Church. But also, about our commitment to live both our vocations fully—mine, as a priest, and Helen's as a single woman.

For her, I come to realize, the sacrifice is greater.

"Tom," she says to me as we drive to the airport to catch our flight home. "If I haven't already, I want to make something clear to you."

"What's that?"

"I want to be clear that I love you. I will always love you. There will never be anybody else but you."

"You've told me that," I say with a smile.

"Yes, but I just need to be explicit about what that means to me. It means that your life of celibacy, your life without physical intimacy, is the life I'm choosing, too."

"Helen," I say, "I can't ask—"

"You're not asking me, Tom. I've thought about it a lot. I won't date anyone. I won't marry anyone. And I certainly won't be sleeping with anyone. If I can't be in your bed, I don't want to be in anyone else's."

Our talk continues on the plane as we make our way closer to home and closer to our dinner with the Archbishop. We know we need to have a plan before we meet with him.

By the time we land, we think we have one.

But it really depends on the Archbishop.

***

We arrive at the Archbishop's residence together, since I'm still unable to drive until Thursday, the day after Ash Wednesday. I asked Dan Conway to drive Nate Rodriguez to Dulles to get my car and drive it back to the Rectory. I was very vague as to how I was going to get from Baltimore to Myerton—or even how I was getting from Dulles to Baltimore in the first place.

It wasn't a secret anymore that Helen and I had been together in Bellamy. Fortunately, the news of my sister's murder and our role in breaking up a human trafficking ring seemed sufficient to squelch any rumors. Even Anna, so rightly concerned about me and my feelings for Helen, didn't bring it up when I spoke to her on the phone except to say, "I'm really glad Helen was able to help you find out what happened to your sister."

The Archbishop's Residence is gorgeous, Georgian brick with three stories above ground as well as a basement. It is about 200 years old and was built when Maryland was one of the only places in America where Catholics could live without fear of religious harassment. I know from experience that the main floor houses both the Archbishop's offices and those of his secretary, a grizzled old priest who arrived to serve as the Archbishop's gatekeeper after the Marine Corp unit to which he was assigned as a chaplain asked that he be sent home for being too aggressive. He is the one who opens the door and invites us in, saying that the Archbishop is finishing saying Evening Prayer in his chapel.

Father Wayne, or as we call him behind his back, Father Duke, leads us through the main reception room and the side reception room into a small sitting room where I have met with the Archbishop in the past. He suggests—or rather, orders—that we be seated, standing in front of the small loveseat and pointing to the other side of the burning fireplace to two wing chairs, as if concerned with what we might get up to when alone.

Father Wayne leaves us, saying pointedly that someone will be stopping in soon to offer us drinks. Again, he's telegraphing that no shenanigans will be tolerated.

Once we're alone, I look at Helen and say pleasantly, "You look nice."

She had insisted on changing out of her travel clothes at the airport from a comfortable denim skirt and sweater into something more . . . conservative, I guess is the word I'm looking for. She's wearing a crisp white blouse buttoned to the neck. Her long black skirt is narrow but has no slit in the side and is so long that there's barely a hint of ankle showing. Over this ensemble, she is wearing a long black sweater with matching black earrings.

The only flash of color is her gold Saint Michael's medal.

She smiles back at me. "Thanks. Nice is what I was going for. Nice woman, nice cop, nice Catholic, not in any way dangerous to the soul of any priest anywhere but especially not to the one sitting beside me."

I stand up as she finishes her statement and the Archbishop strides into the room. He is a big man, more than six feet tall and obviously someone who enjoys good food. He takes my hand and shakes it as Helen also stands.

"Father Tom, so nice of you to join me tonight."

"I am the one who is honored," I say, as my mother trained me, and then, "Your Eminence, may I present Detective Helen Parr? Helen, Archbishop Walter Knowland."

"It is a pleasure to finally meet you, Ms. Parr. Obviously I have heard many nice things about you."

Helen begins to blush as I quickly add, "Yes Archbishop, the press has been very complimentary."

His Eminence, who never misses anything, no doubt noticed her blush and my rescue.

Oh well, it's probably for the best. He'll at least have some suspicions by the time we talk.

At this point, the evening becomes a blur. A young man and woman, each clad in matching wait staff attire, moves in and out of the room as we talk and enjoy a drink and some small canapes. From there we go to the small dining room, just the three of us and Father Wayne, who proves to have several rather humorous tales of being under fire to share with Helen.

After dinner, which is as elegant as the occasion demands, we retire to the Archbishop's study for coffee. Father Wayne remains with us for about a half-hour before excusing himself, leaving Helen and me alone with the Archbishop.

"Well, Tom," he begins, "you said you have something you want to discuss with me? Will you be hanging back after Ms. Parr leaves or is she to participate, too?"

Taking a deep breath, I say, "Ms. Parr would like to remain for this discussion."

"As I'm sure she could have told me herself," he says with a smile. "So, I will assume that you are the one who will get the ball rolling."

I shoot a quick glance at Helen, who smiles at me encouragingly.

"Your Eminence," I say, "you see before you a man who is a priest and determined to remain one, but who has fallen in love with a woman."

"I see," he says, years of training and experience making it easy for him to keep a poker face. "Go on."

"Well, Your Eminence, that's the problem, I don't know how to go on. That is why I'm here tonight."

To my surprise, he pulls out his phone and taps a few keys before turning his attention to Helen.

"Ms. Parr," he says carefully, "Am I correct in assuming that you are the woman in question?"

"Yes, Your Eminence, I am."

"And that you are a Catholic, a member of Father Greer's parish?"

"Yes, Your Eminence."

He then turns to me and says calmly, "Father Greer, would you excuse us, please? Father Wayne will keep you company in the other room."

Thoroughly confused, I can only mutter, "Sure," as the door opens and a habited Sister walks in. I leave and nearly run right into Father Wayne. He turns on his heel and without a word leads me to another small sitting room down the hall.

We remain there for the longest twenty minutes of my life.

When I am finally escorted back to the room, the sister is leaving and Helen is as white as a sheet.

I look at the Archbishop, fury welling up in me that he has somehow hurt her when he says, "Have a seat, Father Tom, everything is fine."

I look at Helen, who is beginning to get some color back in her face as she says to me, "Yes, Tom, everything is fine, at least so far."

I take the seat next to her and sit, staring at the Archbishop.

"Father Tom," he says with a grave tone and expression, "you seem confused, but if you'd think about things for a minute, you wouldn't be." When I don't respond, he continues, "Ms. Parr is a member of my Archdiocese. That makes me her over-shepherd and very responsible for her spiritual health and safety. As her priest, you hold a certain amount of authority over her. Therefore, my first task—my most important task—in this situation is to make sure that you have in no way coerced or taken advantage of her in any way. She has assured me that you have not, that your relationship has been completely consensual, and that there has been no serious physical intimacy between you."

Finally getting my breath back, I say, "That is correct."

"So, I understand that you want to remain a priest. Do you also want to continue to have some sort of relationship with Ms. Parr?"

"Yes, Your Eminence."

"And you with him?" he says, looking at Helen.

She nods, a slight smile on her face. "Yes, Your Eminence."

"Well, it is not unusual for a priest to find himself in the situation of having fallen in love. In fact, I've hardly known any who has not at some point during his ministry. Traditionally, the solution has been to relocate the cleric in question to another parish or sometimes even another country. What would you two think of that idea?"

I open my mouth to speak but he cuts me off with a wave of his hand, saying, "Ladies, first."

Helen takes a deep breath and says in a voice I've only ever heard her use when giving testimony in a trial, "Tom and I have discussed that possibility and we agree that while we do not feel it is necessary in our case, we will both bow to your judgement in this matter and do as you order."

"Order is a very strong term, Ms. Parr. Besides, while you are right and I could order him to a new assignment, I could not order you to stay away from him. Other than the walls of the Vatican itself, there are few places on Earth I could send him that you could not follow, if you were determined to do so."

"That is probably true, Your Eminence. But you see, I am determined not to. We both understand that his vocation to the priesthood far outweighs our own feelings, even for each other. So, in a twist on words that I use now with knowing irony, where you send him, I will not go. Where you lodge him, I will not lodge. But," she pauses and takes another deep breath, "His God will be my God."

"Beautifully said, Ms. Parr. You two have certainly given me much to think and pray about."

The Archbishop sits back and rests his hands on his belly, staring at a point on the wall to the side. After a few moments that seem like an eternity, he turns back to us.

"I would like to think about this for a couple of days," he finally says. "Would you be willing to meet with me again, say on Ash Wednesday? I know that's a busy day for you, Father, and a work day for you, Ms. Parr, but if you could swing it, I would be very grateful. How about at noon? I can come to you this time so you could take your lunch hour then. I'm sure you'll both be fasting so you won't need time to eat more than a light snack."

Helen and I look at each other, slightly dazed, and then both nod our heads at the same time.

"Good, then," he says, standing up. "We'll meet at your office, Father Tom, on Wednesday at noon."

He gives us his blessing, then has Father Wayne walk us to the door. We walk out of his mansion into the dark, crisp late winter evening. I realize that Helen is not wearing a coat and go to pull mine off, but she stops me. "No, Tom. What will the Archbishop think if he is watching?"

"Only that I am a decent enough guy not to let the woman I claim to love freeze to death while I wear a warm coat." I try again but by this time we are at the car.

We drive in silence out of Baltimore. We're speeding—and since Helen is driving, I mean speeding—west on I-70 just past Frederick when she breaks the silence.

"What do you think?" she asks.

"I have no idea, Helen," I say, looking out as the dark countryside passes by. "I mean, I guess he could be deciding which foreign mission to send me to."

"Oh, Tom! You don't really think—"

"No, I think he would have told me if he was inclined to do that." I sigh. "We're just going to have to wait and see."

"It's going to be a long day, Tom."

"That," I nod. "It is."

It's almost midnight when we arrive at the Rectory. "Good night," I say before I get out of the car, resisting my desire to hug her. "I guess I'll see you on Wednesday, unless you want to have lunch or something?"

"No," she says firmly. "It's only a day away and we both have a lot to get done. Thirty-six hours apart won't kill us and if it does, then we're better off dead."

I look into her eyes, trying to read what she is saying but there is no bitterness there. Neither is there self-pity or any other kind, for that matter. Instead, her jaw is set and her chin is up. I raise my chin, too. I get out of the car, get my luggage, and stand outside the Rectory watching as she drives off.

Forty-Five

The next day is a whirlwind as I try to catch up on the mail piled on my desk. Thankfully, no one has been born or died while I was gone, nor has anyone suddenly decided to get married, so I am able to devote most of my time to office work.

I'm grateful to find that the vast majority of mail consists of condolence cards from my parishioners concerning Sonya's death. Almost all contain personal notes with assurances of prayers. Many also contain artwork done by various children, usually consisting of drawings of someone floating up to heaven, obviously to meet Jesus. I know I will need to send thank you cards for these, but I figure that will be a good task to take on during Lent.

Afterward, I find myself wondering about our upcoming meeting. Will the Archbishop move me to another parish or maybe to a mission field somewhere? He had said that that was the way it had been done in the past, but he had made no commitment about our situation. If he does move me, where will I go? Back to the Archdiocesan Archives? Maybe Our Lady of the Mount for a long retreat in which I would get my head and my heart straight?

I'm surprisingly reluctant to leave Saint. Clare's. I've come to enjoy being a parish priest—even with all the gossip and, of course, the alpaca incident. After my neglect over the last few months, I really want to have the opportunity to be the pastor these people—my people—deserve.

Anna is quiet but comforting, noting no doubt my lack of any mention of Helen and her absence from the Rectory. She fusses around me, making my favorite foods and doing my laundry. She answers the phone every time it rings and seems to screen my calls, since I often overhear her say that I will have to call someone back but I never get instructions to do so.

Before I know it, it's 8:00 a.m. Ash Wednesday Mass, and I'm carefully placing ashes on the foreheads of the penitents and intoning solemnly, "Remember that you are dust, and to dust you will return."

Yes, this thought really puts me in a very pleasant frame of mind for my noon meeting.

The Mass ends by 9:30 a.m., late for a weekday Mass but then again, there were a lot of penitents present. I get back to my office and try to find something to occupy my mind until noon.

I'm rearranging my books on the shelves by color when Helen knocks on the door to the rectory just a minute or two before noon. Anna shows her in, being nicer to her than she has been recently, probably because she hasn't seen her in almost a month. Still, I notice that she leaves the door open a crack, no doubt so she can hear what's going on inside.

Helen takes a seat across from me and we just look at each other. "Tom," she begins before I can say anything, "I think I need to make something clear. No matter what happens today, I will always love you and always be as much to you as I can, given our unique circumstances. I don't want anyone else and I won't have anyone else."

Her voice cracks and I stand to come around the desk to comfort her but she waves me off. "Please, Tom, for the love of all that is holy, don't try to touch me. If you do, I will never finish this and I have to finish this, for both of us."

She takes a deep breath as tears well up in her eyes and continues, "That being said, I have no intention of spending the rest of my life mourning what we will never have. I have lost the man I loved before and survived that. At least you are still alive, and as long as that is true, we have some hope for something. I will go on and I expect you to do the same. You owe that not only to me and to yourself, but more importantly to the people you will serve, whoever and wherever they are."

Before I can say anything, the door opens and the Archbishop walks in. Helen and I both stand and, in keeping with tradition, I yield my seat behind the desk to him. I am thankful to do it, thankful to be sitting by Helen one last time.

As I sit down, I catch a glimpse of the time on my phone.

12:04 p.m.

He is late.

But the Archbishop is never late. His punctuality is legendary. Had he been standing there, eavesdropping? Had he heard what Helen said?

Before I can consider this possibility, the Archbishop says, "Shall we begin with prayer?" Not waiting for an answer, we each make the sign of the Cross, and he prays a short but powerful prayer for wisdom and enlightenment. We join him in his Amen and then fall into silence.

Before beginning, the Archbishop eyes us calmly for a moment that seems like an eternity.

"Father Tom, Ms. Parr, thank you for bringing your situation to my attention, for expressing such a sincere desire for God's will, and for giving me time to contemplate how best to advise you.

"As I mentioned when we previously met, the traditional way to handle situations like this has been to transfer the priest. However, many in the Church now recognize that plan may have been based on the false assumption that men and women could only have deep relationships if they were romantically connected. In a world where women work as equals with and often superior to men, where they meet and interact in completely non-romantic ways on a daily basis, this assumption seems especially outdated.

"Father Tom, you are in a unique situation compared to other priests in that, even though many seminarians have had intimate and even sexual relationships before they discovered their vocations, few have been married and know the joy and sorrow of daily life with a woman. This is both your gift and your cross, for you knew what you were giving up the day of your ordination. This makes you different from a young man who might come to me with stars in his eyes insisting that his happiness hinges on leaving the priesthood for the love of a woman.

"Ms. Parr, you, too, have been married and, if I may say without any intention of insult, you are old enough to know your own mind. When you say that you wish to maintain a platonic relationship with Father Tom, I feel certain that you understand what it will take to do so, and that you know yourself well enough to make that sacrifice.

"In light of all these factors, I am not going to move you anywhere, Father Tom. Instead, I am going to give you and Ms. Parr a chance to try this new type of relationship that you say you want to forge. Lent begins today and it is by its very nature a penitential season, so any suffering you experience as you make this adjustment will be both magnified and sanctified to God's glory and your good.

"Father, I expect you to send me a detailed account of any interaction that takes place between the two of you during this time. You will also need to make yourself available periodically for us to meet together and discuss how you are doing.

"Ms. Parr," he continues, handing her his business card, "on the back of this card is my cell phone number. I ask you to call it now."

Looking perplexed, Helen does as he asks. He immediately declines the call but then saves the number to his phone. "I now have your number in my phone under your name. If you call, I will answer immediately if I can. If I can't, I will call you back at my very first opportunity.

"If you have no questions for me, please feel free to bow down and receive a blessing." He begins to raise his hand, but I interrupt him.

"But sir," I say, forgetting his proper title. "How are we supposed to work this out? What are we supposed to do?"

With a twinkle in his eye, the Archbishop says, "Tom, you and Helen must do what all people must do in relationships. You must figure it out as you go along."

With that he blesses us and stands, moving towards the door. Pausing there, he adds, "Oh, there is one more thing. Please be assured of my daily, fervent prayers for your relationship, as well as those of my fellow bishops around the world."

Before either one of us can say anything else, he is gone.

Helen and I stand in my office, staring at each other. Finally, we both exhale.

"Wha—What just happened?" Helen asks with amazement.

"I—I'm not really sure," I say, equally amazed. "I think he just said I could stay and we could have a relationship with each other."

Helen starts laughing and crying at the same time. "Oh, Tom! I was so scared he was going to take you away from here! I prayed all night that he wouldn't, but also that if he did, I'd be strong enough not to try to go after you!"

"Oh, Helen," I say, my voice breaking as tears come to my eyes. "I am so happy! I don't know what it means, and I know we still have a lot to figure out, and I'm sure it's going to be difficult, but I am so happy that at least we have the chance to find out together."

"Together," she says.

I look at her. She smiles and nods. I open my arms and draw her into a hug, quietly saying "one-mississippi, two-mississippi, three-mississippi," to myself before letting me go.

"Three seconds," I say. "Just like we agreed."

Helen nods. "Well, I still have thirty minutes left for lunch. What shall we do? I mean, we can't eat."

"I'm not sure I could eat anyway. I have a better idea anyway," I say.

At her quizzical look, I pull out my Rosary. "Do you have yours with you?"

She digs through her bag and manages to locate it without too much trouble. Clutching our Rosaries in our hands, we leave the Rectory and take the walkway to the side door of the Church.

The church is dim, no lights are on. The only illumination is the sun pouring through the stained glass windows, casting a kaleidoscope of color throughout the building, and the candles burning before the Blessed Virgin, Saint Joseph, and Saint Claire.

We approach the center aisle quietly and turn toward the altar. Carefully, we kneel on the bottom step. Raising our eyes together, kneeling before the Lord we both love and want to serve with every fiber of our being, we clutch our Rosaries in our hands, preparing to contemplate the profoundest mysteries of all.

Making the sign of the cross, we pray together in one strong voice that echoes through the empty space surrounding us.

"In the Name of the Father, and of the Son, and of the Holy Spirit.

"Amen."

About the Author

Susan Mathis was born in and grew up in an extremely small town in Alachua County, Florida where her family has lived for more than 100 years. When Susan was still very young, James (J.R) Mathis was born in a somewhat bigger small town about 100 miles south of where she lived. Within a decade, James' small town would become part of Orlando, the biggest tourist destination in the United States. He was not amused. That is how, while Susan was running barefoot, swimming in lakes full of alligators and feeding chickens, James was sitting in his bedroom reading books faster than his father could bring them home from the library.

Were James and Susan to write their love story, it would definitely be an enemies-to-lovers trope. They met in the library where he was working. He found her demands for books that he had to pull and bring to her so unreasonable that he actually turned her into the head librarian. She in turn was so anxious to drive him away that when some friends secretly set them up she laid out an entire speech about how miserable her life was (she is typically very upbeat). Little did she suspect that he had a passionate attraction to misery and they were married just over a year later.

Fast forward 26 years, three children, four grandchildren and 20 years of James working for the Federal government. He was diagnosed with a highly treatable but still very scary form of cancer. As so often happens, this brush with mortality inspired him to do something he'd always wanted to do, write a novel. After the publication of the second Father Tom Mystery, Susan joined him as coauthor. As far as the Mathises are concerned, writing together is the most fun a couple can have sitting at a computer.

Read more at https://www.facebook.com/groups/J.R.MathisAuthor/.